Sadie A. McCaully
66642 E. Bay Rd. Sp. #46
North Bend, OR 97459

W9-AVK-656

Mrs. Mike

The Search for Joyful

Mrs. Mike

The Search for Joyful

Benedict and Nancy Freedman

BERKLEY BOOKS, NEW YORK

A Berkley Book
Published by The Berkley Publishing Group
A division of Penguin Putnam Inc.
375 Hudson Street
New York, New York 10014

The Search for Joyful copyright © 2002 by Benedict and Nancy Freedman
Book design by Tiffany Kukec

Mrs. Mike copyright © 1947, 1975, 2002 by Benedict and Nancy Freedman
Excerpt from *The Search for Joyful* copyright © 2002 by Benedict and Nancy Freedman
Book design by Tiffany Kukec
Cover design by Erika Fusari
Top cover photo by Jake Wyman/Photonica
Bottom cover photo by Steve Edson/Photonica

ISBN 0-7394-5091-3

PRINTED IN THE UNITED STATES OF AMERICA

Mrs. Mike

Acknowledgments

Claire Gerus, for making the arrangements
Susan Allison, for guiding the publication
Anne Sowards, for shepherding the manuscript
Johanna Shapiro, for her insightful literary psychotherapy
Deborah Jackson, for recognizing truth
Hartley John Freedman, for providing technical assistance
Patricia Carroll, for being there

To Nana
and
to the readers of
Mrs. Mike
who asked for this story

To the Readers of *Mrs. Mike:*

This is a love letter, written to say Thank You to three generations of readers who treasured the book, wrote to us, and kept Mrs. Mike *in print all these years. You told us how it affected your lives and what it meant to you. Now it's our turn to tell you that your loyalty resulted in an Internet miracle—this new edition of* Mrs. Mike, *and the writing of a sequel.*

Log on to Amazon.com, search "Mrs. Mike," and see for yourself. These are the e-mail outpourings of affection that moved—not mountains—but the Freedmans. We read your comments and felt you calling us to another effort.

At the time of Mrs. Mike's *original publication, it was a main selection of the Literary Guild®, serialized in the* Atlantic Monthly, *condensed in* Reader's Digest, *appeared on the* New York Times *bestseller list, and translated into twenty-seven languages. In that halcyon year we were besieged by publishers eager to do a sequel. We hadn't much use for sequels. It stands to reason, we thought, that the choicest material goes into the original. We did not consider the idea.*

So what happened?

Half a century happened. We became parents, traveled, quested, wrote, taught, became grandparents—lived a life. And as writers we stored up a fresh fund of experiences that demanded a new book.

We began. The computer keys flew under our fingers; we couldn't get it down fast enough. The Search for Joyful, *to be published in February 2002 in hardcover by Berkley, is the story of*

Kathy, daughter of Mrs. Mike's "more than sister." Written in the style of Mrs. Mike, the new book presents a young woman making a life for herself and finding love in the face of prejudice, discouragement, and war. It will be in bookstores in time for Valentine's Day, 2002.

This new edition of Mrs. Mike, and the sequel to come, are dedicated to you, the readers who kept Katherine Mary Flannigan alive in your hearts. You reached out to us—we reach out to you.

Benedict and Nancy Freedman

One

THE WORST WINTER in fifty years, the old Scotsman had told me. I'd only been around for sixteen, but it was the worst I'd seen, and I was willing to take his word for the other thirty-four.

On the north side of the train the windows were plastered with snow, and on the south side great clouds of snow were whipped along by a sixty-mile gale. There was snow on top of the train and snow under the train, and all the snow there was left in the world in front of the train, which was why we were stopped.

"They're sending us snowplows from Regina, no doubt," the old Scotsman said.

I looked out the window, but it was no snowplow I could see, nor the road to Regina, nor even the coach in front of us, but only whirling, boiling, rushing gray-white snow.

"You'll be telling your children you were in the blizzard of 1907," the old man chuckled. "I was speaking to the conductor a while back. It's forty below and dropping. No, we'll not be in Regina *this* week." He opened his book and began to read.

We'd left Montreal March 5, eighteen days before, eighteen days spent mostly in pulling the engine out of drifts and scraping ice off the wheels.

It was because of my pleurisy I was being sent to Uncle John, who lived in Calgary, Alberta. Up till 1905 Alberta had been part of the Great Northwest Territory, and it gave me a real thrill to go to a place that had been officially civilized for only two years.

My mother had her doubts about letting me go into such a wilderness. We looked it up on a map of North America, and Alberta seemed awfully empty. Our part of the country, which was Boston, was covered with winding black lines meaning roads, and barbed-wire lines meaning railroads, and circles of all sizes meaning cities and towns. It was so crowded with these proofs of civilization that there was no room for the names, which were stuck out in the Atlantic Ocean. In Alberta there was none of this reassuring confusion. A couple of thin blue rivers, a couple of crooked lakes, and the map maker was through. My mother found the circle that was Calgary and carefully compared it with the circles of Massachusetts.

"A fine black dot it is, but not to be mentioned in the same breath with Boston," she said. Boston was a very distinctive city on our map, being a large dot with a ring around it. "And you'll bear in mind, Katherine Mary," she added, "that's as far north as I want you to go. Don't be letting your uncle take you up into this." She waved in the general direction of Mackenzie and the North Pole. "My own mother lived and died in the house where she was born, and all the traveling she did was to the oatfield and back."

We both sat and wondered at the size of the world until she folded it up and put it in the bureau drawer.

However, the doctors said the cold dry climate of Alberta would be good for my lungs, and Uncle John said it was a long, long time since he had seen one of his kin, and so at last my mother gave in and let me go.

She put me on the train in Boston, and for the twentieth time I promised I'd dress warm and keep dry and not go out into the night where there were bears.

"Now, there's a lot of snow up in those north places," Mother cautioned me, "and you'll always remember to wear your woolen socks. And when there's a cold wind blowing, on with your shawl and button up."

"Yes, Mother," I said. She kissed me, smiled and cried, and the train pulled out. Now here I was in one of those "north places" and the old Scotsman was calling to me from across the aisle.

One of the trainmen had wiped off the frost from his window. The Scotsman pointed, and there against the stock fence along the right of way were hundreds of cows and steers, blown across the prairies by that icy gale and packed densely along the fence, frozen and dead.

THERE WAS FROST all over the window, except in the corner where I'd scratched a clear space to look out, and except for KATHERINE MARY O'FALLON printed underneath, and except for where I'd drawn Juno's ears. Just then the train gave a jerk and started slowing down, making twice as much noise as when it went fast. They always do, and I can't figure out why.

I'd put Juno in the big lunch basket Mother'd given me. I had to keep him in there during the day because dogs were supposed to be kept in the baggage car and there was a mean porter on this train. Juno was the worry of my life. He had broken a strand of wicker, and I was always in terror that he'd stick that black nose of his out the hole.

The train was just about stopped now. I thought maybe it was another snowplow come to clear off the tracks, so I looked out. There wasn't much to see; snow on top of everything and not too many trees. There was a red silo and a house, and I was glad I didn't live there.

The basket with Juno in it started moving around in a very un-basketlike way. It finally fell off the seat and started rolling toward the aisle. I grabbed it back fast, opened the lid, and gave Juno a couple of slaps on the nose. This Juno wasn't like Mother's Juno; he was only a puppy and couldn't be expected to be as wise and smart yet. All our dogs were named Juno, and they were mostly cocker and black. The Irish Juno who had come to America with us had been red. I didn't remember that one because I was only two then. The first Juno I remember was the white and brown one, the one that howled when Uncle Martin played the violin. Uncle had his violin and his bagpipe (the Irish kind) from Denny Lannon, the great storyteller, whose great-grandniece I am. Mother used to say that Denny Lannon had a song and a story for every day in the week, and two for Sunday.

There I was thinking of Mother. And I mustn't. Otherwise how could I keep going through this white world of pale sky and frozen earth?

The wheels started again—the wheels that took me away from the three-story brick house and Uncle Martin's new sign saying in gold letters that we let rooms. But the room on the third floor Mother never let to anyone. It was the prettiest room in the house, always full of flowers. It was kept for someone down on his luck who would need a pretty room and flowers to cheer him up. Many a down-and-out actor had lived there, once a janitor out of work, and once a lady who took in sewing but couldn't do much any more because her eyes were bad.

I felt sorry for the lady whose eyes were bad, so sorry that I began to cry. I wasn't crying for her exactly, but for all the sadness in the world. And because right now, if I were home, I'd be feeding

Pete, Mother's canary. But I wasn't home and someone else was feeding him, Mary Ellen or Anna Frances.

I blew my nose because I was determined to stop crying, but that didn't stop it. So I opened Mother's cookies. I'd been saving them for an emergency, and they were pretty stale. I ate them and cried some more because they were my favorite kind, small and brown and lumpy with bits of chocolate. *I* made that kind, too, only not so well. Mother said I didn't mix the dough thick enough. Anyway I sat there and ate cookies and cried. After a while the cookies were all gone, and there had been two dozen of them, so I knew I'd been crying a long time.

"Regina! Regina!" Sure enough, we'd come to a town, a big one with yards and houses coming right down near the track, dogs and people and a little boy standing waving at the train. The little boy had so many clothes on and the top jacket was stretched so tight it looked as if it would split if he kept waving. I wanted to cry about the little boy too, but I couldn't. He was too fat to be hungry and had on too many clothes to be poor.

We stopped, and I followed the people who were getting off to walk around and stretch their legs. It was awfully cold and I'd forgotten to put my sweater on under my coat. Mother never let me go out in such cold weather for fear it would make my pleurisy worse. I hoped it wouldn't. I was afraid I'd be sick when I got to Uncle John's. I stared at the postcards on display, hoping that the scenes of sunsets and mountains and oceans would cheer me up. But I kept thinking of Mother and wondering if I'd ever be home again. The postcards blurred, and so did the station of Regina as I ran along it to the train, which was smoking and almost ready to go. I climbed on the nearest coach and walked through to mine.

My berth had been made up, and I didn't see Juno's basket. I climbed in and searched frantically, looking into the most impossible places, under the pillows and behind the curtain. I ran down the car. I ran back and, throwing myself on my stomach, peered under the berth. There was the basket, tucked away next to my valise, but even as I pulled it out, I knew it was empty.

The wheels began to turn, and an awful feeling stabbed into me that maybe he was under them. I began a frantic search under seats, between bags, and around legs. A gray-haired man stopped me. "If you're looking for a black cocker spaniel, the porter has him. Carried him down that way." I started running. He was still talking, but I couldn't wait. Maybe they'd put him off. Maybe he was out there on the track, wandering lost around the station. The wheels chugged faster and faster.

I was at the end of the coach and pulling at the heavy door when I stopped. On the other side, the frightening covered part where the cars join, was Juno. He was sitting up on his hind legs because the mean porter was holding little bits of meat for him. I looked hard at the porter, and anyone could see that he wasn't mean, but only sad and thin.

I'd been sad and thin all day, too. But now I was only thin.

THEY CALLED ME early, but I was already awake. This was the day we'd be getting in, and I had a lot to do. First I got out the red plaid dress I'd been saving. I was sorry now I hadn't worn it because it was all in little lines that wouldn't fall out. It had been thirty days in that suitcase.

I combed Juno and then gathered up my clothes and took them into the ladies' room. I thought I looked very well in my new dress, even if it was wrinkled. People with red hair as a rule look awful in red, but my hair has enough brown in it to be called auburn. I tried to put it up in the figure eight my mother wore low on her neck. It was harder to do than I expected because my hair is curly and wouldn't cooperate. But when I had it up I looked at least eighteen. Too bad I had to spoil it by putting a ribbon on. That was the way Uncle John was to recognize me, by the big blue ribbon in my hair.

When I got the bow tied there was still a couple of yards of ribbon left over. Back to my berth for my scissors, and then back to the ladies' room where they had the mirror. And all the time it was getting later. I tried the bow on one side and then on the other, on the front and on the back. Wherever I put it, it looked queer with my hair up. And it was so big.

People began coming in to dress. I was fascinated by a very fat woman dressing inside her nightgown. She had her hands underneath and pulled everything up from the bottom.

It was getting crowded near the looking glass, and the ladies began pushing. I had to decide where to put the ribbon. I fastened it on the right side and started back to my berth. The Scotsman shook my hands, both of them. "It's been a fine trip. I hope you meet your uncle all right. It's been a pleasure knowing you, Miss O'Fallon."

I said good-bye to him and felt sad, the way you feel when you've shared something with someone whom you'll never see in this world again. When I got back to my seat, I tied a piece of the leftover ribbon on Juno. By now everyone on the train knew I had him, so there was no use keeping him in the basket. The train began to slow down. The windows were frosted over again so I couldn't see, but I knew it was Calgary.

Uncle John, Uncle John . . . I tried to fix the name with a body. Tall and dark, a lean face, Mother had said. What if he wasn't there? What would I do? What if he was there and didn't recognize me, and went away? What if he didn't really want me to come? What if he didn't like me?

The train was stopping. I grabbed Juno and put him in the basket. What would I say to him? What would we talk about? Should I call him Uncle John, or Uncle, or . . . ? Would he really be here? I couldn't believe it—John Kennedy, my mother's brother.

And just supposing he was here, would he know me? I put my hand up to the ribbon; it was still there. But he might not have received Mother's letter about the blue ribbon. Some people said I looked like my mother. I hoped he'd recognize me. I took a mirror out of my purse and changed the ribbon to the left side.

Ten minutes later I was standing on the platform, and a tall, dark, lean gentleman with eyes just like my mother's was smiling and saying, "Katherine Mary?"

Right then and there I put my arms around him and kissed him. Then I looked at him again. "I hope you're my uncle John," I said.

"Yes, I'm your uncle John." Then he looked at me hard. "Just like your mother." He kept looking at me. "Is it the custom," he asked slowly, "for young women in Boston, America, to wear two hair bows on their one head?"

"I added the second hair bow at the last minute because, Uncle, I didn't know which way you'd be coming from."

Uncle John had a big coon coat for me. I put it on right over my other coat, and it felt good. I climbed into the cutter, sat on a buffalo robe, and had another thrown over my knees. The buffalo robes excited Juno. He took a corner of one in his mouth and rocked back and forth, growling way down in his throat.

We started up. All Uncle did was pick up the reins, but those horses knew. It was like flying. We started up the snow on every side, and the wind blew a challenge. Juno was completely subdued and lay against me with his nose under my arm.

I snuggled into the furs and took a couple of quick looks at Uncle John. He was dressed in a coon coat too and fur mittens. And a fur cap pulled down over his ears.

"What kind of fur is that?" I pointed to the mittens.

"Beaver."

I could see Uncle John wasn't much of a one for talking. "And the cap too?" I asked.

"Yes."

Well, that subject seemed to be exhausted. I was about to settle back and look at things when Uncle surprised me. "How did you leave your mother, Kathy?"

"Mother's fine," I said. "She sends you her love."

Uncle John nodded his head and grunted. I tried to figure out what feeling that expressed, but I couldn't. So after a while I gave up and just watched the town go by. Once I saw a street lighter reaching up with his long pole and making a light.

"And your sisters?"

The words startled me, coming out of the dusk and the silence with no other words behind them for two or three miles. Then I realized that two or three miles between words in this vast country was equivalent to a pause my mother would have filled with, "And who will have another biscuit?"

"And Frances and Mary Ellen are very well. Anna Frances poses for magazine covers. Mary Ellen is engaged. And I tap dance. . . ." I paused, but not for any two or three miles, just long enough to think if there were any more accomplishments we possessed as a family. There weren't. I glanced around for another subject. It was getting dark and pressing all around us were the silhouettes of buildings. "Calgary's a big city, isn't it?"

"Yes," Uncle said, "mighty big."

That was that. I tried another tack. "How far is it to your ranch?"

"Two days."

I nodded and leaned over the edge of the cutter to feel the wind in my face. We turned a corner and went down a hill, and Uncle finished his sentence, ". . . . but we aren't going there now."

"We aren't?"

"Well, no."

I waited patiently for him to go on. But I was about ready for another question when he spoke again. "We're stopping to see a woman."

This was interesting because Uncle John was a bachelor. "Who?" I asked.

"Name's Mrs. Neilson. Margaret Neilson."

The "Mrs." spoiled it. Except maybe she was a widow. I was still thinking about this possibility when we stopped. I shut Juno up in his basket and ran after Uncle John.

"Now remember, Katherine Mary, she just got out." Uncle John said this in a strange tone, as though he meant to say something else.

"Out of what?" I asked.

We walked up on the porch and Uncle rang the bell. "That's what we call it, Kathy. Coming out. It means out of the north country."

A middle-aged woman with a dirty dressing gown flapping around her opened the door. "Yes?"

"We'd like to see Mrs. Neilson."

I could see the woman's eyes light up with curiosity. "She's in her room. I'll show you."

"If it's the same one, end of the hall, I'll find it."

I followed Uncle John down the hall. The woman muttered something as we passed. Uncle stopped in front of a door. He turned and said, "Now remember, Katherine Mary."

What was I to remember? I didn't find out because the door opened, and a beautiful young woman stood looking at us.

"Mrs. Neilson . . ." my uncle began, and then stopped.

She was staring at me with large startled eyes.

"I'm Katherine Mary O'Fallon," I said.

"My niece," Uncle added.

Her eyes dropped to her hands. She wore a delicate little wedding ring. She turned it around and around. "Come in." And she smiled in a way that made my heart go out to her.

The room was dark and shabby, and I felt bad that she had to stay in it. But, as my mother would have said, she was a lady. She treated us as though we were in a palace.

When we were all seated, my uncle reached inside his coat, and then inside his jacket, and finally inside his shirt and took out an envelope. "It's your ticket."

She smiled.

"Your ticket," he repeated.

"You've been very good to me, Mr. Kennedy."

Uncle John didn't seem to know what to say to that. He took out his pipe and then put it away again. He cleared his throat. "Well, you'll be getting back, Mrs. Neilson. And that will be a good thing."

"Where are you going?" I asked.

"She's going to New York," my uncle said.

"I've been there. Mother took me."

"We were married there." She said it very softly.

"Is your husband there, or is he here, too?"

"He . . ."

I looked at Uncle John, and then I knew it was my fault no one was talking.

Margaret Neilson reached over and took my hand. Hers was like ice. "It's hard. It's a hard country. Men fight it. Men like to fight, but a woman . . ." Her voice got small and then stopped altogether.

Uncle stood up. "Mrs. Neilson, it's time we started. I'm taking Kathy up to the ranch."

She walked to him and took hold of his arm. "Don't go. Not yet." She looked at him in a pleading kind of way. "Have some tea first. I insist."

Uncle John sat down, a little limply I thought.

"Thank you, that will be real nice."

She smiled at that and hummed a little tune while she put the water to boil. Uncle took out his pipe, remembered, and put it back again. This time she saw him. "Mr. Kennedy, smoke your pipe. Please, I like a pipe."

She poured out the tea and served it to us in broken china cups. And then I saw it wasn't tea, just hot water. She must have forgotten to put the tea in.

"Sugar and cream?" she asked my uncle. "Or do you take lemon?"

"Lemon, please."

And there she was squeezing lemon into the hot water, and there he was stirring it around. Shouldn't someone mention that there was no tea in it, or was that impolite?

"And you, Katherine Mary, how do you like yours?"

With tea, I almost said. But I was glad I didn't, she enjoyed entertaining us so much.

"I'd like sugar," I said. And she gave it to me, two spoonfuls. I glanced over at Uncle John. He was drinking his. So I began to sip mine. And, holy St. Patrick, there's nothing worse tasting than hot water with two teaspoons of sugar in it.

Then she got her own cup and sat down. It's so silly, I thought. Now she'll find out, and wonder why nobody said anything. She'll think we're crazy, sitting here drinking hot water. I looked away just as the cup reached her lips because I didn't want her to see me staring. I waited for her to say something. She did. She said, "You must take Katherine Mary to the hotel tonight. Then she'll be fresh for the trip up tomorrow." She took another sip, and this time I watched her. She didn't seem to notice anything.

We sat around drinking our hot water and not saying much until it was time to say good-bye. She kissed me, and there were tears in her eyes when she did it. "I couldn't pull him out," she told me. "I couldn't."

We left early the next morning for Uncle John's ranch. Uncle tucked me into the cutter and started the horses on a fast, silent trot over the snow-packed road. For a long time I said nothing. I watched the clouds light up and the sun rise slowly and the snow gleam. I saw tracks of wolves and mountain lions crossing the road. I showed them to my uncle. He sucked at his pipe and said, "Rabbits."

I felt the inside of the buffalo robe that wrapped me and wondered how it felt on the buffalo. I breathed the sharp morning air and smelled the horses. But all the while in the back of my mind I was troubled. "Uncle John," I said, ". . . about last night . . ."

"Yes?"

"I felt strange in Mrs. Neilson's house. Didn't you?"

"No."

"Mrs. Neilson seemed so dreamy, and I always had the feeling she didn't hear a word we were saying."

"No great loss," said my uncle John with a puff of smoke. This shut me up for a while, and I took to looking up at the clouds and figuring out animals and ships and islands there. The cutter skimmed along more like a sailboat than a sleigh, and the wind blew in our faces. I watched my uncle's pipe to see if he was angry, and finally I asked, "Have you known Mrs. Neilson long?"

"Eight months."

"Was she always like this?"

"No," Uncle John said. "People change." The road began to wind uphill. The horses slowed to a walk. "She was a bride when she came," my uncle said. "Neilson was a strong man, but stubborn. Did things his own way and never asked advice. Capable, though. Did everything himself. Wife adored him."

I nodded eagerly, but it was several minutes before my uncle went on. I tried to picture Mr. Neilson, the strong man but stubborn. I could see his big shoulders and heavy hands, his square chin. Did he have light hair or dark? I never knew.

"Built his barn himself, no help. And a kind of shed, a milking stand on the west wall. People laughed at him for wanting the cow to get up on a stand to be milked, but Neilson was stubborn. He did things his own way. And after a while nobody gave him advice.

"Well, he went back East for a girl. You've seen her, Kathy. Pretty, but delicate, with scared eyes. Those women are not made for this country. Anyway, the house was all ready, and he brought her out to Lesser Slave Lake, and one night there was a blizzard. Snowed three days without a letup. When it snows like that, you can stick your head out of the window and all you see is the nearest snowflake. You can walk two steps out your door and never find your way back to the house. But the stock in the barn have been three days without feed, so Neilson gets up and says he's going to the barn. His wife doesn't say anything, just looks at him scared. So he gets a little angry because he doesn't want to catch her fright, and he says in that stubborn way he has, 'There's two horses and a cow and a steer and two pigs—and I'll be damned if they'll starve!' Now she looks at him, pleading with her eyes. I suppose she wants to say, 'Forget the animals, I want you!' But you can't say that to a farmer. He'd die twenty times for those matched bays. He opens the door. Now, most of the fellows up here run a rope from the house door to the barn door during the blizzard season. When you have to tend to the stock, you don't need eyes; that rope is your compass, your chart, and your navigator. Neilson didn't rig a rope. I don't know, maybe he was too stubborn. Maybe he thought he was being kidded. A lot of the men around here were mad at his stubbornness, and they'd tell him things to do, like to plant wheat under the Northern Lights for a big crop, or to set out bowls of milk for the bears so they wouldn't pick up chickens, and a lot else, to see if he would bite. So when they told him about that rope, I guess he laughed and said he'd seen snow before."

My uncle John looked down at me. "Comfortable?" he said.

"Go on," I said. "That's not the end. Go on."

He smiled. "All right. Neilson opens the door. He can't see the barn, but he knows exactly where it is. He's been to that barn ten thousand times. He pictures the barn. He pictures the door in the barn. He pictures the road to the door. And then he runs as fast as he can, so he won't swerve. . . . After two steps he disappears, and the snow is blowing in her face and she can't see or hear him, so she closes the door. She sits down, but her eyes never leave that door. She didn't even get a chance to kiss him or smile at him before he ran out.

"In her mind she follows him down the path to the barn, and she sees his hand reach out for the door, pull it open, pull himself in; she hears the horses whinny a welcome. 'Don't come back,' she prays, 'don't come back. Stay in the barn till it blows over. Stay where you're safe.' Two hours go by, and he doesn't come back. And suddenly she begins to tremble. She knows he isn't in the barn, he's lost, he's crying for help. She leaps up; she puts on her sweater, her coat, her boots, her gloves, her hat, she opens the door. . . . She stops. She almost laughs. He is there, he is surely there, safe in the barn. And here she was going to lose herself, wildly, uselessly. She can see him coming back slowly to the house in the final ebb of the storm to find her lying frozen in the drifts. Taking command of herself, she closes the door, sits down on a straight chair, and tries not to think. But after a while she knows he is dead, long dead, and she moans, and sobs, and screams. And there are still eight hours of night left.

"At seven in the morning the wind died. Half an hour later the snow stopped. Mrs. Neilson buckled on her snowshoes and went out. In a drift about four yards from the barn door she saw a boot. She pulled at the boot, but it wouldn't come. She went into the barn, harnessed a horse, and brought it out. She tied a rope to the horse and looped it around the boot. When we came by that afternoon, checking up, she was still trying to get him out."

IT TOOK US two days to get to Uncle's ranch. We were almost there when I noticed a difference in the air. It seemed warmer, and the sky flushed a deep rose. The glow spread over everything. "Uncle John," I said, "my face feels warm."

Uncle smiled. When I say he smiled, I mean he smiled with his eyes. They twinkled and wrinkled, and that's about as much of a smile as he could manage. "It's going to chinook," he said.

"What's that?"

"You'll see soon enough, Kathy." After three days I knew my uncle well enough to know I'd hear no more about chinooks. I puzzled over the word a long time. It sounded Indian, I thought. Or maybe Eskimo.

"Well, we're here," Uncle said.

I looked around. We had turned off into an icy path, and I could see a fence. But that's all I could see.

"Up ahead." Uncle pointed.

Yes, there was smoke. Soon I was able to make out a large square house, log-built. A man waved and shouted and ran up to us. Juno began to bark excitedly.

"Hello, Jim," my uncle said. "Where's Johnny?"

Jim didn't answer. He was grinning at me. He even started to remove his beaver cap. Uncle looked at me with twinkling eyes. "I thought it better not to tell your mother that there's only one other white girl in these parts. This is Jim, one of the hands. Miss O'Fallon, my niece."

"Pleasure to meet you, I'm sure." Jim was still grinning.

We got out of the cutter, and it felt good to be standing on solid ground.

"Where's Johnny?" Uncle asked again.

Jim's smile broadened. "Out celebrating the Boer War."

Uncle grunted, and we went into the house. The contrast in temperature between indoors and outdoors was so great that I ripped my furs off before I said a word or looked around or did anything else.

Uncle showed me over the house. It had two bedrooms, a big kitchen, and a front room. It was very comfortable. Uncle had ten hands working the place, mostly looking after cattle. "They sleep in the bunkhouse," he said.

"Is one of them named Johnny?" I asked, because I was wondering about what Jim had said.

"No." Uncle took out his pipe and lighted up. "No, Johnny lives here with me. Does the cooking."

"Where is he?"

"You heard what Jim says, he's out celebrating."

"But Jim said he was celebrating the Boer War."

Uncle John puffed a while. "Yes," he said at last, "that's right. You see, we were in it together. That's where I knew Johnny."

I thought of all the snow outside, and the miles and miles of nothing. "But how does he celebrate?"

"Humph!" Uncle said. And that's all I could get out of him about Johnny.

I HAD GONE to bed with Juno and a four-stripe Hudson's Bay blanket. Uncle had given me a white one because the Indians said the white were the warmest. But that night it chinooked, and I threw off all my blankets, for it blew hot and warm. The red glow deepened in the sky. In twenty-four hours the snow disappeared. I was glad to see the last of it, but that was because I didn't know.

"Uncle," I asked, "what's happened? Over night it's spring."

"Chinook," he said. "It's a current of air from the west, warmed by the Japanese current. It moves in over our mountains and down. It gets warmer and drier as it comes. And when it reaches the prairie, the thaw sets in."

At first I ran around and looked at everything. The earth was bare, with little grass blades pricking at it. What I had thought was field melted, and the Red Deer River ran its course. Juno and I took a long walk along its banks, looking into the swift, turbulent waters and listening for the different tones as it rushed at stones and boulders. We watched the ice break and disappear. The larger chunks were carried past like white rafts. It would have been a wild journey for anyone riding those ice cakes, for they whirled and stuck . . . and for a moment lay in the shelter of the shallows before another eddy spun them on again.

We left the river and wandered up near the cut banks. They were low beds that once had been mountain streams. Now they were dry, and cattle were grazing there, thousands of them. Juno barked and barked, but not one of the shaggy heads lifted to look at us. It is very fertile in these canyons, and the cattle graze all year around, even in the winter, for the long thick bull-grass comes right up through three feet of snow.

But today the snow had gone. Everywhere, from all things, there fell a constant drip: from branches, from roots, from boulders, from eaves. I went to sleep my second night on the ranch to the uneven rhythm of that wet, pattering sound. In the morning the sun shone on the moisture-soaked earth, and a rainbow was made. The sound of wet air shaking itself into the Red Deer torrent made a subtle kind of counterpoint. This magic land . . . this was the North.

I walked again to the river. It was much higher than the day before. In some places water ran over the prairie, keeping pace with the strong current of the river. I saw men at a distance, driving cattle. They shouted and waved at me. But the wind carried their words away, and I couldn't hear. One of the figures separated itself from the group and came riding for me. It was Uncle John. "Back to the house," he yelled. "Get back to the house."

I wasn't used to being shouted at. Without answering, I turned and walked back.

No one was in the house. No one came for lunch either. I got awfully hungry, and when I couldn't hold out any longer, I looked around the kitchen and ended by eating some dried fruit. It was four o'clock by then, and I was feeling very lonesome and neglected. Even Juno was no company. He kept whining, and every once in a while let out a sharp bark. That made me nervous.

At first I thought I imagined it, but then I sat very still and listened, minute after minute. I was not mistaken. A low mournful sound vibrated through the house.

It was after dark when the men came trooping back, tired and silent. I'd been mad at all of them, but when I saw them, the anger went out of me. I put some coffee on the stove. It was hot and black, and the men relaxed.

"How many you reckon we lost?"

"Hundred head, maybe."

"MacDonald's lost more," Uncle said.

"What happened?" I felt I could ask it now.

Uncle John gulped down more coffee. "Stock drowned."

"Drowned?"

"The men have been rounding them up for three, four days, since we first knew it was going to chinook. But there were a couple thousand head to get out."

I still couldn't understand. "But how'd they drown?"

"Ice jammed. Blocked the river. Flooded the prairie. We were working in three feet of water, and it was rising all the time."

I tried to shut out the picture of thousands of beasts helpless in the flood.

"Let's have more coffee, Katherine Mary."

I filled up the cups all around. They drank and warmed themselves for a few minutes. Then Uncle John went on, "You know how water seeks its level. Well, it did this time. Went rushing and foaming into the canyons where the herds were grazing. We rounded them out at fast as we could. Got most of them. Got more than some. MacDonald lost five hundred head."

I closed my eyes.

"Happens every year, Miss," one of the men said. "Most times we get 'em out. Sometimes we don't. It's the chinook does it."

I felt sick. Only that morning I'd seen them in the arroyos, red and white patches of them going on for miles.

I knew now what that strange monotonous vibration had been— the lowing of panic-stricken cows and steers struggling for a foothold, thrashing and churning till the water turned muddy. Men shouted at them, horses nudged them, water lashed over them, and their fear burst loose, stampeding them. The young fell and were trodden. The muddy waters turned red. They cried their soft low cry of terror, and the walls of the room had sounded with it. I looked at the eleven men sitting there in soggy boots. This, too, was the North.

Two

I WAS IN the kitchen, making seven berry pies. They were currant—dried currants, at that. I'd never done this much baking before, and I was up to my elbows in flour. There came an awful knock at the front door, as though someone were kicking instead of knocking. I walked into the living room and stood uncertainly looking at the door. The thumping continued.

"Who's there?" I asked. An extra kick was the only answer. I didn't know what to do. Uncle was out shooting, and I was alone in the house. "Who's there?" I asked again.

"Open the door—or I'll leave him on the porch!"

My first thought was that Uncle John had been hurt. I opened the door. A tall young man in a bright red jacket strode in. He carried a man on his back.

"Holy St. Patrick!" I cried. "Tell me quick, is he dead?"

The young man laughed and dumped his burden down on the couch. "Smell him," he said.

I did. The odor reminded me of John L. Sullivan, the fighter. He used to stay at our house. He had a watch with diamond shamrocks on the back, and every time he'd come in smelling like this, there'd be one less diamond shamrock on that watch.

"Who is it?" I asked.

"Johnny Flaherty."

So this was the missing Johnny. "Will you turn him over, please." I wanted a good look at him. He turned him, and I saw a little man with a big, shaggy mustache and a pale face with a yellow tinge to it.

"He needs some black coffee. You'd better be putting it on."

I whirled around. I was five feet, four and one-half inches, but I had to look up, way up. "I thank you kindly for bringing him back, and I'll thank you to be on your way again, for I'm taking no orders from an English soldier."

"An English soldier, am I? And what gave you that idea?" He frowned down at me, and he was very good-looking.

"With that red coat, you're either off to a fox hunt or you're a British peeler, or maybe you're both."

"You little chit—look at the size of you and you insulting the uniform!"

That made me mad. He could have noticed my naturally curly hair or my eyes, instead of my size.

"Well, if you're not an Englishman, who are you?"

"I'm Sergeant Mike Flannigan, of the Northwest Mounted."

I never could really have thought he was an Englishman, not with the lilt he had to his speech.

Johnny Flaherty moaned from the couch. I had almost forgotten him.

"Miss O'Fallon," the sergeant said patiently, "will you get the poor man some coffee?"

I decided to let this Irish cop know whom he was dealing with. Without a word I walked off into the kitchen. I heard Mike Flannigan singing in a good, and certainly big, baritone, something that went, "Heave ho, heave ho!" at the end of every line. I paid no attention but started the coffee. In a moment he came in with Johnny Flaherty on his back again.

"Whatever are you doing?"

Mike backed up to the pump and slid Johnny off his back, then whirled to catch him as he sagged limply on the floor. The sergeant braced him with a knee and a hand against the wall. With the other hand he pumped. "Got to sober him up before your uncle gets back."

The water came in a sudden stream. He pushed Johnny's head under it and continued pumping. For a moment there was no reaction except a feeble sputtering. Then suddenly Johnny let out a whoop and began thrashing wildly in all directions and using the same words John L. Sullivan used.

Flaherty's arms and legs flayed out at every angle. The only stationary part of him was his head, which Mike held relentlessly under the pump. Profanity and water ran down the dripping mustache into the drain. And all the time Mike soothed him in a low soft brogue.

"Shut your mouth, Johnny Flaherty, there's a lady present."

"To hell with her!" bubbled out from the pump.

Mike gave him a good ducking for that. But his words came all the more gently. "I'd be ashamed, Johnny Flaherty. Just as John was counting on you to help him welcome his only niece."

"To hell with him!" yelled Johnny, getting his head free of the pump for a second and glaring savagely around with water-clogged bloodshot eyes.

Under he went again. It was funny and sort of pathetic to see the little man squirming while the one big hand of Mike Flannigan held him under. Mike went on in a mild, reproachful voice, "So you've let him down, and now look at the sorry impression you're making on the young lady."

"To hell with you, you son of—" He didn't get to say it. A full minute passed. He began yelling something that sounded like, "I'm drowning!" But if he was, it didn't seem to disturb Mike. He went right on pumping and lecturing. "What have you to say for yourself, Johnny Flaherty? I suppose you'll be telling me next you were out celebrating?"

Johnny sputtered something that Mike took to be an answer.

"Don't tell me you were celebrating an honorable historical event like the Boer War by getting completely and disgustingly drunk?"

"That's what I was doing," said Johnny. "I was celebrating the war." His speech was no longer thick, and he didn't slur his syllables so much.

"Yes?" asked Mike, who still held him firmly by the collar. "And what's it an anniversary of, this time?"

"Mafeking," Johnny said. "The Battle of Mafeking."

"Uh-uh," Mike said. "You celebrated that last time, only six weeks ago. How many times a year does a date come around?" And he began pumping again.

Johnny watched him. "Kimberley," he said desperately. "It was the glorious Battle of Kimberley."

Mike laughed. "I sometimes wonder if you were really there at all. Kimberley was fought in February. What month is this?" His pump hand started working, "What month is this?" he repeated evenly.

"Isn't it February?" Johnny asked. "That's right," he screamed, with his head halfway to the pump. "It's April! Must've got mixed up for a moment."

"You must have," Mike said, and then, in his most beguiling tone, "What did you say you were celebrating, Johnny?"

"The victory of Magersfontein," Johnny said, and they both started laughing. I remembered vaguely from history class that Magersfontein had been a Dutch victory. Johnny grabbed a towel and started rubbing his head and face, and then wound the towel around his neck.

He turned to me and gave me a sheepish grin. "I feel rotten, Miss Katherine. Besides which, your uncle's going to be like the black Satan for the next few days. I hope you can bring yourself to overlook the disgusting spectacle I've made of myself, and not be too hard on me."

"She shouldn't forgive you, you old toper, and that's a fact."

"Keep out of this, Sergeant," snapped Johnny, without taking his worried, red-veined eyes off me.

"Mr. Flaherty," I said, "I'm sorry to learn you're a drinking man. My mother always said it was the curse of the Irish, but if you like your coffee as strong as your drink, it's ready for you."

He seized the cup avidly in his hands. "And God bless you for this and for your forgivin' ways. It's an angel, in truth, has come to live with us." He drank the coffee down without taking breath. "I'll have a second cup, Miss, and then I'll go to bed."

Johnny drank down his second cup, as he had his first. The front door slammed. "It's your uncle!" Johnny was terrified. "I'm in bed! Tell him I came home peaceful and went straight to bed." And Johnny was out the one door before Uncle John was in the other.

Uncle walked right up to Mike Flannigan and shook him by the hand. "It's good to see you, Mike. What brings you into our part of the country?"

"Well, John, rumor has it that a young lady has been seen in these parts, and I thought I'd better check on it." He laughed and flashed his eyes at me to see how I was taking that.

"He came to bring Johnny home," I said.

Uncle stopped laughing and his mouth clamped into a line. "Johnny home?" he asked.

"Yeah," Mike said, but he didn't seem to want to say anything more than that.

"Come home walking?"

"Sure," Mike said.

"Sergeant Flannigan," I began, "you know very well—"

"I'm not saying he didn't need a little assistance," Mike put in, and looked at me in a way that made me know I'd better shut up. I did.

But Uncle John was mad. Plenty mad. He didn't say anything. Just walked into the room he shared with Johnny. We could hear them in there going at it. Uncle John would start quiet and end shouting, and then Johnny would shout too, so that neither one could hear what the other was saying. And that was probably just as well.

I was embarrassed that Sergeant Mike had to be here to hear it. But he seemed to be enjoying it. Every time there was an extra loud "God damn" or "bastard," he'd throw back his head and laugh.

I went on preparing the dinner and setting the table and pretending I didn't know what those words meant, although I did from John L. Sullivan. I was getting madder and madder at Mike Flannigan, so mad that I put two sets of spoons on the table and no forks. He noticed when I took off the extra spoons and laughed harder.

I stopped squarely in front of him. "What do you find so amusing, Sergeant?"

"A young lady like yourself in Alberta Territory."

I didn't know what he meant by that, so I looked at him sharply as though I did know. "Will you please tell my uncle that dinner is ready?"

"What about the hands?"

"They've eaten, all ten of them." I must have sounded tired, for he went for Uncle right away.

They came back, Uncle John not saying much. I didn't say much either because I was mad, and Mike didn't say much, because he was eating. After a while, when I'd stood it as long as I could, I asked my uncle, in a very polite voice, if he'd care for more potatoes. He put down his fork. "Katherine Mary," he said, "I think you're not too favorably impressed with my friend Johnny Flaherty?"

"I'm not," I said.

"Well," my uncle said, "he takes a lot of putting up with, but it's worth it to have the best cook in the Northwest."

I remembered the mud on Johnny's clothes and hands, and his face going from green to purple under the pump. "He can cook," I said, "but it's a question in my mind if I'd care to eat it."

The men smiled. "You're a very fine cook, yourself," said Sergeant Mike, though I noticed he hadn't touched the currant pie. "But all the women in the world and their grandmothers couldn't cook the way Johnny Flaherty does. Why, he learned the trade from the fiends themselves, the way they cook the sinners in the volcanoes."

They both laughed, but I turned to my Uncle John and said, "It's funny now, but a few moments ago you weren't laughing, Uncle John. You were telling Johnny Flaherty to go to—to where he learned to cook." I wound up blushing, because Mike's eyes were on me.

"True," my uncle nodded.

"And how often does Mr. Flaherty celebrate?" I continued.

My uncle sighed. "Ah, there never was a war like the Boer War. A battle nearly every day, and all critical."

"And you get mad every time they bring him home?"

My uncle nodded soberly, but Mike was roaring at some joke I didn't see. His laughing made me angry. "Then why do you put up with it at all?"

My uncle took a bite of currant pie. A strange look came into his eyes, and he laid the fork down.

"Hmmm," he said. What he meant by that I don't know, only he ate no more pie.

"If it was me," I muttered to myself, "I wouldn't let him come back."

"Kathy," said my uncle, "do you know what a flapjack is?"

"It's a pancake," I answered with some contempt, "made with eggs and flour, nothing very special."

"Tell her about Johnny's flapjacks," Uncle John said to Mike.

"My mouth waters and tears come into my eyes to think of it," said Mike solemnly, while my uncle listened with a very pleased expression on his face. "It is a pancake to make the deaf and dumb speak and the Irish women, God bless them, to eat and be silent. Johnny's cakes are as rich and fine as the food of the saints, and so light that when you throw 'em in the air they stay there. I wish I had a dozen now."

"You may think he's exaggerating about Johnny's cooking," my uncle said, "but I'll tell you a story to prove it. Johnny and I were buddies in the Boer War. He's a little man now, and he was a little man then, and not a hair on his face but that mustache like a kind of cord to hang him up by.

"We were out on patrol, and a Dutch column, horses and wagons, came down the road and cut us off. So we lay down behind a boulder in the field and put mud on our backs and lay still as stones, which in truth is what we seemed to be at fifty yards. Our heads and arms were up close to the boulder and pretty well hidden from the road, so after a while Johnny says, 'Are you hungry?' I snorted. 'And so what?' I asked. Johnny pointed to a flat stone at the edge of the boulder. The sun had been beating down on this stone all morning, and it was hot. 'We'll make it hotter,' says Johnny, taking out the captain's field glasses, which we had, being on patrol.

" 'What are you thinking of, Johnny?' I asked.

" 'Flapjacks,' says Johnny.

" 'You are mad with the heat, Flaherty,' I say. 'Let's eat our condensed rations.'

" 'Condensed rations!' says Johnny, and spits.

"He was right, so I spat too, being careful not to move the mud on my back and legs. On the road they were pulling field pieces past, and Johnny and I kept count.

" 'Of course,' says Johnny, 'this is not the five-burner stove me mother had in Ireland, and it will not accommodate large pancakes. But I will roll them thin.' So he reaches into his knapsack.

"You understand, Katherine Mary, it was the patient work of a half hour to move his hand to his knapsack. But out come dried eggs and pancake flour and condensed milk. Well, he mixed the batter in the palm of his hand, which added to the flavor, I'm thinking, and he rolled it out thin with his forefinger, and cooked it on the hot stone with the captain's lens. And they came out flapjacks no bigger than a shilling, but tasting like manna from heaven. And all this time we moved nothing but our hands and our mouths. Our hands very slowly and our mouths very fast.

"It got dark and we started to make our way back, but there was a sniper waiting for us in a tree. The first we knew of him, there was a shot, and we both rolled into the ditch. It was not exactly a ditch, but a damp stream bed, wet and dirty.

" 'Did you see where it came from?' says Johnny.

" 'No.' I had not. Neither had he.

" 'Then we stay here to eternity,' says Johnny, 'because he knows where *we* are.'

"I looked at Johnny and said, 'It is not the fate of a Kennedy to spend the rest of his life with his face in the mud. I'll stand up and draw his fire, and you kill him.'

" 'A very good plan,' says Johnny approvingly, 'but it is I who will stand up. I am a smaller man, and there are not so many places to kill me.'

" 'That may well be,' I replied, 'but as it was my idea, it is my right to try it.'

" 'Like a Kennedy to hog all the glory,' Johnny snickers. 'You invented the plan, I will carry it out.'

"I began to be worried. I saw the prospect of a long, lonely hike back to camp, with nothing to eat but condensed rations. 'Johnny,' I said, 'if he kills you, there will be no one left to make the pancakes. And your pancakes are my only satisfaction in this hot and dirty land ten thousand miles from Ireland.'

" 'And much good it will do me to make pancakes,' says Johnny bitterly, 'if you are too dead to eat them.'

"So the argument continued, and finally we threw dice to decide it. But they were Johnny's dice, and he could make them come out thirteen if the mood was in him, so it was no surprise to see that he won and stood up and was shot in the shoulder before I brought the Dutchman down.

" 'Are you all right, Johnny?' I yelled.

" 'My left arm,' he says holding it.

" 'Praise be to the Mother of God,' I said, 'it's not your flapjack arm,' and we got up out of the ditch."

My uncle pushed back his chair, and so did Mike. "Wait till you eat them," he said. The men stood up.

I was getting used to my uncle's stories. I soon learned that when it came to spinning a yarn or telling a tale, he had a touch of the genius of Denny Lannon the storyteller, whose grandnephew he is. And I suppose the reason he was so sparing with words in between times is that he was saving them up for his next story.

"Well," said Mike, "when are you going to teach Kathy to shoot?"

"You mean go hunting?" I couldn't believe it.

"Johnny bought her a twenty-two in town," Uncle said.

"You won't be needing any ammunition," Mike said, and grinned at me.

"Why not?" I asked.

"Well, you can use the currants in those seven currant pies you baked."

Was there really something wrong with the pies? I'd been saving mine for later because I was full. But I walked to the table and took a big bite to show him. It was as if I had pebbles in my mouth. I wondered what was wrong. But I wasn't going to ask them because they were laughing at me and because my mouth was too full of that currant rock pile to talk. To spit them out would be defeat, so I made a fake gulp and tried to hold my mouth naturally as if I had swallowed them.

Mike said good-bye. I didn't answer because I couldn't. He took my hand and leaned toward me till my hair brushed his cheek.

"Spit 'em out," he said softly, "and next time, cook 'em."

I DID NO more cooking for a while. Johnny was back on the job, and he would only let me in the kitchen to sniff. But I made him promise to let me get the dinner if ever Sergeant Mike Flannigan returned.

Oh, it was a fine revenge I was preparing for him! I would make currant pies with currants so soft and juicy they would melt in the mouths of the men, but his I would fill with buckshot. And while the others ate and enjoyed, he would break his jaws. Then I would say, not to him but to the walls, "It is weak teeth these redcoats have."

Or maybe he'd come knocking at the door in the middle of a storm, with mud all over that fine uniform, and a slow step, and weariness in his eyes (for he had ridden night and day without rest), and bleeding from a wound in the shoulder, where a crazy 'breed had shot him. I'd help him in and take off his boots, and give him hot tea and whisky, and get him into his bunk. He'd say, "Thank you." I'd say, "Oh, I'm just a little chit." And I'd laugh carelessly to show it didn't make a penny's difference to me, one way or another.

Sometimes I brought him home with a bullet in his shoulder and sometimes limping from frostbitten feet. But today his leg was broken where a horse fell on him. He was leaning on me and I was helping him to the couch, when a girl rode up on a pony and banged on the door.

I opened it, and she strode in, tall and blonde and swift-moving. She was the first white girl I'd seen since Calgary.

"I'm Mildred MacDonald," she said. "And you're Katherine Mary. You're very pretty. You don't resemble your uncle John at all. I would have come over earlier, but I was in Calgary. Do you like it here? Have you seen Johnny Flaherty? Can you ride?"

I said, "Yes," meaning I could ride. As for the other questions, I'd lost track.

I guess she'd lost track too, for she snapped back, "Then let's go. That's my pony outside. Name's Squaw."

"I'll go get Rosie," I said. "It'll just take a minute."

Mildred went into the kitchen to talk to Johnny, and I went to the stable to saddle Rosie.

Rosie was a red-and-white Indian cayuse, and Uncle John had told me Rosie was mine for as long as I stayed with him. But he hadn't told Rosie. She was more trouble than a bag of wildcats. Some days she acted as if she had swallowed a pint of pepper. She dashed here and there, trotted and galloped and jumped ditches, whether I wanted to or not. The next day she would mope. A slow walk was her fancy now, a slow walk that grew tireder and tireder and at last stopped altogether. If I kicked her, she'd go into a bumpy jog, two steps walking and two steps trot, and the moment my attention wandered, Rosie stopped.

Hard as it was to ride Rosie, it was harder to saddle her. I threw a blanket and saddle on her back. That was easy. But the moment I threaded the end of the cinch strap through the rings, Rosie's eyes met mine, her nostrils twitched, she sucked in an enormous breath, and her stomach swelled up like a sausage balloon. Pull as I would, I could barely fasten the strap. I mounted her, out came her breath, the saddle slithered around, and the blanket worked loose. I'll be lucky, I thought, if a stirrup doesn't come off.

It was this, I think, that lost me the race. It's a hard thing to race a horse when you're running a private race yourself to stay on her back. Rosie was faster than Mildred's Squaw, but more independent. And when Rosie zigzagged, it was all I could do to make me and the saddle zig and zag with her.

If only Rosie had let me saddle her right, and had run fairly straight, and not stopped once to take a quick bite out of a shrub, I could have won the race long before my pleurisy got me. As it was, Mildred was sailing ahead on Squaw when my pleurisy stabbed my side and chest with long twisting pains.

Mildred caught Squaw up short and wheeled her around. They came galloping back. She reined the pony in. "What's the matter, Katherine Mary, don't you feel good?"

"I'm all right," I said. "I'm just not used to riding. I bounce all over." I slid off Rosie's back. I felt shaky, and the pains were still in my chest.

"Put the reins forward over her nose." Mildred got off Squaw. "They think they're tied then and won't bolt for it."

"Will they just graze here?"

Mildred nodded. She was still breathless from the chase. I sat down with a rock to lean against. The meadow and the sky were fuzzy, as if they were made out of cloth, and they leaned at a queer angle. I closed my eyes, and when I looked again, the meadow was level and the sky was where it ought to be.

Mildred flopped down beside me. "That was fun. I love to ride. So does Dick." She stopped, looked at me, and laughed.

"Who's Dick?" I asked, because I saw I was supposed to.

"Dick is Richard Carlton. He's a lawyer with brown eyes that I'm going to marry."

"Are you really going to get married?" She seemed more wonderful to me now than ever.

"He lives in Calgary, and we've been engaged for three weeks."

"How do you have to feel about someone, to marry him? I mean, do you think about him all the time and try to remember how he looks and what he's said . . . ?" I stopped. Mildred was looking at me in a strange way.

"Are *you* in love?" she asked.

I felt my cheeks getting hot. "Of course I'm not in love. Why, I don't even know what it feels like. That's why I asked you."

"Well, you gave a pretty good description of it."

"I just thought you'd have to feel something like that if you were going to marry someone." I felt I was stumbling around so I quit talking and watched Rosie and Squaw munch grass, then amble slowly, still chewing, to a more tempting spot, pull up and digest the most tender of the young blades.

"Dick has his practice in Calgary," Mildred went on. "I was in last week with Mother, and he took us to lunch. Dick knows your uncle John."

"Does he know a lot of people?"

"Oh, Dick knows everybody."

"Well," I hesitated, "does he know Sergeant Michael Flannigan?" There, it was out and said. Mildred didn't seem surprised. It was just conversation.

"Of course he knows Mike. So do I, so does everybody in Alberta, I guess. In fact, Mike and I had a long talk about you in Calgary."

"Oh!" I tried to seem casual. "What does he do in Calgary?"

"He's on some sort of detail work. Anyway, he said I was going to have a girl friend, a very pretty one, at that."

"Oh, he didn't! He thinks I'm skinny."

"I'm just telling you what he said, Katherine Mary."

"Well, he thinks I'm skinny too, because he called me a little chit. As a matter of fact . . ." I pulled two wide grass blades, placed them together and tried to whistle through them, but it didn't work.

"As a matter of fact, what?" Mildred asked.

"Oh, nothing. I was just going to say I don't think much of Mike Flannigan."

"Why not?"

I considered. "Well, for one thing, he's too cocky."

"And he's a big brute of a man too."

"Oh, I like a man to be big." Then I saw she was teasing me. "Mildred," I said, "don't you ever tell him I said that."

She smiled. "I won't, Kathy. Why, I'd bite my tongue off before I'd repeat a thing like that to Mike Flannigan or any other man. They're conceited enough as it is." She squeezed my hand. "But you do like him a little, don't you?"

I thought about that for a while. "Well, I like some things about him."

"What things?"

"His eyes."

"They are nice," she agreed.

"Mildred, they're so blue you could swim in them."

Three

WE WERE IN the kitchen. Johnny had shot a deer and was skinning it. It was bloody and messy, and I tried not to look. Johnny tossed a piece of fur at Juno, who dragged it into a corner and worried and fought it.

The other men would go off on long hunts, be gone all day. But not Johnny. He'd go out to the ravine about a mile behind the house and just sit there until a deer came by, and then shoot it. He was telling me that moose meat was better, that it tasted like beef, and that next time he'd bring down a moose.

"Especially the nose; great delicacy, the nose."

"I don't think I'd like to eat anything's nose," I said.

"Yes, you would. You'd like moose nose. An Indian dish, great delicacy. Another favorite with the Indians is bear paw. They bring in beautiful bear skins to the Hudson's Bay Company, but all the paws are cut off. Could get a lot more for their skins if they wouldn't mutilate them—but they'd rather take less and eat bear paws." He took the carcass outdoors. Juno and I followed him and watched with great interest as he tied it in a tree.

"Keep the flies from it."

"Don't they fly as high as that tree?" I asked.

But Johnny was more interested in food than in flies. "Tell you something else that's a great delicacy, that's beaver tail. Yes, sir, that tail is real sweet. On the other hand, a porcupine tastes terrible."

I followed Johnny back into the kitchen.

"Ever make a mulligan stew?" he asked.

I had to admit I hadn't. "What do you put in them?"

"Everything. You can watch me." He took pride in his cooking, just as any artist would, and it was a treat to watch him. He let me collect the vegetables for him while he cut up the meat. Everything in one pot. That was the principle, Johnny explained. I watched enthralled as caribou, grouse, pork, rice, potatoes, dehydrated corn, canned tomatoes, macaroni, and celery followed each other into the pot. Johnny laughed.

"The more the better. Everything flavors everything else in a real mulligan." Johnny stopped talking to stir. Soon the smell of it was in the air, and the look on Johnny's face was one of reverence.

"What about the deer in the tree? Is it going to be a mulligan too?"

"No, it's going to be pemmican."

"What's that?"

"Just dried moose or deer meat."

"I haven't seen Mildred for ten days." I said "Mildred" but I was thinking "Mike" and there must have been something in my voice because he stopped stirring and looked at me.

"Is a moose like a deer, only bigger," I asked quickly, "with bigger antlers?" That wouldn't have fooled a woman, but it fooled Johnny. He was right back on moose.

"They're not the same thing at all, different animals. Take a moose, now. It will never gallop like a deer. Just swings along at a sort of pacing trot. But it can outdistance the fastest horse going."

Had Mike gone back to the country he'd come from without stopping to see my Uncle John? Or was he still on duty in Calgary? Would he be coming by the ranch again? I suddenly realized that Johnny had stopped talking. The last word I'd heard had been "moose," so with a great deal of interest in my voice, and none at all in me, I asked, "Is a moose a clever animal?" It sounded like a stupid thing to say, even to me, but it was enough for Johnny to be off again.

"Well, now, clever—it's hard to say. It's got poor sight. But it's clever enough when it comes to smelling or hearing." He interrupted himself to put a spoonful of mulligan in his mouth. With his cooking and eating and eating and cooking, it's a wonder to me so much ever came to the table.

I began to think of the time that I had cooked and Mike had eaten. But it was hard to think around Johnny when he was telling stories, and he was telling one now.

"It was a blizzard storm I was out in. Mighty trees such as fir and spruce crashing down and branches breaking off and flung by the wind great distances. It was in such weather and on such a day that I was stalking a giant moose with an antler spread of fifty to sixty inches. Now, mind, he was over a hundred yards from me at the time, and all around were the trees and the branches crashing to the earth. And here I was sneaking up on him, trying to get my sights on him. But there was too much brush between us, and he was taking cover in it, not because he suspected I was around, but because that's their instinct. Well, I was moving gently as I could through that gale—but didn't my foot step on a twig and snap it! Well, it was a little twig, and mighty trees were splitting and falling, but the big fellow heard that twig and he let out a 'bell' and was out of sight before I could get my gun to my shoulder. That's a true example of their powers of hearing."

I guess it was true, all right, and a little more than true. But that's the way Johnny tells things.

"Help me dish out the mulligan." And Johnny reached down three bowls.

"There's only two of us." I started to put back the third bowl, but he stopped me.

"Mildred's here," he said.

"What!" I ran to the window. She was tying Squaw to the porch. I turned and looked at Johnny. He was grinning.

"Heard the pony," he said. "Our men would've come in all together."

"Johnny, you've got hearing like a moose."

Mildred came in and ate mulligan stew with us. It was wonderful because, as I said before, Johnny was an artist. He would no more let anyone drop a vegetable in his stew than Michelangelo would have let a student sculp the finger of one of his statues. No, you could not help Johnny cook. About dishwashing he wasn't so much of an artist. He let Mildred and me help him. And then pretty soon he was off altogether.

We were glad to have the kitchen to ourselves. Up to then we'd just been skirting around things and giggling when we got too close to the important ones, as when Mildred said, "Done any more swimming, Katherine?"

Johnny said, "What do you mean—any more? There ain't no place to swim around here."

We both laughed, and Johnny looked kind of disgusted, and that's when he said he had chores.

Mildred was just waiting for me to ask her something, and I wouldn't. Finally she had to say it herself. "I was in Calgary again to see Dick."

"How is he?"

"Who? Dick?"

I thought that was mean of her. "Of course, Dick. Isn't that who you were talking about?"

Mildred smiled. "Oh; he's fine; in fact, he's wonderful. Mother and I shopped in town all day for my trousseau. And then in the evening Dick took me dancing. Oh, it was fun!"

It sounded like fun. I imagined myself shopping with Mother and picking out a beautiful filmy white gown because Mike and I were going to be married. And then in the evening Mike took me dancing.

"You're so quiet," Mildred said. "What are you thinking about?"

I realized I'd been drying that bowl for an awfully long time. "Nothing. Just about what a good time you must have had."

"Oh, and guess who we saw?"

My lips formed the word "who," but I don't think I ever got it out.

"Ted Russell. Oh, that's right, you don't know Ted, do you? Mike Flannigan was there too."

"Where?"

"At the dance."

Words, just plain words, strung together in a sentence can slash to pieces the make-believe and the dreams. They cut into mine. The black wavy hair and the tall red coat were the same. But those eyes, those blue eyes that had been smiling at me, smiled now at someone else.

"What was she like?" I must have asked out loud because Mildred answered, "What was who like?"

But now I didn't want to know. What did it matter whether she was tall or short, thin or fat? I wasn't she, and never would be. It would be this girl I didn't know, but who was much prettier than I, who would bandage Mike when he came in wounded. It was she, this girl who maybe had wavy black hair and blue eyes too, who would cook surprises for him, who—

"Katherine Mary, who were you talking about?"

"Nobody," I said and threw a shower of knives and forks into the drawer. "Let's go out on the porch." I thought this would change the subject, but I was wrong.

We were out there and sitting on the swing when she asked it again. "I know you were talking about somebody. Now who was it?"

"I was just wondering about the dance, and what you wore and what Mike's girl wore."

"Mike's girl?" She gave me a blank look.

"Well, you said he was there, didn't you?"

"But he didn't bring anybody. He just called the dances. Why, he didn't dance once."

Words, it was just words again. Or maybe it was in myself. I had made the unhappiness, and now I made the glad feeling that was all through me. I thought about it for a while. Words that I could spell, and a few that I couldn't, were back of all feelings that anyone in the world had ever felt.

"Mike asked about you." These words were so wonderful that they bounced me right up in the sky.

"He did?"

"Yes, he thinks you're awfully pretty."

"He does? Did he say so?"

"Well, he didn't say it exactly like that. He said he'd never seen such a head of hair on any female."

I was a little disappointed.

"But, Mildred, that doesn't mean he thinks I'm pretty. That just means—well, that I've got a lot of hair. And anyway 'female' isn't a very nice word."

"What's wrong with it?"

"I guess there's nothing wrong with it. It just sounds like animals, that's all."

Mildred laughed. "You should be glad 'cause that shows he doesn't go around saying nice things about all the girls. 'Cause if he did, he'd know how better." I thought that was a very fine bit of reasoning and my affection for Mildred increased considerably.

"He said something else, too."

"What?"

"He said your eyes were as gray as the breast of a dove."

That was poetry, and it thrilled me. "Did he really, Mildred?"

Mildred hesitated. "Well, he said gray as a whisky-jack."

"A what?"

She looked at me helplessly. "A whisky-jack; it's a bird too."

"But not a dove?"

She admitted that it wasn't a dove, but a thief and a scavenger.

"Wherever did it get such a name as whisky-jack?" I asked.

"It's the kind of call they have. It sounds like they're asking for whisky."

Well, I didn't know whether I liked Mike's compliments or not. Of course, you had to take into consideration that he was a woodsman, and it would be natural for him to compare a girl with things he knew. He'd probably never seen a dove, and a whisky-jack he saw every day. Even so, working hard at it, I couldn't make myself like it. Then, suddenly a terrifying thought struck me, and I looked at Mildred. Why had he mentioned my eyes, the color of my eyes, unless . . .

"Mildred, you didn't tell him?"

"Tell him what?" She asked it right out, as if she had nothing to hide. But now the suspicion had entered me, I could not be sure. "You know, what I said about his eyes being so blue you could swim in them."

Mildred looked hurt. "Why, Katherine Mary, you know I'd never breathe a word. Why, I'd bite my tongue off first."

The way she said it made me feel very ashamed and unworthy of her friendship. But still I couldn't help thinking it was funny he'd said anything about my eyes.

Mildred stayed all night. I was supposed to ride her back in the morning, but we slept pretty late. And then Johnny took his gun and went toward the ravine. It was a perfect chance. We decided to make apple pies. I knew how to do that. Mother had taught me. I intended to make twelve of them all at once. I figured I'd have to, with that many men eating them.

"We've got a case of apples, Mildred. How many do you think are in a case?"

"About thirty pounds," Mildred said.

I looked inside and held up a very wrinkled-looking object.

"Is this an apple?" I asked Mildred.

"Of course. It's a dried apple."

I'd never used dried apples before, but I proceeded as if they had been regular apples like the ones Mother bought in Boston. I put the thirty pounds of apples into the washtub in relays and soaked them. Then I put them on to boil.

"Haven't you got an awful lot of apples there?" Mildred asked as she watched me fill container after container with apples and set them on the stove.

"Don't forget I'm feeding twelve men," I said, and that shut her up.

I was sorry I had snapped at her, and I said, "I suppose you're a good cook yourself, Mildred."

"I've cooked for Dick lots of times when he was up at our ranch. I think that's one of the reasons he proposed to me." She laughed, and then stopped all at once. There were tears in her eyes. "Oh, Kathy, I don't know when we'll be married."

"Why?" I asked, slipping my arm around her. "What's the matter?"

"Oh, nothing. It's just that—well, it's harder to marry a lawyer than a Mounty."

"What's so hard about it?"

"A Mounty can't marry till he's been in the service five years. And a lawyer can't marry till he can feed a wife. At least that's what Dick says. And it's hard to get started."

"It's always hard when you're young," I said, and I said other things that we had both heard people say. They seemed to comfort her. Not the words, but that she knew I was sorry about her and Dick, and that I wished they could get married right away.

Mildred snatched off her apron. "Come on," she said. "That's enough. You can ride me home now."

We raced each other over the low meadowland, and that seemed to restore her spirits. But I kept thinking about something she had said—that a Mounty had to be on the force five years before he could marry. I wondered how long Mike had served.

I didn't stay at the MacDonald ranch because of the boiling apples. On the ride back I just let Rosie lope along. I only pulled at the reins when she stopped to eat grass, which she did as often as she thought she could get away with it. Suddenly I jerked her up so hard and short she rolled her eyes and flicked her ears at me. I hadn't meant to, but coming over the hill to the north of me was another rider.

In such wild and open country you rarely meet anyone, but it wasn't that that made me pull at Rosie. It was that even at that distance I could see that the rider was tall, and that he was dressed in red. I told Rosie that there were other Mounties in the world, and it probably wasn't Mike at all. But I didn't believe myself, and my heart pounded fast and made more noise than Rosie's hoofs.

He was close enough now for me to see it was a uniform—red jacket, dark blue riding breeches with a yellow stripe, long brown boots, spurs, holster, beaver cap on top of black waving hair, and blue eyes, the bluest I had ever seen.

I looked up into them and kept on looking. No words came to my head. The way I'd planned it, I was going to bandage him or feed him, but here in the hills, I couldn't do either. So I smiled the smile I'd practiced in the mirror.

"How do you do, Sergeant Flannigan?"

"Get off your horse," he said. That was certainly not the way to greet a young woman you hadn't seen in three weeks. I gave him what I hoped was an icy look and dug my heels into Rosie, who shot off.

Mike wheeled his horse and took after me. It was a short race because he rode that big black horse of his right in front of Rosie. She stopped short; I went pitching forward and, would have fallen if

Mike hadn't reached out and grabbed me and set me back in the saddle.

He dismounted. "Get down," he said.

I sat there with my lips pressed hard together, thinking things I could only have said if I'd been Johnny or John L. Sullivan.

Sergeant Mike reached up, put his two hands around my waist, and lifted me down. For just a minute I was standing awfully close to him, and for that minute I couldn't do anything.

But I pulled away. "Mike Flannigan," I said, "you're not to push me around and pull me off horses. I'll tell my uncle, and he and Johnny and the ten hands will ride you down and even if you are a Mounty, they'll hog-tie you and—" I had started out in a low, frigid voice, but by now I was yelling, and he stood there and watched me, slightly amused, as if I was putting on a show for him.

"Katherine Mary, you're the hardest girl in the world to do anything for."

I looked at him a little uncertainly. "What did you want to do for me?"

"I want to teach you to manage a horse."

There he was telling me again.

"I know how to manage my horse."

Mike laughed. "If you could have seen yourself bouncing all over, like a jack-in-the-box, you wouldn't think so."

"Mildred says I ride very well."

"You would if you'd tighten your cinch."

"But Rosie—" I changed my mind. I wasn't going to give him the satisfaction of showing me or telling me anything more.

"But Rosie blows out her stomach when you go to pull it tight. Is that it?"

"How'd you . . . ?" Then I saw the grin on his face. "Yes, that's it."

"Well, look. Here's what you've got to do." He undid Rosie's cinch and held it ready to tighten. Rosie took her usual big breath, blowing out her belly till it looked like a barrel. When she had it completely extended, Mike cracked her across the back with the flat of his hand. Rosie was so surprised she gave a sort of gasp, and all the breath went out of her. Her sides deflated like a punctured balloon, and in that moment the cinch was pulled in and tightened.

"There," said Mike. "Now you do it."

I tried to, but the first time I didn't hit hard enough, and the second time I forgot to pull the cinch, but finally I got it.

"Did I do it right?" I asked, knowing very well I had but wanting a little praise out of him.

"Now, another thing," said Mike. "You're riding English on a western saddle. You've got to let out those stirrups." He fiddled around with them and slipped them in a lower notch. "Try that," and he handed me up.

"How is it? Comfortable?"

I had decided to say it was all wrong, but he asked me so eagerly that I had to let him be right. "Yes, it's much better."

He looked at me and smiled, not that teasing grin, but a sweet, gentle, kind smile.

We looked at each other for a few minutes. Then I began to realize neither one of us was talking. And that he was looking at me in a queer way. Of course, the sun was in his eyes, and it might have been that.

"It's a lovely day," I said, "but warm." And before he could answer, I let out a cry that startled all of us, including Rosie, who started off like a mad thing. I kept her going, too, urging her ahead.

Mike never did catch up to me. He had to catch his horse first; it had bolted when I shrieked. He kept shouting questions, but at the speed Rosie was going there wasn't enough breath in my body to answer him. Besides, how could a man understand what it is when you've left your apples boiling too long!

I pulled up in front of the house and jumped down. The dried apples met me at the door. They had boiled up and over. The floor was covered with the messy things. I stood aghast, looking and not knowing where to begin.

Mike came up behind me and looked too. He didn't say anything, just took off his coat, rolled up his sleeves, and went to work. We filled a washtub and a bucket with puffed dried apples. I was embarrassed that a thing like this had to happen when Mike was here. But it was funny, and I couldn't help laughing. Mike laughed too when he saw me laughing. I guess he didn't dare laugh before, for fear of hurting my feelings.

He reached for the last apple, but it slipped out of his hand almost at my feet. I stopped to get it just as he did, and we bumped heads with an impact that sent us both sprawling. We really laughed then. We laughed so hard we couldn't get up. Uncle John and Juno must have heard us because they came in to see what was going on. There we were, Mike and I, lying on the floor and roaring. Uncle looked down at us, and we looked up at Uncle. It was a long way up Uncle John's six-foot-three of height, and by the time you reached his face you were at a psychological disadvantage. I suppose Mike thought so too, because he got to his feet.

"Hello, John." He said it a little breathlessly, but with one of his most ingratiating grins, which Uncle John did not return.

"Katherine Mary," my uncle said, "you will please get up from the floor."

Mike came forward to give me a hand, but Uncle stepped in front of him and helped me up himself.

Mike looked upset. "We were just—er—picking apples." He waved toward the linoleum and repeated the word "apples." Uncle John looked at the linoleum too. But all the apples were picked up, all but the one we had fallen down over, and Juno must have eaten that because there wasn't an apple in sight. Uncle, Mike, and I stared at the blue and gray linoleum.

"We were picking apples," Mike repeated stubbornly.

"Hmmm," Uncle said.

And that was all he said until dinner, when he told Johnny that in *his* day they picked apples from trees.

MIKE WAS BACK in a few days. He stood in the doorway holding out a present.

"You didn't need to bring me anything," I said, but was very excited that he had, so excited that I couldn't get the string untied.

"Here"—he took it out of my hands—"I'll do it." He snapped the cord and handed the package back to me. I opened it, looked at Mike, looked at it, and looked at Mike again.

"Well, put them on," he said.

I lifted out a pair of heavy mackinaw pants. "But they're men's," I protested.

"Put them on. I'm not taking you hiking in *that.*" And he pointed scornfully at my blue polka-dot dress.

"Are you taking me hiking?"

"Yes. Hurry up and change." I grabbed up the trousers and started for the bedroom. Then I remembered. After all, they were a present.

"Thank you very much," I said. "They're lovely."

Mike grinned. "Put 'em on."

We tramped along a stream, past the foothills and up into the mountainous country. I liked the way Mike walked. I liked the freedom in his body. I kept up with him too because he had just said that he hated to walk with women who minced along. Mike led the way up the path. For a while I watched the tops of the tall silver trees, but I stumbled, and then I watched the ground. It was dappled with moving dark shadows of leaves and with bright sunny patches. It was a strange day. The air would be very quiet, and then up ahead you would see a fluttering of the leaves. A moment later the little gust of air would pass you, and it would be still again.

We entered the gorge of a mountain stream. The sides loomed steeper and steeper. Rock ledges shot up to meet perpendicular cliffs. A sharp black shadow shrouded our path. The sun and sky disappeared and leaning out over us at a crazy angle was a giant gray bluff.

Mike looked back over his shoulder. "Notice the sheer rock faces. See how one juts out above the other. I think the Indians must get their patterns for blankets and baskets from the design in these rocks."

I was glad, though, when the cliff didn't hang over us, but slanted back the way it was supposed to and let us have the sun again.

"Thirsty?" Mike asked.

"Yes."

He flopped down on his stomach on a low flat rock and, reaching into the stream, cupped water into his hand and drank. I lay down on my stomach too and cupped my hands and filled them with water, but the water dripped through my fingers, and by the time I got my hand to my mouth all I could do was to lick a slightly wet palm.

Mike laughed. "I guess you'll have to get your face down in it. Inch forward a little so you can reach it."

I looked at the frothy swirling water. "I'll fall in."

"No, you won't."

"My hair will get wet."

"I'll hold it." He caught back my hair, and I got a very good drink. I stood up laughing and blinking water out of my eyes. Mike opened his hands slowly, and my hair fell back around my shoulders.

"Is your hair red?"

"It's auburn," I said and tossed my head a little so he could see the lights that auburn hair has.

He turned away. "Come on."

I followed him back to the trail. He'd thought my hair was pretty; I knew he had. Why wouldn't he tell me?

We passed a tiny tree growing out of a solid mass of rock. "Look, Mike."

Mike slowed down and looked. "It's got guts," he said. "In another twenty years it will be a spruce."

We walked on again, and I swung my arms like Mike. Up ahead he stopped and held a brier that would have snapped back and struck me in the face. He watched me as I came up to him and ducked under the branch.

"You walk like a boy," he said. I knew that was meant as a compliment, the first compliment that Mike had ever paid me. I was glad now that I had strained every muscle to keep up with those long legs of his. But after a moment I had to lean against a rock to catch my breath.

"I wonder what makes a mountain?"

"Upheavals in the earth, but it's the water that cuts the levels and ravines and determines the character of the mountain."

I loved to hear Mike talk. He put himself in the place of whatever he told about. When he told about mountains, he was the mountain talking. I glanced up at him. He was shading his eyes and looking upstream. There'd been something on my mind, and for days I'd been thinking of ways to ask it. Finally I decided the best way was to ask it straight out. Then it would seem to be a question like any other, or at most a desire to make conversation. So I said it.

"Mike!" He turned and looked at me. "How long have you been a Mounty?"

"Since I was a kid. Let's see, it's been about seven years." He looked at me with a question in his eyes.

"I was just thinking," I said hastily, "that that's why you know about mountains and what makes them, and things like that."

"Well, when you live in 'em, you get to know 'em. As a person knows his house because he lives in it."

I nodded, but I was thinking . . . seven years. And Mildred said all a Mounty needed was five years on the Force. I stopped myself right there. My heart pounded the blood into my face.

"Let's go on, Mike," I said, but he caught my hand and pulled me back.

"We've got to go quietly from here on. Follow me and don't make a sound. I've got something to show you where the stream bends up there."

"What?" I asked, but he motioned me into silence and, leaving the trail which branched away from the river at this point, made his way silently and nimbly over the stream bed. Those wet rocks were slippery, and slimy moss grew on them, so I followed much more slowly, and he waited twice for me to come up to him. The second time he nodded toward the forest of silver trees scattered among the rocks and thickening into a dark tangle of woods.

I looked and at first could see nothing. Then I noticed one or two and finally a dozen trees that had been felled in the oddest manner. The stumps were not sliced straight across as a saw would leave them, but were whittled into a conical shape, the tip ending in a sharp point.

"Beavers," Mike whispered.

"Is that what you were going to show me?" I whispered back.

"That's the way they cut trees. One working at each side. They slice the wood through with their teeth. Their dam's just ahead."

We crept forward a few feet more. Mike pulled me down beside him on a rock ledge, and I stared at the blockade of wood, stones, twigs, and mud that dammed the stream and turned it into a large pool.

We were silent a long time, waiting and watching. My foot began to cramp under me, but I didn't dare move it. And then, up to the surface of the pool bobbed a beaver. He swam across, using his tail as a rudder. He scampered up on shore, and we lost him among the rocks. He was about three feet long, and one-third of him was tail. His hair started silky gray and became a coarse, thick, reddish brown. When he jumped to the rock, I saw that his hind feet were webbed.

"We were lucky to see him." Mike's voice was very low. "In the spring they are usually off roving the forest, but there is a break in the dam. See, where that little trickle of water is coming through." Mike stopped talking suddenly and jerked his head toward where the beaver had disappeared. Here he was, back again. He came walking on his hind legs, carrying stones and pebbles in his paws.

"He looks like a little man," I whispered.

"That's what the Indians call them, 'the little people.'"

The beaver walked out on top of the dam and, reaching over, stuffed his stones into the opening and patted mud carefully around. Mike reached impulsively for my hand. I followed his eyes, and there at the foot of a large elm was another beaver. She was chewing busily at a branch and didn't seem to be helping in the construction work at all.

"They eat the pulp of branches, and water-lily roots, leaves, things like that, and berries too." Mike's hand was still over mine, and I wondered if he knew it.

"How many beavers do you think there are?" I whispered.

"Usually there are about four adults and eight young."

"How old does a beaver get?"

"Oh, they live to be twenty or thirty years old."

The beaver that had been eating dropped her branch and came down to the edge of the pool to watch her mate. You could see that she carried young. The little fellow working on the dam had dived in the water. He was submerged for several minutes.

"They have a lodge down there with dozens of rooms that are connected by water. They're very busy, these little people. They fell trees in the summer when they're building a new dam, and when the tree's ready to fall, they whack the ground, with their tails. It's their warning, like a lumberman yelling 'Timber!' Then in the fall they build their lodges. Sometimes there's as many as a hundred of them working, laying in supplies of wood for food and building material." Mike smiled at me. "In fact, they are the only creatures, besides man, that do so much building and engineering. They like to change the looks of the world, and so do we." He stared into the water. "They are very human. I have heard stories of Indian women losing their babies, who have suckled young beavers to bring them comfort."

I saw the dark head of the beaver as it broke the surface. He swam the pool and climbed up on the bank beside his wife. And what a performance he went through after his bath! He squeezed the water out of his coat with his hands, much as we would wring out laundry. It was very funny to watch him, and I almost laughed out loud. Then the two of them began to tussle. They wrapped their arms around each other and rocked back and forth, then round and round, but never sideways. They looked like fat little furry men wrestling. I looked at Mike to see if he was laughing, but he wasn't. He was looking upstream, and his face was angry. He jumped up. The beavers stopped romping, stared at him, and scampered off.

"Mike!" I got up too. I was mad at him for frightening them away.

"Stay here, Kathy." He spoke so emphatically that I did what he told me. I stood watching as he made his way along the rocks by the beaver pool.

But I was curious to see what he was after, and anyway why should I stay here just because Mike Flannigan told me to? So I followed him over the rocks and sand, past the pool, and then I saw what I couldn't see before because it hung gray against gray slate rock. A pole like fishing pole had been set low over the water. It had a clamp on the end of it. A mother beaver had swum into it. The trap had sprung, swinging the pole high into the air. And there the beaver hung by her forepaws, whimpering. A large hawk swooped low, and I cried out. Mike wheeled around.

"Get back!" I saw then what he did not want me to see. The eyes of the beaver had been torn out of their sockets. Mike broke the pole and laid the animal on the ground. Then he carried me into the edge of the wood. There he sat me down with my back against a tree. He had faced me in the other direction, so I heard him go but did not see him.

That note of distress was in my ears. I sat there seeing the empty sockets ooze blood. Then I heard the shot, and my hands unclenched themselves. I heard Mike coming back, but I couldn't stop crying. I could see the toes of his boots standing beside me. He bent over and touched my hair, very lightly.

"The hawk did it, and the beaver was still alive!" I sobbed through the woods.

"Kathy, don't think about it. I never thought—" He stopped, and when he went on his voice was calm again. "No real hunter would trap, this time of year. An Indian wouldn't. Most others wouldn't either."

I shook my head because I couldn't talk.

"They wait till June anyway, when the young are born." I knew he wanted me to answer him, but I couldn't. I just couldn't.

"And it isn't like this, as a rule. Almost all the fellows set traps under water, that either drown the beaver or let it get away without mangling it. These spring poles are nasty contrivances, and not many use them. Really, Kathy."

"How—how long had it hung there?" I choked over the words.

"Not long." But I knew he was lying because the blood had clotted.

"What did you do with it? Just leave it there?"

Mike looked embarrassed. "That paw that it was caught by was almost pulled out anyway, so I put it in the beaver pool."

I looked at him in horror. "You mean you cut off its foot and put it in the pool?"

Mike avoided my eyes.

"It's one of those crazy Indian customs that white men that live among Indians fall into. You feel sorry for the beaver you've had to trap, so you leave part of him, any part you can spare, in the place where he has lived, so the spirit coming back will find it and understand that the hunter made what reparation he could." Mike spoke as though he believed this. What a strange man he was!

"I've known trappers who have worked hours boring a hole through the ice of a beaver pool to give back to the spirit a portion of what he had taken."

A furry body hanging by a mangled forepaw, a hawk biting and tearing away the helpless thing's eyes . . . His words had fallen gently, like a curtain shutting those pictures from my mind. He took both my hands in his. He felt badly. I knew he did. And we had been having such a nice day. I forced a smile and then looked up to show it to him, I hadn't known he was so close. My face was streaked with tears, but he reached down and kissed it. I let him kiss me. It was something I had not known, this melting away into feeling.

FOR A WEEK I had been after Uncle John to get his permission to go to the O'Malleys' dance with Mike. And all I could get out of him was, "I'm thinking it over."

I made a face to myself, but he caught me.

"And what's the matter, Kathy?" he said. "Don't you believe I'm thinking it over?"

I fired up. "You've been thinking it over night and day for a week," I said. "It's a wonder you've had time to attend to the cattle and the house and the accounts."

"Well," he said, "when's the dance?"

"Tonight."

"Your mother might not be wanting you to run off to dances at your age, even if it is with a Mounty, so I'll have to continue to think it over." He turned toward the door. "But get your clothes ready, just in case . . ."

When Mike came to pick me up, Uncle John was still thinking it over. He said he'd let me know his decision when we came back.

We laughed together as we saddled our horses.

"Your uncle John," said Mike, "never says anything straight on. Always hits it sideways."

We rode off over the muddy road. A light irritating rain was falling, and I kept reaching down to make sure none of it was trickling off Rosie's back into the saddlebag. In that saddlebag was my dance dress, very carefully folded, with round twists of newspaper in the folds to prevent creases. In my mackinaw pants and beaver coat I looked like Mike's kid brother, but bouncing on Rosie's side I had a dress that would remind him that I was a girl. Blue and shining it was, with heavy ruffles and a slender waist; and my blue shoes that matched were at the very bottom so as not to crush anything.

The O'Malley barn could be heard long before it could be seen. As we rode up the hill we heard the shrill notes of a fiddle start up, and the laughing and talk die down. Two Indians galloped by us in a wild silent race. The rain stopped for a while, and there was a pale gleam in the west where the moon was trying to break through. Mike stopped at the barn and told me to go up to the house to change. But I wanted to look in at the dance first.

Four or five Indians were standing around the door. They were dressed in dark blue suits; and, although the suits were all the same size, the Indians weren't. Mike opened the door, and I peered into the huge dimly lit room. A few smoky oil lamps hung from the rafters, throwing long, flickering shadows on the floor. They were dancing a fast and furious square dance, but as far as I could make out there were ten men to every woman on the floor, and a few hundred more men lined up along the walls. Three fiddlers played wildly in the back, and near them a tall ferocious 'breed with a dirty handkerchief around his neck plucked at a guitar. I heard the caller yelling above the racket, "Join hands round for a Birdie in the Cage! Get your partner and swing her off the floor! Join hands round— Birdie fly out and Hawkie fly in! Hawkie fly out, give Birdie a swing! Everybody join hands and swing her all around!"

A space cleared in the center of the floor, and I watched a heavy-shouldered giant of a man swing his partner around and around with everybody clapping and stamping. Her beaded moccasins barely touched the floor, her skirts billowed out, and her head was thrown back, eyes closed. I was frightened and excited and anxious to join the dance myself.

"I'll run up to the house and change," I told Mike. I walked out, and the four Indians in their blue suits looked at me and grinned. Mike appeared, glaring.

"I'll take you," he said.

When we came back to the dance, it was even more crowded. White trappers, 'breeds, and Indians fought over the few Indian girls. I felt eyes staring at me from every corner. Before I threaded my way through the first square dance, I had received twenty proposals, including marriage. I was the only white girl there.

I never had time to sit down and catch my breath. Sometimes in the patterns of a dance I would be swept away from Mike. Arms would tighten around me, and faces would flash by—dark Indian faces, gleaming with sweat and grease; red Scottish faces shining with heat; small French faces secretly smiling. The music flew by in wild, erratic rhythm, the laughter was loud and excited, and the floor of the barn shook under the heavy steps of the men.

Unexpectedly I heard Mike's voice in my ear. "Come over to the side," he said taking my hand. "There's going to be trouble." I followed Mike's eyes and saw a pale man standing uncertainly by the door, scrutinizing the dancers. Some of them stopped and watched him curiously. He had a vague abstracted look that made you think of a sleepwalker or someone who had been lost for a long time. And yet he was young, and his hair was black and thick, and his face would have been handsome had he smiled.

"George Bailey," Mike said. "And Bull MacGregor is here with the girl."

"What girl? Who's Bull MacGregor? Where?"

But my questions were answered quickly. Nearly everyone had stopped dancing, and a path opened. At one end of it I could see the giant who had whirled his partner in the air during "Birdie in a Cage." A six-foot-four Scotsman he was, with dirty red hair and an uneven beard. At the other end of the hushed dancers stood George Bailey. He didn't look at Bull MacGregor or the slender Indian girl, half his size, who stood next to him, staring at the floor. Instead, he looked over at Mike, and you could see he was annoyed by the attention he was drawing. There was whispering and talking from the crowd. Someone snickered, and the musicians went at their fiddles in an effort to start the dance again.

Mike and I watched Bull MacGregor swagger insolently past George Bailey on his way to the door. His girl half-ran, half-walked along with him, Bailey did not move; his hollow face showed no expression. MacGregor opened the door, and the wet air blew in. But the girl had turned around and stood staring at George Bailey. Her face also was expressionless, but her whole body was tense and expectant. MacGregor tapped her on the shoulder, but she did not feel it. He said something in a low voice. The girl didn't move. He flushed from his forehead into the neck of his open shirt, and he hit the girl in the face, a hard short blow.

We all watched George Bailey. He was crossing the floor, slowly, steadily. His mouth was slightly open and his hand trembled, but he didn't quicken his pace.

"No knives, George," said Mike.

Bull MacGregor waited, leaning forward, swinging his huge fists, heavy as sledges. The girl scrambled to her feet and seized his arm. MacGregor flung her off, and she fell toward me and Mike. Her lip was bleeding, and there was a long purple welt on her cheek.

"Do something, Mike!" I pushed him. "Put him in jail."

"Yes, yes, in jail," the girl sobbed, clinging to me. "He kill him, he kill him!"

George Bailey was about ten feet away. He stopped uncertainly, hesitated, but MacGregor rushed him with a bellow that made me understand why they called him "Bull." There was a flurry of punches. Mike and two other men stepped into the struggle, and it was all over in a second. Bull's right arm was slashed and bleeding, and Bailey lay on the floor, shaking his head queerly. The two men helped him to his feet and pulled him away, while Mike stood in front of MacGregor talking in a low voice.

"I'll forget the scratch," Bull said, "but if I see him around again, I'm going to let the dirty 'breed have it."

He turned toward the girl. "And now *you*, come on!" He put his hand on her shoulder and sprayed blood all over us both.

She held my hand and repeated hysterically, "No go! No go! He kill me!"

"Let her alone," I said. "Let her alone, you big coward. It's easy enough for a man the size of a buffalo to beat a little mite like this." And I put my arm around her, though she was a bit taller than I.

"Sergeant Mike, put him in jail," the girl pleaded. "He beat me, he choke me, he try kill me! Look . . ." and she started to undo the collar of her dress.

"Let her alone for tonight, Bull," Mike said, "and go home."

MacGregor growled something and turned toward the door. The blood was still trickling down his arm, but he ignored it.

"How's the cut?" Mike said.

MacGregor pushed his way out without answering.

"Don't let him go!" the girl screamed.

"Shhh," I said. "What's your name?"

"Mart'."

"It's all right now, Mart'," I said.

"Please, Sergeant Mike, put him in jail."

Mike had an annoyed look on his face.

"Mike," I said angrily, "do something for her. That big bully! I'd just like to have seen him lay a hand on me."

Mike grinned. "All right," he said to the girl, "he beats you?"

"He try kill me all the time."

"And you're through with him for good?"

"Yes, yes, through, finished."

"All right. Come in in the morning and sign a complaint, and we'll arrest him."

"Yes! Yes!"

"And you can stay here tonight. I'll speak to the O'Malleys. They'll put you up."

Mike signed to an older woman, who came over and took Mart' away. Her fingers clung to me, and she repeated, "Yes—in jail, in jail!"

I watched till the door shut behind her. The fiddles started up with renewed vigor, trying to erase the impression she had made. But I wasn't interested in music or dancing any more.

"Mike," I whispered, "you *will* put that man in jail?"

He smiled. "She won't come in to sign a complaint. She won't even stay here tonight. In an hour she'll go home to Bull."

"No!" I cried, horrified.

"It's happened before," Mike said calmly. "They always go back."

"Well," I said turning a little red, "if any man ever struck me, if he just laid his littlest finger on me, I'd get the biggest sharpest knife in the kitchen, and I'd whet it all day on the grindstone; and it's my belief, Sergeant Flannigan, that man wouldn't sleep long in my house."

Mike burst out laughing and swung me onto the dance floor.

It rankled in me. I mean, I didn't like Mike's callous attitude, and I didn't like that bully's roughness, and I didn't like her weakness if she went back to him, and I was just irritated all around. So I guess I acted a little cool to Mike, and soon he seemed to draw into himself and become dignified, and then we were riding home in silence.

Finally I said, "It was a very nice dance, and I thank you."

And he said, "Yes."

I said, "I certainly enjoyed all the people, and the Indians, and the music."

And he said, "Yes."

I kicked Rosie, hard. We began to trot.

"You're not much for talking this night?"

"No."

"And what is on your mind, Sergeant Flannigan?" I said.

He turned his head and looked at me, and began to talk, fast and earnestly. "You think I'm hard and cynical, that I'd stand by and let a man strike a woman and do nothing about it, but you don't know the story behind it, so I'll tell it to you, and you're not to interrupt until I'm done." He reined in, and the horses settled down to a walk.

"The girl's name is Marthe Germaine. Her mother was pure Indian, her father some kind of mixed 'breed, a man no one liked—

neglected his wife, neglected his kids, ran off and disappeared one day. You remember that man who knifed Bull MacGregor? George Bailey, he's called. Part Indian. Used to be a very nice fellow, but he's changed a lot. Anyway, then he was young, good-looking, a hard worker, made a lot of friends. He fell in love with this girl, Marthe, took her up north to his trap line, made her his girl. They didn't get married, there's not many marriages like that. I mean it's rare for a man to marry an Indian girl with the priest and everything. But George loved her and was good to her, and she adored him, and worried over him, and mothered him, the way women do. George had a partner, this Bull MacGregor you saw, and as long as George was there, he kept away from the girl. MacGregor had nothing but contempt for George; he could crumble him with his bare hands. But the man was his partner, and MacGregor had his own peculiar code.

"Well, one day George had to go down for supplies. Supposed to be back in a month. Didn't return for six months. Ran into all kinds of bad luck and trouble. Bull waited two months, then he took the girl. I guess he figured George was never coming back, so she was his by inheritance. Of course, he never asked *her* how she felt about it, and if she made any objection, I suppose he smashed her in the face. After all to him she was just an Indian *klooch*. But Marthe was pretty, and capable, and MacGregor grew fond of her; so when George Bailey came back, Bull wouldn't give the girl up.

"Now, here's where the story gets peculiar. Marthe hated Mac-Gregor, hated him as close to murder as an Indian woman can think, and she loved George. But she was afraid, if it came to a fight, that George would get killed. So she told him she didn't love him any more, that she'd always loved Bull, and she sent him away. That was that, for five years.

"Then Bull brought her down here. She was miserable. He knocked her around the way you saw tonight. Well, one day Bull beat her up worse than usual, left her unconscious, and a neighbor sent for Constable Vincent. He locked Bull up for the night, and I told the girl that if she wanted to, she could sign a complaint, and I'd hold Bull there for a month, and she could clear out. I tried to convince her that in a month she and George could lose themselves, and that Bull would never follow, it didn't mean that much to him.

"She thought it over, and then said she was going back to Bull, he was her man, he brought her food, he built her house, she was his woman. And then she said something very funny. She said she hated George because he hadn't the courage to fight Bull like a man. Now, that I haven't figured out to this day. After all, *she* was the one who stopped George. And yet, tonight, remember the way she looked at him, as if daring him to come on? Well, I don't know how it's going to end, but someone's going to get hurt."

"Well, all women aren't like that," I said.

"No." He smiled. "But they're unpredictable creatures, all of them. For instance, right now you're sulky, and in a minute you're going to laugh." And he leaned over and squeezed my hand. I laughed. I couldn't help it.

But then that was all. He didn't say another word. He didn't squeeze my hand again or try to kiss me. We just rode ahead under the dark clouds. And what *I* say is, men are unpredictable creatures, all of them.

Flashes of lightning ripped the heavens, and a torrent of rain blinded our horses. I turned my face to the sky and laughed because the things you enjoy can't hurt you. That's what Mike always said. In spite of that my boots felt soggy, and the wet penetrated my heavy mackinaws.

I thought about the Indian girl and wished George Bailey would fight for her and get killed. I thought about Mike too. He kept looking at me in a worried way. I know he didn't like my being out in this downpour. Oh, yes, he was fond of me. There was no doubt about that, but he was fond of his horse too.

Once we had passed the broken-down fence that marked Uncle's property, the horses took heart and began to gallop.

"Ride right up on the porch," Mike shouted. "I want to get you out of the rain." So I rode Rosie under the shelter of the eaves and got off.

"I'll take them around to the barn," Mike said. "You go to bed."

"I've had a very nice evening," I said.

"Katherine Mary, get in the house and out of those wet clothes." I went into the house, but I gave the door a good slam. And there was Uncle John sitting up.

"It's a quarter to one," said my uncle.

"It's a wonder we ever got here in this rain. The horses almost got mired."

"Where's Mike? Didn't he come in with you?"

"He's seeing to the horses."

"We can't let him go on a night like this. He'll sleep in the bunkhouse."

There was a long pause. I waited there, miserable and shivering, because I wanted Mike to come in and see that I hadn't done what he told me.

At last my uncle said, "Did you have a good time, Kathy?" I went over and kissed the top of his head.

The door opened and slammed, and Mike strode across the room, leaving puddles of water behind him. He nodded to Uncle. "I told Kathy to get into some dry clothes."

I faced him. "I was just saying good night to my uncle. Any objections?"

Mike was looking grim, and Uncle interrupted. "He's right, Kathy. You're wet to the skin."

What were the two of them—a couple of grandmas? I flounced out of the room.

"You can say good night in the morning," Mike called after me. I didn't even turn around.

I dried all over with a rough towel. It felt good. Then I got into my nightgown. I was still chilly, so I put on my robe too. Then I got into bed and pulled up the covers. I didn't feel sleepy, and my behavior troubled me. After all, Mike had taken me out, and I'd had a wonderful time. And poor Uncle John waiting up till all hours. Then I'd acted like that.

I got out of bed and opened the door to the living room. Uncle was still there by the fire, and I could see a section of Mike, a section of kitchen, and about an inch of stove. I came out and walked to the fireplace. Mike stuck his head around the corner of the kitchen door.

"I'm cold," I said, and held out my hands to the fire. I wanted to say, "I'm sorry," too, but Mike started yelling because I didn't have any slippers on, and when he got through I didn't feel like saying it any more.

"What are you doing in there anyway?" I asked him. "I thought you were supposed to be in the bunkhouse."

"Well," said Mike, "I was warming up some water for a hot bath. But as long as you're still up, you're the one who's going to get it." I simply laughed.

Mike said nothing more, but poured the heated water from the kettle into a large washtub. Uncle John watched with interest. I pretended to be staring dreamily into the fire.

Mike came to the door. "It's all ready," he said.

"Uncle John, can you make out any salamanders in the flames?" I punctuated that sentence, with a shriek, for Mike lifted me off my feet, carried me to the chair, set me down in it, rolled back nightgown and robe till they reached my knees, then stuck my feet into that tub of water.

"It's too hot!" I yelled.

"It's good for you."

"Uncle, Uncle!"

Uncle was shocked into movement, not much, but a little. He stood up. "Mike, I think this has gone too far." I think he meant Mike pulling my clothes around my knees.

"It has, John," Mike agreed, "and I want to talk to you about it right now." He looked down at me. "You stay where you are." He walked out of the kitchen and shut the door behind him.

I stepped quietly out of the tub, dried my feet with a dish towel, walked without one creak of the floor to the door, and stood listening, hoping to hear Uncle John bawl Mike out. But it was Mike who was doing the talking. I listened to one sentence, then another, and then I realized what he was leading up to, and then I heard him say it. At least I think I did because Mike pushed the door open.

"I thought I told you to stay in that tub." He scooped me up and set me down again with my feet in the hot water. I had my arms around his neck, and I didn't let go.

"Mike, do you?—do you?—"

"Yes," he said, and put my hands back in my lap. He walked over to Uncle John, who was shaking his head and talking to himself. Mike stopped in front of him. "Well, John?"

"I can't give my consent, Mike. The girl's too young, only sixteen. And she's not well. She was sent here because of her pleurisy, and her lungs aren't too strong."

"I'll look after her, John." And we both knew he would.

"You'll be going back to your wild North, and you can't take a delicate girl like Katherine Mary into a country like that. You know you can't."

Mike looked from me to my uncle. "There's two ways of thinking, when it comes to that. To my mind, the country would harden her, make a strong woman of her."

There was silence between the men.

Finally Uncle said, "There's no man I'd rather give her to than you, Mike Flannigan, and you know it well. But she was put in my charge by her mother. And her mother would not approve. She's too young yet, and she has no strength. I'm thinking she could go back to Boston."

I stamped my foot, forgetting it was in the tub, and the water splashed all over. "Have I nothing to say about this?" I asked the two of them.

Mike looked at me reproachfully. "Your uncle's too good a friend for me to be talking a matter like this behind his back."

"And what am I? I hope at least you think as much of me as of my uncle."

"Kathy, of course I do."

"Well, then, you just say it. If you love me, you tell me right here and now. And if you want me to marry you, you ask me, and then maybe I will and maybe I won't."

Mike came over to me and crouched down by my chair so he could see my face. He spoke low so my uncle couldn't hear. "I love you, Kathy. I always have, and I think you've always known it."

I couldn't stand the look in his eyes, the earnest almost pleading look. I turned away from it. I, a sixteen-year-old, had demanded that this sergeant of the Northwest Mounted humble himself, and he had.

"I'll make you happy, girl. I'll give my life to it. I want you for my wife." He didn't touch me. Didn't even take my hand. But I felt and knew only Mike.

"I'm going to marry you. I'm going to marry him," I said to my uncle. But my uncle was no longer there. Mike stood up, drawing me with him. We held to each other, and I had never had him so close.

I SHUT MYSELF in my room. All night long I went over it and over it with Mother, and sometimes she cried and sometimes she laughed and sometimes she didn't do anything at all. And that's what I was most afraid of. I could see her opening my letter. She would read it twice, because the first time she wouldn't believe it. Then she'd know I wasn't coming home, that I was going to marry someone named Sergeant Michael Flannigan and go up to those "wild north places" with him. I had to stop her worry and her fear by telling about Mike. "He's a man," I wrote, "twenty-seven years old, responsible, who'll look after me." To know he was kind and good and capable—that would help her. And she would hear the same thing from Uncle John, who had promised to write also. Maybe I could make her know about Mike; but about the country he was taking me to—never.

And when would I see her? I knew Mother hadn't the money to come for the wedding—and Mike already had his orders; we would leave immediately for Hudson's Hope. The pain of a separation that would be for years, and maybe forever, must run between us the length of the Saskatchewan.

Things would be different between my mother and me. I would be Katherine Mary Flannigan, a woman, and my mother would be Margaret O'Fallon, another woman. The mother and the child were somehow gone. But these things couldn't go in a letter. We must tell

each other the good things and the things we hoped would be good.
I looked down at the words I had just written . . . "We will be married
here at the ranch on October 20, that's this Sunday. Uncle will give
me away, and Johnny will be best man. I have a beautiful dress, all
white with lace at the throat and on the sleeves."

I couldn't put it off any more. I began a new paragraph, writing
the words that had to be written. "Then we are going to Hudson's
Hope, where Mike is stationed. We'll take the train from here to
Edmonton. From Edmonton we must travel seven hundred miles by
dog sled. Mike says the trip will take two or three months."

I looked over what I had written and crossed out the part about
seven hundred miles and the words "two or three months." Then I
crossed the whole thing out and started over.

"Hudson's Hope is quite a way from the nearest city, Edmonton,
but we will make the trip in easy stages."

Then I told her that my pleurisy didn't bother me any more, and
that I was much stronger. I thought writing it down like this would
help make it true. Because I really was a little worried that I would
fold up on Mike somewhere along those seven hundred miles to
Hudson's Hope.

I put that thought away, along with worries about what to take
with me, what kind of punch to serve at the wedding, and what if
Johnny didn't stay sober long enough to stand up with us when the
time came.

I returned to my letter. It was slow work, choosing the words to
hurt my mother. If only I could have written about Mike's hair, and
eyes—and his straight nose, and how tall he was. Well, I had, a little,
but I knew she was interested in other things about him. So I told
her how the Canadian Government supported us, gave us house,
clothes, horses, food, and a little money. I thought it better not to tell
her what Mike said about money not being much good up there.

"Everything is trading," he had said. "Food you can eat, horses
you can ride, skins you can keep warm with. But what can you do
with a paper dollar?" Yes, I knew my mother better than to speak
disrespectfully of money.

"I want for you to be here so much," I told her, "but I know you
can't leave the house, and that anyway the trip would be too expensive. And we have to leave right afterward because those are Mike's
orders."

I felt important, writing about orders. It was all new and strange.
"But you'll come and see me when we're up there." I continued.
"And then we'll come to Boston to see you."

While I was writing it, I thought it was true. But then I looked at it and knew it wasn't. It was far, across a continent. I felt afraid. No one would know that, not Mother and not Mike. I'd keep the fear pushed down inside of me, and no one would know it was there.

"I'm awfully happy," I wrote.

I was. Awfully happy and awfully in love, and tomorrow I was marrying Mike.

ive

WE HAD TO leave Juno. He was too civilized to live on the trail. The sled dogs would tear him to pieces, Mike warned me. "I'll get you another Juno when we get to Hudson's Hope," he said, and I left Juno with Mildred. He was the last tie with Boston and home. From now on the Northwest was home.

We took the train from Calgary to Edmonton and set out for Lesser Slave Lake as part of a dog-sled caravan. There were thirty-six sleds of traders, trappers, and Hudson's Bay Company men.

Two nuns were riding on the sled of a trapper named Baldy Red. They were bound for the Mission at Peace River Crossing and had no visible money or supplies. The older one had come to the camp where the caravan was assembling and asked if there was room for herself and the other sister. The men talked it over for a while, but no one seemed able to spare the space. Each sled was heavily laden with equipment and goods.

At this point Baldy Red walked into the meeting. He was a short, stocky man with a fringe of bright red hair circling his bald spot. His neck was red, his face was red, and his nose was bright red. He wore his shirt open at the throat, and no cap was on his head or mittens on his hands. He pushed his way through the group of men and walked, or rather lurched, over to the nun. Mike said he was drunk, but he didn't speak like a drunk, and I thought what he said was nice, and nicely put.

"Sister," Baldy Red addressed the nun, "my friends here say there's no room. That's a true word. But I will *make* room. It's women like yourself this country needs. To bring the word of God to the heathen, and the hand of mercy to the sick. And God bless you for the good work you're doing, and, God damn me—I mean God help me—I'll make a place for you and the other holy sister on my sled."

And the Sister said, "Thank you." She looked him over carefully and then asked, "Are you Catholic?"

"Sister," Baldy said, "I don't know. My parents never told me. I've never gone to a Catholic church. But," he added appeasingly, "neither have I gone to any *other* church."

The nun smiled a little. "My friend and myself will be glad to ride with you. God reward you for your courtesy."

Baldy Red with a very gallant air led the nun to his cutter, and they drove in for Sister Magdalena.

"Well, I'm glad of that," I told Mike. "I was getting ready to ask you if we could take them."

"We're loaded to the brim," Mike laughed. "If we had another passenger, I'd have to harness you with the team."

"He's a very nice man," I said. Mike said nothing, but he smiled, I thought, queerly.

The next day we started. Baldy Red made a seat out of two packing cases and up-ended three more to make a back rest. He covered the cases with buffalo robes and seated Sisters Margaret and Magdalena on their improvised throne.

The day was cold, fifty below zero, and no amount of covers could keep me warm sitting on the sled. So I'd get off and run until I was warm and tired, and then get on and ride until I was rested and cold.

Baldy watched over the nuns as if they had been truly his sisters. He found them extra robes and made ear muffs for them out of a pair of old mittens.

"Something's up," Mike told me. "That old rascal never spoke to a nun in his life."

"You don't like him," I said.

"Sure I like him," Mike said, "but I don't trust him. That old Baldy has never made a straight move in his life. Even if he blows his nose, there's something crooked about it."

"I don't believe it." I said.

"There was the time he sold a Dutch farmer his horse," Mike said thoughtfully. "The farmer, Humbert his name was, paid Baldy eighty dollars for the horse; for, while it didn't look any too handsome, being sort of mottled brown with white spots, it was sound in wind, fast, and well trained. Humbert bought the horse, and he says for a day or so he watched that horse with fear in his heart, waiting for its teeth to fall out, or for it to go lame, or get vicious or come down with the glanders—because, you see, he knew Baldy.

"The third day he went in to brush the horse, and the horse was gone. He rode to town, and Baldy was gone. Humbert didn't waste any time, but came to the barracks and swore out a complaint, charging Baldy Red with the theft of one six-year-old horse, brown with white spots.

"A week later we caught up with Baldy. He had two horses. We brought them both back. One was a ten-year-old gray mare. One was a six- or seven-year-old brown horse, brown but with no spots. Farmer Humbert stood a long time looking at his horse, and then he started to swear. Claimed Baldy Red had stolen the horse and covered up the white spots somehow. Baldy just laughed and said the old guy was crazy, this was a different horse. Humbert opened the horse's mouth and said he recognized the teeth. Baldy sneered and asked him did he see any spots before his eyes. Well, we were stuck. Humbert had identified the horse as brown and white, and this horse was brown all over. We washed and scrubbed him with soap and turpentine and naphtha, but brown he was and brown he stayed. Humbert nearly went crazy. He said he recognized the teeth, the ankles, the eyes, and the gait of that animal. But, as Baldy pointed out, that's not much good as evidence from a guy that can't tell the difference between brown and white. So we had to let Baldy go."

"Well, then Baldy *was* innocent, and you were just picking on him," I said. Mike looked at me, and at the glee in his eyes a doubt grew in my mind. "Where *did* the other horse go, the brown and white one?" I asked.

"There was only one. The brown part went with Baldy," Mike said, "and the white part went with a little paint remover."

The first village we came to was Athabaska. The weather was changing; there was a tension in the air, and heavy clouds piled in the east. The sun was already low when a circle of pale, silvery light sprang up around it. A little later, within this giant loop, four smaller shining circles appeared. In each circle a small unreal but gleaming image of the sun shone. Looking up at the five tangent suns gave me a weird and alien feeling. I seemed to be on the plains of a distant planet, gazing into a dream landscape. The silver circles became hazy, the mock suns flashed evilly, the daylight seemed to flicker, and then the vision vanished, and the true sun sank into a mountain of dark clouds. Even the dogs seemed upset, and we rushed on at a furious pace until we whirled into Athabaska, and I tumbled off the sled, my face stiff and my eyes dull with staring.

"Sun dogs, they're called," Mike told me. "I've seen as many as sixteen surrounding the sun, like puppies around a bitch, and shining every bit as bright as the big one. Sun dogs. The Indians are scared of them. They think they are evil stars trying to kill the sun, and they beat pans and raise an awful racket to scare the sun dogs away. It generally works. The whole illusion is in the atmosphere, and I guess the noise shakes it. Anyway, when you see those things, ten to one there's a blizzard by the morning."

There was. We were stuck in Athabaska two days. In that time I saw a lot of Baldy Red.

The cabin we occupied was long and rambling, with two stoves and twelve beds. The one assigned to Mike and myself was at one end, and Mike hung a blanket as a sort of curtain because, he explained to me gravely, we were newlyweds. The nuns slept next to us. As a mark of respect. Baldy Red had dragged in three of his heavy chests and improvised a table where the nuns took their meals, away from the men. When I saw Baldy, face purple and sweating in the sub-zero cold, lug those six-foot packing cases into the cabin, half break his back propping them up so that the three cases would make a level surface, and then cover it all with a gaudy cloth he'd dug up somewhere, my heart went out to him, and I turned to Mike and said:

"There's a man with a kind heart. I think it's sweet and pathetic the way he built that table for the nuns. He even thinks that horrible rag is a pretty tablecloth. And look at the way he worked, dragging those heavy cases in."

"They *were* pretty heavy," Mike said, and winked at me; why, I didn't know.

I set about making friends with Baldy Red. First I spoke to the nuns. They were overcome by his attentions.

"And yet they say he has a bad reputation," said Sister Margaret.

"Evil tongues!" said Sister Magdalena.

While the blizzard roared outside, and I chatted with the nuns, Mike and the men were grouped around the big stove discussing the weather, though, as far as I could see, that didn't change it any.

Baldy Red came over to ask the sisters if there was anything they wanted, and I took the opportunity to talk to him.

I guess the story Mike had told me was on my mind, because right in the middle of a perfectly innocent conversation I asked him if he'd sold any horses lately.

"I sell horses right along, Mrs. Flannigan," said Baldy without hesitating in the least.

"I'm not the best judge of horseflesh in these parts," he went on grinning, "but I'm the best judge of who's the worst judge . . . and that's the way I keep body and soul together."

Throwing a pious look at the nuns, he made his way back to the stove. He smiled at us all the way, with his cheery, innocent red face, but I was beginning to doubt him too.

I went back and threw myself on my bed. I could hear the wind beating against the walls. I pulled back the curtain over the one tiny window in the north end of the cabin and looked out into flying snow. It reminded me of that terrible night when the train had been stalled before Regina, a long time ago. I couldn't make myself believe that it had been less than a year. It seemed as if I had lived the longer half of my life since that day. I was suddenly overcome by the same loneliness and hatred of the cold and snow as on that night, and to comfort myself I began to draw a dog's ears, Juno's ears, in the frost of the windowpane.

Well, another Juno was behind me. The train Juno would be scrambling over Mildred's ranch. The Boston Juno would be curled up in my mother's bedroom, where her grandmother, the Irish Juno, had had her first pups. And I was going to make Mike give me a Northwest Juno as soon as one of our sled dogs had a litter. For a second I was worried because it seemed to me that only male dogs could do that hard-sled-pulling. But then the only dogs I'd seen in the North were sled dogs, and if they were all males . . . so I reassured myself and went on drawing Juno.

It had taken a long time to get used to these northern dogs. Not dogs, but half-tamed wolves they seemed. Pat one on the head, and you'd lose a finger. I've seen Black-Tip take a bite out of the one in front of him while pulling the sled on the dead run. The greatest and most unbelievable confusion in the world is when dog teams go at each other, and snarl the traces like a wet fishline, and pile the goods in the snow, and mill around in growling fury.

About the only one with a gentle disposition was Black-Mittens. The half-breeds and the Crees seemed to think highly of the black parts of a dog, and so they were named Black-Ear, Black-Foot, Black-Socks, Black-Mittens, Black-and-White, Black-Patch, and so on, up to the magnificent leader of the team, Black-All-Over.

In the morning we were on our way to Jussard. Baldy Red was snowshoeing beside our sled and joking with Mike. "And what are they sending Sergeant Flannigan into our territory for?" he said. "Is it to give him a rest?"

"Why, to put down crime," I said, a little proudly.

"Crime!" Baldy laughed. "There's no crime to speak of in the Northwest. Oh, a few shootings, and once or twice a week a throat cut over a woman . . . or maybe Scotch Bobby taking a pint too much and burning down a house. But as for thieves and pickpockets, and such bothersome rascals, we've none of them." He grinned at me. "Why, Lady, you could take a sack of gold from here to Fort St. John, and not a man would stop you. You're as safe as in the Lord's pocket."

"A place *you'll* never go, Baldy," Mike said.

"Now, there's a houseful of redcoats at Jussard," Baldy Red continued, "but what use in the world are they but to smoke the government's tobacco and eat the government's food, and interfere with the movements of the government's best citizens?" This meant himself, for he shook his head in a self-righteous way.

"Redcoat is a name I don't like," Mike said stiffly.

"You'll not deny if you fell on your knees you'd look like the sun setting over the hills," said Baldy with a wink at me.

"Some day you're going to get your whiskers singed, Baldy, my boy," Mike said. "And it's a pity I'm not on duty this trip, or I'd do it for you."

"Would you now?"

"Yes," said Mike. "And the first thing I'd do would be to have a look in those wooden chests of yours, if it wouldn't be disturbing the comfort of the holy sisters."

"Oh, but it *would* be disturbing their comfort," Baldy said, with what I thought was a kind of weak smile. "And the Lord knows that's the least we can do for women that bring such a blessing on this God-forsaken country. Have you ever heard of the Mission at Grouard?" He turned to me.

"No," I said.

"A wonderful place," said Baldy, and launched into a description of the Mission, the nuns, the school, and the gardens.

Mike waited till he had finished. Then he grinned and said, "Baldy, you're so fond of the nuns, why don't you give them something? One of those chests of yours would make a beautiful seat for the schoolroom. Yes," Mike said, warming up, "five or six kids, maybe seven if they were small enough could sit on them, and if they didn't kick their feet too hard, they couldn't be breaking the glass."

"What glass?" Baldy Red shouted, and it was comical how pale his face could become and yet leave his nose shining red above.

"Why, I have a picture in my mind of your chests being filled with rows and rows of bottles."

"The only bottles I ever carry north are empty bottles," said Baldy solemnly, "for castoreum." He turned to me and explained that this was a panacea made by the Indians from two small glands under the beaver's tail.

"In that case, everything is okay," Mike said. "There's no law against bringing in empty bottles."

"The bottles are empty," Baldy said stubbornly and returned to his nuns on their chests, where he sat down and eyed Mike and me suspiciously.

"What's wrong with bringing in full bottles?" I asked immediately.

"To Baldy Red, the only full bottle there is, is a bottle full of whisky. And the law says—no whisky north of the fiftieth parallel."

"Are you going to arrest him?" I demanded, thrilled because I had yet to see Mike make an arrest, and yet a little sorry for Baldy, who seemed so nice and friendly and had taken all the trouble to explain to me about the Mission and the beaver-tail medicine.

"No," Mike said. "I'm just guessing. Besides, I'm not on duty. We'll see what the boys at Jussard will do."

But the Mounted Police at Jussard couldn't cope with Baldy and the nuns. They searched the sleds of the caravans thoroughly for liquor, firearms, and other contraband, but they gallantly refused to disturb the two nuns on their cases of whisky. And so the five packing cases that made up the sisters' throne were untouched, and we pushed on to Peace River Crossing. We were starting our three-hundred-mile trek upriver to Hudson's Hope in the morning. Since Baldy would be starting earlier, we said good-bye before turning in. The crimson old man winked back slyly. "Like I said, Sergeant, empty bottles—just empty bottles."

That night, our last at Peace River Crossing, Mike whispered to me, "It's a shame to let all that rotgut liquor poison the Indians, and it would be a worse shame if that noble Baldy Red were a liar." So Mike sneaked out of our cabin, and what he did I don't know, but after we came to Hudson's Hope, word reached us that Baldy Red had spoken the truth after all. When he came to open his five cases of bottles, they were, in truth, all empty.

Six

MIKE SAID THE air was so cold he was afraid it would freeze the lungs of the horses. Maybe that's why every breath hurt me. I was tired. The going had been slow all day, and Mike was up ahead with the runner. Another mile, and he dropped back to my sled.

"How goes it, Minx?" he asked, and squeezed my hand.

I laughed and said, "Fine."

He gave me a sharp look and then began telling me what a good rest we'd have tonight. "This isn't a trapper's cabin. The Howards have a big home with an organ. They had it freighted in."

"Have you stayed with them before?"

"Sure, they've put me up whenever I've been in the territory. Everybody's glad of company up in these parts; they try to get you to stay on and on."

"Who are the Howards?" What I really wanted to know was: was there a *Mrs.* Howard? I thought how nice it would be to talk to a woman. Mike jogged along by my side, and his forced breathing punctuated his speech. "Howard's a lumberman. Got a mill up there at Taylor Flats."

"Is he married?" I asked.

Mike laughed. "Well, all I know is they've got four sons."

I smiled to myself. I was a married woman, and Mike said things like that to me sometimes. But the smile went out of me, for the cold was cutting at my insides with every breath. Pain was white, white and cold, and it was around me like a winding sheet. Something beat at my ears and dripped into my mind. At first I thought it was snow, but after a while it made sense and I knew it was Mike talking.

"We'll be there soon . . . soon, darling."

By breathing very regularly, I was able to push away the white and see the troubled blue eyes of Mike Flannigan. "Did Mildred tell you what I said about them?"

"What, Kathy? What, girl?" He bent very close to me because my words hadn't come out as loud as I thought them.

"I told Mildred. I said, 'His eyes are so blue you could swim in them.' " The words poured out on a swell of pain, but it was suddenly important. I had to find out. "Did she, Mike? Did she ever tell you that?"

"Yes, darling. She told me. Now don't talk. Rest. We'll be there soon."

"But what did you think of me?"

"I loved you, Kathy."

I sighed and turned my face in against his furs. I tried to remember when he had gotten into the cariole with me—but after a while I forgot to wonder, and then I think I slept.

The motion stopped. I sat up and looked around. We were in a clearing. Ahead of us was a house, and a charred barn stood a little to one side. All over the clearing were neat stacks of firewood. Mike picked me up. His steps shook me and hurt.

He set me down inside, and the sudden heat almost choked me. There were a lot of people, all talking in whispers. A woman helped Mike undo my furs. "The poor child," she said.

I remember being put in an iron bedstead, and Mike feeding me soup and then lying down beside me. I thought it funny he had on all his clothes and wondered why he didn't come under the covers.

WHEN I OPENED my eyes it was daylight, and Mike wasn't there. I sat up carefully to see how I felt, and I knew I was much better. My clothes were folded over a chair, and I began to put them on. I saw the door handle turn very softly, and the door open very slowly. Mike looked in. "Kathy," and he was over by me in a step. He was so close that his worry and his fear and his love were mine too, and in me.

"I'm all right, Mike," I told him before he could ask me. "Shhh," I said, "It's all over. I'm well now."

Mike laughed shakily. "You'd think I was the one who had been sick."

I laughed too. We sat on the bed and laughed with relief that things were better, and not worse.

Then Mike went into the other room and came back with something that looked like a dog harness.

"What's that?"

"It's for you," Mike said. He looked at the leather straps in his hand and then at me. "A Mounty's got to be a bit of everything, Kathy. Up in this country, where there's no judge, no policeman, no forest ranger, I have to be those things. I have to be a doctor too." He looked at me and smiled to reassure me. Then he said, "You've not been well, Kathy. And I think it's a collapse of the right lung you've got. Now, don't look scared, darling—because I've got the thing here that's going to help you." And he waved the dog harness.

"That?" I asked.

"It's a brace that will keep your shoulders back. Haven't you noticed how you're leaning forward all the time? Why, the air your lungs are meant to be filled with never gets where it should, on account of your hunching your shoulders forward." I must have looked unconvinced because he added, "A good posture will keep you from getting so tired, Katherine."

"But, Mike, I don't want to wear a brace."

"You'll give it a chance, won't you?"

"Well, if I can wear it under my clothes."

"Sure and you can. I've made it that soft it won't chafe."

I took off my shirt and undid the top buttons of my underwear. "You'll have to put it on me, Mike. I'll never figure out how it works."

"Lift up your arms, then, and I'll slip it on." I did. But instead of slipping it over my arms, it was himself he slipped between them. He kissed me in the hollow of my throat, and it was a long time before we got those braces on.

I rested in my room all day, and that evening I met the Howard family. Mike had spoken of the Howard "boys," but the youngest was five years older than I.

I went into the kitchen to ask Mrs. Howard if there was anything I could do. She was shocked at my wanting to help. "Eyes and hair," she said, "that's all you are; eyes and a mop of hair. The only thing you can do that will be of any use is to wash up for dinner." So I pumped water over my hands and then looked around for a towel.

"Up there on the wall." Mrs. Howard pointed. "We got one of those roller towels. Henry brought it back when he was out about a year ago."

I could see that the towel had not been changed in that length of time. It was black and grimy, and as it hadn't occurred to Mrs. Howard to change it, I could hardly suggest it. I took hold of the towel with as small a grip as it was possible to get and still spin it around. As it whirled I looked for a clean spot, or at least a light gray one. There didn't seem to be any. I turned it again, very slowly, to make sure. By that time, my hands were dry.

"Ma," one of the boys called in, "where's dinner?"

Mrs. Howard looked harassed. She was stirring four or five pots and keeping a weather eye on twenty pairs of socks that hung over the stove. The line was strung too low, and every time she reached for a dish, the socks flapped in her face. The main course was beans, and she let me put them on the table. They had a very long table, and the Howard men and Mike were seated at it. Everything in the room was homemade—except a gilt organ. It was highly polished, and a candle gleamed at either end, giving it the appearance of a shrine, which is what it was to this family.

Beside each man was a brass spittoon. The six of them lolled back on hind chair legs, chewing tobacco and spitting. The idea seemed to be not to spit in your own spittoon, but in your neighbor's. There must have been some skill to the game because the floor was spotless. Mike looked up and gave me a sly wink. "What are we eating?" he asked.

"Beans."

A chorus of groans went up. "Ma," Mr. Howard called to the kitchen, "is it beans again?"

"Never you mind, Henry Howard." She came in with meat in one hand and a pot of prunes in the other. "We got dessert tonight." She set the prunes on the table. "These here are known as lumberman's strawberries."

"You see, they're dried," Mike explained. "Easy to keep up here."

"Aw, heck," one of the boys said. "I thought when you said dessert, you maybe meant candy."

"Now where would I be getting candy?" his mother asked as she set some dried eggs beside the dried prunes. "It's all gone three months ago." She turned to me. "Last time Henry went out, he was supposed to bring me some cups. My china ones I started housekeeping with all got broke. And all we got left is that tin one you see."

I looked where she pointed and was horrified to see a tin mug of water making its way toward me. Each man gulped thirstily, wiped his greasy lips with his hand, and passed the cup on. It was refilled at frequent intervals. It came to me; a bean was floating in it. I tried not to think how it had gotten there, but passed the cup quickly to Mrs. Howard. "Aren't you thirsty?" she asked.

"No," I said.

"Well, anyway, I was telling you about how we haven't got no decent china. Know what this Henry done? He bought candy. Now, some men can't be trusted. They'll go on a drunk as soon as they hit town. Well, Henry'll go on a spree, too, only with him it's candy. What does he do but eat it and stock up on it until all the money is gone, including the money set aside for my cups."

"I hated to touch that cup money," Mr. Howard interrupted, "but it's a terrible craving, Mrs. Flannigan, just terrible."

He had called me Mrs. Flannigan, and I glanced significantly at Mike. He still wasn't used to my having the same name as his mother.

I was startled by a low wailing cry that rose to a shriek. No one seemed to notice it or even look up. But it started Mr. Howard on a new train of thought. "Hear about our fire, Mike?"

"Noticed your barn was charred. Lose anything?"

The wail had been taken up and answered again and again in a maniacal crescendo of sound. I shuddered with it long after I stopped hearing it. Then I was hearing it again, a low minor wail that built and built until the final shriek tore through you.

"What is it!" I knew from the way the heads swung toward me that my voice was out of control.

"It's nothing," Mrs. Howard said. "A wolf pack's out there crying to get at the bodies of the horses. They smell the cooked flesh, and it's driving them crazy not being able to get at it."

"Yes," one of the boys said, "we lost five horses. Barn was ablaze before we knew it. Couldn't none of us get near it. The horses just roasted, that's all."

"It was terrible," Mrs. Howard said. "You could hear the poor things screaming."

The screaming of the dead horses and the screaming of the wolf pack blended, swelled, receded. I followed the curve of the rising inflection, and when it reached its shrill wailing peak, I screamed too. I jumped up and screamed on the same note as the wolves and the horses.

The men looked at me. I screamed and screamed.

There was a frantic rush for the door. Chairs overturned as the men fought to get out. Away they went, every male Howard, into the night. Mike was on his feet too. He took me by the shoulder.

"Katherine Mary, stop it!" He spoke with a sternness I'd never heard before, and I did stop it. But the wolves didn't. They kept it up. The shrill note of their cry hung in the air, faded and came again. At the window I saw the frightened faces of the Howard men. I began to laugh, it was so funny. They could listen to tortured horses and wolf pack in full cry, and it didn't bother them. But a girl's screams had chased them from their home in stumbling panic.

"Katherine Mary, stop it!"

I tried to say, "It's all right—I'm just laughing," but I was laughing too hard to say it, and Mike didn't like my laughing any more than he had my screams. Tears were running through my fingers. I guess I was crying too.

Mrs. Howard went to the door, "Freddy!" she called. "Come on in here and play something on the organ. It will calm her." There was no answer from the outside.

"Freddy?" she said again. And Freddy slunk in. He gave me a quick furtive look and sat down at the organ. The tones came low and mellow, but the howling pack held their pitch—making weird dissonant chords. The boy began another song, "I Wandered Today Through the Hills, Maggie." It was my mother's song, one she sang as she fixed flowers for the best room and hummed when she hung the clothes to dry. Maggie was the girl's name in the song, and Maggie was my mother's name, too, Margaret Kennedy O'Fallon, but everybody called her "Maggie."

And then I knew what it was all about. The cry of the wolves had the loneliness in it, and that was why I had to scream and cry with them. I was lonely too because I didn't have any mother. The two-storied house and Uncle Martin and my sisters and Mother's canary—and even Uncle John and Johnny and the little Juno I'd left—were in my thoughts, but under my feet these two months had been only the trackless white of this dead and frozen land, empty with loneliness.

Mike could see that the music wasn't cheering me up any. He leaned over me and very gently lifted me to my feet. "We'll get you to bed, Kathy," he said.

Upstairs I tried to tell him that it was just that I hadn't felt well, that it really didn't mean anything. Mike's face was full of misery, and I knew an unhappy determination was in him. But he held it in and would say nothing. I put my arms around his neck. "I'm happy, Mike. I love you and I'm happy."

He pushed my head against his shoulder and stroked it.

"Really, Mike," I whispered into his jacket, "I am happy. I don't know why I act like this. I guess I'm crazy."

Mike still stroked my hair. "I'm taking you back in the morning, Kathy."

MIKE AND I lay awake with our own thoughts. And in the morning he took me on, not back. It was that night that I really became his wife, for I knew that this white land and its loneliness were a part of Mike. It was a part I feared, that I didn't know or understand. But I knew that I had to know it and understand it, and even love it as

Mike did. Because I wanted to be like Mike and then, after our lives had been lived, maybe I'd be Mike.

When he held me, we were crushed into one, one body with one heart beating through us. And that's the way it had to be with our minds and our feelings. It was much harder because they get tangled in thoughts and caught in emotions. But in the end that's the way it had to be.

So I lay there, my second night in Taylor's Flat, and told myself, "If you love Mike, you'll love the things that go with him. And if you can't love them, you'll understand them—and until you do you'll keep the fight to understand them in yourself, and not be carrying on and worrying him like you did tonight." I was cold and trembling under my covers for fear I'd talked to myself too late, that Mike would really send me back.

But Mike must have been talking to himself as hard as I was to myself, and he must have decided that I was still worth the trouble I caused, because in the morning he said nothing about sending me home.

One night cannot dispose of a feeling or settle an attitude, and many a night on the way up to Hudson's Hope I had to fight back thoughts of my home and my mother and the tears that came with them.... Yet it was a happy time and an exciting one, full of love and adventure and a new life opening up. The fears grew smaller, and all they could do was peck at my happiness.

The country, as we approached Hudson's Hope, became more beautiful. We traveled up the frozen river bed, and hills large and small rolled away from us on either side.

Mike told me I was stronger. I knew I was.

"The brace helped me."

"And you've adjusted quickly in a country that is usually too hard for women." He was proud of me, and he acted proud in front of the men because where were *their* wives?

On the north side of the river there were few trees, but on the south side there were forests of poplar and jack pine, large sections of which had been lumbered over. The river bed sank deeper and deeper and finally became a gorge with cliffs of white rising up as walls. We left the ravine and traveled on higher ground over a trail Mike said he knew well. Our dogs were climbing.

"When we reach the top you'll see the flag. Then we're there, Kathy."

There was a flag in front of every Hudson's Bay Company in the Northwest. It meant hot food, rest, fresh supplies, conversation, people, a little oasis of humanity and comfort before going on through the white void. Only this time it would mean more; it would mean our home. After almost three months of travel, we'd have a home. We hadn't reached it any too soon, either. For it was February, and the thaw set in during March. There was no traveling in this country in spring and summer, except by canoe. But we had made it in time. There was the flag coming into view, showing that the log house behind it was a branch store of the Hudson's Bay Company, not one of the half-dozen trappers' cabins that hid themselves among the drooping, snow-laden trees.

I took Mike's hand without saying anything. It was beautiful. The few cabins were grouped on a plateau, and below them hills rolled away, carrying white armies of poplar and pines on their backs. To the north and facing the village was a fifty-foot drop where in spring and summer the Peace River ran the gauntlet of bluffs.

We pulled up in front of the store, and Mike pushed against the door just as it was thrown open by a big brawny giant. The two men collided, laughed, and gave each other a couple of pokes, the way men do. He was as tall as Mike, only thicker and bulkier. He was half in and half out of his furs.

"Son of a gun, son of a gun," he kept saying, and all the time hitting and poking at Mike with his big beaver mitts. Then suddenly he caught sight of me. "I'll be . . ." he said and stood there staring. I got out of the sled and came over to them. Mike took my hand. "Kathy, meet Joe Henderson." I smiled at him and said, "Hello," but the big man was without words.

Mike laughed. "How long are you going to keep us standing out in fifty below, Joe?"

Joe mumbled something in his beard and kicked the door open. No sooner were we in the house than Henderson found his voice.

"Uaawa!" he bellowed. "Uaawa!" A dark Indian woman appeared from the back room and stood poised like a wild thing.

"Where the hell did you go running off to?" And then, as she continued to stand there with frightened eyes, "We'll want some tea, so get busy!" His voice lowered from a bellow to almost a whisper. "You see," he said to me, but without looking at me, "you've got to think out every step for them. We'll want food too, and she could be getting that while the water's boiling. Only you can't never explain that to them."

He sighed and sat down on a packing case, leaving the two chairs to Mike and me. I looked around curiously. The woman worked in the center of the room over the stove. I looked away at once, for she seemed to wince under my glance. I concentrated instead on the room. There was the usual counter with shelves mounting to the ceiling behind it, and a tangle of goods piled and stuffed and jammed into the shelves. Wild masses of cascading flowered cottons tumbled over jelly glasses. Knives speared spools of wire, and a rusty alarm clock sat on top of twelve cans of beans. On the floor were piles of soft, gleaming pelts, and on one of these a naked baby slept, its tawny body blending with the skins.

"What a beautiful baby! Is it yours?" I asked the woman at the stove. She lifted her head to be sure I meant it, to be sure the white woman spoke to her. When she saw that both these things were true, she smiled, a half-smile that came into her eyes.

Henderson reached for an empty bottle. He had thrown it at her, and she was picking up the shattered pieces before I realized what had happened. A cut over her eye bled onto her hands as she worked. Henderson had not watched to see whether his bottle had landed a blow or not but had turned back to us.

I stood up. "Mike," I said, "I want to see our house."

Mike stood up too.

"But wait." Joe Henderson was upset. "You must eat. You've come a long way today."

I walked toward the door and began putting on my furs. Mike stood uncertainly. No one said anything. The woman looked across at me and then back to the water which had begun to boil. It was to the water she spoke.

"It bring much honor to house if Sergeant Mike and Mrs. Mike eat."

I unbuttoned my jacket and sat down. Preparations for the meal went on. But the woman did not speak again.

After a while the child on the pelts stirred. I took him on my lap, but he wriggled off and walked on fat, unsteady legs to Joe Henderson. I caught my breath as I saw him grab hold with a small brown fist to the giant's pants leg. The child said something, whether in Indian or gibberish I wasn't sure.

"Does he talk?" I asked.

Joe Henderson gave me a strange look.

"Yes; in the language of the Beaver Indian, he calls me 'Father.' " There was a mocking note in the man's voice, but it was very gently that he stroked the dark head of his son.

"Tell the lady your name."

The child turned in his father's hands and regarded me a moment with serious eyes. "Siwah," he said.

Henderson scowled, then turned to the woman, speaking unpleasant sounds in her tongue. She gave no answer, and the motions of her hands were not interrupted. He turned to his child. His voice was no longer harsh, perhaps it was the change back into English. Again he said, "Tell the lady your name."

The reply came promptly. "Tommy Henderson."

"He's a fine little fellow," Mike said.

I was surprised. I didn't know Mike liked children. There were so many things about Mike I didn't know. But about this I was glad.

The Indian woman served us silently, but did not eat herself, and Henderson did not ask her. I was glad when it was over and we were out of the hot room with its smell of food.

Mike grinned down at me. "Which way do you think our house is, right or left?" I looked in both directions. Coming in from the top of the hill I'd seen some cabins, but now a forest of pine hid them.

"Right," I guessed.

Mike laughed. "Right it is. Come on." But I still stood there.

He looked back. "Excited?"

"Yes," I said. "But that Joe Henderson, he mistreats her. Why, you could kill a person with a bottle like that, couldn't you?"

"Well," Mike said, "maybe."

I could see he was disappointed because he thought I wasn't excited about seeing our house. So I put Joe Henderson and Tommy Henderson and the Indian woman into the back of my mind. And I put my fur mittens into Mike's fur mitten.

"Mike, are you really taking me to our home?" He looked at me with blue eyes shading into all the blues there are.

"And does a little chit like you have a house and a husband? And do you think you're going to set up housekeeping with us?"

I laughed. Then I stopped because he had.

"Kathy—I hope it will be all right, the changes I have made in your life!"

"Mike, I love you." It wasn't an answer to his words, but it was the one he wanted.

"It's been all right so far, hasn't it?"

"All right?" I threw my arms around him. "It's been wonderful."

"Come on then, I'll race you to the house."

He's shy, I thought. Yes, he really is, that big hulk of a man. But I said, "How can I race you, when I don't know where it is?"

"Follow me," and he was off on long legs.

"This isn't any kind of race," I said, running after him.

Mike turned into the pines. Ahead of us in a clearing stood a cabin. I stopped running. I approached it, trying to know it all at once, the trees and the rocks, the ground rolling under my feet. This was home. Mike put his arm around my shoulder.

"Don't look so awed, darling, it's just my office."

"Office?" I repeated the word blankly.

"Well, sure. I've got to have some place to lock up the criminals. Unless you want to keep them in the spare room."

He pushed the door open, and there was a large shabby desk and two chairs, one comfortable and one uncomfortable. There was a cupboard too, all padlocked. It didn't look anything like a jail, and I couldn't see why the prisoners couldn't get out of the windows.

"Do you really keep prisoners here?"

Mike laughed. "Never have. In the first place, there's very little crime. The Indians never give trouble unless there's been liquor smuggled in. The 'breeds are a little wilder. Every once in a while there's woman trouble, squaw stealing. Then I bring 'em in and put them to work."

"What kind of work?"

"Oh, usually cutting me a winter's supply of wood."

"Well, if nobody's locked up in it, what do you need an office for?"

Mike made a serious face. "Katherine, you don't realize I'm a big man up here. That's why I stay here. Sit down, girl, and I'll tell you all about it." He pushed me into the comfortable chair.

"This office is the Hudson's Hope court and hospital." He unlocked the cupboard at the back. It was filled with rows of neatly labeled bottles.

"Medicines?"

"Not much. Quinine, disinfectants."

"You mean people really come to you when they're sick?"

Mike said slowly, "We're seven hundred miles from civilization or a doctor."

"But do you know anything about it?"

"Not much. I bought some books in Calgary."

I looked at this man that I had married. There was more here than a red coat.

"Where's the house? I want to see that."

"It's behind the office." He caught my hands as I started for the door.

"Kathy, I hope you won't be disappointed in it. It's just a house, you know; Government-built."

"I'll love it, Mike." And I did. It was set cozily among the trees, and through a side window I could see Mike's office. There was a large front room and two bedrooms. There was a combination stove and heater, the kind they all had in this country. Logs to keep the room warm were shoved in the back, and the front was a wood stove for cooking meals on. The chinks in the wall were stuffed with moss. Over the bed was a buffalo skin.

"They still have them in these parts."

"Buffalo?" I asked.

"A few herds. Wood bison, we call them, but they're dying out."

I forgot to answer. I ran around and looked at things and planned the cleaning I would give everything, and how I would have more room by moving the table against the wall, and that I'd make new curtains. I whisked by Mike with a head full of ideas, but they were spilled out, for he reached out a sudden hand and caught me to him.

"Like it?" he asked. But how could I answer, with him kissing me so hard?

The rest of the day was spent in cleaning, scrubbing, and scouring. Top and bottom we went over that house, and we went to bed very tired and happy. We were excited, too excited to sleep. We lay there whispering to each other how it would be.

"You'll make me a book case."

"Yes," he said. "In the summer there is the river, and in winter we walk on snowshoes over the white world." I was feeling very drowsy and contented. I closed my eyes and snuggled under Mike's arm. But a face came before my eyes, the dark sullen face of the Henderson woman. I closed my eyes tighter to send it away. I was happy and sleepy, and I didn't want any ugliness from the world to get into our cabin. I couldn't keep it out. I saw again the flash of the bottle as it left Joe Henderson's hand—saw the blood falling in a thin stream to the floor.

"Mike . . ."

"Hmmm?" said Mike in a sleepy, faraway voice.

"Is that Indian woman Joe Henderson's wife?"

"You might call her that."

"But he acts as if he hates her."

There was a long silence. I thought Mike had fallen asleep.

"Yes, I think he does," Mike said slowly, into the pillow.

"Hates her?" I asked.

"Yes."

"But why?"

"Because of the boy. Everything is because of the boy."

"Tommy?" I asked.

"Yes," said Mike, and then he added, "There were two Tommys." I lay still in the dark, waiting for his voice to continue.

"You see, there are many reasons why a man comes to live in a wild land like this. We come, you and I, Katherine Mary, because here we can live the real life, the life men were meant to live. But there are men who are used to the cities, who would never leave them except they are driven. Joe Henderson was driven when Tommy died.

"He had only the one child, and he idolized him. But the boy was not strong, and Joe quarreled constantly with his wife—I think her name was Isabel—because he thought she ran around too much to parties and lunches—and didn't give Tommy proper care. Well, maybe she was a bit flighty, but it certainly wasn't her fault that Tommy caught diphtheria. The child came down with it, that's all. Well, I guess the little fellow didn't have much resistance. He was really just a baby, about two or three years old, the size of this Tommy. Anyway, he was dead in four days. And Joe Henderson never spoke a word to his wife. He looked at her when she cried and sobbed and held the little body—just looked at her.

"From that day on he was driven. He drifted through cities and towns, working only to eat and never long at one thing.

"It was only when he struck into the Northwest that any peace came to him. He seemed to take a sort of satisfaction in the rigor and the hardships. At least he had something tangible to fight—the cold. He prospered for a while, and he did pretty well. He came to be known as a steady man, one that left the Indian women strictly alone. Every three or four months, of course, he'd go on a binge. Then he'd talk about Tommy to anyone who would listen.

"Well, the Hudson's Bay Company needed a man here, and Henderson got the job. He's been here four years now. The first year he lived alone. He hated women—you couldn't trust them. Hadn't his own wife killed Tommy? But you've seen him, a big fiery man with red blood in him.

"I was glad when I came in from a couple of months on the trail to find Uaawa with him. I thought it might soften him a little to have a woman around again. And it did, for a while. But as soon as the baby was born, he changed. Of course, he shouldn't have called him Tommy, but he did. And I think it hurt him every time he looked at the child, to see the dark Indian face of him. The other Tommy had been fair.

"He blamed Uaawa for a lot of things—for the boy's black hair and brown face. Then she is a woman, and he didn't trust her. He questioned how she dressed him, what she fed him, where he played. The woman is Indian, and maybe that saved her from going out of her mind. She didn't fight back, not when he beat her and kicked her around, and she didn't go back to her people. That wasn't her way. She was too Indian. And she chose a typical Indian revenge, or maybe it wasn't revenge at all. That's the trouble with the Indian mind, you can't understand it.

"She began by giving this child, this Tommy Henderson, an Indian name. Of course Joe was furious. But in spite of the beatings he gave her, she continued to call little Tommy by his Indian name. When Joe isn't around, she speaks to the child in the Beaver language, and the boy has come to understand that language. He knows the myths and legends of his mother's tribe. There's no doubt the woman is making an Indian of Tommy Henderson.

"It's probably very simple. She sings the songs that were sung to her by her mother, and tells her son the only stories that she knows. Or it may be a pride in her own people. Perhaps she doesn't want the boy to be ashamed before white men. Yes, perhaps it is only that she wishes him to understand her people, to have pride in them. Or perhaps it is as Joe Henderson says—the woman is jealous and spiteful. The child has all his love, she none of it. For the child, Joe will do anything. He's Tommy, and he loves him. Being Indian and being a woman, Uaawa knows this giant of a man who kicks and curses her can be made to suffer through his son."

I thought it all over, a long time.

"I think he's made a mistake. I don't think he's fair to the Indian woman. You're right, though. It's all because of the first Tommy, and you can't help but be sorry for Mr. Henderson."

Mike didn't say anything. The complicated, tangled pattern of lives, where they touch and intertwine—it's impossible to unravel it. I was sorry I had tried. Who can know anything about anything? Especially when they're sleepy.

$\mathcal{S}$even

MIKE LEFT EARLY for his office. I promised to be over as soon as I'd done the dishes and help him straighten up out there. Well, with only two of us it didn't take long to get the dishes out of the way. Then I had a good idea. I thought I'd put up a lunch, and we could eat in the office. It would be fun, a sort of indoor picnic.

I began slicing bread for sandwiches. Suddenly I whirled and faced the room. There was nothing there, of course, but I felt that there was, and I worked uneasily. The feeling of being watched became stronger. Again I turned, this time toward the window, and I laughed with relief; for there, staring in, was a round-faced girl about six years old. I opened the door gently and smiled, so she wouldn't be afraid. But she bounded off like a deer, stopping a safe distance from the cabin to turn and stare.

"Wouldn't you like to come in?" I called.

She just stood there regarding me silently with enormous black eyes.

"Come on," I coaxed. But as she didn't move and it was cold with the door open, I shut it and went back to making lunch.

She came silently, so silently that I hadn't really heard her, but I knew she was out there. I went to the door again, this time with a sandwich in my hand. I opened it and held out the sandwich. She looked at it and held out her hand. I gave it to her, and she fingered it carefully all over, then stuffed the whole thing in her mouth. I had decided that she knew no English, so I motioned to her to come inside. She watched my gesture with intent, curious eyes. But the only response was the continued chewing of that sandwich. Again the cold drove me in.

I counted over the sandwiches and tried to guess how many Mike could eat. I felt a cold gust on my back. The door was open. I continued working and waited for the slight click the door gave when it was closed. The click came. I smiled to myself.

I didn't hear her move, but pretty soon the dark head was at my elbow and the dark eyes on the food. Excitement throbbed in them at the sight of the thick, buttered bread and the slices of meat. I reached down another sandwich to her. Again it was fingered all over with wonder and awe before it was popped whole into her mouth. Two other sandwiches followed. But the last one was not eaten. She carried it off. Stealthily, quietly, she was gone from my elbow, and when I turned to look, gone from my house. My stock of sandwiches being pretty well depleted, I started to work on some new ones. I had finished and was wrapping them when my door opened again.

A brave in full Indian dress with much beadwork nodded solemnly at me, stalked to the best chair in the house, and sat down. Behind him followed aunts, sisters, uncles, and cousins. Each gave me a nod or a grunt and then sat in my chairs. The last chair was finally occupied, and still they came, seating themselves ceremoniously on the floor.

When they were all in, you couldn't have stepped for Indians. They sat there regarding me steadily and silently. I didn't know what they wanted or why they were here, or what I was expected to do about it. Some fifteen children were gathered in the doorway, chattering excitedly, and in the middle of the group was my little friend, waving her sandwich triumphantly, and at the same time protecting it from the sudden onslaughts of the other children.

"Holy St. Patrick!" I said aloud and stared hopelessly at the thirty expectant faces and the sixty hungry eyes that stared back at me. Could it be that they expected me to feed them?

I couldn't just stand there with my mouth open, I had to do something. I was Sergeant Flannigan's wife. I had a position to keep up in the community. I thought of a speech, saying I was not settled yet but that we'd all have a nice party soon. But, looking into the rows of swarthy, stolid faces, I was convinced that they wouldn't understand my speech, that the only thing they'd understand was food. It was plainly my move, and thirty people were waiting for me to make it. I did. I put on a gracious smile.

"What a lovely surprise! I am very glad to see all of you here."

While I was saying this in a loud voice, I was rapidly counting noses. Twenty-eight grownups and twelve children. I had seven sandwiches. By cutting each sandwich into four parts, I would have twenty-eight pieces, each an inch long. Well, Mother had served *hors d'oeuvres* that weren't any larger than that. And there was still a little meat left. The children could have that. I would put on tea. That, at least, there'd be enough of, except, of course, they'd have to drink in relays because there were only ten glasses.

Well, it was the strangest and silentest tea party ever given. I cut up the seven sandwiches and passed the pieces around. They were accepted gravely and gravely swallowed.

But the ice wasn't really broken until tea was served. Then the noise of much sucking, smacking of lips, and gusty sipping—I took this to mean my guests were enjoying themselves. So I smiled and beamed and asked who would have some more tea. This was the only thing I said that they seemed to understand.

When they had had all the tea they could drink, the gentleman who had led the procession rose. This was the signal for general departure. The women smiled shyly, and when the last one had pushed the last child out before her, I had to keep looking at the ten glasses, the crumbs, and the spot in the corner where one old crone had kept spitting to assure myself that I had just given a tea party.

IN MARCH THE thaw set in. The snow had become pockmarked. Millions of tiny, shallow holes appeared in it as it sweated. The winter was almost over. We had missed the last mail delivery. There were only two during the winter, and when Mike told me there were none at all during the summer I cried.

But whenever I got awfully homesick and lonesome for Mother, something happened. And something happened now to take my mind from thoughts of home. I stooped down in the snow and examined the prints carefully. By putting my fingers close together and jabbing them into the snow, I tried to imitate the impression there. It wasn't a dog track because it came in from the woods and circled the house again and again, each time drawing in closer. I remembered how the dogs had whined last night. I was excited now, and I ran back to the house.

"Mike! Mike!" He came to the door. "Look at the tracks! What is it?"

He bent down as I had, to study them. But to him they meant something.

"Wolf," he said, straightening up. "You wouldn't think he'd come so close to the house. But you never know what a wolf's going to do. I saw one once that seemed to be dying. He just staggered along, and overhead a raven watched him. Finally the wolf sank down in the snow and lay still. The raven swooped down, settled on him, and prepared to eat—only it was the wolf that ate the raven."

"You mean a wolf is smart enough to pull a trick like that?"

"Yes, and I wonder what deviltry brought this one so close to the house."

Mike looked up. Overhead the trees had lost their silvery-white finery, and their bark was black and wet where it had melted.

"How'd you like that hike I've been promising you, up to the Bull? The snow's gone now except for these few inches."

I had been wanting to go to the Bull. I'd heard about it from the Indians who dropped in regularly once a week for their treasured tea parties. It was a gigantic rock shaped exactly like an enormous buffalo head. It guarded the entrance to the Ne Parle Pas Rapids a few miles up. Whenever I teased to go, Mike had put me off, saying the snow was too soft and treacherous for our snowshoes this time of year.

"What do you think about that wolf coming so close?" I asked as I swung off with Mike.

"It's an interesting thing." And it was interesting to me that he could talk and walk at such a pace. "But it's really the prairie chickens that are making them so bold."

"Prairie chickens?"

He grinned. "Rabbits to you."

It made me mad, his making such a mystery of it. "Go on," I said.

But he didn't go on. We had struck the high ground above Hudson's Hope. And from there the eastern Rockies could be seen, Backbone-of-the-World, the Indians called them. There they were, range after range of them, shading from purple to the faintest blue. The mist rose about their base, making them look like sky islands. Mike held my hand very tight. It was wonderful to share things like this, especially as I always got kissed.

We walked on. The spruce rose in dark towers above us, and everywhere and from everything the snow was going. After a while I remembered about prairie chickens.

"Well, every seven years or so there's a disease that breaks out among them. It seems to be some sort of head and throat infection. Anyway, they die off like flies. And of course both the timber and the black wolf feed mostly off them. So when the prairie chicken gets scarce, the wolf goes hungry."

"But can't a wolf eat other things besides rabbits?" I asked.

"Oh, yes, they hunt caribou herds, picking off the young, the sick, the crippled. And if they're ravenous, sometimes they will attack a full-grown animal. They go after mountain sheep and goats and even moose. But those herds are always on the move, and if they don't happen to be in the same vicinity, old wolf gets vicious. He has to be either ravenous or mad to come into the post."

"Do you think ours is mad?"

"I hope not," Mike said. "I don't want our dogs coming down with hydrophobia."

I must have looked pretty sick when he said that because he reassured me at once. "Don't worry, Kathy, I'll put out meat with a little strychnine rubbed through it. That ought to get him."

But I didn't like that either. Now I was sorry for the wolf.

"Maybe he'll go away," I said, "or die naturally."

"Wolves don't die except three ways—mange, distemper, or poison."

"Can't they be shot or trapped?"

"Not as a rule. They're too clever. They're so trap-shy that hunters can keep them away from a carcass of a deer by laying a piece of metal on the ground."

"I still don't like it. I hate to poison him."

"If we don't," Mike said, "he'll start ripping our dogs to pieces."

I sighed. Things weren't like this in Boston.

"But, Mike—" My hand was gripped so hard the bones ached. I looked at Mike. He relaxed his grip and pointed. I followed the direction of his arm. I saw nothing. Just a snow bank. But I kept staring at it very hard. I knew there was something there, and I wanted to find it. I wanted to be a woodsman like Mike. Then I *did* notice something, a thin stream of vapor rising from the drift. Mike led me away. When he considered we were far enough from the drift, he stopped.

"You saw it, didn't you, Kathy?"

"I think so. That little bit of moisture rising up?"

"That's it!" Mike was jubilant. "And can you guess what it is?"

Well, I couldn't, so he told me. "It's a bear hibernating. The thin little trickle of steam is his breath. He'll be waking up any time now, though."

I marveled at Mike. He had the sharp sight and the cunning of an Indian.

He pointed out the Bull to me, and, sure enough, the great rock was a perfect buffalo head, even to the shaggy neck which we began to climb. It was fascinating, this world of Mike's. But I was too much of a stranger in it yet.

A crunching like glass splintering filled the air. What now, I thought, and looked at Mike. He gave a triumphant shout into the face of the Bull. And the Bull threw the cry back to us. Again and again we heard it sounding in the crevices.

"Now you're going to see something." And Mike pulled me up to the top.

Below us a long strip of white earth heaved like a huge writhing snake. White sandstone cliffs looked down as it pushed up on itself, splitting cakes of ice loose. In the open space water moved. It was the Peace River crunching and gnawing at the ice layer that covered it. Blocks of ice and frozen snow were beginning to pile up on themselves, and a chunk as big as my head was struck from both sides and sent catapulting thirty feet into the air. Then larger pieces went flying and popping—one ice block the size of our double bed jumped past us into space and then fell back, cutting a jagged hole through which water foamed and spurted. Tormented, the river strove to free itself. Faster and faster now the cakes were being shot into the air. All around they leaped and fell. The noise was deafening. For miles up and down, the Peace spat out gleaming ice that flashed a moment in the sun, then crashed heavily back.

"The river's angry," I whispered, but even through the din Mike heard me.

"Not angry. It shakes winter off as we rub sleep from our eyes."

"How did you know, Mike?"

"About the breaking up? It comes about this time every year. And when you've been in the country as long as I have, you can usually hit the day."

"But how? I don't see how."

"Well, the snow starts to melt, and when there's just a bit left and it's just so soft, well, then you figure it's time for the breakup."

I had to laugh. He sounded just like Mother, a perfect cook who could never tell anybody how she made things.

The barrage of ice blocks continued as more and more river broke loose. In half an hour it flowed freely, carrying the melting blocks along. The ice cakes still jostled and whirled against each other, but only occasionally now did a piece get lifted into the air.

This experience made things different for me. Things I had thought of as static, lived, had a violent insurgent life of their own. The river was like the bear; it hibernated for the winter.

I tried to tell Mike a little of what I felt about it.

Mike was a woodsman. He understood. "All of it, the forests and the mountains and the rivers, they've got their moods and their feelings, just like a person. The Indians recognize this—just as they know some places are good and some are evil. Why, there are places in the forest you couldn't pay an Indian to go into."

"Because they're evil?" I asked.

"Yes, or cruel, like the rapids *qui ne parle pas*. That means the rapids that don't talk. That's why they're so treacherous. Usually you hear the murmuring of rough water well in advance and are able to do something about it. But here there is no sound, no warning. The first thing you know you're in them. The water drops two hundred and forty-three feet in a couple of minutes, and no one has gone through it alive. Once they put an empty boat in the rapids and waited down below to see what happened. Not even a board or a splinter of that boat came through. It must have been pounded to pulp."

I looked down into the freed water. It was swift-moving, even here. I drew back from the edge.

We walked over the rock to the side we had climbed. Climbing down is always harder than climbing up, and Mike gave me a hand to hold to. But I won't climb down unless I see where I'm going. So I faced out and waved my foot back and forth in hope of finding some place to set it. Mike was watching me and laughing very hard, which was one of the reasons he didn't see them first. The other reason was he was climbing down with his face against the side of the Bull the way you're supposed to. Anyway, men, dogs, and sleds suddenly appeared over the hill.

"Mike, Mike, look!"

We climbed back up and watched the men and teams surging over the plains below us. More and more sleds spread out over the valley until there must have been fifty men racing each other over the waste.

"Those are our neighbors, Kathy. Hudson's Hope men, all of them."

I stared down curiously at them. They were coming home after a winter's trapping. That would bring the population of Hudson's Hope up to about one hundred thirty-five people, including the Indians on the reserve.

The sleds were piled with dark furs.

"How much do they make from a winter's trapping, Mike?"

"I'd say six hundred dollars is a pretty fair season. But most of them owe a good part of that to Joe Henderson. He outfits the men up to a hundred and twenty dollars . . . on credit."

"That's very nice of him."

"It's business," Mike explained. "He won't trade with them until he gets paid."

'Breeds, whites, and Indians ran forward beside their sleds, waving their arms and yelling. I turned to see what they were yelling at, and from the other direction came the women, running all together.

As the two groups neared each other, I began making out the faces of the women. There was old Ookoominou, who had spat in the corner at my first tea party. There was Ninalakus, running on light feet ahead of the others. I tried to guess to which man each was calling. A tingling thrill of anticipation was in me. These women had not seen their men for seven months.

The tension grew. The men and women were close enough now to recognize each other, and eyes passed quickly from face to face.

A few caps went sailing into the air, and a few hurrahs were heard from the men. The women stopped running; one or two walked forward slowly, and the rest stood still.

The men were among them now, circling in and out and through them. Here and there a man ran forward and caught a woman to him. But when that happened, the man was always white, and the woman always young.

For the most part a woman would walk to the man's side and he, many times without a word to her, would toss heavy pelts from the sled into her arms. She, bracing herself, received skin after skin until her body bent under the weight of them. Then the man raised his whip and the dogs started, the woman keeping pace.

Bit by bit the women fell behind. Once again, men and women were in separate groups.

I couldn't understand, and I couldn't keep it in me any longer. "Mike, why do they do that?"

Mike didn't look at me. "Their dogs are tired from the long trek. They wanted to lighten the sleds for them."

"But the women!"

Mike said nothing. I followed his eyes and couldn't believe what I saw happening. An Indian had unhitched one of his dogs and was harnessing his wife to the team.

"Mike!"

"His dog's gone lame," Mike said.

I couldn't answer him. I watched, horrified, as the woman strained with the beasts, and the sled moved slowly after the others.

"Indian women are toughened to it, Kathy. That's all they've known for a thousand years. Why, it's only recently the braves have even turned professional trappers. Used to be the men only hunted to eat. There was no such thing as profit. And the occasional hunting they did was their only contribution. The women have always done the work, the lifting, the hauling, the skinning, the cooking and home building."

"But it's terrible. What kind of a life is that?"

"It's changing," Mike said. "Very slowly, of course, but it *is* changing. When the Hudson's Bay Company first came into this territory, it was the squaws they had to hire to bring the furs those seven hundred miles into Edmonton. They often carried a hundred and fifty pounds of goods on their backs, over fourteen-mile portages without a rest. Now, of course, the men have taken over, and there's come to be plenty of 'breeds and whites too. But at least it shows there is hope, that things are gradually changing for the women."

They'd have to change a lot more, I decided, and I was busy with plans and revolutions all the way home. I didn't do any talking because I was thinking hard. Uncle Martin was always discussing the exploitation of labor, and he said organization was the only way to fight it. To Uncle Martin organization meant strikes. I considered the idea of getting the Indian women to go on strike against the men. But I decided they weren't advanced enough. They were savages, and they wouldn't understand.

I would have to devise something else. If I was going to live among these women, I was going to do something for them. I didn't know what yet, but . . .

Mike broke in on my thoughts. "Did you have a nice walk, Kathy?"

I looked at him surprised. Is that what we had done today, taken a walk? A walk here didn't mean around the block on a cement sidewalk, as it did in Boston. It meant wolf tracks, bear breathings, rivers throwing ice at you, and Indians, and . . .

"Yes," I said. "It was a very nice walk."

ight

MIKE HAD SAID of the mosquitoes, "They are the first to come and the last to go." But I hadn't realized what mosquitoes could be. I hadn't realized that every act of ours would be governed by them. When winter ended, I looked forward to getting out of my heavy mackinaw pants and into skirts once more. But I was never to wear skirts in this country; for spring and summer, and all during the mosquito months, I wore overalls as protection against those vicious swarms of insects. Mike tacked a fine cheesecloth over every window. The mesh of ordinary screening was not small enough for those tiny, whining pests. The dogs were made miserable. We had to keep smudge pots going, and all day long they huddled about them. Even wild animals were sometimes driven mad by the swarming, biting hordes. The nights were cold, and it was then we had our only relief from mosquitoes.

Mike had given me gloves to wear when I worked in the garden. I decided privately not to be bothered with them, but ten minutes out of doors, and my hands were red and swollen twice their size. So now I never went out without them. Another necessary piece of mosquito-fighting equipment was my hat, a big hat with a wide brim from which hung a cheesecloth veil that was carefully tucked into the neck of my waist.

As I bent over my field peas I was conscious of the thin whine of a thousand small wings. The sound was so constant and so monotonous that usually I didn't hear it, but now for some reason I did. The mosquitoes lay in dark shifting clouds over everything, and I was proud of having outwitted them with so many clothes.

There was something in my red clover patch I decided not to pull up because there was just a chance it might be red clover. I'd have to ask Mike when he came. He should be here pretty soon because he was taking me to the Indian Reserve. I straightened up. This gardening was hard on the back.

"Kathy!"

I ran around to the other side of the house and watched Mike come to me over the tall grass.

"Are you ready, Kathy?" he called. I was, and fell into stride beside him.

"I know it's longer by the river," I said, "but it's prettier."

Mike smiled, and we turned toward the river.

"How long do you think it will take me to speak their language well, Mike?"

"Not long. You're picking it up fast."

"The grunting I can do already," I said, "and the solemn looks."

Mike laughed. "Let's hear the grunting."

But instead I showed him a wild canary. It was pale yellow with black on its wings, not at all like Mother's canary. Mike had pointed one out to me a few days ago, and I wanted to show him I remembered.

Mike stopped me suddenly with his hand.

"What is it?"

"Nothing. You look pretty against a Manitoba maple. It sort of goes with that red hair of yours."

"Auburn," I corrected.

I was very happy, and I was doing good too—doing the kind of work missionaries and people like that did.

"That cheesecloth is going to make a big difference in the lives of those Beaver Indians, isn't it?"

"It should," Mike said.

It struck me this wasn't a very enthusiastic reply. But I forgave him because last week he had spent two hours talking to the Indians in their own language, telling them that the mosquitoes could not get through the cheesecloth I had brought them. He had explained patiently that it would be sanitary and comfortable, and they would have less sickness if they fastened this thin stuff over their windows and across the entrance of their tepees.

"What messages of civilization are you going to bring them today?"

Mike was teasing me, but I answered very seriously, "I'm going to teach them to wash."

"Wash what?"

"Everything. Themselves, their children, and their houses."

Mike laughed from there all the way to the river, when he got interested in telling me how we could make a million dollars. He pointed to the low island formed of sand, gravel, and silt that collected behind log jams and in other sheltered places. He stooped and picked up a handful of the sand.

"There's gold here," he said, waving it at me.

I poked at it with interest and turned over a few bright-flecked pieces that might have been gold. "Why don't we mine it?"

Mike threw the handful away.

"Too fine, no profit for hand panners. Some day, though, somebody will invent a machine for mining this stuff and make himself a million dollars."

We walked on silently, thinking about gold. After a while Mike said, "It would ruin the country, though. All those prospectors coming in." And then, without change of inflection, "Watch that elk, Kathy."

I looked out across the river. It was narrow at this point, not a quarter of a mile across. In the middle, heading for the shore, was a giant elk breasting the water majestically. His antler stalk rose from his head like a young forest.

"Look, he's treading water. Something must have frightened him."

"Maybe he saw us or smelled us."

"No," Mike said, "the wind's the wrong way, and elk can't see at this distance. But he's scented something he doesn't like. He's turning back."

And sure enough, the animal turned and headed back for the opposite shore.

"There's the fellow that scared him. Look, Kathy, over there on the other side of the shoal."

I shaded my eyes and peered across. A large brown bear was making hooking motions with his paws in the water.

"Is he fishing?"

"Sure. See him? He's throwing the fish up on the bank."

Mike was right. Every few seconds the bear would scoop up a squirming fish and toss it on the shore.

"That's what the elk scented, all right."

"But Mike—" I watched as the beautiful creature swam toward the bear.

"They'll do that," Mike said, "every time. I've seen it happen with deer and with wolf too. When they're startled midstream, they'll swim back to the side they started from, no matter how close they are to the other bank. Even if the danger comes from that original side, back they go."

The elk veered again and swam on a slant. He landed well upstream of the bear and plunged off into the woods. The bear never looked up; he was busy devouring his catch. We watched as he poured the wriggling, flipping things down his throat.

"They're whitefish," Mike said.

I gave him a quick glance. He couldn't possibly see what kind they were, clear across the water.

"You see," Mike explained, "they were coming in the shoal water to spawn. That's the only reason the bear was able to catch one after another like that. And it's the season for whitefish."

I reached up and kissed him through the cheesecloth. "You're wonderful!"

"It's my business," Mike said seriously.

"To be wonderful?"

"To know these things. It's a business just as banking or farming is a business."

"But you know it well," I said.

"Sure I know it well," he agreed.

While we had been kissing, the bear had gone away. We walked on beside the river. We were close to the Indian village when Mike pointed. "Another fisherman."

There was an Indian boy in the bottom of a canoe. He leaned over, his head close to the water, and peered down intently. In his hand was a dart, poised and ready.

"They spear the fish," Mike said. "Look, Kathy, he's got a partner." Up above circled an osprey. Suddenly his wings folded back, and he dived, or rather dropped, into the water. He came up gulping and swallowing the last of a still-thrashing tail. Mike called something to the boy, who grinned and held up a fish in either hand.

"What's he fishing for?"

"Anything he can get—pickerel, trout, giant pike. We'll go fishing with the Indians some night. They burn torches at the end of the boat to lure the fish."

The boy in the canoe shouted a shrill word to us. It sounded like "Muskinongi." Mike jumped to the edge of the water and stared down. I ran over too, just in time to see a dark sleek head dive beneath the surface.

Mike laughed. "Muskrat." Although we stared for several seconds, it did not reappear.

We left the river. Some Indian children were racing each other in the woods. They played silently. Heads looked out curiously from houses and tepees. The women and the children stopped work to watch us. Inside, the braves reached for their eagle headdresses and then stalked out to greet us. As we walked toward the house of Mustagan, the chief, the group around us swelled. Boys left their arrow-making, young men put down the paddles they were fashioning, girls left their spinning and their beadwork. Mustagan came forward from his door to greet us. He was a tall, strong-looking man. And behind him moved Oo-me-me, his wife. She was soft and pretty, and her name meant "Little Pigeon." Mustagan spoke words to Mike and raised his hand in ceremonial greeting. He led the way to his house, a cabin very much like ours.

Oo-me-me spread two bright blankets on the ground outside. Mike and Mustagan sat upon them, and the other men squatted in a circle around them. Oo-me-me brought the pipe to her husband. It must be passed around and smoked. It was beautifully carved, with a long eagle-plumed stem and a smooth bowl. But I didn't like the strong, acrid stink of it. I tried not to think of the mouths it had entered and the teeth it had lain between. Mike got a second puff at it, and as there were thirty or forty men, I was glad he was accorded this privilege.

Still, there was dignity in these men, hunters of the tribe, warriors. The circle was impressive, dark bodies rising naked out of velveteen cut from Joe Henderson's bolts. But over the store-bought goods were laid trappings of beadwork; images and colors flared against copper flanks.

On the nearest copper flank a mosquito settled, gorged its fill, and flew away. Mike said the Indians and the mosquitoes had lived here so long that they were used to each other. The 'breeds suffered like the whites, but the full bloods seemed more or less immune. But they weren't immune to the diseases that go with the fly and the mosquito, and I looked at the windows of Mustagan's house. No cheesecloth of mine was hanging there, and the only curtain was made of the beating wings of insects.

"Oo-me-me," I said sternly.

She looked at me with smiling eyes. I beckoned her away from the council of men and into the house. I pointed at the bare windows. "The netting, the cheesecloth Sergeant Mike put up, where is it?"

She smiled again and spoke her Mission School English slowly. "Him much fine, much pretty."

"Yes," I said, "but where is it?"

She looked at me a moment as though trying to understand what it was I wanted. "Me bring, yes?"

"Yes." I was glad that at least she still had it. Mike would have to hang it again, and I would have to explain again. "These things take time," I said to myself—"and patience," I said to myself, only harder.

A whimpering sound came from the room Oo-me-me had entered. I walked to the doorway and looked in. A baby lay in a nest of clothes that had been heaped on the floor for it. It waved its chubby legs, driving a flock of mosquitoes and flies into the air. On one leg was an open cut, angry and red. When the leg stopped twitching, the insects settled down on it again, biting into the flesh.

Oo-me-me had found what she was looking for. She returned to me with an armful of what the French call *parflêche*. It's a kind of dried hide, and half a dozen skirts, mostly velvet and velveteen, were wrapped in it. She undid the package with care, and I saw that each dress was edged with a thin strip of cheesecloth.

She was so pleased and proud of her dresses that I didn't say anything. Then I looked at her baby, turning and twisting under its covering of biting bull flies and mosquitoes.

"Oo-me-me," I said, "you have done wrong."

She understood that word. She must have known it at the Mission, for a hurt, puzzled look came into her eyes.

"It is not yours, that netting. It belonged to the windows."

She looked sullenly, almost defiantly, at the windows. "For what they want pretty dresses?"

At that point Mike came in. I showed him the dresses and started telling him the whole thing very fast, so that Oo-me-me wouldn't follow it. I don't think Mike could have followed it either if the dresses trimmed in cheesecloth hadn't been there as evidence. I could see from his expression that the whole thing struck him funny, and I think he would have laughed if my voice hadn't gotten a little shaky at the end. Instead, he called in Mustagan and told us about Father Lacombe and the garbage can.

"You see," Mike lit his pipe, and began in Beaver, slowly, so I could follow. Mustagan's eyes never left his face. An Indian is the most patient listener in the world. "Years ago, when the first Mounty rode into Calgary, there was nothing there but a tent. The tent belonged to Father Lacombe, the first white man to come into the Territory. That little tent was the first Mission in the Northwest. Well, the Indians there were Blackfeet, and Father Lacombe taught them and lived among them and became a brother to them, and spoke to them much of their elder brother who was God's son, whose name was Jesus. Also he spoke to them of other things. There was one habit in particular that he spoke against, and it was this: when food and filth filled a tepee so that a bad smell came, and there was no place to step, the Blackfeet would leave that house and build for themselves a new one that was clean and fresh—for a while.

"Now, in the nation from which the good Father came, it was the custom to collect waste foods and bones into a neat pile, to hunt out the dirt from all corners of the lodge, gather it together, and burn it. He spoke to the Blackfeet of this white man's custom, telling them it was good medicine. But to the women this custom brought more work, and as it was the day was not long enough for their labors. So, though they listened with pleasure to the voice of Father Lacombe and watched his gestures with admiration, still did the waste matter and the filth lie on the floors of their tepees.

"But the Father did not despair of teaching them, for he knew the ways of women, and that their hearts followed after beauty. So he wrote on a piece of paper. And this paper was carried by dog sled and runner into the city that is called Regina. And back into the wilderness came a large thing of *cylindrical* shape." Mike's hands molded a cylinder in the air, and Mustagan nodded. "It was wrapped in many layers of heavy paper and guarded always by ten braves, for it was known to be the good medicine of Father Lacombe. And after many months it arrived in the camp of the Blackfeet. The drums beat, and the people of the tribe gathered around. Father Lacombe stripped the wrappings from it, and a great cry went up, for the thing flashed silver in the sun and was beautiful to behold.

"The Father then showed them how the top came off, easily as the scalp from an enemy's head. And the tribe filed by and looked within. When he saw that the eyes of the women glowed to behold this thing of beauty, Father Lacombe spoke and named the thing of shiny silver, *'garbage can.'* He explained that within its mouth would lie all the decaying food and gnawed bones in the camp.

"The Blackfeet were well pleased with this silver gift and wished to make gifts in return. But the Father would not take their skins, their bows, or their weapons; he said only that they must put his gift to good use.

"Now there was sickness in another tribe, and Father Lacombe journeyed ten sleeps away to bring them comfort and medicine. When he returned he went, before taking rest or sleep, to look at the floors of the lodges. Great was his disappointment, and bitter were the eyes he turned upon the Blackfeet; for still did the filth lie ankle-deep in the tepees, and nowhere did he see the garbage can.

"He went then to the chief and asked that the council fires be kindled. And when the blankets were laid and the people assembled, great was his surprise to see two braves enter the circle with the garbage can in their arms. It was placed in the center of the council, and the chief took his seat upon it.

"For a moment the Father knew not what words to call upon. But finally he asked why they had not filled his gift with trash, as he had asked them. And the chief made answer for the people, saying they would not fill so beautiful a gift with such dishonorable objects.

"We would no more throw bones at the present of Father Lacombe than we would throw them at the Father himself."

Mustagan nodded in silent approval.

"And so," Mike concluded, "the chief ceremonial seat in a Blackfoot council is known still as *gabajcan.*"

Oo-me-me looked with awe and wonder at Mike. And Mustagan said, "A storyteller, him bring gladness to all hearts."

I was feeling better too about the cheesecloth. Greater and wiser people than I had not succeeded any better. How clever Mike was! He would not offend Mustagan and his wife by mentioning the cheesecloth directly, but had hinted at their error with the involved circumlocution an Indian loves. I wondered if Oo-me-me had understood the parallel.

I said, "Next week when I come I will bring you more cheesecloth."

Oo-me-me looked puzzled. "But no more have I dresses to put it on."

A brave entered the house. An Indian never knocks on the door, not even on the door of his chief. Though he held his voice low, the words that he spoke to Mustagan came from him in a sort of pant. The man's excitement spread to the others. Oo-me-me stared with wild eyes at his face. Even I, who could not hear him, felt trouble.

"How long ago?" The words burst from Mike in English. He changed them quickly into Beaver. The Indian answered, and Mike stood up. Mustagan also rose, and the Indian, taking it as a sign of dismissal, darted off.

Mike turned to me. "Chief Mustagan will send someone back with you, Kathy."

"What's happened?" I couldn't keep the fear out of my voice.

Mike hesitated. "A white woman lost on the trail."

"A white woman around here?"

"Maybe not. We don't know where she is. She and her husband started by boat from Peace River Crossing. I know him slightly, a Frenchman, Jacques Jellet. He's a trapper."

"How did she get lost?"

"They'd been traveling four or five weeks, camping at night. They didn't want to overload the boat with provisions, so he shot their meat on the way. Well, three days ago he went off a ways hunting, and when he came back she was gone. He saw the fire was low, nothing but a few embers. So he figured she'd gone after wood. He waited a half hour or so, then he began calling her.

"Two days later he stumbled into a Cree camp, still calling her. At first the Crees ran from him. They thought he was some kind of spirit. His clothes were half torn off him, his body was cut and bleeding, his eyes were wild, and over his head he waved a burning torch."

"Was he mad?" I asked.

"No, mosquitoes."

The Indian who had brought the news was back at the door with a horse. Mike took the reins from him.

"How did our Beaver Indians hear what had happened in the land of the Crees?" I asked.

"Haven't you heard of the moccasin telegraph?"

"Yes," I said, "I've heard of it, but I don't know what it means."

"It means," said Mike, "that the print of the moccasin is on every trail, and by the moccasin comes the news." He swung into the saddle.

"Mike, be careful."

"She couldn't have gotten far," Mike said. "There's really no chance she could have wandered as far as my territory, so this is just routine. They'll find her body a hundred miles east of here."

I caught his leg and looked at him. "Her body? But, Mike, she couldn't be dead! She's only been lost three days. You can't starve to death in three days."

Mike looked grim. "She's dead, all right."

"But how?"

He paused, then said the word again, "Mosquitoes."

Nine

THEY HAD TAKEN the Union Jack from in front of the Hudson's Bay Company and were flying it down by the pier. It waved good-bye and so did we to the men in the boats. There were three large canoes piled with the winter's catch of furs. The men would take the pelts three hundred miles by water to Peace River Crossing, from where they would go by overland trail another four hundred miles to Edmonton. That trip had taken us three months in winter. In summer, traveling by water, it would be longer. I felt sorry for the wives of the men who were leaving. They did not talk or wave as much as the others.

The trappers crowded the pier, pointing with pride to the canoes, identifying their own furs, laughing and telling stories of how that beaver and that mink tangled with their lines. "Look how low is *bateau* in the water, eh! Heavy with the winter's work. *C'est bon.*" And they waved their sweaty, bright-colored handkerchiefs at the Indians in the canoes, and yelled messages at them: "Tell that little *klooch* at Grouard that I'm still thinking of her!" Or, "You get to Peace River Crossing, you tell one Baldy Red I cut his heart out he no pay me that five bucks!" I laughed out loud when I heard that. I'd almost forgotten Baldy.

Mike undid the ropes and shoved off the first canoe. A great shout went up. It shook the air, from every throat it burst—that is, from every throat but one. Atenou sat glumly, his face in his hands. I watched him as Mike shoved off the second and third boats. His expression of woe did not change. His eyes stared mournfully as the canoes flashed past him, but he did not move his head to follow their passage.

Something was wrong. This was not like Atenou. He was one of Mustagan's best hunters, a man whom the Indian women watched with their slow eyes, for he had not yet taken a wife.

I walked over to him. "Atenou, is something wrong?"

He lifted his eyes to me, then they closed from the exertion.

Maybe he's sick, I thought, but I didn't want to ask that because Indians are very susceptible to suggestion. Instead I said, "What is it?"

A low moan, that was all. It frightened me, and I called Mike.

"What's the matter with you, Atenou? You look like the last rose of summer."

Atenou answered Mike as he had me, with a wavering moan. Mike tried again, this time in Beaver. Atenou took his hands away from his face, and one cheek was swelled out like a balloon.

"Toothache." Mike pronounced the word first in English and then in Beaver. Atenou held onto his jaw again. Mike forced his hands away and his mouth open. He asked questions which the Indian answered with grunts and groans. Mike's hand was in Atenou's mouth by now, and he did something inside it that brought a bellow. A pretty half-breed girl going by asked, "Atenou is singing with the toothache?"

Mike turned to me. "An abscess. The one in the back. All I did was press on it." He hauled Atenou to his feet. "Come on!" He marched off, piloting the brave toward the office.

I ran after them. "What are you going to do?"

"It's got to come out," Mike said.

"But . . ." Mike's look warned me into silence.

Atenou was completely docile. I guess he thought nothing worse could happen to him than what he was feeling now. But he was wrong.

Mike sat him in the big chair. "It's your wisdom tooth," he said. "It's got to come out."

Atenou gazed dully at him and made no answer. Mike went to the back of the room and unlocked one of the cupboards.

I followed him. "Mike," I whispered, "you don't know how to pull teeth!"

"Shh!" Mike whispered back. "Do you want him to lose confidence in me?"

"Oh, Mike, I don't think you should try it."

Mike got out a bottle of liquor and rummaged around until he found a whisky glass. "Here, pour some out for him. Give him as much as he'll hold."

I took the bottle from Mike, and maybe my hand shook or maybe I looked a little white around the mouth, because Mike grinned at me and said, "Pour yourself a glass too." I ignored the suggestion.

Atenou looked very surprised when I handed him the forbidden firewater. But he drank it down and asked no questions. Every time I asked if he would have some more, he grunted acceptance. I don't know how many glasses of whisky I poured him. Finally I got tired and left him the bottle.

I walked back to see what Mike was doing. He was very busy. In front of him was spread a case of vicious-looking instruments supplied by the Canadian Government. Also supplied by the Government was the thin paper book of instructions which Mike was reading.

"What are you doing?" I asked with disapproval.

"Trying to find out if it's a bicuspid."

I recognized that dogged note in his voice, and I knew that Atenou's tooth was as good as out.

"All right," I said. "How do you go about it—just pull?"

Mike consulted the book. "Pull with a twisting motion, it says here."

"Twisting?" I asked dubiously.

"Certainly. You know what twisting is—a, a twist."

Poor Mike, I could see he was scared. Well, he's got a right to be, was my first thought. My second was more wifely: "What can I do to help?"

"You can help me tie him if he's drunk enough."

He was drunk enough. He lolled back in the chair, humming a war chant and hiccoughing. We passed the rope back and forth over and under Atenou's body until, as Mike said, we had him hog-tied.

Then Mike told me to bring him the case of instruments. The sight of those dozen sharp hooked implements seemed to bring Atenou out of his drunk. Mike nodded toward the whisky, and I poured another two glasses down his throat. On the third glass his head fell back, his eyes clouded over, and the stuff dribbled down his chin.

Mike took off his jacket and rolled up his sleeves. We walked silently to the pump out back and washed our hands.

"Open a fresh roll of cotton," Mike said. I nodded and followed him into the office. It took an awfully long time to find the cotton, and almost as long to open it. When I brought it to Mike, he was rereading the directions in that thin paper book. There was sweat on his forehead. He fingered through the instruments and picked out a pliers.

"Open your mouth," he said to Atenou. But Atenou was too drunk to understand him even when he spoke in Beaver.

Mike turned to me. "Hold his nose, Kathy."

"What?"

"Hold his nose. He'll have to open his mouth then to breathe."

I could see Mike's point, but I didn't relish holding the nose of that drooling, drunken Indian, even if he was tied.

"Hurry up!" Mike said.

I moved close and bent over Atenou. The smell of him was indescribable, part whisky and part—I don't know what. I took a deep breath, which I intended to hold until that tooth was out, and pressed the end of his nose between my thumb and forefinger. Nothing happened. I pressed harder, and the mouth fell open. In went the silver pliers and Mike's hand up to the wrist. In a moment they were both out, but there was no tooth between the pliers.

"Holy St. Patrick, did he swallow it?"

"No," said Mike. "I haven't pulled it." He looked away from me. "I was thinking—" He stopped.

"Yes?" I said.

"I was thinking that maybe I could do with a small gulp of that whisky myself."

It somehow pleased me, seeing Mike Flannigan in need of a drink like any other Irishman. Well, he had one. And it was no small gulp that he had, either.

"Now it's your turn, Kathy."

I looked at him, then I looked at the dark shining nose I had to hold again. I took it straight from the bottle like a man. I coughed and choked and made a face, but a warm comfort spread inside me. I grabbed Atenou's nostrils and squeezed. Again the mouth dropped open, again the pliers and Mike's hand entered. I saw it give the twisting motion and the pull. I saw it give the twisting motion and the pull again. Mike braced his foot against the chair—twist, pull, a jerk, a yell from Atenou—and the tooth came out in the pliers. Mike waved it triumphantly in the air. I guess maybe he was a little drunk. I guess maybe I was too, but whether from whisky or relief I don't know.

But Atenou was sober and feeling gingerly around in his mouth with his tongue. When he came to the hole, he let out a cry that could be heard in the Red River Valley.

Mike and I rushed to him, untied him, bathed his face, gave him whisky, and plugged the vacant spot with cotton. All this time he never stopped yelling. Suddenly I realized the impossibility of yelling with your mouth filled with cotton and whisky. I looked at Atenou. His mouth was closed. The screams were coming from somewhere else. Mike must have reached that conclusion too. He ran to the door and started yelling, "Drop it, you damn fool! Drop it!"

I ran to the door too, but Mike pushed me back. I ducked under his arm and looked. The horse I saw seemed to be one of the four escaped from the Apocalypse. Its coat shone with sweat, its eyes rolled in terror, its lips were flecked with foam, its ears were flattened and twitching, its nostrils flaring. The screams of the man were mixed with those of the animal. For there *was* a man on its back, a man clutching something wildly, desperately, in his arms. I strained to see. Even Atenou watched with interest from the window. What the man seemed to hold was a ball of fur. It couldn't be that. I craned forward and before Mike pulled me back I had seen it. A bald-faced grizzly was running almost at the horse's flank. She was the same coloring as the fur ball the man held—her cub, of course. Now I understood Mike's hoarse cries of "Drop it! Drop it!"

The man turned toward us a ghastly face. Mike cupped his hand. "You idiot, drop that cub!"

For a moment it seemed that the man had not understood, for horse, rider, and grizzly streaked by us. I caught my breath, for the grizzly was gaining on them. Its bared teeth were even with the mare's thin, white-stockinged shanks. But the man *had* understood, for his arm went out from his body in a queer jerking motion. At the end of them the cub dangled and was dropped. It rolled over and over. The mother grizzly turned to it, nuzzled it with an inquiring nose. Then, picking it up in her mouth, she set off at a dignified trot for the woods.

The horse stopped and whinnied uncertainly. The man went limp in the saddle. He seemed to have caved in from the stomach up. His shoulders dropped, and his head sank between them. Mike ran for him. "Katherine Mary, get out that whisky."

There was no need to get it out. It was still sitting on the table. I filled the glass full. When Atenou saw me at the whisky, he clapped his hand to his cheek and groaned pitifully. I poured him a glass too.

Mike returned with a pale-faced young man leaning on his arm. The stranger crossed the room unsteadily, smiled wanly when Mike introduced me, and fell into a chair. Mike handed him the whisky. He drank it down obediently in one gulp, as though it were medicine.

He coughed a little, but already the color was coming back to his face.

Mike sat on the edge of the table and lit his pipe. He blew a few thoughtful puffs into the air. "Now let's have it."

"Have it?" The young man looked startled. "Oh, you mean about the bear?"

"No," said Mike. "I mean about you. We'll get to the bear in good time."

"Oh, me?" The young man smiled a rather ingratiating smile. "Peters, Ralph Peters."

"All right, Mr. Peters. What are you doing in this part of the country?"

Mr. Peters sat up straighter in his chair. "Just passing through, Sergeant. I'm a prospector."

I followed Mike's glance. He was looking at the young man's hands. They were well kept. The nails were cleaner than mine and had been buffed until they shone.

"How much prospecting have you done?" Mike asked in a slow drawl.

Mr. Peters seemed embarrassed. He shifted slightly in his chair. "I guess I exaggerated a bit when I called myself a prospector. I haven't done any mining as yet, I'm on my way north. Yukon, matter of fact, to try my luck."

"You must have got in this afternoon. That's the only way I figure I could have missed you—in all that confusion when the fur brigade left."

"A good guess, Sergeant. I came in just afterwards. Met the canoes about a quarter-mile before sighting the dock."

"You're American, aren't you?" Mike asked.

"Why, yes, Detroit."

"And what did you do in Detroit?" Mike was still looking at Ralph Peters's hands. They seemed to fascinate him.

"I sold shoes. Thomas & Bailey's main branch, Tenth and Church streets."

Mike grinned. "Well, I guess you can tell us about the bear now, Mr. Peters."

At the mention of the word "bear" the color drained from Mr. Peter's face, and he reached for the whisky glass. I filled it for him, he took a sip, coughed, and set it down.

"It was a terrible trip, by canoe, you know. I thought I'd stay here a week or so and get the cramps out of my legs. Well, first thing

I did was borrow that horse and ride around a bit. Wanted to see the country."

"It's a beautiful country, isn't it?" I asked.

He looked at me a little blankly. "Oh, yes. But full of bears."

Mike laughed. "It's the season for them. Summer and spring."

"Yes," the young man said slowly, as though marking those seasons definitely in his mind. "Well, I was just walking the horse, so as to see everything better, and as you say, ma'am, it *is* pretty country, rolling and mountainous, and the leaves new and fresh. I was remarking to myself that things are a lighter green when they first come out, sort of a lime or yellow-green, I guess you'd call it."

"Where'd you find the cub?" Mike asked impatiently.

Mr. Peters looked at him reproachfully. "In a yellow-green thicket. You see, the horse had stopped to browse when suddenly its ears went back, and it stiffened up. At the same time I saw a movement in the thicket. Well, I was curious. I pushed back the bushes with my gun. If it was anything dangerous, I figured I could shoot it. But all it was was a little bear cub crouching there. When he saw me he made a noise in his throat that was supposed to be growling. He was awfully cute, you know, round and chubby like a chow puppy. I got close, for a better look at him. He whimpered a little when I picked him up, but he didn't put up much of a fight. Had the thickest fur I ever felt in my life. I thought it would be fun to take him back to camp.

"My horse smelled bear and didn't want to let us up, but I finally got me and the cub on her back. I'd just turned her and headed her for home when a whirlwind of fury crashed through the thicket at us. The horse lunged forward like a crazy thing, but it couldn't pull away from that she-demon of a bear.

"Do you know, we must have galloped five miles with the creature at our heels. I could hear it panting. Once I looked back at the blur of mottled fur, at the open mouth drooling saliva, at the bared teeth. The lips were rolled back and the teeth snapped, closing on air, but always snapping closer. I thought I would fall from the horse. Only the thought of falling under that creature kept me on its back."

"Why didn't you drop the cub?" This from Mike.

"Drop him?" said Mr. Peters. "I didn't know I had him. I didn't know anything but those blazing red holes of eyes. My head was filled with a terrible screaming. I guess it came from me."

"It did," Mike said. And then he made a practical suggestion. "Finish your drink, Mr. Peters."

Mr. Peters raised his well-cared-for hand to his mouth. It was white, and the blue veins stood out in a strongly marked pattern. He thought it held a drink. It didn't. There was no doubt of it. Mr. Peters was badly shaken.

To take his mind off bears, I began to talk about Atenou's tooth. Atenou listened appreciatively as I told about his pain and his courage. He was beaming by the time I got to the extraction.

"Where is that tooth, anyway?" Mike asked.

I looked at the table. The pliers were still there but the tooth was gone. I turned to Atenou. He grinned and pointed to his chest; there, on the end of a buckskin thong, swung a small pouch.

"It's in there?" I asked him.

He dumped the contents of the pouch into his hand. First came a silver button, then a packet of herbs tied together, and finally the tooth. The blood was now dry on it. Atenou lifted the tooth carefully in two fingers and extended it toward Mr. Peters.

"The tooth of wisdom," he said slowly.

"Wisdom tooth," Mike corrected.

"Same thing. Yes?" Atenou asked.

"Well—"

"Yes." Atenou decided for himself.

Mr. Peters drew back slightly from the tooth. "What do you want to carry it around with you for?"

"It good medicine—powerful."

Mr. Peters laughed. "Indian superstition."

Atenou, who did not understand such a long word, was nevertheless pleased by it. "Yes," he said. "Much strong. It make cure of pain between bone."

"Rheumatism," Mike explained.

"Oh, really?" Mr. Peters winked broadly at us. He was beginning to enjoy himself. "And what else does this tooth do?"

"It make love in heart of loved woman," Atenou declared gravely.

Mr. Peters thought this especially funny.

"Him also great protection against bears."

Mr. Peters stopped laughing. "Really?"

"Strong medicine against grizzly."

Mr. Peters turned to us. "You know, I sometimes think these native superstitions are worth looking into. After all, they live in these places and have survived."

"Bear no come where is this tooth. No like, strong medicine."

I was proud of Atenou, the chief hunter of Mustagan. He drove a shrewd bargain with the shoe salesman from Detroit.

Ten

"UP HERE," MIKE said, "there are no signposts or traffic cops. During the day you've got the sun, and at night the stars. From them you'll learn to tell time, direction, and to some extent, the weather."

It was my first astronomy lesson in the clear black night of Hudson's Hope, and the stars crowded in on us, a million times brighter, closer, and more real than the stars of Boston. The Big Dipper I knew, and that was all. Somewhere, I was sure, there was a Little Dipper, but it was hiding. "About the only other thing I recognize is the moon," I admitted.

Our necks were stiff from craning, so Mike laid out a blanket and we lay on our backs, gazing up. I remembered the verse from my mother's Bible, "And God made the firmament. . . ." This was the first time it had really looked like a firmament.

"The two end stars in the bowl of the Dipper, they're called the Pointers because they point to the Pole Star." Mike's hand traced out the line. "Roll your head closer to mine so we'll be looking the same way," he said.

I smiled. "Are you flirting with me, Sergeant Flannigan?"

"Not at all, Mrs. Flannigan," he said, putting his arm under my head. "This is an astronomy lesson, and you'll kindly point out the Pole Star for me."

Well, that wasn't so easy because, to tell the truth, for all it has such an important name, and is (Mike says) the basis of navigation and direction-finding, the Pole Star is a pretty mediocre-looking star and hard to find.

"There's the Big Dipper," I said, "and there's the Pointers, and there's the Pole Star." And, glory be to the saints, just as I pointed, out jumped the Little Dipper, hanging from the Pole Star like a pot on a hook. "And there's the Little Dipper!" I cried out, much to Mike's amazement.

"So you're learning by yourself, redhead," he said, and hugged me.

Then he showed me the Dragon that curls around between the Dippers, and Cassiopaeia's Chair, and the Hair of Berenice, which the Indians call Owl's Eye, but which I would call Dinner Plate, because that's its shape.

"You're to remember," Mike said, "that the Pole Star is the North Star. It's in its place every night, all night. The North Star never moves from there, but all the rest of the stars turn around it.

"Why is that?"

"Shall I give you the scientific explanation or the story the Beavers tell?"

"It's too lovely a night for the scientific explanation," I whispered. Mike sighed and smiled, but he knew I was right. This cold, clear, enchanted night was no place for mathematics and physics. Right ascension and declination and the ecliptic would have to wait for an evening with an indoor star chart. On this black, bright-jeweled chart that was flung over our heads, only magic and mystery could move.

Mike said, "The story was told to me by an old chief of the Beavers, on my long patrol three years ago. I heard it twice after that, once among the Blackfeet, once in a different version among the Crees. But it always began:

"It was in the days of before-the-before. Before the day of the first chief of the tribe, before the builder of the first tepee, before the father of the first Beaver. Yet even in those days there were men on the earth, and they hunted. And when they died, they went to the plains-above and hunted there forever.

"Now, then there was no sky, and the sun lighted up the plains-below and the plains-above equally. On the plains-below men hunted buffalo and moose, and on the plains-above the spirits hunted smoke-deer and bison of fire. It happened that the men on the flat of the earth became discontented, as all men do, and took to watching the hunts of the spirits and envying them. And it's not hard, my darling, to see how that was. For what is buffalo meat and moose meat and the skin of the beaver compared to the magic meat of the fire-bison and the flashing skin of the sky-eagle! One day Onowate, a man with the strength of three bears, threw his hatchet into the air and killed a sky-eagle. The spirits were angry and complained to the Great Spirit. And he hid the plains-above from the eyes of men with a blue curtain.

"During the day the sun shone on the plains-below, and during the night it shone on the plains-above. And men continued to hunt deer; and the spirits, deer of smoke.

"At that time there also lived Ayoo, a woman with the cunning of three mountain lions. And she was curious. She wished to see the hunt of the spirits in the plains-above. So she urged the men of the tribe to climb the trees and cut holes in the blue sky-curtain. Now, beloved, the trees then were not like the trees now. They were as large as a mountain, and tall. A hundred men holding hands could not circle the base of such a tree or see the top. The upper branches of these trees rested against the sky-curtain. And the men persuaded by Ayoo's cunning, the cunning of three lions, these men cut holes in the sky. And when night came and the sun shone on the plains-above, the light leaked out and twinkled.

"The men spent their evenings peering through the holes and spying on the hunts of the spirits, and Ayoo sat on the highest branch feeding her curiosity. One night, Onowate, the man with the strength of three bears, reached through his opening and caught a fire-bison by the leg and pulled it through. Onowate's arm was seared to the shoulder and two of his fingers turned to ashes, but that night he feasted on the dinner of the spirits.

"Once again the spirits complained to the Great Spirit, but the Great Spirit refused to repair the curtain. It seemed that he was angry with the men and yet pleased by their audacity. But at last he yielded to the pleas of the spirits, and with a twist of his hand set the sky-curtain spinning.

"No longer could the men look through the holes they had made. No sooner would one put his eye to the opening than it would begin to move, and he either stopped looking or fell off the tree. Of course, the spinning has slowed down by now, but keep your eye on the stars, and in half an hour you will notice that they have shifted.

"So the men on the plains-below gave up their gazing and returned to hunt buffalo and moose and the skin of the beaver. And Ayoo was unhappy because her curiosity was not full.

"Now, Ayoo was a woman with the cunning of three mountain lions, and she had a plan. She went to Onowate, the man with the strength of three bears, and whispered her plan. And one night he went to where a tree grew that was the greatest tree on the flat of the earth, and its name was Gorikan, which means 'unbendable.' This tree Onowate climbed. And when he came to the top he took the highest branch of the tree Gorikan and thrust it into the nearest hole in the sky. And it stuck there.

"Round and round that branch the sky-curtain whirled, but that point never moved. For it was held there by the tree that was unbendable.

"Then the spirits that hunt in the plains-above became angry. They complained once more to the Great Spirit. But this time He laughed at them. And so they sent fire.

"The fire burned the man's skin, and it burned the woman's hair, and it burned the bark of the tree. But Onowate beat out the fire, and Ayoo put grease on his wounds, and Gorikan stood straight.

"So they sent water. The water loosened the man's grip, and it filled the woman's mouth, and it rotted the trunk of the great tree. But they held firm.

"So they sent stones, and thunder, and iron, and lightning. Nothing worked. The tree stood, and still the sky went whirling around that one point, and Ayoo fed her curiosity.

"In the end, the spirits aroused the terrible Snow Spirit that lives in the below-the-below. And he came with his winds and his rains and beat upon the three. Ice formed on the arms of Onowate, and even with the strength of three bears, he could no longer lift them. Hail beat against the head of Ayoo, and even with the cunning of three lions, she could not think. And snow and more snow piled on the branches of Gorikan, until with a great crash the unbendable tree broke, and fell, and all were buried beneath the snow.

"Yet to this day the sky-curtain turns around that one point in the north. And sometimes at night Ayoo stirs under her blanket of snow and whispers cunning into the ears of Onowate, and with his great strength he starts to lift the tree once more so that she may look in on the hunt in the plains-above. And then the spirits unchain the terrible Snow Spirit and rout him out from his cave in the below-the-below, and we have such storms as make men tremble."

I lay very close to Mike, and we looked up into the sparkling holes in the sky-curtain and dreamed of the man and woman buried beneath the snow since the days of the before-the-before.

"You are very strong, Mike," I said as he tightened his arm around me. "You have the strength of three bears," and I hugged him back.

"And you, little one, have the strength of one bear, or maybe half a bear," he laughed.

"I am much better now," I said. "I'd forgotten." And I suddenly realized that I was healthy and strong, so healthy and strong that for weeks I had forgotten all about my chest and my cough and my pleurisy. I had even forgotten to put my brace on.

And so I thought this would be a wonderful time to tell him, now that I was well, and the sky was full of stars, and his ear was close against my lips.

"Mike," I said, "we're going to have a baby."

He jumped a little. "Is it true?"

"I've known for some time," I said.

"Well, you certainly kept it hidden from me," he said.

I laughed. "That wasn't hard."

"You imp," Mike said joyfully, "you have the cunning of three lions."

And we looked up and watched the sky turn.

Eleven

A WIND HAD sprung up—Meyoonootin, "fair wind," the Indians called it. I'd been working in the garden all morning. I was a little tired and didn't want to overdo because of the baby. I leaned the hoe against the house and sat on the steps. I shaded my eyes and looked out across the hills. Meyoonootin bent and lift the grass in rhythmic waves like the waves of an ocean, a green sea breaking around the roots of a forest.

A little gray mole ran out from the grass at my feet and scurried blindly up on the porch. He ran first one way and then the other. I didn't want the dogs to get him, so I cornered him and set him free again. The grass shook and trembled as he made his way through it, then fell again into its easy indolent motion.

The air was heavy and full of haze. The sun seemed half obscured, but it shone with more color. It was a strange, flaming orange. I took in a deep breath. Smoke, that's what it was. Not haze. There was a fire somewhere. It had been such a dry spring. Things were brittle. A fire now would be bad. I felt uneasy. I wished Mike was around. I decided to get him.

As I ran toward the office, I heard one of the dogs behind me. I turned to call it, but it wasn't a dog. It was a cat, a giant cat with a tawny coat, and only a few feet behind me. I braced myself to meet it, my arm lifted to protect my throat and face. The animal's tongue lolled out over its teeth, the eyes were glazed. As it came abreast of me, it veered slightly and raced on. I fell against a tree, bewildered. A small striped badger scurried after the lynx. I began to laugh. There was something wrong with the laugh. But there is something wrong with everything when a wild cat is chased by a badger.

I caught my breath, for I realized now what it was that forced the wild things of the forest to take suddenly to the paths of men.

Only one thing could make the badger run with the lynx, and that one thing was fire.

I ran on toward the office, and three gray rabbits ran with me. The smoke was thicker now, and hot ash and cinders sifted down on the path. But the animals were running *with* me. That meant the fire was behind us. I wondered if it would reach the house. Why hadn't I brought the dogs with me? But they were smart. They'd run the right way.

I saw the red of Mike's jacket as he ran toward me. He didn't say a word, just grabbed me tight against him.

"Thank God!" he said, over the top of my head. Then he pushed me arm's length from him.

"Get to the river, Kathy. Its widest point is just opposite the store. Wade out to the middle and stay there." His hands tightened on my arms. "Stay there till I come for you. Promise me you'll do that."

"Yes," I said. "I will. Oh, Mike, is it going to be bad?"

"There's a wind," Mike said, "and a forest fire's never any joke."

"What about you? Mike—I'm so frightened you won't be careful!"

Mike pulled me to him; his hands were in my hair a moment. "I'm fine. You know that. You do just what I tell you, Kathy. Don't be frightened, don't get panicky, and don't leave the river. No matter how bad it looks, don't leave the river. It's safer there than anywhere else, and the minute it isn't I'll be there to take you out."

He gave me a push. "Hurry, Kathy!"

I ran so that Mike would see that I would do everything as he told me. The brush broke behind me, and in a moment Mike was running at my side.

"I'm going with you, girl—as far as Henderson's. He's going to be worth ten men to me now."

I stopped running. "But, Mike, he's not there. He's hunting."

"Damn! That's right, went south, didn't he? That means he's cut off. All right, darling, I'll leave you here then."

"Be careful and—a blessing, Mike." But already he was gone. He had left the path and struck out in the direction of the reserve. I stood and watched the red of his jacket as it moved through the filigree of laced branches and brush that already separated us. I turned away.

"Dear God, don't let anything happen to Mike! Please, God. Please, please, please!" And by God, I meant God and the woods and the mountains and the unknown old gods that the Indians knew. I walked in that prayer all the way. The air was a blue blur, and the rest a dark blur full of many colors, all blending—and I was alone, knowing for the first time in my life, knowing through anguish how I loved Mike Flannigan.

I saw the flag in front of the Hudson's Bay Company. I saw it clearly and distinctly, and everything else came into focus for me. Women, dragging children, pulling children, holding children, were crowding the river banks. Some had waded into the river and were standing waist-deep. The children cried and whimpered and stared with frightened eyes past the store, where clouds of smoke circled up and bright flashes leaped among the pines. Two little boys were not crying. They thought it was fun to be in the river. They made faces at the dark column of smoke and then dived under so the smoke couldn't get them. I went down to the bank and walked into the river. The water was cold, and I waded up and down the edge until my ankles were used to it. The hottest day cannot warm water the ice has imprisoned all winter. It felt strange, sloshing into my shoes. I thought of taking them off, but the bottom was too rocky.

It was terribly hot. The wind was no longer Meyoonootin, fair wind, but Sou-way-nas, the fierce south wind. It blew hotly over us, bringing us gray ash that was our homes and our forests.

There were more people crowding down to the river. Oo-me-me waded out in water past her waist. In her arms was the child. I went over to her. "Oo-me-me," I called.

There was no response. Her eyes were on me and were very quiet. She had resigned herself. She was waiting for the known or the great unknown.

"Oo-me-me," I said again, "did Sergeant Mike tell you to come here?" There was no answer.

I had to know where he was. "Oo-me-me, please! Was it Sergeant Mike who sent you and the others down here?"

Her eyes were past me now. As I looked into them I saw reflected the smoke and the darting flame. Nothing more.

Of course it was, I said to myself; it's Mike directing things. He's sending everyone where he told me to go, the widest part of the river. But maybe he hadn't reached them. Maybe something had happened to him. The Indians would probably come here anyway.

The wind whipped the smoke wall. It beat the flames and made them dance. They reached out golden arms and leaped into new places. I strained my eyes. Little black figures darted among the smoke, but whether one of them wore a red coat I could not tell. I remembered my prayer and began saying it again.

Someone was calling my name. It was Lola, the 'breed wife of one of the men who had left with the fur brigade. She held a baby in either arm, and a third at her skirts, crying.

"Mrs. Mike!"

"Yes," I said. "I'll take him."

I lifted up the baby that sat crying in the water. I rocked him in my arms and talked to him. After a while he forgot to cry, and then he fell asleep. It was good to hold a baby in your arms and to have quieted him.

It was terribly hot. I waded deeper into the river. Lola followed me.

"Why did everyone come here? Did Sergeant Mike tell you to?" I asked.

She shifted one of the babies onto her shoulder. "No, him send three fellers to tell everybody come and be safe in river. One, she go reserve; me, I live by there, so I hear, too. Other two, they warn cabins. One go east, one west, tell all women, children, come."

It was good to hear this news of Mike, to be able to follow his movements, to know that then, at least, he had been all right.

"You think we die in damn river?" Lola asked.

"No, Lola, we won't die. Sergeant Mike has all the men together by now. It looks to me like they're going to try to stop the fire at the lumbered-over spot behind the Company store. See, you can see them over there, a little to the left of the big smoke." It helped me to hear these words even if I had to say them myself.

"Look!" said Lola. A red fox dived into the water from the cliff above. The wind brought to us the smell of his scorched coat. He swam until he was just within his depth, and there he stayed completely submerged, with only the top of his nose showing. There were twenty or thirty dogs around, but they paid no attention to him. I looked for our own dogs and saw Black-Tip, the team leader. I called to him but couldn't coax him past where he felt bottom.

The fire had entered the back door of the Hudson's Bay Company. The building broke into flames; fire poured from every chink and opening. The roof fell in. They had not checked it at the clearing. The river was the next natural barrier.

The wild things, hesitating at the brink of the river, hesitated no longer. Moose, deer, otters, mink, bears, wolves, lynx crowded into the river with the humans. The smoke thickened. The only sky to be seen was a dense, thick, curling, shifting gray. The baby woke gasping. I waded farther into the river. The current was swift there, and

I had to brace myself against it. I bathed the child's face and wet his hair, but still he cried.

"I do not see Ookoominou, my mother," Lola whimpered. The smoke stung my eyes and obscured the faces around me. I could no longer see who was here and who was not. But there were not as many as there should have been. This threw me into a panic. If they were not all here, Mike would try to get them through, and it was no longer possible.

The flames shot up along the river like a ragged fringe. Everything was bright, terribly bright, but because of the smoke I could no longer see. I closed my eyes, but I couldn't shut away that brightness.

The child screamed terribly. I lowered him until the water was at his chin. Hot ashes were falling and burning me. The air blistered my face. My eyebrows and lashes were singed. My face and throat burned; my body was numb with cold.

The fire danced on the edges of the river; the water was gold. Ripples mirrored the flames, glittering red and orange. Everything was intensified. Color! There had never been such color. The world writhed in searing, burning color!

Sound was the only thing that could travel through that color and live. Animals and humans cried with the forest, with the trees as they strained, as they broke, with the trapped creatures.

I tried to guess how long it had been, how long I had been in the river. Was it day or was it night? I could not see the sky. I did not know. I only knew the torturing heat and the smoke. I tried to figure it out by deciding whether I was hungry. But the skin of my face seemed to throb and swell, and food was a word I remembered from a long time ago.

I saw the fire leap the river. It burned, a bridge of flame, from shore to shore. That was farther up, where it was narrow, but it was blowing down on us. The heat cracked my skin open. I couldn't stand it. Mike! I thought: Don't let this happen to Mike. I covered the baby's nose and mouth and ducked both of us under the water. It felt wonderful, cold and wonderful on my blistered face, and if I was dying I didn't care. The child struggled, but I kept my hold until there was no breath in either of us. Then we came up, gulping for air, but the air hurt. I clapped my hand over the baby's face before he could breathe out. Once again we were under. I lost count of the times we came to the surface. I'd wait until my lungs were bursting, then up, to let the burning air rush in through nose and mouth. The child still struggled, so I knew it lived.

I don't know when I realized the air no longer hurt to swallow. The smoke and fire were still there. But hadn't they always been? Wouldn't they always be? I was too tired to think about it. I only knew that for some time I hadn't cooled our faces in the water. The river went past, went past, went past—it was time moving by. It flowed without stopping, it was silvery now with no brightness in it.

Mike picked me up. I don't know where he came from. He picked me and the baby up. He was taking the wet clothes off me. When he came to the shirt, I tried to help him by holding my arms up, but I couldn't. I was too tired. With his hunting knife he cut the clothes from me. The next thing I remembered was feeling warm, under blankets and drinking hot soup. I was dressed again, this time in skirts, Indian skirts and a man's shirt. It was day, a different day, the next day, Mike said. I looked at everything; there was a sky over my head, not a roof. My blankets lay on the ground. A smudge was burning at my head.

"Am I all right?"

Mike grinned. I don't know how I knew it was Mike. His face was black with streaks of skin showing where the sweat had run down. The red coat had gone and the shirt under it. He laid a hot compress over my face and throat.

"It hurts," I said. "What is it?"

"Tea, strong tea. Best thing in the world for burns. The Indians use it."

"Mike, Mike!" I sat up and threw my arms around him. "Mike, Mike, Mike!" I wanted to say, "Are you all right? I love you. Were you careful?" I wanted to tell him, to ask him about the baby, the fire, what had happened; but the only thing that came out was "Mike."

Mike held me. He whispered little words to me, pet words. He told me I was fine and that the baby was fine. "You were just tired, Kathy. Chilled and tired, and you got second degree burns on that pretty face of yours."

"Yesterday," I said, "you just went to the office. We might never have seen each other again. . . . Oh, Mike, it can happen like that!"

Mike's blue eyes looked hard. "It has happened like that for some of them."

I had forgotten there were others. For a moment there had been only Mike and me, but now suddenly there were those others, almost a hundred and fifty of them.

"Mike, were many—" I stopped. The drawn look on his face told me.

"It's not your fault, Mike."

He looked at me for a long while. "I don't know," he said slowly. "I haven't been able to think that out yet. I don't know yet if it was my fault, but it was my duty to protect the people against this country."

He had told me once he was a policeman, not against man, but against Nature.

"Tell me about it, Mike." I knew it would be better if I could get him to talk.

"We got the fire under control in fifteen hours. It's still not out." He was reciting facts, making a report. He was judging now, and his voice was impersonal.

"I needed every man if I was to stop the fire at the river. I wasn't able to do that. At one place the fire jumped. But where the Peace is wide, there at the bend where you were, Kathy, we stopped it. I had forty-seven men. I needed a hundred of them. I sent three, took them from their stations. Young Eagle I sent to the reserve with orders to evacuate all women and children to the river. Pierre and Scotty I sent to cover the outlying cabins. Pierre went east of the store, Scotty west. Scotty got through."

"Pierre?" I asked.

Mike shook his head. "He never came back."

"Mike, you can't blame yourself."

"I should have sent two men," he said. "One would have gotten through."

"But you couldn't spare them."

"No."

I put my hand over his big one.

Atenou walked toward us over burned ground. Mike rose to meet him. One question was asked and answered. Mike turned to me.

"Will you be all right, Kathy?"

"Yes," I said, and tried to get up to prove it.

Mike pushed me back. "Rest, Kathy. You've got to be careful. It's been a shock and a strain on you."

"Where are you going?" I asked him.

He hesitated. "I'm going to the cabins east of here to see what can be done."

He kissed me swiftly.

"Be good, Minx."

I rose up on my elbow and watched him stride off. I'd forgotten to ask him about our own home, if it was standing.

"Atenou."

He looked down at me.

"Our home, Sergeant Mike's home, is it burnt?"

"Burnt," he said.

"Completely? I mean, there's nothing left?"

"Him burnt."

Somehow I couldn't picture it. I saw it as I'd seen it last. My wedding dress from Calgary hanging in the closet, Mike's map of Canada tacked to the bedroom wall. That big iron stove, *it* couldn't be gone, I thought. And my garden. The field peas were just coming up.

"What about the reserve?" I asked Atenou.

"Some place fire eat up. Some place strong medicine, fire him no go."

That was good. At least the village hadn't been completely demolished. It could probably be rebuilt.

I came to the question I feared. "And the outlying cabins?"

"Many gone, some not."

"And the people who weren't in the river?"

"On gray wings went they."

"How many?"

Atenou told off the names. He held the endings, drawing out the sound of it. The effect was a chant, a death chant. I shuddered. Most of the names meant faces to me, sometimes words, sometimes laughter. Children and women, all of them, and all from cabins east of the shore. Atenou stood like the angel of death, slowly intoning. He must have counted off forty names, a third of the people. The last named were men who had died fighting the fire. There were only three of them, and the last was Pierre, the man Mike had sent to the east.

"They found him?"

"Found," replied Atenou. "Him under tree on way to cabins, him back crack like kindling."

"But didn't the people try to do anything when they saw the fire coming?"

"Ground show some get through to river. Fire she come between—those who were afraid to go; now they cannot, they take children, go hide down wells, in root cellars."

"Did—did that save any of them?"

"Sergeant Mike him take bodies from there now."

I turned my face against the blanket. It was rough. It hurt my skin, it made me cry.

My arm was seized in a powerful grip. I was half shaken to my feet. The face I looked into was mad.

Joe Henderson twisted my arm under me. He glared at me from green glittering eyes over which were neither lashes nor brows. Both had been singed from his face. His lips were cracked and swollen, they were caked with blood. They twisted and grimaced before the word came out. The word was "Tommy!"

Still I could only stare. The clothes had been torn from him. His body was a network of gashes. He must have crawled miles on his hands and knees; they were pulp. And his side, his entire right chest was burned and blistered.

His mouth twisted itself for another effort. "Where's Tommy?"

"There were so many people, such confusion . . ."

"He was in the river. He must have been. You saw him." He commanded me to have seen him, but I hadn't.

"There was so much smoke I couldn't be sure." A film spread over Henderson's eyes.

I tried to reassure him. "But he must have been there. That's where we were right in front of your place—" I stopped suddenly and remembered something from a long time ago. No, from yesterday morning. Uaawa taking an east trail with little Tommy.

Joe Henderson's burnt mouth got ready to say "Tommy" again. I couldn't have stood it, so I told him, "Yesterday morning you went hunting, Joe. I know, because Uaawa came past my house with Tommy. I called to her, and she said you'd left and she was going to visit her sister."

"Her sister—the Bonnard cabin. East—she took him east into the fire. Tommy . . ." His voice broke over the name and he started running. He staggered like a drunken man, he almost fell from the cliff into the river.

"Mr. Henderson!" I called. "Joe!" He didn't hear me. I got up. I felt pretty good, just dizzy, and he couldn't go alone. He was in no condition to. It wasn't hard to catch up with him because he wasn't walking straight. I took him by the arm, and I think several times kept him from falling.

It was witches' country, black, burnt over. Trees stood hollowed, empty of their life, with only stark charcoal wrappers left. It was hot underfoot; the fine ash burned through our shoes.

Along the dead shore and over the smoldering ground a woman walked, looking into the Peace River and calling. We came closer. The woman was Lola, and it was my own name she called, "Mary!"

"What's the matter, Lola? What are you doing here?"

She did not take her eyes from the water. "Did you come by river, Mrs. Mike?"

"Yes," I said.

"Did you see my baby, my Mary, Mrs. Mike?"

"Oh, Lola!"

"The river took her, damn river. I held them both. I slip on bottom, on damn rocky bottom, and river take her from my arms. You no see her, no?"

"No," I said, and turned to Joe Henderson, but he was not there. I plunged into the forest of black stumps.

"Mary!" called the woman on the shore. "Mary, Mary!" I ran from the sound.

I came to the clearing. There should have been a cabin there. There wasn't. I ran on. I almost fell into the foundation of a house. The root cellar was half-filled with smoking ash. I heard voices now, somewhere a man crying. Two Indians passed me carrying something charred and black in a blanket. I didn't know what it was when I looked at it . . . but when I thought about it, I knew. I saw Joe Henderson standing in a knot of Indians and 'breeds. I walked to them. I had run all the way but now somehow it took me a long time to reach them.

They were gathered about a well whose stone sides were blackened like an outdoor oven. From down inside the well came Mike's voice, hollow and full of echoes. "Give me a hand there!"

Mustagan bent over the edge and stretched out his hands. A brave reached to steady him as he received the burden. With a grunt he lifted the body over the side and laid it on the ground. There was a general movement forward. Only Henderson stood rocklike, his eyes rested a moment on the figure. It was a woman's. There was no face. Joe Henderson looked back toward the well. One of the men called down to Mike, "Anyone else?"

It was a moment before Mike answered. "Yes, two, I think. I'm sending up the child."

Again Mustagan reached into the well. This body was very small. He laid it at Henderson's feet. This time no one moved. They were like a well-trained chorus, their eyes fixed on Henderson, waiting for him to cry or sob or scream. But he didn't do anything.

Mike handed up the third body, again a woman's. Joe didn't look at it, not once. He didn't lift his eyes from the body of the child.

Mike climbed up from that death hole. I was almost surprised. The rule, I thought, was that Mustagan had to lift you over the edge and that you had to be dead with your face burnt off.

Mike looked angry when he saw me, but he just said, "Sit down, Kathy."

There was no place to sit. The ground was too hot. There was only the wall of the well, and I wasn't going to sit on that. I shook my head, and Mike turned a little wearily to Joe Henderson.

"I'm sorry, Joe," he said.

The words seemed to rouse Henderson. For the first time he looked away from the boy, looked straight at Mike. He spoke very quietly. "It's not Tommy."

Mike didn't say anything.

I looked down again at the boy. Of course it was Tommy. The face was there, all but—Anyway, there was enough to see. There could be no doubt that it was Tommy Henderson.

"It's not Tommy," Joe Henderson said again. Then all at once he fell beside Tommy and grabbed him in his arms. The small blackened shoulder turned flaky and crumbled under his touch. He didn't seem to notice.

"Don't be scared, Tommy. Don't be scared. I won't let anything happen to you, not this time, not again! I saw the smoke, Tommy, I came up by canoe as far as I could. But it crossed the river, Tommy, cut me off. But I went by land, Tommy, right through it. So don't be afraid, Tommy. Tommy?" He let the body fall from his hands. "No, that's not Tommy. I won't let it be Tommy!" And he turned up an agonized face. He saw me. He began explaining very fast.

"You see, my store is right by the river, the widest part of the river. Uaawa would bring him to the river." He repeated the name Uaawa to himself. Dark shadows swam in his eyes. Then they became still with uncertainty.

"Uaawa," he said again, as though that explained everything to him. He looked over at the body of the second woman, his hands clenched at his sides.

"So she sneaks out as soon as my back is turned—takes Tommy to her sister. They talk to him in Beaver, sing to him in Beaver. They feed him Indian food, tell him Indian stories. She tried to make an Indian out of my son, out of Tommy Henderson."

He stopped and laughed, or maybe cried. It was a strangled sound in his throat.

"She hated me, all right. She knew I had no use for her, and she hated me. The damn *klooch!* She knew she could get at me through Tommy. I was a fool. I should have known she'd do this. But he was hers too, and I didn't think she could."

Mike took him by the shoulder. "What are you saying, man?"

"That she murdered my son."

"You mustn't be thinking things like that."

Joe Henderson spoke again.

"The many times I told the woman what to do in case I wasn't here, and Tommy was bit by a snake! What to do if he cut himself, what to do if he got sick on those tins they send us, and what to do if there was a fire. 'Put him in the river,' I told her, 'right in front of the cabin it's deepest and widest.' "

Mike spoke soothingly to him. "She didn't know there would be a fire, Joe, when she started off."

"It was hate that made her take Tommy to that Indian cabin. Hate that made her put him down the well."

"Joe! Joe, it was too late by the time she saw the fire. It was between them and the river. She did what she could for Tommy. He was her child too."

"Hate was her child. Mine is dead."

The graves were dug all day. I worked with the women. Thirty-seven wooden crosses we made and whitewashed. We cooked mush in the cabins and tepees that were left. The fire had skipped around like a child playing hopscotch. Without reason it had taken and it had spared. Mike fell asleep while he was eating the mush. I shook him and he finished. Mustagan asked us into his cabin. He shook hands with Mike after the custom of white men. "The Sergeant, him save the people of Mustagan."

That was all, but it was enough.

welve

I TRAILED MY hand in the water. It looked like the hand of a sea nymph who had somehow drifted into the Peace River. The current was carrying our canoe along swiftly, and the Indian in the bow held his paddle upraised, watching for snags. I let the water run through my fingers and kept my eyes on the woods, hoping I'd see a bear. I loved to watch bears—from a distance. The day before, I had nearly sat down on one. The men had pulled the canoe on the bank for some minor repairs. I walked over to a flat rock, curled up on it, and there was a black bear eating red willow berries. He backed away, but stopped to turn up a rock and lick off the insects and bugs clinging to the bottom. That's when I jumped up and ran. A bear that will eat grubs off the bottom of a stone will eat anything, I reasoned, and that anything might be me.

Mike wasn't impressed. He said black bears were friendly, lumbering old cusses, and that the only ones I need worry about were grizzlies. Just the same, it was a shock seeing it, and from then on I was doubly careful. I didn't want my baby born with a face like a black bear's.

Mike thought I was becoming unusually scary and fanciful. "It'll be a good thing when you have the baby and get over all this," he'd say.

But I continued to give way to my moods, and right now it was my mood to take my hand out of the water and flick drops in Mike's face. He grinned down at me and splashed me with his paddle.

"How's my cabbage?"

That was his new name for me. He said that's what I looked like, a little round cabbage. I dipped down for more water to splash back. He laughed, caught a crab, and almost lost his paddle.

I lay back among the cushions and half-closed my eyes against the sun. It was lazy and peaceful after the excitement of leaving. Ours was the last boat of the season, and already Hudson's Hope was weeks away.

We had been rebuilding our house on a new site. The other was too charred; it would be years before anything grew back. Mike had dug the foundation when the letter with Government seals came through to us.

"We're transferred to Grouard," Mike had said. "Well, at least we don't have to worry about packing."

And that was a true word. We had the clothes on our backs, and that was all. The fire had cleaned us out.

One by one, 'breed and Indian, they came, and at our door each left a gift of food. The canoe was given us, and enough provisions for the six weeks it would take us to reach Grouard; and these people faced a long, hungry winter.

Everyone came down to the river to see us off. The flag was flown at the pier just as it was the day the fur brigade left. At the last, Mustagan stepped forward and presented me with a suit of white caracul. To Mike he gave an ornately beaded quiver full of flint-tipped arrows. We shoved off, and I looked back at the waving hands, at the waving flag.

Tonight, as I laid our blankets on somebody else's bed and hung that somebody else's blanket up as a partition, I wondered about all these cabins we'd been sleeping in for the last few weeks. The owners of them we rarely saw. But on the wall or over the stove was usually a crudely painted sign. The one here said, "Make yourself to home, stranger, and shut the door when you leave." In the North no one ever locked his door, not even when leaving for the winter.

Every night we stopped in a cabin where wood had been stacked, matches left, and canned goods laid out for the chance traveler. All the unknown host received in return was a scribbled note giving our thanks, any news we could think of, and our names. This whole system of northern hospitality was a gigantic chain, for while we were eating this man's beans, he was undoubtedly farther up the trail, eating somebody else's.

I lay awake listening to the snores of the Indians who were rolled in their blankets on the other side of our partition. The baby was moving in me. It moved a lot now. It was strange to think I had a person in me, a person who some day . . . I snuggled in against Mike. It was then I felt my first pain. The cramp grabbed hold, turned and twisted in me like a live thing. I clutched Mike.

He was awake instantly, bending over me. "Kathy!"

"It's the baby!" I tensed myself against the pain, but it had stopped. I began to cry.

"Kathy, darling; girl, what is it? What's wrong?"

Nothing was wrong now, but I was scared. So was Mike.

"Kathy, are you—? It's bad?"

I cried harder, but against his arm, so the Indians couldn't hear.

"I don't want to have my baby here! You promised me we could get to Grouard, you promised me."

"Darling, I thought we could."

He began stroking me. I jumped away from him and said very viciously but very quietly. "You keep away from me!"

"Kathy." Mike said it in a stunned sort of way.

"You lied to me," I said into the pillow, "and now you can just leave me alone."

I knew I was unreasonable, that Mike had done his best. But I couldn't help it. I wanted a woman to help me. I would be ashamed in front of men. Oh, Mike was all right—but not those two Indians.

"Kathy," Mike said soothingly. "Kathy, girl."

"You've got to send those Indians away. I'm not going to have it if they're here. I won't, that's all. I just won't!"

Mike took my hand. "I'll send them away. I'll take care of you myself. It won't be anything, kitten. All women have babies. Haven't I always looked after you? And I will now. Don't be afraid, girl, trust me."

"I don't trust you," I said, and pulled my hand away. "You said we'd get to Grouard, you said I didn't have to have it on the trail. You promised."

"Kathy." There was decision in Mike's voice. "Tell me exactly how you feel. Do you have any pains now?"

"No."

"And how many did you have before?"

"Well, one."

"You'd be having them fast and close if you were near birth. I can get you to Peace River Crossing by morning. There's a Scottish woman there, Mrs. Mathers, who used to be a trained nurse. Do you want to chance it?"

I threw my arms about his neck. "Mike, you're so good to me!"

In less than ten minutes we and the two bewildered sleepy Indians were in the canoe. Sometimes I slept and sometimes I looked into the dark water. It was a silent, unreal trip. The paddles dipped together. An owl hooted through the forest. I would rather have my baby beside the river, with the wind blowing clear and sharp, than have it in that close and musty cabin. But there were no more pains. I dreamed that all the Junos we'd ever had were leading a beautiful little girl toward my mother and saying, "This is Katherine Mary's child." And I kept saying, "No, no, she hasn't been a baby yet, she hasn't been a baby."

When I opened my eyes the stars had faded out and the sky looked soft and pink. I reached up and kissed Mike's hair.

"Where's that baby?" he said and laughed.

We were no longer running in a gorge, but beside a grassy bank rising in terraces from the river bed. It was sunny meadowland, and there were wild flowers, blue and red, and after a while a yellow kind. It was four hours before we came to Peace River Crossing. The Indians call it Eteomami, which means "Water Flowing Three Ways," because here the Hart, the Smoky, and the Peace come together.

"It's civilization," Mike said. "They've even got a telegraph."

He helped me out of the canoe. The ground felt unsteady under my feet. I held onto Mike and thought of one thing: getting to Mrs. Mathers's house. Twice Mike's name was called, and both times he answered without stopping.

"Here we are," he said, and we walked onto a porch that squeaked and moaned with every step. Mike knocked, and we stood there waiting. He knocked again, and the door opened a grudging crack.

"What do you want?" The voice was high-pitched and querulous.

"It's Sergeant Flannigan, Mrs. Mathers. I've brought my wife to you."

The door opened farther, and at first sight I didn't like her. She was a woman of fifty, with a lot of flesh, loose and gray. I tried to do away with my impression. Mike says it's a bad habit of mine, judging people right off by the way they look. But it wasn't the way she looked, exactly, it was her voice too.

"You poor dear," she said. "Come in."

The house looked like her—big, rambling, and untidy. It smelled of food, and not only of today's food, but as though every meal had left its grease and its smell behind. She was telling me to take off my things. I did, but I felt uncomfortable the way she was looking at me. "This is silly," I told myself. "The woman's a trained nurse, she's got to look at me if she's going to help me." So I smiled and told her how we'd traveled all night to get to her.

"My dear," she said, "I don't know how you stood the trip. I know of many a miscarriage brought on by less than you've been through."

Mike frowned, but she didn't seem to notice.

"Bed's the place for her, Sergeant. I'll let you know when she's all tucked in and comfy."

Mike gave me a reassuring grin as Mrs. Mathers led me off.

She turned back the bedding and smoothed the rumpled covers. I stood and looked at the room. A cracked slop jar and basin, a dark dresser, and a straight-backed chair were the only furnishings.

"Do you want me to help you out of your things, dearie?" The plump fingers reached toward me.

"No," I said, drawing back a little. "I can manage fine, thank you." But I didn't, not with her watching me. I fumbled at every button. I'd taken off my boots and my mackinaws when she came toward me with a string in her hand. At the end of it was tied a button.

"Now," she said, "stand still, Mrs. Flannigan, and we'll see something."

"What?" I asked.

"Well now, we'll just see," and she hung the string in front of my stomach and stilled it with her hand.

"If it's a boy, the string will move forward and backward. If it's a girl, it will swing right and left."

"Oh, please, I'm so tired. I want to get into bed."

She was indignant at that. "Well, if you're not even curious!" She handed me a flannel nightgown which from the size of it was hers and watched me as I slipped it on.

"You're not built right," she said.

"What do you mean?" I felt frightened.

"You're just not. Too small all over."

I got into bed and pulled the covers up high.

"Some women aren't made for child-bearing, and you're one of them."

"My grandmother had fourteen children," I said, "and my mother had three."

"What did I tell you? See how they're dwindling off?" She brought her face against mine. "It's a bad month too. August is the eighth month of the year."

I made an effort to overcome the repulsion I felt. "Augustus must have thought it was lucky when he called it after himself."

"Too many eights," she said. "Eighth month of 1908 . . . and to-day, do you know what today is? The twenty-*eighth!* It's bad luck, terrible. I doubt if we'll take that baby out of you alive."

I shrank back against the sheets. "You mean I'll have a dead baby, a stillborn baby?" Just then it moved in me, and that tiny precious movement gave me the strength to lash out at her. "Don't you say things like that! Don't you dare! My baby's all right. My baby's alive!"

"Of course your baby's all right. What are you talking about, Kathy?" Mike stood in the doorway. "Kathy, what's wrong?"

I tried not to cry, but I did through every word. "She said I can't have a baby. She said—"

"What?" The word dropped from him like a bomb.

Mrs. Mathers began talking very fast. She scuttled over the words like a fat prairie chicken. "I said it would be a hard confinement, Sergeant. There's no use fooling ourselves, it will. And I was telling your wife that we always try to save the mother. If needs be, let the child go and save the mother. So you see, there's nothing for her to worry about, nothing at all, if the worst comes to the worst—"

"Get out!" Mike said, and his lips barely moved.

Mrs. Mathers stood and looked at him as though she hadn't heard right. Mike didn't say anything more. He didn't have to. Just looking at him made me want to hide under the covers.

Mrs. Mathers must have felt that way too, because she said, "Humph!" and started for the door. It wasn't until she was safely out of the room that she muttered something about "my own house!"

Mike closed the door and came back to the bed. He spoke in a stern voice. "Forget that nonsense."

"Mike," I said, "she's the one you're mad at, not me." But even this wouldn't make him smile.

"Of all the fool, ridiculous things to tell a girl!"

"But maybe she knows. Maybe she's right. After all, she's a trained nurse, Mike."

"You see, she's got you half-believing those bogey stories. You'd think a nurse would know better. But I guess being a nurse can't change a person's character. She's a gray woman with gray sayings."

"A crape-hanger."

"Yes," Mike said.

But I couldn't keep it up, not even for Mike. My baby was going to die—and I wanted it so much. I turned away from Mike and cried for the little Mike, the woman's words repeating themselves in my mind.

Mike took my hands away from my face and kissed them. "Listen, Kathy. This idea of bringing you down here wasn't so good. But it was because I didn't know anything about the woman—just that she was a trained nurse. That impressed me. I wanted you to have a trained nurse. I want you to have the best. And, by Heaven, you're going to get it."

I tried not to smile. "Another idea, Mike?"

"And this time it's good, kitten. I'm going to telegraph Mrs. Carpentier to come up from Grouard and look after you."

"Mrs. Carpentier, who's she?"

Mike smiled. "Mrs. Carpentier is a good witch, a fairy godmother. You'll love her, Kathy."

"But who *is* she?"

"Well, she's Cree, full blood, married to Louis Carpentier, a 'breed trapper. Wonderful person. Been midwife to every woman within a hundred-mile radius."

Anything was better than Mrs. Mathers. I couldn't have stood her handling me. "Could she be here in time?" I asked.

"She'll have to be."

TWO NIGHTS LATER my pains began in earnest. Mrs. Carpentier was somewhere on the trail. Mrs. Mathers sulked in the next room, and it was Mike who sat with me. The pain ripped and tore me. I'd hold onto his hands and scream. He tied a sheet to the bedpost. I'd pull on it and pull until it stopped. Then I'd lie panting, gathering my strength to meet it again. Mike would wipe the sweat from my face. Sometimes I remember a cool cloth on me.

It was one of these times when I lay exhausted, gasping for breath, that she came. I didn't notice that the door had opened. She was just standing there, looking down at me. Sarah, I thought, it's Sarah, from the Bible. I sighed and closed my eyes. I felt peace. The fear had gone.

It began again, seizing, grabbing, tearing. Then she spoke to me. "Sarah . . ." I tried to say, but only wild screams came.

Her voice went on, like an undertone of river water, slow, strong, and clear. I clung to the sound. I held to it. The pain swept me into a black gulf that was wet, that was sticky, that was blood, that was sweat. But I knew that in the voice and behind it was the world. If I held on, I could get back to it, into it, through to it.

The pain let go of me then, suddenly and completely. I didn't open my eyes. When you're as tired as this, you've got to be dead. And a weak tear rolled out because I didn't want to be dead.

Something fragrant, slightly pungent, was in front of my nose. It smelled of the woods. I opened my eyes to see. Sarah was holding a glass for me. I drank. It was bitter and yet sweet.

The pause had been shorter this time. It grabbed me faster. The words stayed with me, they were telling me, "Grow in the moist soil . . . running streams." Swirling pain, rising pain, but it could not pull me down into the darkness.

"Yellow flowers," she said, "small, bloom in June." I was being broken, split into two pieces.

"Mike, stop them!"

"From root come medicine. Make nice baby come fast. Make mother strong. Grind the root, crush . . ." Crush! That's what they were doing to me, crushing.

"Mix with water. Name is squaw root. Squaw root for help squaw with baby." That was all. I lost the words, everything. Then Mike was kissing me, stroking me, putting the wet cloth on my face again.

"Darling, it's all over. We have a girl."

I smiled at him. I could hear Sarah moving. After a long time I was able to turn my head and watch her. She was rubbing oil on a tiny mite of a baby. They put her beside me, tucked her in my arms.

"A lovely girl baby," Sarah said.

I looked at Sarah. She was big, big as a man. Six feet tall and strong. There was a grace and dignity in her, and a kindness and a knowing that sixty years had brought. I thought of what Mike had called her, the good witch.

The little thing in my arms stirred. The movement gave me a happiness and a joy I had never known. I smiled at Mike, I smiled at Sarah.

"Tell me about squaw root," I said.

"It have seed like big pea, can make much good drink . . . like coffee."

The little mouth opened against my breast.

"What else can it do?" I asked.

"Squaw root beside make well the squaw, make well the hands-swell-dropping sickness, the shaking sickness, the laugh-and-cry-without-reason sickness, and the pain-in-joints sickness that is called rheumatism."

I touched the baby and touched Mike. My family, I thought. I was so happy. I didn't want to spoil the enchantment this good witch had brought, so I asked her, "Tell me more about squaw root."

But instead she told me about my baby. Moss, she said, was softer than cloth. And she diapered it in moss, held in place with little pants. Talcum powder you couldn't get up here, but she knew something better, pounded tea leaves.

"You must have had a lot of children," I said.

"Seventeen of my own. Many others, maybe hundreds, I brought into the world."

"So many?" I asked her.

She nodded. "I brought my sister into the world when I was ten years old. And always after that, more children, and more. I never lose mother, and I never lose child, except once . . . in this house."

"In this house?" I held my own baby tighter.

"Yes," she said. "He was dead baby I take from Mrs. Mathers."

Mike's hand tightened over mine.

$\mathcal{T}$hirteen

WE CALLED THE baby Mary Aroon, after my grandmother, Bridget Aroon. Mary is the sweetest, most beautiful name there is, and I was always grateful to my own mother for squeezing it into my name.

Sarah left for Grouard two days after Mary Aroon was born. It was the day she went that I showed her the name Sarah in my Bible. I told her how Sarah had been the mother of a race. I told her that in my delirium, when I saw her standing in front of me, I had felt she *was* Sarah. Her hands had been strong, her voice gentle, and for me she had been that ancient mother of Israel.

"Mrs. Carpentier," I said, "I want to call you Sarah. May I?"

She ran her finger over the name in the book.

"It is the name between us," she said.

In a week I was strong enough to make the trip. Mike bought a cart and padded it with blankets. I lay in it and bounced the long way to Grouard. Many times I told Mike I'd rather be riding the horse, but he would smile and tell me I had a fine view of the sky.

I had never before looked forward with such eagerness to a place as I did to my new home, Grouard. When I had come in to Peace River Crossing, my only desire had been to lie down and hide. Now all my fears were turned inside out, a new life opened before me, and I knew that when I came to Grouard I'd start living it.

Sarah had told me how I would come to the village: "First up over Black Bear Hill, and down below, way on the ground, is piece of shining rock like stone for arrowhead, only rough around the edges. It is far, far away, and when the wind blows you see it is not a rock, but Lesser Slave Lake. The Crees, they call it Slave Lake because the Blackfeet, that once lived here, made slaves of captured people. And tears of slaves make this great lake. When you see it, you will soon be in Grouard, and your friends will be there, Mrs. Mike."

And so it was. The hill, the lake, and new friends to welcome us. Two men came riding up the trail to meet us. Constable Cameron had seen the smoke of our last campfire. The Indians, as usual, had known all about it even before he did. They told him it was Sergeant Mike, Mrs. Mike, and Mike's girl-child. So as we came over the top of Black Bear Hill, Ned Cameron came galloping up the other side, pulled in his horse, and saluted.

"Constable Cameron, sir. And this"—pointing to the slim youngster who rode behind him—"is Timmy Beauclaire, and I think, Mrs. Flannigan, he has a present for you."

"A puppy," the boy said. He pulled it out of his jacket. "Like it?"

"Very much," and before I knew what I was doing, I showed him the baby, bundled in her fur bag. "Like it?"

He nodded, and we both laughed.

Mike and Ned Cameron walked their horses and exchanged news. Timmy leaned from the saddle and handed me the puppy.

Timmy Beauclaire was about thirteen then, very thin and eager, with curly brown hair and sharp eyes of the color people call hazel, but really twinkling blue, brown, and green. I was his friend from the first minute and mothered him in a way that was laughable when I remembered I was only a few years older. Truly I felt that I had lived a hundred years and could give advice to my own mother now.

Timmy asked me what I would call the pup.

"Juno," I said.

"That's a funny name."

"It's Irish. All my dogs were called Juno, and it's brought me pretty good luck, and so this one is going to be Juno too."

"Don't you want to see whether it's a him or her first?"

Well, I did, but not with him around, so I said, "Makes no difference. He's still Juno."

"You mean *she's* still Juno," Timmy grinned, and Mike came up and we drove off for Grouard.

The part of Grouard I saw first was the little white cemetery on the hill, and it was so bright and sparkling it hardly dampened my spirits. The crosses were whitewashed and salted against the rains; this I knew from Sarah. The tall gray stone cross was Black Eagle's, the first important chief converted to Christianity; this Timmy told me. I thought the cemetery quaint and pretty, and only for a moment did a shadow of the future fall over me. There was the tiny distant figure of a woman walking through the graveyard gate, and for a second I thought it was me. Then we turned a corner, and the cemetery was gone. Cabins began to appear, and Ned Cameron shouted to me, "Grouard!"

We passed the boat landing in the cove, the Hudson's Bay Company store, and the trail turned into a hard-packed dirt road.

"There's a friend of yours, Mike." Cameron laughed as we came upon a most curious building. It was a gigantic cage made of saplings stuck in a circle in the ground and bent in on themselves. In one corner was a little shed or lean-to, and next to it a heavy gate. A man stood in front of the shed, grinning and waving at us. It was Baldy Red.

"Our jail, Mrs. Flannigan," Cameron said.

"What's he done now?" I asked.

"Baldy? Oh, he's back to his old trick of letting cows follow him. Other people's cows."

Baldy had come to the edge of his cage. "Welcome to Grouard, Mrs. Mike; and you, Sergeant, I'm counting on you to get me out of this thing."

"See you in the morning," Mike shouted back. We were past the jail, past the barracks, and driving up to a little cabin in a hollow.

There were half a dozen people standing in front, waiting for us. There were tall trees bending over the house. And there was a garden of the strangest, most beautiful flowers I had ever seen. This was home.

Sarah was the first to greet me and help me out of the cart. She took the baby from my arms and led me into the house.

"You sit down, rest first," she said. "I have soup ready and tea. Plenty of time meet everybody. Madeleine take care of baby." Sarah handed Mary Aroon to a dark plain girl of fourteen or fifteen.

I sank back into a chair, but I wasn't tired, just taking everything in—my new home, my new friends . . . and the flowers. I could see them through the window, row upon row of colors, soft and bright. And not one of them could I recognize. Who, I thought, had been caring for my garden? Who had planted and cultivated these lovely flowers months before I came? I wanted to ask Sarah, but she was too busy feeding me and introducing my guests.

"This is Timmy's mother, Mrs. Beauclaire. Mrs. Constance Beauclaire and Mr. Georges Beauclaire, her husband, and Madeleine and Barbette are her daughters, and the baby—of course the baby is yours," Sarah concluded gravely.

Georges Beauclaire twitched his mustache, grunted something, shook my hand and left, clearly relieved at the chance to join the men outside. He was a heavy, broad-shouldered man, rough and awkward in his movements, yet with a certain good-natured big-bear grumpiness about him that almost made me laugh. Beside him Constance Beauclaire seemed delicate, shadowlike, and almost as young as their daughters. There was a foreign grace about the way she stood and walked, and her soft eyes had a veiled, preoccupied air that you find in people who live in the past. When her husband left, she drew up a chair and silently took my hand. The light fell more fully on her face, and I saw the strength and character I had missed. I saw a small, proud mouth, a slender straight nose, as rare in the north as a princess's coronet, and deep, brooding eyes of an unearthly blue. It was the lavender-blue that lights a lake for a moment after the sun has set. This was no trapper's wife.

"Katherine Mary," she repeated my name softly, and it sounded unusual and elegant in her liquid French speech. "I would have wished to know you ten, twenty years ago. You will never understand, I hope, what it is to be one white woman, *the* one white woman." Constance smiled. It was more the remembrance of a smile than a smile itself. "You must tell me about Winnipeg and Montreal and Boston. Not much, what you can remember. They are not the cities I remember, but they will do."

"My mother lives in Boston," I said. "You are very much like her."

Sarah was bending over me, another bowl of soup in her lean hands. "Nice party?" she asked me.

"Yes," I said. "The best there ever was."

The sun was low, and its rays spread across the room, twinkling in the dust of many feet. Almost in a dream I spoke to Constance, and Sarah, and Sarah's husband, shy silent Louis Carpentier, and the McTavish brothers, and Old Irish Bill, with his long hair and elfin eyes ("the finest mathematician in Canada," Constance said), and Madeleine cradling my baby and scolding Barbette, who wanted to play with her too, and Mike standing behind my chair, smiling at them all. When they had gone I went to the window and looked at my enchanted garden with its rows of flowers that never grew in a garden before.

"It's been lovely," I whispered to Mike. "They were all so sweet, even poor Baldy in his cage. And I'll never finish thanking the one who planted this garden. Mike, who was it?"

Mike seemed uncomfortable. "They say it was Mrs. Marlin. She wasn't here tonight. She's not very—she's not very well." Then abruptly he said, "Look, Kathy, don't get upset about those flowers," and he started to explain something. I never heard it. I'd fallen asleep in his arms.

It had been an evening of magic, but the morning was quite down to earth. The baby woke me, squalling; the puppy, Juno, got into a sack of flour; and a bear off with a bucket of milk I'd hung outside the window. I walked out into my garden—and they were all dead, every single flower, lying dead and withered on the ground. The enchantment was gone, the fairy wand broken. I ran into the house and shook Mike awake.

"Mike, my flowers!"

"I know, Kathy." He dressed quickly and drew me out to the garden. "Look." He pulled up one of the poor faded things. It came right up out of the ground. No roots, no stalk, no leaves. It was just a blossom, cut and stuck in the earth.

"She's not right in the head, this Mrs. Marlin," Mike said unhappily. "She thought it would be a pretty welcome, Kathy," he said. "They're mostly wild flowers. They grow in the woods, in swamps, in very difficult places. She must have spent all day finding them, and then she put them in the ground to make you a garden."

I pressed his hand tightly. Suddenly I knew the enchantment hadn't gone. I thought of these people. None of them knew me. Yet Timmy brought me a puppy, and Sarah saved my life, and Old Irish Bill sang old Irish songs for me, and crazy Mrs. Marlin spent a day in the swamps so that I might have a pretty garden for an hour. I kissed Mike hard and walked back into the house. I picked up the baby, and she stopped crying. I dusted the puppy off and gave it a piece of dried fish. And as for the bear, if he liked my bucket of milk, he could have it!

Fourteen

CONSTANCE BEAUCLAIRE HAD come to borrow liniment for her husband's sprained foot. The baby woke up and began to cry. Constance bent over the crib and lifted her into the air. Mary Aroon laughed, and Constance laughed back. I had never seen her laugh freely before. Constance lowered the baby to her shoulder and patted her. Her hands were beautiful, so slender and fragile. It seemed strange to me that such a creature should live in this wild country.

She smiled across the room at me, and again her smile made me sad. "She is very like my Suzanne."

"Suzanne?" I said. I knew she had another son besides Timmy, and then of course the two girls, Madeleine and Barbette, but I hadn't heard of Suzanne.

"Another daughter?" I asked.

"A baby like this. It was a long time ago." She laid little Mary gently in the crib. "My first family."

I didn't understand. "Your first family?"

She looked at me with those great lavender eyes. "Katherine Mary, you are so young."

That was no kind of an answer. "I'm almost eighteen," I said.

"Almost eighteen," she repeated, and she smiled that smile full of pain and tenderness. "I was almost eighteen when I came from my country, from France."

France, yes—that's where she belonged, rare perfumes, and full swishing skirts, a box at the opera, a carriage with plumed horses.

"We came over on a small boat, my father and mother and five sisters and brothers. It was strange how it happened. The sailors blamed the captain, and the captain blamed my father, and he—well, he was dead by then, and so were the others."

"They died on the boat, your family?"

"Yes."

"All of them, the five sisters and brothers?"

"All of them. You see, my family had been well-to-do. We lived in Paris. I went to convent school on the Riviera. Later I had a governess, English."

This woman of faded beauty sitting before me in heavy mackinaws and a man's shirt, worn and mended, had known things of another world, another life. I hadn't dreamed them up, the opera and the horses with plumes; they had existed.

"My father speculated and lost everything. Of course, I didn't know that then, I just knew we were going to America. I thought of it as a holiday, and so did the others. I didn't even look back at the house because, you see, I was almost eighteen, and looking forward. When we came to the ship—it was a large sailing vessel—the captain was pacing the deck, and when he saw my father he began cursing. My father was very angry and ordered us below so we should not hear the captain's words. Later, when my father came down, he said the captain was an unreasonable ruffian. And that was all we could get out of him. But my brother, Renè, who wished to become a sailor, and who was always bothering the crew, said the captain's temper was due to my father's arriving three hours late. To my father time was of no concern, he was master of it as he was of everything else. But the crew was surly. The maledictions called down on my father's head would bring bad luck.

"We were two days out when Florence, my youngest sister, sickened. My father insisted it was the food, but it was smallpox. When she died, the captain slipped the body overboard quietly at night so the crew wouldn't know. We were forced to keep in our quarters. Food was left at the door for us. The hands were told we were quarantined for measles.

"Then we began dying inside our cabins. I shared a room with my two remaining sisters. The morning of the fifth day, I found they'd locked us in. From then on we did not know if our parents and our brothers were alive or dead. When my sister Viola died, I pounded on the door and screamed for my mother. No one came, no one answered me, no one brought food. The whole ship is dead, I thought. And I held onto Jeannette, who tossed and moaned; and begged her to stay with me. But she died too. I covered her with one sheet, and Viola with the other. But I was frightened of the still bodies, and I began throwing myself at the door. I dug my nails into the wood and screamed."

She turned her eyes on me, soft, wounded eyes. "I hadn't eaten in two days. It was hot in that little cabin, and the smell of death was there. I closed my eyes and prayed to die fast. When I opened them I was lying on the berth, and there was a tray of food in front of me. My sisters were not there. I got up and tried the door. It was open. Suddenly I knew it wasn't real, that I had dreamed it, that I alone had been sick and dreamed these things. I ran to my mother's cabin, holding to the wall of the passageway. I tried the door, and it opened. There was no one there; even the trunks were gone. I ran on to my brothers' cabin. The berths were made up. It was neat and tidy, no clothes around, nothing." She stopped talking and looked at me.

"That's the way it was. It had struck the men too. They had fallen from the ropes and the rigging. A third of them died. The whole crew had been demoralized. They had forgotten our food, they had forgotten everything, had prayed and sung and wept. The boat somehow looked after itself.

"It took two months to reach America. And, as I said, the crew blamed the captain for the curses he had called down, the captain blamed my father, and he was dead."

Constance smiled at me. "Don't look like that, Katherine Mary. It happened such a long time ago, twenty-five years. I can talk about it now, tell it as if it were a story, because so many years of living have passed between me and that little French girl. She was called Constance too, but the language she spoke is not my language. The things she learned on the Riviera I do not remember."

"What did you do, all alone?" I asked her.

"I got a position as a maid. A housemaid. I was very fortunate. Did I tell you even the trunks had been thrown overboard, for fear of contagion? But I was fed and clothed and given a day off once a week. I would go to church, and then walk. I walked and walked all over the city because there was only a small empty room to go home to. One day, on my day off, while I was walking, I heard my name called. I recognized him at once, Georges Beauclaire. He had been our groom. A great man with a horse, my father said. I was so glad to see him I almost kissed him. It was as though a part of my family had been restored to me. He knew my name, he knew theirs. When he asked me about myself, I cried. I had not been able to cry all that time.

"I married him that afternoon. He told me he had nothing. Well, that nothing of his was enough to get us into Canada. Georges dreaming of this immense wild country where a man worked for himself and had no master. And because I had no dreams of my own, I shared his. At Edmonton we bought a horse and loaded him with our supplies. He went lame in two days and had to be shot. We spread out our goods there on the trail. Georges took a gun and cartridges, a knife, matches, and a fifty-pound sack of flour. I took a fifty-pound sack of sugar on my back, and we walked. We walked till our shoes fell apart, and then we walked barefoot. We ate the berries along the way, and at night I cooked the flour with sugar and water. It kept up our strength.

"We'd been on the trail six weeks when the first snow fell. We had no other clothes. We had nothing. We thought we would have to die. But we didn't say that to each other, we didn't say anything, we saved our breath for walking. And came to a trapper's cabin. He was a Russian. Gorgin his name was. He was leaving for his winter's trapping, and he took Georges along as partner. I stayed seven months in the cabin alone. My first baby was born there. It didn't live."

"Oh," I said, "was that Suzanne?"

She shook her head. "No, the first was a boy. I never named him. What was the use?"

She got up and walked to the window. A dying sun lit her features. My mother told me there were people in this world born to sorrow. Constance was one of them.

"You asked me about my families. Women up here speak of their first family, their second family, their third family. Counting the baby boy I lost that first winter, I've had four families. Nine children. They're out there." I knew what she meant, the little graveyard we'd passed on the way in.

"When Georges came back that winter, we had money for clothes, a team, and provisions. We came here to Grouard. We built our house. The Indians helped us. And I had my second family, three children. It was the little girl, Suzanne, that reminds me of your Mary. I raised one of the boys, Paul."

"What happened?" I asked, glancing nervously at Mary Aroon, who was asleep in her crib.

"Measles, that time. Whole tribes were wiped out with it."

"But the other times? You said you had nine children."

"Once it was scarlet fever, and once it was typhoid. The winters are hard up here. There is no doctor, but I raised four. You saw my girls. Paul is married; he lives in Edmonton. And Timmy you know."

She turned from the window. "A nice family. It's enough for any woman. But sometimes I think of the others."

I didn't know what to say. I closed the window and fastened it, to give me something to do. She watched me, and when I had finished she said:

"Katherine Mary, we're going to know each other very well, for many years, I hope. You'll see, you'll come to understand. These big things, these terrible things, are not the important ones. If they were, how could one go on living? No, it is the small, little things that make up a day, that bring fullness and happiness to a life. Your Sergeant coming home, a good dinner, your little Mary laughing, the smell of the woods—oh, so many things, you know them yourself." She took my hand.

"You know I didn't come to talk about myself—but you are the only woman to come in in all these years; the others, the 'breeds, the Indians, even my own daughters, have never been out. It makes a difference, so you'll forgive me."

"Oh, no, it's been . . . I mean, you've been—" I stopped. I wanted to say, "How wonderful you are, how beautiful . . ." But I didn't know how. She picked up the bottle of liniment.

"Thank you, Katherine." She walked toward the door and then paused.

"You haven't seen the Mission. Perhaps you and the Sergeant would enjoy the midnight mass. I usually walk. The woods are very peaceful at night."

Before I had time to answer, Mike kicked the door open. He and Constable Cameron were half-supporting, half-dragging Timmy between them. Constance rushed past me. The boy was sobbing. She lifted his head and looked into his face.

"Is he all right?" she asked Mike. Mike nodded. They brought Timmy into the house, and Mike pushed him into a chair. None of us looked at him. He was trying to control his crying, and long rasping breaths shook him again and again.

"You went to my house first?" Constance asked Mike, and I was amazed how calmly she spoke.

"Yes," Mike said. "Georges was there, soaking his foot. He's got a pretty bad sprain. Anyway, he said you were with Kathy."

Constance turned to Timmy. His dark, tousled head was in his hands, but he seemed quieter.

"What happened, Tim?" she asked.

"Mish-e-muk-wa . . ." the word was muffled by his hand. Mish-e-muk-wa was the Cree name for bear. The Indian word startled me.

I thought of what Constance had said—none of her children had ever been out.

"As near as I can figure it," Mike said, "Tim was out hunting with Jerry West. They were on their way back with a few rabbits when they bumped into Doug and Ray Lamont and Dennis Crane. They'd been fishing, hadn't they, Tim?"

"Yes." Tim choked out the word without looking up.

"So they all walked back together," Mike went on, "and the men were kidding Tim and Jerry about their hunting, asking them why didn't they really bring down something, like an elk or a mountain lion, when all at once Doug lets out a whoop and grabs Tim's rifle, for there's a grizzly. You see, they were coming back along the lake, and this grizzly's on the other side of Miller's Cove. So Douglas says this is his kind of game, and he lets the grizzly have it. It's at long range, clear across the water, but he hits the bear.

"But he didn't kill it." Timmy looked up at us, his face streaked with tears. "It went into the water and swam toward us, right across the cove. And Doug kept pulling the trigger and it just clicked because it was empty, but he kept pulling it anyway."

"Didn't the others have guns?" his mother asked him.

"Fishing poles." Timmy's lips twitched, and for a moment I was afraid he was going to laugh.

"It kept coming, and Doug kept clicking that empty gun at it. And Jerry, he dropped his rabbits and started running. The bear wasn't swimming any longer; he was touching bottom. His neck and shoulders were out of the water." The terror in Timmy's eyes grew.

"Don't tell it, Tim," Constance said. But he had to tell it.

"We ran, all of us. There was a shack, no one lives there now, they used to make liquor in it. You know, Mother."

Constance nodded.

"We ran for that and—Jerry fell—" Timmy looked at his mother, faced her as though he were facing God. "I didn't stop. I could have picked him up, but I didn't." The anguish that darkened his eyes darkened hers. She didn't say anything.

Mike spoke up then. "The others didn't stop, Mrs. Beauclaire. Grown men, and none of them stopped. There wasn't time."

"Yes," said Timmy, "there was. We ran into the house, and Dennis slammed the door. Then Jerry got up and ran to it. The grizzly was behind him, its mouth open. Jerry grabbed the door and tried to pull it open. But they held it. I tried to open it; they pushed me away. Jerry was pounding at it and calling to me—to me! And I couldn't make them open it. I begged them, I begged them . . . and then Jerry began to scream."

Constance put her hand on his shoulder. "Timmy," she said. But Timmy didn't hear her, he heard Jerry screaming.

"He's dead?" Constance asked Mike.

"Yes," Mike said.

"God, you should have seen him," Constable Cameron said. "His face was torn apart."

"Ned!" Mike said. And Constable Cameron stopped talking, but bears were on his mind, and I was sorry when he said he would go to the Mission with us for midnight mass.

It was, as Constance had said, very peaceful walking in the crisp cool air. Timmy walked silently, his eyes on the ground. Mike was talking to Constance, but talking so Timmy could hear.

"When you're overwrought like that, things go on happening, and it seems that they're taking a long time about it. But really everything took place in a matter of seconds."

Timmy's hands clenched. "Mike," he said, "cut it out."

"All right, Tim. I just want you to know that after talking with the others, I'm convinced that it had to be done like that." Timmy didn't say anything, and we walked on. It had been a long evening. Mike had visited the shack, and he and the Constable had made out a report. Supper had been silent. I looked up. Black trees against a midnight sky.

"Sure," said Ned Cameron, "it was just a case of one or all." No one said anything. The leaves stiff with frost crackled under our feet. It was again Cameron who spoke.

"Yeah, a wounded grizzly's a mean animal. Ordinarily they're pretty easygoing and shy. But they're desperate fighters when they're wounded or when you get them cornered. How big was this one, Tim?"

Tim didn't answer.

"Remember the one McTavish got last summer? Weighed over a thousand pounds. I never was lucky enough to get one of them big fellows. Mine have always been right around four hundred pounds. But this fellow the McTavishes got, front claws were six inches long. They trapped him, you know. It's pretty easy, once you find a bear trail, because a bear will always step squarely in the print of his own tracks, so there are well-worn footsteps, almost like stairs in the hills. But the ground between isn't broken down at all because it's never walked on. So what you do is set the trap right in the middle of a print, and you got your bear."

I glanced at Timmy. Shadows crossed his face and lay in his eyes; from the trees, I thought.

"Another thing about real bears. That's what the Indians call 'em, real bears . . ."

"Ned," Mike said.

"I was just going to say, it's too bad it isn't six weeks later. The whole thing could never have happened then because they hole up about the time the first heavy snows hit us, and that's usually November. Have you noticed there's frost on the ground already?"

We came into a clearing, and the moon struck Timmy's face. Constance was watching him anxiously. I slowed my steps and smiled at Constable Cameron.

"Mike showed me once where a bear was hibernating in a drift."

"They'll do that, north side of a snowbank. But usually they den up in a watee about five feet high, six feet wide, and say ten feet deep."

I had stopped to pin my scarf tighter. We were far enough behind now so Timmy couldn't hear.

"You notice the grizzly didn't eat the kid, just mauled him up. As a rule, you know, they'll eat anything. But about a month before they den up, they quit eating. They go into hibernation with a clean belly and intestines. Their stomachs are drawn up in a solid lump like a chicken's gizzard." I gulped and nodded.

"That grizzly may be wounded worse than they think. I'm going to have a look around tomorrow. If the fur's in good condition, they fetch quite a price."

I was glad when we reached the Mission. It was the largest building I had seen; in fact, it looked a little like a fort. It had a stockade surrounding it, and inside were gardens.

"They raise their own food," Mike said. "They took the prize last year in hard wheat. Bishop Grouard is a fine man, Kathy. I'm anxious for you to know him. Grouard's named for him, of course. This Mission was the first building on Lesser Slave."

"It took God to beat the Hudson's Bay Company," said Cameron, and laughed.

"There are eighty children living here now, and they keep the place up. Each one has his job, gardening or sewing or whatever it is, and they take a pride in it, as you can see by the look of things."

The service had started, and we slipped in quietly. The pews were logs split in two. They rested at right angles to one another, forming seat and back. Candles made little pools of light, and shadows wavered on the rough-hewn walls. They were strange shadows, pointed and long—an eagle headdress . . . rounded shadows like a turkey's back, made by the women as they pulled their blankets around them. But the dark faces were lifted, their bodies yearned forward, and the words reached quietly into the corners of the chapel. The softness of the Cree language, with its deep musical notes, was very restful. I felt peace steal over me. I looked at Tim. There were tears again on his face. But the words drew me, and I turned toward the altar.

The bishop was a white-haired, vigorous-looking man. Thick hunter's boots showed beneath his black cassock. He stood straight, like a sturdy old oak, and when he prayed it was a gentle conversation. Closing my eyes, I felt the answering response. In the hush and the quiet I felt I couldn't pray. I could only feel a happiness and a contentment. I opened my eyes and looked into the face of the Mother of Sorrows. She was carved in wood. The work was crude. It looked as though it had been done with a hunting knife. But the face was not cold, like expensive marble faces. A great beauty was there, a great love and sincerity that made you forget its awkwardness and the strangeness of its proportions. The purity of the expression haunted me, the sorrow of the eyes, the sweetness of the mouth. I knew it. I had seen it before . . . I turned away, but the face was still in front of me. No, it was Constance Beauclaire, and her eyes rested on Timmy. Mother of Sorrows, I thought; and now my prayer came.

$\mathscr{F}$ifteen

MIKE WANTED ME to take a girl from the Mission to help with the house and the baby. I had completely forgotten my pleurisy, but every now and then I would catch Mike watching me with a worried eye. I still didn't stand straight enough or breathe deep enough to suit him.

"You don't have to take too much on you, Kathy," he said. "You can have one of the young girls at the Mission give you a hand with the housework."

"How young?" I said.

Mike laughed. "Fourteen, fifteen, sixteen," he said. "At what age do you get jealous?"

I gave him a push. "Who's jealous of you? You think you're such a dashing figure of a man in your red coat and all!" I looked him over and I had to admit, "Well, you are."

"Now look, Kathy," Mike said seriously, "you think I don't know about your sneaking down to the cage, taking Baldy Red things to eat, and squeezing in through those saplings to fix up his shed. If you want to do it, that's okay. But pampering Baldy Red with hot meals and clean sheets adds to your work."

I was mad that he had found out about it. I lashed out. "It's disgraceful! That filthy place, and the horrible things he cooks for himself!"

Mike didn't answer me, so I gave in a little. "If I have a girl to help me, can I go on fixing up Baldy's cell?"

"As long as I don't know about it officially," Mike said.

So we decided to get a girl, but somehow I didn't get around to it, and then Baldy was released, and it wasn't until he had been clapped back into the coop right after Hallowe'en that I finally went to the Mission.

I knocked at the door. It was opened by a cheerful-looking, red-faced Sister.

"I'm Mrs. Flannigan," I said.

"Don't stand there in this chill weather, child. Come inside."

She wouldn't let me talk in the hall, either, but took me to an inside room. Tea was served by an Indian girl of twelve or thirteen, primly dressed in long black stockings and a gingham pinafore. It was not until Sister Teresa had poured me a second cup that she felt she could ask my errand.

"I want to bring a girl home with me. I have a baby, and my husband says I should have a girl to help me in the house. I'll take good care of her, and we have an extra bedroom."

"I see," the Sister said. "Would you want her to do the cooking?"

"Well, I don't really care. It would be nice if she could do a little of everything, cook and keep house and look after babies. And then we could trade off doing things, take turns at it."

The Sister nodded. "You'd want one of our older girls, then. Well, the best thing to do is to let you meet them." She rose, and I followed her into the hall. "We've eighty children here at the present time. All ages. We've classes every morning. They're taught reading and writing. And Old Bill gives them a lesson in music or mathematics whenever he can spare the time. A good man is Irish Bill."

We entered the kitchen. Four girls were at work there. They smiled shyly at me. But when the Sister told them why I was here, they stole little glances at each other. And I was afraid that as soon as I left the room, they would laugh. When we were in the hall again, I asked the Sister to what age they kept the children.

"Until they're eighteen," she said.

I was glad of that, because I was eighteen already, and it was with more assurance that I walked into the next room. Here there were thirty or forty children, all sizes, all ages, and all busy. There was cleaning and scrubbing going on. There was a lesson on the blackboard, there were looms, there were girls knitting, sewing, crocheting. There were children with books, and children with games. There were big girls looking after babies. The Sister explained that this was the recreation room. All those who had no classes or special chores at this hour played here.

"It's supervised play, of course. They are taught useful and instructive things." She stopped by one of the older girls.

"Amy here is an expert needlewoman." She held up a patchwork quilt. The stitches were tiny and regular.

"It's beautiful work," and I smiled at the girl.

She looked at me appraisingly with black shoe-button eyes and did not smile back.

We walked to another group. The eyes of the children followed. Some of the little ones laughed and pointed. The bigger ones looked down at their work as we came up to them, but their heads lifted as we passed, and I felt them staring after me.

"Louise is very good with children," the Sister said. "Quite dependable." She spoke of them as if they weren't there. Louise looked away, then back shyly, uncertainly. More girls, trustworthy, good housekeepers. I was getting them mixed up. Smooth braided hair, dark eyes, black stockings.

The Sister opened a door at the back of the room. Wails and sobs came from the dark interior, and I drew back nervously.

"It's punishment row," she explained.

The room was a linen closet with only one window very high up. A bench was placed in the center. On it sat three small children crying their eyes out, and a big girl looking pensively at the floor. At that moment Sister Teresa was called back. As soon as the door closed behind her, the children stopped bawling, and began pulling at the big girl. "Go on, go on, Mamanowatum!"

The girl looked at me and smiled.

"What did Fleet Foot do then?" one of the little boys asked her.

"He went then alone into the forest. At his side ran the black wolf—" The door opened, the cries went up from the three simultaneously, and Mamanowatum's eyes rested modestly on the floor.

The Sister went right on about punishment row. It seemed Gerald had stolen from the apple bin, and Luke and Veronica had kicked each other and called names. The Sister hesitated when she came to Mamanowatum. "And Anne," she said, "has acted in a very foolish way."

I realized then that their Indian names weren't used. If I had named the girl, I wouldn't have called her Anne, but something light and wild and full of laughter.

"We rarely find it necessary to punish the older children." She looked reproachfully at Mamanowatum, and turned toward the door.

I said suddenly, "I'd like to take Anne home with me."

We were all surprised, the nun, Mamanowatum, and I. But the Sister recovered first. "She has a lovable disposition. But I feel I must warn you, Mrs. Flannigan, she's wayward, and her needlework isn't what it should be. Still, she's very good with children." I pretended not to see the twinkling glance Mamanowatum shot at me.

"How old is she?" I asked.

"Fifteen," the Sister said and, clearing her throat, she added, "I think it would be best if you discussed your choice with our Mother Superior."

"Of course," I said. "But I want to ask Anne— Would you like to live with me? You could have your own bedroom, and there won't be too much to do."

The girl looked at me earnestly. "Yes," she said, "please."

I sat alone in the room where the Sister and I had had tea. It was important to me now. I wanted Mamanowatum. I was afraid they wouldn't let her come because she was being punished. Then I wondered why she was being punished. I didn't think she would steal or kick people on the shins, but of course I didn't know.

The Sister came back, accompanied by the Mother Superior, a tall austere woman. "Mrs. Flannigan?" she said and nodded courteously. She sat and motioned me to be seated.

"I'm glad that you have come to see us. I'm sure you will give one of our girls a fine home."

"Yes," I said "Anne."

"I have already been informed of your choice." The voice was cool and level, the eyes were cool and level.

"I'm curious, Mrs. Flannigan; what made you choose Anne? In so short a time I would think it impossible to judge if she possessed more virtues than the others, or more talent."

"I don't know," I said, and I didn't. I mean I wasn't clear in my own mind why I wanted her, but I did . . . enough to fight for her. "I like her," I said.

The Mother Superior seemed puzzled. "My dear," she said, "I think perhaps you were sorry for her."

"Oh, no!" I had interrupted her. That immediately made me young and impulsive-sounding. The Mother Superior appeared not to notice. I admired her for that.

"Mrs. Flannigan, I think you are a very generous person. I think you felt pity—" I started to deny it, but she stilled me with a glance. "Pity is one of the greatest qualities with which the human soul is endowed. Do not be ashamed of it."

"As I say, you felt sorry, seeing Anne sitting in punishment row along with the four- and five-year-olds. Having aroused such an emotion in you, naturally she stood out in your mind."

The shrewd gray eyes fascinated me. Was she right? Was that the way I felt? Then into my mind popped the merry face of Mamanowatum and the story she was telling about Fleet Foot.

"Well, my dear?"

I looked at the Mother Superior. "Can't I have her?" I asked.

She smiled at me; even the gray eyes smiled. "Mrs. Flannigan, I'm determined this conversation shall proceed in a logical way. If you don't intend to ask why Anne is being punished, I shall have to tell you."

I must have looked surprised, for she said, "My dear young lady, perhaps this girl is an incorrigible liar or a thief. In that case it would be as well to know it before taking her into your home."

"Of course, you're right." I was angry with myself. I'd been acting like a child.

"Well, to put your mind at rest, she is none of those things. She is intelligent, charming, and completely capable. In fact, she is admirably suited for your purposes."

The woman was twisting me in her words.

She went on, "Anne has a fault, however, a serious fault—that of being too young."

"It's a fault she'll outgrow."

The Mother Superior didn't notice my joke. "Anne is young enough to imagine herself in love."

"She's in love?" I asked. And then, "Is that why she's being punished?"

"We have no reason to believe Anne has been immoral. Otherwise we couldn't keep her here among the other girls. I believe that she is merely headstrong."

"Is she too young to marry?" I asked.

"She's only fifteen."

"Yes," I said, remembering that I had been only a year older.

"Of course, Indian girls mature early and marry young. If it were anyone else, well, maybe. But as it is, it's quite impossible."

"You know the boy?" I asked.

"He's Jonathan Forquet," she said, as though that explained. "Son of Raoul Forquet." And then, a trifle impatiently, "My dear, you've heard of the Riel Rebellion?"

"Yes."

"Then you know it was an uprising of the half-breeds against the Canadian Government, an attempt to set up a government of their own in the Northwest. Riel himself was apparently a mild-mannered man. In fact, he was a schoolteacher. Nevertheless, he was the brains behind the revolt. But in the massacre that followed he lost the reins, was merely swept on in something he lacked the power to stop. He became the figurehead in whose name blood flowed and crimes of all descriptions were perpetrated." The Mother Superior looked at me from beneath severe brows. "Forquet, Raoul Forquet, the father of Jonathan, was one of the brigands who seized command. He was relentless, unfeeling. Completely so. He murdered, destroyed—and called himself a revolutionist. Of course, the whole thing was impossible without the Indians, and the Indians refused to join the 'breeds. So it ended as those things usually end, with the hanging of the leaders. Then men soon lost heart and disbanded. However, in this particular section they did *not* disband, for Raoul Forquet had not been caught, and he was still carrying on a war with Canada and Great Britain. A handful of lawless, ragged men followed him in his private war. But some were caught and some ran off because Raoul Forquet, to do him justice, refused to allow them to pillage and steal." There was a pause.

"That's all," the Mother Superior said. "When he was caught, there were three followers and an Indian girl with him. The men were hanged. I tell you this so that you may understand Jonathan's character. And why it is not possible for Anne to marry him."

I thought about Raoul Forquet. "He was a very stubborn man."

"Exactly, and Jonathan is like him, very like him. I don't know when he saw Anne first, but he began waylaying her. I understand he has even met her inside the Mission walls. Perhaps," the Mother Superior said, "all this strikes you as romantic. Perhaps your pity is again aroused for the two lovers. But I wish to tell you that I have talked to Jonathan Forquet here, where I am talking to you now. I made every allowance for him. I granted the fact that he is three-quarters Indian, that he was raised in squalor by an Indian mother, that this same mother undoubtedly fed him on tales of his father's greatness. But nothing could excuse his arrogance, his defiance. He laughed and refused to answer my questions. Only when I asked him to leave Anne alone did he answer, 'She be my *klooch.*' That's what he said, and that was the word he used to me, '*klooch.*' Mrs. Flannigan, I can't tell you what I felt. It was as though his father were standing before me. The same relentless determination." The Mother Superior unfolded her hands and then folded them again.

"I wonder if you realize what the word *klooch*, as Jonathan used it, implies? Tragedy for our Mission-trained girls. The tragedy of filth, dirt, ignorance, and superstition. Our girls read and write. Can you turn them into pack animals, to live in tepees, to haul and lift all day for a man who kicks and beats them? You see the impossibility of it. You see the tragedy of it. You see why Anne cannot marry Jonathan."

"Yes," I said, "I see."

"Now that I have explained the situation, Mrs. Flannigan, the decision rests with you. And the responsibility, of course, if you decide to take her."

I knew I was getting into trouble. When you see trouble as plainly as I saw it, there's no excuse to go walking out to meet it. But I remembered Mamanowatum, and how grave her pretty, happy face had gotten when she looked up at me and said, "Please."

The gray eyes of the Mother Superior made me hesitate, but I knew I was going to do it.

"My husband, Sergeant Mike, can take care of that Jonathan. And I'll look after Anne."

The Mother Superior rose. "Very well, Mrs. Flannigan. I hope both you and Anne will find happiness in the arrangement."

Before I could thank her, she was gone. The plump Sister, after telling me she would get Anne packed and ready and send her down to me, trailed after her. I was alone now with nothing to do but think about what I'd done.

$\mathcal{S}$ixteen

I WAS CONGRATULATING myself on how well everything had turned out, when it happened. In the first place, everyone had taken to Mamanowatum. Mary Aroon cried to be picked up by her, and Juno followed her around the house. Mike was pleased with himself for having thought up the idea—and she was a great deal of help, but mostly she was a great deal of fun. Mamanowatum, her Indian name, means "Oh-Be-Joyful," and that is what we called her.

When I told Mike what the Mother Superior had said about Jonathan, he just laughed. "I don't think we'll have any trouble in that direction."

But he was wrong.

It was about an hour after he'd left the house that I went out to shake the rugs. And there on our front doorstep was a pile of the most beautiful skins I'd ever seen. Beaver, mink, otter, and lynx were stacked in a neat, gleaming pile. I couldn't believe my eyes. There must have been two hundred dollars' worth of pelts there. While I was standing, staring, Oh-Be-Joyful came out too. She gave a little cry and gathered the skins in her arms, burying her head in the soft pelts. She whispered into the warm fur in her Cree language.

"Oh-Be-Joyful, do you know whose furs these are?"

She lifted shining eyes to me. "Yes, Mrs. Mike, they are mine."

"Yours?" She hugged them to her before she would answer me. "Are they not beautiful?" she asked. "Are they not the best of furs?"

"Yes," I said. "They are. They're expensive. Too expensive to be lying around on the porch."

Oh-Be-Joyful examined each pelt, stroking it and exclaiming over it.

"So young is the season for so pretty furs. He is clever, no?"

He? So that was it. "Oh-Be-Joyful," I said sternly, "where did these furs come from?"

She looked at me with such happiness that I was troubled.

"From Jonathan," she said, and when she said it the name was beautiful, the most beautiful I'd ever heard.

"Who's Jonathan?" I asked, to gain time.

"He called Jonathan Forquet. He is maker of canoes. From the land of the Blackfeet and the land of the Beaver come men to buy from Jonathan the canoes."

"Really," I said in my coolest tones.

"The *bateau* sings the song of the currents, and the waters race to catch it. For Jonathan, he know the time to cut the birch bark. In the almost summer does he make the cut beneath the lowest branch, and another above the roots. With his knife he makes the line between, and with the flat side of his knife lifts the birch bark and takes it away in one piece, without breaking. This I have seen him do."

I didn't want to take her pride and her happiness from her, but the word *klooch* made me do it.

"When did you see him making canoes?"

"In the almost summer." Her hands were still in the furs.

"When you were at the Mission?" I asked.

Now she understood. We looked at each other a long time.

"Why did they call me 'Anne' at the Mission?" she asked slowly.

"I don't know. Why?"

"Because they did not wish me to be joyful."

"No," I said, "that's not the reason. They name all the children with the names of saints, so they will try to be good also."

She shook her head. "They did not wish me to be joyful," she said again.

"They did not wish you to be bad or wicked; they did not wish you to be a *klooch*."

Her black eyes studied me. "Mrs. Mike, I *am klooch*. The word, she mean woman, Indian woman."

"Oh-Be-Joyful," I said almost angrily, "you're neither a *klooch* nor a woman; you're a fifteen-year-old girl."

Her full lips went stubbornly together, but she made no answer.

"And while the good Sisters at the Mission took care of you and taught you, it was wrong to sneak away and be with Jonathan."

Her eyes were round with wonder at such a thought. "When I first look on him I know my home is where he is. He tell me of the four winds, he tell me of the forest spirits, on the hill he dance for me the dance of good harvest."

This Jonathan that told such stories, that danced on hilltops, was not the cold, relentless young man I had pictured. I could only think that Oh-Be-Joyful was a child yet and no judge of character.

"Are you happy here, Oh-Be-Joyful?"

"I love you," she said.

It wasn't easy to harden my heart against that, but I wasn't going to let this pretty, bright-faced child become the squaw of Jonathan Forquet.

"Then you must promise me that while you stay here with us you won't see Jonathan." She bowed her head and did not answer.

"Promise me, Oh-Be-Joyful, and I'll never mention it to you again. We'll forget the whole thing."

She raised sad eyes to mine. "Can I forget him who brings me the joy my mother, who is dead, want me to feel?"

I was angry, but I made myself remember that she had never defied me before. I said as quietly as I could, "If you don't promise, I can't keep you."

"I love him," she said.

I went right on, "I'll have to send you back to the Mission. They will keep you for three years yet; they'll watch you."

She smiled at that. "Jonathan, he go where he want."

"I want you to stay with me, Oh-Be-Joyful. And all I ask is that you promise me."

"No," she said.

I was afraid I was going to cry in front of her. I turned away and walked to the end of the porch.

"I'll help you pack. There are some things of mine I'd like you to have." Saying that made me realize I was sending her away. I felt awful.

"If you change your mind," I said and stopped, because I was choking over the words. Oh-Be-Joyful began to sob. I ran back and put my arms around her.

"Oh-Be-Joyful, don't cry!" But she cried harder.

"Do you really love him so much?" I asked.

"Yes."

"Oh, dear," I said, "I wish Mike was here."

It occurred to me that we would look pretty silly to anybody walking by, holding onto each other like that and crying. It was up to me to pull myself together. I did, and decided that as I couldn't do anything with Oh-Be-Joyful, Mike would have to handle Jonathan, scare him away from the place or something.

When I thought about it a while I was sure that Mike could manage it, and that Oh-Be-Joyful wouldn't have to go back after all. But of course I couldn't tell her that I intended to get rid of Jonathan. So after I had jumped up, feeling everything was solved, she continued to sit there staring down into the pile of furs.

I wanted to get her busy at something. "Help me tie up these pelts. We'll take them over to the Company store, and they'll give them to Jonathan next time he's in."

She gathered the furs in her arms. "They are mine," she said.

"Oh-Be-Joyful, the furs are Jonathan's. You can't accept a present worth several hundred dollars from him."

"When brave lay gift before door and woman take it in, it mean she have him as husband."

"Then you most certainly will not take it in."

"I take," she said.

"Oh-Be-Joyful, you give me those furs!"

Her grip tightened on them.

"You're a mean, ungrateful girl, and it will serve you right if you marry Jonathan Forquet. You'll have no one to thank but yourself."

There were tears in her eyes, but she said nothing.

I walked back into the house. I felt confused. I wasn't so sure that the Mother Superior had been right. And I wasn't at all sure that Oh-Be-Joyful was wrong. I'd once heard an Indian refer to me as the Sergeant's *klooch*. If having a baby and a little home made you a *klooch*, it wasn't such a bad thing to be. It seemed to me that it all came to this: what was that relentless, stubborn, determined boy, that maker of canoes, that storyteller and dancer on hilltops, really like?

I walked back out on the porch. Oh-Be-Joyful still sat there, her eyes big with misery. I put my hand on her head and stroked the thick black hair.

"What's he like?" I asked her.

She caught my hand and pressed it. "He tall and straight as young fir tree. He walk in the ways of our people. He hunt alone, no brother sit at his campfire. He is silent like the woods, and when he speaks it is with knowing. With much care he take bark from tree, that tree is not hurt. Yet great fierceness is in his soul, and around his neck hangs the teeth of Mish-e-muk-wa. I want much, but never he speak love to me. Now today he lay the furs before the door as my father lay furs before the tepee of my mother. Should I send them back to the lonely campfire?"

"Oh, dear," I said again. "I wish Mike was here."

But when I thought about it, I was glad he wasn't. What I needed was a chance to talk about it with him alone. So I packed up a lunch and took it to his office. There was a great deal of loud talk coming from the office, and as I passed the window I glanced in. A swarthy 'breed with a dirty yellow handkerchief knotted around his head was saying, "He try kill me every night."

"Now wait a minute," Mike said. "Let's get this straight."

I decided I'd better not interrupt them, so I sat on the step and waited for yellow handkerchief to go. But he was a long time about it, so I took out a sandwich and began to eat. Also I wondered who was trying to kill yellow handkerchief, and why, and if they would succeed. They must have moved nearer the window because their voices became suddenly audible.

Mike said, "Then you don't know why Jonathan wants to kill you?"

At the name Jonathan, I choked on my sandwich.

Yellow handkerchief's voice was surly. "I tell you, no. Him hate me very much. Him make up this lie."

"About you stealing from his trap lines?" Mike asked.

I was so excited and upset that I opened another sandwich.

"Yes," yellow handkerchief's voice came again, "him tell that damn lie to my face."

"You're sure it's a lie?" Mike asked.

"You think I steal from trap line?" yellow handkerchief roared. "You think I thief? Then good-bye!"

I drew myself to one side so as not to be crushed as he stamped out. But he didn't stamp out, for Mike said quickly, "Now look here, Cardinal, let's not be so touchy. If your life's been threatened, I'm on your side; but I've got to know how matters stand before I can take any steps."

"How they stand?" Yellow handkerchief was beside himself. "I told you how they stand. That snake Jonathan Forquet come every night to my house and shoot at me with arrows."

"How many nights has he done this?"

"Three."

"And how close does he come?"

"Damn close. He pin my sleeve to table, him let fly arrow one-half inch from my head. Last night arrow she knock a spoon out of my hands."

"It sounds like he might just be trying to scare you," Mike said.

"He try kill me," yellow handkerchief said with conviction.

"Well, whether he is or not, he can't go around shooting at people."

"I tell you, him try kill me. Him come and say to me, 'I kill you, Cardinal, you dirty dog, you steal from my traps.' And it is a lie and he knows it, but he shoot anyway. Every night he try kill me."

"All right," Mike said. "I'll bring him in."

"What that mean, you bring him in?" yellow handkerchief asked suspiciously.

"It means, Cardinal, that I'll handle it my own way."

"You put him in jail, yes?"

"Now look, Cardinal. I want you to keep out of this. I'll talk to Jonathan and see what I can get out of him. But if he sees us together, he'll shut up like a clam."

"Okay, okay, so long you put him in jail."

"I'm not promising that."

The door opened so suddenly that it almost knocked me off the step. Yellow handkerchief's boots left gray prints on the thin layer of November snow.

Mike looked at me sternly. "Kathy, what's the idea, sitting out here in this rotten weather?"

"I had to talk to you about Jonathan."

Mike walked back in and sat down with a sigh. "Then you might as well have joined the party. That's all I've been doing, talking about Jonathan."

"Is he really a killer?" I asked.

Mike grinned.

"Well," I said, "I couldn't help but hear some of it, with yellow handkerchief yelling like that."

"Yellow handkerchief?" Mike laughed. "Oh, Cardinal."

"Listen, it's no laughing matter, because Oh-Be-Joyful loves Jonathan."

"Yes," Mike said, "you told me about it."

"But now it's worse. Today he dumped a whole bunch of skins on our porch."

At last Mike looked concerned. "He wants to take her off, huh?"

"Yes," I said. "That's what it means. And I couldn't get her to promise me not to go. You've simply got to do something about it, Mike. You've got to talk to him, tell him to keep away, and put the fear of God into him so he'll do it."

"Jonathan doesn't scare easy," Mike said.

"That's too bad for him. Then you'll have to put him in jail as Mr. Cardinal suggested."

"Good God, Kathy, I can't put a man in jail because he's in love!"

"But he's dangerous. Suppose he kills Mr. Cardinal, how would you feel? And how would I feel? Because by that time he would have run off with Oh-Be-Joyful too. Mike, it makes me just sick to think of it, a potential killer."

"Kathy, you're working yourself up over nothing. In the first place, I don't believe Jonathan is a potential killer. I think that Cardinal *did* rob his traps. And Jonathan took this way of scaring him off. Trap-stealing is the most serious crime in the Northwest. You can see why. It's a man's livelihood."

"Then why didn't he come to you?"

"He's Indian, that's why."

It seemed to me Mike was being unfair. "You're taking Jonathan's side against Mr. Cardinal's," I said.

Mike said very evenly, "I'm trying not to take any side until I know more about things."

"You don't like Mr. Cardinal."

"Of course I don't like him. He's got a reputation that smells like dead fish, a whole stinking trail of it, from here to Calgary."

"What's he done?"

"Laudanum," Mike said.

"What's that?"

"It's a drug. They use it for anaesthetics; it puts you out. Cardinal served a year in Calgary for peddling it. I've just checked with the Calgary authorities because someone's been bringing Laudanum into my territory."

"Oh, Mike, how do you know?"

"You remember the day Jerry West was killed by the grizzly outside that old shack?"

"Yes."

"You remember I went down there to investigate? Well, on the way I met Cardinal. He was carrying a box of fishing tackle, but no pole and no fish." Mike's voice sunk lower. He was talking to himself by now.

"I'd give anything if I had opened that box of tackle. But I didn't suspect then. It was only as I walked toward the shack that I noticed it was where Cardinal's footprints had come from.

"Now, the way I figured it, Cardinal must have heard what had happened with the bear, and while I was taken up with Tim he went to the cabin and probably took something away in that box of tackle. So I had a look around, and I noticed a peculiar thing. The window by the door was knocked out, and there were pieces of glass lying on the ground. It made me wonder why Jerry West pounded at the door until the grizzly got him. Why didn't he jump through the open window? The only reason I could think of is that the windowpane wasn't knocked out then. I began to suspect it was Cardinal who had knocked it out. But why?

"Then I noticed an interesting thing: a few pieces of the window had shattered and fallen inside the room. I bent down to examine them and found that they were not window glass at all. They were tinted a light green. I became conscious then of a sweet sickish smell. I felt around, and the floor beside the green glass was damp.

"Then of course the whole thing came to me. I was sure the smell was laudanum."

"What I think happened was this: Cardinal had hidden his supply in the shack. The shack was used as a distillery in the old days, but since that was broken up, no one's been near it. A perfect place to hide the stuff. Of course, when he heard about the grizzly killing, he knew I'd be down to investigate, so he had to beat me to it. He did. He packed up the vials of laudanum in his tin box, and in his hurry one of the bottles broke. He kicked the glass into the corner where no one would be apt to notice it. And if they did, so what? The place used to be a distillery. But the smell was noticeable in the shack, so Cardinal knocked out the window, and it was dissipated in the fresh air." Mike looked at me and grinned.

"Why don't you arrest him?" I asked.

"It's all supposition," he said. "I haven't got a fact in the world to back it up with. But it makes a nice story."

"And you make a nice detective." But after I'd thought about it a while, there was one thing I didn't understand. "What do people in this country want with laudanum?"

"On first thought you can't see it. Mountaineers and trappers don't seem the type to take to narcotics. But there are plenty of snowbirds up here, and plenty who aren't, who like to have a supply of the stuff on hand. The reason for it is a pretty grim one."

"What is the reason?" I asked.

"Well," said Mike, "a lot of miners pass through here on the way to the Yukon, and miners travel alone and work alone. Anyone who thinks he's onto a rich vein doesn't want a partner around to cut his throat. Then there are plenty of trappers who work alone, too.

"Now, there are many things can happen to a man alone on the trail. And the man who falls and breaks his neck is a lucky man. But suppose you don't break your neck, suppose you just break your leg? The vulture starts circling, and the wolves stand in a circle, and every time you look they're closer. You can keep them off for a while until your ammunition's gone or until you fall asleep. Well, that's when the little three-ounce phial you wear around your neck's going to stand you in good stead. Because it's going to put you to sleep, painlessly and soundly asleep. You won't feel it when the hungry circle closes in. You won't feel the first crunching bite. You won't feel the others rending and tearing and fighting each other for your still-living flesh."

"Oh, Mike, it's horrible!"

"Not with laudanum," he said.

We sat in silence for a moment, then Mike reached for the lunch basket.

"How can you eat?" I asked him. "I feel absolutely sick."

Mike opened the basket and looked in. "Sure you do," he said. "You've eaten all the sandwiches."

I couldn't believe it. Not even when I saw the empty lunch basket. "It's a nervous habit," I said with dignity. "I always eat when I'm upset."

Mike set out the next morning to find Jonathan and bring him in. I don't know how Oh-Be-Joyful knew it, but she did. We were silent and avoided looking at each other. When I fed the baby, there was no calling back and forth about the new tooth, or any laughing over the way she talked to herself. Oh-Be-Joyful used to pretend Mary Aroon was speaking Cree, and she would answer everything the baby said. It was very funny, but there was no fun in anything today, and no happiness. While I was peeling the potatoes for dinner, I came across one that looked just like a little fat man with big ears. I held it up.

"Look, Oh-Be-Joyful, at my little man."

I thought that would make her laugh, but she burst into tears and ran from the room.

It had been such a long day, and now it was past suppertime and no Mike. So many things can happen to a man on the trail. Especially if he's out to bring someone in who, maybe, doesn't want to be brought in.

Pictures crowded into my mind. Mr. Neilson, a strong man but stubborn, his boot sticking up out of the snow and the girl with the delicate wedding ring pulling at it. Burnt bodies lying by a well. A beaver with its eyes gone, swinging from a pole. Timmy sitting in the little church, his face wet with tears. I lighted a candle and set it in the window. It would be a welcome to Mike. It would make things more cheerful.

Oh-Be-Joyful came silently into the room and sat in the corner most filled with shadows.

"I wonder what's keeping Sergeant Mike," I said. And just then I heard him clumping with his snowshoes on the porch. I opened the door, and a gust of snow swirled in my face.

"Mike," I called. He grabbed me to him in a rough snowy kiss. Not until he bent to unstrap his snowshoes did I realize there was someone with him, standing silent in the dark.

"Come in," I said. The Indian boy followed closely behind Mike. I slammed the door shut against the wind and turned to them.

"Kathy," said Mike, "this is Jonathan Forquet."

Jonathan nodded courteously, but there was no smile on his lips. I noticed this because I noticed his mouth in particular. It was full, with a clean sweeping outline. He held himself well, proudly or perhaps defiantly. His long dark eyes swept over the room. They came to rest on Oh-Be-Joyful who stood in the farthest corner, hardly breathing. Jonathan's face did not soften. He gave her no sign, but he looked for a long minute.

It was Mike who roused him by demanding dinner in a loud voice. I was angry with Mike, terribly angry, for having brought Jonathan to the house. I wanted a chance to tell him so, so I said, "You have to help me carve the meat," and I led the way to the kitchen. As soon as the door swung to behind us I turned on him, blazing mad.

"Mike Flannigan, what on earth are you thinking of, bringing that boy here? Didn't you see the way he looked at Oh-Be-Joyful? Oh, you're crazy, just crazy!" The tears that had been close to the surface all day spilled over, and I wiped them away furiously with my apron.

"Kathy, I brought him here because I didn't know what else to do with him. And I think," he added slowly, "that that's what you would have wanted me to do."

"Oh, Mike, if they hear about this at the Mission, they'll take Oh-Be-Joyful back. They'll think you're deliberately encouraging it. And you are."

He took me by the arm, but I shook him off. Then he grabbed me tight by each shoulder, so tight I couldn't have shaken his hands off or pried them off either. He swung me around to him.

"You're going to listen to me, you little minx. I brought Jonathan here so you could put a meal into him. The boy is starving. He fainted on the trail coming in."

"Is he really starving, Mike?"

"When I found him, he was peeling the bark from a jack pine and sucking at the sap. You've got to be pretty hungry to do that."

I couldn't believe it. "But if he could shoot at Mr. Cardinal, why didn't he shoot food for himself?"

"He's sick," Mike said. "That's why it took me so long to bring him in. He's too weak to travel, really. But he's a plucky kid. Jumped away from that jack pine like a shot when he heard me coming. Afraid I'd guess what he was doing. And on the trail, not a word out of him. I didn't realize there was much wrong, he walked along with me quietly enough, and then all at once just crumpled up on the snow. He lay there as if he were dead. I built a fire and erected a kind of lean-to to shelter him from the wind, and all that time he didn't move. I started chafing him then and loosening his clothing. I noticed that his skin was discolored around his waist. I opened his shirt and found that his whole body was terribly bruised. For a while I thought that one of the ribs was broken. He must have been kicked fifty times in the side. That's the only thing that could account for it. I began to see why he was shooting at Cardinal."

"But if he was so weak, how could he?"

"I had a look around Cardinal's cabin on my way to pick up Jonathan. The cabin's on the hill, and I noticed a wide strip of underbrush had been crushed and tufts of weed and bush pulled up by the roots. At the time I couldn't understand what could make a track like that, but after I saw Jonathan, I knew. He's crawled up that hill every night for three nights. Where the vegetation's pulled up by the roots, that's where he rested or maybe fainted. How he could hold on like that I don't know, but he must have."

I thought of Raoul Forquet and his war with Canada and Great Britain, and I understood how Jonathan held on. "You think that Cardinal beat him up?" I asked.

"Yes," Mike said, "that's what I think. I visited Jonathan's trap lines, and there were signs of a scuffle. There have been heavy snows since then, but once a man sets foot, or in this case, snowshoes, on a snow-covered rock or a fallen tree, he leaves an impression no snowfall will obliterate. And that's what happened. There were the close-footed prints of the Indian Jonathan. And the impression of white or 'breed steps, wide apart, straddling on the web of the shoe."

"But Jonathan's a 'breed. That is, his father was a 'breed."

"He's Indian for all that," Mike said. "More Indian than many a full-blood. When he found his traps had been meddled with, he lay in wait. Cardinal came by to take a look at the traps, and Jonathan caught him at it, confronted him, and probably demanded the stolen skins. Cardinal must have knocked him down. I think one blow did it. Jonathan must have struck his head on something, or maybe the blow knocked him out. But if there'd been any real tussle, his face would look like his body. It's a pretty ugly picture, Cardinal standing over an unconscious boy and kicking him. If Jonathan had been white, he would have died in the forest. But, being Indian, he ate the sap of the jack pine and lived. Not only lived, but crawled to the house of his enemy every night to shoot at him."

"He just meant to scare Cardinal, didn't he?"

Mike shook his head. "He meant to scare him, all right. But a cat scares a mouse, worries it, before she pounces. Jonathan may be intending to pounce."

"Well, that brute deserves to die, and I wouldn't blame Jonathan a bit for killing him."

Mike looked at me with that teasing smile of his, and then his face grew grave. "If I could prove Cardinal was a trap-robber, the whole Northwest wouldn't be big enough to hold him."

"But it's proved," I said excitedly. "Jonathan's your witness. He actually saw him."

"That's what I *think*," Mike said. "But that's not what Jonathan says."

"What does Jonathan say?"

"Nothing."

"You mean when he came to, he wouldn't tell you how he'd gotten hurt?"

"He wouldn't," Mike said.

"But why?"

"Because of that devilish pride of his. He got the worst of things, didn't he? First Cardinal robs him, and then he beats him up. Jonathan wants revenge, and he doesn't want me spoiling it by sending Cardinal to jail. My job is plainly to keep the boy from becoming a killer."

"And mine," I said, "is to feed him before he faints in my living room."

I carried the dishes to the table. Jonathan stood leaning against the door. He spoke a low word to Oh-Be-Joyful and she jumped up to help me. In the kitchen, Oh-Be-Joyful caught my hand in hers. "Jonathan, he is sick, yes?"

"He'll be all right," I said, "once he gets a good dinner in him."

"You are sure, Mrs. Mike? You are sure?"

"Of course I'm sure." But I wasn't. I didn't like to see Jonathan leaning against the door that way. He wasn't the kind to lean if he could stand. I set down the platter of meat.

"Well," I said, "I guess we eat."

Mike turned to Jonathan. "Pull up a chair."

Jonathan smiled slightly and shook his head.

"Come on," I said. "Things will be getting cold."

Jonathan did not move. He said, "Already I eat much today."

"Of course you have," I said, "but you've been out on the trail with Mike for hours. I know Mike's always starving when he's been out all day like this." I cursed the evil little luck that made me use the word "starving," for Jonathan said, with that half-smile on his face, "Me, I do not starve."

Oh-Be-Joyful spoke softly to him in Cree, but he would not look at her.

"I'll feel very sorry if you do not accept my hospitality, Jonathan," Mike said.

"And my cooking," I put in. "A cook likes a little appreciation, and the best appreciation is eating."

Jonathan held that little mocking smile on his face and said nothing.

I sat down abruptly with my back to him. It was a terrible meal. Who could eat anything with that hungry boy watching us silently? Oh-Be-Joyful didn't touch a thing. Mike ate steadily without once looking up from his plate. I stood it until the meal was nearly through, but when Oh-Be-Joyful pushed away the stewed plums which were her favorite dessert, I pushed back my chair and said, "Jonathan Forquet, you've spoiled everybody's dinner by your stubbornness, and I hope you're satisfied!"

His eyes met mine. They were young and troubled. "I—I did not know," he said.

"Well, you know now. Next time I cook a meal, and you're around, you're going to eat it whether you like it or not."

"Kathy," Mike said.

"I don't care, it's perfectly ridiculous. Jonathan is pretending he isn't sick or hungry, and we're pretending with him." Somewhere in the middle of this I heard Mike groan, but I went right on, "I'm going to feed you, Jonathan, and then I'm going to put you to bed. And in the morning when you wake up, I'll ask you if it was all right that I did it."

Jonathan moved from the door and stood straight and tall in front of me.

"I don't care," I said again. "It's your own fault. It's the only way you let a person treat you."

He smiled at me, and his eyes were friendly. "Mrs. Mike, I ask you, please you give me to eat, yes?"

"Nothing's hot now," I said, "but the meat's just as good cold."

He sat at the table and ate my dinner. He ate with his left hand. It was stiff, and he had difficulty raising it, but the other hand hung at his side, unusable. He ate slowly and very little. When he had finished he looked to Mike and me and said gravely, "I have eaten in the house of my friends."

"Yes," Mike said, "you have."

Oh-Be-Joyful was filled with delight by what had happened. She smiled secret smiles to herself and moved busily around the room. Jonathan watched her with pleasure.

"She is too young," I whispered. "You will let her stay a while with me." I waited.

The words came so low from him I scarcely heard them. "It is well."

There came a rapping at the door that somehow shattered the peace and the friendliness. Mike opened it, and Cardinal stepped inside. He wore the same dirty yellow handkerchief, this time under his cap. He looked quickly around, and when he saw Jonathan he grinned in a very unpleasant way and clapped Mike on the shoulder.

"Ha!" he said. "You got him. Good!"

Jonathan jumped to his feet. He looked from Cardinal to Mike. There was a curious expression in his eyes.

Cardinal crossed the room and planted himself before Jonathan. He stuck his neck out, bringing his face very close to Jonathan's. The boy did not move.

"So!" Cardinal said. "Sergeant Mike, we did good to arrest this fellow, no?"

"Arrest!" Jonathan looked at Mike.

"Jonathan is not under arrest," Mike said.

"Him murderer!" Cardinal cried. "Him try kill me all the time."

Jonathan watched, apparently indifferent, but Mike was mad.

"I thought I told you to stay away, Cardinal. You're not doing any good here."

"I know what you want, Sergeant. You want by nice talk get out of him how he try kill me. I know better way." Again he brought his face close to Jonathan's. "You tell Sergeant Mike you shoot arrows at me."

Jonathan looked past Cardinal at Mike. He spoke slowly for the thoughts forming in him were painful. "Sergeant Mike light fire on trail to warm me. In his house him give me food. Is it that he want I speak of shooting arrows so he arrest me? Tell me now, this thing is true?"

Mike returned Jonathan's steady gaze. "The thing is not true. If I had wanted to know about the arrows, I would have asked you. There was no need to ask. I knew you had shot at Cardinal. But I had a different reason for bringing you here, Jonathan. I wanted your side of what happened between you and Cardinal. Of course, I must also warn you: there must be no more shooting."

"No!" bellowed Cardinal. "This is all wrong. Him try kill me. How I know tomorrow night he won't shoot straighter? Do I got to be dead before you put him in jail?"

Mike spoke to Jonathan. "There's to be no more shooting. I want your word on that."

"His word! What you think he is? Some damn good schoolboy? Him murderer, murderer!"

It was difficult to ignore Cardinal, who was practically frothing at the mouth, but Mike did ignore him.

"Well?" he asked Jonathan.

Jonathan looked fiercely ahead of him at nothing.

"I can't let you go around shooting at people," Mike said.

Jonathan stood there without answering.

"Jonathan," Mike said, "if you shoot at Cardinal again, I'll be forced to arrest you."

Jonathan's gaze rested almost gently on Cardinal. "Then my next shot, she be my last."

Cardinal turned pale. "It's a lie about the trap lines! It's a lie!"

Jonathan did not answer him. Instead, he said, "One moon ago, I follow Mother May-Heegar, gray wolf, to den. She lie down and die of wounds. From inside come little May-Heegar. Them cry like puppies. I take skin from Mother May-Heegar and eat her. I give pieces little May-Heegar. They eat her too. When skin of Mother dry, I put in den. Little May-Heegar like sleep there. Then I tie my shirt over opening. They scared of shirt, no go out while it still there. Next day I come, feed little May-Heegar. Them so little, I must chew food for them. After we eat, I paint little May-Heegar faces with bright paint, like I paint canoe. That show they mine. Every day now I go play with them. But one day I take rag from opening, they no run out. They dead. They mostly eaten. I feel bad. I look around, see mark of Pee-Shoo. Follow track into forest, see Pee-Shoo spring into tree." Jonathan touched the chain of bear talons that hung around his neck. "Mish-e-muk-wa die with one arrow through heart. But Pee-Shoo, big cat, killer of cubs, did not die, but went with beating heart through forest. My arrows, they follow him, they let him not to rest.

In terror must he live now until the day my pity, she guide arrow into the wicked, frightened heart of Pee-Shoo."

Jonathan looked at us. He did not look longer at Cardinal than at the rest of us, but when he had gone, Cardinal fell heavily into a chair.

The next morning we heard that Cardinal had left Lesser Slave Lake. He had gone in the night to do his winter's trapping farther north.

Seventeen

WINTER WAS LONG and quiet. The men were away from the village, trapping. The women stayed in their houses. In my own I had made a new friend—my daughter, Mary Aroon.

Now that she was over five months old, Mary Aroon had decided to take charge of the household. She had an uncanny eye for spotting things I needed, and yelling till I gave them to her. That was the end of my red pot-holder, and my green taffeta ribbon, and my spool of coarse thread, and nearly the end of Mike's shaving brush. Mike himself had to interfere to save this and argue it out with Mary Aroon.

This love of bright colors she got from me, along with her red hair. But her appetite came from Mike. Better than a clock, she was. Did I wait two minutes past her feeding time, she'd bang on the walls of the crib; that was warning. Next minute the house would be filled with screeches that should have come from a mountain lion. There was no answer to that. Mary Aroon was fed.

I expected another baby sometime in July. I was determined that this one would be just as strong and healthy as Mary Aroon. The bitter pessimism the women of Grouard had adopted didn't touch me. I wasn't resigned to losing six children to raise three. Every one of mine was going to grow up!

This was good country, I felt. I had come here weak and pale, coughing, hunched over, with shooting pains in my chest. Now I was well, I ran my own house, I had a child and would have more. Surely in this cold clean air of the North my children would thrive. I tucked the blanket up over the back of my baby's neck, kissed the top of her head, and gave her a nice bright green piece of cloth to play with.

Sarah had given me a small bottle full of brown powder. I secretly gave Mary Aroon a pinch in a little water, once a week. I was afraid Mike would disapprove. After all, I didn't know what the brown powder was. Probably a doctor from the outside or a pharmacist would have laughed and said it wasn't anything, meaning anything in their books.

But Sarah told me, and I believed: "Better, Mrs. Mike, to give medicine for sickness before than after. This way, when sickness come into baby, medicine is already there waiting."

So I took the scratched little bottle, which from its shape was probably once an iodine bottle in a prospector's first-aid kit, and I put it on the back of the shelf behind the salt and pepper and sugar.

"Sarah," I had asked her, "how do you know all these things?"

"Mrs. Mike, I know from my mother and from many old men and women who knew from before; I know from trying and mixing, myself; I know from the look of the plants; I know from things I am told when I sleep. You give your baby this now, she will have good stomach, good liver, she will never be sick. And you come yourself," looking at me critically, "come in January, and I start giving you squaw root. By the time your new baby comes, it will be quick and easy, like that!" And she brushed one hand swiftly against the other.

Therefore in January I dutifully walked down to the Carpentier's cabin on the lake and called for Sarah. She appeared at the entrance of a shed which ran along the south side of the cabin. She looked very tall and commanding. "Come up here," she said.

I had been down to her cabin only three or four times, and I had never been in the shed. I had never wanted to go into the shed.

Things grew and hung in that damp musty place that belonged at the bottom of swamps, under rocks, or in nightmares. From the door I could see thick, fleshy stems, slightly hairy, spread over a rack to dry. On the ground in front of me was a long-dead stump with strange warts on its dried-up roots and unhealthy-colored toadstools attached to the sides. One of the toadstools, thin and crumbling in its rottenness, was carefully supported by a network of string. Along the side of the shed was a long table, completely bare except for a dead muskrat pinned to the wood. The air was full of the smell of decay. Even the sunlight was transformed into a weird silvery light by the curtain of cobwebs which hung over the lattice. I shivered a little as I stepped into Sarah's workroom.

"Sit down, Mrs. Mike." She pulled a chair out of the shadow for me. I sat down, looking around me nervously. I wondered if I was imagining things moving in the dark corners.

"My plants," Sarah said. "Beaver oil for put beaver smell on trap, I sell to trappers. Rub on trap, lay trail on ground, fool wolf. Wolf not get man smell, get beaver smell, come fall in trap. White trapper use musk, fish oil, other things, but beaver oil best."

I turned my head, and something curved and sharp swung against my cheek. It was a clawing foot with nails protruding. It hung from a buckskin thong.

"Nothing," Sarah said. "A lion's claw. When bad things grow in the body and swell it, it is good to hang this claw by the bed and pray to the maker-of-claws to tear out the evil."

She reached under the table and picked up a large tin can. She tilted it to show me the pale brown chunks it held.

"Touch it," she said. I touched. It was rubbery, yet soft. "I take plant, squeeze out milk, dry in sun, becomes like this—good for heart, good for liver, makes to cough." She pinched off a piece, swallowed it, and coughed, a dry sharp cough. She smiled broadly and offered the can to me. I shook my head.

"No, I don't feel like coughing," I said, trying to laugh. The next moment I jumped. Something had moved in the gray corner across from me. I couldn't see well. It was in the shadows, but it seemed about the size of a puppy, it hopped like a toad, and a hoarse cry came from it. Sarah picked up a large packing case and put it over the thing.

"Nothing, an animal," she smiled.

"Yes," I said.

"Mrs. Mike," she said, taking my hand, "never be frightened of things because of their looks. Ugly mud flower"—she tilted the can again—"make well the heart. Pretty root"—and this time she picked up a long curling tuber—"kill a man."

"You don't like this room," Sarah continued, "because she smell a lot, because she is dark, because these things in it not your friends. But I like smell, I like dark, and all things here my friends—even him." She reached out her heavy foot and gently touched the box. There was an answering thump from within, and again that cry. The animal under the box began moving around restlessly. Was it a beaver being prepared for an operation to remove the precious castoreum? Was it a monstrous toad whose withered skin was a prime ingredient in magic? I was afraid to think about it. I forced myself to look away.

"You told me to come, Sarah," I began.

"Yes, you think of your next baby. I have ready for you." She reached over the table and fumbled in an open cupboard. "Many hundred babies I am the first to see. And only one die. Every one I save with squaw root." She chuckled. "You take every day, and I tell you, when baby come you not even know it, no! Once I play good joke on Louis, my husband, I am near my time, big like vinegar barrel. I am cooking dinner. I say, 'Louis, we need wood!' He say, 'We have plenty.' I say, 'Louis, chop wood!' He look at me and shrug his shoulders. I turn my back, take big chew of squaw root. He pick up ax, walk out. Let me tell you, when he come back with split wood, there is twins in the bed, and I am back cooking dinner. But he is a man, he is blind, he sit down and eat. 'Coffee strong enough?' I say. He say, 'Yes.' Then both babies cry. He look around! *'Sacre bleu!'* he say French. He run to bed. Where they come from? He hit his head with both hands. It was good joke, Mrs. Mike, best joke I ever make."

Sarah handed me a little box made of bark. "You laugh now, Mrs. Mike?"

I smiled. The atmosphere of the place had changed. It was still a witch's den, but a den of white magic, sorcery that ended in a joke. I followed Sarah down the shed while she exhibited her treasures: bearberry leaves drying on a plank, starweed soaking in a bucket of water, peels of slippery elm bark stacked in a corner, stalks of trumpet weed crushed in a stone bowl. Here were remedies for sore throat, for rheumatism, for snake bite, for unreturned love, for headache, for a broken leg, for a balky horse, for bad hunting, for all the ills and afflictions of man. Sarah's catalogue fascinated me so that I forgot all about the wet cobwebs, the toadstool, and the animal under the box. Curiously I asked her if she had any deadly poisons.

"Much easier to kill than make well," she said. "Anyone can pick up rock, crush in head of a man. Take wise man to fix. I could go in wood, pick here, there, many poisons. What for? I don't need. In pot here under table I have a little bit musquash—beaver poison—I keep covered so dog won't eat. This grow in wood, and anything come along and eat, little by little legs get stiff, body get stiff, no move, no breathe, then die. Once I remember deer eat, but not much. Get all stiff, lie down, look like dead. Along come Indian boy, cut off hide of deer. Get deer three-quarters skinned, suddenly deer him wake up, deer run off—without skin, no—not this much!" Sarah spread out her hand.

"No!" I burst out. "That's horrible!"

"It happen. Musquash bad medicine."

"Good! I come for bad medicine." A woman stood in the doorway at the other end of the shed. She leaned forward in a half-crouch, taut and intent.

"What you want?" Sarah said harshly.

"I just come to talk," the woman said, and edged into the shed.

"I already tell you no, many times. What you want talk for?"

"I . . . Mrs. Mike," the woman caught sight of me and raised her head. "How are you, Mrs. Mike? I am Mrs. Marlin. I just come by to talk," she added defensively.

"Mrs. Marlin!" I cried. "I've wanted to see you, to thank you."

"Thank me?"

"For my flowers. They were lovely."

She lifted a thin hand to her face and looked at me wonderingly. Mrs. Marlin had that fragile exotic beauty that comes of the mixing of many races. Her eyes were deep blue, yet the sockets they were set in were slightly slant. Perhaps a Russo-Chinese prospector had met the French-Indian *klooch* that was her great-grandmother, and touches of Scottish and Irish had been added since. There were faint echoes of all races in her beauty, and this made the whole in some way inharmonious. It was an alien loveliness that delighted the eye but disturbed the soul.

"Flowers?" She paused. "I remember. I planted garden for you, Mrs. Mike. It is pretty, no?"

I stood looking at her, trying to think of something to say.

"They die?" she said. Then, nodding her head. "They die. I knew. What I touch . . . it dies."

Sarah stepped forward. "You go now!"

Mrs. Marlin sat down stubbornly on the packing case. The rustling inside began again, but she didn't appear to hear it.

"I think she wants to speak to you alone," I said to Sarah.

"She not belong here. You go!" Sarah shook the young woman roughly.

A heavy cloud passed over the sun, and it became suddenly dark in the shed.

Mrs. Marlin spoke in a sly simple way. "You make death medicine, give me."

"I have no death medicine," Sarah said. "Who you want kill?"

"No man . . . no woman," Mrs. Marlin crooned.

I leaned forward. Under the table my foot kicked an iron pot. Beaver poison? I remembered. Little by little the legs get stiff, the body gets stiff, you look like dead, then . . .

"Law get you if you kill. Redcoat get you." Sarah was saying.

"I no kill person . . . just . . ."

"Animal?"

Then, after a long pause, "I think I know who is this no-man-no-woman," Sarah said ironically. "No. You right. Law not get you. Redcoat not get you. Very easy . . . if I help." Slowly Sarah's large hand closed on the woman's shoulder. With a jerk she pulled her to her feet. "But . . . I not help!"

Mrs. Marlin shook herself free. "I ask you ten, twenty time," she said bitterly. "You not help, I do myself, with knife maybe, with this hand maybe . . ." And she held out her trembling right hand, the fingers clawing in a terrifying gesture.

They stood there facing each other, motionless, silent, eyes expressionless, a violent wordless battle going on between them. I saw Sarah's face fall slack, saw the heavy wrinkles in her cheeks deepen.

"Yes," she said at last, in a voice so low and husky that I could barely make out the words, "I give."

Mrs. Marlin said nothing. Her lips parted slightly and bared her clenched teeth, her eyes widened, and she turned the clawing hand palm up. That was all.

Sarah took a jug out of the cupboard, fished around for a small bottle, and carefully poured a sticky black syrup from one to the other.

Mrs. Marlin seized the bottle and silently fled.

Sarah immediately lit a fire in the stove. After a few minutes she choked it down and covered the hot coals with a bunch of dried sweet grass. Thick white scented smoke poured out of the stove, and Sarah passed her hands through it again and again with a washing motion.

"What are you doing?" I asked.

"I make myself clean."

After a while she said, "You should know what this about, Mrs. Mike."

"I don't want to," I said. "I think I'd better go home. I don't feel very strong."

"Mrs. Mike," Sarah said gently.

"Well, I'm afraid for my baby," I said defiantly. "This has been a strain."

"Don't worry about your baby, Mrs. Mike. You love, you want to have, you will get. She too, that woman, will have child. But she hate, she don't want. She tell you herself, she want kill it. Kill it before it begin to live. Not one look does it get at world, at bright sun. No, not one yell does it make for show its own strength. No, into ground she put it, before it have one chance to walk on ground." Sarah stopped and added heavily, "Me, I help."

"No, you can't," I whispered. "Take back the medicine."

"Many times before, woman come ask me for to help kill baby. I say no. I bring maybe five hundred baby into light, only lose one. I not help kill them. All right. Two, two-three year ago, Indian woman come. Have some reason, not want baby. I say, no help. She go away. She do nothing. Just sit and hate child. Hate all day. Not sleep. Hate all night. Day come when child is born. She reach down to kill him, to choke him. Pull him out by head. Twist head. Break arm. Crush little fingers. Bend soft back. Old, old woman take away broken baby."

The packing case was moving. Sarah put her hand on it, to steady it. But the rustling inside continued.

"Old, old woman give me child. I keep. I try fix. But can't fix good."

For the first time I noticed the air holes punched in the case. Then I understood. That's where she kept it, that broken, misshapen child. I watched, horrified, as the case rocked and swayed. I leaped up as it overturned.

The thing sat there. It was a giant frog, blinking at us. Sarah took advantage of its surprise and clapped the box over it again.

"What did you do with that baby?" I asked. I was shaking all over.

"The baby? Oh, him not live long." The good witch sighed. "Just as well, I not fix too good."

ighteen

THE BIG EVENT of the winter was the Edmonton mail. I had a letter from Uncle John, and a letter from my mother, and a package that was marked DO NOT OPEN UNTIL XMAS. It was the first package I'd had from the outside since my marriage and, as Christmas was long past, I opened it. First I untied the string and put it in my string bag. Next I unwrapped the paper and put it in the cupboard. Then, when I couldn't draw out the excitement any longer, I permitted myself to look into the box. Out came handfuls of corrugated cardboard padding, and something at the bottom flashed. It was a mirror—the size of a baking pan, with a Boston label pasted on the back, and my face smiling up at me in front. I could hardly recognize myself. The face in the glass was my mother's, younger and stronger perhaps, but not at all like that of the skinny child who had come to Calgary for her pleurisy. In the box was a little note: "My darling, Merry Christmas and a Happy New Year to you both, Mother."

I opened my mother's letter.

She wrote of many things: her new curtains, the hot summer, the coat she had had remodeled, the scarcity of eggs, the mysterious disappearance of two good silver spoons, the bronchitis my sister had in August, the trouble her stove was giving her, and the way Boston was getting dustier all the time. She didn't say she missed me, she didn't say how badly she wanted to see me; but I felt it, and in all the chatter about eggs and spoons I saw my beautiful mother standing in the doorway waiting for a girl who would not come, who was raising her own family in a cabin four thousand miles away. As I read, my life in the North wavered and flickered. It seemed to me that it was a wild dream, with all the inconsequence and crowded incident of a dream. My mother and our home were suddenly so real and present to me that I almost heard the clatter and roar of traffic in the streets of Boston.

Mary Aroon wailed, and Boston vanished.

To almost every cabin of Grouard the winter mail brought a warm breath of the civilization south of us. Mike had a circular from Winnipeg warning against an epidemic of smallpox moving east from British Columbia. Along with it came a case of vaccine which he was to put in cold storage until further notice. Louis Carpentier got a package of dried dates from his cousin in California. Mrs. Marlin received a check from her late husband's family. Old Irish Bill received six months' issues of the *London Mathematical Gazette*. There was a postcard for Baldy Red threatening him with half a dozen kinds of destruction if he should ever show his face in Edmonton again. It was signed "Emily." And there was a heavily sealed letter for Mr. James McTavish informing him that he was an earl and peer of Scotland.

The McTavish brothers lived in a tiny cabin down by the lake. They were extremely poor and unlucky. If James McTavish went fishing, the other boats put in to shore; no fish would bite that morning. If Allan McTavish trapped a rabbit, it would be sick; if he shot a moose, it would rise and charge when he came up to it. Their credit at the store was good, but their accounts were always on the debit side of the ledger. An amazing piece of good fortune like an earldom could not fall to *our* McTavishes. We were all sure it was a mistake.

But Mike examined the papers with the stunned brothers, and when he came home that night he told me it was true.

"James McTavish is an earl, all right, Kathy. And he's the owner of a castle and a whole village in Scotland."

"Lord McTavish," I said. "Somehow I can't picture it."

"It took a remarkable number of deaths," Mike said, grinning, "but one way or the other all the other heirs are gone, and only James McTavish and his brother are left."

"And what is Allan, now that James is an earl?"

"Why, just the younger brother of an earl. That's all."

We both laughed. Allan would never get used to that. He was the younger brother in fact, but not in spirit. In the early days the brothers had taken turns at trapping and housekeeping. One did the hunting, the other cured the skins; one caught fish, the other cooked them; one drove the sled, the other mended the harness. Gradually James McTavish began to shift the active labor to his brother's shoulders while he sat home with his books and his pipes and his domestic duties. True Scot, he kept his house as neat as a pin, and there were even some who called the little man Mrs. McTavish behind his back. Now he was an earl, and his domineering athletic brother was only an earl's younger brother. It wouldn't last that way. We all knew it.

In the morning the brothers called on me to say good-bye. They were leaving for Edmonton immediately, thence to Winnipeg, Montreal, Liverpool, Edinburgh, and their earldom.

James showed me a threadbare plaid skirt, carefully patched. "The tartan of the clan," he said. "I expect to wear it at the ceremony."

"What ceremony?" I said.

"They will ask me to take an oath of loyalty to the king, I have no doubt."

"Not in that rag, Jamie," said his brother. "It's not fitting for an earl to have patches in his pants."

"I'm not ashamed of honest poverty," James replied stubbornly.

"You're not poor," Allan went on. "You're the owner of a castle and a mountain and a glen and a village." He turned to me with a worried expression. "We've been racking our brains, Mrs. Flannigan, trying to figure what that comes to. Ten thousand pounds, would you say?"

"I don't see how I can possibly guess unless I know how big the mountain is, and how many houses are in the village, and I'm not even sure what a glen is," I answered helplessly.

"Mrs. Flannigan," Allan said, "the letter said there was a castle. Not a cabin, mind you, which is one room, or a house, which is three to ten rooms, but a castle, that's at least fifty rooms. Now, a fifty-room castle is a valuable piece of property."

"There are castles in Scotland," James said sourly, "which are just rocks falling into the road. The rats wouldn't give you three cents for the lot." He grimaced. "I have a feeling it's just such a castle we've got."

"Fine talk for a new-crowned earl!" his brother stormed. "And the mountain and the glen? What of the mountain and the glen?"

James smoothed the worn tartan with his dry, spare, hand. "A mountain and a glen! And who is to buy a mountain and a glen? What market is there for mountains? A mountain is worth that—" He snapped his fingers. "This is no mountain such as are in the Yukon, full of silver and gold. It's a Scottish mountain, full of furze and wild goats. That's the kind of mountain we've got!"

"But a village, Mr. McTavish," I interrupted. "A whole village full of people is worth something!"

"That's what I tell him, morning, noon, and night," Allan said.

"Precisely what *is* it worth?" James said. "Am I to sell the people? Mrs. Flannigan, a Scottish village is a liability. School, church, poorhouse, infirmary—money out of my pocket, that's all; money out of my pocket."

"Ridiculous!" Allan said.

"You'll see, Allan. That's all this village will be, money out of my pocket." Lord James McTavish shook his head dolefully.

I was half-convinced. "Maybe it isn't such a good thing to become an earl," I said.

"There have been earls of Scotland, leaders of a thousand men, so poor a bowl of porridge was food for the day," James said emphatically.

"Mr. McTavish," I said, "maybe it would be better if you didn't go."

"My duty, Mrs. Flannigan, my duty to the clan."

Allan broke in with a roar. "It's all a lot of nonsense! He has every intention of going. Do you know what it's all about, Mrs. Flannigan? It's all about that miserable tartan. Fifteen dollars I want him to spend for a new one in Montreal, that's all, and he says he can't afford it."

"I have no the money!" James said.

"What about the old coffeepot?"

"There's nothing in the old coffeepot but twenty dollars to bury us when we die."

"We'll be earls before that! You'll have enough money to bury yourself twenty times over." Allan furiously snatched the plaid from James's hand and thrust it at me. "Look, Mrs. Flannigan, the earl's dress, with a mark on the seat of the pants they'll see as far as London!"

In truth, it was badly patched. The material was the same, but the stitches were large and loose, and the stripes weren't lined up right. I looked at James McTavish, but he only looked down at his feet and muttered, "I have no the money."

So it came about that I patched the tartan of an earl and lord of Scotland and sent him off to his coronation.

I WAS GIVING Mary Aroon a bath, and it was quite a job. Oh-Be-Joyful poured in the third kettleful of water. I tested it with my elbow. Mary Aroon sat and watched the whole process. She knew all this preparation was for her bath. And it pleased her to see her big giants running around like this. When I finally decided the water was the right temperature, I lifted her in. She laughed and chortled and waved her little fists. She loved her bath, as she always had an audience. Today it was Oh-Be-Joyful who leaned over the tub and swirled the water around in exciting ripples and splashes that made Mary Aroon gasp and gabble in that unknown tongue of hers. She was a plump, healthy baby who kicked her legs at you with energy. Her little back was strong now, and she sat in the tub by herself, my hands an inch away but not touching her.

She was in the midst of her bath when an Indian threw open the door, letting in cold drafts of air.

"Shut the door!" I yelled. But he didn't, so I jumped up myself and slammed it to.

"Sergeant Mike, Sergeant Mike!" the Indian said in a voice of terror.

"At the office."

"Him not there." The man opened the door.

"What is it?" I cried.

"Larry Carpentier, him in bear trap!" He was gone, the snow closing around him and covering even his tracks. I sat down slowly.

Larry, Sarah's boy! They'd be taking him to her cabin. Oh-Be-Joyful lifted Mary Aroon from the tub and wrapped her in a blanket. She came to me holding the baby.

"You go?" she asked.

"Yes." I got into my furs, my fingers working automatically at the buttonholes.

"You think him hurt bad?" Oh-Be-Joyful asked.

"I don't know. Get the baby dressed, Oh-Be-Joyful. Feed her at four."

I walked on snowshoes out into the white crisp world. The sky was a pale winter one. The trees were hung with frost lace. Icicles like sharp daggers pointed down at me. I tried to hurry, but the snow was so soft I was afraid of floundering.

Poor Sarah, seventeen children, six raised, and now this! A bear trap. They had them at the Company store. Terrible things. Two sets of steel jaws with teeth six inches long that interlocked, that bit in, that mangled. I tried not to think of Larry, of anybody, even a bear, walking into the pan, the flat part of the trap where the powerful springs are concealed. Forty pounds they weighed, the ones in the store. I shivered inside my buffalo jacket seeing the jagged jaws closing on the flesh and bone of Larry Carpentier. Odd, too. It wasn't the season for bears. It must have been an old trap someone set and forgot, or couldn't find.

And it had to be Sarah's son. Big strong Sarah, her back was used to bending under troubles. And Larry. It seemed to me that Sarah spoke more of Larry than of the others. He was a mild-mannered young man of twenty-five. He caught wild horses up in the Yellow Pass and bred the strongest sled dogs in the North. He had a well-stocked barn, and cattle. In the summer the trappers bought the fruit he raised, especially plums and strawberries.

The smoke of the Carpentier cabin darkened the sky in front of me. A scream, a terrible scream came from inside, then another. I tried to undo my snowshoes. My hands trembled. The mittens were stiff with ice. Again the screaming. A man's screams are terrible. With my heart beating so it choked me, I pushed open the door and stood, staring.

Larry lay on the table, and all his blood seemed to be beside him. From his foot to his knee, he was held by a rusted steel trap, the teeth of which clamped together, cutting entirely through the leg in thirty different places.

"Water," Sarah said, without turning around. "Boil it."

I couldn't move because then I saw what she held in her hands. It was a saw. She raised it. Larry's eyes followed the motion. She set the saw in the groove she had already made in the flesh above the knee. Back and forth. I saw the sweat break on the boy's face. I heard the crunching of the leg bone. Again the screams. The terrible agony of his screams.

"Water," Sarah said.

I moved forward. I pumped, I filled a kettle. I lifted it to the stove. The cries drew me back. His nails dug long furrows in the wood of the table. His dark eyes rolled back under his lids, leaving white, unseeing holes. The smooth muscles moved in Sarah's arms. Back and forth, back and forth. The trap bumped and clanged against the table. Sarah's strong man's hand pressed the saw's teeth deeper into the wound. It quivered, it quivered like jelly. A strange laughter stirred me. Mother and child, I thought. Mother and child. Then Sarah began hacking. The bone chipped and splintered. I looked at her face, at the clamped lips! I looked at her hands. I thought, how can she do it! I looked again at her face, relentless and calm. Then I understood. Sarah had gone mad. The good witch was evil. Her boy lay under her hands, twisting, screaming, while she hacked at him calmly with a saw. I stared at a flap of hanging flesh. It grew, it grew until it covered the whole room and had wrapped me in its soft bloody folds. The color deepened. It turned black, but I knew it was still blood. The screams faded, receded, became a buzzing that turned into a voice. It was a voice I knew, that I had heard before. I felt comforted. I wanted to understand the words, that came over and over again. It was my name, "Mrs. Flannigan."

I opened my eyes and looked into the face of Bishop Grouard. I struggled to get up, but his firm hand on my shoulder kept me down.

"You're all right, my dear. Easy now. That's it."

I raised myself slowly into a sitting position, and he propped a pillow behind me. There were no more screams. Only a low moaning came from the boy on the table. For he still lay there, and beside him lay his leg.

Mike stood over him with the saw in his hand. As I watched, he lowered it, wiped his face with the arm of his jacket, and turned to Sarah.

"It's off."

Sarah nodded, dabbed at the stump with water, cleaning and washing. Then she wrapped it in a steaming flannel poultice which she clamped into place.

Mike walked to the head of the table and put his hand on the boy's shoulder. "You'll be all right now, Larry." Larry tried to speak, his face convulsed with the effort, but no words came.

Mike made a shrewd guess. "Don't worry about a thing. I'll look after your stock until you're up and around." The boy sighed. His face relaxed. Mike moved softly away. "Don't worry," he said to Sarah in an undertone.

Sarah was heating another poultice and measuring clear drops of fluid into a dish filled with something that looked like mustard. She nodded when Mike spoke to her, but did not look up from her work. Poor Sarah. My heart overflowed for her. I hadn't been any help to her. Not any. What strength was in her, in her hands and in her soul! I was ashamed. Not for having fainted, but for having been mad myself, and I must have been, to have had such thoughts about her.

Mike walked over to me and helped me to my feet. The Bishop rose too, and the three of us went out together. We buckled on our snowshoes silently, without looking at each other. We had gone maybe a quarter of a mile, when Bishop Grouard said, "A wonderful woman. A heroic woman."

"Amazing strength," Mike said. "That leg bone was really hanging by shreds when I took over."

"Where were you?" I asked.

"Out on line inspection. The telegraph was on the blink most of last winter. I want it open the year round, and I thought if I kept check on the wires . . ." His voice trailed off, and we walked in silence.

"You mustn't worry, Mrs. Flannigan," the Bishop said. "We'll take care of them. We'll see that Mrs. Carpentier has a hot supper tonight, and Larry too, if he's ready for it. And for as many nights as there's need."

"Oh, no. I want to do that for Sarah. I *want* to. She saved my life."

"Sorry, but I'm going to be stubborn about it, Mrs. Flannigan. You see, we cook *en masse* up at the Mission, and another dish or two to fill is nothing."

I didn't say anything. I didn't even thank him. He must have seen that I was crying, because he said, "We'll have him up and about. I feel confident of that. So confident that I'm starting to work on a wooden leg."

Mike shook his head. "I don't know. He's weak, to say nothing of shock. Must have been a couple of hours in that trap before they found him. He'd started up to the Yellow Pass about a week ago. So no one missed him at this end. In fact, I didn't expect to see him for months.

"The way the Indians found him, they heard a gun go off and went to investigate. Larry was lying there, shooting into the bush. He said he was being attacked by a lion. He was off his head delirious by that time. His leg was already turning black and gangrenous. The Indians tried to pry open the trap, but it was old and rusted. They thought from the condition of the thing that it had been set a couple of years ago and lost. That sometimes happens. They're so cleverly hidden. Anyway, they wrenched and pulled and jiggled at it until Larry passed out. That scared them, and they decided just to bring him in as fast as they could, trap and all. Which was probably the smartest thing they could have done, because they had no disinfectant, no way of stopping the bleeding even. So they brought him in, and it wasn't too tough on him because the leg was partially frozen. They brought him to my office first, and when they couldn't find me, they took him home. His mother saw at a glance that the leg was past saving. So she did the smart thing, the thing one in a million could do. She cut it off. She made a clean job of it too, and if anyone can pull him through, it's Sarah."

I knew Mike was right, of course, and no one had more faith in Sarah than I had. But I couldn't see how that boy could live with that poor mangled leg—and the blood that had poured out of him."

"Has a man ever been caught in one of those traps before?"

Bishop Grouard sighed. "Plenty of times, my dear, plenty of times. Fifty or a hundred years ago the English designed a mantrap twice the size of this one, with teeth nineteen inches long and weighing about ninety pounds. It was used on large estates to catch poachers."

I held onto Mike's arm. "Did they—did they always die?"

"Usually. At least they were always maimed and crippled to such an extent that future poaching became impossible, and that's what the owners of the estates were interested in."

Things moved. A gray rabbit hid behind a bush, the clouds blew into each other in their hurry, and the collision was without sound. We ourselves moved noiselessly along. Everything was smothered and blanketed by the snow. The only sound I could remember was the low moaning in the cabin we had just left.

Thinking of Sarah's child brought to my mind the picture of Mary Aroon as I had left her, kicking her plump little legs in the bath water. I remembered how those legs waved in the air and danced. Then I thought of taking a saw . . . No, I couldn't. Not even to save her life, I couldn't. And I knew I was not the woman Sarah was. And not the mother, either.

"Kathy, what is it?"

"Nothing, Mike." I smiled at him, but I guess the smile wasn't much of a success because he wrapped a big fur arm tightly around me.

When we came to our house, I asked the Bishop in, but he shook his head and held out a fur mitten to us. "It was good of you, Sergeant, to put the boy's mind at rest, but just the same you've cut out a job for yourself, looking after the stock."

"All in the line of duty. Article 37, Section C, in the Mounties' *Handbook of Regulations*. Anyway, you're the one that's taken on the big job . . . making him a wooden leg. Are you really going to do it yourself, Bishop?"

"Oh, yes. All in the line of duty. See the Gospel according to St. Matthew, Chapter 25, Verse 40." Bishop Grouard smiled at us and walked on.

"He's a fine man," Mike said, looking after the snow-encrusted figure of the old man.

That night, when the supper things were cleared away and Mike was out tending to Larry's stock, I got down the book of *Regulations* Mike had referred to. I thumbed through it carefully and then shut it with a smile. There was no Article 37, Section C.

I peeped in at Mary Aroon. She was sound asleep, and that was good because there was still another book I wanted to look in. I got out the Bible and opened it. There *was* a Chapter 25 in the Gospel of St. Matthew, and at Verse 40, I read:

"Inasmuch as ye have done it unto one of the least of these my brethren, ye have done it unto me."

$\mathcal{N}$ineteen

WE OWNED HALF a cow. Larry tried to give us the whole cow, but Mike wouldn't hear of it. After an hour's arguing in which Larry threatened to take off his new leg and hit Mike over the head with it, they finally settled on half a cow. The cow gave ten quarts of milk a day, and five belonged to us. Mike insisted that I drink a glass at each meal, and one before I went to bed, while I was carrying the baby. I think he bullied me a lot because whatever he wanted me to do was somehow tied up with the good of the baby, and of course he'd get his way.

By the middle of May, Larry was quite comfortable on his wooden leg, and whenever I went over to his barn to milk Bessie, he was there, walking about, testing the leg, grinning, stroking Bessie's head, and telling me wild stories about her: how in the icy winter of 1907 her milk froze in the pail, and he carried it home in a piece of paper or a pan.

One day I invented a game for the walk home. The object was to see how far I could swing the milk pail without spilling a single drop. But as I came within sight of the house, I saw a strange Indian sitting on my porch. I changed the pail to my other hand and walked on slowly to meet the trouble I was sure he brought. He stood up when he saw me.

"Sergeant Mike?"

"He's not here."

"Big trouble. Must find."

I set the pail down. "What *is* the trouble?" I asked.

"Must find Sergeant Mike quick."

I saw there was nothing more to be got out of this fellow, so I gave in. "He's at the reserve. I'll take you."

"Me find." He walked down the steps.

"I'm going with you," I said firmly.

I looked at him out of the corner of my eye as we walked. He had the light springing step of the woodsman and the keen eyes that noted automatically how soft the ground was and how old the rabbit tracks.

"Where are you from?" I asked.

He pointed in a northerly direction.

"What tribe?"

"Blackfeet."

"That's a long way away. Sergeant Mike has no authority over the people of the Blackfeet. You must have a sergeant of your own."

The man grunted. I thought a while. We had heard that there was smallpox among some of the tribes. In fact, that's what Mike was doing today, vaccinating the whole Indian Reserve.

"Have you sickness?" I asked.

"No sickness," the Indian replied.

He's probably lying, I thought. They've sent him for help, and he's afraid to tell me. Well, if it was sickness, Mike wasn't going. I wouldn't let him.

"Sergeant Mike's not a doctor," I said. The Indian said nothing.

We walked in an unfriendly silence to the reserve. I noticed as we approached that the village was awfully quiet. There were no children playing in front of the tepees. There were no old men squatting in the doorways smoking. No women's voices calling, laughing. No sound of loom or kettle, nothing. It was a dead village.

I looked into the tepees, throwing back the heavy entrance skins. Nothing, no one. But things looked natural, as though they had been left but a moment before. The fires were not out, needlework was left on the floor, dogs bristled and growled at us. I opened the doors of the cabins, but again everything was deserted.

The Indian peered over my shoulder. He was evidently frightened, for he fingered the charm pouch around his neck, and his eyes rolled nervously. He must have thought the entire tribe had been spirited away by Gitche Manito. And even so, his deductions were more positive than mine because I simply didn't know what to think.

I was wondering where Mike was. I peered into the shadowy forest that crept up to the edge of the village, and I distinctly saw a face watching us from behind a bush. Was it a child playing a game? It couldn't be. This face was lined, was old. As I looked, the bush trembled and the face disappeared. I stared into the woods.

Dark shapes glided like spirits among the trees. And though there was no wind, bushes and leaves rustled in the strangest manner. The Blackfoot at my side was walking very close to me and casting terrified glances at the shadow shapes.

I felt eyes on us, many eyes, the eyes of the village. I was walking fast now, as fast as I could without running. Suddenly I heard a welcome sound. A baby was crying. The noise that came from somewhere in front of us was not a spirit wail, but the wail of a very real human baby, bawling at the top of its lungs. I turned toward the sound, into the woods; and there, behind the last tepee, was Mike. Beside him sat the crying baby, and three feet in front of them was the mother.

Between Mike and the young mother was a large jagged boulder. Mike was talking to the woman, and as he talked he slowly circled the boulder toward her, and she just as slowly circled away from him. It took them five minutes to complete the circuit, and all the while Mike kept up a steady one-sided conversation. The woman stared at him with large black eyes, not at his face, but at his hands. I looked too and saw that in one hand he held a small glass tube and a piece of cotton. In the other he clutched a shining scalpel which he pointed straight at the young woman. I didn't blame her for backing away, and I didn't blame her for not listening to Mike's soft words.

"It won't hurt," he was saying. "It won't hurt you at all. It's good medicine."

And all the time the sharp, wicked-looking blade chasing her slowly around the rock. Suddenly Mike stopped circling. The girl stopped too. Mike smiled reassuringly at her from his side of the rock. The young woman watched him warily, trying to determine what that smile meant. She reached her conclusion a moment too late, for Mike took a running jump onto the rock and dived off the other side on top of her. As they went down, I heard him pant, "This won't hurt . . ."

He had her pinned flat with his knees and arms. All she could do was roll from side to side and bite when his hand got close enough. His knife scraped on her upper arm. She yelled and screamed and tried to draw away from the uncorked vial, but in spite of her wriggling, Mike managed to get most of the fluid into the scraped place. When she saw he had succeeded, the woman's screams redoubled.

Mike got up from on top of her and removed his cap. "I'm sorry," he said, "but everybody's got to be vaccinated. It's orders."

The young woman rocked back and forth, holding her arm. Her baby had stopped its crying to listen to hers. And the baby was not the only spectator. Curiosity had brought the distant shadow shapes in closer.

Mike carefully wiped the scalpel and walked to a tree stump on which his supplies were laid out. He selected another tube and tore off a fresh hunk of cotton.

"Who's next?" he asked, looking into a bush that shook nervously.

"Come on out, Johnny, you're a brave boy. There's nothing to this. It won't hurt." Mike advanced slowly on the bush. Two bright eyes watched not him but the gleaming knife and the mysterious glass bottle. Mike pounced, but Johnny was quicker. He bolted from under the bush and dashed into the forest, paused at a safe distance, and looked to see if he were being followed. He was. Mike decided to use psychology. He put the scalpel and the glass tube behind his back.

"Johnny, Johnny," he coaxed.

I could see he wasn't going to get anywhere with Johnny, so I called to him.

"Kathy," he said, coming toward me, "what are you doing here?" And then excitedly, "Darling, I'm so glad you've come."

"Why?" I asked suspiciously, for I didn't like the way he was brandishing that scalpel.

"Why, now I can vaccinate you, and they'll see there's nothing to it. They just cry from fear."

"They do? Well, I'd like to oblige you, Mike, but you see I've already been vaccinated."

"Oh." And then his face brightened. "How long ago?"

"Well, I don't know exactly. Why?"

"If it's more than seven years, you need a new vaccination," and he started uncorking that little glass vial.

"Oh, no," I said hurriedly. "It wasn't that long ago. It was just recently. Just before I came out to Uncle John's."

"I thought you didn't remember when it was."

"Well," I said, "I remember now."

Mike put the cork back grudgingly, then his eye lighted on the Blackfoot. He smiled at him ingratiatingly.

"Now, there's nothing to this, nothing at all."

"Mike," I said, "you can't. He's not your Indian. I mean, he's a Blackfoot."

The word caught Mike's attention, and the Indian was saved.

"Blackfoot," Mike repeated, and looked at the man with interest.

The conversation that took place between them I couldn't follow. It was in a dialect I didn't understand, but every now and then I caught a Cree word. And then I caught a word that meant something more to me. The word was "Cardinal," and what it meant was trouble.

Mike put an arm around me. "Well, Kathy, I'll be leaving as soon as we can get me packed up."

"Oh, no, Mike."

"I'm afraid so, darling."

"But why?" I said, hanging onto him. "Is it on account of that Cardinal?"

"Yes." Mike started packing up the vials.

"You should have put him in jail when I told you. What's he done now?"

"Same thing."

We started back through the still-deserted village, the Indian following us.

"Trap robbing?" I asked.

"Yes. A refinement of it. He substitutes poor fur for good."

"Are you going to arrest him?"

"Yes. This time I've got all the evidence I need against him."

"But why can't Constable Cameron arrest him?"

"He's got to stay here and vaccinate these people." There was grim satisfaction in Mike's voice. "If he can."

"I don't see why you don't finish vaccinating and let Cameron bring him in."

"Because," said Mike, "if I were betting on who'd outsmart who, I'd bet on Cardinal."

I sort of agreed with Mike, although I didn't say so.

When we got to the house I had Oh-Be-Joyful feed the Blackfoot while I got Mike's supplies together. Tins of beef and tea and another pair of mittens, an extra buffalo robe, for he was going into the Far North.

I walked out front and watched Mike strap the things to his horse. He would ride to Peace River Crossing, pick up another Mounty there, and make the rest of the trip north by canoe.

"When will you be back, Mike?"

Mike cursed under his breath at a slip knot that for some reason didn't slip. "Two months, Kathy, for sure."

I reached out a hand and steadied myself against the porch rail.

"I'll put in a few more tins," I said and went into the house.

Oh-Be-Joyful was washing dishes in the kitchen, so I closed the door of the storage room behind me. I looked up at the rows of cans, trying to select those that would be most nutritious. But the bright labels blurred and swam in muddy colors before my eyes. I leaned my head against the edge of the shelf and cried silently.

Months didn't mean anything to him. He'd said it just like that . . . "I'll be away two months." He was going because he wanted to, because it was adventure. He didn't think about me, about us, that it wasn't so easy to have a baby, that maybe I'd be dead even.

"Mike," I said his name out loud, "Mike, don't you love me any more? Don't you care that I'll be alone, that I'm scared?"

I dried my eyes with the hem of my skirt. I had to be getting back. He'd be wondering why I was so long. I took down three more tins of beef, some soup, and more tea. "He's a man," I told the girl in the sunbonnet on the box of tea. "He hasn't even thought about it yet. It hasn't occurred to him. He'll feel awful when he remembers. He loves me." The girl on the label kept smiling. "He loves me," I said again and began to cry.

"Kathy!" It was Mike calling. I rubbed my tears away and took a deep breath before I answered him.

"Here I am," I called, "in the pantry."

I listened to his steps as he crossed the kitchen, and I couldn't help smiling a little because he's such a big man.

He opened the door. "What are you doing in here, kitten?"

"Getting more food. It would be awful if you ran short."

"Darling . . ."

"Yes, Mike?"

He reached out his arms to me. When he was through kissing me, I still stayed there with my head against the red of his jacket.

"Kathy, if you don't want me to go, I won't."

"Really, Mike?"

"Of course, really."

I reached up my arms and slid them around his neck. "No, I don't trust Cameron to bring him in. You have to do it yourself, Mike."

Mike held me very tight. "Kathy."

"Of course," I said, "you're his superior. If he fails, the blame is on you."

"Remember the other time, Kathy?" He was speaking very softly, his lips against my hair. "Remember I promised you you wouldn't have the baby on the trail?"

I nodded.

"Well, I'm going to promise you something this time. I'll be with you. I'll be back. If I wasn't sure that I would be, nothing could drag me away from you now, understand?"

"Oh, Mike."

"In the meantime, Oh-Be-Joyful will be with you. And in case you or Mary Aroon is sick, there's always Sarah, thank God. We've very good friends here, Kathy. Don't be afraid to go to them."

"Mike, it's just you I'm worrying about. Be careful."

"Listen, girl. Don't come out. It's no good standing and watching a man ride off. It gives you a lonesome feeling."

I was glad Mike said that because I hated the idea of seeing him swallowed up by the outdoors. Here in my own house I could pretend that he hadn't really gone. I closed my eyes and lifted my face.

"You're beautiful," Mike said.

"You never used to say that before we were married."

"Well, you weren't beautiful then. You were too skinny, and had too many sharp places, elbows and things."

"What things?" I asked.

He laughed and seized me. "But you're beautiful now. Ever since the baby, you're softer and lovelier all over."

His mouth was warm and rough and wonderful. Then he pushed me away from him, looked at me, and drew me back again by the shoulders. This time he gave me a big brother hug that meant, "Be good, Minx, take care of yourself."

I knew he was going now, but I wouldn't let him, not just yet, just a minute more.

"Mike," I said, "will you still love me if I say something?"

"What?" he asked.

"Damn Cardinal!" And bless Mike, I said. Only not out loud, because men don't like that kind of thing.

He smiled at me with those blue eyes and ruffled my hair with those big hands. Then the pantry door banged to, and I was alone.

MIKE KEPT HIS promise. He was back in six weeks, with Cardinal riding beside him, the same dirty yellow handkerchief knotted around his neck.

That first evening was a happy one. I'd fed Mike a big dinner. After such a trip I felt that even our criminal deserved a real meal, so I sent Constable Cameron over to the jail with a supper for Cardinal.

Mike sat in the big arm chair with Mary Aroon on his lap. I curled up on a buffalo robe with my head on his knee. Mary Aroon began to laugh, for Mike was making shadow pictures on the wall for her. He made a rabbit that wiggled its ears, and he made a billy goat that wiggled its long beard.

"Tell me how it was, Mike."

"How what was?" And he made a little old woman with a pack on her back.

"About how you captured him," I said.

"Oh, that. I just went up to his shack."

"Did you have to do any fighting or shooting?"

"No; he saw me coming and beat it. But he didn't go far. I heard him walking around the cabin that night. And in the morning I saw the tracks he'd made. There was still a thin layer of snow up there. Well, there was a night and two whole days that he stayed out with no food and no blanket. But the second night he called to me from outside the window."

"What did he say?"

"He said if I didn't go away he was going to shoot me and then burn down the house. I asked him, 'What about the buttons?' And he yelled in, 'What about them?'

" 'Well,' I said 'they won't burn, and if there's a button left, or a tooth or any part of a bone, you'll hang. Because everybody in Grouard knows I came to bring you in.'

"He didn't say anything, so I figured he was thinking that over. I fanned up the fire nice and bright and put on a kettle of tea. As I did it, I was thinking what a good target I made. When the water started boiling, I walked out on the porch and looked into the darkness where he'd been talking. I couldn't see a thing, but I talked as though he was right close by that first pine. 'Come on in, Cardinal, and have some tea. We'll talk it over.' And he did. He stepped out from behind that pine.

" 'You're right, Sergeant, about those damn buttons,' he said.

" 'Yes,' I said, 'I guess I am.'

"So we had tea and after a while dinner, and then sat around the rest of the evening. That's all. In the morning we started home."

Mike crossed his legs and slid Mary Aroon along them until she was sitting on his foot. He held her tiny hands in his big one.

"Now we're going for a ride." He swung his foot out and back very gently, out and back, and began to chant, "This is the way the ladies go, nimety-pin, nimety-pin." And then, swinging his leg with more force, "This is the way the gentlemen go, gallopy-trot, gallopy-trot." By the time he got to how the farmers go hobbly-hoy, he was wiggling his foot all over, and Mary Aroon was bouncing around as though she were riding a bucking bronco. She shrieked and yelled her delight and got red in the face from excitement.

Mike stood up and lifted her into the air. "Now you're flying," he said.

Just then the door burst open, and Cameron stumbled in.

"He's dead!"

The shout brought Oh-Be-Joyful from the kitchen. We all stared at the man.

"Murdered! There's a hunting knife stuck clear through his throat."

"Just a minute," Mike said. "Who's dead?"

"Cardinal. That's what I'm telling you. I walked down there with his dinner, and he's sitting on the bench with his head thrown back against the bars. I thought he was sleeping. But when I got close, I see he's been stuck right through the throat. What a mess! And the knife still in him."

Mike got into his jacket.

"You should have seen it," Cameron said to me. "He was laughing. His mouth's wide open in a kind of twisted laugh."

"Laughing?" Mike said, and then, "You said it was a hunting knife. Have you ever seen it before? Do you know whose it is?"

"It's got Jonathan Forquet all over it, plain as though it was written."

"What do you mean?"

"The handle's all carved up. A whole hunting scene winding along. It's Jonathan's work, all right. You know he can't keep from whittling. He cuts designs in everything he owns."

"All right," Mike snapped and gave a quick look at Oh-Be-Joyful. "Let's not jump at conclusions." He started for the door and then turned back to us.

"Oh-Be-Joyful, I want you to think hard and answer me truthfully. Have you ever seen a hunting knife such as the Constable describes in Jonathan's possession?"

Oh-Be-Joyful stared straight in front of her. "No," she said.

"There's plenty of people around here can identify Jonathan's work," Cameron said.

Mike opened the door. "Come on, we'll take a look at things."

Oh-Be-Joyful continued to stare at nothing long after they had gone.

"Jonathan didn't do it," I said. "He wouldn't kill a defenseless man." But I knew that by tribal law Jonathan had the right. "Besides, he's too clever to leave his knife there." But at the same time I thought: Isn't that just like Jonathan to boast silently with a knife, to leave it as a taunt? I tried to reason myself away from the thought. I reasoned out loud to Oh-Be-Joyful.

"Even if it is his knife, that doesn't mean anything. Everyone knew of his quarrel with Cardinal. They'd know he'd come under suspicion. So they'd steal his knife and leave it at the scene of the crime."

I thought myself that that conclusion was a little weak. It would be no easy matter to steal from Jonathan.

Oh-Be-Joyful said suddenly, "When they bring the knife, it will be Jonathan's."

I looked at the girl. She stared through the walls of my house. Across a mile of grassy path she stared into the cage. The cage was before my own eyes too. The last time I had been in it was when Baldy occupied it. I shuddered to think that through those bars, the bars I had so often slipped between, a killer had struck. I remembered Cameron's voice. "Through the throat," he'd said. "Clear through the throat."

"Jonathan didn't do it," I said again, and this time with conviction. Because the picture wouldn't come. I could put the knife in Jonathan's hand, I could even raise it, but I couldn't make him stick it in. Not Jonathan. A shadowy deformed shape took over at that point.

"If he did," Oh-Be-Joyful said, "if he did do it—" She had to stop. "If he did," she said again, "they would put him in jail forever?"

"But he didn't do it," I said.

"He didn't do it," she repeated after me. Saying the words out loud like that helped her believe them.

I was not surprised that, when Mike and Cameron returned, Jonathan walked between them. The three men entered without a word. Mike took off his jacket and flung it over a chair. All eyes watched his movements.

"Well," he said, "it's got to be talked out."

"You've got it," Cameron said.

Mike reached into his pocket and brought out a carefully wrapped object. He held the paper by a loose edge, and the weight of the knife brought it tumbling out of the wrapping onto the table. I stared at it. The blade was clean now, but a dark spot stained the head of the stag that ran around the handle. In fact, I noticed with a shiver that it stained the stag's throat.

"Oh-Be-Joyful," Cameron said, "look at the knife."

So that was why they'd brought Jonathan here instead of to the office. They meant to work on him through Oh-Be-Joyful.

"Look at the knife," Cameron said again.

Oh-Be-Joyful looked first at Jonathan. But he made no move, gave no hint. Her eyes traveled slowly, unwillingly to the knife, then back to Jonathan.

"Well, it's his, isn't it?" Cameron asked.

She looked beseechingly at Jonathan, but he only smiled at her. She turned to me. "Mrs. Mike!"

I stepped up and put my arm around her. "It's all right, Oh-Be-Joyful." I looked defiantly at Mike. "You don't have to answer if you don't want to."

Cameron got red in the face.

Mike said, "I think Jonathan will answer any questions about the knife himself." And turning to the boy, he asked, "Is it yours?"

Jonathan did not hesitate. "Yes," he said.

Oh-Be-Joyful slipped out of my arms and went and stood by Jonathan. Together the two of them faced us.

Mike said, after a pause, "Sometimes you make knives to sell, don't you?"

"Yes."

"Is this one of those?"

Jonathan regarded us with that crooked smile. "No," he said. "It is mine."

"Have you loaned it to anyone recently?"

"No."

"Has it been constantly in your possession?"

"You think I kill Cardinal?"

"I don't know. Somehow I don't think you'd do it that way."

"Why wouldn't he?" Cameron asked.

"My hunch is all the other way." Mike was watching Jonathan closely.

"In fact, if you tell me you didn't do it, I'll release you and look elsewhere." Mike paused, but Jonathan said nothing. "Otherwise I'll have to hold you on a murder charge. That will mean spending the summer in the cage. I couldn't take you out before the snows next winter."

We all looked at Jonathan. Mike had given him every chance. Surely, if he was innocent, he would speak now. He didn't.

I walked over to him, closer than I would if I thought for a moment he was a killer. "Jonathan Forquet, would you have us believe that you cut that man's throat while he slept?"

"I did not say that."

"No," I said, "but you didn't say you didn't, either."

He didn't answer me. "You heard Sergeant Mike. All you've got to do is tell him you are innocent."

"Yes," said Mike, "that and an account of your actions this evening will satisfy me."

Cameron grabbed Mike's shoulder. "Sergeant, you're crazy! What's to prevent him—"

Mike threw his arm off, and the movement silenced him.

"Well, Jonathan," Mike asked, "what do you say?"

Jonathan was not smiling now. He looked coolly at us, one after the other. Then he spoke.

"When north wind forget he north wind and blow from south— when the mad sickness of the wolf come on me, so that I run in circles and bite my own flesh—then will I make account to Sergeant Mike."

"That was a pretty speech," Mike said, "and you'll have all summer to sit and remember it. You're under arrest."

"No!" Oh-Be-Joyful sprang between them. "He did not do it," she said to Mike.

Jonathan looked at her almost tenderly. "You good *klooch*. You do not want me spend summer in cage with mosquitoes, with bull fly."

"Tell them you did not kill him."

Jonathan looked at her thoughtfully. "Did I not?"

"No," she said, but her eyes were not on his.

"Think," he said. "My knife and my hate. Did I not?"

Oh-Be-Joyful stood with her head down, and her tears dropped on the floor.

Twenty

THERE WERE A lot of things on my mind. Sarah kept telling me to relax. I tried to. I watched the northern lights dance outside my window. They flashed and quivered, forming arcs and ribbons of colors.

"The spirits are dancing there," Sarah said as she set the kettle to heat.

Oh-Be-Joyful came to the door with the sweet oil Sarah had sent her for. Her eyes were wide and frightened. Sarah took the bottle from her and chased her out.

I was very sorry about Oh-Be-Joyful. I had tried to tell her how I felt, but she wouldn't let me. It had lain between us these weeks. She did what I asked her and more than I asked her, but silently, with no words and no laughter. When she was not in the house, I knew she was standing before the cage. She would stand for hours pressed against the bars, but they never seemed to talk together.

"Take deep breaths, Mrs. Mike. Relax."

"Mike," I said. "Mike!"

I felt him take my hand in his. Love is pain, I thought, all love, and I cried out against it.

I heard the sobs, I felt the tears. I thought they were my own. But in a little bit, when I was easier, I saw that Oh-Be-Joyful had her cheek against my hand, and that the tears were hers.

"Mike didn't want to arrest him," I said.

"Me, I am crazy. I thought everyone against him."

"You're crazy now to say such talk." And Sarah lifted her to her feet. "Mrs. Mike must rest."

But Oh-Be-Joyful still clung to my hand. "Oh, my sister," she said to me in Cree, "oh my more-than-sister, forgive me."

I smiled at her. She seemed very far away. The northern lights made a robe for her. A curtain of colors shone between us—shone between me and the world.

The bright pain, the dazzling, screaming pain of many colors entered me, was tearing me. A new life. I was exultant, I was despairing.

A wailing filled the air and a moaning. I heard Oh-Be-Joyful's voice from the other side of the door, angry, pleading. But the sounds of wild grief, of lamentation, continued.

Suddenly a woman flung herself on the bed beside me. Mike's hand slipped from mine. He's taken her out, I thought, and then I wondered who she was.

A mosquito whined in the air and kept settling on me. I turned and twisted and writhed. Mike came back and killed it. I wanted to ask him who the woman had been, but I began to breathe the pungent odor of the woods, and I heard my good witch say, "Make nice baby come fast."

It did. For the next time the sky-curtains closed over me, throbbing with gold and purple pain, with agonizing violet and red—the boy was born. I lay with my eyes closed and let Sarah's hands work over me. They kneaded me into shape, they soothed and cleansed.

When I opened my eyes next, my son lay in the shelter of my arm. Mike was standing over us. He put a big finger down to the tiny bundle, and the baby grabbed hold. With the movement he grabbed hold of my heart too.

Sarah smiled broadly. "The northern lights danced for him at his birth," she said.

Mike laughed. "It is a good sign. He'll wear a red coat too, this little one."

Suddenly there came a high, piteous wail, followed by the moaning I had heard before. I wasn't out of my mind now, surely I wasn't. I clutched Mike.

"No, Kathy," he said, "it is nothing. Poor Mrs. Marlin is out there wanting to see your baby. We sent her away once, but she must have come back. Oh-Be-Joyful is stationed just outside the door. She won't let her in."

"Did she come in the room before? Did she lie down on my bed?"

"Yes," Mike said, "before anyone could stop her, but she didn't mean any harm. She just wanted to see the baby."

"She shall see him," I said. "Sarah, let her come in."

Sarah shook her head. "Too much excitement no good. You rest."

"Please, Sarah. I want to show him off."

Sarah grunted an Indian grunt of disapproval and opened the door. Mrs. Marlin stood on the threshold, her voice uplifted on a keening note, her body rocking in sorrow. The opening of the door confused her. She broke off her wailing and peered uncertainly at us.

"Mrs. Mike say you come see baby."

"Oh, can I see too?" Oh-Be-Joyful asked.

"No, too much."

I smiled at Sarah, who stood like a watchdog over me.

"Let her, Sarah."

At my word, Oh-Be-Joyful bounded into the room. She looked with wonder at the blanketful of baby tucked in my arms.

"Oh," she said. "The little brave, the little warrior."

"You can hold him," I said because I saw she did not dare to ask.

She darted a quick look at me to see if I meant it and then, with her breath held, lifted him.

I sighed a little. I felt sleepy and contented. I watched with half-closed eyes as Mrs. Marlin timidly approached Oh-Be-Joyful. Something about her caught my attention. She moved slowly as one in a trance. Only her eyes were awake and alive. They were bright and large and swollen from crying. But it was the look in them, the avid, hungry way they fastened on my baby, that frightened me. I tried to tell Mike, but I wasn't quick enough. The suddenness of the woman's movement paralyzed me. With a darting gesture of the hand she took the baby from Oh-Be-Joyful.

Mrs. Marlin backed toward the door, the baby in her arms. But Sarah reached it first and blocked it with her body. Mrs. Marlin edged to the far wall, keeping us all in front of her.

"What the hell!" Mike jumped up and strode toward the woman. In her fear she clutched the baby tighter. I half raised myself against the pillows. "Mike, don't!"

My words stopped him. "Yes," he said, "you're right."

Oh-Be-Joyful looked questioningly at me. I nodded to her, for I saw that Sarah could not leave the door and that the woman was afraid of Mike. I watched the girl approach. Mrs. Marlin watched her too. She crouched against the wall, ready to spring, to rush them all.

Oh-Be-Joyful stopped within five feet of her. She smiled and held out her arms. "Give me the baby."

Mrs. Marlin didn't answer.

O God, I thought. She doesn't even understand.

Oh-Be-Joyful still smiled. "The baby is not yours," she said gently.

This seemed to rouse the woman. She strained the child to her.

"Mine," she said.

"No, the baby is not yours." Oh-Be-Joyful said it slowly and patiently as though she were teaching the words to her.

Mrs. Marlin began to cry and rock her body. "Mine," she moaned. "Mine."

But in another moment she was smiling and telling Oh-Be-Joyful that she was going to have a baby.

"In July," she said. "Isn't this July?"

No one answered her.

"Yes," she said slowly, "it is time." She turned dark eyes on Sarah. "Where is my baby?"

I remembered the black liquid she had carried away from Sarah's shed last January.

"Where is my baby?" She was no longer asking it. It was a song to her now.

She cradled my son close in her arms. She crooned to him. "My baby dead. You are my baby. My baby went out from me when black medicine went in. My baby's spirit go into you not yet born. You are my baby."

Mike edged a little closer to her. Oh-Be-Joyful held out her arms again. The woman laughed at them and jiggled the baby up and down. The movement slowed to a rocking motion, and she began to moan again. Her tears spilled onto the baby's white blanket. Her voice was a broken murmur.

"Dead, all dead, everything dead. Baby dead, father dead. Everything I touch dead. Dead, dead, dead." She sang it to the tune of an old French nursery rhyme.

"I'm not *klooch*," she said, turning on us, "not Indian. I got married in a church to American husband. American man. But he died of coughing sickness. Everyone die. I'm not *klooch*, not Indian for every dirty 'breed put hands on. I tell him go away, leave alone. I'm widow of American. But when him drunk, come roaring into my house, throw me on bed, sometime on floor. Then he don't come no more. Maybe go trap line. I got baby in me, his baby. I'm not *klooch*. What should I do? I go to Sarah, get black medicine for kill baby. But when I'm home I think little baby, pretty baby, want live. I think I want baby, soft little baby to hold. I put bottle away. I think, when he come back I tell him I no *klooch*, him marry me in church maybe. Then pretty soon he come back. Sergeant Mike bring him, put him in cage. I go see him. I say, 'I'm not *klooch*, not Indian.' I tell him how his baby make me big. He sit down close to bars, he say, 'You all right. Government she pay five bucks a year for kids born on reserve. You stick by me, I make you rich woman!' He throw back his head and laugh. Laugh at me, but I no *klooch*. My knife she lie in my belt. I take, I stick, like I stick my pig last summer in the throat. Red bubbles come out his mouth. The mouth she still laugh. I go home and drink black medicine. I get much sick. My little baby gets dead. Dead, dead, dead." She sang the words as a lullaby to my baby.

"Cardinal," Mike said.

"Cardinal," she repeated and spat.

Oh-Be-Joyful looked at Mike with shining eyes.

"Wait," he said. "She may have imagined it. Where did you get the knife?" he asked her.

"Knife?" She no longer remembered what she had told.

Mike said, "You're not a *klooch*. He laughed at you. You stabbed him with the knife. Where did you get the knife? Think. Where did you get it?"

"My knife," she said, "mine."

"Jonathan Forquet stacked wood for you this winter."

"It's not his." She began to cry. "He gave it to me. He said I could have it."

"Yes," said Mike, "you can have it. If you give me the baby, you can have it."

"To keep?" she asked.

"To keep."

She handed him the baby.

𝒯wenty-one

IT WAS THE time of the first fruits of the corn. The Indians were preparing a great feast, and I had undertaken to be on the food committee. During the last week every Indian for three villages around had come to me and asked me to write down his name on the list. After his name would come the food that he pledged: half a deer, a whole deer, two beavers, or maybe seven rabbits. But, as all these animals had yet to be trapped and killed, it was really difficult to determine what our exact menu would be.

The children had been gathering firewood for days, and this was now neatly stacked under the great iron pots that hung from poles in the clearing.

The food began arriving. Black Feather was entered for one brown bear. He brought me two ducks and a string of fish. Strong Bow, who was down for half a moose, came in with a long story and a baby porcupine. But I didn't care as long as the food piled up. The women arrived before noon, and the carcasses were divided and apportioned among them for skinning.

That evening I laid out the lynx-paw robe lined with red velvet that Mike had given me when Ralph was born. I didn't have any relatives called Ralph, and neither did Mike. We just called him that because it was the prettiest name we could think of. I also got out the suit of white caracul Chief Mustagan had given me when we left Hudson's Hope, and called in Oh-Be-Joyful.

"Would you like to wear it tomorrow?"

She smiled and shook her head.

"But look," I said. "It will just fit you."

She ran a caressing finger over the white fur.

"Try it on," I suggested.

She shook her head. "I don't think I go."

"Of course you're going," I said. "Everyone is going."

"I thought I stay with the babies," she said.

"Well, you can't stay with them because they're going too. Besides, you don't want to miss the games and the feasting and the dances. It's going to be fun."

She didn't say anything. I pretended not to notice.

"Try it on," I urged again.

She did, listlessly and indifferently. But when she saw herself in the mirror my mother sent me, a little color came into her cheeks. She did look beautiful with the white fur framing her face and throat. With a sigh, Oh-Be-Joyful turned away from her reflection.

I wondered, as I'd wondered the month Jonathan had been out, what was wrong between them. When he had been in jail she had been with him every hour she could spare, but since he had been released, she had not seen him. Once he had come to the house, bringing a wild pheasant, and she had stayed in her room. Once he had stopped by and talked to me of a small herd of bison he had seen in the vicinity. He had spoken with his eyes on her door, but it had not opened.

Oh-Be-Joyful slipped out of the caracul suit and folded it carefully on the bed.

"Take it into your room," I said.

"Thank you," she said. "It is so pretty."

I turned back the bed and laid out Mike's slippers. "I suppose Jonathan is in the games," I said, fluffing up a pillow.

"I don't know," she said, and fluffed up the other one.

"What's happened?" I asked.

She sat wearily on the bed. "In summer the deer stand in river many hours. The bear roll in mud until it coat its body. Why?"

"Why?" I asked, a little impatient at this Indian indirectness.

"So deer fly, bull fly, and mosquito do not make them mad. Why then you think Jonathan sit in cage through the hot days, his body bitten, his feet taking two steps, then back, then two step? He whose feet go in all the paths of the forest?"

This was not a new question. I had asked it of myself many times.

"Well, it's hard to know Jonathan," I said. "Hard to understand his reasons. He lives by some inner law of his own. Of course he didn't tell Mike he had given Mrs. Marlin the knife because he didn't want her punished. He didn't understand that she wouldn't be killed or imprisoned. And you couldn't make him understand because he's never seen a hospital. He didn't know that she'd just be taken care of."

Oh-Be-Joyful shook her head impatiently. "Yes, about the knife. You understand about the knife. But Sergeant Mike he say to Jonathan, 'Tell me you do not do it, and you go free.' "

"He's stubborn, that's all. Mike wanted an accounting of his actions, and rather than give it to him, he went to jail. It doesn't sound reasonable," I admitted, "but it sounds like Jonathan."

Oh-Be-Joyful seemed to speak to herself: "I thought he kill Cardinal. Jonathan, he know what I think. And that is why he say nothing, why he went to sit in jail."

"I don't understand it yet."

"He would not say, 'I don't sneak up on man in cage, I don't bring him to the bars with my talk, I don't kill man with knife, who has no knife'—these things he would not say. He wanted that I should *know* him. But I did not know. I know only Cardinal is his enemy. I know the knife in Cardinal's throat is his, and most I know the never-forgotten anger in Jonathan."

I began to see into Jonathan's mind, to follow the circuitous courses of his thought. His conception of love seemed strange and mystic. He wanted his woman to understand him, not with her intellect, not with her emotions, but directly, soul to soul. The things he had done, the things he would do, she must know as well as she knew his face. She must know he would kill Cardinal, but not murder him. Jonathan would not help her to this knowledge. Instead he let

Mike put him in the cage, where he sat, proud and haughty, under the stinging swarms of insects. He remained motionless for hours at a time, staring into the cool distant green of the forest, but when Oh-Be-Joyful came, bringing fruit and milk, he said nothing to her. He waited for the day when she could speak, when she would say to him of her own accord, "You did not kill Cardinal."

Much of this Oh-Be-Joyful understood now. And she was ashamed before this man of stern pride whom she loved. Indirectly his days of stubborn suffering had accomplished what she had desired: Oh-Be-Joyful "knew him," as she put it. But between them were still the days of torment and suspicion, and the insult of her long-unresolved hesitation.

I tried to comfort Oh-Be-Joyful. "He wanted you to know him all at once," I said. "But it takes years of living together to really know a person."

"If I loved him enough, I would have known *then*. How can I look at him? If he sees me, he must think of those weeks, and I must think too."

"You mean a great deal to him, Oh-Be-Joyful. It was for you he did it. It will be all right again."

She raised dark eyes to mine. "How can I know him when his spirit dance on the mountaintops?"

I laughed at her. "He's no spirit," I said. "He's a willful, stubborn boy who follows his own paths."

"But you like him?" Oh-Be-Joyful asked anxiously.

"Yes, I do."

She smiled and gathered up the white furs.

I WOKE IN the morning to the throbbing beats of a drum.

"Happy first fruits of the corn," I said and reached over to kiss Mike awake. But he answered me from across the room. I opened my eyes at that and saw that he was already half-shaved.

"How come?" I asked, sitting up and yawning.

"I've got to be on the spot when the Indians and the 'breeds start drifting in from the other territories."

"If I hurry like everything, won't you wait for me?"

He kissed me on the head.

"The games won't start till about nine-thirty. You could wait for me if you wanted to."

"Kitten," he said, "did you ever hear of the massacre of 1897? Well, it was the feast of the dog. A feast very similar to the feast of the first fruits of the corn. Only instead of opening with foot races, it opened with the medicine man tearing a live dog to pieces. Then followed feasting and ceremonial dances. You see, it's much the same program laid out for today. Only there was liquor snuck in, and by evening there were sixty-eight scalps taken."

"I don't believe it," I said, "but I'm not the one to stand between a man and his work. You'd better get down there and keep an eye on things."

Oh-Be-Joyful and I hurried the children through breakfast, but even so the foot races had begun by the time we reached the village. There were a dozen young men competing. Oh-Be-Joyful looked quickly from one to the other, then her interest in the game was over.

But the excitement of the shouting crowd got into me, and I found myself yelling, *"Kenipe, Kenipe!"* to a young man who didn't *kenipe* fast enough, and came in fourth.

After the races there was some shooting. It was done with rifles, the marksman shooting down a pine cone or breaking a stick tossed into the air. One boy missed repeatedly with his gun. Grabbing up his bow and arrow, he waited for another chip of wood to be thrown and pierced it before it reached the ground.

Somewhere a solemn chant started. It was taken up by the men, who formed themselves into a long line.

"What are they singing?" I asked Oh-Be-Joyful.

"It is the gambling song. They are going to play the wheel-and-arrow game."

The men began divesting themselves of bows, bracelets, headdresses, belts, and placing them in piles in front of them.

"They are betting those things."

I watched as a large wheel was rolled along the line of men who attempted to toss an arrow through a spoke as it passed them. If they failed, the little pile of trinkets at their feet was taken away. If they succeeded, they received fur for fur and bead for bead what they had bet.

A drum broke up the gambling and summoned the people to a gigantic lodge erected for the occasion. It had been built of willow boughs.

Mike was outside holding on to a bottle and arguing with Baldy Red. "Now, you know better than this, Baldy."

"Sergeant, you haven't a legal leg to stand on."

"How's that?" Mike asked tolerantly.

"This here's three-fourths tobacco juice. Now, there's no law that says you can't drink tobacco juice above the 50th parallel."

"How about the other one-quarter?" Mike asked.

"Hell," said Baldy, "that's flavoring." But in spite of his protests, Mike kept the bottle. He guided us into the lodge and sat us down in a corner. While the people filed in he told me about the ceremony.

"It began in the old days when Earth Man, who was the first man on the earth, heard the first thunder. After the thunder came the rain, and the rain ripened the first fruits. Since that time, whoever hears the first thunder calls for a feast."

Everyone had crowded into the lodge, and all eyes were turned expectantly toward the entrance. An old man came in, he who had heard the first thunder. He walked to the center of the lodge and squatted beside a rectangular pit. Handfuls of sweet grass were passed in and placed in the pit. A fire was lighted there, and the old man purified his hands by holding them to the smoke. When this was done he began to unwrap the pipe. It was covered with many layers of furs, and there was a song for each layer, so it took quite a while to get it unwrapped. The stem was brilliantly plumed with many feathers. The old man pointed it toward the sun, toward the earth, and in the four directions of the world, asking health and happiness and long life. Now five hot stones were passed in and laid upon the smoldering sweet grass, one in each corner and one in the center.

"They represent the thunders," Mike whispered.

An ear of corn was set on each stone. Then the old man dipped a blade of grass into the water and sprinkled the corn and the stones. He sang four songs, and the people sang after him.

The giver of the feast invoked Gitche Manito and gave thanks that men ate corn. The sun was asked to work faithfully to ripen the yet-unripened stalks; they reminded him that he was put there for that purpose. The thunders were asked for rain, and the earth was asked to bring forth more corn, that the children of men might grow old.

The lodge door was opened. We walked out and received an ear of corn from the great kettles that were used only on this feast day. The people drifted into groups, eating and talking. A little boy ran around holding his stomach and crying, *"Meesook, meesook."* Everybody laughed. The word meant dinnertime. The women were busy turning spits of buffalo tongue and deer meat. I felt responsible for the food and was relieved to see that, no matter how many times they went back for more, there was more there. At last even the hungriest were filled up.

Stories were told, and little knots of listeners formed. The women exchanged the gossip of the villages, and some who had come farthest spread out their blankets and slept. The children both napped, so I decided we could stay for the dancing.

Dusk was setting in when the weird gambling chant arose again. Mike took part for a while and lost a knife. This time it was a game played with two bones, one painted red and one black. You try to guess in which of your opponent's hands the red one lies.

"Funny," Mike said. "The colors are the same as roulette," and after he'd lost the knife, "and I always had rotten luck at that too."

The pulsating beat of the drums led us away from the games and up to the circle of dancers. All day Oh-Be-Joyful had followed me around. She bent her head over Ralph and moved silently through the festivities. Nothing touched her. She did not see the glances of the young men. Her feet did not quicken to the throb of the drums.

The first dance called for the maidens and the young men of the tribes. The girls gathered at one end, and the young men faced them across a circle of space. A girl ran up to us and caught Oh-Be-Joyful's hand.

"Mamanowatum," she said.

Oh-Be-Joyful shook her head, but now a dozen young women were around her.

"Come, come," they said, "the eagle moon is filling out," and they pulled her unwillingly into the dance.

She looked back at me. "Mrs. Mike!"

But I would not help her.

The line of girls danced forward to the line of boys. On toe and heel they moved, and Oh-Be-Joyful moved with them. Then the line of girls swept back, and the young men surged forward, step, hop, step, in exaggerated rhythm.

A harmonica, playing "The Red River Jig," cut in upon the austere pattern of drumbeats. The 'breeds and whites had started a dance of their own. A little way back they cut pigeon wings and did the double shuffle, leaping and springing in the air. They drew a crowd of their own, that clapped hands and thighs in time to the harmonica. A fiddler joined them.

I turned back to the Indians. The commotion had no effect on them. They pounded their feet into the ground in unbroken measures. Oh-Be-Joyful, dancing in her white furs, was transformed with joy and beauty. She did not laugh or smile, but she could not keep the excitement from her eyes. The young men and the young women rushed together and fell back. Jonathan was dancing with the men. Fiercely, exultingly, he leaped and crouched in the prescribed positions of the dance. A murmur ran through the watchers. I heard an old man tell another, "Like a thistle he leaped among them."

Suddenly the line broke. The women wove among the men. As Oh-Be-Joyful passed them, boy after boy called to her. But she moved as swiftly as the restricting patterns of the dance allowed. She stopped in front of Jonathan and, lifting the scarf from her head, threw it around his shoulders. The other girls did the same, each catching a young man with her shawl. Everyone laughed and whooped and shouted.

Most of the couples broke up, a few walked away together. But Jonathan and Oh-Be-Joyful stood where they were when the drums stopped. I didn't see him ask the question. I didn't see her answer it—but when Jonathan walked across the village, she went with him. At the edge of the wood he stopped and caught some branches from her path. They swung back into place, and she was gone. She had followed her maker of canoes. He would build her a tepee of willow; they would lie on balsam and on furs. She would follow his steps through the paths of the forest.

Oh be joyful, Mamanowatum.

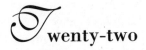

Twenty-two

I SAT DOWN to darn socks and wondered where the time went. Here it was January 1911, and I hadn't heard from Oh-Be-Joyful for nearly a year and a half. I'd had less trouble over her disappearance than I expected. Mother Superior had sent plump Sister Teresa to see me. Over tea and bannocks she mourned that even if we found Oh-Be-Joyful, it would probably be too late, didn't I think so?

"Too late?" I asked.

"Well, you know what emotional creatures they are."

I nodded gravely and admitted that it probably was already too late.

That was two summers ago. I couldn't expect Oh-Be-Joyful to visit me, or even write. Who was there to carry her letters? But I kept hoping there was some way she could let me know she was all right, and that Jonathan—that Jonathan had made a life for her as Mike had for me.

At the desk Mike was making out his semiannual report. It was only nine in the morning, but he was working by candlelight. In winter our mornings were dark until eleven. I didn't like getting up in the dark. I'd just as soon have been as lazy as the sun. But the babies woke up at seven-thirty, and that was that. I finished the dishes and settled down to mend a pair of Mary Aroon's overalls.

"Damn!" Mike said. I was startled. Then I heard it too, the low, drawn-out howl of a wolf. I bent my head over my sewing because I didn't want Mike to see me laughing. But it was really funny—Mike and that wolf. The wolf had been hanging around for a couple of months. I'd seen him several times, a big fellow with a silver-gray coat and a limp. What he wanted at our place I don't know. We had no cattle at all, our half of Bessie being kept with Larry's half in Larry's stable. In fact, Larry did a good deal of complaining. After visiting us, the wolf would drop by his place for dinner. Apparently he had learned the sound Larry made when he called his turkeys. The wolf would hide behind the trough or a barrel halfway between the feeding ground and the turkeys. Then as they streamed by he'd pick off any loiterers.

Mike had said, and this was two months ago, that he would come over and help Larry shoot the marauder. So he went, and sure enough, as soon as Larry gave his turkey call, old wolf hove in sight. However, this time he didn't come up to the trough, or even as far as the apple barrel. In fact, he didn't come into the clearing at all, but slipped back and forth, a gray shadow among the trees. Mike said he was gunwise and wouldn't come in while they were holding rifles.

To test this theory, the men put their guns in the kitchen, and while they were gone the gray wolf got another turkey.

Since then Mike had made up his mind to get him. He knew this was a wise old wolf, and he prepared his bait accordingly. He set aside a plump juicy rabbit and carefully stirred three-eighths of an ounce of strychnine through its flesh, blood, and entrails. Mike wore gloves while doing this to kill his scent, and as a last artistic effect he bought a vial of oil of anise from Sarah and sprinkled a trail of it leading up to the poisoned carcass. Turning in, that night, he said with satisfaction that he estimated the wolf would give up the ghost approximately two hundred yards from the bait.

The next morning he took care to be out early so the dogs wouldn't get sick eating the dead wolf. But the rabbit lay undisturbed where Mike had put it. There were wolf tracks, though, and Mike was partly consoled because they did come in along the oil of anise trail he had laid. Apparently the wolf had drawn in close to the bait, had circled it once, and then hoisted a leg over it. Mike pointed out the yellow stain in the ice.

"Look at that!" he said indignantly.

"Maybe he had to," I said.

"He didn't have to. He did it to show what he thought of that trap. It's a typical wolf way of expressing contempt."

"Mike," I argued, "wolves are just like dogs. I'm sure there's nothing personal in it."

"There is," Mike said, "and I'll be damned if I'll let a wolf sneer at me."

"Mike," I said, "it's ridiculous to get worked up over what a wolf thinks of you. Besides, animals don't know how to sneer."

"Oh, no? I once saw a couple of male wolves fight. As soon as one went down, the victor stood over him and deliberately lifted a leg."

"But how do you know he did it maliciously?"

"I could tell by the look on his face," Mike said stubbornly. And from then on he was doubly determined to get the big silver wolf.

He consulted with the Indians and dug pits. They were carefully constructed pits and represented a good deal of labor, as they were five feet across and twenty feet deep. But, although gray wolf investigated them and expressed his opinion of them in the usual manner, he never fell in. Mike returned the taunts of the wolf with craftier traps and more tempting poisons. But in the morning the gray wolf's contempt was clearly discernible in the snow.

In spite of Mike's efforts, the lame wolf had adopted us. One morning I saw him cavorting around our back yard with a thistle in his mouth, shaking it furiously, dropping it and capering after it again. He was such a handsome creature that I was secretly glad Mike hadn't succeeded in killing him.

We'd always know when he was around because the dogs went crazy. Especially Juno, who returned howl for howl in a way that made me wonder how far back you had to go in her ancestry to find a large silver wolf.

Mike went on with his report. It was going slowly because he was using his best penmanship and literary style. The wolf continued his sad wailing call, and Mike frowned deeper in an attempt to concentrate.

Ralph began to cry. Mary Aroon had taken his rag doll away from him.

"Mary Aroon," I said, "shame on you for taking the baby's doll. You give it back to Brother like a good girl."

She regarded me silently, and I saw her little fist tighten over the doll. She ran to Mike and threw herself against his knee. The impact was so sudden that the tail of the "Y" he was writing went shooting up into the clear space between the lines.

"Kathy," Mike said angrily, "can't you keep her away when I'm busy?"

I felt hurt. I couldn't be expected to run after her every minute, especially when I had a lap full of sewing.

"She's your child too," I said and hauled her back. "Now you keep away from there, Mary Aroon. Your father's busy." I went back to my sewing.

The baying of the wolf sounded closer. Juno lifted her head off the hearth and sang out a dismal answer. Mike said he could detect the difference between a wolf and a husky howl. But I couldn't, and it startled me to hear the answering cry come from behind my back. Poor Juno! I turned to watch her. She was going to have a litter any day now, and I suppose that's why a wolf in close to the house worried her. I bent down and petted her, but she still whined nervously.

A wail of despair came from Mary Aroon. I whirled around.

"Now you've done it!" Mike yelled.

And it was true, she had done it—the bottle of ink was rolling uncorked across his carefully made out report.

Mary Aroon raced past me screaming bloody murder and making for the bedroom. Mike made a half-hearted attempt to blot the paper, then jumped up and ran after her.

He never had spanked the children before, but I knew by his face he was going to now. I was so scared that I ran after Mary Aroon, Mike right behind me.

Mary had thrown herself face down on the bed, a strategic error. With some vague notion of protecting her, I threw myself, face down, on top of her. Mike didn't hesitate an instant. I don't know if he even knew who was on top, but I got the worst spanking of my life.

I cried, Mary Aroon cried, and Mike—well, there were tears on his face and he was making some half-smothered sound and shaking all over. I thought, and I've always thought he was laughing. But when I accused him of it he became very grave and begged my pardon. I remained sulky. He went further—he promised to devote the afternoon to me. What did I want to do?

I thought about it and decided I wanted to take the children out in the new sled he had made for them.

Mike dressed Mary Aroon because, being older, she stood still better and was easier to handle, and I dressed Ralph. We stripped them to the long wool underwear that went down to wrist and ankles. Over this came the outdoor underwear, which was red flannel and covered the other completely. Next came the little lumberman's shirt which I made by the dozen from Mike's. Then miniature mackinaw pants. Sometimes I longed for ruffles and bows, the dotted swiss and fine linens that my babies would never wear. We tugged on hip-length beaver coats, beaver caps, and beaver mitts that came to their elbows and had a string through them so they couldn't be lost. Then came the footwear. Three pairs of wool socks and over them the larrigans.

By this time the children were panting, and we set them down outside to wait till we got dressed. They looked as roly-poly as a couple of little fat bears.

While Mike was pulling on his red flannel union suit over his white wool one, I began to laugh. He looked like a red gander. I kept on laughing. I fell down on top of my furs and laughed till my stomach hurt. When I feel like laughing, all the funny things crowd into my brain together, and the funniest thing of all was my spanking.

"Did you know who was on top?" I asked him.

"No," said Mike, "and I didn't care." He pulled my cap over my ears. "Come on."

The snow was hard-packed and icy. It made wonderful sledding. Our sled was an old wagon Mike had found in the back room of the store. He'd taken off its wheels and put on runners. The only difficulty had been that, because of its tall wagon sides, only three of us could get in at a time, and even then the grownup had to sit crossed legs. But Mike had remodeled it by cutting a foot-high hole in the back side. Then the way we worked it was this: First Mike would get in, lying full length on his stomach, his legs sticking out the hole. Then, with the baby in my arms, I would flop on top of him, my legs also going out the hole, just on top of his. And Mary Aroon would climb in and squeeze down wherever she could, usually in my ribs. We were ready then for the flight downhill. It was really a long gentle grade, but with Mike whooping and the wind stinging our faces and whipping our clothes, it seemed wild enough. The children arrived at the bottom breathless and glowing.

"Give me this apple," Mike said, pinching Mary Aroon's red cheek.

"No!" she shouted.

"Well, what about this little cherry?" and he pulled her nose. That was her cue for the attack, and she pushed him into a snowbank.

They wallowed and rolled until I decided they had enough snow in their mouths and down their necks for one day. I bundled the children into the sled, and Mike and I started for home at a brisk pace. Mary Aroon began fussing. I told Mike not to notice it. But he was afraid she was cold and went back to see if the robe was tucked around them.

"Holy St. Patrick!" he said and pointed. Ralph was sitting playing in the snow about ten feet behind us. He had evidently fallen out the hole. I rode the rest of the way in the wagon. I held the baby tight in my arms and tried hard to explain to Mary Aroon why this time she got praised for crying.

We hadn't started for home any too soon either. The Windmaker was driving gusts of snow into our faces.

"Look at that," Mike said as we came into our yard. He kicked with the toe of his boot what I thought was dog dung and muttered, "Wolf!"

"It's probably one of the dogs," I said to soothe him.

Mike stood down and examined it. "There's hair in it," he said. "That's the way you tell the difference between wolf and dog. A wolf's has the hair of game animals in it." He straightened up.

"I don't like it. Why, he came in practically to our porch. I'm going to quit fooling around and really get that guy."

As if in answer, there came a lonesome bay. We strained our eyes in the direction of the sound. On a rock overlooking the frozen level of the lake stood a gray wolf. He was excited by the storm and calling a challenge to it.

"Is it our wolf?" I asked.

Mike snorted at my phrase. "It's the wolf I'm going to get, if that's what you mean."

"Maybe it's a dog," I said, peering through the confusion of snowflakes, "a renegade dog, one that's gone wild and now he's sorry and wants to have a home."

"Katherine," Mike said after a tense pause, "there are ways of telling a husky from a wolf."

"What ways?—I mean, other than . . ."

"Take the kids inside," he said, "and hand me out my rifle."

I did, and while I was rubbing Ralph rosy, I heard the report of Mike's gun.

"Dear God," I said, "make him miss." I wondered if I'd said it fast enough, or if the bullet had already struck down that beautiful and wise creature.

Mike came in, banged the door, and stuck the gun in the corner.

"Damn poor visibility," he said.

Later, when the children had been kissed and tucked in for their naps, Mike decided that maybe it would be a good idea after all to instruct me in the difference between wolves and dogs, just so I wouldn't be giving bones to the wrong animal.

"It's in the tails," he said. "A husky's curls. The ears are different too. A husky's droop, and a wolf's stand erect." He took several preoccupied pulls at his pipe.

"Do you realize, Kathy, that a ranch loses ten percent of its net income a year because of wolves?"

"Really?"

"Ten percent on an average-size ranch; that would mean a thousand a year."

"But, darling, there are no ranches around here."

"Larry Carpentier has turkeys. And what about Bessie?"

"That wolf hasn't bothered Bessie," I said.

"Kathy," said Mike, patiently, "have you ever seen the pitiless way in which a wolf kills a cow?"

"No," I admitted.

"Well, the cattle are in a tightly packed circle. The wolf makes a lunge at one of them, say Bessie, and frightens her away from the others. Then, when he has her separated from the herd, with one bite he disables her legs and pulls her down. Now, you wouldn't want that to happen to Bessie, would you?"

"No, and I don't see how it could. Bessie is just one cow, not a herd of cows. I don't see how you could separate her from—"

"My God," Mike said, "you've no imagination."

"Yes I have."

"But you don't picture it. The fangs of that wolf closing over Bessie, Bessie's eyes rolling. It's wanton killing. It's not as though the wolf were hungry. One meal a week or twelve meals evenly spaced all winter is enough to keep a wolf going. Why, I've known wolves to kill a cow for the sake of the calf she's carrying."

"All right," I said, "kill it. If you think you can kill it, kill it!"

Mike relit his pipe and asked me if we had any unskinned rabbits. He knew perfectly well we had because Bishop Grouard had brought us three.

"I've just remembered an old Indian method that I've never known to fail. It doesn't involve poison, Newhouse traps, or pits." He looked at me expectantly.

"What is it?" I asked.

"Just this," and he took out his hunting knife, "imbedded in the bait. When he satisfies himself that it's free of poison, he'll tear into it, and the knife will cut his mouth and tongue."

"That won't kill him," I said.

"No, but it will draw blood, and the smell of blood will draw in other wolves, maybe even a mountain lion. A wounded animal doesn't last long in this country."

Mike began pulling on his clothes. "You can't tell what will happen when they get infuriated by blood."

"When who gets infuriated by blood?"

"The animals."

"The ones that aren't there yet?" I asked.

"Never you mind," Mike said, "there's liable to be three or four dead wolves out there by morning."

He went out with a rabbit, a knife, and the last of Sarah's oil of anise.

While he was gone, Juno had her puppies. She gave little short high yelps when I took my hand away, so I stroked her and talked to her. And four blind wet puppies were soon nuzzling her. She had a fine time cleaning and licking them, turning them over and knocking them down.

They were plump active bits of fur, and I could hardly wait for Mary Aroon to wake up and see them. I'd been promising her these puppies for weeks.

I heard Mike outside stamping the snow off his boots.

"Mike!" I yelled. "Mike!"

He opened the door and looked in. "What's the matter?"

"We've got puppies!"

He grinned and came over, shedding clothes as he came. He looked at those puppies a long time, and the grin slowly faded from his face.

"Hmmmmm," he said at last and buttoned up his jacket. He reached for his cap and his gloves.

"Where are you going?"

"Out to bring in that bait."

"But—"

"Kathy," he said, "it just wouldn't be right for me to be killing the father of Juno's puppies."

Now it was my turn to stare at the puppies. They were gray, all four of them, silver gray. And their tails, what had Mike said? A husky's tail curls. Well, theirs stood out straight and pointed. And their ears were erect, not flopping over like Juno's.

"Holy Mother of God," I said and sat slowly. "We've got wolves in the house."

"They're only half wolf," Mike said.

I looked dubiously at Juno. "Three-quarters."

"It doesn't matter. A lot of the Indians purposely mate their dogs with wolves to keep the breed fresh. You remember Louis Carpentier had a full-blooded wolf in his team for a while. It didn't have the stamina, though."

"But these were to be the children's."

"We'll call them theirs. They have to be kept outside anyway, the kids won't see much of them this winter, and in the spring there's bound to be more puppies."

I nodded, watching the little gray wolves nurse. A low sad howl drifted in to us, and Juno pricked up her ears. It came again and she answered.

"You better get out there, Mike, before he finds the bait."

I helped him into his coat. The air was almost solid, and in a moment it had dropped a curtain of snow between us. I walked back to Juno and her little wolves, smiling. For two months he had tried to catch that wolf. He'd laid some ingenious traps too. But now I knew he would always think of himself as saving that wolf's life; although why this particular trap should work when for two months none of the others had, I didn't know.

*T*wenty-three

THE McTAVISH BROTHERS returned to Grouard dressed exactly as they had left, with nothing to show the change in their fortunes except a case of books. It was rumored that they had a fat account in a Winnipeg bank—the proceeds of the sale of the earldom. This James McTavish angrily denied.

"Not a penny did I get out of the whole transaction," he would repeat. "And I'm out a hundred and twenty pounds passage money."

However, it was noticed that the brothers began to live a little better, and that instead of his semiannual sprees, Allan permitted himself to get drunk once a month now.

James asked me to come down to their house and pick out any books I might want to read through the winter. There were about fifty volumes spread out on the floor in black, brown, and russet leather bindings, some with titles stamped in gold. I had never seen books like that. I opened a copy of Burns's poems, and stared fascinated at the elaborate end-papers covered with swirls of color and flashes of silver. The paper was as thick as cloth, and the initial letters long and curled.

"There's Sir Thomas More, and Shakespeare, and Tyndall on *Sound*, and Bobby Burns, and four or five Bibles, and Knox's *Sermons*, and Carlyle, and Johnson's *Rasselas*," James said.

"It's wonderful just to touch them," I said.

"You can have any you want, Mrs. Flannigan."

"Are all these from your castle in Scotland?" I could not repress my curiosity.

"Aye, and the only thing worth more than a lead two-bits," James said, and started to spit. He looked at me and checked himself. "That damn pile of stones," he added bitterly.

Allan McTavish put down the fishing line he was unsnarling and squatted down beside the books.

"And what good these are going to do you is more than I'll ever know," he mocked his brother. "Sir Thomas More and Shakespeare! You that's been reading paper-backed novels all your life."

"They're good books," James said, "and tooled leather covers, and after crossing three thousand miles of ocean, I'd be a brainless fool if I didn't get something out of it."

"Well, you got to be an earl, didn't you?" I said.

"No, I did not."

"But you said . . . and I mended your tartan, and everything . . ."

"I turned it down, Mrs. Flannigan. I changed my mind the day before I was to sign the papers. It wasn't for me, Mrs. Flannigan. To sit in a pile of stones on a poverty-stricken hill, and the only company a score of dead McTavishes in the Mausoleum, and the people speaking a murderous Scottish it would take me ten years to figure out. No. My shack in Canada looks better to me than that pile of stones ever did!"

"For once he's right," his brother said. "There's something in this country that nails you down and keeps you here. But lugging the case of books was a fool stupid thing."

"Pay no attention to him, Mrs. Flannigan, but take what you please. It'll be good reading these winter nights. Take one with pictures."

I searched carefully and was tempted by a beautiful brown and gilt edition of *Famous Scottish Judges*, and by a sturdy *Complete Works of John Milton*, but I fell when a book opened to a five-color map of Manchuria and Inner Mongolia. I never could resist maps of strange places, and I walked home from the McTavishes carrying *The History of China*, Vols. I, II, and III.

Mike was astonished. "Couldn't you find anything lighter?"

I told him that China interested me very much, and that I was going to read the whole thing from Mythical Times to Modern Times.

"Well," he said helplessly, riffling the pages, "I suppose you know what you're doing. But why China? I should think you'd be more interested in a history of Ireland or Canada."

"China," I said, "is the seat of the world's oldest civilization."

Mike burst out laughing. "So you already read the introduction on the way over."

I had, and I could hardly wait to get into the first chapter. That night I lit a bear-grease candle and opened to the "Age of the Five Rulers."

For weeks I lived in two worlds. I felt that if I stepped out of my door I would see, not the Alberta prairies, but the plains of Fukien. Jade and lotus and porcelain were words I murmured to myself while I worked. I cannot explain the overpowering fascination that dry, long-winded history had for me. Perhaps it was that so much time had passed since I had read any book. Perhaps it was the pictures of cloudy mountains and twisting rivers that rewakened the desire to wander in far places that always slept in me. Or perhaps the amazing people I could be while smoking meat and making soap.

One day I was the tyrant Shih Huang Ti, who built the Great Wall and burned the great books and in the end was laid to rest on a bronze map of the empire flowing with rivers of quicksilver. I ruled my brood with a strong hand that day and demanded of Mike an accounting of his actions as sternly as any monarch interviewing his chief general.

And the next day I might be a Taoist priest or a young beauty from Szechwan waiting to be married to the Crown Prince. But most of all I enjoyed playing the life of Yang Kuei-fei, a "subverter of Empires," a charmer of princes, whose feet were washed by the Emperor, whose candy was fetched by an army from the other end of China, whose parrot was buried in a silver casket to the accompaniment of Buddhist hymns.

I was working fourteen hours a day, and it made it easier to fancy myself a silken favorite lounging in the royal summer pavilion and scattering jewelry on the floor that my courtiers might help adorn me.

I hummed Mary Aroon to sleep with a patchwork tune which I pretended was Yang Kuei-fei's own song. "The Rainbow Skirt and Feather Jacket," but which in truth sounded much like the "Londonderry Air" with bits of "Killarney."

It was my delight to imagine that outside my bedroom window spread the gardens of the Emperor's summer palace. The rustling of the wind was to me the noise of the artificial brooks winding through a conventionalized landscape of miniature hills, set with marble benches and carved stone birds. The tall pines were stately pagodas, and Lesser Slave Lake was covered by lotus flowers. I was Yang Kuei-fei, imperial concubine, jeweled and scented, dressed in rich silks, surrounded by musicians and lantern-bearers, supping on jade-tinted fish, and casually listening to my praises sung by the revered poet Li Po. This Li Po gaily defrauded out of his due measure of rare wine granted him by the Emperor. As reward for his verses, Li Po was to have two-score cups of the treasured imperial cordial, unbelievably ancient, and the color of peacock's eyes. I, Kuei-fei, gave the cellarer a jewel-encrusted false-bottomed cup to measure out the wine with. Li Po received only two-thirds of his due, and I appropriated the rest for the delectation of myself and my Mongol lover, An Lushan.

One night Mike asked me why I was so abstracted. Or to be more exact, he said, "Come out of that daze, Kathy." I didn't dare confess my double life, but I told him the story of Yang Kuei-fei, hoping that it would charm him as it had charmed me. Mike only laughed.

"Kathy, it's a great career you'd have had on the stage if you'd stayed in Boston. When you talk about China, you almost make me believe those people are your relatives and close friends." He put his arms around me. "Surely it's not so serious that they buried the white parrot, that tears have to come into your eyes."

"But I—I mean Yang Kuei-fei loved it so much. It's sad, isn't it?"

Mike shook his head. "Try as I can," he chuckled, "I just can't work up a tear over a fifteen-hundred-years-dead parrot, white, black, blue, or yellow. What really interested me was that trick with the wine cup. Now that explains a lot." He winked at me and lit his pipe.

"That explains what?" I said after a while, knowing that I would have to ask him.

"Well," Mike said, "Irish Bill down at the Hudson's Bay store gives four cups of sugar for a beaver skin. Now, all of a sudden, James McTavish is offering the Indians seven cups. I thought it was kind of generous of him, but now . . . I would like to take a look at the bottom of that McTavish cup."

"There!" I said. "That shows. It's not so different, after all, China and Grouard. People are really the same everywhere. McTavish's cup isn't covered with jewels, but I'll bet it has the same kind of false bottom as Kuei-fei's cup."

"Which goes to show . . . ?"

"Which goes to show that people are the same all over the world, and that as far as actions and feelings are concerned, there isn't much difference between here and there, and that I wasn't so silly imagining myself in China."

"It doesn't show that at all, kitten," Mike said. "It only shows that James McTavish read the book before you did, and"—Mike grinned—"he got more out of it."

THE CHILDREN WERE in bed. Mike was laying out his favorite game of solitaire. He never won it. It was the kind where you lay out the deck three cards at a time, suits are built down in the array and up on the aces, and only the bottom card of each triplet is movable. I glanced from the picture on the cards, a lady with a lunch basket standing in front of a bicycle, back to a reproduction in the Chinese history. I'd finished the book a couple of nights before, but I was still acting the people and their lives, repeating the strange beautiful names. This morning, while I brushed my hair in front of the mirror, I pushed my eyelids slightly up and back. I didn't look Chinese, of course, with my red hair and blue eyes, but I did look exotic, maybe Mongol. Genghis Khan had red hair and Kubilai, his grandson, who ruled Cathay, had blue eyes.

I looked down again at the book. It was a painting, white against black. At the bottom, in print it said: "A Reproduction—The Sung Period—Attributed to Li Lung-mien." This picture wasn't new to me. I knew what it was about, a mountain waterfall. Just rock and water and a tenacious tree that grew from the rocks. Up the grade a man climbed. You didn't see him at first. He wasn't important. He blended with the scene, his back humping into the shape of the rocks around him. He was like the tree too. His fingers clung to a staff, and the tree's roots clawed into the earth, but the brush strokes were the same, a clinging to life. Yet the man didn't stand out, he was part of things.

I couldn't have the picture because it was in the McTavish's book. But I looked around the walls, imagining where I'd put it if I *did* have it. I saw that over the table was a magazine illustration of a fat baby. Sometime or other I must have tacked it up there. I didn't like it any more. I didn't like the pink and blue cover it lay on. I didn't like the yellow curls and the doll-like face. I got up, took down the picture, and threw it in the stove. Mike looked up from his card game.

"I got tired of it," I said. I stood at his shoulder a minute, watching.

"If I could only get that jack out. Look at that, the ten of diamonds in the middle, and I can't free the jack."

"I don't know why you play that game, Mike. You always get mad."

"If I could only get rid of that five of clubs."

I saw he couldn't, so I walked back and picked up the book again. Only I didn't look at the picture. Not yet. I was a sage, a philosopher. I looked with satisfaction at the bare wall. I was austere in my tastes. I owned this print in the McTavish's book. No, I owned the original. My good friend Li Lung-mien, the poet-painter, had given it to me. I kept it wrapped in a parchment scroll. I took it out only to contemplate it. I turned the book over, only allowing myself to look at the abstract beauty of individual brush strokes.

There was a curious sound at the door. Someone was pushing at it, hitting it with bare hands. Mike opened it. Wiya-sha stood there.

"Sergeant Mike," she said, "my baby sick. My baby choke."

The history of China fell shut in my lap. The woman stood outside, waiting; little sobbing breaths came from her. I brought Mike's jacket and coat.

"The gloves are in the pocket."

He nodded. "I'll be back as soon as I can. Don't wait up."

He brushed his lips quickly across mine and followed Wiya-sha into the night.

I hated these nights when pain and death took Mike away: sickness, a woman stolen, or a man shot. The shadows from the fire seemed longer, darker, they moved more violently, I didn't want to sleep until Mike was beside me. I moved around making things tidy and straight. I scrubbed a kettle. I set out the breakfast things. When there was nothing left to do, I undressed, folding my clothes over the chair. I went quietly into the children's room. They slept soundly, Ralph with his mouth slightly open. I was worried about that. I hoped he didn't have adenoids. He was a handsome little fellow. He had

Mike's dark hair. But Mary Aroon was the real beauty. I just hoped the freckles on her nose would go away by the time she was grown up. I thought of Wiya-sha, of her sick baby. Thank God my two were healthy; they had never been sick.

I walked back into the front room. Mike had been gone two hours. I stirred up the fire and put on tea. He'd be coming home cold and in need of something hot. The floor was icy. I got into bed and curled myself into a ball. I felt lonesome. I wished Mike was here. I mustn't go to sleep—the fire's lit. I closed my eyes. I was warm now and drowsy.

Suddenly I was awake, very awake and listening. Someone was knocking. Mike wouldn't knock. I got out of bed and into a bathrobe. The fire was ashes and embers. There was someone at the window—Mike.

He called to me, "Don't open it, Kathy."

I walked to the window and stared out at him.

"I don't want to come in," he said. "Wiya-sha's baby just died of diphtheria. I'll sleep in the office."

"But, Mike . . ." I couldn't grasp it.

"If this is an isolated case, it will only be for five or six days. You'll walk down and leave my meals for me, okay?"

"Yes," I said "but—"

"If you need me, just hang a sheet out the window."

"You're sure it was diphtheria?"

"Pretty sure. Listen, darling. Don't worry. About the only precaution you can take is to swab your throat and the kids' with iodine."

"How?"

"With a feather. Dip it in the iodine bottle."

The glass was between us. A red coal smoldering in his hair made me think I was dreaming. But then I saw it was a reflection.

"If you need me, hang out a sheet."

"Yes."

"But when you bring the food down, don't come in. Just leave it on the porch."

"Will it be bad?"

"Maybe not. We'll know by morning."

By morning broken cries and lamentations drifting in from the village woke me. Mary Aroon was frightened and began to cry. I shut all the windows and locked the door.

"It's the wind," I told Mary Aroon.

"Why is it crying?"

"Eat your cereal."

I drew pictures for her, and she colored them with her crayons.

"Mama," and she held up my attempt at a hen which she had colored with barbaric reds and purples.

"That's very nice," I said, "but try to stay inside the lines."

She went at it again. I washed the breakfast dishes and threw out the cold tea that no one had drunk the night before. I splashed the water and rattled the dishes and tried to hum an Irish lullaby, but now and then a wild, despairing cry reached us, and always the moaning underneath. I found myself straining to hear it. Maybe it *was* the wind, or maybe it was the low, sad notes of old Bill's organ.

I put on Mike's breakfast. While I waited for the toast I looked out at the office. There was no sign of him. But there was a flash of movement over by the group of birch. It was a man running. He was naked. Naked in below zero weather. As I stared, he flung himself into the snow, buried his hands in it, pressed it to him like a covering. A woman ran to him, half-raised him. He reached his arms back longingly and plunged them into the snow. She pulled him to his feet, and, supporting him, they walked a few uneven steps. But his strength had been spent in that first wild flight. He sagged suddenly in her arms; his head fell across her shoulder. She lowered him to the ground, and with her hands under his armpits dragged him past scrub brush and trees until they were hidden. My toast was burning.

"Mama," Mary Aroon held up a pink tree.

"Yes," I said. "It's very pretty!"

By the time Mike's new piece of toast was done he was at the window knocking. Mary Aroon ran and held up the tree and the hen for him to see.

"Kathy," he said, "you've got to help me."

"Mike, are you all right?"

"Fine, but it's everywhere. They're lying four in a bed. Half of 'em don't have food in the house. Those who do can't stand up to get it. Get your biggest pots. Fill 'em with water and boil a couple of pounds of beef and a couple of pounds of rice in 'em."

"Yes," I said.

"When it's done, signal with the sheet and I'll come get it. Put it out on the porch. If you can spare any bread, put that out too."

"Mike!" I yelled it and beat the window because he was turning away. "You've got to have breakfast."

"Later."

"No, now. You're exposing yourself to all those sick people. You'll get sick too if you don't keep up your strength. It's all ready."

"All right." He walked away. I opened the door a crack and set out the food. When the door was safely shut, he came back and began to eat. I told him about the man in the snow.

"Poor devil, fever. Sometimes they do that."

I asked him what he was doing for them.

"Nothing. I passed out all the quinine I had. Now I'm giving them alcohol. It's a stimulant, and that's what's needed. But food is the best. If we can keep their strength up."

He left, but was back in an hour for the soup. I passed out the three pots. It took all my strength to lift them off the stove. I dragged them across the floor and set them on the porch. Mike carried the first two off. On his way back for the third, he told me the Mission was giving food too. It was closed and no one allowed inside. But Father Grouard set out food as I did.

"Sarah and Constance?" I asked.

They were all right, and tending the sick.

"Did you swab out the kids' throats?" Mike asked.

"Yes."

"Well, do it again." And he walked off toward the reserve.

The day dragged on. No one came near the house. Mary Aroon and Ralph took their naps early. They'd played hard and were ready for them. I tried to keep busy. There was a lot of mending to do. I dumped some miscellaneous socks from my work basket into my lap.

I don't know how long I worked. I don't know how long I sat there not working. I realized my fingers had stopped, and that I was listening. I had determined not to listen, but the low drone was hypnotic. It was grief. They were crying for their dead. I tried to picture grief, but I couldn't. Death was the long, black-robed figure with the head of a skull that stalked through posters. But you couldn't make a picture of grief. Grief was negative, not having.

The room darkened and I looked up. There at the window, with her back to the sun, a woman stood looking at me. Her hair was all undone, and the wind whipped it against her face and body. She held out a bundle to me, and her eyes pleaded.

I walked to the window. I could see how pale she was. Her eyes burned hollow with fever. I couldn't remember her name. I had seen her last week at the store and before that in the village. She lifted her bundle against the glass of the window. It was a baby. Dead and already stiff.

I ran to the door and started to undo the series of bolts I had fastened. Mary Aroon padded in from the bedroom, tripping over her long flannel nightgown. I snatched her up in my arms and threw myself against the door. It was still held by the latch. I set the baby down and frantically shot the bolts. Mary Aroon tagged after me as I ran to the window. I pushed her away. I didn't know—maybe she could catch it through the glass.

"Please," I shouted to the woman, "go back home. I can't let you in."

She remained motionless, holding out her baby as though that answered me.

"What do you want?"

The woman swallowed. She tried to speak. The effort made her choke. She spat in the snow, saliva with queer gray flecks in it.

"Go home. Lie down."

She pushed the dead baby toward me. Her mouth formed a word, formed it again and again. At last I understood.

"Medicine." She wanted medicine for the child.

"Go home," I said. "You're sick, go home."

She mouthed the word at me again, "Medicine."

She continued to look at me. She waited expectantly. She didn't understand.

"Go to Sergeant Mike. Sergeant Mike will give you medicine."

Her eyes dulled, and she shook her head slowly. She's been to Mike; poor Mike, the liquor must have given out too. Or maybe the baby was already dead then. The woman still watched me. I was the white woman. I was expected to do something. I couldn't stand it.

"I can't help you. Go away, go away!"

She turned obediently and walked off my porch. She walked unsteadily and when the choking seized her, she fell. It was terrible to see her protect the dead baby from the jar with her own body. She made no effort to rise. Her face contorted as she struggled for breath; her body twisted and jerked. Strands of her hair beat at her like lashes. The spasm was still on her, but she looked straight at me and pointed up.

An owl flew over my house. I looked back at her. Was that what she meant, the owl? Her lips drew back, she was laughing at me. No, poor thing, it was only a gasping for breath that didn't come. She fell forward in the snow, across her child. The wind lifted her hair, it crawled uneasily about her.

I turned away from the two dead people in my front yard. I picked up Mary Aroon. She mustn't see. She . . . and all the time the face of the woman was before me. Why had she laughed? I felt it was a curse on me, an unclean thing. If only she hadn't laughed.

But it wasn't her laughing that frightened me so much, it was that bird. What was there—something about an owl—then I remembered. An owl flying over the house brings death. An old Indian superstition.

Twenty-four

RALPH WOKE CRYING. The glands under his jaws were swollen. His throat looked red. I put Mary Aroon in our room and hung out the sheet. By the time Mike came, there were large grayish patches in his throat.

"Mike," I said, "do something."

Mike kept hot towels on the baby's throat, and he had me boil water on the stove so the room would be moist.

"Feed him all he'll eat, Kathy."

"No, I want some medicine," I said, and shuddered at the word. That other woman, she'd wanted medicine too.

"There's an antitoxin," Mike said.

"Do you have it here?"

He shook his head. "Take two or three months to bring it in, and the stuff's got to be fresh."

"It's not fair! Just because we don't live in a town."

Mike leaned over and felt the baby's pulse. He didn't say anything when he took his hand away.

I made soup, and when I brought it in Ralph was turning from side to side. Mike held the bowl, and I tried to feed him. But the pain in his throat wouldn't let him swallow.

"Ralph, baby, this is the train we're going to see Grandmother on. It goes to Boston, and this is the way to Boston, right down the little red lane." Only it wasn't a little red lane. White patches covered it, and it was turning a thick yellow. I drew back frightened.

"It looks like leather."

"It will be all right, Kathy. The disease is just running its course."

"Don't lie to me, Mike," I said.

"I won't, girl,"

Ralph choked. He was fighting for every breath.

That night Mary Aroon held onto her throat and cried. "Mama," she said, "Mama!"

I tacked up her pink tree and the purple and red hen where she could see them. I put the gingham bear on her pillow and fed her.

Ralph began to cough saliva; it had gray flecks in it. The little body twisted. Every organ in him strained for air. Why couldn't I put my own breath into him? Why?

The hoarse rasping sound gave way to a gurgle. Ralph struggled and lay still. Mike bent over him. When he raised his head, I knew. I guess I'd known before. He put his arms around me, but I broke away.

"No!" I said. "No, no!"

Seven hours later, we lost Mary Aroon. I told her we'd go on the sled again, that she could keep the puppy in the house, that he could sleep on her bed. I promised her anything, anything. But the yellow membrane grew in her throat, choking her. I kept the compresses hot. But, suddenly, the writhing stopped.

"Kathy," Mike said.

"But she's never been sick! She's never been sick a day in her life!"

He tried to lift me up, but I clung to her, still promising her the puppy, a rag doll, stories.

"Kathy," he said, "Constance's girl, Barbette, she's been sick since yesterday."

I didn't answer him. I cradled Mary Aroon, I whispered pleading words to her.

"Kathy, don't!"

"All right." I stood up.

"Darling, you can't do any good here. Go to Constance."

Mike, this was Mike, wanting me to do something. I loved Mike, so I packed a basket, I put in the right things; but all the time anger throbbed in me, a terrible anger against this country, this Grouard.

"Mike," I said, and I was careful not to look at him, "if we'd been in a town—"

"Don't, Kathy. You mustn't think like that."

He walked with me, carrying the basket. I couldn't believe they were gone. My babies. Where had they gone to? Was Mary Aroon wandering through a hazy unreal world looking for her mother? And the baby, he was too little even to do that. Or was that the end? Were they only allowed to live a few months and then, nothing? Why? What was it about? I thought of the Chinese painting, the little man, the unimportant man.

"No, it couldn't be like that."

"Kathy, shhh! I love you."

I didn't know I'd spoken out loud.

We walked to Constance's house.

Madeleine sat with Timmy on the steps; she was blue with cold. They watched us go in but didn't say anything.

The fire had gone out. I shivered. Barbette lay on a bed at the far end of the room. Constance was on her knees beside her. She got up slowly and smiled a weary smile.

"Yes," she said. "The food. You brought food. We will take it into the village. There is no need here."

I leaned against the door. It seemed natural to me that Barbette was dead.

After a while Constance spoke again.

She started to ask me about my children, I could see that she did, but she stopped. Mike stood slightly behind me. He must have made some sign.

She put on a sweater, a jacket, and a coat. Mike went out and I heard him say to Tim, "Stick around, I'm going to need you."

He was back in a moment with a couple of sticks. "If you're going into the village, Kathy, I want you to take these. The dogs are dangerous. They haven't been fed for a week."

I nodded and took the sticks from him. There was an ache in me for Mike. I thought of myself holding him, kissing him, drawing the pain out of him. I thought of it, but I knew I wouldn't do it, that I couldn't do it. I went out with Constance. Timmy came around the side of the house with a shovel in his hand. I tried not to see.

We walked on a long way.

Once Constance said, "My dear—" and then, "O God!"

Once I changed the basket to my other hand.

The crying and the moaning closed around me. The first house I walked into, they were all dead but an old woman who sat on the floor, her head covered by a blanket, mourning. I put a half-loaf of bread beside her and went out.

The scene outside the next cabin held me. It was like a drawing I had seen in one of the McTavish books—a vision of William Blake's—and everyone knew he was mad. Out the window hung a pair of legs. And in the snow a young man kept clubbing a snarling phantom of a dog. I grasped my stick in both hands and walked toward them. The dog turned on me. I struck it on the nose and it backed off, whining. Another dog, lean and gaunt and ragged, crawled as close as he dared, on his belly. The two watched, their saliva dripping, while the man lowered the body of a girl into the snow. Lifting her, he climbed on the roof and laid her down.

I looked at the roofs of the other cabins, and for the first time saw the rows of feet. I saw then that there were bodies lashed to the trees too. That's the way Mike kept our meat in the winter. Best refrigeration in the world, he'd say. Only you had to be careful to pick a thin-trunked tree or a sapling so a cat or a bear couldn't climb it.

Here and there what I thought was a shadow detached itself from shadow and jumped, yelping at the trees. The creatures would fall back whining their disappointment and their hunger. Luckily most of the dogs were away with the trappers. Only the females with pups had been left, but now these pups were half-grown, and starving. The Indians fed them twice a week, which was only enough to keep life in them. But who could do even that now? Who could fish for them when sickness was a whirlwind among the people?

The mangy animals at my feet had inched forward. I flailed out with my stick and they cowered. The young Indian slid down from the roof and turned into the empty house. I put the other half-loaf of bread inside the door. He shook his head. "Where her shadow go, I follow."

The soft Cree words hurt his throat. He choked. Why had I not seen how gray his face was? He stumbled and half-fell onto a bed of skins. I rekindled the fire, went to him, but he motioned me away.

"Let me at least bring you warm soup." He shook his head. I sighed and turned away. As I reached the door, he called me back. "Mrs. Mike!"

"Yes," I said. "Let me make you easier."

"The dogs."

I didn't understand.

"The dogs," he said. "They break in maybe."

"I'll wedge the door."

"Yes," he said, "for I must lie here many days. Sergeant Mike, him have one, two, maybe three men help him. We die too fast . . . is not enough."

I wedged the door. I remembered that for the ever-after world of the Crees, they must keep their bodies intact. It would not do to appear before Gitche Manito mauled and torn by huskies.

I hurried past the rows of bodies waiting for Mike's shovel, and into a tepee where three children lay tossing. I hauled water, I set it to boil. It was a poor home; they had only manure to burn. I wrung out compresses. I forced soup down swollen throats. Sometimes the little dark faces blurred, and it was my own two I was fighting for.

A child twisted into a terrible knot and died. The mother covered her head and moaned.

"On the gray wings of dawn she went."

Yes, the sun was up, but the light from it was cold. The dead in the trees looked at us. The living writhed and choked and spat. And I moved among them, empty. Pain, tiredness, nothing touched me. Once a pair of little arms reached out to me, and I thought: Why these? Something hurt in me when I looked at the two children who were going to live, that were getting better.

I went for more water. Famished shapes slunk after me, but they kept at a distance.

I should have felt sorry for these starving animals, but I didn't. I didn't feel anything. "Poor dogs!" I said, and I remembered that I had always had dogs and always loved them. But it meant nothing to me. And then I couldn't remember what meant nothing. I just knew the pail was very heavy. I followed my own footsteps back. I filled, poured, dipped, wrung, cooked, fed.

An old man carried in the body of an old woman. "I been to hill of white crosses," he said. "Snow much deep, ground much hard for old man."

His daughter, the mother of the three children, said without turning, "Put her in tree."

Tears ran down the old man's face. He picked up his burden again and went shuffling out. A moment later there was a cry. I looked out. A dog was tugging at the small shrunken corpse. The old man pulled and fought, but it was torn out of his hands. The dog ran off, dragging his prize, growling in his throat. The old man stumbled after him. The dog dropped the body, and with his eyes on the old man, began rending and tearing it. The old man, sobbing, flung himself on the dog, beating it with feeble hands.

I came at the dog with my stick, but by the time I reached him, the old man was mangled.

A gray dog moved in and fought the tawny one, and while they fought I pulled the old man away. I dragged him to the tepee, but he was dead, and the gray dog was dead. I turned away from the sight of the tawny one as he stood bristling over the shriveled corpse.

Some time after that, Sarah found me. She took me back to Mike. Part of the way she carried me.

$\mathcal{T}$wenty-five

THE CRIBS WERE gone. I never asked Mike what he had done with them. Mary Aroon's crayon drawings were gone, too. I waited until Mike was out and then hunted the house over for them. I guess I was glad that I didn't find them.

Mike was gone every day. He and Tim and Tim's father, old Georges Beauclaire, buried half a village that week. It was mostly the children that went, and the old people.

The second night Mike had taken me up the hill. We had walked between the rows of white crosses. Was the sorrow of other days like the sorrow of now? Did each neat whitewashed cross mean empty pain?

A little past the summit of the hill, a new row had been added. These crosses had not yet been stained or salted. But cut into the wood I read the name Mary Aroon Flannigan, and next to this, Ralph Flannigan. My two babies lying on this bare, windswept hill! I knelt down and laid my hands on the snow. I remembered the day, almost three years before, when Mike and I and our baby daughter had ridden into Grouard. I remembered seeing this hill and the bright crosses. Hadn't I known then for a moment? Hadn't I seen myself wandering through the rows that stretched horizontally, then end to end, and then crisscross in shifting geometric patterns?

I had been afraid when Constance told me of her children, the one she hadn't named and the others. What warning could be plainer than her words, "The women here speak of their first family, their second and third families." Why hadn't I taken my children then, away from this country that had killed them? Why hadn't I taken them to antitoxin and doctors, out of these frozen winters?

I got up and followed Mike home. What had happened to us, to Mike and me? I wanted to reach out to him, but I couldn't. At first I didn't know why, and then I realized that I was blaming him. Did he feel it? Did he feel the thoughts that lay there, heavy and unspoken between us? He had very little to say to me. He was sweet and kind and patient, only he'd look away from me. And when he thought I was busy with something else, he'd stare at me. I couldn't sleep because of the way he'd look at me. But there was a bitterness I couldn't force back. He'd known. He'd lived in this country. He'd seen what it did to families. Every winter he'd seen children die in epidemics. He knew how virulent even a simple disease like measles was among the Indians. And he knew that in all the Northwest there was no help. He hadn't had the right to bring a wife into this country. He hadn't had the right to have children.

Eight days later the last of the graves had been filled in. I went with the women to whitewash and salt them. I moved, I worked in a kind of horror. I was beginning to realize my children were under there.

It was almost dark when I got home. I stopped outside the house in surprise. There was music coming from it. Such longing was in it, such hunger and desolation, that I stood there crying.

When I went in, I hurried past Mike, not wanting him to see my face. It was an old accordion he was playing, the accordion which had hung in Irish Bill's store for over a year. When he saw me, he stopped. The thing dangled awkwardly from his knee. I don't know, maybe if he had spoken to me then— But he went back to his music. I noticed it was a different song, that he played more self-consciously and made mistakes.

That night I knew I had been living in a daze. Mist and fog had mercifully wrapped themselves around my thoughts. All the time I had been listening for laughter and voices that I would never hear again. Why had I delayed giving away the children's clothes? Why did they still hang in the closet?

That night and for two months after I sat in the room with him. I don't know what he found to do in the daytime, but he kept away from the house. I wanted him, I longed for him, I couldn't stand the loneliness. Sometimes I counted the minutes out loud. Then he'd come.

"Hello, Mike," I'd say.

"Hello, Kathy." And if dinner wasn't ready, he'd go and get his accordion.

While I scrubbed the potatoes and put them on to boil, I went over the things I was going to say to him. But when I was sitting facing him, my heart pounded and I would jump up for salt or to bring milk to the table, or maybe I'd forgotten the napkins. Anyway, what was there to say? Everything went back to four years shared and known together. Each day, even the happiest, was now an entrance into a labyrinth of pain and bitterness.

After dinner I'd sit and listen to him play. He brooded in his music. I brooded in myself. I was alone. Mike was lost to me as surely as the children were. Night after night I listened to his music, hating it. Night after night I stared into the snow, hating it. I watched it melt. I watched the trappers come home. They gashed their feet and ankles and covered their heads with their blankets. The sound of mourning mingled with the sound of that damned accordion.

Spring came. A birthday present, four months late, came from my mother. I was twenty years old. Most girls of twenty were engaged or brides. I laughed when I thought of it, because everything for me was dead. Mike looked up when I laughed, but didn't say anything.

The accordion was driving me mad. When I was alone with it in the daytime, I wanted to smash it, break it into pieces. It had taken the children's place in his heart, and my place.

It was another night. I watched him reach for it again. I knew I was going to stand up and scream. I didn't because they brought a man in just then. They were carrying him on a door. I washed the blood off his face before I saw his eye was almost out, just hanging. I cut the jacket and shirt off him. Mike worked over his face. And somehow Sarah was there and putting on poultices. He was Randy Nolan, new in the territory. He'd come in with the trappers. When I looked at him again, his eye was in place, and Mike was bandaging it. One of his ribs was broken off and sticking through the flesh, and across the others were long, bloody slashes.

"Bear?" Mike asked.

Steve Brooks slumped into a chair. "Where in hell's your whisky?"

I got him some. He didn't bother with the glass I'd brought. When he'd had a long pull at the bottle, he asked Mike, "Well, what do you think?"

Mike didn't answer. He was occupied with an arm that hung at an odd angle from the socket. Steve Brooks went at the bottle again.

"Save some," Mike said. "I want to bring him around when I've got this arm set."

"Listen," Steve said, "I was with him, out in the canoe, shooting ducks." He paused for another drink. "Joe there was with us." He pointed at the Indian who had helped bring Nolan in. "He'll tell you what I said. I said, 'Don't shoot that damn bear.' Yeah, there was a bear on shore, a grizzly, sort of a yellow one. Reared right up when he saw us. Made a good target, except we was in a lurchy old canoe."

He had another go at the bottle. "Where was I? Well, it don't matter. Anyway, Randy shot him and the bear rolls over dead. Don't move or nothing. So we paddle in, and Randy jumped out before we're even beached and goes racing up to where that bear is lying. Well, you can see what happened."

I insisted that he should not be moved, and Sarah agreed with me. I welcomed that work the sick man brought me. I had something to think about, something to do. The first week he was unconscious most of the time. The second week he lay moaning. I didn't think much about whether he'd live or not. I thought more about giving him sweetened warmed milk with bread softened in it—or about making the broth nourishing. After a while Sarah let me change the poultices. It was amazing to see how they drew the angry red from the newly formed scar tissue.

Then he began to talk to me when I came into the room. He hardly spoke above a whisper. He talked of cities, Chicago. He'd been born in Chicago.

"Been all over," he said. "Once I been to Los Angeles."

"Have you ever been to Boston?" I asked.

"Sure. Got a sister living there." Before I knew what I was doing, I was telling him about my mother and Uncle Martin and my two sisters.

"She always has a canary, and his name's always Pete, and the dogs are always Juno. And there's a room on the top floor full of flowers, and she keeps it just for—" I stopped, ashamed of myself, for I could see I'd tired him.

But we talked again. In the morning when I brought him poached eggs, it was parks and theaters and restaurants we discussed. I described the block I'd lived on, and the house, red brick, and even the stone steps leading up to it. He told me that his sister was married to a traveling man. That she was lonesome and always writing him to come, and that she had a kid he'd never seen.

"Randy, she calls it. Named it for me. Can you beat that?"

He'd always been a rolling stone, he said. But he cursed the day he'd ever rolled into this devil's country, begging my pardon.

Finally he was able to have a pillow under his head, and then two. But he didn't get his strength as he should have. The wounds were closed and no longer draining, but he lay listlessly week after week. Sometimes he'd curse the country and sometimes the bear, but usually he'd just lie there. It was plain he'd never recover the full use of his arm, but his face was not going to be disfigured as I'd thought at first. I was glad of that. It would have been a shame in such a young man.

He thought I was wonderful to take him in and care for him. He didn't know the gap it filled for me. He didn't know I would slave night and day just to hear him tell about the concert he'd heard at Symphony Hall, and what the latest things in clothes were, and that almost everyone had a motorcar now. They went awfully fast, twenty-five miles an hour. And the day would come when they wouldn't have to be cranked, either.

I had a plan that excited me and frightened me. I led the talk back to his sister.

That night before dinner I sent a telegram to Agnes Lentfield, Boston, U.S.A.

The next afternoon Mike came in with a wire for Randy Nolan. I acted surprised and said that someone must have written his family.

Mike said, "Kathy, don't you trust me any more?"

"I don't know what you mean."

Mike looked steadily at me.

"Oh, for Heaven's sake, Mike, what if I did send the boy's family a wire? Someone should have sent it long ago. They've got a right to know. Why act so tragic about it?"

He didn't say anything, and I was glad because I didn't want to quarrel. I wanted to know what was in that wire. I walked into Randy's room with it.

"It's from your sister," I said.

He took it from me and tried to open it, fumbling with his good hand.

"I'll do it for you," and I tore it open. Purple block letters: RANDY DEAR STOP MUST COME WHEN FIT TO TRAVEL LOVE AGNES.

"She wants you to come." I showed it to him.

"Well, I don't know," he said.

"What do you mean—you don't know? Of course you know. That's what you've been wanting."

"Yeah," he said, "but what about her kid? Probably won't get no rest with a kid around. And, anyway, I don't know if I'm fit to go yet. It's an awful pull from here to Edmonton, to Boston."

I persuaded him that he was fit. I reminded him that little Randy was named for him. That he was his own nephew whom he'd never seen. At last he agreed to the trip.

"Say," he said, "how'd Agnes find out about me?"

"Oh," I said, as casually as I could, "she was your nearest of kin. We notified her, of course."

"But she isn't my nearest of kin. I've got a mother and—"

"I know, but she's your favorite."

He started to protest.

"Look," I said, "I'm not going to hear any more out of you. Too much excitement is a bad thing."

So I settled him for sleep and went in to have it out with Mike. He was polishing his accordion, and for once I didn't care. I poked up the fire a bit.

"The telegram was from his sister," I said.

He didn't say anything.

"She lives in Boston," I went on.

"Boston?"

"Yes, and she wants him to come right away."

"You mean to Boston?"

"It would be the best thing in the world for him."

"Would it?" He was looking at me strangely.

"I think so," I said.

"Why?"

"Well, it would be good for him to get out of this country."

"What's wrong with this country?"

"He ought to have medical treatment. He ought to see a doctor."

"He's doing all right."

"Considering he's tormented by mosquitoes and insects and a hundred kinds of flies."

"I hadn't noticed any in the house."

"Well, they get in every time the door's opened and— Oh, what's the use, Mike? It's the country that's killing him. How can he get well here? How can he possibly get well here with the memories this place holds? . . . I mean, he ought to get in the sun. You can't put a sick man in this sun. The mosquitoes would kill him. But summer's short, and then it will be winter. And you know what that means. Dark all morning and the terrible cold and the glare. Then if there's sickness, it's the weak ones that go."

Mike looked at me for a long time. "He can't go by himself."

"I know." I talked very fast. I didn't look at him. "I thought I'd like to take him out. I haven't been out for almost four years. It would be a grand chance. I'd take him clear through to Boston, and see Mother and—"

Mike got up. "If you have to do this, Kathy, go ahead. God knows, maybe it's best. Maybe it will be good for you."

"It's not on my own account," I said.

"I know. I know. When will you go?"

"As soon as I can."

Mike lit his pipe.

THERE WASN'T MUCH to do. I packed my clothes and the first-aid kit. Randy was able to sit up, but Mike made a stretcher for him so that the trip wouldn't tire him more than need be. This time almost the whole journey was to be made by train. No more waiting for the winter freeze; spring or summer you could go now, because the Edmonton and British Columbia Line was pushing deep into the Northwest. Of course they were still quite a way from Grouard.

Mike was explaining to me that the best way would be across Lesser Slave Lake to Sawarage, a hundred miles away. "There'll be a fifteen-mile portage that won't be easy with Randy on a stretcher. It might be smart to get a horse and wagon in Sawarage and make it with them."

"Whatever you say."

I looked at the trunk that stood open in the middle of the floor. It was packed with heavy rough shirts and men's pants, small size. I thought of myself in Boston explaining to my mother that I wore pants all the time I unpacked.

"Well," I said, "I'd better leave a clean house for you. Sarah's going to get your meals and keep an eye on things."

Mike didn't say anything, but spread an old map out on the table.

I was happy, awfully happy, at getting away. And I told myself that, as I dusted and swept and scrubbed. I also told myself that Mike didn't seem to mind my going very much. He could have said more than he did.

"How far are you going with us?" I asked.

"I'll see you on the train, Kathy."

"That's very sweet of you, Mike. But I don't want you to have that long trip. It isn't necessary."

"It *is* necessary, it's necessary to me." He folded up the map and stuffed it into his pocket. He walked to the window and stood looking out.

"God damn it!"

"What?"

"I don't want you to go."

"But—"

"Listen, we haven't even talked it out. You haven't told me how long you're going to stay yet, and I have a feeling—"

"What, Mike? What's your feeling?"

"What's the use? You're going, aren't you?"

"Yes." What else could I say when he asked it like that?

That was in the afternoon. He went out to make arrangements about the boat. At supper Randy joined us. There could be no talk then. And after supper Constance dropped in. She was terribly excited about my going "out." She insisted upon giving me the kerchief she wore on Sundays. It was real linen. After she'd left, Mike said we'd better turn in, that it would be a hard trip for me and I should be resting. I agreed with him.

I brushed my hair out in front of the mirror. I took a long time over it because Mike loved to watch me. I looked at him in the mirror and saw that he was watching me now. I smiled at myself in the glass. We would say our real good-byes tonight because in the morning everyone would be there to see us off—Sarah, the Beauclaires, Old Bill, everyone. But tonight it would be like in the old days; he'd kiss me and hold me and all the silences would be broken through.

He didn't kiss me or hold me. He said, "Good night, Kathy," very gravely.

I lay beside him for hours wondering whether or not he was asleep.

In the morning there was a lot to do. I already had the makings of sandwiches laid out. I just slapped them together. All right, I thought, that's the way he wants it. He hadn't spoken to me of the future, of when I came back. That was all right with me. I'd be glad never to set eyes on this country again. But maybe he thought there was still time; maybe he didn't realize these were our last moments alone. I finished packing the hamper and snapped it closed.

"I guess there'll be a crowd down at the lake," I said. But he was lugging out my trunk. I wasn't even sure he heard me.

Everyone was at the dock, and everyone had instructions for me. I was to look up a girl in Los Angeles and somebody's mother in Detroit.

"But I'm going to Boston."

So, I was going to Boston, it wouldn't be much out of my way, and they loaded me down with names and addresses and presents. If I got to New York there was a little restaurant on Seventh Avenue . . . And the things I was to bring back—dresses, pipes, pictures . . .

The sick man was lowered into the launch. Tim kept begging Mike to let him go as far as the train.

"If it's all right with Constance," Mike said.

James McTavish gave me a list of books I was to pick up second hand if I could.

"But, Mother, I've never seen a train." That ended it. Constance gave in, and Timmy came with us.

Bishop Grouard shook my hand, gave me his blessing, and if I got a chance I was to look up Father Grady at St. Anne's. And somehow, all the while, through the confusion, I was conscious of Sarah. She watched me as I smiled and joked, and her eyes were mournful. At the last, when Mike was holding out his hand to me and Timmy was yelling, "Get in, Kathy!" Sarah came up to me.

"Mrs. Mike," she said, "come back. You must come back."

Mike lifted me into the boat. I turned and waved, but the faces blurred into a wall of faces. And the shouting, calling, and well-wishing reached me as noise from which I could not separate a word. All the time I was thinking: How could she know?

The water cut me off from Grouard. I looked at the hill. We were too far away to see the crosses. Don't stand here, I told myself. Walk to the front of the boat. It would be symbolic, a looking forward. But I didn't go forward, not until I felt Mike looking at me.

There were wild geese honking and flying overhead. They flew in a pattern, making a V across the sky. There had been patterns for me too. A red brick home, mother, sisters, a yellow Pete and a Juno. I had broken that pattern for Uncle John's. Then Mike had carried me into a wild white pattern that had turned gray and frozen.

Randy and Tim and I laughed over my many and varied commissions. Mike smoked and listened. It took us ten hours to reach Sawarage. We were all cramped and tired. We split up for the night, various families taking us in. And in the morning we followed Mike's plan of renting a horse and wagon. The rail lines were only fifteen miles away. But what a fifteen miles!

The men who had taken us by boat kept on with us. We couldn't have done it without them, for the trail was muskegged. We wallowed in mud, the four men pushing the wagon from one watery rut into another. They laid boards and tried to keep the wheels on them. But every few minutes the horse would get bogged, sinking to his knees in the marshy places. By the time he had been pulled, coaxed, hauled, and kicked out of it, the slime had oozed over the boards, and once again the wheels would go slithering off. To make it worse, Randy gave advice from the wagon. I saw the boatmen look murder at him, more than once. We ate lunch mired to the wheel hubs, and floundered on again. I couldn't believe train tracks had been laid on ground like this.

"Maybe it's a rumor," I said. "After all, have any of you ever *seen* the train?"

And then, there it was. In the midst of nowhere stood an engine, a caboose, and a car with seats. We investigated and exclaimed over everything. But not as much as the men who came out of the station exclaimed over us. I guess we were a sight, solid mud up to our hips, and the rest of us smears and splashes.

The railroad men were very hospitable. They took us into the station, which was a derailed box car, and fed us black coffee.

Mike asked them if it was true that, in bringing the line in, they followed the old buffalo trails. They said they did that as nearly as possible. The buffaloes always chose the easiest grades and cleared paths in heavily timbered sections.

They discussed the country, and Mike said it would open up once the railroad was in. "In ten years there'll be tourists and hotels for them to stay at. The vacationing bankers and holiday lawyers will ruin the hunting and trapping, God help us!" The railroad men nodded and spat and agreed with him.

"Although," said the engineer, "you raise mosquitoes in this country like they raise cows in Jersey, and they'll keep the tourists out better than anything." And he swore to us that the summer before he had seen big mosquitoes who couldn't get through the netting themselves, push the little ones through.

Mike laughed politely and asked about the fare. It was they who laughed then. "We can't charge you for the kind of ride the young lady will get. She travels as our guest, but at her own risk."

And though Mike argued till I was afraid they would change their minds, they didn't.

About that time we missed Timmy. Mike found him in the engine, fondling levers, gloating over switches, touching buttons and knobs.

We made a bed for Randy in the caboose. And Mike brought my trunk in. The small overnight case he carried into the car with seats. From deep inside a pocket he pulled out ten ten-dollar bills.

"Not so much," I said.

"I'll feel better if you have it. You may need it, you never can tell," and he stuffed the money into my hand.

Tim and the boatmen came up and said good-bye. Suddenly I realized Mike was saying good-bye too.

"I think you were right, Kathy, that the change will do you a lot of good."

The conductor looked in on us. "We're pulling out, Sergeant."

"Kathy . . ."

"Yes?"

"I want you to have a good time."

"I will."

"Sergeant!"

"All right. Kathy, I—" His arm went around me, clumsy and uncertain. I watched him walk away, and then he was outside and we were smiling at each other through the window. The train jerked forward. Mike walked along under the window. My last picture of him was standing alone, against the whole Northwest.

I stared out at the wet dripping country, my heart aching with the things said and the things unsaid.

The first hour the engine jumped the track twelve times. At each derailment the crew tumbled out and lifted it back on. It took us two days and one night to go two hundred miles. But there were a lot of diversions. There were contractors' tents all along the way where we'd stop for food and talk and black coffee. Then on again. If I got tired of sitting, I'd get out and walk beside the train and talk to the engineer about all the things I was going to do in the city. Every once in a while the ground became slushy, and water covered the tracks. Then I'd hop on and look after Randy. I began to enjoy the trip, to look forward to Boston.

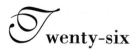

wenty-six

CAUSEWAY STREET. THE North Station. Boston. There it was, gleaming in the rain, familiar and yet unreal. I had the same uneasy feeling you have in a dream when you speak freely and yet a bit dubiously to someone you have loved and who is now long dead. All through the trip with the sick man I had been fretting impatiently, burning to see my home and Mother. Now I was afraid.

My sister, Anna Frances, and Randy's sister, Mrs. Lentfield, met us at the station. There were introductions, talk about baggage, and hasty good-byes. Randy had stood the trip extremely well, and he was happy, confident that Boston surgeons would have him walking again. I felt I'd been right to bring him.

My sister had been watching me thoughtfully and saying very little. Mother was home, nursing a cold. Mary Ellen hoped to get down from Rhode Island. There were none of the questions I had been expecting about Grouard and Mike. Instead, my sister took my hand as we rode home in one of the new trolleys and said, "Mother is very happy you've come home."

"I want to stay a long time," I said carefully.

"As long as you want," my sister said. "This is your home."

If my sister was strangely silent, my mother was even more strangely talkative. She kissed me and smiled at me and spoke of a thousand and one things—of the elevated railroad they were building, of my sister Ellen's baby, of the awful weather, of guess whom she had run into at the library, of the good and bad habits of the boarders, of the difficulty they had finding out when my train was to arrive—in short of everything under the sun except my four years in the Northwest.

My mother was looking remarkably young and gay. She insisted her cold was much better, just seeing me had been the tonic she needed, so we ended up going out to lunch and taking in the town. Mother knew her Boston, and I had to admire everything, even the new bank building. After a while I was carried away by her gaiety, but even so I felt there was something forced and nervous about it.

The second day there was a homecoming party for me. Boys and girls whose faces I vaguely remembered crowded into my mother's living room. Someone played "Alexander's Ragtime Band" on the piano. I missed Uncle Martin's bagpipe, but he ruefully explained that the boarders couldn't stand its "outlandish noise," and it was gathering dust in the attic.

A tall pale youth called Dick or some other equally colorless name invited me to dance. My sister served sherbet and small delicate cakes. I ate them greedily. The food was the only thing that tasted real to me.

Dick made me sit down next to him at the piano while he sang "Oh, You Great Big Beautiful Doll" in an exaggerated comic style, looking at me and grinning after every chorus. A din of chatter and gossip filled the room. I got up and walked out on the porch. I couldn't stand so many people so close to me. I was overpowered by the noise, the perfume, the decorations, and by the glare of the electric lights. After the soft glow of candles, everything seemed harsh and artificially bright.

On the porch the air was cold and wet. It felt good. I strode into the drizzle. I turned my face up, and the rain caressed my cheeks. The subdued secret patter it made on the pavement soothed me.

"Kathy, what are you doing out here?"

Dick was standing on the porch, testing the rain with his out-stretched hand. He drew me back under the eaves.

"Aren't you enjoying the party?"

"Oh, yes, it's nice," I said.

"I know how you feel. I like to get away from the crowd too." He looked me over curiously. "You're liable to catch cold. It's raining, you know." He laughed and leaned on the porch rail beside me.

"Well, how does it feel to be back in civilization?"

He edged closer and put his hand on mine.

"You'll think I'm kidding, but it was quite a blow to my young life when you moved away."

I drew back, feeling suddenly uncomfortable in my sister's full-skirted party dress.

"You're teasing," I said, trying to match his gay air. "Aren't you, Dick . . . it *is* Dick?" Now I was really confused and hardly ready to resist when he took both my hands and began to speak earnestly and rapidly.

"Kathy, you have no idea how beautiful you look in that gown. I'm quite an expert on color harmony, and take it from me, chartreuse is the perfect thing for your eyes and hair. I will always remember you as you are now."

I wanted to say this is my sister's dress, and I generally wear trousers, sometimes two pair if it's cold enough, and this talk of color harmony is ridiculous, and you know you don't mean a word of all that chatter, and please let go of my hands . . . But a numb bewilderment was on me, and in a moment he was drawing me closer. When I saw that silly face bending down toward me, however, the spell broke. I laughed and pushed Dick away. I could see that he was as surprised as I was at my strength and roughness.

"Go in and play with the girls," I said. I opened the screen door and walked upstairs. I was gleeful. In Alberta I had been delicate, even pampered. Sarah kept a continuous eye on me. Mike saw that I had nine hours' sleep. Everybody knew I had to be careful because of my pleurisy. But down here in Boston I was almost indecently healthy and strong. For the first time since I'd left, I allowed myself to think of Mike. There were no men like him in Boston. Tall, yes, but not solid. Brilliant, but not enduring. I sat on the bed in my sister's room and smiled proudly. After a while, I cried.

The door opened softly, and my mother stole into the room. She put her arms about me. "Katie," she said, "you're lonely."

"It's all over now," I said. I rubbed my eyes with my hands and stood up. "I'd rather not go back to the party, Mother. I'd rather just sit here and talk to you. We really haven't had a chance to be alone."

"I wanted you to myself too, Katie. But I thought, after all those years, you'd like some fun . . . some gaiety."

"Mother," I said abruptly, "I love him. I always will."

"I know."

"I wish he were here."

My mother smoothed my hair. "We can work that out," she said. "I don't want you to leave home for a long time." She looked thoughtfully down at the floor. "Perhaps . . . Sergeant Flannigan would like to come to Boston."

"For a visit? He couldn't do that."

"I mean permanently," my mother said.

"No, Mother. In Boston, Mike would be just a cop."

"Katherine Mary." My mother spoke in a new firm voice. "The last thing I would ever do is to interfere in my daughters' lives. You were married somewhere off in the wilderness to a man I never met, and you've lived four years in a place I never heard of. I always dreamed of the day when you would have a big church wedding with your sisters and myself by your side. Well, that can't be helped. It's a wild thing you are, just like your father that went off to Australia and came back with a parrot on his shoulder. But it's not my happiness I'm thinking of now. You've lived hardly like a woman, stuck in a little cabin with snow outside and mosquitoes inside, with not two dresses to your name, and not a white woman to pass the time of day with, nor a doctor to care for your babies when they lay dying, far from your friends and your family. No one should be made to do that. It's not right. I'm an old-fashioned woman, Katie. I believe a woman should stick by her husband. But this time it's different. If your man wants you, let him come here and get you. It's no blame I have for him. A man lives the life he has to. But I'm your mother. And I'm not letting you go north again to loneliness and the graves of your children!"

"I don't want to," I murmured.

"And now," my mother said brightly, "you're to forget all this. You're to remember you're only a child of twenty years, and you're to cheer up and smile. Surely you've worked hard enough and suffered long enough. Now, let's go back to the party."

"All right," I said, "I will."

So I went down and danced and talked and sang and drank punch, and though I didn't believe it was possible, my spirits began to lift, and when I went to bed that night I was too exhausted to think back or brood; so I went to sleep content, if not happy.

In the morning I gave my sister back her party skirt, and Mother took me out and bought me one.

"Would you like to go to the theater tonight?" she asked.

"Yes," I said. "Tonight, and tomorrow night too."

There were weeks of plays, operettas, and musical comedies— color, movement, and song reaching out from the stage and holding me entranced. *The Red Mill, The Dollar Princess* . . . It was after *The Chocolate Soldier.* Mother and I were riding home on the "L." The tunes I had heard were running through my head, the full taffeta skirts were still whirling. Mother was speaking of the boarders, and I wished she wouldn't. I wished she would let me waltz and coquette with the twelve tall, gold-braided, uniformed men and sing with the pretty powdered women. It was about Miss Ivy that she didn't know what to do.

"She has a perfectly good position. Why, she earns more than Mr. Monts. Of course, when I took her in she wasn't earning, but now it's different. She can afford to pay for her room; after all, it's the nicest in the house, and I think she should."

The blue painted sky with its white clouds gave place to the real one, black, wet, and drizzly.

"Why don't you ask her to pay, Mother?"

"Well, I've hinted at it. But you're right, Katherine Mary, and I'll be asking her straight out."

I was ashamed of myself for being so thoughtless. Mother'd done so much for me since I'd been here. It wasn't right. She was middle-aged and working hard for the little she had. When we went to *The Pink Lady* and *Quaker Girl,* I took Mother. We saw *Peg o' My Heart* too, so sweet and Irish, with love going all the wrong way till the end.

We went to all the shows, and there were plenty, for Boston was always the big try-out town. But the most thrilling evening was the one spent at the Boston Theatre. Sarah Bernhardt was playing, and the Washington Street entrance was jammed with pushing sables and prodding minks. Mother and I went around to the side and into the theater by a sort of tunnel. The galleries were steep, and we climbed to the very top, so high that I got vertigo and pictured myself crashing into the orchestra. Funny, at Hudson's Hope I scaled the highest, most dangerous bluffs and wasn't afraid.

Well, I couldn't tell you much about the play, but every move-ment of that woman is engraved upon my mind. She was tall and very slight, with a mass of red hair piled high on her head. She hypnotized the entire audience. We strained forward to catch each inflection of that clear, high voice. The other actors annoyed me. I waited for them to finish, that she might answer. What a night! After that I piled my red hair high on my head.

"I TELL YOU, I left it in my room." I paused on the stairs uncertain whether or not I should go down. I didn't like Miss Ivy. She spoke in a shrill excited way, and since she had been paying Mother five dollars a week it seemed that her voice had gone up another octave. Mother'd already seen me, so I walked on down.

"I'm sure you've mislaid it," Mother was saying.

"Good Heavens, is something missing?" I asked.

Miss Ivy ignored me. "I couldn't have mislaid all *three* of them."

"Three of what?" I asked.

"The *Atlantic Monthly*," my mother explained. "She saves them, and now she can't find the last two issues, and—"

" 'Can't find' is one way of putting it. Why I never even laid eyes on this month's copy. That is, just barely. I hate to accuse anyone in this house, Mrs. O'Fallon, but it seems plain that someone has entered my room, and do you know, I had left a gold ring on the wash stand. It was just fortunate they didn't see it."

My mother looked very pale and very angry. "I refuse to listen to such insinuations. There's been nobody in your room except myself, to clean. And I think it's just possible that in clearing up after you, I threw out the papers you're missing. If I did, it's your own fault for keeping the room in such a litter."

"Litter! Well, I like that! Not only is there no privacy here but—"

I mumbled something about going down to the corner and shut the door on Miss Ivy's list of injuries. It was good to get off by myself and not have to look at graveyards and Emerson's home or Julia Howe's or Booth's or anybody's, but just wander without bothering to *go* anywhere.

There were bicycles on the street, but not many. Mostly there were shining black motorcars that honked impatiently at nervous, traffic-leery horses in blinders.

I hesitated which way to go. I'd seen the downtown district with its steel and cut stone and marble. I'd walked along the Back Bay Fens and wondered why the houses all had their backs to the water. So now I turned toward Beacon Hill. I looked in through tall iron gates at expanses of green lawns, at stone mansions. I passed brick walls that towered over me and imagined the lawns and the houses.

I caught glimpses of wonderful flower beds and shaded walks. Once some elegant young ladies were playing croquet and missing the wickets. Once a gardener nodded to me, and I nodded back.

From the other side of a fence a black spaniel kept pace with me, barking. I laughed when I thought of this little dog beside my Juno, or imagined his shrill yelp lifted against the baying of a deep-chested wolf.

It was getting awfully warm. I felt hot and thirsty, and there was nothing around me but estates. Well, I thought, I guess they can spare a glass of water. I had to walk another quarter of a mile to find one that had no wall. I turned in at the driveway past all the "Private" and "No Trespassing" signs.

Rows of flowers lined the drive. They were beautiful, but you hadn't the pleasure of hunting for wild violets under their leaves. These violets were planted to be looked at. There were no surprises, either; in the pansy row there were pansies, and in the jonquil row, jonquils.

The drive took me up to a gigantic stone house, very massive and very ugly. I hesitated about which door to knock at. I wasn't going to go around to the back, yet I didn't like the looks of the front door. I just knew it would be opened by a butler or a maid in a frilly cap. I decided to try the side door. But I might as well have saved myself the walk, for it was opened by an elderly man in evening dress, white gloves, and a green striped shirt who lifted one eyebrow, a trick I had practiced but never perfected.

"You wished something?"

"A glass of water, please. I'm thirsty."

"I'm terribly sorry, Miss, but didn't you notice the signs? Madame would not—"

"All right." I walked down the steps.

"But if you're really thirsty—"

"Never mind." I walked back the long flowered path and back the five miles to Mother's. I couldn't understand. The water was free, it was supplied by the city. I thought of the hundreds of trappers' cabins throughout the Northwest, the doors left open, the food there for you, the wood cut and stacked.

When I got home I found they were waiting lunch for me. Mother was in the parlor adding and re-adding the items deductible from her taxes. In keeping house, I had never had to bother about rent, mortgages, taxes, assessments, any of those things.

Anna Frances told me to hurry down, everyone was hungry, and she was putting on the toast.

As I washed my hands and face I noticed that they needed it, which proved there was as much dirt on Beacon Hill as any other part of the city. The thought restored my spirits.

A wail from Anna Frances brought me to the head of the stairs. "Oh, Mother, weren't you watching the toast?"

"Why, no. You put it on, dear."

I ran down. Everyone was at the table. I slid into my place, but not quickly enough. My sister waved a black square of scorched toast at me.

"You could have hurried. I told you I was putting it on."

Mr. Monts turned to Miss Ivy. "She's always burning the toast."

"I've never made toast in this house before, so I don't know how I possibly could have burnt any."

"Why don't you scrape it off?" Mother asked. "It's not so bad when the black part's scraped off."

"Oh, it's no use!" Anna Frances carried the toast into the kitchen and dropped it into the sink.

Mrs. Ellison shook her head. "It's wicked to waste food like that."

"I took a walk to Beacon Hill," I said, smiling around on everyone. But it didn't work because Miss Ivy, who had sat drumming her fingers on the table in an effort to think, said suddenly, "You did too make toast, Anna Frances. It was three weeks ago Friday, when that young gentleman friend of yours was at the house." Then, turning to Mr. Monts, "I knew she had. And you're right, she burnt it then too."

"It's not the burning of it," Mrs. Ellison said, "it's the waste."

"If toast can't be a light, even brown," Mr. Monts grumbled, "it's better to eat bread."

Anna Frances began to cry.

"For Heaven's sake!" I said, jumping up so hard my chair fell on the floor. "All she did was burn a piece of toast. So you'll go without—or if you must have toast, you'll toast it yourselves."

"We don't have kitchen privileges," Mrs. Monts said haughtily.

Mother said, "Sit down, Katie." And I would have, but just then Miss Ivy began fanning herself and saying the smoke from the burnt toast in the kitchen was just reaching her, that it was making her ill. That she was sensitive to smoke.

What would she have done, I wondered, if she had stood all day in the river with her skin blistering? That smoke she couldn't have waved away with her hand.

I turned from the table and the faces of the boarders. With a third of a village dead there hadn't been this much commotion. When you've seen bodies lifted from the wells and root cellars that were charred as black as the toast they complained about, when you've seen little Tommy Henderson with his skin flaking off in cinders, and then hear the same words that describe those memories describe the smell of a kitchen or the condition of a gas range—then you realize many things. I knew now how alien these people were to me, how different their whole pattern of thought. Even my mother and sister were irrevocably separated from me. They could never know any part of my life up there. They could never know my children or my husband.

My husband. That was why I was crying. I'd been seeing Mike as I'd seen him last, standing alone against the Northwest. I understood now. It was the country, the country I was homesick and longing for, that made him *Sergeant Mike Flannigan*. I'd been unjust, I'd been wrong. I knew it now, and I had to tell him. I had to have his arm around me and his voice telling me the wonderful things about the stars and wolf dung. But mostly I had to explain, to get him to understand the things that had piled up in me. I had to tell him that after the children died I thought I couldn't stand it, that I had to get away.

"BUT THE ONLY thing I can't stand is not being with you, not being yours again. Mike, you must let me come back into my own place. I'll never leave you again. I couldn't, you're my life, this is my life . . ." And I spread my arms taking in the miles of endless snow.

He met me at the train. He had put bells on the dogs. Wrapped in a buffalo robe was a little new Juno the Second, whose eyes were hardly open yet. And the big Juno, the team leader, had almost broken the traces to get at me.

And now I was beside Mike in the cutter. Mike! His voice was low and choked up. He'd start to say things, and then he'd stop and just look at me. Then I'd forget what I was saying and just look at him. After a while I told him about Boston and the boarders. He laughed when I came to the toast and said, "When little things are so important, it's because there aren't any big ones."

"But everything's big here. Why, look at those firs and all the miles between things, and, and—look at you," I added. His arm tightened around me.

I tried to tell him how wrong and confused I'd been about everything. But he wouldn't let me. He kept kissing me, over and between and through all the words. He was so good to me and wonderful that it made me cry. I cried, too, because of his lonely nights with no children and no Kathy. My tears turned to sleet, and Mike had to stop and wipe my face.

"Mike, promise me, we'll live together all our lives and never be away from each other."

He held me. The reins dropped, and Juno had to pick her own way.

"We'll start over, won't we, Mike?"

"Sure." And he made me imitate Miss Ivy again.

I had to know all about Sarah and Constance and Timmy and old Georges and the McTavishes, and could you get more things at the store with the train so close.

All of Boston now seemed as unreal to me as the plays I'd seen there. After landscapes that were trimmed and raked and pruned into existence, it was thrilling to skim across unbounded open country. The snow shone and sparkled. The sun struck here and there among the fine particles, touching them with cold fire. I didn't think how beautiful it was. I thought how many times I had watched it before. And now for the first time it was familiar; I recognized it just as I recognized the way the air smelled.

Mike had been watching me, and now he said, "How does it seem to be home, Kathy?"

That's it, it was home.

That night at Sawarage I woke myself up to make sure I wasn't dreaming, that Mike was really beside me. I kissed the pillow close up near his cheek because I didn't want to wake him. He opened one eye and grinned at me.

"Don't waste 'em, kitten."

IT WASN'T UNTIL late the next day that we got home. Icy branches arched like crystal domes above the cabin.

"There's nothing so fine in all of Boston." I jumped out of the sled and ran up on the porch, but Mike got to the door first.

"Listen, Kathy. It's in a bit of a mess. At first glance it won't look very good. I guess I'm not much of a housekeeper."

"Don't be silly," I said. "It can all be straightened out." Mike looked dubious, so I prepared myself for the worst and pushed the door open.

The house was scrubbed, polished and shining. I looked at Mike to see if he had been joking, but one glance at his face convinced me that he hadn't. Everything was in its place, and on the table was a steaming hot dinner.

Just then I heard the back door close. We ran to the kitchen in time to see Sarah striding off. We called to her, and she raised her arm above her head to show she heard. But she wouldn't call back or even turn to look at me.

Coming from the crowding, pushing, noisy world, I was impressed again by the delicacy of the Indian women. Sarah did not understand politeness; she understood that we must be alone—that this return was Mike's and mine.

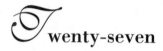

wenty-seven

AUGUST 1914, AND war. Mike got the news by telegraph the eighteenth of the month, but we had known it was coming since the fourth, when Britain had declared herself at war. It seemed strange that guns we couldn't hear and events we knew nothing of could reach into our remote settlement—but here and there men left their trap lines, sold their equipment, and rode the train into Edmonton.

It was by train that we got our month-old newspapers. We read them and were shocked, as the rest of the world had been weeks before. The news we received by telegraph in cold, blunt statements made it hard to picture blocked roads of streaming refugees and armies like juggernauts closing in. But these first war editions blazed with atrocities and published photographs of blurred dead bodies and emaciated living ones. I had never seen such tension and excitement as they caused. There were fifteen or twenty people waiting their turn at each copy.

More deserted trap lines, more secondhand equipment to be bought cheap at the store. Timmy came to say good-bye and to ask Mike to look after his pony.

I couldn't help saying to him, "Tim, think of your mother."

"Father'll be with her. Besides, Paul, my brother in Edmonton, has enlisted, and he's got a wife. Besides, I have to go."

I looked at Tim, a young man now. I sighed and kissed him. The pony whinnied and nickered, and Timmy turned to wave. He wrote to Constance from Camp Valertier, from Quebec, from England, then from St. Nazaire, France. Mike and I got a postcard of the Loire River and one of a cathedral.

By the end of winter I had delivered five wires, "Missing in action," "Killed in action." I took them on snowshoes into the village and twice off to lonely cabins. I never said anything. I always tried to. But when I handed over the envelope, a man died. Even before it was unsealed, he died. There are no words against death. Death just is.

Sarah came into the office one day.

"Make me a cup of tea, Mrs. Mike."

That very ordinary request frightened me, for in all the time I'd known her Sarah had never asked anything of anyone. I put the water on and sat with her. Mike worked at the desk without looking up. I wondered if Sarah was ill. The water bubbled. I added the tea and let it simmer.

"Will you have some?" I asked Mike, but he shook his head and I poured only two cups. Sarah drank slowly and steadily.

"More?" I asked, getting up.

"No. It is enough." Then abruptly, "Constance's girl, Madeleine, she have babies, she die."

"Madeleine died?"

"I take two babies from her. She bleed. I make it stop outside, but inside she still bleed."

I watched Mike lay down his pen. "She had twins?" he asked.

"Yes. A boy and a girl."

No one said anything. We sat and drank tea. Mike returned to his ledger. It grew dark.

Three hours later the telegraph began to click, that click I had come to associate with death. It almost seemed as if we had been waiting for it. Sarah raised her head and watched Mike closely as he copied the message.

"MARCH 27—MR. AND MRS. GEORGES BEAUCLAIRE ... REGRET TO INFORM YOU ... KILLED IN ACTION ..."

Mike stood up. "I'll take it over."

"No, I'll take it." He handed me the telegram. I wanted to crumple it, destroy it, tear the words to pieces. "I'll take it to Constance." I turned to Sarah. "Does she know about Madeleine?"

Sarah nodded. "She was with her. By now she home."

"Why? Why does it happen like this? Why both together and why to Constance?"

Before they could answer me, I went out. I knew there was no answer, and I didn't want any more of that silence.

Poor Constance, mother of sorrows. Already she was grieving, and then I'd come. But it might help her if it's me, I said to myself.

Maybe she'll cry or say something then. It was strange: two taken and two given. Twins. No one had suspected it would be twins, not even Sarah.

Finally I was there. I knocked and went in. She came toward me. "Constance . . ."

I was going to prepare her, to say wise and gentle things, but all I could do was to hold out the telegram. She stood looking at it, but she wouldn't take it. I put it on the corner of the table. I was glad to look away from those violet eyes, from the marble face.

She spoke through stiff lips, "Which one?"

"Paul," I said.

NEXT SPRING IT was Timmy, and again I carried it to her. It felt unreal. I had done it all before. I couldn't be doing it now. She was preparing the babies' bottles; she turned to me smiling and saying, "Kathy."

I stood there where I had stood in the winter, by the corner of the table. Under my hand lay the first wire. It was unopened and thick with dust. She had never touched it. I put the second wire on top of the first and went out without looking at her. I guess it helped her not to have to see it written. Words made you know. They made it harder to dream and pretend. I know all about dreaming and pretending. Sometimes at night I still held Mary Aroon and Ralph in my arms.

It suddenly seemed strange to me, that silence about the dead. Mike and I never spoke of our children. All this time I had drawn back from any reminder of them. I had forced my thoughts away, flinching if they got too close. Only recently had I allowed myself to think of them, and the pleasure had been more than the pain.

Now suddenly I wanted to laugh with Mike again about the time Mary Aroon got her head stuck in the porch railing. It had been awful getting her out, and later, when I was telling Oh-Be-Joyful about it, Mary Aroon put her head in all over again to show how it had happened. When we told Mike at dinner he had all he could do to keep her from going through still another demonstration.

I almost wanted to go back to Constance and tell her that after a while she would be able to think of Timmy, and each time the hurt would be less. Then I remembered her families, her lost families of children, and I felt ashamed. The day my own two had died, on the way to the village, she had tried to tell me something, had started to say something. It was this, of course. I smiled and told myself, "Katherine Mary, you are like a baby that is so pleased with himself for standing up that he doesn't notice anyone else has learned to stand too."

Mike was staring out the window. Timmy's little cayuse stood in the pasture with her nose laid along the fence. Mike walked to the stove and knocked the ashes from his pipe into it.

"Sarah was here. I don't know how the devil she knew, but she asked about Tim."

"Did you tell her?"

"She said, 'When they're little, sickness. When they're big, war.' "

I remembered the first time I'd seen Timmy. He came riding up with Constance Cameron. "He held the puppy up for me to see, and I held up Mary Aroon."

"Yes," Mike answered. "Remember that? She was bundled right up to her nose." He broke off suddenly and looked at me carefully for a long time. Then he smiled.

"Mike," I said, "it just came out. I was thinking of it and then I'd said it." He reached for my hand.

"On the way home I was thinking about the time she got her head caught in the porch railing. I wanted to talk about it, but I didn't know I was going to."

We sat together, the memories holding us silent. When words came we hardly noticed, they were so much a continuation of our thoughts.

"You used to say she was a born actress. Remember, Mike?"

"She was too. Remember the time Ralph fell off the bed, all the attention he got?"

"And a couple of hours later Mary Aroon fell off too!" We were both laughing now.

"Kathy," Mike said, "you're crying."

"No, I'm not." He held up his hand. It was wet with my tears.

"I didn't know it," I said.

We sat a long time watching the shadows of the trees stretch over the grass.

THE WORLD OUTSIDE, the noisy quarreling world that sent us the wires of death, sent us a new death. Born in the dirt of European trenches, in the fall of 1918, the flu spread into the Canadian Northwest. And we died, again without doctors, serum, or help. Even the wild forest creatures died. The bear was the only red-blooded animal to escape it. But then, as Mike says, nothing affects bears.

I followed Sarah into the bedroom of the Beauclaire cabin. She closed the door and we stood in darkness, listening to the soft voice of Bishop Grouard. It came to us indistinctly from beyond the door, a low murmur, rising and falling in benediction, in prayer. His deep tones were punctuated by feeble responses, barely audible. The pauses were awful. They might mean she hadn't the strength to answer, or they might mean she was dead. I was getting used to the dark. I saw the big square shape that was a bureau; I saw the twins asleep in their bed.

Sarah's voice came out of the shadows. "Too bad. She live enough just to see her children dead." I couldn't answer her, and the darkness was thick between us.

After a while the Bishop called to us. He was pulling on his coat. In the corner by the door an Indian child stood crying.

The Bishop sighed. "I am needed in another home for the same purpose." He turned for the last time toward the bed, but Constance lay with eyes closed, unmoving, unknowing. He went out, the child following him. Death was everywhere.

Georges sat huddled by the bed. But it was many hours before Constance moved or spoke. Once she opened her eyes and said, "I know I'm dying. But, Kathy, I'm so tired I don't care." Georges jumped up and began to plead with her. But Sarah only nodded. "She does not care. I know. At the end there are only the children, and when they go . . . nothing."

I smoothed her pillow. It was made from a flour sack. I smiled when I remembered the way I had first pictured Constance. What a shame to have put her in satin skirts heavy with brocade. I realized now that there was no place for the sapphire rings in golden settings that I had wanted for her. You would not encumber hands with jewels and have them mend and wash and handle babies. Constance's hands had always fascinated me. They lay, slim and brown, against the covers. You would not think there was the strength in them to make such a life, dig it out of nothing.

Why was I thinking everything in a new way? Where was the Kathy who had longed for finery and romance? Because she had once been me, was she closer to me now than any other?

More hours. I heard my mother saying, "There are those in this world born to sorrow." Why had I always pitied Constance? I couldn't understand it now. She had had sorrow: her family, all her children—gone. But death does not stand at the end of life, it is all through it. It is the fear of losing, the knowledge of losing that makes love tender. I remembered what she had said about the little things being the important things. I felt closer to her than I ever had. So much of what she had said came back to me. I remembered how she had talked to me that first day in Grouard. I hadn't liked it then, her emphasis on the fact that she and I were white, the only white women. There were already strong ties of love and friendship between me and my Indian neighbors. I had Sarah. But now I understood. It wasn't *that* she meant. She had tried to say, "You and I came to this country. We have known other things. The rest were born here, so they live here. But we chose it, you and I, and we are the only ones."

I bent over her. I wanted to say, "Yes, now I see. I understand you. And I can be a better friend than I ever was." But she lay so still.

We sat through the night. I felt stiff and cold. Sarah got up to prepare a fresh broth of herbs. But Constance remained motionless. Her lips were parted, and her breath came and went too gently.

I watched it grow light. Mike came to take my place, to beg me to sleep. She opened her eyes again, looked at all of us, knew us.

"Mike and Kathy, take the twins."

Georges threw himself across the bed, sobbing, clutching at her with his red hands. She patted him absently, as she would a child. She spoke. "It's cold," she said. And then, "Timmy, light the fire."

That was all. I cried against Mike's coat for one of the dearest friends I ever had.

All the while I was conscious of Sarah moving about, silently doing the things that must be done. She grieved, but who would lay out Constance's blue cotton dress, who would wash the body and prepare it, if not Sarah? So she went sorrowing from one task to another. At first I didn't try to help her. I didn't want to touch Constance. The body of a loved person is a terrible mockery. It says, "Look, I am still here," when you know she is not there. I had held those hands and kissed that mouth and combed that hair. I didn't want to do it again now.

Sarah passed me with a kettle in her hands. Her back was terribly bent, and her motions were slow. I had never before seen how old she was. But she didn't stop working. Her love for Constance wasn't wasted like mine in mourning and grief.

I shook off my numbness. I opened the door and went into the other bedroom. Two little figures stood on the bed. One had a shirt over his head which Mike was trying to pull past his ears.

"Here," I said, "you've got to unbutton another button."

"Then you'd have to take the whole thing off," he protested.

"There are times when it pays to start all over again, and this is one of them."

The child's feet started prancing, and a muffled sob came from behind the plaid shirt. I took it off and smoothed back the tousled brown curls.

"Were you scared in there?" I asked.

The boy shook his head.

"He was!" I turned from little Georges to little Connie. I was terribly startled to see the large lavender eyes of her grandmother looking out at me from that baby face. I had never realized how alike they were. Little Connie had the same delicate features, a haunting sweetness in her mouth. I wondered if I would find my Constance again in this four-year-old.

Although she was only standing in her underwear, I whispered to her that we could beat Mike and little Georges. We did, and then watched Mike struggle with her twin's coat. Every time Mike put it on, the sleeves of the baby's various shirts and sweaters were carried up into such a knot that the coat sleeve couldn't be pulled over it. Connie and I helped by putting all sleeve ends firmly in little Georges' hands. The coat went on.

We hurried them through the front room and out of the house. I went back to tell old Georges that he was to come to see the children all the time—that they needed their grandfather. I don't think he heard me. His eyes were sunken and almost closed. He seemed dazed. But maybe he was just thinking a long way back. Maybe somewhere in his mind a young man with a fifty-pound sack of flour on his back trudged barefoot beside a beautiful young girl with lavender eyes. I went out as quietly as I could.

Mike had kept the children busy building a snow man. We couldn't persuade them to leave it except by promising them a new one when they got home.

That night Mike played he was a bear. And when we went to bed the house was in a litter, a wonderful exciting litter of cutouts and spilled jam and cookie crumbs. Mike caught me around the waist while I was cleaning up.

"Well, girl?"

"Oh, Mike—" I couldn't say anything else because I was crying and getting kissed all at once.

Twenty-eight

IT WAS WONDERFUL having children in the house again. The long hours Mike was away were suddenly filled for me. The twins played well with each other. Of course it was up to me to get them started. But once I had set out chips and blocks from the kindling, they would spend intense hours piling them in stacks. I taught them little French songs that I had heard Constance sing. And at night when they rough-housed with Mike, I worked on a blue dress for Connie to wear Sundays. I thought I would make a blouse for Georges out of what was left. I worked late over it. Long after the children were in bed, Mike and I discussed them and planned for them. Mike thought it would be nice for Georges to be a Mounty, and I thought that maybe Connie would be a nurse. We decided that Old Irish Bill would give them music when they became six. The picture of a pretty white-starched nurse faded, and I saw Connie bowing instead to an audience at Symphony Hall and seating herself at the organ for another encore.

The blue dress was done. Connie hopped up and down impatiently while I buttoned it on. Then she stood back for me to see. I looked at her and burst into tears.

"Come here, Connie. I've got to take it off you."

Now it was her turn to cry. I promised her another dress, much prettier, any color she liked, only not blue. In blue she became her grandmother, her eyes became the same strange lavender. It broke my heart. I traded in the blue material for red, and that night started a new dress. While I worked, Mike read me the poems of Bobby Burns that we had borrowed again from the McTavishes. I loved to hear him declaim, "A man's a man."

It was one of these evenings when Jonathan Forquet walked into the room, holding in his arms a solemn-eyed baby.

"I come to my friends." He said it half-defiantly.

Jonathan was Jonathan. It had been eight years, but he had the same proud way about him.

"Is it your baby?" I asked, coming toward him. "Is Oh-Be-Joyful with you?"

He looked at me and answered slowly. "Can you not see that she is dead?"

Then I did see it. I saw it in the black eyes that looked hopelessly into my own. The lids were heavy . . . Jonathan had cried.

"The sickness?" I asked him. "The flu?"

"The sickness, it took her, Mamanowatum." He lifted the baby toward me, and before I knew it I had her in my arms. Jonathan watched me as I held her.

"From ten sleeps away I bring you. Mamanowatum, she call her Kathy. She want this winter come show you girl-child, come show you happiness. Now she no come ever. Only I come, say, 'Keep baby.' No want Mission for keep her. They not like me. They not like my father."

Mike came over to me. "We'll keep her, won't we, Kathy?"

"Yes," I said. "Of course."

Jonathan nodded "You are my friends. I knew. I come, bring furs once, twice, in the year. You sell. Feed, make clothes for girl-child." He hesitated. I knew there was something else.

He spoke in Cree: "Mamanowatum . . . many winters we are together, always the canoe sings in the river and the paths we walk are of happiness. You will say that to the girl-child? You will tell her of the joyful heart of Mamanowatum!"

Mike patted him roughly on the shoulder. We stood in the doorway and watched him walk into the night. He was alone, as he had been before he knew the gentleness and the love of Oh-Be-Joyful. The baby reached out after him, but the little fist closed on emptiness.

I turned to Mike. Oh-Be-Joyful, the girl with black stockings sitting primly in punishment row . . . I saw her laughing, scrubbing a pot with the same intensity with which she had clung to that pile of pelts, Jonathan's present. I heard again the story of Fleet Foot, heard her chattering to Mary Aroon in Cree.

Mike crouched on his heels and looked earnestly at the round copper face of the baby. "She's a cute little mite." He ran a finger lightly under her chin, and she dimpled all over. Mike grinned back, "Hello, Kathy." He winked at me, "We can't have two Kathies. Let's call her Kate."

Kate. This brown Indian baby had my name, perhaps part of my destiny. "My more-than-sister," Oh-Be-Joyful had called me. And her child was closer to me than my own sister's. I murmured the name, "Kate." I pictured Oh-Be-Joyful saying it, bending over her child, thinking of me, whispering my name. She lived in the wild world of brilliant summer colors, she walked through the clean pine woods of

the North, among the cries, the calls, the flapping of wings, the sway-
ing of bush, surrounded by life, part of it, free in it; at the height of
her happiness, her child in her arms, she had thought of me.

"Mike," I said, "it's very strange . . . and I want to understand.
What does it all mean?"

"Well, there's a pattern," Mike said. "The baby is Kate and you
are Katherine, and it's right that you should have her."

"A pattern?"

"Yes. I don't mean the names exactly. But Oh-Be-Joyful was
part of the pattern of your life, and things like that don't just stop.
Things from her life will come into yours, into ours, as long as we
live."

I knew what he meant by this pattern. It wasn't something you
could put into words, but you could sense it behind everything. If
you tried to talk about it, all you could say was something trite, like
water is always watery, and leaves are like leaves. But it did have a
meaning. You could see that events were like the people they happened to. Oh-Be-Joyful's life had always had that intense emotion
and pathetic grasping after happiness that my mother said was char-
acteristic of those "who are not long for this world." Perhaps on
another day I would laugh at this and consider it superstition, but this
day, watching Oh-Be-Joyful's baby in Mike's arms, I saw the pattern
too.

Stretched on the loom was the huge white cloth of the North.
We were the threads. Short and long, our ways stretched across it,
bright and dull: Oh-Be-Joyful, born here, loving it because it was her
home; Constance, coming because she hadn't a better place, because
she must make a new life for herself; and I—I had come thinking I
was different, that I could choose my own place in the world; but I
was woven in as firmly as the others. There was a time when I had
tried to run away. Everything up here had suddenly become too big
for me. The great sweeps: winter, cold and white, the coldest and the
whitest; summer, the northern lights hanging terrifyingly in the air. I
had tried to escape, like Mrs. Neilson, who had gone back to New
York, or Mrs. Marlin, who had gone insane.

But when I left Mike, I left myself, I left the Katherine Mary the
North had made. I was part of Grouard. Sarah had nursed me; I had
nursed Randy. Constance had mended my clothes; I had mended
James McTavish's plaid. Oh-Be-Joyful had cared for and loved my
children, and now it was I who was to care for and love hers. Mike
was right: the pattern of a life isn't a straight line; it crosses and

recrosses, drawing in and tying together other lives, as I do when I gather in the ends of my thread to make a knot.

"It's strange," I said, "but love for a place has to grow in you, the same as any other kind of love."

"Do you really love it, Kathy?" Mike said in a low voice, playing absently with the Indian baby. "You've had a hard time up here, and perhaps not a very happy one, and I can't promise that it'll be any different."

"I don't want it any different if it can be with you." I didn't move. I felt too much in love to touch him or even look at him.

"Mike, I feel almost like when I was a kid and ate all the Easter candy before my sisters got up. Look at me. I have everything. And then think of Jonathan with only emptiness in his life."

"He had what he wanted, and still has a part of it. And so did Oh-Be-Joyful."

"But for such a little while."

"They had it, and that's what's important!"

Mike reached up and pulled me down on the floor beside himself and little Kate. He rocked us each in a big arm.

"I'm thinking back a way, Kathy. Not very far, when you and I were alone too."

I began to see. The pattern of things half-formed itself against the jumble of incidents before I lost it again.

THERE WAS GREAT excitement the next morning when the twins found out they had a baby sister. We told them they could celebrate any way they wanted. It wasn't hard for them to decide. They'd been after Mike for days to take them out in the snow.

Mike laughed. "Okay, Kathy, dress 'em up. I'll meet you on the porch." And he went off on some errand of his own.

When the last fur mitten was on the last twin, I sent them out to wait while I bundled up the baby and dressed myself.

It was a wonderful winter's day, clear and cold and dry, with the sun shining. I came up close to see what Mike was working over. It was our old sled. I thought he had burned it or hacked it to pieces, but evidently it had only been hidden, probably under the wood pile. He was oiling the runners and rubbing off seven years of rust. The twins were busy rubbing too. Mike looked at me over the heads of the children. "I just came across it the other day, and I thought they'd have a lot of fun with it." I smiled at him, and he smiled back, relieved.

"All aboard. Everybody in!" There was a wild scramble, and more arms and legs than I thought we possessed even collectively.

Mike swung into the wind. It was good to watch him striding through unbroken snow, but I was content—back here in the sled, keeping the children from falling out the hole.

It was a magic cutter. We sailed across a frozen sea. Georges was captain and yelled orders to Connie, who yelled them at the trees and drifts and clouds.

"Warm enough?" Mike asked when we were at the top of the hill.

"Yes."

The twins were pulling at him, demanding a snow fight, but he still looked at me, unsatisfied.

I tried to tell him. "It hurts a little."

"What hurts you?" Connie asked. "A pin?"

"No," I said. "Happiness."

The
Search
for Joyful

$\mathcal{O}$ne

THE WHISTLE BLEW. The train lurched forward. Black clouds of smoke obscured Mama Kathy and Connie. Only seconds before they had been repeating their advice and hugging me. Mama Kathy held to her belief that I was headed for sin city, as she called Montreal. I felt I was embarked on an adventure like her own, when as a young girl she'd traveled from Boston into the wilderness of the Northwest Territory. I was reversing this, going from the prairie to the big city— like Mama, starting a new life in a different world.

As I watched the land speed past in a blur of white drifts, I remembered the times Mama put us to bed with tales of her journey in the blizzard of '07. The train stalled for weeks, waiting to be dug out by snowplows. Wiping the frost from the window she looked out at hundreds of cows and steers blown across the icy fields, packed along the stock fence, frozen and dead.

When I wiped the frost from my window, the vista that greeted my eyes was smiling and sunny, the snow sparkling. I felt buoyant and excited. A call had gone out, and I had answered it. What would come of it, I didn't know.

I tried to disentangle exactly what it was that had propelled me toward this moment. Not one event, but many threads, twisted and woven together. Growing up with Mama Kathy and Papa was the main thing. There was something special between the two of them, kept alive by Mama Kathy's stories of how it had been.

"The Crees called me Mrs. Mike," she'd say, "because they couldn't get their tongues around a name like Flannigan." And I'd beg for more stories about those times. I wanted to be part of them. But the special love, the special joy belonged to her and Papa Mike.

When I realized that . . . the what-ifs began. What if I was really their daughter? What if the twins were really my brother and sister?

The desire to fit in gave rise to all the what-ifs of my life. It became a game, and yet it was more than that. What if I was allowed to keep one of the kittens? What if I could go into town with Papa? What if I was a rabbit and lived in a burrow? What if I didn't have to be "included." *Included* was Mama Kathy's word. "Remember," she'd say to Connie and Georges, "Kathy is to be included."

What set me apart? We were all adopted, so it wasn't that. I didn't guess the reason because they never talked to me about it, and their love protected me from even thinking about it.

Still, I had a sense of uneasiness. In the bathtub I scrubbed my copper skin hard in an attempt to lighten it. Mama Kathy, when she understood what I was doing, scooped me up in a big towel and held me against her. "Your skin is the color of a young fawn because you are Oh-Be-Joyful's daughter. You can't believe how close we were, Kathy. She was my more-than-sister." She told me I belonged to the First Nation people and that my band was Cree. "You are Cree Indian."

The first day at mission school was my first real contact with Indian children. They regarded me with solemn black eyes very like my own. I stared at them, at their heavy straight braids. What if my hair grew long and was plaited, wouldn't it look exactly like theirs? Their skin was the same tone too, the tone Mama Kathy called sun-kissed.

The Indian children kept to themselves. They sent glances in my direction, but didn't speak to me. One girl fingered a pouch of some kind she wore around her neck, looking at me all the time. I did not return her glance; it was too full of things I knew nothing of.

At recess no one talked to me. I stood isolated and alone in the noisy schoolyard. Both sets of children, the Indian and the white, ignored me. I was marked as not belonging.

I watched the white girls jumping rope. I knew how to jump rope. I jumped better than they did. My feet never got tangled up. I continued to watch. Finally I went over to them. "I can jump rope."

Several girls giggled, the rest stared, but no one said anything. There was a short line; I joined it and waited my turn. When it came I stepped into the arc of the rope. It made a fine whooshing sound each time it struck the gravel. I jumped and jumped and never fell out of rhythm.

The Cree girl, who was called Elk Girl, contemplated me with dispassionate eyes and reserved judgment.

I wanted to know more about being Indian. I got Mama Kathy to tell me again how she brought Oh-Be-Joyful from the mission to help with her babies, who died afterwards in the diphtheria epidemic. Seven years later it was the flu, born in the dirt of European trenches, that created world-wide havoc and carried off the twins' mother and grandmother too. Mama Kathy always finished by harking back to her own children. "Mary Aroon and Ralph were taken, but the good Lord gave me you three rascals to raise." Because, when the disease was almost over and the danger seemed past, it claimed a final victim, Oh-Be-Joyful.

I didn't like this part of the story. "Tell me," I prompted, "tell me about Jonathan Forquet." And I recited along with her, "Jonathan Forquet loved her from the moment he set eyes on her.... Now tell who he was." I knew that too, which was what made it such a wonderful tale.

"He was your father." And we hugged each other in delight.

As she related how ill he had been, how despondent after my mother's death, a memory formed hazily in my mind. A strange Indian standing on our porch, his eyes searching me out, just me, from all the others. I was the only one he saw. After gazing at me a long time, he opened his arms.

I wouldn't go to him. I held on to Mama's skirt, but she gave me a gentle shove. "It's your father, Kathy." She chose the word well, because while I couldn't have two papas, a father was all right.

When he held me I thought of pine trees and streams, and smoky fires. He clasped me against him a long time, until I began to squirm. He turned my face so that I looked at him, and said, "I bring you a name."

That seemed an odd thing to say. I had a name. My name was Kathy.

He continued almost without pause. "I traveled a long journey to bring it. Your mother's spirit guided me to the Grandmothers." His voice was taut, vibrant. "Listen to me, child. In the lodges of your people you are named Oh-Be-Joyful's Daughter."

Oh-Be-Joyful's Daughter was my Indian name, but it had never been part of me. I wasn't that girl.

Except . . .

I think it was Oh-Be-Joyful's Daughter who showed me how to fight for acceptance at school. I used a gift I had from Mama Kathy—storytelling. Stories came effortlessly into my head, and I would spin them out for Connie and Georges during long evenings.

Most of my plots were borrowed. When I got to high school I learned this wasn't such a bad thing. Shakespeare borrowed a lot of his plots too.

An endless source of books was Old Irish Bill. He probably had the finest collection of tattered and dilapidated books in the Northwest Territory and his own library system. You could take home up to ten books at a time, but you had to sign for them. You also had an obligation to repair them to the best of your ability. I spent many hours with brown wrapping paper, paste, scissors, and sometimes cardboard. A special satchel at our house was dedicated to Irish Bill's books.

I grew up with Kim, Robin Hood, and Long John Silver. Those afternoons when I sat on the worn couch in Irish Bill's living room, he would prepare hot chocolate, adding a nip to his—"against the cold," he would say. It was very companionable, he with a pipe, me scattering crumbs as I dunked corn bread.

Mama was a history buff and wanted us to take advantage of Irish Bill's wonderful store of knowledge. She told us she had once spent an entire winter immersed in his prized history of China, which on the flyleaf bore the inscription, "Property of the McTavishes." Georges liked how-to books, on magic and fixing things and surviving in the wilderness. He would explain to Connie, who never opened a book if she could help it, how the world ran, what was wrong with it, and how it could be improved.

Connie had her own fantasy life. Very early, about age six, she planned her wedding, "down to the last detail." A gown of billowing satin, a veil, orange blossoms—she pictured it all against a background of wedding guests. The fact that the nuptials were years in the future, and that no groom loomed on the horizon, bothered her not at all. He would appear, along with a tiered wedding cake, when it was time.

Stories. I loved stories. And stories became my passport.

I sat on a bench in the playground and began my inventions. My audience was a boy with a sprained ankle, who couldn't participate in football practice. The first tale owed a large debt to Jack London's *White Fang*. As I got into it, more and more children came to hear. My great triumph was when Elk Girl joined the group to listen to the saga of Gray Wolf.

Gray Wolf went from adventure to adventure. White Wolf was his mate and everyone knows wolves mate for life. The story continued for months, and then something impelled me to bring disaster on poor Gray Wolf. In fighting free of a trapper's snare he was shot and blinded.

I drew a deep breath wondering how he could survive in the wild. But only for a moment. It was clear to me that White Wolf came to his aid, inviting Gray Wolf to lay his muzzle against her flank and gallop through the forest with her. From then on he ran at her side. She was his eyes.

Elk Girl came up to me later in the week and put a bushy animal tail in my lap. "The spirit of the wolf liked your story. He will be your guardian."

I took the wolf tail home and examined it further. It was gray with a ring of white and one of a darker fur, a symbol of good luck, which through mysterious Indian magic would keep evil at bay.

PACKING FOR MONTREAL, I had put in my old talisman at the last moment. I was glad I had. As the silver and blue Canadian Pacific rushed on, I wondered if I would be the only First Nation person to enroll at Charity Hospital. The only First Nation person to answer the call for army nurses.

The only First Nation person.

I had faced that situation when Connie and Georges began dating. They always double-dated. Even for twins they were close. I watched them whisper together, finish each other's sentences, and laugh at private jokes. They invented a secret cryptographic code—the Twins' Code—that Georges boasted no one could break. Another signal between them was the word *tomahawk*. Whenever either mentioned the word, it meant, "This is boring. Let's get out of here." The problem was working a word like *tomahawk* into ordinary conversation.

I took it all in. I watched as they were caught up in a social life, and realized this would not happen for me. I was already in high school and no white boy asked me out. Although Randy Harrison tried to kiss me when he caught me alone behind the gym.

I took to staring into my looking glass and brooding. Was I pretty, I wondered, studying my prominent cheekbones. My eyes were large and set well apart. My lashes, long and straight. My teeth white and straight, and my mouth full, even when I laughed. My nose? What can be said about noses? Mine wasn't big, it wasn't small. It was just a nose. Did these features add up to a pretty face? I decided to ask Mama Kathy.

"Mama," I said that evening as I took down the dishtowel, "do you think I'm at all pretty?"

"Pretty?" She seemed startled. But I could see she was considering the question. "You've always been a sturdy girl. And thank goodness your health is excellent."

"Yes, yes, but am I pretty?"

"There's a look of Oh-Be-Joyful about you, but I see your father too. You have his strength."

I smiled. It was hopeless.

When Connie came in, I told her I wanted a sister walk. Connie, because she was older, saw how hard it was for me to get things out, so years ago she had instituted sister walks. A sister walk is of course only for sisters. No one else can come along, because that's when you tell whatever is on your mind.

"Connie," I said when we were halfway to the pond where a colony of ducks and a pair of white egrets had made their home, "I want to know, it's important to me: Do you think I'm pretty?"

"Of course you're pretty."

That was a big-sister reply and it didn't satisfy me. "What do the girls at school say about me?"

"They think you're exotic."

"Exotic? That isn't pretty."

"You have a Metis French grandfather, and that strain shows. I'd guess you were Indian, but I wouldn't be sure. Let's ask Georges."

"No," I said, suddenly shy, "forget it."

I got an after-school job at the drugstore. I was stationed behind the soda fountain, where I mixed frothy sarsaparillas and chocolate shakes.

I was mixing and scooping and waiting tables while China was wracked by civil war. I barely recognized the names Mao and Chiang Kai-shek. When the Japanese set up a puppet government in Manchukuo, I was serving Coca-Colas and rainbow ice cream cones.

Two women sat down at the soda fountain and fanned themselves. Saying "I really shouldn't," they ordered double malts. A little kid, scarcely as high as the counter, undid a dime tied into a corner of his handkerchief. A couple of girls from my own grade, in circular swing skirts wearing lipstick, came in. I hardly recognized them out of our school uniform. How hard we tried to pin our middy blouses in a sexy way, emphasizing slim waists and hinting at something on top as well. When the Sisters spotted the new fashion, it was immediately abolished.

Now my classmates were young ladies, meeting boys here. Was I also a young lady?

Elk Girl came in. She had dropped out of school. I hadn't seen her in almost a year. She put money on the counter before uttering a word.

"I'll have a banana split with everything on it," she said as though we had parted that morning.

"How've you been, Elk Girl?" I asked as I sliced a banana, added three scoops of different ice creams and three sauces, sprinkled on nuts, and finished with a dollop of whipped cream and a maraschino cherry.

She followed these preparations with an eagle eye, then put her question to me. "Have you ever eaten one?"

"No," I admitted.

"That's what I thought. You fix 'em, but you don't eat 'em."

I felt uncomfortable. How did she know that, since the Depression, banana splits were considered too expensive around our house?

With great deliberation Elk Girl took out a pack of Old Golds and offered me one.

"No, I don't smoke." I was horrified that she did.

She contemplated me with the look that had disconcerted me since I was seven. "You should smoke, you know. Smoke is holy. Bet you didn't know that."

"Who says it's holy?"

"The Creator." She laughed at my expression. "Can't go higher than that." With concentration she blew a smoke ring in my direction.

I brushed it away.

"Won't your white mama let you smoke?"

I pretended to be busy counting out paper napkins and filling containers.

"Oh-Be-Joyful understood smoke."

This pronouncement shook me. What did she know about my mother?

"I live with a power woman. Sarah is very very old. She is a wind shifter and she knew Mamanowatum."

"Who's that?"

"Your mother, Oh-Be-Joyful. Mamanowatum is the way it's said in Cree. Sarah, the woman I live with, knew her, she knew Jonathan, she knew about you being born . . . and she knew what would happen."

"How? By divination? By magic?"

Elk Girl said complacently, "She looks into smoke and it shows her things."

"What things?" I couldn't help asking.

"Herself."

I frowned over the answer.

"You have to know yourself first, before you can know anything else; that just stands to reason. By the way, how do you get on with your pawakam?"

"My what?"

"Your wolf tail."

"I still have it, if that's what you mean."

She seemed pleased with this answer. "You make a good split." She carried her sundae to one of the tables and proceeded to eat with obvious relish, making sure to get every bit.

"There ought to be a law," one of the girls from school whispered in a voice meant to carry, "no ice cream for You-know-who above the fiftieth parallel."

This raised a laugh from her friends, but Elk Girl did not choose to hear. She had not come for ice cream. I knew enough about magic from my brother to know that. Georges was fascinated by things that appeared to be one thing and were in fact quite different. "The science of misdirection," he called it. Elk Girl had come because of the pawakam.

ELK GIRL WAS my only link with my Indian self. My only link to Oh-Be-Joyful's Daughter. She seemed to know a lot about me. I knew nothing about her, not even where she lived, except it was with a wind shifter called Sarah. Elk Girl had always been aloof, distant, and unknowable, like my Indian heritage. I decided to make her a friendship bracelet. I'd made one for Connie's birthday. It involved a lot of rummaging—tiny glass beads, seed pearls from a pair of outworn gloves, covered buttons from a torn jacket, segments of a broken watch band, strung together. I was still thinking about the possibilities of a second bracelet as I walked home from school. I wondered if I could find enough items.

Because I lived farther out than most of the kids I generally walked home alone. I turned at the sound of my name.

"Kathy!" It was Phil Dunway on his bike. Phil Dunway was the boy at school that I liked. I'd liked him since fifth grade when he stood up for me on the playground. He was a senior now, and after graduation I wouldn't see him again.

Phil caught up to me, got off and walked his bicycle. "Kathy," he said again, "I'm going your way."

I was surprised at his friendliness. At school we didn't speak. "Fine," I said. Neither of us could think of anything further to say, then we spoke at once. I laughed and took a breath. "Are you visiting someone?" I asked, because he'd never taken this route before.

"No." There was a short pause. "I just thought maybe you wouldn't mind."

Was he saying that he took this path deliberately to walk me home? My heart raced with excitement. He liked me. Phil Dunway, the cutest boy in school, liked me.

The pause between us lengthened, and I searched for something interesting to say, but could only come up with, "Lucky you, you'll be graduating in a couple of months."

"Yeah." He smiled but had nothing to add.

"So, do you have something lined up? A summer job?"

"My dad wants me to go into the contracting business with him, but things are pretty slow just now."

"You ought to think about being a Mountie. If I was a man that's what I'd be."

"I'm glad you're not."

"What? A Mountie?"

"A man." And he took one hand from the handle of his bike and laid it over mine. The wheel immediately turned, bringing us to an abrupt halt. "Can we maybe sit down somewhere and talk? If you don't have to get home, that is."

"No, I don't have to be home."

There was shade not far off, and we sat with our backs against the large oak. Phil took my hand again. "This is better," he said.

I let my hand stay in his.

"I never see you with any of the fellows at school." He threw this out tentatively.

"No. I'm not going with any of them."

"That's what I was hoping because . . ." He leaned over and kissed me. He did it very deliberately as though he had been nerving himself to it. Then he did it once more and this time I cooperated.

It felt heady. His touch awakened me to new knowledge of myself. In Phil Dunway's arms I sensed what it was to be a woman. His fingers lightly followed the outline of my cheek, my throat, and, dropping lower, my breasts.

I drew back frightened that I had allowed so much, afraid I would allow more. "I have to go."

"Can I see you again tomorrow?" he asked, getting to his feet. "Right here? Can this be our place?"

I hesitated. I wanted to, but . . .

"I'll be here," he said persuasively, "right after school. Will you?"

Words choked in my throat, but I nodded.

I thought of Phil all night, analyzed every intonation, action, and gesture. In English class I went over it all again. In mathematics I got totally lost, thinking not of square roots but of the soft, waving texture of his hair, remembering my fingers in it.

While I was still debating whether or not to meet him, I found myself there. Phil was leaning against the old oak and at sight of me his face lighted and he came forward. Without a word we put our arms about each other. This time there was no fumbling, his mouth was deliciously open and his hands sure. He continued where he had left off. He slid his hands under my shirt. I rallied from dreamy acquiescence determined to say no.

He didn't ask, just opened my shirt and stared. "I never saw a girl before," he said.

I got to my feet, pulling my shirt around me. "You shouldn't have done that, Phil."

"I'm not sorry, Kathy. I should be. And I apologize. Don't go away sore." He caught up to me. "How'd you like to go to the senior prom?"

That stopped me. I'd never been to a school dance or any other kind. No one had ever asked me. The senior prom. I'd fantasized about it forever, Cinderella at the ball.

"Well?" Phil asked. "What do you say?"

I forgot I hadn't answered him. I nodded before I could get the yes out.

"Can I have another look, then?"

I closed my eyes and stood in front of him, my face burning as he unbuttoned my blouse.

That night I took down my wolf pawakam. I felt it held the answer to my question. "Guardian," I whispered, "does he feel what I feel? Does he love me? Really love me?"

The talisman replied sooner than I expected. Sooner than I wanted. I lived a very short time in my Cinderella dream. After school the girls were whispering to each other, speculating who was taking who to the prom. Some had already been asked, and they preened themselves before the wallflowers.

I didn't say anything. Marlene was keeping count at the drinking fountain. She said, "So far, Ev is going with John Boyle, Gwen with Danny Thompson, and Cindy with Phil Dunway . . ."

She went on, but I didn't hear. I left her standing there and walked down the hall and out to the ball field where I knew he would be playing lacrosse. It was baseball season, but a bunch of the fellows got up their own lacrosse game so they could charge and block and work out their hostilities.

"Phil!" I called. "Phil."

They were taking a break, and Phil was showing off, cradling the ball. He looked up. The other boys did too. They were startled and one of them mimicked, "Phil, oh, Phil, Pocahontas wants you."

He looked at me. It was a long look. Then he turned his back, laughing.

The public humiliation pinned me to the spot. I couldn't walk away from the shame any more than I could walk away from the anger. I wanted to run, but I was chained where I was. I knew I could never tell anyone, not Mama Kathy, not Connie either.

I had brought this on myself. I had forgotten I was Indian. Remembering released me, gave me strength to walk past my classmates looking neither to the right nor the left, my ears closed to comments.

At home I got out the wolf tail and stared at it a long time. I hadn't known who I was. Now I knew. I would braid wolf hairs into the friendship bracelet.

I DIDN'T GROW up until Papa died. He wasn't sick. Something broke inside him and we couldn't get him to a hospital. It had rained for days and the roads had turned to muskeg.

I heard his voice in muffled cries, hoarse and desperate, from the bedroom.

When Mama Kathy came out she staggered against the door. I rushed to her, led her to a chair, and pushed her gently into it.

"The Luminal, Kathy. He asked for it. It's in a small silver packet in the medicine chest."

"Yes, Mama, I'll get it."

"Oh, God, the pain, Kathy. It's terrible."

"I'll get him the Luminal, Mama. It will be better."

She nodded, and I went into the bathroom, found it, and, filling a glass of water, took it to him.

The covers were knotted into a corner of the bed. Papa's eyes had glazed over like a sick cat's, sweat rolled along his face, and his body was rigid. I poured some of the water on a towel and bent over him, wiping his forehead, murmuring as I worked. "I've brought you the Luminal, Papa. It will relax you."

He was in no condition to swallow anything. A spasm bowed his body and blood gushed, splattering the wall, ejected with the same terrible force that had taken over his body.

I rushed to the bathroom for a clean towel, passing the door to my room. There, in the closet on the top shelf, was my guardian. I couldn't see it, but I didn't need to see it.

"Help me," I whispered. "Help him."

When I returned, Papa was stretched out on his back, sleeping.

I stroked his hand, his capable, strong-fingered hand. What good was his strength to him now? What good were dampened towels and Luminal, even if he could swallow it? What was needed was large decisive steps. Something had gone wrong inside. He needed stitching together, he needed an oxygen tent to help him breathe. He needed a hospital equipped to help him.

His eyes opened. He looked at me and said in a voice that I bent to hear, "You'd make a good nurse, Kathy."

Those were his last words to me. Mama Kathy came in. Her red hair was pinned neatly back; she had taken hold. I relinquished my place.

I went out and sat on the porch steps. Connie and Georges came and sat beside me. No one spoke. Then Connie gave a quavering little laugh. "You know what I was thinking? Do you remember, Kathy, when you were little, about five, I think? You use to spend hours making concoctions of dirt and grass, all mixed up with seeds and baking powder from the kitchen."

"I remember that," Georges said.

"Do you remember what it was for?" Connie challenged him.

I knew. It suddenly came back to me. I was making a medicine so Mama Kathy and Papa would live forever. "It didn't work," I muttered.

We learned it was peritonitis that took him, a burst appendix. Sergeant Mike looked after the whole province. If a job needed doing, there was Mike Flannigan of the Royal Canadian Mounted Police to do it. He was game warden, inspected traps and settled disputes. He kept illegal drugs out of his territory and was responsible for immigration violation and sabotage. And when he'd time on his hands, he repaired the telephone wires and vaccinated a village. He would turn his hand to anything, help anyone, and in the end no one could do anything for him.

Elk Girl explained it to me that night. I was exhausted, out of my head with grief, and had thrown myself across the bed without bothering with a cover. Elk Girl came in, covered me, brought the pawakam and laid it beside me, then opened the window and sat there, looking out. She stared up at the stars, and they, serene and wise, looked down on us. Elk Girl didn't speak. She didn't say that the stars were where they belonged—but they were.

WE THOUGHT IT would be a small funeral, just the family and a few friends from the town. But word was carried on the newly extended phone lines and, when these quit, by moccasin telegraph penetrating deep into the woods. People came, white and Indian, from all over the province, people we didn't know but who had known Sgt. Mike Flannigan.

The Royal Canadian Mounted Police were well represented, their scarlet dress uniforms punctuating the somber attire of the others. Among the guests was Jonathan Forquet. He came not only for Papa Mike but to stand beside Mama.

On the day of the funeral she leaned on his arm. He himself was a compelling figure, spare almost to the point of emaciation. His eyes, when he turned them on you, burned with the intensity of a soul about to leave the body, an arrow ready to quit the bow. When the prayers were finished and he spoke I could understand why the Indians regarded him as a holy man.

"This Mountie we lay to rest today arrested me, kept me jailed for a murder I did not do, refused to give his blessing to my marriage. Yet I am here from across Canada, from Quebec Province. Why? Because when I was starving in body and soul he fed me at his table. He travels now to the west where our people have always traveled. But if he was here he'd laugh in our faces. As he saw it, he did what anybody would do. His own kids died in the diphtheria epidemic, and he was still bringing soup and medicine to people too ill and weak to manage for themselves. But don't think he wouldn't go after a trap thief and bring him in, Mountie style. He was there to fight a fire, or pull an abscessed tooth. He entered our lives, one way or another. Look in your heart to see which part of him you carry."

Before he left, my father called me to him. He acted as though he had a right to do this, as though he had been here. But it was Papa. Papa was the one to oil my skates, to show me the beaver dam, to explain the migration of birds—it was Papa's lap that was always there for me.

Jonathan Forquet never bothered about me, never inquired about me. He was never part of my life. He was off somewhere being holy, preaching to unlettered Indians who were in awe of him.

Well, I wasn't in awe of him. I followed him reluctantly, my feet scuffing leaves.

He walked a little way into the woods, and the musky smell of decayed vegetation under loamy earth made me think of the grave.

He began speaking again in an intimate way, as though I was his daughter. "You have grown up well. Mrs. Mike is right, there is a look of your mother about you. There is also a look of sadness. Not only because of Sergeant Mike's death, but it has been in you, I think, a long time. It comes from the way you look at life."

"Don't lecture me. Did you find the beaver dam? Did you fix my skates? I don't even know you. And you don't know me."

"I do know you. I brought you your name."

"You show up once. One time in sixteen years. Well, you know what I wish? I wish it was my papa I was standing here with."

A slight smile hovered about the corners of his mouth. "And that I was where he is?"

I turned away.

"Oh-Be-Joyful's Daughter—"

I stopped. I wasn't used to anyone addressing me by this name.

He went on in a detached tone, but I felt the urgency behind it. "When I think of you, when I dream you, when I speak your name, you are with me. Far things are just as near. Didn't you ever feel this?"

"No. Either someone is here with me, or they're not."

"A namer is never far."

"You were. To other people you brought religion and all that, but there was nothing for me. And you can't start now, I won't let you." I was angry to find I was crying.

He went on as though I hadn't said anything, "You must remember who you are. You must learn to be joyful."

"You haven't the right to expect anything of me. Go take your good works somewhere else." I turned and ran. The joyfulness he tried to force on me seemed dreadful. At school I'm not accepted—it doesn't matter, be joyful. At work I serve sundaes I can't afford to eat—be joyful. My papa, whom I love more than anything in the world, dies—be joyful.

We didn't speak again. I was glad when he left.

Two

AFTER PAPA'S DEATH, we tried to be a normal family. We couldn't talk about Papa at first. We had to and yet we couldn't. It was Jonathan Forquet Mama Kathy told me about. I didn't want to listen because I knew I'd been unfair to him. But I couldn't stop Mama.

"When Oh-Be-Joyful died, he didn't know what to do. He went wild, gambled, made himself ill, almost died. Then he turned to religion, but he didn't find what he needed, not completely. Not until he read the teachings of Handsome Lake."

"Is Handsome Lake a person?"

"He was a Seneca prophet. Before that, like Jonathan, he was a drunk. This brought him close to death, and he experienced a vision in which it is said he was shown the braiding of all things. When he recovered, he wove the wisdom of the Seneca into the wisdom of the Christian Bible. That was in 1799. It is to this man's teachings your father has brought new life. Every second year in the longhouses a ceremony is held recounting the story of Handsome Lake through dance and recitations. Your father leads this."

And I had flared out at him, telling off the great man. Well, I didn't care how great or important he was, or what religions he resurrected. He was still an absentee father.

WHEN MAMA WAS finally able to retell the old stories, I felt better. I think she did too.

She told me how primitive and isolated the Northwest Territory was in the days when she fell in love with a handsome Mountie whose "eyes were so blue you could swim in them." He was about to be posted into wild, untamed country, and he considered her too young to make up her mind properly. So instead of proposing to her, he proposed to her uncle. "The storm still raging, and me standing there, my feet in a basin of hot water." There were tears behind our laughter, and we held each other and cried them.

"Your papa reached out to people in a remarkable way. For instance, Jonathan." Papa, she said, couldn't make Jonathan out. His traplines had been plundered and winter furs—fox, ocelot, and mar-

tin—stolen. Then the man Jonathan accused of the theft was murdered. In spite of the fact that it was done with Jonathan's knife, Papa
did not believe him capable of cold-blooded killing. "I remember
Mike telling him if he'd give his word he didn't do it, he'd release
him. Do you think Jonathan would do this? No. We had to *know,* all
of us, Mike and me—and especially Oh-Be-Joyful—that he wouldn't
murder an unarmed man. He spent the summer in that sweltering,
mosquito-ridden jail because, as he put it, he couldn't read his in-
nocence in our eyes. . . . Yes," she pondered, "Papa was exasperated
by him, but in a way he loved him."

I began to know Jonathan Forquet. I began to consider what he
had said to me on our walk, and to wonder if I could get back to
being happy. Not merely happy as a great many people are . . . but
joyful.

Joyful is past happy. Happy is more a quiet content. Joy on the
other hand is actively seeking moments when you're high on life,
and if those moments aren't there, to make them, to cause them. It
was the inheritance Jonathan Forquet meant for me, and for the first
time I wanted his good opinion. I wanted to live up to my Indian
name.

PEARL HARBOR, AND the planes couldn't get off the ground.

Pearl Harbor, and the sea sent dead to the surface like flotsam.

Pearl Harbor, and suddenly the immensity of oceans no longer
protected us.

Christmas 1941. The angel from her topmost position on the tree
did not signify peace on earth, goodwill toward men. Her golden
wings spread over a world exploding into madness. In Canada we
kept our radios tuned to the news station and scanned the daily paper.

Georges said from the beginning that when Mussolini and Hitler
formed the Axis, all hell would break loose. He bought a map of the
world and tacked it up in his room. A yellow arrow showed Mussolini
gobbling up Ethiopia; a black arrow showed Hitler gobbling up Austria. A year later Germany, on the pretext of defending Sudeten Germans, took over Czechoslovakia. Georges pasted a black swastika on
that country and put a question mark over Poland. Hitler must have
had access to Georges's map, because six months later he rolled into
Poland, and the word *blitzkrieg* entered our vocabulary.

"Hitler's pouring in mechanized troops," Georges confronted us,
as though we had something to do with it. "And how do the Poles
fight back? With horses! Can you see it? Horses charging tanks."

Mama didn't argue, that wasn't her way. "We already fought one war for democracy and found out it was for the perpetuation of the British Empire."

Georges managed a laugh. "There speaks our Irish mama."

The news supported Georges. France and England declared war.

Canada was at war a week later, although Prime Minister Mackenzie King assured us that Canada's role would be for the defense of North America. England could fend for herself. We, along with the United States, would be chief suppliers, but that would be the extent of our participation.

Headlines repeated the P.M.'s promise: NO CONSCRIPTION. "It's a relief to know that no Canadian boys will be sent overseas," Mama Kathy said.

Georges felt differently.

I argued that once the troops of the British Expeditionary Force confronted them, the Germans would be brought to heel. At the same time an irrational fear gripped me that Germany would make an end run around France and somehow rise up off our coast at Nova Scotia.

I listened to Connie and Georges debate, a rare instance because the twins were consistently on the same side in all their opinions. This time I sensed Connie was afraid.

I read the papers and was glued to the radio. Prices zoomed out of sight. We planted a victory garden. Free seed was distributed—lettuce, tomatoes, beans, and carrots. The corn was put in at some distance, because Mama Kathy insisted it impoverished the soil. In spite of these efforts, there were shortages of everything, including good news.

While I watered the garden, there were sightings of periscopes off the Atlantic coast, and an eight-year-old girl was killed in her bed by a lobbed shell. My fear no longer seemed irrational.

The North Atlantic became a hunting ground for U-boats. The liner *Athenia* was sunk by German submarines, the carrier *Courageous* lost, and the battleship *Royal Oak*. Georges made notes in the margin of his map.

The Germans didn't attempt to breach the Maginot Line. They swarmed through the Low Countries and dropped parachutists, half of which were dummies brought to add to the confusion.

France held out a month. In one of the greatest sea rescues in history, every English boat from the royal yacht to fishing smacks cooperated in evacuating 340,000 British, French, and Belgian troops through Dunkirk and other Channel ports.

Paris was declared an open city. The Germans walked in without firing a shot. On the radio we heard Churchill announce that Britain would fight on alone. "This is our finest hour," he said, while London was being pummeled by dive bombers. He vowed to defend the city street by street and house by house. Children and the aged were dispatched to the countryside. England was crying in the night.

Mama Kathy quietly joined the Ladies' Defense Society and began knitting socks. Evenings we huddled around our radio and looked at each other bleakly. For the first time it was conceivable England might lose the war.

"This is it," Georges said, "I've had it with sitting on the sidelines."

We three women, Mama Kathy, Connie, and I, stared at him mutely. He left for Ottawa right after Sunday services to join the RAF. But Saturday evening to cheer us up he gave a farewell magic show.

That brought back the famous magic show when I was seven. Georges rigged a curtain, one of Mama Kathy's blankets, strung on a wire along the living-room rafters. And he gave me a part. I was to open the curtain in the beginning and in the end draw it. We rehearsed all week. The day of the performance Old Bill came and played his Irish bagpipes. Mama baked cookies, which she passed around. Papa's contribution was to applaud. He was an enthusiastic applauder. He showed us how to cup our hands to make twice the noise. And if you jump to your feet and clap your hands over your head, it makes for a deafening ovation, especially if you add cries of Bravo!

I was seized by stage fright and when the time came for me to close the curtain, I pulled the wrong way. Of course I was only pretending to pull. Connie was actually making it move, which it did—the other way.

A huge laugh from the audience made me realize my mistake. I had ruined the show. Disgraced and in tears, I ran from the room.

Georges was after me in a flash and took me in his arms.

"It's all right, Kathy. It's like the curtain is magic and goes its own way. We're going to keep that in the show from now on."

Connie came and gave me a hug. "Are you crying because of that stupid curtain?"

"I used to be crying about that. Now I'm crying because . . . because . . ."

"Because why, honey?"

"Just because!"

She placed her cheek against mine.

This sent me into a fresh paroxysm. "Why can't I be a twin?" I wailed. "Everybody else is."

If Georges wanted to smile, he didn't show it. "It's like this, Kathy. Most people, God gets right the first time. He did with you. He looked at you and said, 'This is a good kid.' "

Georges, where are you? His hope of the RAF didn't work out. Myopia was enough to disqualify him. But he applied for and was accepted into officers' training, somewhere in England. Connie whispered not to worry, he wasn't in the front lines.

Connie would know. They had stayed up the night before he left reviving the Twins' Code.

THE WAR HAD been going on for two years. But it took Pearl Harbor to make me realize it was my war too. My war, because there was a push to corral the dark and dusky peoples of the world, to force them into labor camps—who knows, perhaps they were death camps. And my skin was copper.

I'd thought a good deal recently about being dark. In Germany the gypsies, along with the Jews, were rounded up, arrested, stripped of their possessions. Gypsies, because Hitler hadn't any Indians. But the civilized world couldn't allow the Nazis to declare themselves a master race and the rest slaves. Here in Canada we weren't all fair-skinned. We played and sang and worshipped in dozens of languages—French, Russian, Plattdeutsch . . . and Cree.

Only England, fighting alone, stood against this genocidal policy of the Third Reich. True, England had done its share of conquering the dark peoples, but it didn't enslave them and it didn't annihilate them.

Now that England was fighting for her life, and Canada too, I knew I had to act. Oddly enough, I knew what I would do. In some subterranean compartment of my brain I had worked it out. Without a word to anyone, not telling even Connie, I applied to a nursing program given in Montreal at the Daughters of Charity Hospital and sponsored by the Royal Canadian Army. The letter of acceptance lay in my pocket all week, while I got up courage to tell my family. After graduation I would be an army nurse and go overseas to join the war effort.

So this other self of mine, this dark, generally silent Oh-Be-Joyful's Daughter, stood up at Christmas dinner 1941, under another brave little tree with its dyed loops of macaroni, Papa Mike's homemade wooden ornaments, and the store-bought angel—stood up and told her family of the personal commitment she had made.

"Montreal?" Mama's cheeks flushed, and the light caught in her red hair. "You're going to Montreal, Kathy?"

"Yes, Mama."

Like a torpedo slipping along underwater, my announcement did not immediately explode. It was into silence I continued, "There's a serious shortage of nurses, and I've been accepted into a two-year course at the Daughters of Charity of St. Vincent de Paul Hospital. It's under the auspices of the army, and when you graduate you automatically receive a commission." I picked my words carefully. I didn't say I'd see action. But I would.

Connie was the first to recover herself. "It sounds like a marvelous opportunity."

"But Montreal," Mama protested. "It's a French city. To all intents and purposes, French."

For Mama this implied gambling, drug trafficking, and worse.

"The Daughters of Charity, Mama—it's a very fine institution. Ordinarily I couldn't afford the course they offer, but it's subsidized by the army."

"You'd come out of it a nurse and an officer?" I shot Connie a look of gratitude as she plunged on. "Just think of it, Mama, we'd have to salute her."

"I *am* thinking of it," Mama Kathy said, "and I know Papa would not have approved. It's sin city, Kathy. That's what he always said, full of vice, and as a Mountie he was in a position to know."

I didn't say anything. Although I could have said that he was the one who told me I would make a good nurse in the first place.

Connie intervened in her older sister way, as though she somehow sat above the fray, "This is the first time since the world was made that women are being called, asked to help, to be part of things."

"You're right about that," Mama agreed, and then made what I considered a concession. "It would mean pulling up stakes. And," she added with asperity, "it would mean Montreal."

"They say those things about any city, Mama."

"Not about Boston they don't."

Boston was where Mama was born.

"A nurse," Connie mused. "How long have you been thinking about it?"

"Since the beginning of the war, really."

"A nurse," Mama echoed, by which I knew she was thinking about it too. Then, "There must be a lot of wounded to patch together."

I jumped up from my place to hug her.

THESE WERE THE skeins responsible for my being on this silver and blue train, speeding toward what would be my life. Each taut thread played its part, but I wondered if it wasn't Oh-Be-Joyful's Daughter who gave me the courage to actually be on it. It was six years from Papa's death, and the whole world had to dissolve in chaos, blow itself apart. Clark and Iba Airfields in the Philippines had to be taken out, British air power in Hongkong destroyed, Bangkok occupied, Malaya invaded, Burma seized, Canadian boys in Hongkong made to surrender to the Japanese, and of course Pearl Harbor—for me to be sitting primly in a coach of the Canadian Pacific, looking out the window while the silver train streaked by farms, forests, lakes, and towns, the speed flattening the earth and carrying me into my dream.

I was convinced Papa knew about the dream. At the moment of death you must see things, know things that otherwise you don't.

Classes started in less than a week. The future was open as it never had been. Connie was right, it had become a different world, where girls were encouraged to go into the workplace, share in opportunities. A career as a nurse allowed me to be on my own, take charge of my life. It was time.

I straightened in my seat, while the Canadian countryside framed itself in my window, and investigated the box lunch Mama Kathy had packed. She must have used her own ration coupons because there was a chicken sandwich. I munched with a sense of well-being.

That night I went to sleep in a reclined Pullman chair with a white doily under my head and my shoes kicked off. The porter came by with a pillow and a thin gray blanket. The engines pulsed through me; I fell asleep and woke to the sound of the rails. Sleepily I put up the window blind and was shocked to see a pressing blackness.

We had entered a tunnel. Across from me two women exchanged stories about the tunnels they hated all over the world, the worst being the New York subway under the East River. The one we were in was under Mont-Royal, a long way from fresh air and blue sky. I also did not care for tunnels.

We emerged, and there it was, stretching in every direction . . . Montreal. I looked out on broad streets, which, in spite of gas rationing, were crowded with automobiles and stolid horses pulling ice wagons, milk carts, and bread trucks. Mainly it was alive with people.

I had never seen so many people. A sense of energy seemed to fill them, and they moved to a quick rhythm.

A porter came through the cars singing out, "Montreal, Montreal! Ladies and gentlemen, *mesdames et messieurs*." I was thrilled by the French even though it was all I could do to count to twenty and puzzle my way through irregular verbs. We circled the city, approaching the station through Ouest Montreal.

The train slowed. With a last look to make sure I hadn't left anything, I squeezed into the crowded aisle and moved forward. We pulled in to Windsor Station. I stepped down portable iron stairs and caught my breath.

In school I'd pored over illustrations of the Taj Mahal and St. Peter's in Rome, but this was the most magnificent building I'd ever seen with my own eyes. A palace for trains. Elegant covered sheds for embarking and disembarking. Lofty ceilings. Commodious waiting rooms, spacious restaurants, busy offices. The concourse was like a Roman temple, with fluted columns and ornamented capitals.

And people, people everywhere, rushing, strolling, pushing, waiting in line, talking, yelling in a dozen languages. Soldiers, sailors, officers of every rank and service. Young women being kissed and kissing, both hello and goodbye. Nuns and priests robed in brown, white, gray, some wearing scarlet sashes. Children racing around, playing improvised games in all this turmoil, one lost and shrieking for his parents, another methodically banging her brother's head on the marble floor.

Some of the women were clearly not passengers. With carmine lips and matching fingernails they approached unattached males. Sin city.

I was looking for the exit, when the crowd carried me to a cigarette stand, an edifice with its own fake Roman columns and cornices. It purveyed nuts, dried fruit, gum, candy, cigarettes, cigars, pipe tobacco, knickknacks, gifts, magazines, newspapers, travelers' kits. While I stood there taking it all in, I heard someone ask for a pack of Juicy Fruit, please. I was transfixed. His voice reverberated like bass organ pipes. It was unmistakeable. I looked around. Paul Robeson, Old Man River himself.

The next second the human current carried me away, and I saw for the first time a sailor with his sleeve sewn together above the elbow.

The city of Montreal was pushed against foothills that rose to an imposing summit. Mont-Royal, its steep slopes indicating volcanic origin, softened into richly planted terraces. At its pinnacle, rising from rock and mountain, was an enormous cross. It protected the city and in some manner, I felt, protected me.

I made my way outside, clutching my directions, and stood waiting for the tram. When it came I was told it was the wrong one. My instructions were correct, but I was pointed in the wrong direction. The conductor advised me which way to go. Unfortunately, merely crossing the street wouldn't do it. I was to go around the block and take a left at Dominion Square, which I could recognize by the Sun Life building.

A bit bewildered, I left the fortress of Windsor Station and passed the Alberta Lounge, which advertised the Johnny Holmes Band featuring Oscar Peterson, the Brown Bomber of Boogie-Woogie. Again I asked my way and finally succeeded in finding my tram not far from the Archbishop's Palace behind St. James's Basilica.

The tram came along on rail tracks with an overhead wire charging it up. I liked its reassuring noisiness, and boarded, making my way by the backs of cane seats. Straps hung suspended from the ceiling and gaudy posters warned: *Loose Lips Sink Ships.* Demonstrating this was an enormous hand with a swastika armband pulling under a ship of the line. I sat beneath "Rosie the Riveter" and laughed silently. The last few days Mama Kathy and Connie had been talking about the premium wages being offered to women by shipyards and aircraft factories in Vancouver. It wouldn't surprise me if after all they did pull up stakes.

Opposite me was an ad for Wrigley's spearmint gum, and scribbled across it in black crayon—not the KILROY WAS HERE that showed up wherever servicemen congregated, but Francophoned into KILROY ICI.

This was Mama's French city, the city founded by Paul de Chomedy de Maisonnueve. This was sin city, beautiful, overwhelming, and subtly foreign.

I glanced again at my instructions. At the third stoplight I got off and found myself facing a stark, sprawling complex stretching several city blocks. I walked along the gray stone walls trying to imagine living behind them. Were they ever breached by sun? I passed an entrance marked Emergency, and a flight of stairs with a ramp beside it for wheelchairs. This seemed a good bet. I started up, my shoes clattering on the steps and my heart racing.

Inside I hesitated. There were statues of saints in niches, and at the rear a long counter under a wooden crucifix. A Sister was stationed there busily thumbing through sheets of documents. I waited for her to notice me.

"Student nurse, are you?"

"Yes, Sister."

"You're in the wrong annex." She directed me to a smaller building partway down the street and a door marked Staff.

With fears and hopes in abeyance, I proceeded toward it. For better or worse here I was and here I would have to stay. "For the duration" had become a slogan. It was mine too: *For the duration.*

I followed a red arrow, painted on the floor, which led to basement stairs. There I paused to glance around a large bare room. Plank tables and benches were pulled out of the way against the wall, making room for half a dozen desks manned—I should say "womanned"—by middle-aged, overworked secretaries and a couple of supervising nuns. The desks were labeled A to F by little cardboard signs.

The Sister in charge was a jolly soul who welcomed me as she looked up from a ledger. "Yes, here you are. Forquet, Kathy. You've been assigned room 212. You'll be rooming with Amanda Brydewell. The young lady checked in this morning. A double is rare. We've had to put as many as four girls in together. Your room is small, but you won't be spending much time in it. If you'll look at your schedule of classes—" Here she broke off, waiting for me to look.

But I had none.

"Didn't you pick one up at table B?"

I shook my head.

"My dear girl, if you would simply follow the arrows—well, don't stand there, get one now."

I ran over to table B. But there was a queue, held up by one well-dressed young woman who was holding the schedule as if it was a menu and she was trying to decide which entree to order. I could feel Sister's eyes boring into my back. Crouching a bit, I filched a stapled batch of mimeographed pages with a pink cover sheet.

While the Sister busied herself with my application, I checked the course list. Chemistry, Psychology, Anatomy, Biology, Pharmacology, Medical Ethics, Principles of Hygiene. Additional subjects had been added: Map Reading, Gas Warfare, Casualty Evacuation, Principles of Triage, and History of the Canadian Army. The blank spaces which at first I thought indicated free time, I saw, reading more carefully, were allocated to visiting the wards and making rounds.

I was amazed that from the outset we would have daily contact with patients. This was exciting, the best part. Perhaps Papa was right, perhaps I did have an aptitude for nursing. I hoped so. Athough we were two years into it, for me the war had just begun.

Sister Eglantine—I'd deciphered it from the scrawl on her name tag—gave me a key and pointed out the elevator. I could count on the fingers of one hand the times I'd been in one—and then there was someone with white gloves sitting on a stool running it. I pressed the up button; grilled doors opened and I stepped inside. What an amazing world this was. Trolley cars and elevators, telephones in so many public places. And if I was to believe the pictures in magazines, electric refrigerators were replacing iceboxes. What next, I wondered? Of course, hand in hand with these amazing inventions were depth charges and land mines, torpedos and dive bombers, more deadly than anything in the last war.

Standing in front of room 212 I tried to insert the key, when the door swung open. Amanda Brydewell peered nearsightedly at me. "Kathy?"

"Amanda?"

She laughed. "It's Mandy."

It was a relief to like her. I liked her pretty face, I even liked her horn-rimmed glasses. They took the curse off her being so pretty. And here I'd been torturing myself with what-ifs—

But I could see she was a genuine person and really nice, even though she'd taken the bed by the window.

"Are you a First Nation person?" she wanted to know.

I laughed at her directness. "Yes," I said, "I'm Cree."

"How exciting. I've never known an aboriginal."

"We don't paint our faces anymore," I pointed out. "We're just like anybody else."

She, it turned out, was the daughter of a prominent Toronto family. "If it weren't for the war I wouldn't be here. My family would never permit it. But I made it a point—'service to my country, doing my bit,' that kind of thing. And it won the day." Her voice dropped to a confidential note. "I suppose I shouldn't say it, I know it's terrible of me, but I love the war." Seeing my expression, she added hastily, "By that I mean of course, I love what it's done for me. Being on my own is going to be so great."

"Have you seen the schedule? It looks to me that we'll have our nose to the grindstone most of the time."

"On the other hand, there are all those young interns."

Yes, I definitely liked the irrepressible Mandy.

Sister was right about it being a small room. The furnishings were minimal: army cots, two straight-backed chairs, one desk with student lamp, and a battered dresser of four drawers. At first we divided them, but she had so many more things that I wound up giving her three drawers and most of the closet.

"The bathroom's down the hall," she said. "We share it with the entire floor. Isn't that the pits!"

Things here were regulated by bells. When the dinner bell sounded, I discovered the dining hall was the room in the basement where I'd registered. The plank tables and benches had been dragged into the center of the room. A Sister presided at each table. We drew Sister Mary Margaret, who ran what she termed a "taut ship." Voices, she informed us, were to be modulated and good manners observed. Since we were seated at the far end of the table, Mandy didn't adhere to these rules too strictly.

Before the meal was over she knew everyone. Totally at ease, she talked to the girl beside her and the one across from her and, reaching over to a girl several places removed, engaged her in conversation too. I watched with a certain wonder. Of course Mandy was a white girl among white girls. I, on the other hand, knew it was only the war that made my being here acceptable. Even so, how did the others regard me? I felt I had a friend in Mandy, but did I imagine it, or were there hostile stares and whispering behind my back?

I took my cue from Mandy and laughed along with her when she made jokes about the food. Fortunately there was a lot of it, which in some measure made up for the fact that it was very plain fare: wholesome porridge, good-for-you vegetables, and a filling potato. There was a gravy that I thought best to avoid, and bread, butter, and jam for dessert. On weekends, Trisha, who had been here longest, reported, this was varied with puddings—tapioca, caramel, and butterscotch. She was waiting for a chocolate day, but so far it hadn't come.

I was grateful to Mandy for sticking with me. We sat in the student lounge, chatting and laughing. Shedding my what-ifs, I joined in, enjoying the adventure with them.

What a nice group they were. Mandy's contribution was to say we were all in the same boat. "Not a U-boat!" they protested, laughing. Almost 400,000 tons of Lend-Lease shipments had been lost. The best thing was to joke and make light of it.

It seemed I shared in Mandy's instant popularity. What good fortune to have drawn her as a roommate. I tried to sort out my impressions of the other girls. Ruth, good-natured, with a mouth full of braces. Ellie, a bit on the plain side but with pretty auburn hair. Trisha, somewhat reserved. All starting out like me to help in this global emergency, to test our wings as persons, to take flight. This was a good place, I thought, to start doing something I hadn't succeeded in yet—being Oh-Be-Joyful's Daughter. The banter and small talk continued until the second bell.

AT NIGHT, CONSCIOUS of a Sister patrolling the corridors, we whispered from one bed to the other. Mandy was an only child and had had a nanny. Imagine! A child to have her own servant. And of course as a teenager she hadn't worked. No drugstore for her; she sat on the other side of the counter. She and I would never have met if not for the war. Her father was a corporate lawyer, and they lived in a two-story house and did not, I'm sure, associate with Indians.

She was right about one thing: the war forced you to think in bigger terms; it brushed away prejudices and there was a feeling of equality as all were needed to pull together. We talked so late that it seemed I barely closed my eyes when the morning bell got us up. In robe and slippers I went down the hall to the bathroom. I was stopped by a piece of notepaper tacked to the door. WHITES ONLY.

Shock imploded in me as though I'd taken a depth charge. I ripped the paper from the door, balled it, and, entering the bathroom, threw it into the wastebasket.

"What was that?" Trisha asked, with a mocking grin.

I turned on her. "The Cree," I said, speaking slowly, articulating carefully, "do not speak ill of anyone. They may take their scalp in the night, but they do not speak ill of them."

The other girls watched from a distance, in an uneasy clump.

I continued in the same tight voice, "I will just say this one thing. I intend to stay here and become a nurse."

Mention of our common goal broke the spell. To my amazement the girls crowded around me, stumbling over words in their anxiety to get them out, assuring me all together that they were behind me a hundred percent. Trisha, I noticed, slipped out to remove a similar sign pasted on the drinking fountain. I saw her crumple it in her hands. I went back to my room, my heart still pounding, still turning the incident over in my mind.

I didn't tell Mandy, but by lunch she knew all about it. "I'm so proud of you, Kathy, for standing up to them. And most of them don't feel that way, you know."

"I don't really care how they feel, as long as they don't interfere with my plans." I heard myself say this and thought, Wow! a new Kathy. I felt a flush of excitement. Was this new Kathy possibly an aspect of Oh-Be-Joyful's Daughter, which had eluded me such a long time?

"Tell me about First Nation people," Mandy was saying. "I really want to know, to understand."

I couldn't. I didn't know that much about them. I disappointed her by having a white mama and papa and a white brother and sister. "The twins have lighter hair than you do."

Mandy's questions set me thinking. It was too bad to know nothing of the traditions of my own people. If I was to be persecuted as an Indian, I should at least understand why.

$\mathcal{T}$hree

OUR FIRST CLASS was a lecture, and we trooped into a large auditorium. There was a brief swearing-in ceremony, at the end of which we were told we were now privates, subject to the rules and regulations of the Royal Canadian Army. Our grades would be monitored, and we would have to maintain a passing average. But on graduation we would be commissioned as second lieutenants. I was conscious of a new feeling, pride and a sense of responsibility.

The assembly was turned over to Mother Superior, who welcomed us, first in French, then in English. The audience settled into respectful silence.

I hadn't realized she was a small woman. Strength and energy seemed to overflow and escape her body.

She paused to look us over with piercing black eyes. When she had made her assessment, she launched into the body of her speech. "The history of nursing in Canada is in a very real sense the history of women in Canada. Marie Rollet Hebert was the first woman to provide nursing care. In 1642 another woman, Jeanne Mance, established the first hospital here in Ville-Marie.

"Our order, the Daughters of Charity of St. Vincent de Paul, eventually added an orphanage and dispensed free health care, funded in part by philanthropy, but mainly through a brewery and a freight company that the Sisters organized and ran themselves." She paused, daring us to laugh. No one did.

"The next hundred years saw nurses trained to serve as administrators, doctors, surgeons, and apothecaries. Canadian nurses first came under fire in the Riel Rebellion."

I pricked up my ears at the mention of Louis Riel. I knew from Papa that my mostly French grandfather, Raoul Forquet, was his lieutenant. But I judged it would be as well not to mention that here. The past was very much part of the present in these cloistered walls. It would be prudent not to trumpet the fact that I was the granddaughter of a revolutionary.

"By the last war," Mother Superior continued, "more than three thousand nursing Sisters served as officers. They were stationed in England, France, and Belgium, and around the Mediterranean. Forty-seven died under combat conditions."

She paused while this sank in.

"Because you young women are to be serving in a wartime situation, the entire program has been accelerated. Instead of the normal three years, it has of necessity been compressed into two. And if you inspect your handouts, you will note that instruction in military matters has been added to the established nursing classes. It will require diligence and hard work on your part, but it is our hope that you will follow the tradition of your chosen profession with the honor and dedication that is the standard for the Daughters of Charity. I ask you to remember that the eyes of your country are on you and on this institution."

Although I laughed and joked about it afterward with the others, the sense of awe remained. I explored a bit on my own, trying to memorize the layout of the hospital. Plaques on the wall each carried the name of a donor, and one, I noticed, honored a Brydewell. Was that my roommate's father or grandfather?

The second lecture of the day took place after lunch and was given in the same hall. I tried, as I had last night at supper, to count heads. My best guess was there were around sixty aspiring nurses. We filed in and took our seats with a buzz of anticipation. The lecturer was not only a medical man, but a distinguished professor at McGill University. He strode onto the podium, a white-haired gentleman obviously brought out of retirement. "One of your young interns," I whispered to Mandy.

He greeted us pleasantly and stated that he was going to commence with a test, "which is by way of determining both your courage and your observation. Now then," he continued smoothly, "I have before me a beaker of urine. Observe it closely."

No one ever in my memory had used the word *urine* in public. It was indicative of coming to grips with the functioning of the human body. Which of course as a nurse I would have to do.

"Now," the professor's voice filled the auditorium, "please watch carefully because I am going to ask each of you to come to the podium in turn. At which time you will do exactly what I am about to do. Observe." With that he dipped his finger into the vial of urine, then brought the finger to his mouth and sucked it.

A murmur of horror went through the room. Ignoring it, he invited us in the most cordial terms to come up by rows and repeat the experiment. Like stricken sheep we mounted to the podium and one by one dutifully filed past the urine in its clear glass receptacle and imitated his actions.

Each in turn, wincing a bit, stuck her finger in the urine and with a final shudder licked it. When my turn came I immersed my finger and, repressing a gag reflex, proceeded to lick the substance off.

When we returned to our places the professor rocked back on his heels and, brushing aside his white coat, hooked his thumbs in his waistcoat pockets. "Well, young ladies, you deserve an A for courage, but an F for observation. I stuck a finger into the urine right enough. But it was the finger next to it I put in my mouth."

A gasp followed this announcement. Mandy and I looked at each other and burst out laughing.

There was more hazing from second-year students, whose chores we ended up doing, including bedpan duty. But I was not again singled out. The story of the Whites Only incident had spread through the hospital, and it won me, if not friends, at least respect.

THE HOSPITAL WAS a massive network of services. There were the pre-op and post-op patients, on which everything from appendectomies to bowel resections were done. There was a trauma center and a burn center. Of course, as first-year students we weren't allowed near the serious cases unsupervised.

My first job was to clean the needles and syringes that had been used during the day. Our limited supply of autoclaves was strained past capacity by the influx of new cases. We had to fall back on the old-fashioned procedure of washing instruments in ether, then plunging them into boiling water. But, as I discovered the next morning, making rounds under the careful eye of a doctor, the ends could become plugged. When I jabbed the needle into a patient's arm sometimes nothing came out. This was unpleasant for the patient and for me. I guessed that the problem was the hard water I'd washed them in. So I did what Mama Kathy would have done—after dinner I went outside and collected snow. Melting it took a long time with very little water to show for it. And I didn't get to bed until after the bell.

However, I had soft water in which to sterilize my needles, and next day when the resident had me start an IV, my needle glided in smoothly without sticking. Afterward, the girls wanted to know my secret. When I told them I had gone out and collected snow, they said I was crazy.

I had collected snow before. When I was little I made ice cream by taking Mama Kathy's vanilla and shaking it into newly fallen snow. Thinking this, I realized a week had gone by with no word from anybody. Just as I began to worry, a whole packet of mail arrived, two letters from Vancouver and one without stamps, meaning armed forces. I was most surprised hearing from Georges. Georges dear—I remembered him in his magician's cape (which was Mama's apron worn inside out but with a Georges flair), waving one of Papa's good dress handkerchiefs and, over his protests, making it disappear. Georges, Georges, can't you make the war go away? Georges dear, where are you? North Ireland with the 80th? Libya? Egypt?

Mama Kathy and Connie were embarked on their own adventure. Mama had consented to pull up stakes after all. They were in Vancouver machining spare parts for planes at thirty-six dollars a week. With wages like that they could put by for the rainy day Mama was always expecting.

But there was sad news as well, the kind that was in almost every letter these days. The Clacks' youngest son had volunteered and was missing in action. I paused a moment to remember his pleasant, freckled face and readiness to laugh.

Then turned to the lively descriptions of life in Vancouver. They had found a comfortable apartment, but with no growing thing about. Mama had lugged in a flower box, in which they planned to raise a tomato vine. Down the street in the schoolyard a section had been set aside for a communal victory garden where they donated what free time they could.

I felt the love behind the ordinary sentences and drank in every word. Both Georges and Connie asked if I'd heard from the other. I knew how hard it was for them to be apart.

My own free time was Sundays and a half day on Saturday. Mandy and I went to the library at the first opportunity to find out about Indians. We carried several volumes to the table; Mandy sat on one side, I on the other. My tome started back in 1763 when the Crown laid claim to all unoccupied land.

I leaned across to Mandy and read the paragraph in an undertone, adding, "The Indians, being nomadic, didn't occupy any land at all."

"So the Crown took it all. Pretty neat if you can get away with it."

"Oh, they were fair—according to their lights. Indians were allowed the *use* of selected lands. 'Selected lands' is code for reserves. And here's something they don't teach you in mission school: even today the Indians don't hold legal title to their reserves."

"I tell you what," Mandy said. "When we've finished off the Germans, we'll go to Ottawa and march on the Canadian government, make them give it back."

"Here it tells about the welfare system instituted for the aboriginals. Instead of justice—handouts."

"That fits with what I'm reading. Two and a half times more poverty among Indians, three times the prenatal death rate."

"But they're starting to fight back. Listen to this. It was proposed in one of the tribal councils that they stop thinking of the money as charity and call it rent, rent owed them on the land."

We'd done enough digging for one day and absorbed all we could of Indian rights. Mandy was hungry, and when she mentioned it, so was I. We splurged on sandwiches and a soda.

"In school," Mandy said thoughtfully, "I remember reading how the tribes escaped extermination in the States by fleeing to Canada, where they were discriminated against but not slaughtered in those terrible Indian wars."

"You don't have to fight a war," I responded, "if you can get it all with a forked-tongue paper."

We didn't go back to the library. Mandy had other things to do, and I didn't like the feelings of anger and resentment that had been stirred up in me. That was no way to be joyful.

The next fortnight I was assigned to blood draws, which entailed going up and down the rows of beds taking blood, smearing the plasma onto glass slides, and labeling and keeping them straight. The second-year nurses complained at this acceleration of our training. We had been promoted from bedpan duty much too fast, in their opinion.

The number of patients on crutches distressed me. They were so young, these boy-men without feet or legs, the lucky ones in casts. I watched my chance and slipped into the stock room to try crutches myself. I spent half an hour swinging about on them. At the end of that time I was exhausted and my armpits were sore. As a result I sewed additional padding onto those waiting to be used, and sprinkled them liberally with baby powder.

Mandy kept a diary in her underwear drawer. It had a vellum cover and tiny gold chain and key. I wondered what she said about me. I think she was disappointed that I wasn't more fun, that I had my nose in a book all the time.

At night, instead of chatting, I sat late, memorizing bone and muscle structure for hands and feet, and I was working on the neck. There were no plots or stories in these books, but after a while I managed to weave the charts and graphs into tales of saving lives.

Besides Saturday half days we students had all of Sunday to allow for church attendance. This, I often thought as I turned the pages of my hymnal, is the sin city Mama Kathy worried about.

Mandy was asked out a lot. Several times we double-dated. But I had the feeling that it took a good deal of manuevering on Mandy's part. I was invariably self-conscious and uncomfortable and finally persuaded Mandy that I preferred a good book, or listening to Frank Sinatra and the Andrews Sisters, or studying French by puzzling my way through *Le Devoir*. Also I was familiarizing myself with the big bands, Tommy Dorsey and Benny Goodman. They set your feet tapping—that is, until they broke off the music for news flashes.

General MacArthur withdrew to Bataan. They used the word *withdrew* but it didn't fool anyone. It was a retreat, a rout, and the rich oil fields of the Dutch East Indies fell to the Japanese. They took Singapore and the struggle was now for Java. In the Java Sea on February 27 we lost five warships in a seven-hour battle. The Japanese sustained slight damage to one destroyer. By March 9 the last Allied troops in Java surrendered.

I gave up reading the papers. It didn't do to think of all those young men dying horribly out there on unknown beaches or winding up in ward B without faces, without limbs. They put their lives on the line and it wasn't enough. We were losing, losing badly—over six million tons of shipping in the Atlantic and endless square miles of territory in the South Pacific.

A new load of wounded were brought in from ships sunk in the North Atlantic, some off our coast. The protective attitude the Sisters had endeavored to maintain for us new girls was a thing of the past. We were, you might say, posted to frontline trenches and found ourselves in the thick of things.

The first time I was called on to hold down the head and shoulders of a patient in the throes of a gastric bleed, whose body contorted and whose blood splattered my uniform and my shoes, I almost passed out myself. Instantly I was in the little back bedroom, and it was Papa. Somehow I managed to stay on my feet and, afterward, in the bathroom, splash water over my face. I dabbed at my uniform and shoes, making a solemn resolution as I did. A resolution I broke the very next day.

I was present at an amputation. It was all right when the form was swathed by a sheet, but then a mangled leg was sterilized and a surgical saw—which was nevertheless a saw—bit into flesh and began to cut. I swayed on my feet . . . that wasn't a human being under the drapes . . . this wasn't happening to a human being. The room swirled. I passed the bandage roll I was holding to the person next to me and raced for the bathroom.

I slammed the door shut and leaned against it. The gastric bleed, now this. At the first sight of ligaments and tendons, I'd given way. I hadn't the stuff to make a nurse. I couldn't look at dismemberment in a cold, professional way. I'd blown it.

"Don't feel too bad, Kathy."

I hadn't noticed Sister Eglantine washing her hands in the corner.

"Compassion is very important in a nurse. The very best nurses have it in good measure. If you can look for the first time on an amputation unmoved, you're not much of a human being. And you have to be a human being first."

I took my hands from my face. Sister Egg, the girls called her, because she was a good egg. Short, dumpy—everything about her could be drawn with circles, even to her rimless spectacles.

"It comes in time," Egg continued, "standing up to it, seeing it for what it is, a lifesaving procedure."

"You think, in time—?"

"My dear, if I were a betting woman, I'd go right down to the East Side and I wouldn't stop till I got to the funeral parlor on St. George. But I wouldn't go in there. I'd go next door to the basement and take a seat at barbotte and roll my dice, and I'd wager everything on you—your guts, your gumption, and the fact that you'll make a fine nurse someday." She folded her hands over her stomach and grinned broadly. "How's that for confidence?"

Sister Egg swept away self-doubts. She had seen girls come and go. She knew. She knew the ones who would make it. "Besides," she said, "it's really the fault of the accelerated program. Ordinarily, a first-year student would not be exposed to such a drastic procedure. But there's no help for it. It's the war."

This seemed reasonable to me. With renewed confidence I went back to the surgical area and stood up to the lecture on professional conduct I received from the surgeon, Dr. Bennett.

To prove to Sister Egg she had not been wrong about me, I took to reading to my amputee patient. It turned out he was British. He told me he didn't want to go home. He couldn't face the pity and especially the way they would try to hide it. "They'd be so damned understanding," he said.

I discovered he was fond of poetry—"To hold infinity in the palm of your hand, eternity in an hour." That evening he had a hemorrhagic discharge under the skin. Dark purplish areas became less as I applied compresses, but I still shuddered at the twenty-three stitches with which the leg came to an end. ". . . Eternity in an hour," I repeated to myself.

Mandy was busy weekends, so I took to going to the movies with Sister Egg. We went to the old Roxy Theater, the Palace, and Loew's. Like me, Egg could never get enough. We sat through double features, short subjects, Fox Movietone, and Pathe newsreels.

The newsreels were hard to watch. Wounded stacked like cordwood waited to be moved to aid centers. Suffering looked artificial on young faces. They were my own age and younger.

Another clip showed the result of the blitz in one London back street, a dazed grandmother emerging from an air raid shelter. She walked a block to her home. It wasn't there. Nothing was there. Then she spotted something, a pan, a little bent but still serviceable. She began to sift through the rubble, saving a torn quilt, a cracked mirror from her life. I chose this time to get popcorn. Egg didn't comment on these absences, but nothing got by her.

We only had a single movie theater in my out-of-the-way home in Alberta, and I didn't go on a regular basis as I did here. Weekly I blew my nose through hopeless romances and parted lovers.

Egg leaned toward me in the dark. "Go ahead, you're entitled to a good cry. After all, we don't permit you girls to show emotion no matter what lies under the bandages you unwrap. This is one way of crying for the boys on the ward."

Bull's-eye! I hadn't known it myself. How had Egg? She had lived three times longer than I, and behind her childlike face was a world of knowledge.

Then I caught her before the lights came up, dabbing at her eyes. "We're two of a kind," she admitted. "But don't blackmail me with the girls."

We enjoyed a good cry, but we laughed too, at the Schnozz and the antics of Jerry Colonna. I stored up prat falls and slapstick situations for the moments I dressed a septic arm or wrote lies for the British boy who had lost a leg. Although there were others in the same condition, I suppose I empathized particularly with him because he was so far from home. And then of course I'd been there when it happened.

Our long winter was almost gone, and one Sunday in early March Mandy suggested ice skating at Berry Pond. I was glad to fall in with the idea, especially as the first thaw would bring an end to a sport I loved. This was a typical Montreal day—cold. I double-dressed, hoping to keep warm that way. Mandy put on two sweaters under her skating outfit but, twisting and turning before the mirror, decided the extra padding made her look fat.

But Mandy was more complicated than anyone gave her credit for. Before we left the room I was wearing her best and warmest sweater.

It was good to be outside, good to leave the hospital behind. We ran down the stairs, our skates over our shoulders, and walked briskly, swinging a free arm, making footprints in the crusty snow that was starting to soften under the sun. We blew our breath before us in frosty puffs.

There were already quite a few skaters on the pond. "It looks like a postcard come to life," Mandy enthused.

We dusted off one of the logs that had been pulled up as improvised bleachers, and sat down. Then began the job of fastening on the skates. Mandy was finished first. Her skates belonged to her, while mine were borrowed. As she waited for me, Mandy studied the skaters. "Look," she exclaimed, "there's that cute intern that transferred in last week. Robert. Robert Whitaker II."

"How do you know? Have you met him?"

"I looked at his application—a picture is enclosed, you know. I'm not so nearsighted that I can't spot a good thing. You have to admit he's attractive. Six feet tall, from Nainaimo on Vancouver Island, son of Dr. and Mrs. Robert Whitaker. He's twenty-six years old—"

"And he's had mumps and measles and his tonsils out," I snapped. Now I understood the reason for this excursion. "How'd you know he'd be here?"

"You're not angry, are you? I overheard Dr. Finch giving him directions."

I finished tying my laces and stood with a bit of a wobble. I'd been on ice since I was three, but this was the first time this year. I followed Mandy and cut myself a nice line to the middle of the pond, tried a turn, then several. It was exhilarating—only, my teeth were cold. Other people get cold ears and noses. With me it's teeth, and as far as I know they don't have tooth-muffs.

I realized I was here simply as window dressing, and I watched Mandy's maneuver with interest. Her plan was simple. She skated backward and plowed into him. They both wound up sitting on the ice. She begged his pardon and introduced herself. Robert Whitaker II or III or whatever hadn't a chance.

Skating straight for me, they came to a T-stop, and I was introduced.

I liked him. And I certainly saw why Mandy did. He was nice looking and had a great build.

"Imagine," she said, "Robert's joined the hospital staff!"

"Really?" I tried to sound as though I were processing new information.

They glided away to "The Skater's Waltz." Mandy looked marvelous. Her cheeks were pink with the cold, and her smile dazzling. I fought down a twinge of jealousy. Sometimes it's hard being the roommate of the prettiest girl in the program.

I lowered my head into the wind and, with my hands clasped behind my back, took a racing stance and zoomed twice around the pond to their once. It was invigorating to be on ice, with your toes and your teeth freezing.

They came alongside. "Robert's invited us for hot chocolate."

Steamy hot, it opened a path of warmth inside. Robert told us he came from a large family, two brothers and a sister. "My dad's just a small-town doctor. What there is has to stretch. So I mostly worked my way through school, did KP at the frat house, drove an ambulance, got by on a scholarship. You know, scrounged. Managed one way or another."

He got by with Mandy too. She had met her intern, and from then on they were very thick. She kept saying it wasn't serious, but it looked to me that it was. She spent every available minute with him.

The nursing staff was constantly being rotated and I was transferred to what I was told was a responsible job, but one I didn't like as much as it had nothing to do with nursing. While I preferred being on the wards and felt I did more good there, I realized of course that someone had to receive medicines and store and dispense drugs. I discovered the job was largely a matter of keeping records. We were short on supplies and once, when we ran low on disinfectants, were told to add salt to water and use it. Before my time there'd been some kind of scandal regarding drugs and they were very security conscious, doing everything by the book.

Shortly after I'd logged on, the driver of a lorry came in with boxes and crates which he began piling in front of my desk.

"You have to sign for it, miss."

The voice had an odd lilt, almost an accent. I looked up into eyes that could have been my own, except they were crinkled in laughter, and were in fact joyous.

I smiled back into a face as dark as my own. The driver, in spite of army fatigues, was Indian.

He had apparently craned over and spotted my signature on the papers before me, because he said, "Right here, Kathy."

I tried to remain businesslike. "Yes," I said, taking up a pen.

"What's your Indian name?" he asked.

"Oh-Be-Joyful's Daughter." It came out spontaneously, as though that's who I'd been all along.

He nodded. "That's a beautiful name. What band are you?"

"Cree."

"Cree? You're a long way from home. I suppose it's the war?"

"Yes," I said, "it's the war," and returned his receipt.

He shoved it into his pocket but didn't go. "Are you always here at this hour?"

"For a couple of weeks."

"Then I'll see you again." This time he got as far as the door and came back. "I forgot to tell you my name. It's Crazy Dancer."

"Crazy Dancer? Is that really a name?"

"I'm a delight maker, you know, a clown."

I must have looked puzzled.

"I see you went to mission school and had a white man's education. You don't know about our people, do you?"

"Well," I hesitated, "I did go to mission school, but . . ."

"That explains your not knowing. But don't worry, I'll teach you."

"Teach me? Teach me what?"

"To be an Indian." He gave a quirky smile and left.

I looked out the window and watched him below in the parking lot. He moved to an inner rhythm as though he scouted along rushing streams and wild forest places instead of back alleys. He swung lightly into the driver's seat. I could see he was a dancer, a crazy dancer.

I suppose it was what he said about being Indian, but I couldn't get him out of my mind. My impression was that he possessed a kind of kinetic energy. Was he handsome? I wasn't sure. Would Mandy think his nose too high-bridged? It was an aquiline nose compared to the flatter noses of whites. But in any culture his face was arresting. In those few seconds a dozen moods had sat on it. He said he was a clown; I believed it. His mouth was ready to smile, his eyes to squeeze together in laughter. Yet there was dignity, almost a haughtiness in the way he carried himself.

Had I imagined more than was there? My Indianness was a part of me I had never explored. And Crazy Dancer wanted to teach me Indian things. I found I was looking forward to the next delivery of medicines.

I'd had an unusual relationship with young men—that is, none. Or practically none. Mostly it was fending off patients in the ward. If they weren't too ill or distressed, they were full of banter and a kind of flirting talk. After all, they were young, they were young men. They were fond of telling me all the things we would do when they got out of here. Once they were up and around, it would be dinner out and then we'd take in a movie, and then . . . And we would both laugh at the innuendo, confident it would never happen.

These fantasy romances were accompanied by an attempt at hand-holding, and frequently my patients essayed more. All this phantom attention was bittersweet. Some of the boys were nice looking, and some persuasive. Others were pathetic and I was careful not to draw away. But at night when I closed my eyes many times there were tears on my lashes because I was playing my old game *What if. . . .*

MONTREAL, MAMA KATHY'S sin city, was a wartime city, filled with soldiers and sailors, some on leave, some waiting to be shipped out. Guys were always trying to pick me up. But they'd try that with anything in skirts. Once by a drinking fountain I was tempted. The sailor was cute and had a nice smile. "Here, let me hold your hair back." I walked away.

But I was disturbed by my reaction. When I analyzed my life, I had to admit it was lonely.

Two days later Crazy Dancer piled more boxes in front of my work station. "Hi!" His smile possessed his face.

"Hi," I said.

"Oh-Be-Joyful's Daughter," he continued formally as though he were proposing, "I have borrowed a car for Sunday. Will you go with me to a drive-in movie?"

"Yes," I said, without hesitation.

"One o'clock white man's time. In the parking lot."

"All right."

"Kathy!" The sisters moved about so quietly you never knew they were there. Sister Magdalena had come around the bend of the hall. "We're waiting for these items. Haven't you checked them yet?"

Crazy Dancer, not at all abashed, stared at her curiously.

"Well, young man, haven't you wasted enough time?"

"Perhaps, if you mean clock time. But there are other kinds."

He would have left then but Sister detained him. "What kind of time are you referring to?"

"Personal time."

"What a strange young man," she said when he was gone.

"Oh, I don't know, he's Indian," I said airily.

THE DRIVE-IN MOVIE was in the country, and the gas coupons must have cost a bundle.

"It's probably our last chance. The rumor is that they're going to black out the city," Crazy Dancer said.

I'd heard that too and was glad they'd held off. I'd never been to a drive-in and was curious. There were dozens of spaces. You drove into one, dropped your money into a slot, and were hooked up to the picture. Instantly the sound of a love scene flooded the car.

"Haven't you ever been before?" he asked.

"No. It's strange—the sound right in the car with you. You feel as though you're part of the movie."

"Actually"—he hesitated briefly—"the movie isn't that important."

"It isn't?"

Crazy Dancer draped an arm casually over the back of the upholstered seat, and gradually lowered it to my shoulders.

I moved nearer the door. His other hand dropped to my thigh.

"What are you doing?" I said, pushing him away.

"What everybody in all the cars are doing." He reared back and gave me a penetrating glance. "Don't tell me you don't know what drive-ins are all about?"

I looked wildly around at the other cars. No one was watching the movie.

"Stop right there, Crazy Dancer. Because if you don't, I'm going to walk home."

"All I had in mind," he protested, "was, you know, a little making out. You don't mind a kiss, do you?"

"It depends," I said tentatively.

"One like this maybe. . . ." And he pressed me so close that I felt the door handle in the middle of my back.

I sat straight up. "If it comes to this kind of holding and this kind of kissing . . . it's not going to be in a borrowed car. And don't tell me you're being shipped out and before the week's over you'll be at the bottom of the ocean floor."

Crazy Dancer regarded me with grave eyes, but his mouth was laughing. "How well you make my argument for me."

I asked, suddenly frightened for him, "Is it true?"

He shrugged. "Who knows?"

We sat and looked at each other, while lovers vowed vows in our ears. I felt ridiculous sitting there, while all around us . . .

"I'll take you back," he said, and put the car in gear.

When we arrived at the hospital parking lot, he didn't open the door, but continued to sit there. "If you didn't make out with me . . . ," he said slowly, reasoning it through, "does that mean you don't make out with anyone?"

"I feel like an idiot," I said. "Any other girl would have known when you suggested a drive-in."

He was still unraveling a skein of thought. "Would you call what we had a disagreement or a fight? With a fight you can kiss and make up," and he shot me a glance.

"A disagreement," I said emphatically. He looked so disappointed that I reached over and gave him an emphatic kiss. Then, jumping out, ran for the nurses' entrance.

THAT NIGHT AS I lay on coarse hospital sheets rinsed in disinfectant, I wondered at myself. I had said one thing and then turned around and undid it in a moment. Why had I kissed him? And what would he remember, the lecture I'd given him or the kiss?

I knew, of course, and hugged myself in the dark as I listened to the litany Mandy insisted on most nights. I didn't mind her going on about Robert Whitaker because I'd found out quite by accident that she'd had the chance to room with someone else but elected to stay with me. That obligated me to hear more examples of her young intern's sterling character. As she enumerated his peerless attributes, I thought—Crazy Dancer has none of those. In the first place he hasn't a proper kind of name. Robert Harley Whitaker II, now with that name one could be a banker, a trial lawyer, the head of a corporation, an admiral in the navy, or the first-rate surgeon he would become. Someone named Crazy Dancer couldn't aspire to any of those positions.

"Robert's such a gentleman," Mandy went on.

I laughed inwardly at the thought of Crazy Dancer being a gentleman.

"And he dances divinely. . . ."

Ah, here we were on common ground. Or were we? I visualized Robert Whitaker with Mandy on his arm doing a box-step fox trot; I could see his black polished patent leather shoes treading lightly.

What did Crazy Dancer wear when he danced? Probably he painted his body and wore a corn-husk mask and bells on his ankles and moccasins scuffing the earth and maybe a breechclout. This time I laughed out loud.

"What are you laughing at?"

I could see Mandy was offended so I changed the subject.

ANOTHER NIGHT LATER in the week, with our window wide open and spring in the air, Mandy whispered from her cot to mine. Robert had three tickets for Delormier Stadium. They were hard to come by and expensive. So when she urged me to go with them I was tempted. I figured out I would have to miss three Saturday movies to see a game. But I was pretty sure Crazy Dancer would show up, so I said no. It crossed my mind once or twice to wonder how Robert was able to afford such things. Supposedly he was a poor boy from a poor family. But somehow he seemed always to have money.

Toward the end of the week we had another bed-to-bed talk. Mandy had gotten to know a lot about Montreal. Robert was alert for any local color and passed it on to her. There was a section in the French quarter that no respectable girl would venture into. Certain hotels rented rooms for twenty minutes at a time all through the night. The town, according to Robert, was wide open—sports betting, lottery tickets, chemin d'fer, baccarat, roulette, blackjack, craps, and barbotte. While even the war failed to put an end to drug smuggling. But the Daughters of Charity of St. Vincent de Paul said their novenas, sang their prayers, and kept sin away. They attempted to do the same with the wounded and dying—but they kept coming.

I had expected to hear from that crazy Indian, Crazy Dancer. I hadn't. Mandy too was without a date for Saturday night, as Robert had been preempted by Dr. Finch for an evening at his home. "To meet his ugly daughter." Mandy made a face and mounted a campaign to get me to go with her to the canteen that was set up in a high school gym. "It's not the Victoria Rifles' Ball or the debutantes' coming out or even the St. Andrew's Annual, but for heaven's sake, Kathy, it's all there is, and I don't want to go alone."

I agreed, mainly to get some sleep. Next day I discovered she wouldn't be alone, Ruth was going too. Mandy lent me a flowered scarf to dress up my outfit, and we started off.

Harsh unhooded lights revealed an upright piano, but no visible player. A handful of servicemen hung around a couple of card tables. They held paper plates with potato chips and not much else. A Crosby record was wobbling on the phonograph.

We stood uncertainly in a bunch. Two sailors homed in on Mandy. I didn't blame them. Mandy was the girl next door, or at least what they wishfully remembered the girl next door to be.

Ruth, on the other hand, was self-conscious about her braces and the cheap silver fillings, which she was replacing out of her meager army pay. Her main worry was that Mr. Right would come along before she was finished. Each Saturday morning she spent at the dentist, returning with all sorts of dental horror stories including the one her dentist told on himself. The reason he had chosen that particular profession was because as a kid his wisdom teeth came in at an angle and stuck right through his cheek.

Ruth had joined us with a great deal of perturbation, afraid she would be asked to dance and afraid she wouldn't. She'd be asked, was my guess, because if she neither laughed, smiled, or spoke she was quite attractive.

Tonight, hopefully, she'd find something other than teeth to talk about.

I put my arm through hers. "Let's get some potato chips."

We started for the tables, but another sailor approached and, with a grin and a few mumbled words, invited Ruth to dance. One glance of panic in my direction and she was whirled away. I held to my course—at least I was going to have something to eat. This time it was a soldier, Canadian army, who came up to me. "There's beer in that wash bucket," he said.

I hadn't noticed the galvanized pail sitting under one of the tables. "No, thank you." I wasn't sure whether he was offering it to me or not.

"Want to dance?"

"All right."

It was a pretext he didn't bother to make too convincing. He held me too close and talked incessantly. I was glad the record was almost over.

"My name's Ed."

"Mine's . . . uh . . . Trisha." I don't know why that name came to mind. I guess the Whites Only sign still rankled.

"Look, Trisha, we've got to go someplace, get out of here."

No, I wasn't the girl next door, I was the girl you took to the nearest drive-in.

"I'm . . . meeting someone." I gulped and looked around for Mandy. I could see she was having a good time, and I didn't want to stand there explaining, so, mumbling that I was going to the restroom, I slipped out. The strains of the newest song on the Hit Parade followed me: "Saturday Night Is the Loneliest Night of the Week."

The next day I was in the middle of a nightmare. That same soldier showed up, the one I'd danced with. I couldn't believe it. I heard him at the front desk asking for Trisha.

There was nothing for it but to intercept him. I plastered a stern look on my face and approached.

The look was wasted. "Trisha!" he bellowed. "I'm so damned glad to see you. What happened last night? Had a devil of a time finding you. I asked all over."

"Did it ever occur to you I didn't want to be found?" I made it as frosty as I could, and anyone else would have backed off. But this guy was impervious to nuances, subtleties, and, I suspected, a hammer over the head. Sister Mary Margaret, trying to be helpful, asked if we cared to step into a private room.

"No," I said as he said, "Yes."

At this moment Trisha herself appeared. "I heard someone was asking for me?" This was addressed to me, as she had already taken Ed's measure. His name had come back to me, and I attempted an introduction, but Trisha was sure the soldier was my revenge, and poor Ed was totally confused by two Trishas. I threw up my hands and left.

I heard later through the grapevine that they had straightened things out to their mutual satisfaction, and ended by going out together. Maybe I did have my revenge.

I WAS MOVED to the trauma center. Duty there drained the life out of you. I saw terrible things, great ragged holes opening in layers, receding deep into flesh.

Sister Egg saved me. Egg was a mother hen to us girls. She caught me in the hall. A severe look lay over her normally good-natured expression. In a clipped, businesslike manner she said, "Kathy, no questions. You are to come with me."

Good heavens, what now? I tried to think which rule I had inadvertently broken as she bustled me out of the building.

"No need to be so somber, Kathy." She burst into smiles. "We are embarked on an expedition to save the caterpillars."

"To save the caterpillars?" I echoed, thinking I hadn't heard correctly.

"Yes, in the park, right across from the elementary school. I fill in teaching the fifth grade part time and I learned to my dismay that the science class is coming tomorrow to collect caterpillars. They intend to chloroform them, stick pins through them, mount them— need I say more? I decided to get to the park first and hide them. And I thought . . . well, I chose you as my coconspirator because I know you have a kind heart."

I laughed until tears came into my eyes. This roly-poly little nun and I made quite a team.

"Tell me, Kathy, am I a good judge of character?"

"The best," I assured her. And when Sister Eglantine, with a guilty look around, got down on all fours, I did the same. The hunt was conducted on hands and knees. We investigated grass blades, wildflowers, small branch stems, leafy shrubs. I made the first find, a lively black fuzzy one journeying along a sunflower stalk. Into Sister's basket it went. Sister found the second and third. It was hard to see the green ones, but I saved several, millipedes I think they were, with so many feet you couldn't count them. It was fun to outwit fifth grade science. It was May and the sun slanted in broad stripes along the grassy floor and, when I squinted, hung in prisms of color.

I needed that day with Sister.

THE NAVAL WAR had turned into a debacle. Wolf packs stalked our shipping in the North Atlantic, mostly sloops, World War I destroyers, carriers with obsolete aircraft, and, it was whispered, insufficiently trained crews. The way it worked, apparently, was that when a U-boat spotted a convoy, it would radio Brest or another French port the Germans had taken over, and word would go out to all the subs in the area. While the original wolf tracked the victims, the rest of the pack converged at high speed, often being refueled and resupplied on the high seas. The packs no longer limited themselves to cutting out stragglers or picking off isolated vessels. They engaged the cruisers and gave battle to the entire convoy.

I read the lists of missing and dead posted in the window outside City Hall and listened when I could to the CBC shortwave in the lounge. It broadcast not only from London but the war fronts. From these sources it was apparent that the losses were dreadful.

Human remnants of these engagements wound up on our wards. To cheer myself I concentrated on the cartoons in the Sunday supplement: a Mountie astride a sinking U-boat, another U-boat about to be devoured by a grizzly bear, and Adolf Hitler with a startled look running from a wild-eyed moose, who had just bitten out the seat of his pants.

It was necessary to laugh when you could.

I didn't know how true that was until Ruth tested positive for TB. This was a test we had to undergo every six months, but it was looked on as routine. Ruth's X ray, however, showed a lesion on her left lung. She was immediately isolated, and her roommate was moved out.

Sister Egg roved the corridors shaking her head and muttering to herself. This was not an unusual sight. Whenever things didn't work out as Egg thought they should, she could be seen roaming the hallways and arguing, whether with herself or with the Lord, no one was sure.

First-semester grades were due to be posted, and, condemning myself for being so selfish when my friend wouldn't graduate at all, I nonetheless kept checking the bulletin board. So far, nothing.

I'd left a patient propped up in bed reading, so I returned to monitor his IV, and my heart pushed into my lungs. A screen had been placed around his cot. I became queasy—I knew what that screen meant.

I came closer and stared at the blanket-covered form. A corpse has very prominent feet because that is the only part that humps up. It wasn't possible. I'd just been down to the basement and back. Finally I got up courage to pull back a corner of the blanket.

It wasn't my soldier but someone I had never set eyes on before. That shouldn't have made it better, but it did. The trouble was, when I started to laugh I couldn't stop.

Mandy found out that in order to play this gruesome joke the senior girls had brought up a stiff from the morgue and simply moved my patient to another room. That evening there were amused glances directed at me.

Why had I been the victim of such a cruel prank? Trisha and Ed had become a twosome, so it wasn't that.

"You goose!" Mandy couldn't contain herself any longer but burst into whoops of laughter. "It's an honor, reserved for whoever gets the highest posting. That's you!"

All thought of grades had been driven from my mind. Mandy took me by the hand and dragged me down to look at them. Kathy Forquet topped the list. Classmates shook my hand, kissed me on the cheek, hugged me. I had been awarded the highest distinction.

MIDWEEK OF THE second week, and I still hadn't heard from Crazy Dancer. Perhaps the kiss hadn't meant anything to him after all. Saturday came and went. Sunday came and went. I decided to forget there was such a person.

I was scrub nurse on a laminectomy, with Robert assisting. When it came to the delicate maneuvering in the lumbar spine, Dr. Finch indicated that Robert was to take over. Finch lived in one of those grand houses on the upper reaches of Mont-Royal, and I'd heard his wife was high society. This morning he was definitely hung over, and I was relieved that he let Robert close. It was reassuring to watch Robert at work. His fingers were quick, deft, and he tied off the bleeders in style.

Good going, I smiled over at him. He was a first-rate surgeon. Mandy would be pleased at this assessment.

There was something else on Robert's mind, however. As we disposed of masks and gloves and washed up, he said, "Incidentally, I've made some inquiries and found this outstanding TB sanatorium in Arizona."

"Arizona!"

"I know. It's expensive. But we want Ruth cured. And they have a great record."

I hadn't heard anything past *expensive.* "How expensive is it?"

"For a year? Several thousand."

"The Sisters could never raise anything like that, even with the doctors contributing and us adding our pennies."

"So," he said with a shrug, "Ruth dies."

"Oh no, good heavens, no."

"There may be a way," Robert said, "if we get Egg on our side." He paused.

"Well, go on."

"You stand in with her. So you should be the one to broach it to her."

"Broach what?"

He smiled a devil-may-care smile. "Bingo."

Bingo was strictly illegal, as was any form of gambling. I stared at him.

He went on imperturbably, "The Sisters don't have money. Bingo is the only way."

"Organize a bingo night here in the hospital? They'd never go for it."

"You're talking about Sisters who ran a brewery. Besides, it's to save Ruth."

They *had* run a brewery. They were pretty tough-minded ladies, and it was worth a try, especially as Ruth was not taking it well. We had all visited her at different times, using reasonable precautions, of course.

"I'm in a state of suspended animation," she had greeted me, explaining that she didn't feel at all ill, didn't even have a cough, and her sputum samples were negative.

"Stop complaining," I said, and we both laughed.

I'd brought a box of chocolates, and she hunted through it for those with soft centers. She was the kind of girl who could put it away and still remain thin as a rail. Her penchant for sweets, however, might have accounted for all those fillings. She mentioned the fund. "I don't have much hope of it," she admitted. "I don't see how they can possibly raise money for a first-class institution like the one in Arizona."

Robert's institution had been investigated by the Sisters. They were impressed, and started a fund in Ruth's name. I'd overheard the Sisters discussing it. It seemed they had all made their contributions, all but Sister Eglantine, who not only had failed to put up her share, but to date hadn't paid anything. "Not a red cent."

Mary Margaret hastened to add, "She didn't refuse."

"No," Sister Ursula conceded. "But we have yet to see the color of her money."

When they toted it up, including pledges by the doctors and staff, even if Egg's contribution equaled the rest put together, it fell woefully short.

That afternoon, Robert and I approached Sister Egg, laying out our suggestion with a good deal of trepidation.

"Bingo?" She regarded us with an enigmatic expression, one that could be interpreted as anger, shock, or possibly dismay. But it must have been her spectacles that reflected these emotions, for she went on to say, "What an extraordinarily good suggestion!"

The fist I had balled my hand into relaxed. I relaxed.

"How do you propose we go about it?"

That, naturally, was why Robert was there. "There are certain elements in this town," he said, "who would be happy to set it up for us, once they understood it was in a good cause, of course."

"Of course," Sister agreed, looking pious. Looking pious is part of a nun's training; they can do it at the drop of a hat. "God works in mysterious ways—" Sister Egg could always be counted on to come through with an appropriate saying—"his wonders to perform."

"Amen," said Robert.

THERE WAS A note at the nurses' station for me. Crazy Dancer had been by, and Sister said he'd written it on the spot. I saw I needn't have worried about that kiss—he was just as confused as I'd been.

The note said:

Dear Oh-Be-Joyful's Daughter,

I think I've figured it . . . certain things that aren't okay for me are okay for you. If that's right, it's okay by me. I've got a surprise to show you, a motorcycle. She was a mess when I bought her, but I've been working on her all week, and she's purring like a bobcat. Let's take her out. How's Sunday? One o'clock in the parking lot.

Best regards,
Crazy Dancer

I was smiling before I came to the end. That's where he'd been, working on a motorcycle. A motorcycle was a good idea. Nothing much could happen on a motorcycle. Besides, tomorrow was Sunday. It was going to be a wonderful day.

IT WAS AND it wasn't.

Services had barely ended when Crazy Dancer was in the parking lot. It was one o'clock sharp. Mama always said Indians were never on time. But he was.

"There it is," he said with a proprietary gesture.

I looked in the direction he pointed. The motorcycle was a three-wheel job and had been polished to a high gleam. It was obviously homemade, and what had been a toolbox was converted into a seat.

"Is that for a passenger?" I asked.

"It's very comfortable. I tried it out."

I wanted to ask, "Is it safe?" But he was so pleased with himself that I couldn't.

"Once," he said with a flourish, "an Indian brave would have come on a fast buffalo pony. But this is now. How do you like it?"

I barely hesitated and said gamely, "I can see you've put in a lot of work on it."

"I have. It hardly takes any gas."

"Really?"

He patted the seat to encourage me. "Try it."

"I just sit on it. Is that it?"

"And hold on."

"To what?"

"To me."

"Oh." I sat gingerly.

"Does it seem all right?" he inquired.

"Oh yes."

"Are you comfortable?"

"I'm fine."

"Good." He threw a leg over the saddle and grabbed the handlebars. "If I go too fast, or you want to stop or you get cold, just holler in my ear. I can hear you."

"You're sure?"

"I'll start up the motor and we'll see."

He did and it was loud. I leaned close to his ear and yelled, "Crazy Dancer!"

He turned, grinning, and the next moment jumped hard on the pedal, kicking it into action.

With a roar and a shivering jolt we leaped forward.

Once under way, the engine transferred its reverberation to me, throbbing through my body. The wind in my face was glorious, my hair flew out behind like a banner. My eyes teared but I made slits of them, taking in the rushing meld of buildings, cars, trams, signs, people. Nothing had its own identity, but blurred into and became part of everything else.

Crazy Dancer and I escaped the city, crossing the Jacques-Cartier Bridge and speeding into a softened landscape of greens and blues. We were riding at the sky, penetrating vast openness, mounting the clouds. It was intoxicating.

Crazy Dancer's waist was my security, that strong, slender waist that I fastened my arms around and clung to.

"Okay?" His shouted word streamed back to me. In answer I hugged him tighter.

We continued to sail along, then something happened to the steering. The motorcycle wobbled. I felt him lean to one side for balance, then tense. I laid my face against his shoulder and braced myself. Crazy Dancer made a last minute effort to spin out and away from the tree.

We struck.

The motorcycle went one way, Crazy Dancer and I another, for I hadn't let go of him. We slid along a grassy embankment and landed in one heap completely intertangled.

Crazy Dancer turned in my arms. "It was to make you joyful," he said.

I intended to say, "Yes, of course," but what came out was a sob.

I saw the concern in his eyes. Indian eyes are not expressionless as I'd often been told; they showed every bit as much concern as blue or brown. "You okay?"

I nodded. "It did make me joyful. I loved it."

"I know what the problem is. By changing the toolbox into a seat I raised the center of gravity. It's too high, I couldn't control the steering. The road turned, but I couldn't force the machine to turn. Are you sure you're all right?"

"I'm fine, just shaken."

"You'll be all right then. I'm going to have a look and see if I can get her going."

He got up, limped over to the machine, whose wheels had only now stopped whirring, and dragged it back to the tree for closer examination. "Well, we popped a tire, number one." He stood the bike up and started the motor. With infinite care he moved the shift lever. A horrible grinding noise came out, but it didn't seem to worry him too much. "Stripped a couple teeth off first, but second seems okay." He laid the bike down again. "The tire I can fix. To patch it I need to pry it off and remove the inner tube. Now, let's see what I can use for a patch." While he looked in the toolbox part of the seat, I rolled my sweater behind my head and made myself comfortable.

"Crazy Dancer, you were going to teach me Indian ways. Remember?"

He shrugged this off. "No one wants them anymore."

"I want them. At least I want to know about them. You said you would. First off I want to know how you look when you're dancing."

"I paint my body different colors, sometimes black and white. My hair is in horns twisted with corn tassels."

"Yes, I thought so. I thought that's how you'd look."

"I've made my diagnosis," he said, looking up. "I got to operate. I'm going to make a patch from that bit of rubber on the seat. Lucky I got a lighter so I can melt it and make it adhere. Lucky I left room for the compact bike pump in the bottom of the seat." He waved the pump triumphantly. "Cost me two bits extra, but I'm glad I made the investment."

"Tell me why you dance."

"Oh, that." He was busy with the rubber, heating it. "I dance because that's when the power floods into you. You seem to be just fooling around, but it's more than that. A clown acts silly, he acts in a contrary manner. He jokes and mocks, even at sacred rituals. You get people laughing and they start thinking in new ways. I teach like that, by bad examples."

"I don't know if my mind is Indian enough to understand. I think I do, but I'm not sure."

"When people question things, that's when they make changes."

"Yes, I see. Your crazy dancing is powerful medicine."

"That's right. You heal the spirit and that sometimes heals the body. Take me. I enter the house where the person lies ill. I have my mask on. I jump about, blow ashes on the sick person. The best kind is nicotiana from inner bark. Cedar is good, it purifies. Sometimes instead of dancing I get someone to play games with me."

"You play games? How does that get anyone well?"

He seemed surprised. "The life force is in motion. Kickball is a good way to release it, or kickstick—even making a patch."

"Don't you have medicines?"

"Of course. But first we put the heart of the healer in sympathy with the spirits. Then we give medicine. Bear gallbladder is strong against poison. Skunk oil is good for sore throat. Rub on grease from a wild goose for cramps or stomach pain. If you can't get a goose, duck is pretty good. Moose and beaver soups boiled with milkweed or red mulberry poured through wood ashes is strong against rattlesnake bite. Brings down the swelling. Even better, if you can catch the snake, cut it up and put it on the wound. Sure we got medicine."

"It all sounds very strange to me and I can't believe it does any good."

"What do you expect? You can't learn to be an Indian in one lesson." He regarded me quite soberly. "Are you sure you want to be an Indian?"

"No, I'm not at all sure."

"You are like me, stuck between worlds. That's why I joined up."

"That doesn't make sense. They're fighting over countries you don't even know about."

"My reasoning is this. I offer my life and perhaps my death in their battle, so I've won a place in white Canada. I have a right to it."

"Well, maybe," I said, not convinced. Privately I thought he would have to scrub at his lovely copper-colored skin harder than even I had and that in the end it wouldn't do any good.

"Will your unit be called up?" I asked.

"Who knows? For now we're detailed to drive lorries and keep 'em running. . . . There"—he straightened and patted the seat of the three-wheeler—"this should get us back. Let's give it a try. I thought we'd start at the top of that grade."

He dragged the machine over to the hill, and in one of those swift movements typical of him had the motorcycle in an upright position. Straddling it, he kicked up the motor. "Listen to that," he exclaimed, "purring like a bobcat."

I approached somewhat reluctantly. "So it was the center of gravity?"

"That's right—when it's too high, the motorcycle wants to steer itself."

"But you won't let it?"

"Now I know this habit, I'll hold it down. Perhaps a regular two-wheeler is better."

"Personally I like four wheels. It seems more stable."

"Four wheels? You're talking a car. You don't like cars."

"Under the right circumstances I like them."

He looked dejected. "A car eats gas and I only have a green ration card." To reassure and persuade me back to the motorcycle, he pointed out a gray and white feather attached to his key ring. "Don't be afraid. The spirit of this bird protects us."

"He must have looked away for a moment," I said.

But Crazy Dancer had his own interpretation. "He reminds me not to try to fly like him, because this is only a machine."

I mounted, my arms once more around him.

To reassure me, he explained his plan for reconnecting with the road. "We're going downhill in neutral and at the bottom shift into second. We'll have to get up to thirty or thirty-five or stall, so hang on."

It was like a runaway roller coaster, but I hung on and we made it.

Crazy Dancer took the ride back a bit more cautiously, because while the motor purred like a bobcat, there was an occasional hiccup.

We stopped at a drugstore for ice cream. It reminded me of the one back home, but this had small round marble-top tables and wire-backed chairs. "I used to work in a drugstore."

"You did?"

"Yes, only it wasn't fancy like this."

"I bet you made good milk shakes."

"I did."

Two white kids came in and were served ahead of us. Crazy Dancer didn't say anything but went to the counter and gave our order there. When he came back he said, "I'll leave a big tip."

"Why would you do that when they ignored us?"

"It is a contrary lesson, one of my bad examples. It makes them think, Why would he have done that? And they will feel bad that they don't deserve it."

I couldn't help laughing at his logic. "Oh, Crazy Dancer, I don't think so."

"My backward examples work. After all, I cracked us up and yet here you are having a malted with me. How do you explain that?"

"It must be your strong medicine."

He laughed, delighted. "Now you are sounding like Oh-Be-Joyful's Daughter."

When we drove into the hospital parking area there were several people about. They sent curious glances our way, taking in Crazy Dancer and his machine. I didn't care what they thought. I'd had a good time. I was happy. In fact I was joyful.

"It will be better next Sunday," Crazy Dancer said.

"Next Sunday?"

"Yes, when you come with me again."

"Crazy Dancer, you forgot to ask me. You can't just assume things, you have to ask."

"I did ask," he said. "Do I always have to use words?"

"Yes, you always have to."

He looked with a very sweet expression, I thought, into my eyes. "Will you come with me Sunday, in the Moon When the Pony Sheds?"

"Yes, I will."

Five

HE CREPT INTO my mind at odd hours during the week. I had a suspicion that he seemed as unconventional to his own people as he did to me. But I liked the unexpectedness of him, the honesty. And I was touched by the fact that he hadn't tried even a kiss. He was feeling his way with me.

He lived by inner laws that perhaps I would never understand. The thrust of everything he did was to bring out the harmony in things. That made him a religious person. And I was reminded of my father, Jonathan Forquet. But Crazy Dancer's God was in everything, in motion, in doing, in being.

A clown, he said, made you think in new ways.

I hunted up Sister Egg to see what she thought.

"That God is in everything? St. Eckhardt in the sixth century wrote extensively on this very point. But scholarship isn't necessary. You just open your eyes and look."

"I'm so glad we think alike. Would you go so far as to say His spirit is in dancing and even soccer?"

"Dancing and soccer? And lacrosse, I suppose? Well, now let me see. God enjoins us to be happy. And since we are happy when we do these things, I would say yes. Definitely yes."

I could have hugged her, I was so pleased.

THE LAST FEW days Mandy was, as Mama Kathy would have put it, a bit off her feed. In anyone else it wouldn't have been noticeable, but I lived with her, and Mandy, usually open about everything, now was abstracted and jumped when I spoke to her unexpectedly.

I didn't pay much attention at first. I told myself she'd had a quarrel with Robert and they'd make it up.

That didn't happen. She continued withdrawn and uncommunicative.

Finally, I blurted out, "Mandy, what is it? What's wrong?"

She shook her head. "It's nothing."

"You're not yourself. Something's happened. Can't you tell me?"

"It's nothing. Really. Just a problem Robert and I have to work out."

It was a polite way of brushing me off, but I persisted. "Is Robert pressuring you to, you know . . . go all the way?"

That made her laugh and for a moment I thought things would be all right. "Oh, Kathy, you are funny, so full of good old-fashioned homespun morality. Robert and I have been sleeping together almost from the beginning. Oh, I know good girls don't. But the war's changed all that. It showed us we have to live in the present."

There was a pause, which I didn't know how to fill, so I put my arms around her. I felt her sag. With a complete change from boisterous confidence, she crumpled.

"You don't think less of me, Kathy, do you?"

"Of course not. It's just that it didn't make you joyful."

"I *was* happy. For a while it was wonderful. It still is, only . . ." She stopped herself and when she continued it was more carefully. "Robert's sensitive, you know. You wouldn't think it, a big, strapping guy like that. But he is. I keep telling him a doctor can't take everything to heart the way he does. He empathizes too much with his patients."

Whatever was bothering Mandy, it was not Robert Whitaker's concern for his patients. I wasn't any closer to knowing what was going on than I had been before.

Sunday came. I dressed with care and scrutinized myself in the mirror. I wanted Crazy Dancer to be proud of me, to think I was pretty. I was in the parking lot at exactly one.

He must have been going on Indian time. He was late.

I watched various vehicles pull up, and leave again. A half hour dragged by in this way before it occurred to me that perhaps he wasn't going to show up. There was a sick spot in my stomach that expanded as minutes passed and it became increasingly obvious that he wasn't coming.

With a last look around I turned on my heel and went to my room.

Who did he think he was to treat me like this? He couldn't have forgotten. He had deliberately stood me up. In some recess of my being I still expected I would hear from him. He'd have some excuse, some story. And I didn't intend to listen, no matter what.

Monday there was no word. Nothing.

When Mandy invited me to go with her and Robert to Harry Sharp's, the casino that everyone talked about but that wasn't supposed to exist, I decided I'd go.

Mandy rarely asked me to join them, and I felt this might mean she was ready to take me into her confidence. Besides, in the mood I was in, I rather looked forward to investigating the darker side of Montreal. And Harry Sharp's casino was as close to Mama's sin city as I was liable to get.

For the occasion Mandy lent me a dress. It was a floaty chiffon in pale yellow. I wished Crazy Dancer could see me in it. I repressed that thought with annoyance.

"You look ravishing, Kathy." The prospect of a nefarious evening brought color back to her cheeks and the old animation. "Have you any money?"

"Not much. Will I be needing any?"

"Well, there's no use going to a gambling casino if you don't gamble."

"You're right," I said. Where and how could I come by money? There was the money I saved during the week for movies, and I might borrow a similar amount from Sister Egg. I shut out of my mind Mama Kathy's reaction to such a scheme.

I knocked on the door of Egg's room. "It's for an emergency," I explained.

The casino was on Cote Street, which everybody called Luck Road. All the swank places in Montreal were subterranean, and this cavern exploded in light and sound. Rapid French struck us from all sides and seemed to accelerate the more plodding English. Other languages intruded. People joked in Russian, laughed in French, and whispered in Armenian. One man wept bitterly in what sounded like Bulgarian or some other Slavic tongue, and seemed on the point of suicide, but allowed friends to restrain him. It was Dante's inferno mixed up with carnival.

The decor was elegant but far from tasteful. There was a crystal chandelier, a gaudy jukebox in conflict with it. Boxed palm trees were scattered about, and, in their shade, spittoons. The floor was marble, disfigured by black heel marks. At one end of the bar an enormous fresco beamed down on us of a woman in extremely high heels, garters, and a feathered boa that covered some essentials, but not all. The room was ringed by rows of slot machines, and people congregated around them. Gaming tables, however, were the focal point from which all other activities radiated like spokes of a wheel.

The crowd around the tables was as eccentric as the room. A conglomeration of expatriates from a dozen countries waved their money, collected chips, and placed their bets. I had a strong feeling they were not what they seemed, that nothing here was. The well-dressed gentleman with goatee, who resembled a French banker, I was sure I had seen driving a cab. It was carny time, and people dressed themselves in their wishes, their dreams.

I was one of them in my borrowed finery.

There were floor-length gowns and women in slacks. Among the men, zoot-suiters in the drape shape with the reet pleat and the stuff cuff mingled with starched ruffled shirtfronts and cummerbunds.

The closeness of the room intensified the sensations my nose picked up—brilliantine, that was a definite smell. It came from a head in front of me that glistened with it. The man turned a hawklike face in my direction. He wasn't looking at me, but at Mandy. It was an insolent look, bold and— He noticed I was observing him and ducked into the maze of people.

Expensive French perfumes were at variance with those picked up in the dime store. The atmosphere was invaded by stogies and cigarettes. Belinda Fancytails from Havana were advertised. They sold everything here.

Sharp's casino imitated both the discreet establishments of Nice and the flamboyance of Las Vegas. Mandy held onto me. We had somehow gotten separated from Robert and were scrutinizing the crowd for him. I followed a strobe light picking out face after face. There in an alcove was the man with the brilliantined hair and hawk face, talking to . . . I thought it was Robert, but the light moved on. When it completed its circuit and swung back, there was the hawk still in the alcove, but alone, nursing a drink. Someone called, "Frankie, c'est va?" and he answered with a smile and a wave of the hand. The smile was unpleasant. One front tooth lay on top of the other, giving him the appearance of a wolverine.

"Here's Robert," Mandy called.

Robert had found us and put an arm around each. He was perfectly at ease. Indeed he was at home in this frenetic strobe-light jungle that pierced you with drums and syncopated music intoned by a beautiful black singer.

"How do you like it? Exciting, huh?" I nodded numbly as he pointed. "Over here they're shooting craps. The dice have to bounce off the rail for the throw to count. If they don't, look out, some thug is apt to chop off your hand." One player was talking to his dice, beseeching them. A woman was kissing hers. Everything was extravagant, exaggerated.

"And over here, Montreal's own game, barbotte. You'll find it played in any alley for penny stakes—and here for enough money to buy all the buildings on the Place d'Armes."

He herded us over for a better look. "It's the stupidest dice game ever invented: five winning combinations, five losing, nothing else counts. A strictly even chance, minus the cut of up to five percent the house skims off on each roll. Played with tiny 'peewee' dice, easy to shave. No skill, no strategy, no technique whatsoever—just plain dumb luck."

Crowded around the table were a raucous and ill-assorted bunch of frenzied gamblers, some dressed to the nines, one who looked as though he'd slept in the bus station. This man, unshaven and reeking of cabbage, was rolling the dice, a mad gleam in his eyes.

"That's Marcel. They call him Magister Ludi, King of the Games. He has more luck than any living person, of both kinds, good and bad. You should have been here last week when he came in without an overcoat. He pawned it for six bucks, lost that stake in two rolls, scraped his pockets for all the change he had on him, lost that, and finally panhandled nickels and dimes from the spectators to make a last two-dollar bet. He won. And won again. Walked away at closing time with more than seven thousand dollars. He bought a new wardrobe, paid a year's room and board in advance at some fleabag inn, and he's back tonight losing the rest."

Making room for the vultures who wanted to savor Magister Ludi's bankruptcy, Robert finally brought us to a table where he was welcomed by players and croupiers alike.

"This is my game," he announced. "Roulette. *Le rouge et le noir.*"

Through the din I heard the croupier calling numbers and colors, the French words an invocation.

"So, little ladies," Robert adapted his manner to the place, "what is your pleasure? What will it be? Red or black? Even or odd? Columns? Rows? Or thirty-five to one on your lucky number?"

"You go ahead, Robert," Mandy urged. "Kathy and I will just watch until we get the hang of it."

"No," I declared. When the pony sheds! Where did he get off, standing me up? "Place your bet, Robert. And I will too."

"Kathy!" Mandy was as amazed by this new side of me as I was. "Are you really going to?"

I laughed and repeated her words back to her, "No use going to a gambling casino if you don't gamble."

"A woman after my own heart," Robert encouraged.

"In that case . . ." Mandy followed reluctantly.

Robert stepped up to the roulette table and placed his chips on Black. The croupier barked his warning call, the gigantic wheel spun, sending out sparks of light, and the money was raked away. Bettors lost and bettors won, their winnings added to the piles in front of them.

I picked a person with a mountain of chips before him, a gentleman with a malacca cane adorned in mother-of-pearl. The handle unscrewed, and out came a small flask from which he refreshed himself in moments of stress. He seemed to be the luckiest one there, and when he put his chips on Red, I emptied my purse and placed the first and last bet of my life.

My last, because after it was explained to me in French that the house accepted only chips, not cash, and the croupier with a resigned expression exchanged my money for a small, very small pile from a store he kept for ignorant females—to the relief of impatient gamblers and a crowd of kibbitzers the lighted wheel could be spun again, the winning number proclaimed, and the long arm of the rake descend to capture three weekends of movies and Sister Egg's ten dollars.

It was gone in under thirty seconds, including the conference with the croupier. The gentleman with the malacca cane barely paused to resupply his hoard. I couldn't do this. Mine was gone. Forever.

I realized a rather dull evening stretched before me. I should have patronized the slot machines, where I could have drawn out the excitement. I realized I was wrong about Mandy too. She didn't seem ready to confide anything to me. Perhaps I'd been mistaken, and there was nothing to confide.

So I amused myself watching as the strobe lights traversed the room, spotlighting one client after another. An elderly woman with a figure like a girl's, who wore both slacks and jewels, a large bald man, who squinted at the light and waved it angrily away—then the light found Mandy. She was watching Robert a few feet away at the roulette wheel. There was an odd expression on her face. When Robert was picked out, I was struck once more by his relaxed, self-confident manner. Was he too much at home here? That might put Mandy's expression into context—it was worry. Or was it fear?

I laughed at myself and inhaled the disgusting smell of brilliantine. With his back to me and shielding himself from the strobes in a row of slot machines was the one called Frankie. He was also watching.

He was watching Mandy.

I DROPPED BY to see Sister Egg with the first of my repayments, and she gave me two letters. I tore open Crazy Dancer's first. A letter from a sister can wait.

Dear Oh-Be-Joyful's Daughter,

    I was transferred, they'd only black it out if I said where. But I'm in Canada, at least for now. I found an engine and a couple of carburetors in pretty bad shape here too.
    I'm writing so you won't forget me. I do not forget you. Let me know if you miss me, and how much. I miss you a lot.

    Sincerely yours,
    Crazy Dancer

There was a P.S., an army post office number where I could write him. On this he abbreviated his name to just Crazy.

I glanced away smiling. He hadn't stood me up. He thought of me, just as I thought of him. He missed me—a lot.

"Good news, Kathy?" Sister Egg regarded me contemplatively.

"Oh yes. From someone I didn't expect to hear from." I had to look away from her gaze to hide the fact that I was out-of-all-proportion joyful.

And she was rewarded for being her good egg self with wonderful news. The Reverend Mother had quietly quashed the bingo scheme. But at the last minute when Ruth was about to be separated from the service and dispatched, not to Arizona but to some inferior institution, one of the radiology technicians admitted she had accidentally splashed some drops of hypo on the film. At the time she hadn't realized what had happened, and only later associated the accident with the diagnosis of lung lesions that had showed up on Ruth's X ray.

I don't think Ruth herself could have been more elated than Sister Egg. "A girl with an appetite like that I knew couldn't have tuberculosis."

I had opened the letters in inverse proportion to their importance. Connie's was the most thrilling.

    . . . Have I mentioned Jeff before? We've been going out quite a bit. Of course I've been going out with other people too. In fact, Mama Kathy made a boyfriend list to tease me. When I saw his name on it, I immediately took it off. I told Mama that he was simply a friend. I think now what I meant was—he was in a different category than the others. You've guessed what I'm trying to say, haven't you?

*We're engaged, Kathy. Engaged to be married. I can
hardly believe it myself. I'm so in love. Someday you'll know
the feeling. . . .*

I stopped reading and hugged the letter. What if "someday" was
now? What if I too—?

I carried the letters back to my room and waved them at Mandy.
"What do you know—my sister, Connie, is in love."

At this announcement of mine, her eyes filled with tears.

I looked away, pretending not to see them. Whatever it was, she
kept it to herself.

I wrote Connie immediately, trying not to let any of the uneasiness I felt about Mandy come through. While I was enthusing to
Connie, saying how happy I was for her, I kept remembering how
happy Mandy had been. Love, I thought, must be difficult.

More about the romance came the next day from Mama Kathy.
Jeff, according to her, was perfect for Connie. And she put in details
that Connie didn't bother with. He was a stress analyst who worked
in the same plant as Connie. His job was on some sort of experi-
mental aircraft. It was very important work. In fact, it struck me that
everything about Jeff began with a superlative. He was very handsome, very talented, very important. I wondered how Georges would
feel about this *very very* person who wanted to marry his twin.

I was answered in the next mail delivery. Georges, in a hasty
scrawl, wanted to know a lot more about "this Jeff character."

Like pups from the same litter, we three were headed in different
directions.

Mama's world had brought me far, given me an education and a
profession. But it didn't accept me. And, what was worse, didn't
admit it didn't. As a student nurse I had gained respect and the confidence of the Sisters and my fellows. During working hours I was
on an equal footing, there were shared jokes, friendly remarks; I was
included. Mama always said—*Kathy is to be included.* Here, at the
hospital, my uniform was a badge of admittance. Out of it, my status
disappeared, and I wasn't included except once or twice as an after-
thought. That's when I remembered how much kindness can hurt.

Looked at fairly, Mama's white world had prepared me, as few
Indian girls were, to take a place in it. But had I left room for joy?
Happiness I long ago rejected as not good enough—it must be joy
that lifted you up to the skies. Joy at seeing, feeling, hearing, joy at
being in the world. Joy became my prayer. The only prayer, Sister
Egg tells me, God wants to hear.

So each day I remind myself I am Oh-Be-Joyful's Daughter, and look for a piece of joy to take to bed at night. I seize on a cloud lighted by a sinking sun, or the pattern in a leaf, or the reds and golds autumn brought, and wrap myself in it before sleeping.

But in the morning I have to face the pain, the useless bravery and hopeless courage in the wards. I couldn't get the ulcer case out of my mind. The ulcer broke through to the stomach, and a naso-gastric tube was used to suction it. That afternoon the patient died.

Not "the patient." *Ralph. Ralph died.* I was hiding from his name. You can't allow names, they make it too real.

No one expected him to die. It was a shock. I kept reviewing the plasma drip I'd been responsible for. But that had gone routinely. I could think of nothing I could have done to keep him alive. So I played a game of dominoes with cot 14, remembering to call him Bob. The dominoes were bone, not wood, and the clicking sound gave him a great deal of pleasure.

"Is there any strategy to this game?" I asked. "It just seems to be matching ends."

Bob's answer was a grin. "You got to beat me before you complain about it being too easy." Midway in the game he said, "No holding out. If you *can* play, you got to."

I gained a new respect for the game. It was like life: you have to play if you can play. And those pieces that were sidelined? You had to forget them and go on.

THE WAR ITSELF was a morass of contradictions, fought from the fogs off the Grand Banks of Newfoundland where wolf packs hid, to the sands of el-Alamein with Rommel falling back to Tunisia chased by Anderson's First Army. Massive German reinforcements arrived, and the battle seesawed.

I don't think in Washington, Ottawa, or London they really knew how the war was going. A victory here offset a defeat there.

Outside Stalingrad German troops were mired by winter. In the Pacific Admiral Halsey mounted an offensive against an island I'd never heard of—Guadalcanal. U.S. and Aussie troops attacked the Japanese in Burma and drove them out of Gona.

Recently there were German prisoners among our patients. I found it difficult to even approach them. There they lay, looking like everybody else. They didn't wear the blue-gray uniform of prisoners, with the large red circle in the middle of the back, a target in case they tried to escape. No, they were in the usual white hospital gowns.

They might look like anybody else, but they were responsible for the shrapnel cases, the amputees, the boy with infected shell fragments in his back. One of them might have killed the Clark boy. And what about cot 19? It was not impossible they had had a part in John's face being shattered, or the abscessed jaw in the corner, with yellow streaks seeping into the fibers of the dressing. They were Nazis, the horde that overran Europe, occupied Paris, bombed London.

The senior nurses were slow in answering their calls and more and more it was left to me. I tried not to think that even now their comrades were trying to kill Georges. Lying helpless on army cots they were just more broken bodies with the same fear-filled questioning eyes. Yet when they cried out, it was in guttural words I didn't understand.

They didn't ask anything of us, there were no requests. It was clear they found their position a peculiar one. While they themselves had been captured, they knew—*we*—knew that in the broader theater of the war Germany was the victor. Everywhere land was taken, ships sunk, populations driven into camps. They must wonder why we inferior peoples didn't recognize that we were conquered. Why didn't we give up and admit defeat?

It must rankle to be so dependent on us.

However, I was a nurse. I administered morphine and pain medication to these examples of the "master race," handled syringes, turned them to avoid bedsores, changed linen, gave baths, and shuddered at their wounds. I couldn't help it. They suffered.

Cot 5 had developed pneumonia. His breath came in weak rales, and it was obvious he was dying. He was very young, eighteen or nineteen. At the end he reached out groping for something, someone to hold on to. I gave him my hand. The name on his chart was Kurt. I was afraid to say it for fear the sound of my English voice would frighten him.

He murmured something in German. "Gott."

That we agreed on. "Yes," I whispered under my breath, "God will look after you."

A second later I closed his eyes and a tear of mine fell onto his face. That's when I found out it was as hard to lose a German as a Canadian or English boy.

One of the men on the ward, with chest injuries and third-degree burns on his hands, thighs, and abdomen, had been picked up from a U-boat. "I would have let him drown," Ruth said bitterly. She had lost an uncle in a U-boat attack.

More than I hated wolf packs and Hitler I'd begun to hate the war.

Whether this burn case would survive to undergo a lengthy series of skin grafts was questionable. We had extracted numerous shards of metal, and were giving palliative treatment. He'd lain motionless in a coma for a week exuding the faint smell of decay accompanying extensive burns and made no better by overlying disinfectants.

I was changing the dressings when his eyes suddenly opened and he looked at me. Gray, thoughtful eyes.

"I hear English voices. Am I in England?" He spoke a cultivated English, better than my own.

"You're in Canada," I told him. "Montreal."

"I always wanted to see Canada."

"Don't try to talk. You're going to come along fine now, but you've been quite ill."

He nodded and slipped, not into coma, but into sleep.

He must be an officer, I decided, to be so well educated, to have such a command of English. I'd forgotten his name, so I flipped the cover page of his chart—Lt. Erich Helmut von Kerll.

I was busy for a while in the other wards, but before I left the floor I looked in on him. He had come around but didn't remember our conversation. He once more wanted to know where he was.

He looked at me and saw me for the first time. "Very kind of you," he said, "an enemy and all."

"You're a patient," I said firmly.

"Very kind," he said again.

I checked the chart of the next bed to make sure he'd been given his evening medication. When I turned back the lieutenant was asleep.

I looked in on him the next morning. He was asleep and his vital signs were stable. His fever, however, remained high and he was continued on intravenous feeding. While I was adjusting the tubing he woke and asked for water.

"It isn't allowed." Nevertheless I brought cracked ice, put a little in his mouth, and passed a chunk across his parched lips. He tried a joke. "Florence Nightingale was some other war, wasn't she?"

I smiled at his attempt.

"What's your name?" he asked.

"Kathy."

He seemed disappointed. "I thought you'd have an Indian name."

"I do. Oh-Be-Joyful's Daughter."

"Remarkable," he said and fell asleep.

*   *   *

EARLY THE NEXT morning before going on duty I stopped by Lt. von Kerll's bed. The night nurse had not carried out her instructions. The edges of his abdominal burns were adhering to the dressings, and it was necessary to moisten them and peel them away. No matter how gently this was done, it was an agonizing procedure.

He grit his teeth. While he said nothing, he sweated his gown through. Gingerly I got him into a fresh one.

"Oh-Be-Joyful's Daughter, I think you don't intend to let me die. I think you intend to get me well."

"I'm going to get you well," I said with resolution.

"I feel much better and I'm hungry."

"That's good news," I said, wondering what I could feed him at this unorthodox hour. Breakfast preparations were not yet under way. Then I thought of the nurses' station—they always kept something on hand. "I'll try to bring you a cup of broth."

I did bring it, but by the time I got back with it he was sleeping. I looked down at him with a pleased warm feeling. The stench of decay no longer hung about his wounds. He was resting comfortably.

RUTH HAD A date and asked me to take her shift in the wards that evening.

When I came on duty Erich von Kerll was awake and slightly propped up in bed. Beside him was soup and a glass of juice, neither of which he had touched.

"Aren't you hungry?"

"I wasn't. I am now."

"Good. What will you have first, the drink?" I held it to his lips. "Now for the main course," and I ladled a spoon of potato soup into his mouth. He took three or four sips then put his hand up.

"Enough?"

"Yes, thank you."

"You'll be able to sleep now. Shall I put the light out?"

"I knew you before, when I was just lying here. I knew when it was you adjusting the machine, changing plasma bags, giving injections, taking my pulse."

"Did you?" I said, trying not to show how touched I was. "I've often wondered if comatose patients don't comprehend more of what goes on around them than we think."

"Yes. Well, I did. When I was in the water I thought, this is when Brünhilde, or one of the lovely Rhine Maidens is supposed to take my hand and lead me to that Valhalla reserved for warriors.

Instead of a maiden of light, waves of oil rushed into my mouth and washed my eyes. And there was fire on the water."

I had forgotten, I allowed myself to forget he was off a U-boat. I recoiled, I couldn't help it.

He read my expression, stiffened, and a look of whimsical grief passed over his features. "I was second mate on the U-186. Our kill was nine merchant ships, two of them Canadian, and a corvette."

I compressed my lips.

Why had he said that? Why remind me we were enemies? I walked from the room.

ix

THE CHRISTMAS SEASON was a busy time here. The saints' days were observed by extra services. I mailed packages to Mama Kathy, Connie, and Georges. Books this year. *A Christmas Carol* for Connie, a beautiful *Audubon* for Mama, and a life of Houdini for Georges. Mandy and I exchanged presents; she gave me earrings, long and dangling. I loved them, although I couldn't imagine where I would wear them, or with what. I found a pretty little pin for her. The Sisters clubbed together and gave every girl a white prayer book.

The Sisters had been persuaded to allow a dance to be held. There were a few regulations: absolutely no liquor on the premises, the affair to be chaperoned, and the hours posted.

We girls, delighted at the prospect of a party, made a trip to the closest woods and brought back fir branches and sprigs of holly. We strung popcorn and macaroni and colored them with leftover cake dye, then turned our attention to the hall.

The tree was symmetric, tall and gaily trimmed with ornaments, some of which dated back a hundred years, and at its base the Sisters laid a crèche. The holy family was represented, the shepherd, the wise men, all the animals, and of course in the manger lay the Christ child, while over him an angel kept guard. I was reminded of the angel wrapped in newspaper a year ago and wondered when the family would be gathered under it again.

I decided to bring a strand of popcorn to the German burn case. He'd undergone a second skin graft and I had not behaved in a professional manner, stalking out as I had. After all, I told myself, it's Christmas. So I went to the foot of his cot.

A tent was arranged to keep the covers from his body. He lay quietly. I thought at first he was sleeping, but his eyes were fixed on the ceiling.

"Merry Christmas," I said, holding out the purple chain.

He turned his head. "Merry Christmas, Oh-Be-Joyful's Daughter."

"You remembered my name."

"Yes, but I haven't had much occasion to use it. I drove you away. My outburst the other day—it came from anger that I can't always control. Anger that I'm caught up in events, tossed this way and that, and find myself a prisoner. The anger spilled out at you simply because you were good enough to talk to me. I am sorry. Can you forgive my boorishness?"

"I don't even recall what was said. My impression was that you were in pain."

"Pain." He shrugged impatiently. "Pain is no excuse."

"No," I said, "just an explanation. . . . You looked so thoughtful when I came in. Were you thinking of home?"

"We generally go skiing. Afterward there's eggnog and Brandy Alexanders with your feet in fur-lined carpet slippers, lolling in front of a fire, roasting chestnuts. Yes, I was thinking of home."

"We used to roast chestnuts too. That was part of our Christmas."

"I begin to think," he said slowly, "that the world is more alike than different."

"And war is old-fashioned and outmoded, and no one wants it anymore."

"No," my German enemy agreed, "no one wants it."

I tied the purple popcorn to the lamp and wandered into the basement to see if anything still needed doing. The staff was assembled and the hall was beginning to fill with groups of sailors and soldiers.

The music started, Sister Ursula at the piano and Dr. Goodwin playing a bass fiddle. In contrast to a few unhappy experiences at school, here I wasn't permitted to sit down. These boys wanted a girl to hold, to talk to. They told me about Maryanne, Aggie, Marie, Patty. The name of the girl kept changing, but they were the same girl.

Dr. Bennett was deep in an analysis of the war. He was explaining to Sister Mary Margaret the psychology behind the latest battle-front moves. "Hitler's egomania is beginning to work for us. He has fine generals, Rommel, for instance, a real professional. But the little madman doesn't listen to him. He doesn't listen to any of them. He knows better. Mark my words, that's the flaw in his character, the fatal flaw that's going to win us the war."

Once Dr. Bennett noticed me, there was no escape—he had found a new victim for his thesis and whirled me away. Dr. Bennett was one of those doctors whom the war had brought out of retirement, energized and given renewed purpose. We had only taken a turn or two when he was tapped on the shoulder and relinquished me to . . .

Crazy Dancer.

I made an effort to keep my feelings in check and said lightly, "This isn't happening. It isn't real."

"It is possible," he conceded, "to dream someone else's dream. But not this time."

"Are you here for an hour, a day, forever?"

"I'm here for the Christmas party." And he swept me into new patterns.

"I didn't know you knew how to ballroom dance. I thought you only danced with a corn-husk mask braided into horns, and stripes of paint on your cheeks."

"I can dance anywhere, anytime, anyplace."

The music called our feet and insinuated into our bodies. Crazy Dancer and I touched a star together.

The Christmas star on the tree was cut twice from silver paper and placed at right angles to itself so that the intersection made it appear to have another dimension. We stopped in front of it, breathless.

"I have a Christmas present for you." He rummaged in his pockets and came up with the gray and white feather off the motorcycle.

"You can't give me this, Crazy Dancer. It's your protection."

"You hold it now for both of us."

"You're sure?"

"I'm sure. That's why I came. I'm only here on a Christmas pass. I came because of what you wrote."

Desperately I tried to recall, to mentally scan my letters. Sometimes you write things you wouldn't necessarily say. Had I signed any of them, "Love, Kathy"? I didn't think so.

He jogged my memory, "The part where you said you missed me. . . ."

"Oh." I was relieved. "I did miss you."

"Missing," he said, "is a powerful wish. You wish someone is with you. Right?"

"Yes. . . ."

"So I came," he finished triumphantly.

I had to laugh at his absurdities. He was a clown who made very good sense.

Mandy, curious about him, dragged Robert over to meet Crazy Dancer.

"I know you already," Crazy Dancer told her. "Sometimes it was you who signed for supplies."

"Of course," Mandy said, placing him. "I thought you looked familiar. Are you posted back here now?"

"No. I came for the dance."

"You came to Montreal for a dance?"

Crazy Dancer shrugged. "—I'm a crazy dancer."

"Come on." I guided him toward the soft drinks and away from Mandy.

The dance broke up promptly at midnight with the traditional "Good Night, Ladies" waltz, and I went with him to the coatroom, where he got into a wool cap, muffler, boots, and a fur jacket. "The cold doesn't have room in the city to spread out. It's pushed together by all the buildings . . . and look what it makes!" He led me to the door and opened it.

Sudden cold, and I burrowed into his furs. There descended flashing bolts of color. The sky, prismatic, rained down pulsating sheets of light. We were part of the changing flamboyant purples, greens, and golds as they illuminated us.

"Don't forget to miss me." He left with a kiss that for me would always be part of the aurora borealis.

GRADUATION FOR THE senior class and the arrival of new student nurses marked my first year.

One of them arrived early. There were special circumstances attached to Emily Champlain coming a week ahead of the others. Emily was a small, dark, serious-minded French Canadian who had been reared by the Sisters of the Sacred Heart in their orphanage. She was past eighteen and they didn't know quite what to do with her. The war had placed a strain on their facilities and space was at a premium. Our nuns were appealed to and here she was.

The only experience she listed in her application was a summer working as an aide in a rundown mental institution for women.

Emily, as it turned out, was my first trainee. Since she had worked around schizophrenics, catatonics, and cyclomaniacs, it was decided to try her in our closed ward. This ward was intended to be a way station in which servicemen broken in mind were evaluated and sent on. In reality it was almost impossible to place these patients, as all suitable institutions were filled past capacity. So the Sisters accepted that the Lord meant this final burden for them, and took it on with what grace they could muster.

Matron Norris, a rather formidable person in her midfifties, was put in charge, and the closed ward became hers. She shared it grudgingly with the psychiatrist, Dr. Bloom, who visited whenever his schedule allowed, which was not too often. Matron Norris used him in lieu of the bogeyman: "We don't want Dr. Bloom to see this behavior, now, do we?" At times she simplified it to: "What would Dr. Bloom think?" Dr. Bloom was a strict Freudian, and I sometimes wondered if a childhood trauma could possibly be at the root of the disintegration of a soldier found cradling the torso of a buddy who had no head.

At any rate I was nominated to work alongside Emily so she wouldn't get into trouble. I showed her around. There was a large room and screened-in porch with bars, as well as a corridor dormitory and bathroom. Seeing these young men, listless, vacant, subject to sudden flashbacks, going suddenly manic, was enough to unnerve the most stable among us. I sized up Emily with some concern. She was so young, just a kid.

"I think the two of us will be able to manage a shift," I said cheerily. "What do you say?"

She looked a bit uncertain, taking in a soldier who roamed about agitatedly, berating an officer for calling in an airstrike using wrong coordinates. I pointed out a burly orderly posted at the door. "As a rule, Matron handles any disturbance. But—"

"*Mais oui,* it was *le meme*—the same—where I worked before."

"As a rule," I assured her, "everything goes along pretty well. The patients themselves are very helpful at times."

She nodded her neat dark head. "They have a way of knowing which will burst out, harm themselves, attack the others."

I was surprised at this insight, and thought she was probably right. "You like nursing, don't you?"

She brightened at once. "Oh yes. The Sisters at the convent always said, 'Take pride in your work. You cannot be a good person if you do not take pride in your work.' "

I nodded absently. She reminded me of myself a long time ago, last year in fact.

Matron Norris sat us both down and outlined our responsibilities. We were to patrol the rooms together and keep on the move, settling disputes, dispensing medication, in some cases feeding—the spoons in this ward were sometimes bitten through, their handles twisted or missing altogether.

Emily raised her hand, as though in a classroom, for permission to speak.

"Well?" the matron asked, not at all pleased by this interruption.

"At the Hotel des Femmes," Emily began in a small voice.

"What are you saying? Speak up, girl."

Emily cleared her throat and looked to me for support. But not knowing what was on her mind, I had to let her go it alone.

"At the Hotel des Femmes where I worked before, they gave the patients the responsibility."

"The patients!" Matron had heard quite enough. "My dear girl, the line between staff and patients is never to be blurred. I want you to remember that." She concluded the interview by saying that any violence on the ward was to be handled by the orderlies. If additional help was needed, there were the MP's. "On no account are you to involve yourselves. Is that quite clear?"

We sat before her and nodded dutifully.

"Oh, and Kathy, as the senior member of the team, I hold you accountable." She dismissed us with "Have a nice day."

But I felt out of sorts. It didn't seem fair to put me in charge and, at the same time, hem me in. Perhaps that's why I listened to Emily.

She hesitated, trying to gauge my reaction in advance, then plunged in, once more relating her experiences at the Hotel des Femmes. "The patients were given responsibility, n'est-ce pas? They themselves broke up fights, and did other useful tasks like . . ." She pondered it. "Like mend the radiator. Your radiators do not function properly," she ended triumphantly, as though that proved her case.

"No," I admitted ruefully, "they certainly don't."

"C'est très froid," and she shivered in her old patched sweater, but the next moment she was all business. "The matron Norris did not talk of suicide. Can we talk of suicide?"

"We try to keep watch on those patients that are acutely depressed," I said uncomfortably, "if that's what you mean."

"But someone, now and then, kills himself anyway. No?"

I admitted that happened. "We can't be everywhere."

"That is where the other system would help. We appoint a patient to watch. Each watches the other. C'est meilleur, two watchers instead of one of us. And those who watch, it gives them esteem of self."

"Importance," I said, liking the solution. But there were several big ifs. Matron for one. And the patients themselves for another—could we trust them? "We *are* terribly short-handed," I conceded.

Emily watched me struggle with the problem. "We'd be taking a chance," I said. "Matron Norris is old school, strictly by the book. If she found out, she'd put us on report. . . . It isn't that she isn't an excellent nurse," I finished. "She is."

"*Je comprends.*"

I knew she did, because her face assumed unhappy lines, and it helped me make up my mind. "Of course, the way I look at it there's no use bothering Matron with such a scatterbrained idea. But we can talk the plan over with the patients and see what they think of it."

"Oh, could we?" The mobile young face exuded sudden joy. The joy touched me.

I only hoped she didn't burn out. I had seen enthusiasm such as hers fade after a few weeks. However, Emily's underground system was worth trying. It didn't hurt anyone and it freed us for tasks we rarely got around to in the locked ward.

The men endorsed the plan whole-heartedly, partly, I think, because it was not officially sanctioned. But in spite of its adoption and even with Matron's disciplined calm, there were certain frenetic times on the ward, such as meals, baths, and bedtime. The bathroom in particular was a place of chaos. Lightbulbs were often smashed and the mirrors soaped, graffiti appeared above the urinals, and there were water fights. Matron always sent us in together to tackle the bathroom.

This evening cot 26 stuffed something into his mouth and was choking on it, so I bent him over and whacked his back. I hated leaving Emily alone and listened for any disturbance. But things sounded normal. My patient finally brought up a three-day-old dinner roll he must have hoarded under his pillow.

I got him into bed and hurried down the corridor to the bathroom.

Shock stopped me at the door. Emily Champlain had our resident catatonic arranged as a towel rack. His rigidly outstretched arms, which were impossible for any of us to move manually, were draped with towels for the men coming out of the shower, and his turned-up palms were soap dishes.

As luck would have it, Matron Norris had chosen this moment to conduct Dr. Bloom on one of his periodic inspections.

At the door she turned catatonic herself, and the good doctor, cyclomanic. He found his voice first and thundered, "How can you treat a human being this way?"

Emily looked stricken. I was about to come to her defense. It wasn't necessary. An eerie voice, rusty from disuse, came out of the towel rack. "On this ward, Doctor, everyone does his job."

At Matron Norris's request I was transferred from duty in the locked ward. I missed working with the innovative Emily and wondered how the patients would fare without the "system." I learned later that Emily herself lay low, but a patient committee met with Matron Norris and argued quite rationally that wartime conditions required wartime solutions. She acceded to patients' demands and reinstated a modified form of "responsibility therapy." I think she got as much pleasure hoodwinking Dr. Bloom as we did hoodwinking her.

THE NEXT MORNING I returned to my old beat and was checking the linen closet with Sister Magdalena, when through the open door to the ward I heard raised voices.

The patient next to the German lieutenant was on his good elbow talking to, or rather *at* von Kerll. Until last week we had kept the prisoners separate from the other patients. But casualties were coming in so fast that we were overwhelmed, and put newly admitted wounded wherever we could find a bed.

A French Canadian sailor, invalided from the Mediterranean theater, was being treated with sulfanilamide administered every four hours. He had responded so well that now here he was belligerently continuing the war.

"*Certainement*, U-boats are floating coffins, *c'est tout*. They're slow torpedo boats on the surface, slower underwater. Slower than a tug in harbor. Once you're submerged, you're pinned down, the easiest target in the world."

The German lieutenant started to defend his submarines, but the sailor cut him off, to heap scorn on the whole German war plan.

Sister Magdalena asked me to pay attention to the linen count, and insisted on adding those in my arms to the ones in the closet. "It doesn't seem to tally," she moaned, and went through it all again.

Meanwhile I tried to glean something of what the sailor was taunting von Kerll with. ". . . And your great Fuehrer with the Charlie Chaplin mustache, what does he know about strategy? He was a corporal in the last war. Okay, so you made a cemetery out of Russia. Winter's here. You know what a Russian winter did to Napoleon. Seen a paper lately? Well, the Russkies have what they call a 'scorched earth' policy. *Vraiment*, they're retreating, but they don't leave so much as a blade of grass for you Krauts. No electricity, no water, no food, no transport, not even a mule. They wreck their own rolling stock, and your trains don't fit their tracks. I'm telling you it was a celebration for us when the little corporal opened the Eastern Front."

Von Kerll retorted that the Axis didn't need Moscow. Capturing the Ukraine meant capturing Russia's breadbasket and controlling the oil reserves of Eastern Europe.

I had enjoyed our sailor giving the German what for. But now that von Kerll was matching him argument for argument, the Quebecois lost his temper. He cursed, first in French, then English, finally he tried German. But von Kerll laughed at his accent.

He became so infuriated that I thought I should intervene. Enough was enough. I left Sister Magdalena in the midst of matching sheets with pillowcases and marched in. "Able Seaman Duprez, I want to know what this means, fraternizing with the enemy."

"Fraternizing?" he sputtered and became so indignant that I was afraid he'd burst open his stitches. "I was just telling that Jerry officer how it really is, *non?* And which way things are going."

"You did a fine job. But now it's time for your shot and a little rest." I pulled the bleached muslin curtain along its track between the beds.

He wanted to continue his voluble defense, but I gave him a glass of water along with a lecture. "You get so worked up you're apt to do yourself damage. Lie back, that's it, and take it easy." I administered a hypo and read to him until he fell asleep. Then I went around to the other side of the curtain to see how my prisoner patient was doing.

I saw he had started a letter and put it aside.

"Can I give you a hand with that?" I asked.

"Yes," he laughed, "a right hand." His own had deep lacerations produced by metal splinters that penetrated the burn. "I'm afraid I'm awfully clumsy with my left."

I picked up the discarded page. "How stupid of me, it's in German."

"I'll start again in English."

"Who's the letter to? Your wife, your girl?" The question was routine. I asked it of everyone.

"I'm not married. At least I showed some sense there. Actually the letter is to my mother. To tell her I'm well and no part of me is missing. That's important. Mother sets a great deal of store on appearance. If I'd been maimed, or if my burns had reached my face, I don't think I'd go home."

"I'm sure you're wrong about that. There was an English boy, an amputee, who felt the same way. It was quite a struggle for him. But when he was discharged, he went home."

"He was brave, braver than I. But then he didn't have to confront the daughter of an Austrian vice admiral. You see, my mother's family is old. By comparison my father is an upstart. When I was a child we used to vacation at my grandparents' estate on the Bodensee. Austria is a land of lakes and that is the largest. Great bathing and boating."

I don't know when it stopped being routine—as he talked I could see a blond boy in a sailor suit wandering the shore, pitching stones, seeing how many times they skipped. More pictures formed. Novels from Old Irish Bill's library, romances by Wassermann, Thomas Mann, and Romain Rolland furnished the background. Gracious hotels looking out on ski runs, summer homes on the lake, picnics aboard the family yacht. And the daughter of this house, I imagined her too. Bobbed hair, of course, after the latest fashion; she'd be quite a beauty. Her little boy longed to climb into her lap, but no one took liberties with Elizabeth Madeleine Hintermeister von Kerll.

"Heinrich, the old gamekeeper, used to take me fishing. Have you ever had rainbow trout? Pike and grayling too. The finest fishing in Austria."

"You're Austrian? Not German?"

"We were annexed in '38, in preparation, I see now, for the war." He stopped, and went on again in an altered voice. "March eleventh at ten in the evening. On the thirteenth Hitler announced we were a province of the German Reich. You can see why. We are the third-largest producer of crude oil in Europe. And we have a modern airport at Wien-Schwechat near Vienna. You don't have to look further than that. The Nazis tore up our constitution. We became a German satellite overnight."

"But Hitler is Austrian himself, isn't he?"

"The house painter?" He snorted. "Yes, he is Austrian. So are the cattle in our barn, if being born on Austrian soil makes one Austrian. But the heritage is something different. Our Academy of Science goes back to the Middle Ages. Architecture, poetry, music, the Vienna waltzes and operettas of my grandparents' time. The Burgtheater is the best German-speaking theater on the continent, and then there's the Viennese Staatsoper, the state opera. Music was born in Vienna. Haydn, Mozart, Schubert, even the moderns, Schoenberg, and Alban Berg. And our museums have a wealth of Old Masters down to the cubist painter Oskar Kokoschka, who naturally has fled. But that's Austria, the heart and soul of her."

My mind had caught further back. All thought of a little blond boy throwing stones into the water disappeared. "It was a plebiscite," I said.

"What?"

"A month after the Germans took over Austria there was a plebiscite. Austria voted to go along, voted for the—what is it called?"

"The Anschluss." His voice had dropped so low I could scarcely hear him. The next minute he rallied. "You have to understand. It was called a plebiscite, it was supposed to be the will of the people. The will of the people was to live, and that was the only way we could manage it."

"Still, you left that part out."

"You're right. I apologize. I wasn't deliberately misrepresenting. I wanted you to see Austria as she had been, as I know her."

He spoke so sincerely that I relented a bit. It had not occurred to me that not all Germans or Austrians supported the war, that some, like Erich, were caught in its net.

In the days that followed, his Austria became very real to me. Years of reading . . . Schnitzler, Franz Werfel, Mann's magic mountain down which lovers skiied, made it easy to close my eyes and see a line of sloping meadows and craggy peaks rising behind them, smell forests of beech and larch, and the many streams sparkling their length like unwinding ribbons. To see the mighty Danube moving lazily, a water bridge from Germany to the Black Sea, where the snow of the valleys and the snow of the streams met.

He spoke of *Grunderjahre,* the good times, his life a procession of nursemaids and governesses, whom he ruled with the quick easy charm of his class. When he was nine a tutor was found for him, a tutor who was strict and knowledgeable in science and mathematics.

It had been decided, probably when he was in his first little sailor suit, that, like his father and grandfather, he would be commissioned in the navy. It was easy to picture him sailing his toy boats from the shore of the Bodensee.

The next time I dropped by to check on the malfunctioning Quebec heater in ward B, I found my two patients arguing violently about the war—this time it was the American Revolutionary War. Von Kerll was vigorously defending Benedict Arnold, who he claimed had been unforgivably snubbed, passed over, and insulted by jealous fellow officers.

"No excuse," Duprez declared hotly, "for stealing a cannon and bringing it with him when he defected."

I could see they enjoyed these mock battles so much, I was sorry to see the sailor go. His infection was cured and he was discharged, gleefully promising to visit von Kerll and keep him up to date on the number of U-boat coffins sunk.

I continued to keep my eye on the Quebec heater, which definitely needed surgery, and received further accounts of von Kerll's magical childhood. That bygone era was so glamorous, so far removed from anything I'd ever known. He had been at the Olympic Games in '33, heard Hitler officially declare them open, watched in amazement as the black American, Jesse Owens, sprinted to victory leaving the champions of the master race to eat his dust. "Only my father's warning glance kept me from exploding in laughter."

He talked of skiing in Cortina. Remembering the hot spiced mulled wine drunk afterward by a blazing fire was his way of dealing with skin grafts. I sat and listened because I knew the pain he was in. He told of climbs he'd made. "Class five-nine," he said with a touch of pride. "And at night, in one of those isolated mountain huts, sometimes I'd practice my English on a Brit, American, or Aussie. There's a special camaraderie among climbers. The nationality doesn't matter, just the mountain. The same goes for sailors."

With Erich it always got back to the sea.

"The sea runs in my veins like blood in other people's. In fact I am amazed to hear the way U-boats are referred to, as though they are inherently evil—We don't stand to, we *lurk*. We don't cruise the waters, we *infest* them like some sort of vermin. We don't pursue, we *stalk*."

His grin invited me to smile back. But I couldn't. U-boats did infest, they did lurk and stalk—and kill.

"Even aboard a sub, things aren't what people imagine. It can actually be enjoyable. I remember one occasion, patroling in the St. Lawrence." I gave a start. That was right here, home base.

He went on; perhaps he hadn't noticed. "I've been on it when we took a pounding from aircraft. But this particular day it was so quiet and peaceful that we cruised on the surface with the hatch open. To breathe fresh air was marvelous. And there was a tranquility over the scene.

"It was a crisp autumn morning, very early—about five or five-thirty. I remember a little cabin among pines, smoke curling already from its chimney. The captain called to me from the bridge, 'Looks like home, eh?' At which the engineer pipes up, 'In my hometown the baker lived in a little house just like that. He used to make Brötchen.' "

Erich looked over at me. "You've got to taste Brötchen sometime, it's a roll, very crusty. Freshly baked, it's part of the traditional German breakfast. . . . Slipping along between the banks of the St. Lawrence, that's what we thought of, not of war, not of pursuing or being pursued—but of those warm morning rolls and a mug of coffee or hot chocolate."

"You make it sound so normal," I said grudgingly. "A Sunday morning outing on the St. Lawrence. And torpedoes at the ready?"

"I'm just trying to say that one side isn't all white and the other totally black."

"It *is* totally black. Look around you at this ward."

This silenced him.

His dressings needed changing, all three, abdomen, thigh, and hand. No matter how delicately I went about peeling off the saturated gauze, his breathing quickened, and in a flood of words he began speaking of a great winding staircase with marble balustrade, along which slipped that shadow boy peering down at the party below—"I would sit still as a mouse on the stairs, looking into the music room while they put on amateur theatrics or a musical evening."

The dressing was off now, and he spoke more calmly, telling me that when he was older, he himself played at these concerts. He must play very well because his face softened and took on a distant expression when he spoke of music. "I wonder if I'll ever get this arm back to where I—" He broke off.

"Of course you will. You'll be starting physical therapy. If you're conscientious your arm will be as good as new."

But there was another skin graft to undergo, and to distract himself from the agony of the aftercare, he said very rapidly, his finger indenting the sheet, "I've made a study of boats. Boats of all kinds. But it's the history of the submarine I find most remarkable. Even the idea of a ship proceeding underwater is remarkable, don't you agree?"

Before I could answer he raced on. "Da Vinci designed an early prototype. But then, he designed the first of everything. The sub I like best is from the thirteenth century. Someone submerged himself in a huge glass bottle."

This effort was more than he could sustain. He converted a groan into a laugh, but he had to talk if he wasn't to disgrace himself and cry. "The first suggestion that came near being practical was when William Bourne, an Englishman, considered completely enclosing a boat and rowing it under water. That was never built. It was another forty years before a craft was actually constructed that could be rowed fifteen feet under water."

"What was that like?" I stepped back to let him know I was finished.

He drew a deep breath. "What was it like? Greased leather was stretched over the ship's frame with close-fitting flaps for the oars."

"Those early inventors must have asked themselves what-if a million times."

"What did you say?" he asked, puzzled.

"Nothing." I was suddenly embarrassed. For I had been thinking how extraordinary it was that an Indian girl from Alberta should come to know the history of early submarines. Too bad that fantastic ideas such as glass bottles had to end in worldwide war and destruction.

*S*even

WHEN I GOT back to my room Mandy was sitting on the edge of her bed waiting for me. "You're late again tonight, Kathy."

"You're a fine one to talk. I haven't seen you back here this early in weeks."

"What have you been doing?" It was not said casually, but in an accusatory manner.

"Nothing. Writing a few letters for the men."

"For a particular one, don't you mean? An officer off a U-boat. Kathy, you're spending too much time with him. People are beginning to talk."

"That's nonsense, you're imagining it."

"I'm not. It was brought to my attention and not in a nice way either."

I couldn't believe what I was hearing. "Mandy, if you're talking about Erich von Kerll, he's a patient. He can't use his right hand, so I'm writing home for him. I don't think I'm breaking any international laws or codes of conduct."

"Still, you must consider how it looks."

"I don't care how it looks. I consider it part of my duties as a nurse. Besides, what I do on my own time is my business."

"People are talking, Kathy."

"Let them."

"Have it your way. Knowing you, I know there's nothing wrong with it. Still, it does seem funny, spending so much time with a German."

"He's not German, he's Austrian."

"Big difference," she said with a shrug. "Besides, why be mad at me? I'm just trying to be a friend, letting you know what the scuttlebutt is."

"I'm not mad at you. I'm just telling you not to pay any attention to that kind of petty gossip."

Was it the reflection in Mandy's glasses that gave her a speculative look? "He's the third bed on ward B, isn't he?"

"Yes," I said shortly.

"I thought so. The good-looking one. No wonder they're talking."

Was he? Was he good-looking? I'd been afraid to make such an assessment myself.

"Don't pretend you hadn't noticed." Then a note of real concern stole into her voice. She was no longer passing along other people's opinion but focused on her own. "You've got to remember, Kathy, he's European. Austrian, German, it doesn't matter. They're a lot more traditional than we are."

"What do you mean, traditional?"

"I guess I mean bigoted. I don't want you to be hurt, Kathy."

"Because I'm Indian? Is that what this is about? Mandy, you are so wrong. Things aren't on a personal basis."

"Are you sure?" She peered at me intently and there was no way I could any longer misinterpret the anxiety of her glance.

"Mandy, you think I don't realize the difference between Erich and me? His grandparents have an estate on the Bodensee. It goes right down to the water's edge. He had his own sailboat when he was nine." I stopped abruptly. "I'm not crazy, Mandy."

"But you *are*. You're reckless, like me, when you love. So I had to make sure you weren't edging that way."

Her glasses looked a little misty to me. I diverted her with Erich's stories of early submarines. "Did you know they once sent someone down in a bottle? Then they tried rowing along the bottom."

She started laughing when I told her about the model they built with wheels to roll along the ocean floor. "There's an American version too, the *Turtle,* in the shape of a walnut standing on end."

I had succeeded in distracting Mandy and making her laugh. But I took seriously the fact that I was the subject of criticism. Did they think that while U-boats were sinking our ships, drowning our men, I had been discussing submarine warfare with an enemy?

I was horrified that such an interpretation had been put on our talks, and I searched my mind. Had I been guilty of indiscretion? I felt confused. At the same time, angry. I was not doing my country any harm. Who did I hurt by absorbing the life of an Austria that didn't exist anymore? I had only been listening to an outdated chapter of history.

As for Mandy's fear that I was becoming interested in him—of course that was nonsense.

I WENT AGAIN after chapel Sunday to visit Erich, but I didn't offer to write letters and I didn't stay long. Just long enough to let whoever was concerned know I wasn't intimidated by gossip.

And long enough to settle the question of his appearance for myself. His features were finely drawn, yet there was strength in them. His light brown hair fell forward over his forehead in a boyish manner. But his mouth was set in too hard a line as though he was watchful and on guard. I suppose he was. After all, he was a prisoner and an enemy. And yes . . . he was good-looking.

Why hadn't I noticed that immediately? Or had I, and not wanted to complicate things by thinking it? It took a world war for my kind and his to meet and talk. And I mustn't forget it.

I began to doubt that it had all been as innocent as I pretended. Had I been attracted to him from the beginning, in spite of professional ethics? In spite of a chasm of differences between us?

Mandy had been a friend after all, and quite right to point out the danger I'd been headed for. I would keep this and every other visit short and impersonal and never speak of submarines again, even if they were thirteenth-century glass bottles.

He watched as I straightened the things on his night table, gave him medication, and turned to go. "Must you leave so soon?" He hurried on, I think to prevent my leaving. "I received a Red Cross package today. Amazing when you think of all the frontiers on both sides it had to pass through."

"Was it from home?"

"My parents received the customary letter from submarine command: 'missing in action.' "

"What a shock that must have been. I'm so sorry."

He regarded me levelly; his gray eyes held a question, but he didn't ask it. Instead he said, "I've been awarded the Iron Cross."

"Oh." I could hardly congratulate him. The pause was awkward. "It must be a relief to your family to know you're alive."

He nodded. "I wonder if they'll get the letter you wrote for me before the war ends?"

"I'm sure they will."

"I don't know. I haven't seen a newspaper or heard the radio since I've been here. We were supposed to be winning the war. It was supposed to be over by now. Is it possible that we will lose? I never considered that might happen. What would it mean for Austria? Would my father's party, the old Social Democrats, regain its position, I wonder?"

His talk of war and politics made me nervous. "Is there anything I can do for you before I go?"

He pulled himself from revery to the present.

"Are you meeting someone? A young man? Is that why you're dressed up and look so pretty?"

"Goodbye, Erich."

"Kathy, I'm sorry. Please forgive me. I haven't much to do except lie here and think. I think about you a lot. I wonder what it's like to be an Indian in Canada."

"Not now, Erich."

"Is your young man white or Indian?"

"I don't have a young man. He's Indian," I said over my shoulder as I left the room. I was so flustered that I ran into Sister Magdalena. "Sorry," I muttered.

IT WAS UNSETTLING to have claimed Crazy Dancer as my young man.

Was that how I thought of him? But I hardly knew him. In fact I very much doubted that anyone could know him. And my mind rocketed between two worlds. The only thing they had in common was that both were insubstantial. The pictures in my mind were of an idealized courtly life on the shores of the Bodensee, where Erich played American jazz records till morning. Which didn't stop him clicking his heels and bowing over the hands of ladies. These fragments broke and distorted as pounding moccasined feet trampled them into shards.

But it isn't possible to have a meaningful relationship with someone you see only intermittently. And it had been almost four months. Spring was trying to burst out of its frozen straightjacket, buds were thrusting tentatively but the coldness of the air nipped them back.

It was grand walking weather, and I returned to my room for a sweater. A walk would help clear my mind. I had to sort out my feelings, put things in order. But when I returned to my room it was to find a crisis. Mandy didn't know it was a crisis, but looking at her I knew instantly.

Mandy was dabbing hydrogen peroxide on her hair.

"What are you doing?" I asked, taking the bottle from her and checking the label.

"I thought I'd put some blond highlights in my hair."

"Mandy, this isn't that kind of peroxide. It's medicinal."

"I guess you're right. It hasn't made any difference."

"Just wait," I said.

In half an hour bleached white streaks appeared. Mandy flew about the room tearing at it as if she could tear it out.

"What will I do?" she wept.

"Sit down," I said, and began to brush her hair from underneath where the peroxide hadn't penetrated. The strands blended and, to finish the job, I set her nurse's cap on her head.

"Oh, Kathy," she exclaimed, surveying herself in the mirror, "you saved my life."

I smiled at her extravagance.

"At least you saved me from a tongue-lashing by Sister Ursula."

I agreed that was quite likely.

I took my sweater from the hook on the back of the door and went for the walk I'd decided on earlier. I got as far as the parking lot, when there was a cacophony of sound as a car horn was depressed again and again. I looked over at the distraction and saw it was aimed at me. I stood still, my mind not registering what I saw.

Crazy Dancer leaped from a decrepit car, leaving the door ajar.

"Is it you? I can't believe it."

"I came for our date."

"What date?"

"The one we made last June, the Moon When the Ponies Shed—" He burst out laughing. "I put in for a transfer, and it finally came through."

He looked so jaunty standing there that I joined in the laugh. "I was just thinking about you, and you turn up."

"Were you thinking that Christmas was a long time ago?"

"Something like that."

"I was thinking the same thing."

I walked over to the car. "What happened to the motorcycle?"

"You said you wanted four wheels. So I made a trade."

I surveyed his acquisition somewhat dubiously.

"It's in good running condition," he assured me.

"What about gas?"

His face lit up—he'd been waiting for me to ask. "It doesn't run on gas. Well, just to get it started. Look at this."

I walked around to the driver's side with him. He opened the hood and pointed out a nest of metal tubing and what looked like a second carburetor. "It runs on a mixture of kerosine and gasoline. Mostly kerosine. There's a separate throttle that feeds the kerosine into the engine."

"It won't explode, will it?"

His smile was teasing. "Do you still have the gray and white feather?"

I nodded. "Well, as you say," I conceded, "it has four wheels."

He came around with me while I got in, then walked back to the driver's side. He fiddled with the controls and the engine started up. It sounded just as an engine should and I hoped it would behave like one.

Crazy Dancer shifted his feet. "Here we go!"

As we pulled out of the parking lot I asked, "And it's running on kerosine?"

"You bet."

"Why doesn't everyone use such a device?"

"It's not legal."

I absorbed this a moment, then said, "You're very good at adapting the white man's inventions."

"Pretty good," he admitted.

"You should meet Georges. He likes to fool around with motors, but he isn't as good as you are."

"Georges is your brother?"

"Yes, he's Connie's twin."

"You didn't tell me they were twins."

"I didn't?"

"Twins. Did you know that everything of importance in the world is a twin? Rain is the twin of sun. Mountains the twin of valleys. Hot is the twin of cold. Good the twin of bad. Which is he?"

"What do you mean, which is he?"

"The good or the bad, the left-handed or the right-handed?"

"They're both right-handed."

"That can't be. The right-handed bring berries, fruit, and flowers to the world. The left-handed, nettles and briars. The right hand made all the animals except the grizzly. The left hand made the grizzly to kill the rest of them."

"A fairy tale!"

He shook his head. "Twins balance the world."

"The world doesn't seem very balanced to me."

He looked troubled. "The Grandfathers never dreamed this world. Perhaps it is as you say, fairy tales."

He seemed so dejected at this possibility that I said, "I didn't mean *everything,* only that my twins are both right-handed."

"Perhaps," he probed the question, "it is different with white twins." This explanation restored his spirits.

We were driving past some of the ugliest scenery I had ever seen, acres of nothing but railroad tracks, freight cars, and switch engines.

"Where are we?" I demanded.

"These railway yards are what keeps Montreal in business, and fed also."

We were bound, he told me, for Ile Perrot at the confluence of the St. Lawrence and the Ottawa, with only primitive and deserted dirt roads.

"You picked a rough place to drive."

"No," he said, "it's for you to drive." He stopped the car and insisted I change places with him. "It's your turn," he encouraged.

"I don't drive."

"I thought so. I was testing you out on some of those curves back there."

"What do you mean?"

"I purposely came up to them too fast. If you drove, you'd automatically press your foot to the floorboard like it was a brake. And that's your first lesson. You don't speed up approaching a curve. You speed up *in* the curve. That way centrifugal force gives you more traction, especially if the curve is banked."

I thanked him for the lesson and wondered what was next. It turned out the second lesson was to get the feel of the car, know where it was on the road.

"Most drivers haven't the faintest idea where their wheels are, how close to the shoulder, how close to the dividing line. They make left turns too flat, and they can't back into a parking space unless it's the size of an eighteen-wheeler because they don't know where their wheels are."

I began to protest. "This is supposed to be a fun date." He replied there was nothing more fun in the world than driving, if you knew what you were doing. He said it was like dancing, only with wheels instead of feet.

I made a last attempt to get out of it. "If I'm going to learn, it ought to be on a regular car, not one with two gas pedals."

He brushed this aside. "Start the engine on gas, and all you have to worry about is the kerosine pedal. The trick is to go slow, stay in first, and know exactly where your wheels are." To practice this he fished out of the trunk some beat-up highway cones swiped from a construction job, and laid out a mille miglia on that country road.

Crazy Dancer was right. It was fun doing a slow-motion ballet with an automobile, knocking over cones in the beginning but finally squeezing through them. Until I got the hang of the clutch, I achieved some nasty jerks and stalls. However, I braced myself against the wheel and had the satisfaction of seeing Crazy Dancer get the bumps. He took it gamely, encouraging me with a soft patter of praise, and only when we were headed for a boulder did he grab the wheel.

"A little practice in the city, and you can get your license."

He came by the following day to give me a short course in engine maintenance and how to hot-wire the ignition in case I forgot my keys. We disassembled and reassembled the two carburetors half a dozen times and checked the tubing before he was satisfied. The fuel pump was the next order of business, then how to jump-start a dead battery. Belts and hoses were Crazy Dancer's particular joys, mainly because on this jalopy they were always slipping, wearing out, or leaking.

At the end of the session, with dusk settling in, he sent me back to take notes and draw diagrams. I'd become pretty good at this in my anatomy course and mentally substituted engine parts for body organs. The fuel pump was a heart. Air intake and carburetor were bronchi and lungs. Transmission was muscle, and electrical system, nerves.

Our next date I showed Crazy Dancer my sketches. He was delighted and gave me a crash course in sectioning and dimensioning. I got covered with oil and the muck under the hood, but that wasn't much different from an operating table.

To crown my success Crazy Dancer announced I was ready for the last and final test. It turned out this was to drive an army truck, which a buddy of his had parked up a side street. Other than the fact that everything was outsized, I had no trouble. My reward was a big hug and an old grease-stained race driver's cap which he set on my head.

Back at the wheel of his own car, he drove us out to the Ile Perrot.

"You know," he told me, "I think you are three things: a spider, a turtle, and a lark."

"Is that good?"

"Very good. A spider is industrious. *You* work all day at the hospital. A turtle is wise. *You* ask questions. A lark is sweet singing and happy. *You* are Oh-Be-Joyful's Daughter."

"Yes, but I have to remind myself that I am. That I should try to be."

Crazy Dancer thought about this and did not like it. "No, trying won't do it. You *let* yourself be joyful."

"And if I'm not?"

"Then I'm here to help."

He waited expectantly for my answer. "I don't know, Crazy Dancer. We're so different."

"And so alike. We are more alike than you think."

"I was raised white and I'm trying to learn to be more Indian. You were raised Indian and you would like a piece of the white world."

"I like their cars and their motorcycles. I like engines. But the whites themselves? Sometimes I think they hate everything. They hate the animals and move into their hunting grounds. They hate the forests and cover even the grass, paving it until not a blade shows. They hate water, and spill oil and wastes into it. They even hate air and make it thick with smoke."

"They make war on everything," I agreed.

He nodded sagely. "It is the reason we have two souls."

"People have two souls?"

"You didn't know that? One is linked to the body. The other is your free soul, the one you send into dreams."

"I was sent a dream once, when Papa Mike died."

"Did you know that a soul can get lost in a dream?"

In spite of myself I felt alarm. "Is that true?"

"Sometimes it runs away on purpose. Then a shaman goes after it to bring it back."

"I can understand why it would run away. You can dream so many more beautiful and interesting things than just the ordinary everyday things around you."

Crazy Dancer frowned at me with a stern expression. "Nothing is ordinary. Nothing is everyday. You need practice in how to look.

I have taken you to where the forest comes down to the sea. Let's walk awhile and I'll show you what I mean."

He stopped the car and gave it a little pat. "It did well, don't you think?"

"Yes, very well. You could patent your invention—if it were legal, that is."

He walked ahead of me. Here on the island the trees seemed to grow from bald rock. "We make an earth walk," he said. "I will teach you how to look. First, at this." He rubbed the frost from a boulder with his sleeve. "Once I found a shell in its deepest crease. At one time, I think, the sea covered it. And over here"—he sprang lightly, rock to rock—"here is a tracing, an imprint in the granite itself, made by a piece of fern in the before time. Observe the pines: each has its own pattern on its bark, made by winds, snows, rains, and flowing sap. See the down-drooping needles of the hemlock and the straight spurs of the pines. Now see last year's nest in that one."

"Where?"

Our feet crunched on the last snow patches. At the edges they were melting.

"Where I'm pointing. It was a martin's. Now," he said, "close your eyes and listen to the voice of the forest. Hear the buzz of gnats, the crickets' chirp, the deep note of the bullfrog, the rustling of baby quail. That raucous cry is a jay. These sounds tell you that the forest belongs to anyone who can see and hear and breathe it."

"Is that true for the whole world? How rich I feel!"

He threw back his head and laughed. When he lowered his face to mine, I was conscious of him as I never had been of anyone before. Tamarack, pine, and hemlock were part of him, and a man's scent. I knew I was going to be kissed in a way I never had been kissed.

My eyes closed. Somehow I knew his closed too as he tasted my return kiss. For my arms had gone around him. My free soul climbed out of me into him.

When he stepped back we looked a long time at each other. Each was thinking, Is this the person I love? I wanted it to be Crazy Dancer and he wanted it to be me. But was it?

"Let's go back," I said.

On the return trip we were both rather silent. That kiss I think had been as much of a surprise and shock for him as it had for me. And he too was trying to evaluate it.

He took me to the nurses' entrance but didn't kiss me again. I thought he would, but he didn't. Of course, he was Indian; he had never heard of the custom of the goodnight kiss that white girls granted white boys when they had a nice time. I remember Mama Kathy telling Connie, "Some boys try to persuade you they're entitled to more, but they're not. They've had the pleasure of your company."

I laughed at this, knowing Mandy had allowed Robert much more than the goodnight kiss. Before I was even in the door I was looking forward to next Sunday. And, what was best of all, all week I was Oh-Be-Joyful's Daughter.

FOR SOME REASON the rich images Erich Helmut von Kerll stirred my imagination with no longer made an impression. The childhood he spoke of seemed remote and alien. In fact it seemed a bit artificial. Winters he skied at Cortina del Ampezzo just across the border, where the Hapsburgs' hunting lodge had been. In his parents' time it was turned into a fashionable hotel. He described the tiled stove going to the ceiling with beds built into it on either side to keep warm on winter nights, and fluffy eiderdown quilts to snuggle into.

It was vivid, as portraiture is vivid, but no longer real. A good book was more alive, and at night I turned pages, reading after lights-out by flashlight. Still, I enjoyed Erich's account of the Lippizaners, which he rode in the fall. I could picture him stiff in the saddle, hard hat on his head. I'd seen a picture once in a magazine, a red jacket with black velvet collar, silk ascot, and shiny boots. He'd have a riding crop under his arm.

Then I pictured Crazy Dancer, bareback, bare-legged, hair flying, laughing wildly. And I placed myself behind him, holding him tight as I had on the motorcycle. That motorcycle had had some good features after all.

"You seem so distant," Erich said, "so far away—so happy," he added ruefully.

This brought me out of my daydream reminiscence. "You'll be pleased to know that you're doing so much better that the doctors are thinking of releasing you."

"To prison," was the morose reply.

"It's not a prison. It's a big warehouse that they've converted into a detention center. Lots of prisoners are coming in now. Italian as well as German."

"More than before?"

"Yes, many more. If you count all Canada, there must be thousands."

"So many? Has the tide shifted, then? I don't ask you," he added hastily. "I speak to myself. It's the damn second front, the Eastern Front, just as that little French Canadian said. I am a patriot, Kathy, a good Austrian. Yet if it would shorten the war, even to lose is acceptable. . . . *Gott im Himmel,* my father would shoot me like a dog if he heard me talk this way. And he'd be right." He turned away and flung his arm across his eyes.

"I'm sorry, Erich."

He turned back then, the same unhappy smile on his face. "Tell me about yourself, Kathy. What's it like to be an Indian in Canada?"

"You asked me that before."

"Did I? Oh, God, I don't want to be stuck in a warehouse full of Nazis."

"The war won't last forever, and you'll be going home."

His smile had disturbed me, but now that it was gone there were deep lines in his face. "If you meant to make me feel better, you haven't."

"Sorry."

"That's because the hard part will be not seeing you."

"Thank you. That's very nice."

"I didn't say it to be nice. I don't speak from politeness. I look forward to your visits. They're the only thing I have to look forward to."

"I must tell you I've been criticized for spending so much time with you." I had spoken impulsively. If I could have taken back my words, I would.

He regarded me with an intent probing expression. "And yet you do. Why?"

"Your stories. Mama Kathy used to tell me stories. Then I took over and told them too. But yours are much more interesting. I can picture it all—so elegant, so far removed from my own life or anything I know."

"And that's it?"

"What do you mean? Of course that's it."

"You'll have to forgive me," he said hoarsely. "I'm in love with my nurse. Just like all the others. How many offers of marriage have you had?"

I laughed, but I knew underneath we were both serious. "Less than a dozen this week," I joked, realizing it sounded forced, that I was trying too hard to keep the conversation to something we could manage.

He tugged at a black onyx ring on his finger, pulled it off, and put it in my hand. "In case I don't see you again."

There was a diamond centered in the onyx. I drew away, leaving the ring between us on the covers.

"Think of it as a war trophy, like a German helmet."

"Don't be cruel," I said, closing my hand because he had picked the ring up once more.

"Don't *you*," he whispered.

I turned away and somehow got out of the room. It wasn't until that evening I found the ring in my pocket.

WHEN I CAME on duty next day I discovered Lieutenant Erich von Kerll had been discharged to the general war prisoner population. I flipped through his chart. The skin grafts had taken, and the areas on his hand, thigh, and abdomen were healed.

I didn't know what to do about the ring. I'd planned on returning it to him that morning. Now I didn't know what to do. I couldn't send a valuable ring through the mail. But I didn't know when or even if I would see him again. Connie had described her engagement ring to me in detail, a raised center diamond surrounded by chips, one for each month they had known each other.

A soldier was brought in suffering from shock and internal bleeding. I transfused two pints of whole blood. And so it went.

I grabbed a bite of lunch with Mandy. I told her about the pneumonia case. We'd had to do a tracheotomy on him, and, as Dr. Bennett closed, the patient stopped breathing. "I wrote a letter for him last week, Mandy. He lived on the Bodensee."

"I thought he lived on a farm with his mum."

That gave me a jolt. Why had that slipped out? Why had I mentioned the Bodensee?

No one expected him to stop breathing; he hadn't seemed critical. The EKG went flat. I willed him not to die.

The floor was mopped, the mop ran over my shoe. Linens were changed; doctors continued rounds; nurses dispensed medicine; cot 9's body, covered with a sheet, was lifted to a gurney. I helped in this and watched it wheeled out the double doors. It was happening in another plane, another slice of time. I wanted to take it up with Sister, complain to staff . . . no one should die when they're nineteen.

By 3:30 my feet hurt and my back ached, and there were still two hours to put in. When my shift finally ended, I decided to forget supper, fall into bed, and sleep the clock around.

Someone was sitting in shadows in the corner of my room. "Don't put on the light," someone said.

"Mandy?" I asked uncertainly.

A shaky intake of breath answered me.

"Mandy." I crossed the room to her. She lifted her face and even in the dim light I could see her cheek was swollen and discolored, her eye puffing and closed.

I was so shocked I couldn't speak.

"I hate him."

I think that's what she said, for she could barely articulate.

"Who, Mandy? Was it Robert? What happened?"

"I'm in terrible trouble, Kathy."

"No, you're not, I won't let him near you."

She shook her head and began crying. "It's not that. It's me. It's what I've done. Oh, Kathy, I'm going to get pitched out on my ear."

"What happened?" I asked again.

She tried to tell me, backed up and started again. My heart turned stone cold: It had to do with drugs. Mandy had been stealing drugs.

She was telling it between dry, hacking sobs, but I already knew. She'd tried to back out and he'd sent this goon after her.

"There was a message from Robert. I was to meet him. We always meet in the park, and he knew I took this shortcut through the alley. Well, this, this man sprang out at me. He had a stocking cap over his face, but I think he might be one of those guys that hang out at the casino. I thought he was going to kill me or rape me. Kathy, no one's ever deliberately hurt me before. He punched me to the ground. . . ."

I tried to calm her. "What about the drugs? When did you start taking them?"

"It was such a stupid thing to do. It started with this osteomyelitis case, a patient Robert had grown fond of. I told you how he empathized. Well, he thought the boy needed more medication than was being prescribed. And the boy himself carried on. Nerve damage, you know, there's no pain like it. Robert kept after me to pinch a couple of grams of morphine. So, stupid me, I saw an opportunity and took some. I thought it was just that once, that the boy would get better and not need it, or . . . you know, die.

"But Robert came to me again. I didn't know what to do. I told him it was too risky, but he kept on and on about it. Finally I agreed and looked for another chance. I was almost caught. Sister Mary Margaret came in unexpectedly and I hid behind those sacks at the back of the storeroom. I was so scared. I swore never to do it again. But Robert convinced me it was humane, the right thing. Only, only . . . the boy was transferred to a neurological center in Boston.

"Robert didn't tell me; I heard the girls talking. That's when I realized—the boy had nothing to do with it, or very little. It was money. He'd lost money, he told me that much, and he borrowed. Kathy, I'm sure it's those people at the casino. They won't stop at anything. They're pressuring him to repay. I know that's what it is." She choked on tears. "Maybe it started with the boy, I don't know. But it's over the gambling. He'd never had money before, and he threw it around. It's my fault too, I didn't ask where it came from. . . . Then the tide turned. He started to lose. He knows how rough those people play and he's terrified. That hurts the most—instead of confiding in me, he sicked this lowlife on me."

I didn't know how to comfort or reassure her.

"They suckered him in, Kathy."

Sin city, Mama had said. "Could you describe the man who did this?"

Mandy shook her head. "I told you, he had a stocking cap over his face."

"But height? Weight? Was he French?"

"Medium height, medium build. And as far as being French, he didn't say anything."

"So there's no way you could identify him?"

She hesitated. "By his hair. He smelled of hair tonic."

"Brilliantine," I said, placing him.

"I'm so ashamed and so frightened," Mandy said into her hands. "Do you think the Sisters will find out?"

I hesitated, but there was no avoiding the truth. "When they take inventory the count won't match."

Of course Mandy knew this. Elongated moments passed between us. Then she began speaking very fast. "I thought maybe you'd fudge it for me. You know, *make* it come out. I hate to ask, but I don't see any other way."

"No, Mandy, I won't do it." I saw immediately that she had expected to talk me around. She'd have to have come from my background to know what being a nurse meant to me. It's not only a career. It's having a place in the world.

"Don't refuse. Don't say no, Kathy."

"I'm not even on that service. It's been months since I worked in the dispensary."

"They're always short-handed. You could request it."

"And then alter the books? No, Mandy."

Another pause filled with unuttered argument. "I'd do it for you."

"Then you'd be very foolish. What I *will* do is get to work on this face of yours. We need ice to bring the swelling down."

"No." She drew away from me. "Either you're my friend and help me, or you're not."

"You're not thinking straight, Mandy. They'll come after Robert again. He can't stall. He's got to pay up. And the only way he can do it is through the drugs. He's going to sic this Frankie on you again."

"Frankie?" Her hand grasped mine in a paroxysm of fear.

"Yes, the name came back to me. There's no question that's who it is. The brilliantine gave him away. I saw him huddled with Robert at the casino."

"I remember. Every time I looked up, he was watching me. You really think he'll come after me again?"

"If you don't give them what they want, yes, I do."

"Robert knows I won't continue."

"He doesn't know anything of the sort. He knows that this one beating didn't force you into it. The threat of more might."

"And he'd be right." Mandy grabbed both my hands. "I couldn't go through this again. Kathy, I loved him. That's the worst part, that Robert is behind this."

I could see the croupier bending forward, raking in the chips, *le rouge et le noir.*

$\mathcal{E}$ight

A TRAVELING FAIR was in town. A few stubbled fields had been transformed with whirligig rides that featured a Ferris wheel and calliope. On the Ferris wheel Crazy Dancer held my hand. On the rocket ride he put his arm around me.

The best part was having our picture taken sitting on the moon. Crazy Dancer studied the small strip of pictures carefully. "Many older Mohawks still won't have their picture taken. They believe that this"—he waved the pictures—"can catch their soul." His voice dropped to a whisper. "If that's so, then I give mine to you and keep yours in return." And he divided the pictures between us.

We strolled past tents and sideshows arm in arm. He bought us cotton candy that dissolved into sticky pink sugar as we ate them down to their paper cones. We passed along a row of flag-draped booths, the Canadian Red Ensign, the French Tricoleur, the Union Jack, and the Stars and Stripes. Crazy Dancer stopped to throw balls at a target of moving ducks. We walked on arm in arm. It was almost dusk. No lights were allowed to show, and the carny was closing down. I hadn't realized we had left it behind until we were surrounded.

A gang of French Canadian toughs began taunting us from behind one of the outlying wagons, telling us to go home to the reservation. One of them came toward us. I saw to my horror he had a gun. He was quite drunk and, going up to Crazy Dancer, kept sticking it in his ribs and telling him to fork over his money.

Crazy Dancer pretended not to understand his accent, and asked politely if he would mind repeating what he had said. The guy repeated his demand for money, but Crazy Dancer only shook his head. "Sorry, I still don't understand. What is it you want?"

The gun was twisted in his side. "Money, you dumb Indian. Money. You understand money, no?"

Crazy Dancer seemed to make a great effort. "You lost money? In that case we must look for it. Where can it be?" And he jumped on top of a packing case and peered through the slats. "Not here." Then, throwing himself at air, he did a complete somersault, landing on a side rail that had been stowed out of the way on top of the crates. He walked this backward, pretending to look to the right and then the left for money. He felt in his own pockets and shook his head. "Not there."

A series of flips landed him on the roof of the wagon, and the next second in the midst of the dumbfounded trio. Pulling off the cap of one of them, as though he still looked for money, he exchanged it for another cap, ramming the first on a totally different head. They stared blankly at him. Crazy Dancer pirouetted madly, cartwheeled exuberantly, and, uttering ear-splitting Mohawk war whoops, began to weave in and out, behind and in front and through them.

"This guy is *fou!*"

"Berserk."

"Crazy, man, he's crazy."

"I'm out of here, *tout de suite.*"

"Crazy Dancer," Crazy Dancer announced, taking a bow.

There was no applause. They ran, and I was still shaking from the encounter. "What a performance. My God, you really can dance. It was unbelievable. When you yanked off that guy's hat I thought it was the end of us. But why didn't you give them money? Wouldn't that have been easier? They might have killed you."

"It is a lesson from when I was young, that many times if you do not recognize evil, it goes away. Just as they are going now."

"So you *did* understand what they were saying?"

"The gun in my side made it very plain." He waited for this to sink in. "Sometimes you ignore evil," he explained. "Sometimes you dance to calm it down, and sometimes you make a game and ask evil to join in."

When I asked Crazy Dancer how he knew which to do, he replied, "How do you know which medicine to give?"

"The doctor writes a prescription," I started to say—when it struck me. Crazy Dancer was the prescription for Mandy. It was Crazy Dancer, crazy and fearless, who would bring Frankie into line.

"I need a favor, Crazy Dancer."

"It's not every person I've sat on the moon with," he replied.

I told him about Mandy, all he needed to know. "Her boyfriend had her beaten up, and she's afraid the same goon will come after her again. Could you stop him?"

He considered this only a moment. "In the days of the buffalo a warrior like me would take his hair, a trick we learned from the French."

"And today?"

"Does he work at the hospital?"

"No. He hangs out at the casino. His name's Frankie."

Crazy Dancer clapped his hand to his forehead. "I know him. He stinks of hair tonic. This will be a pleasure," he added. The relish of his tone alarmed me.

"I hope you'll be careful." I said this, wondering if I should have involved him, because I knew very well *careful* was not in his vocabulary.

A PERSON BURST into our room, a person whose tight curly hair glistened with brilliantine. No men were allowed on the floor, but here he was, disheveled and wild looking, yelling. "Call them off, call them off and we're quits."

I reached out and put my hand on Mandy's arm. She had to stand her ground. She had to face down her attacker.

But I was the one he confronted. "Call off the shadows," he said distractedly, "and I'll do anything you want."

"I don't know what you're talking about."

"Oh you know, you know all right. Indian shadows dancing on my walls, and drums and bells clanging in my head. But when I open the door no one is there . . . nothing is there. I might have thought

I'd dreamed it, but this is real enough." He took a tomahawk from under his jacket. "What do you say? Is it yours?"

"No."

"Don't give me that. It's real and it belongs to a real person. No ghost."

"You're right about that."

"Then you know who it belongs to?"

"Yes," I said.

"And it's no ghost, no shadow? It belongs to someone who's going to use it."

"Maybe not. If he uses a tomahawk on you he goes to jail. If he uses ghost dancers there will be no mark on your body."

"Look, this could all be in my head. I don't care whether it is or not. I want it to stop."

"It will stop if you don't come near Mandy or threaten her or let her be threatened again."

Frankie, for that's who it was, fingered the edge of the tomahawk. "This is the end of it?"

"It can be if you stay away from her."

"I woke up this morning with this thing beside my head on the pillow. I don't know how it got there. I don't know how he got into my room. That crazy dancing was bad enough, a war dance with godawful screeches. But a shadow is just a shadow. I figure the tomahawk is something else, it's for killing, and that now he's threatening to kill me."

"I would read it like that," I agreed.

"But it's over? The Indian magic or whatever it was is over, right?"

"It's up to you."

"If it's up to me, it's over."

BUT IT WASN'T up to him, not entirely.

I was about to monitor a labile blood pressure when I discovered I'd left my watch in my room. I went back for it, to find Mandy there.

She still showed the effects of the beating and refused to be seen, giving out that she had a bad cold. My watch was on the dresser, and, as I fastened it on, the door opened a crack, then more fully, and Robert was in the room. He took one look at Mandy's face and sank down on the bed looking as though he would cry.

"I didn't know. I swear to God, Mandy, I didn't know."

Mandy swayed on her feet. She seemed almost to believe him.

"Of course you knew," I said. "You're the one that set the thing up, that had that pervert waiting for her."

Although he answered me, Robert didn't take his eyes from Mandy. "Nothing physical was supposed to happen, nothing like this. Believe me, he was just supposed to let you know they were planning a little accident for me if I didn't come up with the drugs. They've done it before. They like traffic accidents, that's their thing."

"Oh, my God, Robert."

"The hell with them. Let them plaster me all over the sidewalk. I'd rather have that than—than what happened to you. Mandy, please don't hate me or despise me."

"It was so brutal, the way he grabbed me."

"Oh, God." Robert put his face in his hands. "I'll kill him for hurting you. I'll take that little sneak apart."

"He kept hitting me and punching me until I was on the ground."

Robert lifted a stricken face. "He didn't . . . assault you?"

"I was making too much noise, screaming and crying. No one ever hurt me like that before. You don't even beat an animal like that."

"My poor girl. I don't expect you to forgive me. I'd no idea— why, I'd lay down my own life for you, Mandy."

"You may do just that if you don't come up with the money," I interpolated, because it seemed to me Mandy was ready to rush into his arms. And that was one spectacle I didn't want to witness— *Mandy* comforting *him.*

We three looked at each other in silence, trapped in complexity we didn't want to face.

At last I said, "It isn't only the hospital, the army could be involved."

Robert groaned. "If I could keep you out of it, Mandy, I'd confess my part in a minute and get it over with."

"How could you keep me out of it? I'm the one that took the drugs. Besides, if what Kathy said is right and the army gets to know of it, you'd be court-martialed. It's wartime—they could shoot you."

"Not a bad idea," I said. "But I doubt they will."

Robert turned on me. "Oh, you doubt it, do you? Well, all I know is I've got a great choice: to be run down in the street or face a firing squad."

Mandy, stifling a sob, wound up in his arms after all.

When he left, Mandy let me work on her face, and I was able to bring down the residual swelling with ice. Her "cold" improved, and she resumed her duties.

* * *

CONNIE'S WEDDING WAS approaching, and I'd written that I couldn't come. But she telephoned. I heard her ask, and I couldn't say no. I decided on the spot to borrow the money. After all, it was my sister.

The trip was accomplished over a weekend. I traveled, one of the few women, in a train jammed with servicemen on leave or posted to the west coast. The conductor put me up front where he could keep an eye on me, and I kept my nose in a book.

Mama Kathy was at the station. I recalled it later in almost snapshot highlights. Her arms around me made me remember the Kathy I had been. At the church I met Jeff and liked him. He was a big man, sandy colored. Hair, mustache, eyebrows all the same neutral shade.

It was just an impression because Connie was in the priest's private chamber. I stopped at the threshold when I saw her. Mama Kathy had made Connie's childhood dream true. The gown was the one she had described to us for years, the waist tucked with invisible stitches, the scalloped neckline, the filmy skirt cascading over satin. How often had I heard it described! The bouquet she carried, the orange blossoms for her hair—all matched the fairy tale.

I fastened on the beautiful dangling earrings Mandy had given me. The chords of the organ meant a final kiss, and I went with Mama to take my place in the pew.

It played out exactly as it was supposed to. It was her day. Twenty years later, and the groom and tiered wedding cake appeared as if by magic.

IT WAS AN unusually busy week. I must have passed and repassed the nurses' station a dozen times. Sister Ursula came looking for me. "Kathy," she said, "Colonel Boycroft wants to see you."

"What about?"

"It's Colonel Boycroft," she repeated.

This was it. Colonel Boycroft was someone you saw when a complaint had been lodged against you, or you were brought up on charges. Even the room was oppressive, it seemed to close in on you. The colonel, from behind a massive desk, sent a keen glance in my direction. Nothing escaped him, not a strand of hair out of place or a pinned hem you hadn't had time to sew.

He began amiably enough. "Well, Nurse Forquet, you've done very well here. I understand you are in the graduating class. Is that correct?"

"Yes, sir," I said and waited.

"We've all watched your progress with pride."

"Thank you, sir." The more he went on the more nervous I became.

"The reason I asked you to come in is that something disturbing has transpired. Was it last May you did your stint at the dispensary?"

"Let me see, yes, it was . . . ," I was saying on one level. On another I was thinking—It's caught up with Mandy.

"We have just inventoried our accounts and made the unfortunate discovery that the written record and the supplies on hand do not tally."

"You mean some of the medicine is missing?"

"Drugs, Nurse Forquet. This is about drugs."

My heart was pounding. "There isn't a possibility of a mistake in the records?" I asked.

"I wish there were. They've been gone over meticulously. Naturally suspicion falls on those that had access. Now, if you've any knowledge of this affair you'd do well to tell me about it."

I shook my head.

"It's only fair to warn you that the matter is now under official investigation."

"I didn't take the drugs, sir, if that's what you're thinking."

"I'm not thinking that at all. However, everyone who had access this past six months is under suspicion."

"I see, sir," I murmured, because he seemed to expect me to say something.

"My personal belief is that the matter will turn out to involve some outside source."

"Yes, sir," I said briskly, and left his office with a more hopeful attitude. An "outside source" was none of us, but a vague phantom figure to pin the theft on. It seemed to me a good solution. And I turned my attention to my upcoming graduation.

I knew Mama had spent every cent she had on Connie's wedding. I knew they couldn't come, but I wrote anyway. I was glad Connie had her wedding. I remembered how dream-like it had seemed, but I knew Mama Kathy had worked behind the scenes to match it to Connie's expectations. Only Georges was missing from it. But he was showered with descriptions, as we all wrote blow-by-blow accounts. Connie enclosed pictures and a piece of wedding cake.

There were very few times in my life when I was reminded that I was poor, and even fewer that I cared. But for this occasion wouldn't it have been wonderful to send everyone tickets to come to Montreal? What a fine time I would have had showing them the city.

I was graduating six months earlier than originally planned. The ambitious program combining nursing with military training, casualty evacuation, army discipline, all that, had not been feasible. So the military part was postponed, to allow us to become nurses. After graduation we would report to Ottawa to receive a concentrated preparation for battlefield conditions.

The year and a half had passed, one day so like another. Routine melded it together. The faces changed, the names changed, but the cot numbers didn't. The work gradually became more specialized, more intensive, and the responsibility had grown, but it wasn't that different from my first days. Now graduation was only a month away. After that I had no idea what my life would be.

Mandy and I had long conversations on the subject. We agreed that we wanted a posting overseas. After our strenuous apprenticeship we thought it should pay off with actual combat service. Mandy was keen for the Pacific theater. She wanted to see coral sands and palm trees, and experience warmth in winter. It seemed a likely prospect, as the Americans were retaking island after island. But the European front was seeing some of the most hard fought battles of the war. One thing Mandy and I were determined on, we would stick together.

I had sealed up my letter when Mandy came in breathless and flustered. "I just heard, Kathy. They've apprehended someone. But it's all right," she hastened to assure me, "the girls say he's an outsider."

"You mean there really is someone?" I'd convinced myself that Boycroft had tossed that out as a cover for letting things drop. Apparently I had misjudged the situation, and he had no intention of letting it drop.

"Outsider or not," I said severely to Mandy, "we can't let some innocent person—"

"It won't come to that. He's the wrong man. They'll discover that and let him go."

"Maybe," I said, but I knew from Papa Mike that the law could stumble as badly as the rest of us.

"Anyway," Mandy concluded, "Boycroft wants us in his office."

"What, again?"

"Trisha and Ruth too. And maybe some others."

Trisha and Ruth were already there, looking scared and guilty. In real life, I thought, people play their roles backward. The more innocent you are, the guiltier you look.

"Now then," Boycroft began, "it's been brought to my attention that you four were all on duty at one time or another during the tenure of Charlie Smith." He was observing us closely.

Each in turn denied she knew any Charles or Charlie Smith.

"What about you, Kathy?"

"Charlie Smith? I don't know any Charlie Smith either, sir."

"I thought you might. He's an aboriginal. Drives one of the trucks for the army vehicle pool."

"Oh," I said, breaking in on him, "*that* Charlie Smith. Yes, I know him. Surely he's not under suspicion?"

Boycroft tapped the surface of the desk with his pen. "You know what a private's pay is. He had opportunity and motive."

"And he's Indian," I finished for him.

"Now see here," he said, suddenly flustered, but the next moment regained his composure. "That has nothing to do with it."

"Yes, sir." I saluted. The other girls were staring at me. "I'm glad to hear you say so, sir."

This was the point at which Mandy would speak up. She would say something like, "It's Robert Whitaker II you want."

She didn't.

She didn't say anything.

Boycroft dismissed us.

Mandy joined the other girls, forming a small knot in the hall. I ran past them to our room and got the wolf tail from the back of my closet.

"He doesn't have the right kind of name," I whispered into the fur. "The one they call him by, Charlie Smith, won't stand up in court, it won't stand up against Robert Harley Whitaker II. They need to find a guilty party, close the case, get it off the books. A poor Indian called Crazy Dancer fits the bill. You've got to help him."

I heard Mandy at the door and shoved my talisman back on the shelf.

She came in.

"What is the consensus?" I asked. "That the Indian did it?"

She didn't answer.

Without Mandy to back him up there was only Crazy Dancer's word, the word of an Indian.

And if I implicated Robert, put the blame where it belonged? But again it was a question of names, who he was and who I was.

"Mandy, you've got to speak up. Crazy Dancer did you a good turn. You owe him, Mandy. For God's sake, Mandy, you owe yourself the truth."

She regarded me stonily.

Apparently Mandy and I had nothing to say to each other. And this was the friend I wanted to share a war with.

* * *

I MADE ROUNDS in a preoccupied fashion. If I gave testimony, I saw what the consequences could be. We were both Indians, weren't we? Probably in cahoots. For an army nurse to aid and abet was a serious offense. Was that what I had done? How? By putting ice on Mandy's cheek?

On my way to breakfast Sister Magdalena stopped me with the usual refrain, "Colonel Boycroft—"

"I know—would like to see me."

The stiflingly small room held the same young women, but I was scarcely conscious of this. I focused with every sense in my body on Crazy Dancer. He was standing there, looking debonair, even genial. Boycroft, I'm sure, had been affable. And Crazy Dancer would have expanded on his answers. Especially when the girls came in. Had he told about doing a shaman dance? Poor, vulnerable Crazy Dancer. He had no idea how serious the white man considered this, and probably figured that since they were on a wrong tack, the whole thing would blow up in their faces.

Each of us in turn was asked to identify Mr. Smith as the private who delivered the medical supply shipments.

"Yes, he's the one."

"It's him."

I too nodded in the affirmative and uttered, "Yes."

Surely Mandy— But looking at her, she appeared cool, restrained, and in perfect control. "I'd recognize him anywhere" was her contribution.

When it was too late, when a pair of uniformed MPs came in and took out handcuffs, I could see realization set in. This wasn't a game. These people were going to take him into custody, arrest him.

Up to now Crazy Dancer had avoided looking at me, afraid I would spoil his fun. Now, with a bewildered glance he sought me out.

My eyes fell before his expectant glance. His wrists were clamped behind his back, and he was marched from the room.

Mandy was waiting for me in the hall. "Don't worry about Crazy Dancer. It's just to throw them off the track, delay things while we think what to do. I know I can count on you, Kathy. I never doubted your loyalty."

I pushed her roughly into the storeroom.

"As it happens, you're right. I am loyal. But my loyalty is to Crazy Dancer. If you think I'm going to let Crazy Dancer take the fall for Robert, you're wrong. It's Robert's mess, and one of you is going to clean it up. If you don't go back in there and tell Boycroft the truth, I will."

"You're sticking by him because he's Indian."

"There's also the fact that he's innocent," I reminded her.

"That's why it isn't as serious for him as it is for Robert. For Robert it means court-martial—maybe even . . . You can't ask me to do it."

"I'm not asking. I'm telling you, you have to."

"I can't, Kathy. I simply can't do it."

In a way I was proud of her not being able to. Of course she couldn't. She loved him.

"And what about me?" she went on. "If I tell on him, I'm dragged in."

In spite of myself I almost smiled. I had never known Mandy to put herself second before.

"After all, I'm army too. What if I'm sent to prison? I'd die. My family would die. They would never get over it."

"I think they would." But mention of her family shifted my thinking, and I struck out in a new direction. I remembered the Brydewell plaque in the hall. We shouldn't leave her powerful, influential family out of the equation. "You've given me a clue. Your father's a lawyer. You've got to phone him, level with him."

Mandy recoiled in genuine horror. "You don't know him or you wouldn't ask me to do such a thing."

"It's the only way. I'll place the call for you."

"You mean right now? I tell you I can't."

"You can."

"All right, I *won't*. I'd rather die."

She had repeated that once too often. "If that's your decision, very well."

Mandy shot me a wide-eyed glance. I could see she was struggling. But there was no question, we had to have help. And there was no one else.

"All right," Mandy capitulated, "place the call."

We went into a vacant office, and she guarded the door while I dialed the number she gave me and handed her the phone.

It was her father's office, and she was passed through a receptionist and a secretary. I stood beside her as she cleared her voice. She began by asking how everyone was, including the dog. Then in a rush of tears the whole miserable story poured out.

She listened intently to her father's reply. He did not modulate his voice, and I heard enough to know his decision was final.

Mandy hung up and looked at me. "I hate you."

"He isn't coming?"

"He is!"

Mandy walked away without another word.

I had nothing to say. I had answered the appeal in Crazy Dancer's eyes. What else could I do?

NEXT DAY MR. Brydewell arrived. He was the eye of the storm, a gentleman used to having his way. Jurors must have felt this and quailed before him—judges too. He came in, trailing an expostulating Sister who was explaining that there was an adequate waiting room on the floor below, and that gentlemen were not allowed . . . He paid no attention but demanded that we accompany him to the office of the Mother Superior.

Colonel Boycroft was already there. The size of the room and the opulence of the appointments, in such contrast to his own cramped quarters, seemed to diminish his authority. There was no armed guard at the door, but the nun who acted as receptionist was as formidable.

Brydewell was quite at ease in these surroundings. He neither threatened nor bribed. Addressing Reverend Mother with deference, he said how delighted he was to meet the head of an institution that his family had been connected with for years. He let her allude graciously to the gold perpetual donor plaque, and even managed a disparaging gesture.

Turning to Boycroft, Brydewell mentioned his own service in World War I, and dropped the names of a couple of majors and a general. When his daughter telephoned, relaying the salient points of this unfortunate incident, the first thing he'd done was inquire into the reputation of the officer in charge. And he could report quite honestly that he heard fine things about the colonel's integrity and fairness. At which point his mind was much relieved.

Brydewell accepted a cordial from the hand of Reverend Mother, and continued. Regarding the matter at hand, a confused and totally incorrect version had been bruited about. It misrepresented the circumstances grossly. Regrettably, his own daughter, while in the care of the good Sisters and on his, the colonel's, watch, had been abused and physically beaten into taking a part in this wretched affair.

Without mentioning the word *lawsuit*, the implication was there. He left no doubt he considered the hospital extremely remiss in its supervision. If not exactly *in loco parentis*, the institution had a responsibility for young people who volunteered to serve their country.

The fact that the true criminal was a member of the hospital staff and most particularly an army doctor placed the armed forces in an awkward position as well.

Mother Superior listened attentively, offered no defence, gave no advice, and rendered no judgment. However, she radiated a benign atmosphere of reconciliation, so that at the end of the interview both men understood each other perfectly, set down their drinks, and shook hands with great cordiality.

I felt dazed. I didn't know exactly what had happened.

When I got back to our room, Mandy was packing. "They won't let me graduate. After all the work I put in. Isn't that the pits?"

I put my arms around her. "Mandy, you don't know how lucky you are."

She shrugged this off. "My dad isn't going to do anything for Robert. He told me he deserves what he gets. The only good thing to come out of this is they're releasing Crazy Dancer."

"The only charge they could have held him on was being an Indian."

"Kathy, I wouldn't have let anything really awful happen to him. I intended to come forward if, well, you know, if things got worse."

"I believe you, Mandy. You always were soft-hearted."

"Soft-headed, you mean."

"That too," I agreed.

At lights-out, after the final bell, I heard her bed creak. I reached out my hand, but she wasn't there.

I sat up. I could discern her by the glimmer of moonlight. She pulled her skirt on over her head, got into her coat, and came, shoes in hand, to the side of the bed.

"I'm going home with Dad in the morning. And in the morning they'll arrest Robert. But it isn't morning yet."

GRADUATION!

The day came at last. But neither Mandy or I would be seeing palm trees. I'd had an interview with Reverend Mother, in which she asked me, after I finished the three-week officer training course, to return to the hospital as nurse instructor. The position was traditionally offered to their top graduate, and she thought I would be of most service helping train the new crop of student nurses.

I didn't mind. With Mandy gone, the adventurous aspect was gone too. To me war was simply a vast ravening horror that mutilated and maimed. Where I confronted its carnage made no difference. If I was wanted here, here I would stay.

The line of graduates, of which I was a part, straightened in anticipation as Mother Superior welcomed the audience, which consisted of the Sisters, a few ambulatory patients, and a sprinkling of friends and family who happened to be local. I was conscious of the gap beside me where Mandy would have stood.

Poor Mandy, no one spoke of her. They had reprinted the program, erasing her name. I rearranged the yellow roses in my hand as the line prepared to move. This hard-won day, the day I had looked forward to for a year and a half, was not the wonderful, exhilarating event I had hoped for. There was no one here for me. I hadn't expected there would be, but I felt a twinge thinking of Mandy, thinking of Mama, Connie, Georges. I had hoped Crazy Dancer would be in the audience. But he wasn't. The long line began to move.

Then I saw him. Crazy Dancer must be going on Indian time because he was late. This didn't embarrass him in the slightest. He came down front and took an aisle seat. People noticed and pointed him out; the drug debacle was fresh in everyone's mind. And the entire hospital was following the court-martial of Robert Whitaker II. The sentiment that predominated seemed to be: "I hope they throw the book at him."

But that didn't happen. I'm sure that Robert was not the first young officer to stand before an army court, humbled and repentant. The fact that it was wartime loomed large in determining judgment. The accused was a surgeon. They needed surgeons. Especially in North Africa where Rommel was pounding away at Monty's Eighth Army. It was explained to Robert that there was such a thing as hazardous duty, and if he were to volunteer for it, that would go a long way toward squaring things.

Crazy Dancer appeared unaware that he was a subject of interest. He had come to see me graduate. And as I stepped up to receive my diploma from Mother Superior, I felt a surge of—not happiness, but joy. I was Oh-Be-Joyful's Daughter.

With a whoop I sailed my cap into the air, and Crazy Dancer caught it.

I DIDN'T SEE him until Wednesday, which was odd. He never came on a Wednesday.

I ran out to find out what was up. "It's Wednesday," I said.

"A good day," he replied, "to visit my mother."

"Your mother?"

"Yes, I think it is time. She is a whirlwind of a woman, on the council, into politics, and, besides that, a recognized power woman. She will make the blanket ceremony over us."

"The blanket ceremony? Isn't that . . . ?" I stopped, confused, wishing I hadn't started that sentence, hoping he would finish it.

He did, in a straightforward way. "Yes. It is the way we in the First Nation pledge ourselves to each other."

"A marriage. You're asking me to marry you?"

"I am, and in all the ways possible: with Guiche-Manitou looking on, in a courtroom with a piece of paper, in a Catholic church with a priest."

Crazy Dancer loved me. And I experienced the same joy I had when he showed up at graduation. Joy is a feeling that wraps you and lifts you like frosty breath in the air.

But now Crazy Dancer was saying something else. "I want to know that you are here for me when I come back."

My joy bent like a stalk about to snap, and I waited, knowing, but waiting anyway.

"They called my unit up. We are being shipped out in two weeks."

So this was the way it was to play out. I wasn't going overseas, but he was. I'd seen what shells and shrapnel did, I'd seen the pattern of abscesses under ulcerating skin, I'd dug out fragments of metal, probed for spent bullets.

Crazy Dancer said gently, "I see by your worry for me that you love me a lot. You do, don't you?"

"Yes. We traded souls when we sat on the moon."

"And you will go with me to my mother's?"

"If that's what you want."

"It's the way I planned it," he confided. "I sold the car and bought two bus tickets. There's a short walk at the other end, a couple of miles. You won't mind, will you? Because it gives us the price of a dinner out and we can take in a movie. *The Great Dictator* with Charlie Chaplin, how does that sound?" he concluded happily.

I explained to Crazy Dancer that it would take a day to arrange things with the Sisters.

$\mathscr{N}$ine

THAT NIGHT, THE night before I was to get married, I tried to remember—did he actually say, Will you marry me? Did I answer, I will? I smiled and held my talisman against my cheek. This was the last night I would go to bed alone in a narrow virginal white cot. From now on there would be someone beside me, someone waking up with me. I didn't think it would seem strange, because it was Crazy Dancer, and I felt at home with Crazy Dancer.

I was drifting into sleep, and in my dream there was a feeling of loss, as though I had misplaced something. At first I thought it was Mandy I missed. Suddenly, the hairs of my guardian seemed to crisp and stand erect, as they processed a recollection I didn't want . . . making his cot up with hospital corners, settling another patient into it, answering the bell that had been his and no longer was. . . .

Elk Girl said very distinctly into my ear, "What about the onyx ring?"

"It's a keepsake," I said to Elk Girl. "He said so himself . . . a war trophy, like a German helmet." In the same breath he'd said, "I'm in love with my nurse." We kidded about that, they were all in love with their nurses. We took care of them, talked to them, listened to them. Of course they loved us.

My dream shredded into the calm gray fields of sleep. Some time later I looked into thoughtful gray eyes. Elk Girl laughed a harsh laugh.

"It didn't mean anything," I told Elk Girl.

"That's good," Elk Girl said. "Because it wouldn't be very smart to marry one man when you're in love with another."

"It would be a terrible thing to do," I said indignantly. "And I am not in love with an enemy soldier. What kind of girl would fall in love with a German?"

"An Austrian, a gray-eyed Austrian," Elk Girl reminded me.

"I was glad," I told Elk Girl, "when they moved him to the prison ward."

Elk Girl regarded me skeptically.

I reached out my hand to her, knowing it wouldn't touch anything. "It's Crazy Dancer we should be talking about. It's Crazy Dancer. Ask the forces you talk with to look out for Crazy Dancer. They're sending him overseas. Don't let any harm come to him."

Elk Girl continued to regard me with that same unnerving look. "He's in danger all right, but not from enemy fire. Friendly fire is more deadly. It is you yourself who will wound Crazy Dancer and kill his spirit."

"Never! I'd never do anything to hurt him."

"You're marrying him, aren't you?"

Elk Girl faded. She wouldn't stay and listen. So it was Crazy Dancer himself I told. The next morning in the parking lot I said not hello but, "I love you."

His eyes shone, and the spirit in him shone. I set down my suitcase and showed him the guardian wolf tail.

"He travels with us?" Crazy Dancer asked. "Good. He will help us find our way between worlds."

When he kissed me I realized again how far joy is past happiness. Joy is a whole new ball game.

We had a chicken dinner at a colonial-looking restaurant. Afterward we went to the Chaplin film. At first I laughed along with the rest of the audience as I watched Chaplin and his Hitler mustache go through the silly antics of a buffoon. But the laughter dried up. I resented Hitler being portrayed like this, whacky and nutty. One was thrown off guard, no longer afraid. Yet we must be afraid; I was afraid. This fool had reached into the life I was beginning with my young husband, and . . . and God knows what would happen. Separation, that was for sure. He didn't seem to worry, but I did. The thought of being injured didn't bother him. To him bodies, like jalopies, could always be fixed.

Sometimes they could. Sometimes. The film was still flickering on the screen, when I whispered, "Can we go?"

"You want to go?" He was amazed. He'd been having a good time.

Once we were outside the theater I attempted to pass it over, "Instead of watching other people's lives, I want to get on with ours. I want to meet your mother."

"I'll tell her you prefer her to Charlie Chaplin. She'll like that. She says movies are a drug they feed the people, like the old Roman circuses."

"She must be quite a character."

He nodded, agreeing with me. "She's small and her voice is gentle. But she has the soul of a warrior— Tell me," he added, squeezing my hand, "why in God's name are we talking about my mother?"

We traveled most of the night, and slept sitting up in the bus, holding hands.

Starting a day with Crazy Dancer beside me brought it home. Someday, when the war was over, that was the way it would be.

"Good morning," he said.

"Good morning."

"So this is married life?"

"Don't forget. There's a war to get through first."

He dismissed the war with an impatient shrug.

Our stop seemed to me the middle of nowhere. We freshened up in a filling station and for breakfast had Cheez-its and candy bars.

It was his country we were in, and he pointed out rivers and streams, crest lines and valleys. "I've hunted partridge through this area from the time I was thirteen, and I recognize it just as you would recognize furniture from your house. . . . An old bureau with a chip in the third drawer, that would be where the old elm has fallen. Or a scuffed leather armchair, that's the hill to your right, where there's evidence of landslide."

"Would you want to live near here, once we've set up housekeeping?"

He seemed surprised at the suggestion. "I'm at home anywhere. It all belongs to me, remember?—and to you," he added generously.

Grabbing my hand, he twirled me round and round until we couldn't stand any longer but fell into the grass. We didn't try to disentangle ourselves, but lay with the sound of a cricket in our heads and the sun on our bodies.

I loved his body. It was athletic, supple. He lay against me, relaxed, content it seemed with the tip of my ear. But a second later that wasn't enough for him, he made demands that swept us into other patterns. We met on the other side of our bodies.

Crazy Dancer laid the flat of his hands against my shoulders to push himself away. "We must save this magic for our wedding."

"Just remember that," I said.

We proceeded to the village, a poverty-stricken place with rows of subsidized houses, all small, ugly, and the same. I stole a look at Crazy Dancer. Standing at the edge of these hovels he hugged himself. The proprietary smile on his face told me he was the richest man I knew.

Children appeared from nowhere. We were surrounded by them, noisy, laughing, shrieking kids who shouted his name and pulled on him to get his attention.

"Johnny," he said, recognizing one and hoisting him to his shoulders. And then, "Charlie, you've grown a foot." Charlie was caught up in his arms. A third hooted with pleasure and tugged at his pant leg. Crazy Dancer was considerably slowed in his approach and went forward like a walking bush of birds.

The houses came awake, heads appeared at windows, doors opened. An Indian woman came up to me, and her smile reminded me of someone. Of course—Crazy Dancer.

"The prodigal son has returned," she said in fluent English with a trace of French accent. "And brought me his bride."

He was repeating my name to his mother and to neighbors who gathered around. "Oh-Be-Joyful's Daughter." He said it with pride.

For the first time in my life I had the feeling of wholehearted acceptance, as though I too had come home. I realized of course that the special fondness with which Crazy Dancer was regarded had been extended to me. His choice, his woman, would have been loved no matter who she was.

His mother, Anne Morning Light, like mothers everywhere, insisted that we eat. There were several hasty conferences at the door, and small packages of food passed in. With so many contributions we did not simply eat, we feasted. Morning Light watched with obvious pleasure as we devoured cakes of maize with maple syrup, sausages, and potatoes. Quietly, people slipped into the room and took places where they too could enjoy our enjoyment.

As we ate, Crazy Dancer extolled my many accomplishments to his mother. And what did he mention? Not that I was a fully qualified nurse. Not that I would receive a second lieutenant's commission in the Canadian army. Not that I stood at the top of my class. The thing he was proudest of was the skill he had taught me. "Oh-Be-Joyful's Daughter is a whiz with cars. She knows engines like the back of her hand." And on and on, reflecting the times I'd given the right snap to the wrench in changing a tire while he sat on the curb giving directions, or jimmying the door with a coat hanger while he laughingly dangled the keys out of reach.

I don't think Morning Light knew exactly what to make of this unexpected talent. She smiled and began telling us of the wedding ceremony that would be carried out this very day. There were to be readings from the Gaiwiio, the "good words," followed by draughts of strawberry juice, for it was in the month when strawberries ripen that Handsome Lake was sent his visions.

Morning Light must have given some signal, for the people there sprang into action. We were taken, I by the women, he by the men, to be bathed and purified for the marriage. The ritual was explained to me. It was to be according to the longhouse religion, and again I heard the name Handsome Lake. And coupled with it, Jonathan Forquet.

"My father," I said.

"And her namer," Crazy Dancer added.

This produced an astounding reaction—utter silence.

Then, here and there, someone reached out a timid hand to touch some part of my clothing. I felt my own skin prick with awe. Was I really the daughter of such a venerated figure?

"In this day," Morning Light told me, "Jonathan Forquet is our prophet. The Great Spirit has entered him. He is a holder of Gaiwiio. His mission is to keep the Six Nations People together, to interpret the calendar in the old way of Handsome Lake. He relates the myths and teachings of those times to the present, to show us how to live in a white world. We are dreamers and shamans, and we must understand this. While we fight for autonomy, for reparations, for simple recognition, we must never lose our spiritual selves."

"I know," I muttered, "he tells you to be joyful!"

The small brook wound not too distant from the village. There my clothes were removed, and I knelt with Anne Morning Light and several girls in the water, which they splashed over me, laughing.

I splashed back.

"But we're not getting married," they protested.

"Then you should," and I splashed again.

In this way I was prepared for the blanket ceremony. I thought of Connie and the armful of white roses she carried and the orange blossoms for her hair. "Something old": the dangling earrings from off my ears. "Something new": a lovely brooch Mama bought for her. "Something borrowed": a garter one of the girls at the factory contributed. "Something blue": the ribbons trailing from her bouquet.

My bridal gown was also white, the softest white deerskin imaginable.

The slow padded sound of drums shook from my head the strains of Mendelssohn's wedding march. I was led deep into the woods to a natural glen where people were assembled.

I had no one to give me away. But an Indian woman gives herself away.

The drumbeats increased. I saw the ceremony was to be danced inside a large wheel that Anne Morning Light had drawn in the dust. I stepped inside the circle. Crazy Dancer threw a feathered prayer stick that struck quivering in the ground. With a cry he leaped after it, landing beside me. There were bells on his ankles. Stars had been drawn in the dust, and the sun and the moon and many animals. Our feet danced them away. Making an act of power and an act of beauty, a blanket was laid over our shoulders. We surrendered our shadows to each other. He held mine, I held his.

Crazy Dancer carried me to a hut that had been erected close by in the glade. It was freshly built of sweet willow boughs. The floor was draped with skins, and, tossed against them, my old wolf tail.

The flap was lowered, the world left outside.

Crazy Dancer took off my white deerskin dress and held me naked on his lap. "There are parts of your body that I love more than I should."

"Which parts?" I whispered back.

"Here"—he opened my arm—"the soft part opposite the elbow. And here"—with a finger he closed my eyes so he could put a kiss there too. "And your woman parts, which are so mysterious to me." He explored them, telling me as he did so the difference between white and Indian lovemaking. "I've heard white guys say there are forty positions for sex. They're wrong, it's one beautiful dance, and the lovers flow from one to the next, and on and on, like this and like this . . . ," and I thought I would swoon from the exquisite torture-pleasure that we knew, and relinquished to know again.

Church, flowers, orange blossoms, and an organ . . . they were for Connie, not for me. I had stepped inside the wheel of life.

Food and sweets and drink were brought to our door, and left outside for us.

Afterward, Crazy Dancer told me our honeymoon lasted three days and three nights. For me it was something outside time. When it was over and we were once again back in the world, I still moved like a dreamer.

Morning Light handed me a small bucket, and I went with her to cull wild rice that, she explained, grew in the shallows of lakes and ponds. "It is called spirit rice. No one plants it. It just grows."

It was early fall but the weather was summery, and there were marsh marigolds, lupins, and I spotted pasqueflowers, all growing in profusion.

Tucking up our skirts, we waded along the edge of a small estuary. The water was still, almost mirrorlike except where we broke the surface into ripples. Anne Morning Light shook her head over Crazy Dancer's participation in the white man's war. "It comes of sending him to school. I wanted to teach him myself, reading, writing, some mathematics, and lots of history. But he wanted school, so I warned him, if they find out you're literate you'll wind up in the army someday. And that's what happened."

"I wouldn't worry about him. Crazy Dancer does what he wants to do."

"I sometimes think the Mohawk man is born with an extra gene for fighting. They want to get in on the fighting, no matter who's fighting or on which side. Why should we fight the Germans? They never oppressed us. The British did. The French did. And especially good old Uncle Sam. But Crazy Dancer laughs at all that. He thinks he can leapfrog over problems, put together the white man's machinery, and then they'll have to deal with him, man to man. I tell you it's a dream. It won't happen."

"I don't know, Anne. Things change. Maybe Crazy Dancer can help them change." And I remembered the afternoon Mandy and I had spent in the library. As I felt in the water for the clumps of rice, ripped them up, and began to fill my pail, I recalled my own indignation. I saw that Anne Morning Light's sympathies lay with those who advocated independence from the British empire for Canada, and self-rule for the Mohawk/Iroquois nations. I wondered to what extent one chooses one's wars. Or did the wars choose you?

I don't think we had worked an hour when I noticed a canoe with an outboard motor headed straight for us. It was hardly recognizable as a canoe, its prow standing almost vertical in the water. Of course. Crazy Dancer! He came in where we were, jumped out, grabbed me, and plunked me down on the floor of the canoe.

"We haven't finished," his mother shouted.

He laughed, pulled the cord, and we started up. I leaned out, laughing too, and waved goodbye to Morning Light.

"Was I right? Did my mother treat you to the local political scene? She's such a gentle, quiet person, you wouldn't believe how she challenges rules and anything she thinks racist and oppressive."

"Good for her."

"I don't know. I've had to get her out of jail twice. Once for blocking a doorway, and once for disrupting an official meeting."

"She's fighting for the rights of her people. I admire that."

"I don't know what happened to the way women used to be."

It was a mock complaint, to which I replied, "It's the war."

*   *   *

THE VILLAGE SEEMED to have changed, and in some subtle way even the noise of the children was ratcheted down. The effect was almost that of watching a shadow play. A play of the death of an old chief.

It was Crazy Dancer's mother's uncle. On the way to his cabin Crazy Dancer told me, "Sacred Arrow sent a dream. He wants me to show him the other side, put him on the path to the Grandfathers."

I walked beside my husband, proud that I was to share in sacred ways.

We joined a dozen or more people crowded into the small house. The old man's bed had been moved into the living room to accommodate these well-wishers.

I thought he looked reasonably well for someone on his deathbed, but Anne, who had caught up with us, whispered, "His generation still believe they can choose their time of death. It's one of the few freedoms they still have."

Sacred Arrow was glad to see Crazy Dancer and, shoving away several small children who tumbled about him, clasped him against his chest in a strong embrace. "I will tell you more about the dream I sent you," he confided. "Three angels came to me. They carried bows and arrows in one hand and in the other huckleberry bushes, and their faces were painted red."

I would never have recognized from this description that these beings were angels. Which led me to speculate that an angel must appear to the dreamer in a form the dreamer would recognize.

"These three angels told me," the dying man went on matter-of-factly, "that this is a good time to make the sky journey. They told me to dream this news for you." He patted Crazy Dancer's hand. "Thank you for coming. I am in luck to have you here."

"Make the trip in these." Impulsively, Crazy Dancer stripped his moccasins from his feet and fitted them onto Sacred Arrow's.

This signaled a new phase and the shaman took his place beside the old chief and began extolling his life, recalling the fine deeds he had done and bringing to the attention of the Creator his many acts of kindness and bravery. This commentary was intoned to the accompaniment of drums.

We listened respectfully for a quarter of an hour. Then, returning to his mother's home, Crazy Dancer prepared for the responsibility laid on him by beginning a fast. "I must howl to the earth, and dance the map of the other world."

"But you don't know it yourself, do you?"

"That's why I thirst and fast. I must be pure so the knowledge will be given to me."

Toward evening Anne Morning Light returned with me to the old chief's house. By now they had lit a fire in the cookstove, and it was swelteringly hot. Benches had been hauled in and the men sat around chewing tobacco. Tin cans were scattered here and there on the floor as spittoons, but one old-timer, more proficient and more accurate than the others, spat directly from half across the room into the round stove opening. It wasn't a hundred percent, though; a glob of tobacco juice sizzled on the lip of the stove. Children kept running in and out, banging the door. A dipper of water was passed to the dying man, but he waved it away.

The audience waited, I assumed, for the dance to begin. But Crazy Dancer didn't come as a dancer, he came to the accompaniment of mud-turtle rattles, which were pounded on one of the benches. He burst in like thunder, knocked over a bench, rushed to the stove, and, reaching in, scooped up a hot coal which he tossed from hand to hand.

Then, dropping it, he grabbed up handfuls of coal dust and began sprinkling everyone with it. "He is sending the Great World Rim Being on his way," Morning Light whispered. From her tone of voice I imagined this must be the devil. It was a good idea to send such a being far away from where a good man dies.

I watched Crazy Dancer's shadow on the wall. Anne said against my ear that it was the Doorkeeper's Dance. Twirling, leaping, he seemed at times to fly. At others his feet pounded the earth, and he crouched—only to find strength to spring up again. He was a flame of the fire itself, dancing through that night and the next day and the following night. The morning of the third day Sacred Arrow died. He died quietly behind closed eyes.

The children continued to play around the corpse, but Crazy Dancer changed his rhythm. With his feet in the death dust of this world, he led his uncle to the shadow world. Now that Sacred Arrow was traveling west in his moccasins, his obligation was at an end and he danced to lighten the hearts of those who grieved, especially his mother, who was the old chief's favorite niece. He jumped around and clowned and made faces. He was a delight maker and the children laughed their delight while old people blew smoke on him. But in seventy-two hours he'd had neither food nor rest. Still the drums beat. And still he danced.

That was one second; the next he collapsed on the floor, his heaving sides the only indication that there was life in him. I reached him first, going down beside him and laying my head on a rapidly pounding but steady heart. I raised my head, smiling. This man of mine had the heart of a grizzly. A glass of water was put in my hand and I tilted it against his lips. He opened his eyes at once, and they asked, "Have I done well?" Mine replied, "You were wonderful."

We returned with Anne Morning Light to her house, and she busied herself being a mother. She brought food and, when we had finished eating, wrapped up what was left for our journey. Before letting us leave, she cut Crazy Dancer's hair. I understood it was a sign of respect for his uncle. Crazy Dancer had grown up in this house, learned to dance and have fun here, learned the ideals of loyalty to the band and the family. And learned, I could tell by the attention to me, a guest, the strong Indian sense of hospitality.

Going from a wedding to a deathbed seemed ominous to me. But my feeling of premonition was not shared by any, least of all by Crazy Dancer. First Nation people danced and celebrated, almost without differentiation, the milestones of life. Death was simply a further journey.

The kids started a ball game behind the house. Perhaps the old chief stopped a moment to watch.

Anne Morning Light saw us off with something called moose milk, a homemade drink that had much the effect of bathtub gin. One swallow and you felt as though your eyeballs had come loose.

She took Crazy Dancer aside and told him he had chosen *chai-wootcha,* a good woman. I felt a rush of gratitude toward this sweet-faced scrapper, who thought I would be good for her son. She let us go with the assurance that she would dream us. Dreaming, Crazy Dancer told me, connects the world.

We left, swinging our arms and with a light step. He pointed out kinnikinnick, a little evergreen shrub growing by the side of the trail, whose leathery leaf, when dried, was their usual smoke.

"When we get back to Montreal," he said, "we will marry in a church and get that piece of paper."

The truth was I already felt satisfactorily married. I felt the excitement of our lovemaking and, underlying it, the comfortable feeling that we got on like a pair of old shoes.

"I never worked for money," he said unexpectedly, "only at what I liked."

"I know," I teased. "If it had a carburetor, you loved it."

"If I'd known I was going to be in love with you, I would have worked for money."

"You're poor because you chose freedom," I said stoutly.

"But you'll have nothing now but government checks, and they're not much."

"Whatever they are, they're more than I had before."

He stopped walking and looked at me intently. "There is sadness in you. Is it because I'm being shipped out? Because I can promise you no Nazi bullet has my name on it." He laughed. "They never heard of Crazy Dancer. So I'll come back."

I smiled and said nothing. I had seen some of the boys who came back. Their body parts were disposed of with other wastes. To deflect the conversation I told him a story. Crazy Dancer loved my stories.

"This is a true one," I began, because Indians love true stories best and generally begin their tales that way. "It happened last year, on Sister Egg's birthday. You probably noticed there's a marble statue of St. Francis of Assisi inside the main entrance to the left of the staircase."

"Yes, I've seen it."

"It's large, isn't it? I mean, more than life-size?"

"It's large all right."

"Well, we wanted to play a trick on Sister Egg, she's our favorite Sister. We thought of it as a sort of birthday present. So we set about moving St. Francis to the other side of the stairs, the right side."

"But it must weigh a ton."

"That's exactly right. The idea of the joke was to get a rise out of Sister Egg, have her cry out, 'A miracle! A miracle!' I must tell you it was very hard work. We rolled a rug around St. Francis and fastened it with belts. Then with a jury-rigged winch we loaded him onto a piano dolly. It took forever, but when we finally maneuvered the saint into place and unwrapped the rug, he looked as though he had always been stationed there.

"When Sister Eglantine came down the stairs, she noticed nothing, so *we* rushed out, shouting, 'A miracle! A miracle! St. Francis has walked to the other side of the staircase!'

"Sister Egg stood stock still, then went up to the statue and examined it, shaking her head in puzzlement. 'Well,' she said finally, 'he was in his old location a hundred years. I imagine even saints want an occasional change of scene.'

" 'But,' we chimed in, 'it's a miracle, Sister. Shouldn't you notify Rome?'

" 'The only miracle,' she said, 'is that none of you girls got a hernia.' "

en

NOW WE WERE back in Montreal things that should have been simple were difficult, and ultimately impossible. We had stayed longer than we intended. After all, one could hardly hurry a man's dying. But it did not leave time. There wasn't time to arrange for the church until a week after Crazy Dancer was due to sail. Of course, we didn't need to rent the church itself. I suggested the little vestibule off the Father's office. But there were other weddings scheduled, and several baptisms. Time grew short. And suddenly there wasn't any.

"It doesn't matter," I said. "We'll do it when you come home. Connie will be the matron of honor, and you'll get to meet Jeff. And Georges will be best man. You and Georges will be great buddies. And our mamas will meet and not know what to make of each other, and like each other. And they'll both be proud."

He listened with his head cocked in a look of skepticism. "It sounds good, but it doesn't sound real."

After he left, I remembered his saying that, I remembered how his face had clouded over. It sounded like fantasy to me too. But why shouldn't it happen like that? By then the war would be over, and my family would come. And Anne as well. Why did our wedding seem so misty and unreal?

His orders were waiting. He was to sail on the large troopship in the harbor. The only thing he said about that was, "I don't want you going down to the pier and waving."

So I didn't.

We didn't say goodbye. We found a cheap room to rent. But since we wanted it for consecutive hours of day and night, we paid a ransom for it. It didn't matter. It didn't matter that it looked out on an alley, and trash, and empty beer cans.

In the morning I found he had filled my shoes with flowers. I put my arms around him. With his cheek to mine, he couldn't see the sudden tears. That's how his sweetness affected me. We put the flowers in a water glass and admired them. "Look, even when they're the same variety, their faces are different."

I made him breakfast of things that didn't have to be cooked, and did the same for lunch. Dinner was a short foray, and then back to our cave. We had a whole marriage to pack into a couple of days. He washed my hair. I gave him a back rub. We lay on top of the bed and made lazy love. He pulled me down on the floor and we made frenetic love. I showed him the Twins' Code. "Always let me know where you are."

The idea of a code intrigued him, and he coded a love letter to me on the spot. "Every fifth word . . ." he said as he worked laboriously with a pencil stub.

He taught me Mohawk love songs and war chants. We sang the crazy tunes we heard on the radio:

> *Three little fishies*
> *And the mama fishie too,*
> *They swam and they swam*
> *Right over the dam.*

He told me he understood nursing because he had delivered puppies. "I put this soft, clean muskeg moss under the mother. It's absorbent. We use it to diaper babies. You never see an Indian kid with a sore butt."

I agreed that modern medicine could learn a lot from First Nation people.

Next thing I knew I was confessing one of my childhood tragedies.

"I don't have a birthday. Not really. I was born in the forest somewhere. The closest thing I have to a birthday is the date Mama Kathy and Papa signed the adoption papers, August second."

"No," he decided, "that's not when you were born. You were born when we were married."

And so it went, down to the last minute.

He gave me a cheery grin when he left. There were no important last words. Crazy Dancer walked out of the room and closed the door.

I jumped up, ran across the room . . . and stopped. I didn't open the door. I didn't look after him.

It was my turn to close the door on our little room. It was necessary to take a short walk before returning to the hospital. As far as anyone there knew, I had just taken a leave. They knew nothing about my marriage. That was a good thing, as that part of our plan hadn't worked. In their eyes I wasn't married. Later, when I could talk about it, I might tell Sister Egg. But not now. It was too close, too dear, and too painful.

In the little chapel on the hospital premises I found the sanctuary necessary to reenter my life. One prayer I repeated again and again. "Don't let the Germans discover there is such a name as Crazy Dancer."

Back in my room I wrote my first letter.

Dear Crazy Dancer,

Guess how long you've been gone? An hour and fifteen minutes. There are so many things I didn't get around to telling you. Elk Girl, for instance. She gave me the wolf pa-wakam when we were in grade school. Then somewhere in middle school she dropped out. She is a very strange person. She has powers. Sometimes I dream her.

I stopped. My thoughts had taken me down a wrong avenue. Elk Girl had said some disturbing things about our marriage. I crossed out the part about Elk Girl and started my letter again.

I went about my duties writing letters in my head. At night I got down on paper the thoughts I'd had during the day. Silly things, like the time Connie, Georges, and I spent the afternoon gathering bright stones to outline the garden path. We soaked them overnight to bring out their colors. In the morning we hurried to look at our acquisitions. They were gray and ugly, all color leached out of them. Why didn't he write?

Of course he couldn't. He was stuck on that damned ship. I wondered if he'd remember the Twins' Code. Of course he would. Every fifth word represented a letter and he could spell out where he was. If I knew that, if I had a setting to put him in, it would be easier.

Everyone complained about the mail. It came when it came. I told myself I'd probably get a dozen letters all at once. I woke in the morning, my face wet with tears.

By noon there was an extra on the street, the news was all over— the troopship that left our harbor ten days ago was torpedoed in the North Atlantic. All hands were lost. How could a German torpedo find Crazy Dancer? Then I remembered, he was listed as Charlie Smith.

My soul, my being, that inmost self fought the printed word, the many words that buzzed about me in the hospital and on the radio. I rejected them. I rejected the possibility that he could be dead. He wasn't dead—he'd promised me. We'd gone under the blanket to-gether. I'd know if anything had happened.

Then I recalled the tears on my face.

I wonder if the dead know they're dead. Maybe they just keep on, frozen in their bit of time, doing the same things in another reality. I kept to my schedule. If anything, I was more efficient than before. The only thing I had to be careful of was the concern I read in Sister Egg's eyeglasses.

"You're working too hard, Kathy."

"No, I'm not."

She shook her head, and I could tell she wasn't satisfied. "Hear anything from Mandy?" she asked.

"No."

"And what about that young Mohawk, the one who used to pick you up in those odd conveyances?"

"Oh, him. He went away."

"He was called up?"

"He's dead," I said. I jammed my hand in my mouth, but it was too late. The word was out.

Egg took both my hands in hers. "Sit down, Kathy. There. Now tell me."

"He was on his way to the war. He didn't even get there. He was on that troopship."

"Oh, Kathy. I think you were fond of him?"

"There's a big wad of undigested feeling stuck in me."

"My poor girl. How difficult it must be."

"I loved him. I loved him, Sister. But what good was it, our loving each other? No good at all, it didn't mean anything."

"Of course it did. Love is the dearest feeling there can be. You were fortunate to experience it, and so was he. If he knew your love, you gave him a great gift."

I fumbled in the pocket of my uniform. "Here. Here he is. We're sitting on the moon."

She didn't take the picture from my hand but bent over it. "Imag-ine that," she said.

I replaced the snapshot carefully.

"He was a fine-looking young man."

Was, was, how I hated that word.

"You are right, Kathy. Keep busy."

She must have passed the word on. The charge nurse kept me hopping. Once I snapped back, "Can't you see I already have two patients to clean up?" Instead of reading me out, she gave me a look of such tender concern it almost broke my heart. "I'll send Adele in to finish up," she said. "By the way, there's an Indian woman asking for you at the front desk."

It was Anne Morning Light. She had a telegram.

The telegram should have come to me. But of course the Canadian government didn't know about our marriage, and if it had, would have taken no notice of a couple of dumb Indians under a blanket.

Anne Morning Light soothed me with stories of Crazy Dancer as a boy. He had always been fiercely independent, disappearing into the woods for days at a time. He had a ragged paperback, *101 Ways to Live Off the Land,* and built his own wigwam in the woods behind their house. His father made good money as a structural steel worker on high-rise buildings. "He danced too," Anne told me, "at the end of a girder, twenty stories up. He died in an accident. Not falling—a Mohawk never falls. And not from the machinery—machines never betray a Mohawk. No, he did something much more dangerous, he joined the union."

Thinking of that death brought her son's. She broke down, and in that cold, antiseptic, whitewashed waiting room I tried to comfort her. Together, we mourned our loss.

"I don't suppose you're pregnant," she asked.

"No."

"A baby, now. Some part of him. That would have been a comfort."

When she left I went with her. Sister Egg arranged it. It didn't matter much where I was or what I was doing. I moved through empty spaces. Sounds reached me, though, and scenes passed before my eyes. The sun was warm, the sun was good. I registered that. I knew everything that went on around me, yet it was remote, an alien universe.

I took accumulated sick leave and moved in with Anne Morning Light. We didn't so much live together as side by side. We no longer talked or tried to comfort. We knew it was no use.

I went to the stream where I had been bathed and prepared for my marriage. No laughing girls now, no splashing water. The water was still except for a small eddy. I followed it and came to where the ghost rice grew. For a moment I saw his upended canoe, heard his laughter.

I turned away and started back. Here in this forest he had shot partridge, walking softly. If a blade of grass bent, it straightened. And no leaf rustled as they did under my feet. A spring in his step carried him this way where I plodded past the bureau drawer and the rocking chair—those familiar logs and burnt stags and broken boughs. They furnished the world of his growing up.

But looking at them I felt nothing.

"Kathy," Anne Morning Light said to me that evening, "your healing is not here. My healing lies in a return to my life. I'm going to Quebec. They're holding a protest rally for a Mohawk who is under a sentence of death."

"What did he do?"

"It was harvest time, he went back home to bring in the crops. He didn't run off, he didn't hide. The military police knew where he was. They picked him up in his fields."

"Poor thing," I said. "He didn't understand."

"No, he didn't."

"Well, I guess I'll go back to the hospital. It was very good of you to have me—"

Anne shook her head vigorously. "You're not ready to go back to nursing. You need nursing yourself."

I persuaded her I didn't. I persuaded her I was fine. When she left I sat down and didn't get up for hours. Night came and still I sat there. The dark invaded my mind.

Everything was nothing, and nothing everything. Why had that never been clear to me before? I thought not of what I would do, only what I would not do.

I would not go back to the hospital.

I felt I was treading the obverse side of the moon. Vast, dark, hollow. I wandered it. I walked it. Even when I did ordinary things like buying a train ticket, I was wrapped in it. If someone spoke to me, I replied. If they smiled, I smiled back.

But I kept treading the pockmarked face of the moon's far side. Our feet had dangled over the edge, he'd had his arm around me.

Outside, the world rushed by. In the morning, from the train window, I watched the sun come up. It tinted everything a delicate salmon color like the inside of a seashell.

The sun did not come up in my head. It remained dark there.

They called Montreal . . . I made no move. I wasn't going to Montreal.

The train hurtled along. My dark mind looked at the bright fields. My dark mind reached for him. It was one of those soul-shattering moments when it strikes you again, as hard as the first time—I will never see Crazy Dancer again.

He was dead.

Accept it, his mother had told me.

I didn't want to accept it. We hadn't invented a code that would tell me where he danced now.

The darkness grew and blotted out thought, blotted out possibilities, blotted out hope. I musn't trust hope, or possibilities or thought. The far side of the moon is bleak.

The porter woke me, gently repeating, "We're here, miss. . . . Your stop."

Why had I bought a ticket for home? Mama Kathy and Connie were in Vancouver. No one would be here.

Yet it was comforting to recognize—a fenced pasture with the fenceposts leaning and the strung wire sagging—a tree with its center closed over an ancient burn. The tree grew around the black, charcoal wound and continued to live. But when you destroy the center of a person, that isn't possible. Besides, the person may not want to go on. Definitely doesn't want to.

I trudged along the road. I was going home.

No one was there.

I walked all morning and most of the afternoon. I'd forgotten to eat. I felt dizzy and the sun also turned black. When I got to my house, the door was open, so I went in.

Elk Girl surveyed me critically. I wasn't surprised to see her. I didn't ask what she was doing here.

"You look terrible," she said, and put me to bed.

I slept, not through the night, but through several nights. Whenever I opened my eyes Elk Girl was there. She sat beside the bed and did quillwork. "How long have we known each other?" she asked when she saw my eyes open, then answered her own question, "Since we were seven."

She spooned something that tasted of swamp and cattails into my mouth. "Didn't you ever wonder why I was your friend? Why I singled you out? Why I bothered?"

I knew I was not required to say anything. Besides, I couldn't rouse myself, it was too much effort.

"It's because of who you are," she went on.

Who was I? I waited to hear.

"Oh-Be-Joyful's Daughter, the only child of Jonathan Forquet. He came from the mountains and the forests, from the rushing river and the holy places to bring you your name. And with the name he brought you a special gift. He brought you Gaiwiio, the good message."

Clang went the gates of memory, memories that were not mine. They danced just out of reach and beyond recognition. I closed my eyes and slept.

Minutes passed, perhaps hours. Elk Girl took up where she had left off. "Do you want to begin at the beginning of the world, or in the middle with George Washington?"

She herself made the choice. "The Great Spirit has an evil twin. Whatever the Great Spirit makes is wonderful and perfect, and the Evil Spirit comes along behind him and tries to destroy his creation. But he is not strong enough to undo it completely—only partly. For instance, currents. At the beginning of the world currents flowed in both directions at once. There was the *coming* side of any river, and the *going* side. So that you paddled your canoe either way without effort. Evil Spirit tried to eradicate currents altogether, but he was only able to do it one way. And so on until we come to George Washington.

"The Evil Being Who Lives on the Rim of the World, in January, five days after the new moon following the zenith of the Pleiades, whispered into George Washington's ear. And General George Washington ordered a scorched earth policy against the Iroquois for siding with the British. They fled over the border into Canada, miserable and starving. Among them was a Seneca named Handsome Lake."

I turned my head away. I didn't want to hear. I had been married according to Gaiwiio, Handsome Lake's "good words." The trouble was they led to my father. My father who was no part of my life.

But her voice droned on. "Sick and without hope, Handsome Lake turned to drink. And he died."

I drifted off with the uncomfortable feeling that was not the end of it.

When Elk Girl continued it was in a declamatory chant. "My great-grandmother was a witness to his death. She was there and saw it. And she dreamed it into me as I now do to you."

The wooden planks under my feet became a dirt floor. Against the wall, bowed figures mourned an incantation. The man stretched on the bed was not Handsome Lake. For one heart-stopping moment I thought the features were those of Crazy Dancer. But when I knelt, I saw it was Jonathan Forquet. His nostrils were stuffed with ground tobacco leaves. It had been a long time since he had breathed.

I walked with others to the dirge of voice and drum and stopped where they stopped, at a desolate knoll. The grave had been dug in preparation and the wrapped body of my father was laid into it. In the distance a wolf howled.

On the third day the Gaiwiio was recited.

The howling wolf came close. It was white. It went to the grave site and began to dig. It dug and dug. Finally it dug down to grave clothes. But my father was not there.

With a single impulse we turned and there on the summit of a nearby hill was Jonathan.

The people gasped and knelt in awe. Their voices broke and they shrank back afraid.

I was afraid.

He raised his hand in blessing. "I have come from the sky road to bring you a new world. Gaiwiio is old, but I bring it new and full of hope. The prophet Handsome Lake has made known Jesus's warning—not to follow the way of the money changers, the white men, but to take from the before times of our people and mix this with the best of the white world, giving thanks to the new moon that will arrive again in January."

I woke from my vision hardly able to breathe.

"Did you see?" Elk Girl was almost dancing with excitement. "Did you see the death and rebirth of Handsome Lake?"

"It wasn't Handsome Lake. It was my father."

Elk Girl dug her fingers into my shoulders. "You're sure? It was Jonathan Forquet who came? Your father?"

"It was my father I saw dead. It was my father I saw buried."

Elk Girl covered her eyes and fell on the floor.

"And when the wolf dug up the grave clothes, it was he who stood on a hill and spoke."

Elk Girl said from the floor, "Well, that's clear enough." She got up, straightened her skirt, went to the washbowl, and poured water over her hands, face, and the back of her neck. Then she patted her hair in place. "Finish the soup I brought you, Oh-Be-Joyful's Daughter. We must go."

I pulled back as though I had been scalded. "No! Not to my father."

"He has sent us his pawakam."

"No. He abandoned me. I don't care how great a man he is, I can't forget that. I can't forgive it."

"Kathy, you think he hasn't been where you are now? He had to choose between being your father and being father to the rest of us. People come to him from great distances because he has found the answers that are withheld. He has woven the sayings of Handsome Lake into the wampum of life."

IT WAS A bus journey, and we went in the morning. All day and that night we dozed, conscious when the bus slowed that we were passing through cities. Edmonton, Saskatoon, Regina, Winnipeg, Thunder Bay. In Sault Ste. Marie I heard a town clock strike thirteen. On we went, North Bay, Ottawa, Montreal. Quebec I had always thought of as the end of the world. It wasn't. We rode past it into a scruffy countryside, but old-growth forest could be seen in the distance. We got out at a poverty-stricken little town, and had lunch at a place called Ma's. I had two eggs sunny side up. Elk Girl took her breakfast into the kitchen and had a long confab with the Indian who worked there. I had been silent the whole trip and she was put out over this. But I wasn't able to pull myself out of that dark place.

She returned from the kitchen and said in a businesslike manner, "Jimmy Longbow will take you the rest of the way."

"You're going to leave me here?" Somewhere in the world I was sitting on a stool eating eggs, but where?

"You're the one Jonathan Forquet wants to see," she retorted.

"Wait," I said as she turned to go. "Do you think he really did die?"

"Of course."

I looked after her, no longer sure which was dream and which reality.

Jimmy Longbow handed me a walking stick with a leather thong he had fashioned himself and we started out. Before too long we were in the forest I had seen from a distance. The cool autumn air trapped between pines was pungent. The trees went down to the edge of the river.

My guide melted away. There was no need of him. Jonathan Forquet was at work in a clearing. Before him, lifted on a rack, was a canoe; another was pulled up on the beach.

He put down a tool, and, coming toward me, took my hand and looked deeply into my face. He knew. I could tell that. He knew about Crazy Dancer, and that he was dead.

"I don't know what to do," I burst out.

"Sit down here on this stump. First you will have a cup of water."

He watched me drink with a look of satisfaction. "You did the right thing. You can always come to your"—I thought he was going to say father but he said—"namer."

I stole glances at him as I drank. He seemed not to have become older but to encompass youth with age. "What are you doing?" I asked, indicating the two canoes.

"This is my workshop. I make canoes."

"To sell?"

"Of course to sell. How else is a man to live?"

"You're known as a holy person. In India a holy person collects alms and is fed by the community."

"Why should I accept charity when I can make canoes?"

He took me to a small pine lean-to whose chinks were padded with moss. "Sleep here," he said, showing me a pile of furs in the corner, "and tomorrow you will help me and I will try to help you."

Like a child I obeyed my father.

When I woke I could hear the teeth of a bandsaw. I emerged and came closer, inhaling the aromatic scent of birch bark that had been freshly peeled and rolled in large paperlike layers. Its outermost crust was chalk white, deepening to a buff color.

"Paper birch, cut from high on the tree. I strip it off in a single sheet early in summer."

"What wood do you use to make the frame?" I could see he was pleased at my question.

"A hard maple or cedar. This is cedar I'm shaping now. This piece in my hands will be a gunwale. But I've run out of water. It has to be kept wet."

I picked up the pail beside him and, going down to the river, filled it.

He nodded thanks without pausing in his movements. "Pour the water into this trough," he directed.

I did this, wondering if he remembered the way we had parted years ago, and the cruel things I had said. He placed the cedar strips to soak, making them malleable for bending.

"The ribs too," he said, placing shorter strips to soak. "And lastly, the stem. On other boats that would be a keel, but on a canoe it simply divides the building of it."

We left the construction pieces of cedar soaking and went in to breakfast. He pulled apart a home-baked hominy loaf, which we ate with honey and berries.

"When he died," my father said unexpectedly, "it was your death too."

My eyes filled with tears and I nodded.

We went back to work.

The afternoon was spent fastening the gunwales together in the outline of a canoe. "Tomorrow," he said, "we will put on the skin."

Work stopped when the light faded. Jonathan brought out a pipe and sat in the doorway, smoking. He had laid the guest breakfast before me; I saw it was up to me to rustle the other meals. Dinner didn't look too different from breakfast—berries, a substantial slab of hominy grits, which I essayed on his stove, cooking it with what I thought was bear grease. I topped it off with goat cheese.

We ate in silence, but it was a comfortable silence. Companionable.

"Did you ever die?" I asked.

He nodded over his pipe. "Yes," he said, considering each word. "The doctors told me that I did, that my heart stopped."

"And you were really dead?"

"Yes."

"And the rest, that people say about you?"

"People believe what they need to believe."

"I see. And that is the stuff of myths and legends."

He continued to smoke.

By the next morning our framing was pliable and bent easily, assuming a graceful outline. Together we unrolled the birch bark and lashed it to the ribs.

"Do you see the true beauty of birch? How the grain runs around the tree rather than along its length? That enables us to sew the sheets together." As he spoke, he mixed something with the bear grease brought from the cabin.

"What is that?" I asked.

"For caulking. Pine gum and spruce resin with fat."

The afternoon was spent raising the gunwales to the proper height and binding them to the stem. "Canoe building goes much faster today. Today I rely on Phillips screwdrivers. Not that there is a single screw in the finished canoe, but for temporary bracing there's nothing like them. Bandsaws and jigsaws are a lot faster and more accurate than stone implements. The roots of a living thing are in the past, but the buds open in the present and bloom in the future."

"The present is empty," I said, "and I can't even imagine a future."

He didn't say anything.

It was a day in which we waited for the wood to dry. My time was spent sewing. My thread was made from the cores of spruce roots by patiently scraping layers of skin away. Jonathan came over, presmably to check my stitches. They were small and even, as though sewn with fine silk thread. I was proud of them.

Looking over my shoulder, Jonathan said, "Your mother was an orphan."

My regular stitching went awry.

"She was raised in the cold, severe atmosphere of a mission, but her name was a message from dead parents that she was to be joyful, Mamanowatum. So she knew very well the burden she laid on you when in the spirit world she whispered to the Grandmothers—who passed the name to me."

"My life is in shreds, Father. I can never know joy again."

"I haven't finished my story," my father chided me. "Oh-Be-Joyful grew up behind those repressive stone walls. When small children were punished, she relived her own punishments. She began to break the rules in order to be banished to punishment row. This was a dark storeroom, where children sat on a wood bench and cried. When Oh-Be-Joyful contrived to be shut in with them, she told stories and joked and played finger games. Punishment row became the happiest place in the mission."

My father's story was finished, and he went back to work.

What had he been trying to tell me? That even though I could no longer feel joy for myself, I could create it for others? My stories were dried up in me, I had no jokes, I knew no finger games. If anyone still cried in punishment row, I would say, "Move over."

Another day and another night. My father showed me a collection of miniature canoes in a shed out back. They were six inches long, beautifully made and signed by him.

"White man's enterprise?" I asked.

"Of course." A rare smile lit his face. And I realized that the present held an occasional flash where someone else connected with you.

The caulking, when we reached that point, took a great deal of time as it underwent repeated inspections. Jonathan was a scrupulous and careful craftsman. I was reminded of one of Sister Egg's aphorisms: "What's worth doing is worth doing well."

"The ribs," Jonathan said, "give it strength and make it seaworthy."

Prebent and wedged tightly against the birch bark, they formed the hull of the canoe.

Two weeks from the day I arrived we stood back and looked at a lithe and capable boat.

Without saying anything my father took me to the edge of the river. It was as though he felt I had earned a vacation, and this was it. We stood looking at bright pebbles which the water magnified. The current was slow, but in the shallows a runnel had formed, quick moving, rushing on.

Jonathan picked up a small piece of bark. He tossed it into the fast-flowing channel. Our eyes followed its course as it breasted ripples and was carried along. "That was you when you came here," my father said.

"But where will I wind up?" I was concerned for the small piece of bark. I hadn't been concerned about the world at war or the protesters Anne joined—but I was worried about the fate of that tiny piece of bark.

"It doesn't matter where you wind up," my father said, "as long as you are in control. Do not let yourself be carried like that bit of wood, who has no say in the matter, and gives no direction, but allows itself to be swept along, it doesn't know where or how."

"But what can it do?"

"Why, dip a paddle in the water, steer a good course."

"And what is a good course?"

"It is different for each of us." And with that he returned to the canoe. I thought it was finished. But it seemed there was more caulking, and ornamenting and invocations. I made myself comfortable on a tree stump, pulled my sweater more closely about me, and watched. With the completion of the canoe my visit was at an end. I wanted to leave him something, so I picked a bouquet of wildflowers. Vines and vivid poppies and the season's last white columbine.

When several hours had gone by, he took a rest and sat down beside me. I handed him the flowers. "I don't know what this coarse yellow one is, I'm afraid it's a weed."

"There's nothing wrong with weeds. Weeds are generally tougher and stronger than flowers. Take you, you are tough and you are strong."

"Then I am still Oh-Be-Joyful's Daughter?"

"I call you that. And someday you will grow into that name."

"Because I am a weed?"

"Yes. Because you are a free-growing, strong weed."

He had a parting gift for me as well, a couple of the miniature canoes. "Give them to your friends."

"You don't want me to keep them?"

"No." He handed me a scroll of birch bark, plain and unmarked. "This is for you. Make it into anything you like."

$\mathscr{E}$leven

I RETURNED TO Montreal and the Sisters of Charity a whole person. I missed Crazy Dancer. I missed loving him and being loved by him. I missed the life we never had. But the wasteland inside my heart was gone.

I PUT IN for overseas duty and went through a three-week equivalent of boot camp, during which I got my knuckles rapped by a forceps for being slow to hand the operating doctor a scissors and practiced battlefront hospital sterile precautions, including Lane's technique of two gowns, two caps, and two pairs of gloves. When the site was prepared, you stripped off the outer layer of clothing to immediately begin the delicate work in a sterile environment.

There was also strenuous physical training: chin-ups, push-ups, hiking with twenty-pound backpacks, map reading, revolver practice, setting up and dismantling tents, how to wriggle under barbed wire and set fuses. Other hardening activities included firing .303s, with a ferocious recoil that banged you on the shoulder. A brief course in prevention and treatment of malaria and other tropical diseases, and we were posted.

The weather that a month ago still held traces of summer had become a Montreal winter. But my life, which had teetered at the world's rim, was given back. Like Oh-Be-Joyful in punishment row, I would try to snatch other lives from the brink if I could. For this I needed to be in the thick of things, although with the German conquest stretching from the west coast of France to the east coast of Greece, it was difficult to judge just where that might be. Presumably, however, the Royal Canadian Army would know, and I left it to them.

When I said goodbye to Sister Egg, I had no idea where I was headed. She took the crucifix from her neck and with a mumbled blessing placed it lingeringly in my hands. "If you get the chance, Kathy, ask His Holiness the Pope to bless it."

That was her way of telling me she thought it was Italy. This seemed a good judgment call. Our new class of Liberator fighters had given us air superiority in the Mediterranean and the 4th and

16th German Panzers along with an Italian division had withdrawn from Sicily, while Palermo was taken by Patton's forces. This amount of activity made it more than likely that I would be handing Sister Egg's crucifix to the Holy Father.

An old World War I tramp steamer had slipped into harbor under cover of dark. It listed crazily to port and rode low in the water. I sent up a small prayer, "Not that one."

But it was that one, and at 0300 hours, still in the dark, with a light snow falling, embarkation began. Reinforcements were marched aboard, supplies loaded, heavy equipment stowed, and last, as my cold teeth testified, nine nurses, recruited from several hospitals in several cities.

"I'm going to the war you never got to, Crazy Dancer."

The companionways were narrow, and the ship listed so badly we could hardly keep our footing. The steep metal ladderlike stairs which we climbed down resembled the entrance to hell, as the further into the bowels of the ship, the hotter it became. Three stories down we reached our quarters, bunks crammed in so tight you couldn't sit up without banging your head.

The ten-day crossing was not to be a picnic. We had started to unpack our few belongings when an explosion rocketed through our quarters, throwing us against our bunks. Were we under attack before we'd left the harbor?

Whistles blew, restraining a general rush to reach the deck. Order was restored, and much to my relief we were taken topside and marched off, our sailing deferred for three days.

"What happened?" I kept asking. I was billeted back at the hospital and heard on the radio that the ship next to us, a fishing boat out of Halifax, blew up. Her boiler had exploded.

We embarked in broad daylight on another ship, which looked to be a good deal more seaworthy. The same nurses were there and another three had been added. Far from being confined to quarters, we were pressed into instant service dispensing tablets to seasick recruits. We were not immune either; one of our number, Carol Smyth from Nova Scotia, was stricken. I shepherded her up the sequence of ladders to the deck and fresh air. Manuevering her to the rail, I told her to hold on. With people retching, throwing up, and moaning to all sides of us, I felt a bit on the queasy side myself and took my own advice. I held the rail, breathing in gales of good, brisk salt air.

One of the nurses told me that a friend of hers had made the crossing on the *Queen Elizabeth*. "Imagine. They flew her to New

York, and it was luxury all the way. You sank into carpets inches thick, there was scrollwork and gilt and mirrors everywhere. And a grand staircase and ballroom. The staterooms were fabulous, each with private bath. And the you-know-what looked like all the other chairs. They were cane with red velvet cushions, and she went around trying to lift the seats of three or four matching chairs before she found the right one."

This was decidedly not the *Queen Elizabeth,* or even the *Queen Mary.* Typical of a winter passage, the seas were rough. But the rolling water under us and the spume that lashed us were invigorating. And the sight of the twin smokestacks of our corvette convoy, reassuring.

Meals were hearty affairs with no concern shown for civilian rationing or delicate stomachs. We joined the officers' mess, and it was a cheery company. A rufous-haired young doctor speculated on two things throughout our voyage, my virginity and our destination. The latter, I think, was rather generally known, as a chorus of "O Solo Mio" went along with dessert. Why the time expended on tropical medicine I don't know. When I asked this question I was told, "There's your way, my way, the right way, and the army way." Which was all the answer I ever got.

In the morning there was a briefing. We were to be put ashore at Naples, which was completely under Allied control. A map was pulled down which featured a red line labeled GUSTAV drawn across the waist of Italy. These were the German entrenchments, anchored at Monte Cassino. With a pointer the briefing officer indicated a CCS, Casualty Clearing Station, set up on grounds that the Fiat Company had used as R&R for its employees. There was, we were told, heavy fighting at Mignano, just south of Cassino, and we would in all probability be asked to establish an Advanced Dressing Station in the vicinity.

I would be in the midst of it, right enough, and what-ifs crowded my mind, including what if I died. For some reason I had not considered this a serious possibility. But by the time we pulled into harbor, tension had mounted. The constant din of Dakota flying ambulances taking the critically wounded to hospital ships for evacuation to England, and the sight of the destroyed docks brought home the reality of war. The Bay of Naples was a rusting junkyard. The piers had been targeted at various times by both armies, until they were nothing more than enormous chunks of masonry, broken, upended, leaning crazily into partially submerged ships, toppled trucks, and an airplane wing sticking half out of the water.

In order to disembark we jumped onto a platform of planks laid across the hull of a wrecked cruiser, then scrambled into tenders and were brought ashore, where we were taken by jeep to the clearing station.

Impressions revolved with the speed of the jeep. Mt. Vesuvius, stark, rising from distant plains; houses crumpled in disorderly piles in the street, making it necessary to swing onto the sidewalks or cross the middle of a piazza; disabled staff cars, a stripped-down tank, wrecked vehicles of all kinds; the cry of gulls mixed with the sound of scratched gramophone records blaring a dozen songs into a cacophony of noise.

Our driver seemed to make no effort to avoid mowing down groups of drunken soldiers, part of the army of liberation, I supposed. By some miracle no one was hit. There were Off Limits signs everywhere, but, as far as I could see, they were ignored.

We pulled up in an area cluttered by tents arranged in rectangular groupings. Hand-lettered signs hung at the entrances: O.R., RESUSCITATION, X RAY. And several larger tents marked WARD A, WARD B, and so on. A kitchen, an officers' mess, a patients' mess, two QM tents, a dispensary, and a linen tent. Aside from the fact that it was all under canvas, I was going to feel at home.

We were issued rain slickers and hard hats, assigned a tent, and turned in. Throughout the night, planes took off and landed, sirens wailed, and at 0400 hours we came under bombardment. I grabbed my hard hat and jammed it on my head. I slept in it the entire time I was in Italy. A deadly whistle pierced the air, the ground shook, and we got under our cots, calling to each other periodically that it was okay, we'd make it through, and other inane remarks to prove we were alive. This was important to prove, especially to ourselves. Nearby an explosion ripped the air, there was sharp pain in my ears, and for the next few hours I was stone deaf.

From among the veteran nurses here since Sicily, two groups of Field Surgical Units were assembled and moved out as we "slept."

A series of small, sharp flicks in various sections of my body started me scratching. I had never experienced bedbugs. It was worse than the bombing raid. I tried my insect repellent against them, but they were impervious.

In the morning we were broken into teams and stood out front waiting for transport. This was particularly uncomfortable, as a light snow was falling. Where was the Mediterranean sun? I guess it doesn't come out in January.

The jeeps didn't arrive. There was a snafu of some kind. We never did know what it was. However, an officer appeared to tell us we were dismissed till 0200 hours. Three hours to explore Naples. What unbelievable luck.

I set out in the direction of town, but the first vehicle that came along stopped for me. I thought for an instant that the driver was Indian like me. He was Indian, but not like me at all. "I'm Gurkha," he explained, and then, curiously, "What are you?"

"They call us Indians too. I'm a First Nation person from Canada."

"How amazing that we meet here in Italy."

"Yes," I added, "in the middle of a war."

"That part is not surprising. We Gurkhas are the best mountain fighters in the British Empire. We come from the Himalayas," and he laughed deeply into a thick curly beard. He assured me this was the famous Route 6, the Via Casalina, one of the two major highways leading eventually to Rome. Hannibal, if I remembered correctly, traversed it a few millennia ago with elephants. Now it was clogged with transport of all kinds—tanks, trucks, staff cars, road-clearing equipment, and long rows of wounded being passed in stretchers down the grade. Civilians waved, threw flowers and kisses. It was hard to believe they had been implacable enemies just a few short weeks ago.

The atmosphere was almost one of carnival, American servicemen distributing chocolate to ragged little street urchins, and dwarf women vendors shrieking, "Hello, Joe!"

My Gurkha friend refused to drop me off. "These are mean streets," he said, "no place for a woman alone." He turned into cobbled alleys so narrow pedestrians had to flatten against the sides of buildings to let traffic pass. This was my first European city, and I was amazed at how primitive it was, how different. The buildings built into each other, the wash strung across the street and over the traffic, kids everywhere, ragged, ragged little waifs, some with shoeshine boxes.

My driver told me he had been shod. "Like a horse," he said, "in one of these streets by one of those rascals. I ask for a shine, but he tells me the left shoe needs resoling. Before I know what's what, he takes out these nails half an inch long, I swear. He rips off the old sole, slaps on a new one, trims it to fit with a wicked-looking blade—right on my foot. Then come the nails, bang, bang, bang, into the bottom of my shoe. I thought he was going to crucify me, starting with my feet."

He pointed out a pair of ten-year-olds eyeing us from an alley. "You have to watch out for these little beggars, they're multitalented. They also steal anything that isn't fastened down."

I suggested we stop for a bite at one of the small curbside restaurants that didn't look as though it would be too expensive. "You can park the jeep right there and keep an eye on it."

He agreed readily enough, but refused to leave the jeep. "Not fastened down," he pointed out. He warned me against expecting too much of the restaurant. "There's not much food in Naples. If we're lucky there'll be a little pasta, cheese, and some of those sweet rolls, *taralli,* they call them."

I brought some out to him.

The proprietess, a handsome woman with a flour sack tied about her, discussed the entire menu with me, although she knew I didn't understand a word. With many smiles, she explained why each item listed was not to be had. I also wound up with the delicious *taralli* tarts.

For dessert she disappeared to emerge fifteen minutes later with an enormous bouquet of flowers. In the rush of Italian that went with them I caught the word *liberatore.* That's how the people here saw us, as liberators.

I kept checking my watch. There was time to look into the bookstore across the street, if my Gurkha friend was not in a hurry. I saw he was taking a siesta, so I went across to the shop. Bookstore was hardly what it was. They sold guitar strings, maps, tourist guides, and rather pretty jewelry, locally made.

I bought the map, and a bracelet for Connie, not trying to figure out lire, just dumping all my Canadian change on the counter and hoping to get something back. I didn't. My Gurkha friend deposited me at base camp by 0200 hours, where I was assigned to the 7th British Army Brigade, Royal Sussex battalion.

Things moved expeditiously from then on. We were loaded into a truck and I found myself back on Route 6. We passed the little alley we'd discovered this morning, and the *ristorante.* We ourselves must have resembled a rather gray line dusted with snow that followed alongside the Rapido Valley. The ground here resounded with the deep menacing sound of distant mortars. It was borne in on me that we were here to take from the Germans the barrier where they had dug in, variously referred to as the Gustav Line and the Hitler Line. The core of this natural mountain barrier was Monte Cassino. The Fifth Army had taken the Mignano Gap and Monte Trocchio.

Morale was high. It was thought we'd win Cassino by the end of the week.

But I had studied the map I'd bought at the little bookstore. "Why do we need Cassino?" I asked aloud.

A dozen voices explained it was the gateway to Rome.

The final sacrilege: "Why do we need Rome?"

It turned out that Rome wasn't actually strategic, and the Americans had wanted to bypass it. But Churchill was determined on Rome, principally for its symbolism. At least, that was the word that filtered through to us nurses. So, as part of the Royal Sussex, it was Cassino.

Our vehicle, which had been slowed almost to a standstill, now lurched to a complete stop. With a muttered curse, the driver jumped down to see what was going on up ahead. He walked along the side of the road. The explosion wasn't that loud. But mixed with a human cry it was inhuman. The man was splattered with white chalklike dust and blood. A mine had taken his foot off. People came running up. They seemed to know all about this kind of thing. "It's a *Schuh* mine. Nasty little buggers."

Our driver was lifted into the truck. We put on a tourniquet and gave him morphine, and he was passed back down the line for return to Naples.

An MP approached, asking if anyone present had an army vehicle driver's license. No one spoke up.

"Can any of you drive a goddamn truck?"

"I can, sir." Oh, Crazy Dancer, what have you got me into?

I slid into the driver's seat and rejoined the convoy proceeding into the foothills of the Apennines, going north. There were scattered cypress here, myrtle, and a few stunted pines. Beyond these, vineyards were planted with veins of cold blue lava running through them.

The country rose steeply to a mountain grade. We came to another traffic jam. In order to let a tank company through they rerouted smaller vehicles onto a secondary road through the hills, though to me it seemed more rubble than road.

Italians didn't bother with such things as guardrails, or perhaps they had been torn off. On one side of the narrow lane my side mirror clipped daisies off the bluff, on the other was a drop of a thousand feet into the valley. How close were my wheels to the unseen edge?

The palms of my hands were so wet I had to wipe them one at a time on my uniform. All this while we were climbing, but it became steeper, and I shifted into low.

Then, horror of horrors, an armored personnel carrier appeared, coming at me from around the bend. I was going up, they were going down—they had the right of way. I and those behind me would have to back all the way to the bottom.

I put the truck in reverse and crept backward, my huge antagonist honking at my slowness. The very size of the vehicle coming at me made me consider squeezing onto the shoulder so he could pass.

"Come on, lass," the driver shouted. "The war'll be over at this rate."

I held my breath. I prayed. Where were my wheels? I inched backward into the tight elbow and heard the shrubbery scratch the fenders.

The personnel carrier passed us, the driver and a whole row of soldiers giving me the V sign for victory.

"Please, God, no more vehicles."

And we met no more.

We reached the pass without incident and started a gradual descent. The quality of the air changed, becoming moist and fragrant. Pines were replaced by larch and beech. This was the Liri Valley, but we merely passed through a small corner of it before once again climbing narrow back roads. Our goal was to establish an aid station in the vicinity of troops who had bypassed Monte Cassino and would be attacking from the rear while the main force of the British Eighth Army kept up the pressure from the front. At least that's what my passengers were speculating, now that they had somewhat recovered from our first casualty.

The guns that pounded the earth were only a few miles away. I was waved to a stop, then directed to the Field Surgical Unit up a side road, cut so recently that the backhoe was still at work a hundred yards ahead and there was a smell of turned earth. We piled out of the truck and I saw immediately that this was not the standard Advanced Dressing Station with the equipment I had been taught to employ. Except for what we had in the truck we were on our own. When I sat down to catch my breath, my fingers knotted up as though they were still clutching the steering wheel. The light snow had turned to rain and we made it a first order of business to set about erecting tents. This was one instance where my training paid off.

But casualties started to arrive before we were finished.

A convoy of wounded, and the tents were at the bottom of the truck, disassembled. Hurriedly we unpacked disinfectant, plasma, sulfa powder, morphine, penicillin, needles of all sizes, scissors, basins, bandages, cotton wadding, syringes, urinals, folding cots, blankets, sheets, towels, disassembled operating tables, anesthesia equipment—it was amazing what came out of that truck. Finally, under it all, canvas and poles, where some unknown quartermaster, God bless him, had stowed it.

A matron already on the scene had appointed herself triage officer. Priorities one and two were those so badly wounded they must be treated on the spot, with priority one reserved for the men who might possibly be saved. Priority three was for first aid, where bleeding could be controlled, broken bones temporarily splinted in bivalved casts, pain somewhat alleviated. These patients were evacuated to the general hospital. Walking wounded just sat there. Some bravely pitched in and helped fetch and carry.

Traditionally, the leading principle of medical practice in combat is rapid evacuation. The wounded are picked up by stretcher bearers and brought to the unit medical officer, who gives them the minimum attention necessary and passes them on to an ADS, Advanced Dressing Station, where more facilities are available. From there they are transferred to a CCS, Casualty Clearing Station, which is a small emergency hospital where urgent surgery can be performed.

Here, however, the whole carefully planned system was out the window. The bad roads, flooded valleys, constant enemy fire, and the severe nature of many wounds made normal evacuation impossible. Our Field Surgical Unit provided surgical services right at the front, using the generator that came out of our truck.

Surviving members of a tank crew dug privies, "six-holers" we called them, potato sacks piled between them for a semblance of privacy, but they were only waist high.

In back of the last tent was a row of stretchers holding those that hadn't made it. All through the night we kept adding to their number. The burial detail didn't arrive until noon.

Thank God there was already an operational kitchen and warm soup, enough to go around. I know it saved my life. Pea and carrot soup with a little onion will always be a special memory for me. I sat down and drank it slowly while the *ack-ack* rasped from the valley floor.

Restored, I went to help set up the field transfusion unit. To add to our problems, the rain turned to sleet. Our main task now was to get everyone under canvas. We actually hauled up the ward tents over the patients. We spread tarps across the mud and called them floors. The cots sank and we had to do our nursing on our knees.

I encountered a case that at the Sisters' hospital would have been assigned "locked ward." He was waving his rifle about in a wild way, and I was afraid he would shoot himself or someone else. I had to wrestle him for it. The barrel was slippery with blood, but he wouldn't let go. "It jammed," he said over and over, "the damn thing jammed on me."

One of the walking wounded helped me pacify him.

The bright spot was that penicillin was delivered in quantity. It worked miracles and I thanked God for it.

My first sight of Major Farnsworth, the senior surgeon, was with a mop in his hands, trying to mop up the standing pools of blood and rainwater that collected on the canvas floor of the tent so he could keep his footing at the next operation.

I took over for him. He acknowledged this with a brief nod. You didn't get to know people if you could help it. I did ask, however, about the high incidence of eye and head injuries. "It's the topography mainly. Bullets and mortar fragments ricochet off the flint rocks and boulders into eyes and faces. Get used to it."

By the time we had been there three days, we were beginning to function properly. Then orders came through to move. It was like untrimming a Christmas tree. Putting it together, decorating, that's exciting. Undoing it is something else. But we disassembled and packed and tried to get it all back into the trucks, and even retain a vague memory as to where we'd put various items.

The line crawled forward and after perhaps forty-five minutes we rounded a bend.

There was Monte Cassino standing before us like a wall, and, on top of it, the famous monastery. From great ravines, rocky ledges, fierce slopes and jagged crests the dark escarpment rose stark, majestic. We had toiled our circuitous way to this point, and it loomed above us, sheer granite.

I stared in awe. Holding it, the Germans commanded an unobstructed view of the Liri and Rapido Valleys, the mountain pass of Abruzzi, all the way to Monte Trocchio lying like a beached whale along the Rapido River.

Looking at the featureless gray face of Monte Cassino, I asked, "We are going to take that?!" I watched shells hit and splinter on rock, the fragments spraying out in all directions. For days I had been seeing the consequences—raw gashes where eyes had been, skull fractures, depressed scalp wounds. A fly could not get up this formidable precipice, and yet our boys, under German field glasses and German guns, had tried and would try again. And I would give them morphine when I couldn't do anything else.

I continued to stare at that great mass. No trees. No cover. It was absolutely bare. No way to throw up protection. On it one was exposed, and under it, a target—as we were now. I thought of the slow Allied progress, hill after hill, pass after pass, a river to cross, and, at the end, to be met with this. I didn't see how . . . looking back on it, I still don't see how. This was Monte Cassino.

We began to unload, setting up behind the first shelter of rocks we came to, only a few hundred yards behind our forward troops. Our orderly, who was also our cook, provided everyone with a laugh. Yes, even here, in these circumstances, it was possible. We heard a dog howling, and Stan went to investigate. He came back carrying a large German shepherd, left behind by the Jerries because he was wounded. Stan classified the dog priority one and made room for him in the critical care tent. We couldn't spare a cot, but a lot of the boys didn't have one either. And in all other respects the dog was treated as well as anyone. Since he only responded to commands in German, Stan claimed he'd taken the unit's first prisoner of war.

We soon saw why we had been repositioned at the front. By morning the sky was silver with Flying Fortresses, followed by wave after wave of Mitchells. Shells fell all around us, and tracers occasionally zigzagged toward our tents. The din was constant. Everyone yelled, yet you couldn't hear a thing. Our own people were hit. Nursing Sister Lander was carrying a basin of sudsy water. She was hit in the back; the shell fragment went right through her and struck the basin with a ringing tone as she dropped dead.

Wave after wave of shells, punctuated by machine-gun fire, the scream of rockets. Waste bags soon held arms and legs, even fingers. Injured arrived on stretchers, or on the back of a corpsman. The corpsmen, sometimes ridiculed by new recruits for their reluctance to bear arms, were worshipped on the battlefield. They snatched the wounded from beneath streams of arcing tracers, from places tanks couldn't go.

I noticed several of the fellows I'd patched up back on active duty. We worked as fast as we could but boys held their wounds together with their fingers, waiting for attention. Others clawed at infected areas. Burn cases lay and screamed. You could go mad. Some did, and wandered away, only to be picked off by enemy fire.

A few feet to either side, that's all it took to feel eyes from the monastery watching. The weather had taken sides and become a partner of the Germans. The mercury dropped, the snow turned to thin sheets of ice covering the rocks. Fog settled in, and the airstrike that was supposed to soften up the enemy for our forward push was called off. Our troops attacked with no air cover. The fog became wispy, then stringy, and in some places cleared. They were thrown back.

Most of our mechanized equipment was useless. Our tanks couldn't climb these boulders, while below in the valley our vehicles, from personnel carriers to ambulances, were mired in mud. The Germans had opened a dam, flooding the plain, turning it into the kind of muskeg we have in Alberta after a chinook. The only means left for resupplying us in this forward position was by pack mule. So much for modern warfare. We would have had no plasma, no penicillin, and no morphine if not for the mules. As it was, they forgot to send batteries for our radio, and all communication was cut off for two days.

It was clear that the first concerted offensive for Monte Cassino had ended in a complete rout. Allied headquarters finally realized that Cassino was not simply the next range to be taken. It was the anchor of the entire German defense.

What were the boys thinking, whose limbs filled our garbage cans? It was hard to meet their eyes, hard to keep up one's morale, hard to keep our patients from freezing. It was below 30°F and a captured German, who had fought on the Russian front, declared this was worse.

Scuttlebutt had it that there'd been an amphibious landing at Anzio. From there Allied troops were to fight their way through the Germans, and come to our aid in a pincer movement.

It was a brilliant plan and must have looked good on paper. But it didn't work. They ran into the same seasoned German troops our forces had been up against, and had all they could do to maintain their beachhead. I began to think the war fought with globes and pulldown maps bore little resemblance to battlefield positions, and that much of their cleverly worked-out strategy was obliterated by what actually happened, as men tried for handholds on icy slopes and cover where there was none.

All I knew was that the formidable natural fortress before us, was still before us three weeks later, and, according to a report I helped Dr. Farnsworth fill out, we had lost over 1,600 men simply trying to stay where we were.

And where was that?

It did no good to think these thoughts, but they kept coming into my head.

$\mathcal{T}$welve

REINFORCEMENTS ARRIVED, THE 2nd New Zealand Corps under General Freyberg. They were to break into the Liri Valley, swing around, and attack Monte Cassino from the north while we tried again from the southwest. Of course, they never got together on the details.

Orders came from General Mark Clark's staff at Naples to capture Colle Belvedere, a ridge partway up Cassino, take it at any cost, give no quarter. We heard that this threw our General Tuker into an apoplectic fit. "Blasted idiots. Don't they know it's already held by the Free French?" He muttered strings of curses for several minutes before gradually subsiding.

News came that the Germans had mounted a counteroffensive at Anzio. Far from being able to help Cassino, our forces at Anzio were fighting for their lives. This did nothing to improve General Tuker's temper. He took it out on his pet hate, the monastery. "Like the eyes of an oil painting, it follows you. No matter where you are, there it is, looking down at you."

Another directive from General Clark's headquarters had a curious effect on him. The fury that had swept him before was nowhere in evidence. He internalized it, became calm, became frostily correct, became the prototype of a soldier and a gentleman. As though he were ordering a taxi for the theater, he had his driver fuel up his car for Naples.

"Why in the world," I asked, "is he going to Naples? Is it to shoot Mark Clark?"

The corners of Dr. Farnsworth's mouth twitched, and he came as near to smiling as I'd ever seen him. "That would be an acceptable solution."

Before the hour was out, Tuker was back. He was driving the car himself, with the corporal slumped beside him. We helped bring the wounded man in and set his broken arm. The general marched back and forth just out of earshot and unburdened himself to Dr. Farnsworth.

"Nurse Forquet."

I turned, to be told I was driving General Tuker into Naples.

"There are no drivers available," Farnsworth explained. "But I've heard you're an ace with anything that burns petrol."

"Well, I—"

The general looked me over. "You'll do. Let's go, Lieutenant."

Once on the way, he dropped his abrupt manner and offered me tea from his canteen. Then he withdrew into his own somber thoughts, indicating that I was to do the same. The drive south on Route 6 was in striking contrast to the way up. The engineers had cleared and repaired the damage, wrecked vehicles had been towed away or rolled over the side, bomb craters filled and paved, and, wonder of wonders, they had drawn a yellow centerline.

On the other hand, there were the tanks that never reached us, the abandoned trucks with boxes of supplies from soap to bandages, and presumably batteries. All the things we so desperately needed.

When we entered the outskirts of the city, the general began to talk. "There's no way to take Monte Cassino and not the monastery. I requested Fifth Army Intelligence to furnish all available information regarding it. The answer came back promptly. They had none. Nothing at all. It sits atop Monte Cassino, but they had no interest in it. Whether it is occupied by a German garrison no one thought to enquire. Although it has been a thorn in our side from the beginning, no one bothered to discover if the building has been reinforced over the years, and if so, with what."

I kept my eyes on the road. I didn't know how you replied to a major general.

"Therefore," he said, "this trip into Naples has become necessary. In the middle of a battle it is necessary for me to stop everything and go to the library. That, young woman, is exactly where we're headed, the library!"

I hope we get there, I answered silently. Following his directions, we'd left Route 6 and were prowling about in some corner of Naples, totally lost. But generals have plenty of practice in map reading. He calmly spread out a colorful assortment of road maps, on his lap, on my shoulder, on the dash, and got us to the library ten minutes later.

I helped him pull down volumes as old as the librarian, who, once he understood our mission, brought out ancient compendiums from storage. One was in English, and from it I absorbed a bit of the history of the Monte Cassino monastery. Founded in the sixth century by St. Benedict, the monastery was almost entirely rebuilt in the sixteenth and seventeenth centuries, and converted into a fortress in the nineteenth. The only entrance was by a narrow, low archway of stone blocks, each thirty-five feet long. The walls were a hundred fifty feet high, of solid masonry, ten feet thick at the base, and faced with cream-colored Travertino stone. It comprised a cathedral, a seminary, a fully equipped observatory, and a college for boys. Its famous library ran the entire length, with workshops for paper making, illuminating, and bookbinding.

The general sat at a table and made notes. An hour and a half later he closed the last reference book and looked over at me. "I would be pleased if you would dine with me, Miss Forquet."

I gulped only once. "I am hungry," I said.

Outside there was an American four-wheel drive parked next to our car.

"Take that one," he said.

"But—?"

He waited, looking at me quizzically.

"Yes sir." Military necessity, I would say to any American MP who tried to arrest me, a general at Cassino needs a four-wheel drive.

I liberated the American vehicle, hot-wiring the ignition as Crazy Dancer had taught me. This was more like it!

The general had invited me to dine, and dine we did. We were escorted with bows and compliments to the best table in the best restaurant in the city, whose only wall was bolstered by sandbags.

"I don't suppose the menu is to be believed," I said, looking over the elaborate bill of fare.

General Tuker chortled and read aloud such specialties as duck, prime rib of beef, and Yorkshire pudding. I craned to see. These items were indeed listed in a flowing, calligraphic hand.

I looked at him questioningly.

He was delighted to inform me, "Stocked from the senior officers' mess. We have the food, they have the atmosphere."

"What a great idea," I said approvingly as I looked out over the bay. It was a magnificent panorama. Perched on a hilltop, we were unable to see the pulverized destruction.

Wine with the meal, and my tiredness floated away. Alongside the roast beef and Yorkshire pudding was the best pasta I'd eaten before or since, made with mussels, calamari, prawns, and scallops baked in a mushroom sauce. By the second glass of wine I forgot I was dining with a major general and commanding officer of a division. He was a fascinating conversationalist, a scholar, and author of several military treatises. I wondered what he would have to say about Cassino after the war. I hoped he could report that we'd won it.

Over claret he discussed the problem of the monastery. "A thousand-pound bomb, even if well placed, would be quite useless."

"It's a shame that such a beautiful old building must be destroyed at all. You don't suppose the monks still inhabit it? Are you certain they were evacuated? And what about the art treasures and documents?"

"The Germans are good about sparing art and documents. About the abbot and any remaining monks, I don't know. They may have also given shelter to refugees. It's quite possible. And someone thought there was a deaf-mute servant. In any case we'll give notice before we attack, broadcast a warning."

Our American transport got us back to the front in record time.

OUR TROOPS HUDDLED against winter snow turned to slush. A grayness lay over the mountain like a scrim. Below in the valley it was no better: the marsh was a sea of mud. The depressing landscape matched the uncomfortable circumstances in which the waiting men found themselves. They were too miserable to sleep or read. Water was rationed, as it had to be brought seven miles by mule, so shaving was out. Although one enterprising soldier was using the dregs of his tea to moisten his stubble. Several men had settled down to writing letters home. Most sat and stared at the monastery. Everyone knew by now that its total extinction was imminent. We had been told officially that reinforcements in the form of the 4th/6th Rajputana Rifles were on the way. Two more battalions of Gurkhas held the valley.

The objective was point 953, a promontory close under the defending walls of the monastery. It seemed an appalling route to me, but then, as my friend had told me, the Gurkhas were renowned as mountain fighters. Somewhere, although they had not yet arrived, was a company of Maori sappers, also known as New Zealand's "wild Irish." Their job was to remove those deadly *Schuh* mines with which the place was strewn. This was difficult, as they were simply little wooden shoeboxes with a minimum of metal, making mine sweepers all but useless, while the snow hid them from visual detection. When they did show up, the Maoris were a cheerful bunch. They didn't bother with salutes, but waved smilingly at their officers.

With the addition of so many troops the plan must be to attack simultaneously, again from the southwest and the north, a route that had been chiseled out by the Americans in the first, failed attempt that preceded my tour of duty here. But with the seasoned Indian division backed by the 2nd New Zealand, it was felt we had a chance.

The wait now was for all these forces to get into position. If they attacked with strong air cover it might work. I frequently checked the sky—slate and gray, but no shielding fog.

I heard engines and glanced up. Not the Mitchell medium-range bombers we were expecting but Flying Fortresses all the way from Africa. Weren't they early? The troops from India had barely arrived, and the New Zealanders weren't in position yet.

The planes, dipping slightly, flew directly at the monastery. The bomb bays opened. Were the monks still there? Were they kneeling at the altar chanting the antiphon of the Blessed Virgin? The explosions sent up tremendous clouds of brilliant orange, punctuated by smoke and dust shot through with yellow flashes. Had they finished "Beseech Christ on our behalf" before those words were swallowed in this unchristian baptism?

When the smoke cleared, there was a murmur from the troops. It was a miracle. The monastery stood. Seemingly, it had not been affected by this first deadly run. A second pass, and a third. It stood, with no discernible damage. At 1400 hours it was the turn of the Mitchells. As each successive smoke cloud dissipated, the pounding began to show. The windows appeared larger and their frames were jagged. There was a fissure in the walls, and the roof was beginning to look uneven.

Then, as I watched, the west wall of the building collapsed. I remembered the refugees—had they knelt and chanted with the monks? Tuker had mentioned a warning salvo. But there was none. The planes had appeared too early out of the sky.

Demolishing the monastery was only part of their job; they were to provide air cover for the assault. But when the monastery crumbled, they considered their mission accomplished and left, with Tuker shaking an impotent fist skyward.

The fury of the bombing had been fury in a vacuum, wasteful and tragic. That beautiful centuries-old abbey was gone.

The planes had gone too. Whether deliberately or not, Air Command had not been given the full picture. The monastery was the target, they wiped it out, they left. Air cover was not on their agenda. Too many generals, too many egos vying for headlines back home. Egg would have said, "Too many cooks spoil the broth."

Planes or no planes, the attack was ordered, and hell opened before my eyes. They moved out, two platoons, the third following in reserve. They crawled silently along Snakehead Ridge toward point 953. The men set their feet so as not to dislodge a stone or stumble.

It was easy to turn an ankle carrying a heavy Bren gun or a flame-thrower.

The Germans opened up. Withering fire caught the climbers in the open. Machine guns, mortars, grenades—and mines, the area had not been properly cleared of mines. The rubble that had been the monastery now provided ideal cover for German gunners.

Our men were picked off. Stretcher bearers began bringing down the wounded. I passed among them with gauze and morphine. The Rajputana Rifles reached what looked like a belt of scrub. Instead, it was a thicket of thorn, breast high. I began pulling them out of wounds along with shards of barbed wire. I had never seen such vicious lacerations.

Their colonel was shot through the stomach and lay looking up at me. I stopped the bleeding. The morphine was used up. We were short of basic supplies. I had to watch him die. There was one Gurkha stretcher bearer who again and again climbed over those exposed crags to bring in another fallen shape. He must have made sixteen trips into that inferno. This time he was halfway back when the soldier at the other end of the stretcher was hit, and fell, barely fifty yards from me. I rushed out and grabbed his end of the stretcher. He struggled to his feet and tried to help, but ended up leaning on my shoulder. Somehow, the Gurkha and I brought them both in.

The Gurkha nodded at the chaos we had just left. He was asking for my help, and I went with him. A barrage of mortars exploded around us. When it cleared sufficiently to see, the man we had come after was dead. The Gurkha signed that he had spotted someone farther on, but by now I was confused as to where I was and where our lines were.

A shape loomed out of the dust. Another stretcher bearer—only something was wrong. He was wearing the wrong uniform. I stood still, grooved into the rock I stood on. He'd have to kill me, of course. Instead he said, in passable English, "You're lost?"

I nodded. I couldn't speak.

"That way." He pointed. "South of that rock. That's where you want to be."

"*Danke schön,*" I whispered, hardly getting it out.

"English?" he asked.

"Canadian."

"Good luck," he said, and disappeared in the other direction.

"Good luck—" But he had gone.

My Gurkha, who had stood silent and motionless during this exchange, told me such meetings between the lines were not uncommon. Unofficial, unsanctioned, it nevertheless happened as both sides respected a mutual low-level grunt truce and evacuated their wounded.

The attack was repulsed, and the Germans held on to the Gustav Line. It was almost three months later that our forces took Monte Cassino.

I REMEMBER HEARING several wounded praying in Polish. I had come to recognize these brave fighters in their long gray-green coats. They had lost their homeland early on, but now, as the Germans retreated, they had hope for the first time. The final operation itself was spearheaded by a Canadian corps under Major General Sir Oliver Leese. The way it played out, as I heard afterward, Leese, by taking and holding the Liri Valley, strengthened us at Cassino. The combined pressure breached the German defenses in a number of places, and allowed the Americans to push up the coast, while the British entered the valley. Cassino, that great wall, fell to the Polish Corps May 18, 1944.

The Germans could not withstand this concentrated drive and gave way even in the Alban Hills. The road to Rome was wide open.

Many times in these last months my hand strayed to Egg's crucifix, which I wore inside my shirt. On the same chain was tied a gray and white feather. I thought of Crazy Dancer at the most unexpected moments. I think because I expected to be dead by now, and I wanted him to guide me as he had that old chief. I wanted to walk in his moccasins.

It was haphazard, I felt, whether one survived this madness or not. It depended on such things as going for a drink of water or scrounging up more morphine, or deferring getting the bandage rolls that were needed. You were or you were not in a certain place when the shell made a crater of it. Nurse Lander could have asked someone else to dump the basin. Nurse Lander could have stayed in Canada and not volunteered in the first place.

Funny, I didn't know where in Canada she came from, or even her first name. All I remembered—she was the one who kept everybody's spirits up, the first to wade into the mud and help with the plasma. She didn't hesitate to drag a dead soldier to the burial row, her blond hair flying. And her own body had been added to the pile. I hadn't had time to think about her until now. I thought about the German stretcher bearer too. I hoped he'd survived.

I stroked my feather and Egg's cross. I'd been kept alive and relatively sane. Soon I would be entering the Eternal City.

*   *   *

DAYS LATER WE were strung out on the road to Rome. It was a victory march, but probably not recognizable as such. We were a straggling line of exhausted, dirty, exultant beings. Of all the conquerors that over the centuries had taken Rome we were certainly the least likely and the most ragged. Our vehicles were in no better shape than we were. How we could have used Crazy Dancer! Overheated motors, clogged fuel lines, blown tires were the norm. Sooty, blackened, fed a vile mixture of gasolines, they rolled on.

I was driving again, simply because it was assumed I would be. When we got to Rome I planned to apply for a proper army vehicle license. In the meantime I was part of the long line wending its way, with a recalcitrant sun showing itself occasionally.

Then the engine sputtered, the jeep bucked under my hands and came to a stop.

"Get that thing off the road."

"Yes sir." I outranked him, but on the road those directing traffic have ultimate authority, even over generals. Besides, we nurses had never had time to learn army protocol, and it wasn't expected of us. I jumped out of the jeep and with the help of a couple of MPs pushed it into a field of cauliflowers. I opened the hood. Thanks to Crazy Dancer I had seen enough engines to recognize that a wire from the distributor had burned through. I borrowed the foil from a pack of cigarettes a soldier had dropped out of line to inhale. I twisted the ends of the wire around each other and splinted them with bits of foil.

Getting back into the jeep, I tried to start it when a sudden explosion racked the column ahead—where I would have been if the jeep hadn't acted up. A land mine sent pieces of trucks and people showering down. Something penetrated my body.

I thought it was the sound. I didn't realize I'd been hit. But the flying metal fractured my right elbow, all three bones, humerus, radius, and ulna. I was taken back to the same casualty station I'd helped set up. I pleaded with Dr. Farnsworth, who was still with us, to operate there and then. I had seen him perform miracles in the field. Otherwise, it would mean being airlifted to London, and a circuitous route home.

Farnsworth, bless him, agreed without argument, commandeered a surgical nurse, and woke up our anesthetist. My elbow was x-rayed, and he went to work, asking me if I minded baling wire.

"Doctor," I said, "I'm wearing a crucifix. Would you mind taking it to Rome with you? The Pope needs to bless it. And when he does, it's to be sent to Sister Eglantine, Charity Hospital, Montreal, Canada."

"Don't fret," he said. "It's as good as done. I'm sure His Holiness will not refuse a good Anabaptist."

Before the anesthetist clapped the mask over my face, I saw the bolt intended for my elbow.

THE HOSPITAL SHIP was hazy. I'd get used to the roll and then it would start to pitch.

I remember nothing of the crossing. I was in and out of morphine dreams, in which I had tumbled off the world and was trying to climb back on, but the globe rotated and I couldn't manage.

The ship's chief medical officer bent over me, explaining in a kindly voice that I would not in the future have the use of my right arm. "Oh, and practice your signature with your left hand."

A nurse without the use of her right arm?

I FOUND MYSELF a patient in ward B, one of my own wards. They'd put me at the end and curtained it off for privacy.

I didn't like being a patient. Still, I think it should be a requirement for every nurse and doctor. You see things from a different point of view. For instance, the bedpan. The position is antithetical to human beings, but tied into an IV stand it's difficult to get up and take it with you into the bathroom, which was what I did.

Sister Egg popped in every day to scold me. "You're giving us so much trouble, Kathy, that I know you're better."

I confessed to her my fear over the loss of movement in my arm.

"You've seen enough to know what therapy can do. We'll bring you right along."

I redoubled my efforts, squeezing a ball in my hand when I was too tired to do anything else.

The strangest thing about being back from the war was that no one wanted to hear about it. I tried innumerable times to convey my impressions of the other nurses, accounts of the roads, the scenery, what it was like to be under bombardment, how we went about setting up a clearing station, triage, evacuating priority-three patients, having dinner with a major general—bedbugs. So many things. They'd piled up in me with no opportunity to assess them. Even Egg was too busy to listen. Civilians, I thought, deliberately shut out the war. And I remembered myself—hadn't I always gone to the ladies' room or to buy popcorn when the Movietone news showed hospital ships unloading wounded? It was too much to absorb, too much grief, too much anguish, and no frame of reference.

But it was too bad. Because along with the horrors and the glimpses of hell, there were some wonderful things about the war. The way wounded men hauled unconscious buddies into the station. Nurses and doctors forgot the civilian pecking order and helped each other with the most menial duties. Frontline combat erased rank, sex, and color. Not once in Italy did anyone question my copper skin.

A joyous note in the midst of this sere landscape, a package arrived and out tumbled Sister Egg's crucifix and a note from surgeon Farnsworth. He had indeed marched into Rome, and an audience with the Pope had been arranged. The Pope was highly interested in the Anabaptist service and blessed the crucifix on the spot.

The pupils of Sister Egg's eyes rolled up out of sight. It scared me until I realized it was sheer ecstasy.

My arm was becoming more flexible, but I had a long way to go before it could be considered usable. Egg made a mark on the wall. I was ambulatory now, and only the incapacity of my arm kept me from working. I walked my fingers painfully up the wall again and again, morning, noon, and night, aiming for Egg's mark. At times I'd flinch from even starting.

Then it happened: one glorious day my fingers crawled up the wall and touched the mark.

I went flying to Sister. She looked at me calmly through round spectacles and went with me to verify my performance with her own eyes. "Excellent," she said, and made a new mark higher than the first by a good six inches.

Two weeks later my arm was almost well. Follow-up X rays showed that Dr. Farnsworth had been as good as his word. There was the bolt, hammered into the humerus, and the baling wire twisted around the fragments of the two forearm bones. Twenty years down the road arthritis might set in, but the best preventative was to build up the muscles and exercise them daily.

This prescription was exactly what I wanted. I took up my duties as though I had never seen Maj. Dr. Farnsworth mop the blood from the tarpaulin floor, as though I had never performed Miller-Abbott suctions at midnight under flashlights when the generator quit, or transfused with wrong-size needles—the only ones I had—or looked into eyes of anguish and seen eighteen-year-olds meet death calling for their mothers, or had an enemy wish me good luck on the field of battle.

My father had put me back together. I had been able to manage Monte Cassino. Now I must do the same for my life.

hirteen

SOME DAYS LATER there was a melee at the prison compound, the result of a knife fight. I was told to scrub for an emergency amputation, and received the shock of my life. The draped body on the operating table was that of my friend, the Austrian lieutenant, von Kerll.

Dr. Bennett shook his head and muttered, "I don't know if it's worthwhile trying to patch this Boche up."

My training took over. The surgical nurse swabbed the wound and debrided it. I prepared the tray of sterile instruments.

"Somebody had it in for him," the doctor continued. "As I reconstruct it, there must have been more than one. They tried to slit his throat. During the course of which his leg was pinned, and someone went to work on it. The guards heard the commotion and dragged this fellow out. I don't know if it was in time. He's lost four pints of blood."

Involuntarily I checked the plasma bag. A moment later I asked, "Does he have to lose the leg?" I had to ask, even though I'd seen enough of this kind of carnage to know.

The other wounds were superficial. Someone, as the doctor said, had tried to cut his throat, but the slash missed the carotids. I remembered what Crazy Dancer told me about slashings. Dogs bite, it is the wolf that slashes. I deliberately sent my mind off on this tangent, while they took the leg just below the knee. It was a long operation. But at least Dr. Bennett had a sturdy wood floor under his feet and wasn't trying to keep his balance on a bloody tarp. I helped pack the wound, and began to dress it.

"He's a strong fellow. He should make it."

I liked Bennett. He hated working on the Boche, as he called them, but always did a meticulous job, and somewhere during the operation he forgot they were the enemy and began rooting for them as patients. By the end he had employed all his skill to see they made it. They usually did.

I walked alongside the gurney. How could I tell him? I'd almost rather lose my own leg. But I couldn't let him hear it from anyone else.

I remembered his initial relief at finding himself in one piece. It was on account of his mother. What kind of mother was she? She should rejoice that he wasn't at the bottom of the ocean. I reined in my thoughts, as I had taught myself to do. There were fewer and fewer places I could send them.

A student nurse and I accomplished the transfer to the cot. Then I went to wash my face and calm down.

I washed my face, but I didn't calm down. I dreaded the moment he would open his eyes.

Of course, when he did, he didn't realize. I was checking the glucose drip when he spoke quite distinctly in English. He said, as though continuing a conversation, "It must have been a *Zaunkönig*. It shrieked past, exploding my eardrum. The floor heaved, the sides of the ship buckled, lights flickered and flared up. Then nothing. It was dark. I remember this vile taste washing into my mouth. I was floating in an oil slick." He grabbed my hands. "Are they going to strafe us here in the water? Or leave us? Better have it over with." And he switched to German.

Bending over him I said soothingly, "What about the Rhine maidens? The Valkyries protect the ocean-going warriors."

"They didn't come. I called them, but they didn't come."

It was as I thought, he believed he was waking from his first ordeal, that he was just now off the U-boat.

I stopped by ward B again before going off duty and stood a moment by his bed. His sleep was restless, and he murmured, perhaps cursed, in German. I didn't know what he said, but I wanted him to wake up.

No, no, I didn't. I dreaded his waking up.

Erich wasn't lucid until the next day. I came by at noon to check on him. He was lying quietly, resignedly staring at the ceiling. It was a featureless white ceiling. "Kathy," he said in a very gentle tone, "you're here. So it's all right."

"What's all right, Erich?"

"I dreamt I wasn't in the hospital at all, but in prison. Gott, I thought. . . . But you're here. So it must be all right."

I hesitated. "You *were* transferred to the camp. Don't you remember?"

"So it's true?" He closed his eyes, and his jaw set. "It was better to be floating in waves of oil. That was better than . . ." He made himself stop.

We were both silent. It was Erich who finally spoke. "It wasn't yesterday you were sitting beside me? It was months ago?"

"Yes. Eighteen months."

There was a pause while he absorbed this. "And how have things been for you?" he asked politely.

I tried to match his tone. "I'm still doing business at the same old stand."

"And how is that young man of yours?"

"Dead." The word lay between us.

"I'm afraid to ask anything more. I suppose it was the war."

"A U-boat attack," I said, slowly and deliberately, without mercy.

A vein in his neck throbbed. That was all.

Why had I done that? Why had I punished him, I asked myself when I was out in the hall. He'd had no part in it. It wasn't his fault. Cassino, the monastery, it wasn't his fault. Yet it was, it was. He'd been awarded the Iron Cross. They don't do that except for direct kills.

I recognized that I was not in control and ducked into the bathroom, took several successive breaths, and steadied myself. If I didn't go back, someone else would tell him.

He didn't look at me when I came in but turned his head away. He was very angry.

"Hello again," I said, with professional cheeriness. "I thought I'd look in on you once more. Is there anything you want?"

He tried not to ask, but it broke from him. "My leg, if you wouldn't mind. Something for the pain. There's a cramp in my calf."

I deliberately massaged the wrong leg, hoping to get him to realize, to focus.

"The other one, the left. Just at the knee and below." It was that terrible phantom pain, where severed nerve ends scream, and nothing can be done about it.

"If I can just shift you a bit in bed, that sometimes relieves it." I slipped my hands under his shoulders, straightening him. "Any better?"

He smashed his mouth together rather than answer. But he was turning over in his mind what I had said.

"Your young man—when?"

"Soon after you were transferred."

"God, it's a filthy war."

"He called it fish-hearted."

"Fish-hearted? I like that. It's a damn, filthy, fish-hearted war. Will it ever be over?"

"Yes. We're going to win."

"But," he protested, "the Third Reich was to last a thousand years. Hitler was to overturn the Treaty of Versailles, restore the Teutonic spirit, Saxon myths, Skaldic poems, the Hanseatic code written on stone in runic rhymes. *Sieg heil!* With his great sword Gram conquers the giants and the dwarves. Ravens dine on the flesh of his enemies, swans pull the chariot of the sun across the sky— Kathy, give me something for the pain, or I will break down and cry like a child."

I counted my heartbeats. Then I said, clearly, distinctly, and with emphasis, "Which leg is hurting?"

"My left, I—" He stopped.

He knew. Oh, God, he knew.

I listened to the minutes on the wall clock. I'd never been conscious of them before.

"They *had* to take it off, I suppose?"

I was startled to hear him speak so calmly. "Yes, it was practically severed when they brought you in. It had to be done to save your life."

"I see. To save my life." He laughed shortly.

The charge nurse tapped me on the arm. "Cot 14 is asking for you."

I didn't want to leave him like this, but he had withdrawn to his own private hell.

I wasn't able to look in on Erich until the following morning. He seemed deep in thought, but when he saw me smiled deprecatingly, as though too much had passed between us and he was unsure of himself. "It was good of you to come by. Thank you."

"I wanted to, Erich."

"I'm afraid I took the news rather badly. It's one of those situations that don't come up often. I didn't know how to handle it. But I'm getting more used to it now. At least I think I am. I can talk about it, at any rate. And there's something I want to ask you."

"Yes?"

"It's about that British boy, the one who lost his leg. He didn't want to live afterward, did he?"

"No," I said truthfully, "he didn't."

"And then later, when he grew accustomed to it, he didn't want to go home. And he got you to write letters for him, saying he was slightly wounded but on the road to recovery?"

"Yes. Yes, he did. Oh, Erich, I'm so sorry. But it won't make as much difference as you think."

He held up his hand. "I'm not interested in all that. I'm sure they have marvelous prostheses these days. And I know the crutches will only be temporary, until the wound heals. I don't care about that. I'm not interested. I want to know about the British boy. I am interested in him. Did they amputate both legs?"

I shook my head.

"Just one? Which was it? Do you remember?"

"The left."

"Like me."

There was a pause before the uncomfortable interrogation resumed. "Where was the leg taken off? Below the knee? That's where they took mine, isn't it?"

"Yes, yes. But what's the use of—"

"A lot of use. A lot. It's very helpful."

He closed his eyes, and I began to hope he'd drifted off to sleep, when he said, still with his eyes closed, "You wrote letters for him, telling the lies he wanted the family back home to believe."

"I did, but I never sent them."

His eyes opened with a queer, bright, penetrating glance. "You didn't send them? Oh, Kathy. You are very much Kathy, aren't you? Or are you sometimes Oh-Be-Joyful's Daughter? What's it like to have two names?"

"Why don't you ask me something I can answer?"

"All right. Will you write letters home for me, Kathy? And tell them the same lies?"

"If I don't have to send them."

"No. You have to send them."

"But don't you want to know the rest? The British boy changed his mind. He went home, Erich. And he sent me a snapshot, taken at his wedding. It had a happy ending."

"I'm not interested anymore in the British boy." And he turned on his side, away from me.

WITH THE WAR going strongly in our favor, it seemed an odd time for a prison break. Yet one morning sirens screamed and searchlights crisscrossed a sky which was just lightening. I dressed hastily to hear the news. Sometime in the night five German prisoners cut through the barbed wire and escaped. One was captured almost immediately hiding in the granary, and returned. The hunt was on for the others, with snow-tired vehicles, a ski patrol, and dogs.

Before the day was out the remaining four were recaptured, one of them shot and killed.

The excitement produced a complete dislocation in hospital procedure. But I continued my careful supervision of Erich's progress. He was at a critical stage. Physically he was coming along, making an adequate recovery, but he totally rejected his body. The lack of interest he had expressed in the English boy extended to everything. I also was banished, everyone was, everything, including life itself. I'd been in that place. I knew it well.

However, the escape triggered something in Erich. I didn't realize at first when I found him pale and clammy, that it had anything to do with the breakout. His respiration was so quick and uneven that I was alarmed and decided to send for the resident, but Erich put out a hand and stopped me. "Please tell me," he said. "Who was killed? Was it Norbert? Norbert Freund?"

"Yes, I think that was the name. Did you know him?"

"He's the reason I'm here, the reason I don't have a leg."

"I don't understand."

"There's a clique, among the prisoners, of hard-line Nazis. They were suspicious of me from the first—I didn't give their stiff-armed salute at the mention of the Fuehrer's name, I didn't join in their songs of the Vaterland. So I was ostracized. That suited me fine.

"I judged from the influx of new inmates that the war was going badly for us. And this was confirmed—the arrivals were boys of fifteen and sixteen, called up, taken out of school. Old men were among them, the Volkssturm, who were the home guard, air raid wardens, they also wound up here. You can imagine the anger, despair, frustration at being out of it, while comrades, brothers, sons, fathers are dying."

"That explains the timing of the escape attempt," I said, pleased that he was taking me into his confidence again. "Everyone was asking, Why now, when it all seems to be winding down? But that explains it." I hesitated, then asked something that bothered me. "Do you feel that way, Erich?"

"Of course. My countrymen are being killed and maimed. At the same time I can't help wonder—when it's over, what will Austria's fate be? Will the Allies stick by their promise that the old Social Democratic Party and the constitution be restored? Or will she suffer reparations as a defeated enemy? I don't know. It could go so many ways."

I pressed him to tell me what led to the knife fight.

"A couple of weeks ago, during the exercise period, I slipped into one of the small warehouse sheds to write a letter. I was sitting on the floor, my back against a sack, piles of boxes in front of me.

A small group of men detached themselves from the others and stole in, one by one. They didn't notice me there. I realize now I should have stood up, made my presence known, and left. Even then it might have been too late. As it was, they began to discuss an escape."

"They planned the whole thing in front of you? You knew it was going to happen? Why didn't you say something?"

He gave me a long look.

"That was stupid. I'm sorry. Of course you couldn't."

He continued, assuming a detached tone. "One of them took out a cigarette butt. Another jostled him for it, and it dropped. In retrieving it, they spotted me. That was it. They tried to kill me."

"But you wouldn't have said anything. You didn't say anything."

"Because I wasn't a Nazi, they didn't credit me with being a patriot. To them it's the same thing. They don't understand the code that for four hundred years my family has lived by."

Perhaps they didn't understand, but I did. The nuances he saw, the distinctions he made, were those of a thoughtful man who rejected the fanaticism, yet embraced and loved his country. Even now with the war going against him he saw not only defeat but hope. It was a beginning, and I, who had made so many beginnings, saw that my job was to help him come to terms with his disability.

As far as I knew he had never looked at the amputation, and when I tended it, cleaned it, applied lotion, he looked away. If he could have left his leg in my care he would have.

It was time. I handed him the washcloth. He looked at me inquiringly. "I've already washed."

"You haven't finished."

His eyes followed mine, traveling the length of his leg, coming to an abrupt stop below the knee. "No," he said, "I can't."

I waited.

"I find it repulsive."

I waited.

He accepted the washcloth, clenched his hand over it, and, in a single angry gesture, made a pass over the stump. "There. Are you satisfied?"

I took the lotion from the table.

"What's that?"

"It's the lotion I rub you with. You have to start doing these things for yourself, Erich."

"Why?"

"Because the less scarring, the better success you'll have with the fit of the prosthesis, the more comfortable it will be, and the longer you'll be able to wear it."

He grit his teeth and, looking at the ceiling, pressed the lotion into his palm, and made a swipe with it across the wound. Most spilled.

"It's a start," I said. "We'll try again tomorrow."

The next day when I came, he took the washcloth from me and applied it assiduously to the wound. Then, reaching for the lotion, rubbed that in thoroughly. "Did you know," he was talking very fast, not letting himself think about what he was doing, "that D minor is Mozart's key of fate? He was composing the string quartet K421/417B while his wife was having a baby in the same room. You can hear her cries in the music, then the sudden forte as the second octave leaps to the minor tenth. An uproar in the thirty-second bar of the andante quiets to piano. The child is born."

"That's beautiful," I said. "You can pretend the string quartet is playing while you try the parallel bars." I got him to his feet and handed him crutches. Having so recently gone through therapy myself, I knew the physical pain, the emotional ups and downs, but I was living proof of its benefits, and I was determined that Erich should be restored to a normal human being in spite of himself.

He swung along beside me down the corridor. When we came to the therapy room, he confronted the bars, let the crutches clatter to the floor, and negotiated the space between bars by hopping and swinging his arms. What a superb athlete he was. Never once did he grab the bars for support.

I was ready with the crutches at the other end. The effort had exhausted him. He was wet with perspiration, and I insisted on a wheelchair for the return trip.

He didn't like me to show concern. If he'd had a bad day, he was sure to cover it up. But I got to know these ploys. He would talk music then, or philosophy or poetry. "Listen," and he quoted,

" 'You are like a flower, so chaste and pretty and pure. I look at you, and worry strikes me in my heart. It seems to me as if I place my hands on your head, praying that God will keep you so pure and pretty and chaste.' "

He looked at me with a distant smile. "The Nazis burned Heine's poetry, every scrap."

"Who would want to destroy such a lovely thing?" I asked.

"You are very *schön* yourself, Kathy."

"*Schön*? Isn't that thank you?"

"Thank you is *danke schön; schön* by itself is pretty, very pretty."

I gave him his pain medication.

"Why didn't you tell me that while I was in prison you'd seen action?"

"I don't know. It didn't seem relevant."

"Not relevant to be shipped to Italy, to have gone through Cassino, to have been wounded? Kathy, what happened to you happened to me. What you saw I saw, and the men locked in the psychiatric ward saw. It's relevant, Kathy. Believe me, it's relevant."

The day Erich stood for the first time with his artificial leg, a change came over him. Once on his feet he said, "I begin to imagine I am a man. I don't imagine I will do snowplow turns again or a downhill schuss, but the world is definitely meant to be grappled with from a standing position."

I laughed and agreed.

But now the parallel bars were an agonizing obstacle course. He faced them daily and marched along between them, not reaching for them, not even touching them, but, after a step or two, collapsing.

I always caught him. That was my job and I did it. Then one session in the therapy room, it all came together. His strength, his sense of balance—he walked unaided.

He turned to me in triumph. I shared it with him. He didn't want to go back to bed, but sat on the edge of it. "I no longer feel that terrible sense of *Weltschmerz.*" He smiled and translated, "World weariness."

"I know."

"Kathy, you fought right alongside me. I wonder why."

"I'm your nurse," I said, and went about the thousand and one duties that called me that morning. I had asked myself the same question, but always backed away from it as I did now.

Now that I had gotten him this far along, discharge and prison lay ahead. A man with one leg was vulnerable, and given a second chance would that same fanatical clique of prisoners succeed in killing him?

I went with this problem to Egg.

She looked over a mound of work. It didn't matter how high it was. She always found time for me.

"Kathy, I've been so busy I've hardly seen you."

"Sister, can we save another caterpillar?"

She laughed. "Love to."

"Well, then." I sat down and told her my struggle to bring the Austrian amputee to the point where his life seemed worth living again, only to throw him once more to the Nazis.

"Oh, dear." Egg's eyebrows shot up in consternation. "But how can we prevent it?"

I'd been waiting for that question. "We're so short-handed, and he couldn't escape. He couldn't very well limp out of here, even if he wanted to. We could use him in a dozen different capacities. So why not make him a trustee?"

Sister's glasses regarded me keenly. "Well, now," she said, "let's see what we can do."

ERICH WENT TO work for the nuns with a will. He managed his artificial leg with the skill of a skier, and was on his feet for hours taking on the heaviest tasks. Egg in particular was delighted with him. He upended and moved garbage cans, stowed cots, carried the mail sack in, and became our general factotum.

His quarters were an unused storage room, into which he crammed his old cot and a single chair. He added a bookcase, which he built himself out of a couple of bricks and a board he scrounged from somewhere. It was soon stocked with secondhand books the Sisters picked up for him in lieu of wages. I was not surprised to see a copy of Heinrich Heine's poems. I was surprised at a treatise on elasticity.

"Why would you be surprised? I'm an engineer."

"You are? I didn't know that."

"I have a degree, but the war came and I never made use of it."

Another volume also puzzled me, *The Last of the Mohicans*. "Now why would you be reading that?"

"It's a wonderful book. My favorite when I was thirteen. Did you ever read it?"

"I don't think so."

"You'd remember if you had. It's on account of this book that I didn't mind too much winding up in Canada. I always thought I'd like to live in blue sky country."

"You'd miss the city," I said, "the libraries, theater, music."

He laughed and his voice lit with enthusiasm. "I'd live in the forest, but I wouldn't be a hermit. I'd come in for an evening on the town, as the Americans say." He bent toward me. I was sitting on the floor and the door was open. This was something the Sisters insisted on. Propriety was in this fashion assured.

"In all this time I haven't seen you wear the onyx ring. Do you still have it?"

I flushed. "I should have given it back to you before."

"But why? It's yours. I gave it to you."

"I never accepted it. I couldn't accept it. It's too valuable."

"You talk as though it's a Draupnir, Odin's self-perpetuating gold ring from which nine new gold rings drop every ninth night. But this is only an ordinary black onyx ring. I would like to see it on your hand."

"You would?" I asked, suddenly feeling a strange admixture of things.

"You know, *Liebchen*"—he had taken to calling me that when we were alone—"it might even be possible . . . my boyhood dream of living in the wilderness, fishing, trapping, being close to nature. That kind of life must appeal to you too, it must be in your blood."

"Yes." And the few days I had spent with Anne Morning Light obliterated the little storage room. I'd been bathed and purified there, I'd been married. The honeymoon tepee of willow, the soft skins— Crazy Dancer filled my heart and my being. What was I doing here! I stumbled to my feet and without explanation rushed back to my room.

I hardly slept that night. "He's dead, he's dead," I told myself viciously. It was only a year and some months—too soon to allow myself to be involved, even mildly, with anyone. With Erich, some- times I forgot this. I forgot to hurt. What kind of person did that make me? Was I woman first, and person second? I got out of bed, stood in front of the dresser, and raised my eyes, looking at my reflection in the oval mirror.

I saw a woman. Young, dusky, and yes, attractive. I continued to study my face in the glass. *Schön,* he'd said, means pretty.

Deliberately I opened my top bureau drawer. I had wrapped the ring in tissue paper. But a gray and white feather lay on top of it. I put the feather with my wolf tail guardian at the bottom of the drawer and unwrapped the ring. Onyx—black, hard, polished, the diamond not large but magical. As I held it, colors shifted in its depths. The movement in its center made it seem almost alive. I put the ring on the second finger of my right hand. The innocuous hand. My left hand was bare. Indians don't exchange rings.

Crazy Dancer was no longer in the same world with me. I was young and I was "*schön,*" and someone thought enough of me to give me this beautiful ring.

I was conscious of the ring all morning, although no one noticed it. Or if they did, didn't comment.

I ran into Erich by the laundry chute. We each had a load of soiled linen to send down to the boiler room where the wash was done. He saw the ring immediately. But he said nothing.

At noon he caught up to me in the cafeteria. "Let's take our lunch outside," he said.

I fastened my sweater and followed him into the grounds. We sat on a low stone wall and unwrapped our sandwiches.

"It seems," he said, "that the American and British are at the Elbe, only sixty miles from Berlin. It's over, Kathy."

"Yes, I think so."

"And I'm not going back. Not like this. Not as a cripple."

"Erich, no one would imagine that you . . ."

"Not in the fore part of the day. But you know how it is. The damn thing starts to pain me. If I fight it, a sore develops, and the next day I'm a one-legged man on crutches. So, around four in the afternoon I unstrap the prosthesis. My mother generally entertains at that hour—you know, the local dignitaries, perhaps a visiting virtuoso—and I'd be expected to be part of the soiree."

"You've gone through a war, Erich. You have an engineering degree. Get your own apartment, make your own schedule."

"There speaks the new world. The obligation of centuries doesn't rest on you. You're free, independent, young—in a free, independent, young country. Kathy, I want to be part of that."

"You mean, stay here?"

He reached over and wiped a speck of mustard from my mouth. "Stay here with you," he corrected.

"But—" Too many what-ifs tumbled about in my mind.

"I want to transfer the ring, that I'm very happy to see you wearing, to the proper finger. In Europe the wedding band goes over the vena amoris on the middle finger of the right hand. That you're wearing it at all must mean something. Does it mean you feel for me some part of the love I feel for you? That is the question. I've loved you from the moment you changed my first damned plasma bag."

I tried to interrupt, to stop him, but he wouldn't have it.

"How could I speak? How could I say anything? I was the enemy, a defeated man, a prisoner. But things have changed. It would seem for the worse, but maybe it wasn't for the worst. I lost my leg. I thought that meant my life as well. I hoped you'd forget the surgical scissors, leave them so I could cut my wrists. But then I took a more philosophical view. I realized that committing suicide isn't really the first reaction. First you want to kill everyone else." He laughed.

I had tears at the back of my throat, but he could laugh.

"Don't you think that's an amazing insight? I do. I think it's pretty funny. And of course, once I thought that, killing myself was no longer an option. That's how a sense of humor saves us sometimes. Still I knew I wouldn't go home. But that was a negative. Now I see the positive side."

"Which is . . . ?"

"Staying here. Making a new life in the new world. I want it to be with you, Kathy. The things we joked about could actually be true, couldn't they? Please," he said, and put his hand over mine, "make it true. Marry me."

The next moment I was in his arms and we were both crying. Then I pushed myself away. "We have to think, Erich. Can this possibly work out?"

"Kathy, I've done nothing but think about it."

"But there are things you don't know. I'm married. I was married."

"What?"

"Yes, to Crazy Dancer. We were married in the Indian way. It was a blanket ceremony. The Canadian government doesn't recognize it, of course. But I feel married."

"But Crazy Dancer's ship, the troopship that left in the harbor here, was sunk by a U-boat. You told me that. He died at sea."

"Yes, that's true. But I still feel married."

"Of course. I understand. The commander, and Rudolf, one of my shipmates—I can't think of them as dead. I keep remembering conversations. Questions come up I want to put to them. When they're gone suddenly like that, you can't make yourself believe it."

"That's how it is," I said, seeing the plains of Romagna, seeing Nurse Lander, hearing the ping on the wash basin. "You don't quite believe it."

Erich watched me with concern, with apprehension. We had gone through the same things—he'd said that.

"When you were in prison, I found that I missed you. . . . And when I came back from Cassino and you were in my care again, it just happened. My mind and heart are still scrambling to make all sorts of adjustments."

"I'm trying to understand what you're saying, Kathy. You missed me—that's what you said, isn't it?"

"Yes . . ."

"That's enough. It means you have some feeling for me. What? Fondness? Love? Could it be love, *Liebchen?*"

Gray eyes looking into mine. "Yes, yes, it is love. I love you, Erich."

His embrace was total, and my starched nurse's cap fell on the ground between us.

Fourteen

OUR PRIVATE REALITY, the one that from that moment encompassed us, gave way to a public occurrence. April 12, 1945, Franklin Delano Roosevelt died. The world stood still and tried to absorb what this meant. But if the Germans hoped the shock would paralyze the forward thrust of Allied armies, they were mistaken. The Russians, pushing from the east, were poised to take Berlin. Montgomery on the west was trying to beat them to it. Hitler, it was said, had gone to ground in vaults under the city, while above him in the streets there was hand-to-hand fighting. Another terrible rumor that everyone believed because it was so unbelievable was that Hitler, paranoid, watching everything collapse around him, turned on his own people: Many Berliners sought safety from Allied bombing in the railroad tunnels; it was said Hitler ordered the water sluices and valves opened, and drowned them by the hundreds.

Rumors piled one on another. A few days later the story was bruited about that Hitler had married his mistress, Eva Braun, and died with her in a suicide pact, after first poisoning his dog and watching the effect. May fourth, German forces in the field surrendered to Montgomery. The formal document of surrender that ended the European war was signed and witnessed May eighth at Eisenhower's headquarters in Reims, in the presence of French and Russian delegations. Ike, who had just come from viewing the mass graves of Treblinka where men, women, and children were reduced to jutting ribs and pelvic bones, refused to shake hands with the German general. This was no civilized war, and he refused to confer civility on it by a handshake. Americans are great. I love them.

Wild celebration in the streets of Montreal. The great bells of Notre Dame pealed out over the city. The hospital flew the yellow and white flag of the Vatican alongside the Canadian Red Ensign, the Tricoleur, the Union Jack, and the Stars and Stripes. Patients sat up in bed and blew horns and paper favors that unrolled. Everywhere people joined arms. Strangers kissed and sang. Radios blared "La Marseillaise." Bars stayed open and there were free drinks. Erich picked me up and twirled me around, and we both ended on the floor. We stayed where we were, laughing and kissing.

"I'm no longer a prisoner," he said. "I marry you as a free man."

"Hurray!" I shouted.

But when he had a chance to think about it: "It's bad the Russians hold Berlin, after what we did to them at Stalingrad and Moscow."

He cheered considerably as it came out that Berlin would be divided into two zones, and Vienna into four. The *Standard* ran an interesting article revealing that Roosevelt and Churchill had met here in Quebec Province in August of '43 and again at the Octagon Conference September 11, 1944, in which a plan was developed to limit Russian spoils. The editorial page predicted that the Americans would mop up the Japanese in short order. The world would be at peace.

"We lived through history," I said.

"And contributed to it," he replied bitterly.

But this was not the time for bitterness. The future, which had been on hold, was suddenly here, open, and ready for us. We felt the wonderful hope that filled the air, it spilled into our personal lives. Anything was possible. All the what-ifs could come out of the shadows.

We were happy, so filled with new confidence that I didn't want the slightest cloud to mar our wedding. "You must write your parents," I said to Erich. "You must tell them everything, explain your decision, tell them you are getting married to an Indian girl and starting a new life."

He agreed. He too had enough happiness to share.

Neither of us mentioned our coming marriage at the hospital. Though Erich was no longer a prisoner, he was Austrian, and feeling didn't die easily. However, Mama Kathy had to know and, if possible, attend. She, and Connie and Jeff, and Georges if he was back. It would be a wonderful reunion. After Papa died, our telephone had been discontinued. We couldn't afford one. But Mama had moved back home and wrote proudly that a phone line had been installed. It was as though I stepped into a new era.

I felt quite cosmopolitan as I laid out my dimes and placed a call to Alberta. There was no answer from the other end. I was about to hang up when her voice came through the wire. Unmistakably her voice, yet altered. There was no timbre in it, and before knowing why I was asking, "Mama, are you all right?"

I heard her tell me Georges was dead, but it didn't register.

"He was killed two days ago, after the surrender. He was moving from his quarters at Bletchley Park, crossing a field on his way to

say goodbye to a friend. And, you know, they're renovating everywhere, trying to clean up the rubble. There was an earth-moving
machine working above him. It triggered an unexploded bomb, and
the building he was walking by gave way."

I love you, Mama, I love you. Even that I couldn't say. My dimes
were used up. I continued to sit in the phone booth.

I sat in the public phone booth and tried to make sense of things,
collapsing buildings, dying two days after the war ended, never coming home. Thank God Connie was married and had her own life.
Still, I know she thought of herself as half a person. I remembered
Georges from the time I was very little. I remembered he made
shadow pictures for me on the wall, a rabbit whose nose twitched, a
long-necked dinosaur that changed into a giraffe when I got scared.
I remembered his magician's hat, and that he had made reality disappear and replaced it with his own. Please, please. Make this reality
go away, make it disappear.

I walked back to where Erich waited.

"Well," he asked, "can they come?"

"No." I didn't tell him. I was afraid he would try to comfort me.
For things that make no sense there is no comfort.

I DIDN'T WANT to be married in a church. That belonged to another
young man, and young woman.

I put on my best dress, and Erich bought a beautiful spring bouquet of jonquils and sweet alyssum, which I carried, trying not to
remember the flowers I once found in my shoes.

For the occasion he borrowed the onyx ring. "On our first anniversary you'll have a gold band," he promised.

We were married before a justice of the peace in a civil ceremony, one the dominion of Canada recognized. Since we were in
Canadian jurisdiction, the ring went on the fourth finger of my left
hand.

There was no one to stand up for either of us. I hadn't called
Mama back. I hadn't the heart. Erich had been part of the German
war machine responsible for the fact that Georges would not be coming back. I wasn't sure she would feel that way, but she might. And
I didn't want any cloud on this special day.

I didn't know Erich had rented a motel room. It was the first of
the surprises he'd arranged. "I'm going to dress you like an Austrian
bride. Look," and he produced a pair of lace curtains from Mother
Superior's room, that were supposedly in the wash. He draped one

around me in a sort of flounce. The other, a bridal veil, he fastened to my hair with bobby pins I produced from my purse.

He stood back and surveyed his efforts. "The hair is not right," he said critically. "It needs to be up. And, you know, poofy in front."

"I know how to do that," and I imitated one of Mandy's coiffeurs.

He was delighted. "You look like a grand duchess," he said, and wound flowers in my pompadour. I broke one off to put behind his ear. Then we bowed to each other, linked arms, and waltzed around the room. Every time he made a turn he fell down, me on top of him. This occasioned a glass of claret, which was part of his surprise, and a song.

He started with "The Blue Danube." I contributed the latest Bing Crosby hit, "Don't Fence Me In." He took over with *"Röslein, Röslein, Röslein rot, Röslein auf der Heiden."*

He was shy about making love because of his leg, but a sheet tossed lightly over us, and who knew. Who knew, who cared? When he called me *Liebchen* the great Nordic god Thor strode the moment, sweeping us to a Valhalla of storm and ecstasy. We clung to each other. The onyx ring, on my left hand now, said, You are one.

THE SURPRISES CONTINUED. Next, our wedding breakfast. He had paid the manager's wife to shop for and cook the meal, which he assured me was in the finest Austrian tradition.

"There," he said, sitting across from me, while between us was spread bacon and eggs, pancakes, potatoes, and a lavish frosted roll. "Now I feel married." The coffee was steaming hot, and ladled into it, a mountain of whipped cream.

Erich's final surprise was to produce Mandy. She gave me a big hug and kiss. "Getting married agrees with you," she said, "you should do it more often."

Out of her nurse's uniform she looked like a pinup girl fresh off a Petty calendar. Erich, it turned out, had phoned and persuaded her to come after swearing her to secrecy.

"I'm not in touch with anyone from the hospital," she told us. "But Robert made it back. We're engaged," she said, answering my unasked question. Then came a defense and justification of him, which, while it failed to change my opinion of Robert, made me like her even more.

"You can't believe what that boy went through. He was posted to North Africa with the 8th, just west of Tobruk, the Gazala-Bir line. And it sobered him down, but good. Do you know it's absolutely true that the enemy—" She stopped self-consciously. "Excuse me,

Erich. But it's got to be said. They didn't pay the slightest attention to the red cross clearly painted on top of the hospital roof. They strafed everything. Patients were killed and one of the doctors."

"He was with the 8th Army?" Eric asked. "That means they were up against Rommel."

"That's right. The Boche—the Germans," she corrected herself, "held everything from Alamein to Tripoli. The conditions were impossible, a dead horse right outside the building swelled up and gave off an awful odor. The hospital ran short of supplies. Especially water. The patients weren't bathed. Can you imagine, Kathy? Everyone stank, and everyone had heat rash. I mean, they sweated all day and slept in their clothes at night.

"And the birds! That was the other thing, birds flew up and down the corridors, and dogs prowled between the beds licking up anything on the floor. Can you imagine working under those conditions?"

She apparently had put out of her mind that volunteering for these conditions saved his skin. However, I said temperately, "As long as he came out of it okay. So you're engaged?"

"Oh yes. He even got a commendation. And that went a long way toward smoothing things over with my dad." She went on to expound a bit of Mandy philosophy. "Have you ever noticed that when things are meant to be, everything falls into place?"

Not for everybody, I reflected, pushing back thoughts of Crazy Dancer and Georges, and the Gurkhas, trying not to remember British, New Zealand, and Maori boys left on the mountain. Mandy went on. "A surgeon friend of Dad's is retiring and he bought the practice for Robert."

I saw what she meant about things falling into place.

"I don't intend to stay in the nursing profession," Mandy was saying. "You have to be crazy to work that hard. Besides, we're planning a family. We want three children, a boy, a girl, and—whatever. What do you two want?"

We looked shyly at each other. Oddly enough we had never discussed children.

"A whatever," Erich told her.

Mandy treated us to a dinner at the Hotel Windsor, and pulled me into the ladies' room to say, "Remember our first quarrel?—well, almost a quarrel. I told you people were talking about the time you were spending with Erich, and I advised you to cool it. I'm so glad you didn't pay any attention to me."

I hugged her, thinking this was the reason I loved this flighty, irrepressible girl. She was genuinely glad to see me happy. She was a friend.

Back at the table she explained for the second time that Robert couldn't be here. She filled in the picture by adding that he was assisting at a rhinoplasty.

"That's a nose job, isn't it?" Erich asked.

It turned out the practice was in plastic surgery.

"But Mandy," I couldn't help exclaiming, "he's such a talented surgeon. You mustn't let him waste his gift."

Mandy set down her fork and stared at me in her nearsighted way. "I knew you'd say that, Kathy. Every time I'm with you, you change my entire life. That's exactly what I said to Robert, feeling just like you when I said it. But he's not only doing the rich and infamous. Three days a week it's reconstructive work on vets. You remember those 'serviceable' faces we gave them on ward A?"

It was hard to part from Mandy. I didn't know when I'd see her again.

Later that night I sneaked Erich into my room, and under the covers. Money for another motel evening had run out, so in whispers we planned our life. One of the first things Erich did was to apply for Canadian residency. That made it all seem real. The little blond boy in the sailor suit pitching stones at the edge of the Bodensee, a future Canadian citizen.

We worked on a vita for him to mail to various architectural firms here in Montreal and Quebec, listing his schooling and credentials. With his degree in engineering this seemed a good route to try. We worried about the backlash he was almost certain to encounter. But when we thought about it soberly, it didn't seem that a one-legged Austrian naval lieutenant and an Indian woman who didn't know much about being Indian would do too well trapping and living off the land.

He would, he decided, start as a draftsman. "First I'll draw the blueprints, then I'll design them, and then . . ."

"And by then you'll be a world-famous architect and own the company."

"And go into politics," he concluded.

"Politics?" I was impressed.

He seemed a bit embarrassed. "That's the way I would have wound up if I'd gone back to Austria. In my family it's expected."

"Well, here nothing's expected. You do what you want."

After Erich was almost discovered in the hall making his nightly excursion to my room, we rethought our secret marriage and came to the conclusion that we should tell Sister Egg.

*   *   *

HAND IN HAND, we stood in front of her desk. She looked up with candid, round, nearsighted eyes, framed in glasses that mildly distorted them.

Before she could verbalize her question, Erich took my hand and stretched it toward her. Since our marriage I wore the ring on my right hand, on the vena amoris, which pleased Erich—and no one else suspected.

"What's this?" Sister asked.

"We're married," I said, wiggling my fingers so the small diamond flashed.

Egg rose from the chair to make the sign of the cross over us. Her round child's face was flooded with joy. "Bless you. Bless you both." Then, sinking back in her chair, "Imagine, a romance here, within the walls of this old building. It is absolutely delicious to think about. And you love each other very much?" She looked from me to Erich and back again.

"Very much," he assured her. "We love each other very much."

"Good. Good. That is very good. It is also good not to broadcast it. There is very little forgiveness yet for the war. I myself don't want to know anything officially." And she recited one of the little aphorisms for which she was famous. "Never trouble trouble, till trouble troubles you. Now," she said expeditiously, "I will take soundings, ferret out the lay of the land, and let you know when it's advisable for you to make your announcement."

"Isn't she something?" I said to Erich that night under the covers. Sister Egg, heaven knows under what pretext, protected us by changing floors with Sister Magdalena. Even with this added security, we still laughed with our heads under the covers, and when he hummed Austrian folks songs, it was with his lips against my ear.

We found out all sorts of things about each other. He had mixed up the names of colors when he was little. He thought blood was green. And I told him the story Mama Kathy used to tell me, that when I was little I insisted on dressing myself, and the year I started school wore my dresses backward so I could button them.

"Kathy, Kathy," he said. "You were always Kathy."

I told him about my blue-eyed papa. "Mama used to say his eyes were so blue you could swim in them."

Finally I was able to tell him. I hadn't planned it, it just spilled out, the pent-up agony over Georges. "The reason no one came to our wedding is that I never asked them."

"You didn't? But I thought—"

"I know, the phone call. Erich, Mama Kathy just had word. Georges is dead. Two days after the war ended." I was able to cry now, so harshly that my body shook. Now I wanted his comfort, now I could accept it. We had grown close.

What to do about Mama Kathy had been troubling me. I'd been married for six weeks, and she didn't know about it.

Erich resolved the dilemma by saying, "The best thing to do now is just show up."

"You mean, go back to Alberta? That's where she is now."

"Yes. We'll save for it."

I hugged him for having such wonderful ideas.

WE SENT OFF the first job inquiries. Acceptance would bring independence. We could find an apartment, set up housekeeping, and openly acknowledge our marriage. But we worried.

Since Egg had not reported back to us, I could only assume that she still felt a tide of opposition, and did not judge even my job secure. Especially now, with prisoners repatriated, half the cots were empty in many wards. The pressing need for nurses was past. We were treating mainly chronic conditions. Aside from service-related cases of malaria contracted in the South Pacific, hookworm picked up in the Philippines, and an eye condition brought back from the Libyan desert, there were largely civilian disorders, the usual appendectomies, fractures, and infections, and Dr. Bennett had a cholecystectomy scheduled. The hospital was no longer on a wartime footing. I could easily be replaced. So for the moment we left things as they were.

A letter came.

I recognized the handwriting, and something inside me shriveled.

Crazy Dancer.

Crazy Dancer had written me this letter. I looked at the postmark. It was yesterday.

My fingers went at the envelope like a ravening thing, fumbling in their haste. I could only get it open by tearing jaggedly. I didn't read it. I picked out the important words: *Meet me . . . two o'clock in the afternoon . . . Canadian Pacific station.*

After taking in the gigantic fact that he was alive and had written this, I read it. Slowly, word for word.

I was in such a turmoil I couldn't think. An initial rush of joy was extinguished by an avalanche of emotion. Chaotic, undecipherable. My God, what had I done? Marry in haste, Egg would say, repent at leisure. Mama Kathy said a year was a decent interval, a year to mourn the dead.

A year for the dead to rise up again.

It had been wartime. Things happen fast in war. Life, death, it was all on a different scale, a different timetable. You acted or the moment slipped away.

He was alive! Dear, dear, wonderful Crazy Dancer. The first spasm of joy should have been what filled my heart. Instead it was twisted with fear. I thought of Erich, who had wanted to open his veins with my surgical scissors. Green blood, I thought hysterically.

Half formulated recriminations attacked me from all sides. They pounded my head. Was I married to two men? Had I destroyed all three of us?

I had not consciously gone there, but I was standing in front of the chapel. I didn't go in. I was damned, cursed. There must be some evil in me that had brought this about. Why hadn't my wolf guardian protected me? Perhaps he was angry with me for leaving my Indian self behind. My only possible justification was that it had all come about through love. At that moment Elk Girl's dream warning returned to me. She had said I could wound Crazy Dancer, and when I denied it, tossed back cryptically, "You're marrying him, aren't you?" Friendly fire, she called it.

My soul hid from black dancing eyes, and from gray thoughtful ones. What had I done?

I SCRIBBLED A note to Erich. I told him I had a headache. I did. Instead of turning in, I walked. My thoughts kept pace with me. The only explanation that fit, he must have been a prisoner. But the telegram—lost at sea. And the newspaper—TROOPSHIP SUNK WITH ALL HANDS.

I don't know where I walked. Mont-Royal loomed above me. Buildings seemed to lean in on me. It was hard to breathe. Thoughts I didn't want to remember seared themselves into my head.

At some hour I threw myself into bed. Tomorrow when I saw him—what? At two o'clock in the afternoon he would know I hadn't waited for him.

I avoided Erich all morning. I knew his routine, so it was easy to do. At twenty of I left for the station, that great hub of the CP Railroad. Wealth from furs and mines had built a nineteenth-century palace. The railroad tied the land together and made it a country. Who had told me that? Of course, it was Erich. In a few moments I'd be trying to explain about Erich.

I could see the tracks now. The train would be coming into view, blue and silver. Knots of people craned for a sight of it. Baggage carts rolled past, porters directing them. The air vibrated. The crowd strained forward. The juggernaut appeared, snorting as its tail followed. I pressed myself against a marble pillar. I heard a mother trying to explain to a son why there was no third rail. "It's a diesel." But he felt cheated of the third rail, the deadly one. They spoke in French, "*Mort.*" I saw him. There he was! Crazy Dancer! I wanted to run up to him, kiss him, hug him, laugh with him. I clung to the pillar, hardly able to keep upright.

He stood still and looked around. He's looking for me. I'm right here, Crazy Dancer. But I didn't move.

There were so many people. I saw him look through them, past them. Streams of passengers that the train disgorged funneled to either side of him. Then he saw me. An electric charge passed between us.

He covered the space in a second. The next I was in his arms, being held and holding. He murmured my Indian name over and over, "Oh-Be-Joyful's Daughter."

I couldn't say anything. He put me at arm's length and looked long and lovingly into my face.

I had to speak. I had to tell him. "I thought you were dead."

"But they didn't know my name, remember? None of their death devices could be marked for me."

"There was no word. You didn't write."

"I wrote. . . . You never got a letter?"

I shook my head. "The ship you were on, the troopship, sank with all hands. That's what they said: with all hands."

"I was never on it. There was an officer waiting for me. They assigned me to a special engineer detail."

"You were never on the troopship?"

"Not that one. The ship I was on was a floating repair shop. They put me to work fixing defective torpedoes. We were attacked off the coast of France, rammed by a U-boat. The ship broke up. You can live six hours in the waters of the North Atlantic, did you know that? Anyway, I was picked up by the Resistance, and hidden in a farmhouse. I wrote you all this."

"Crazy Dancer, I'm so happy, so grateful that you're alive. But I'm married."

"Of course you're married. That's one of the first things we'll do, have the wedding in the church; our mothers will sit in the first pew and cry. It will be beautiful."

"You don't understand," I said.

"I do. I understand how bad you felt to think I was dead. But I'll make it up to you, beginning now. Let's get out of here, go someplace where we can be alone."

"Crazy Dancer, you didn't hear me. I'm married."

The dancing lights went out of his eyes. They returned a blank stare. "Go on," he said.

"I thought you were dead."

"You said that."

"I thought you were dead," I said again.

"Oh-Be-Joyful's Daughter, tell me what you have done."

"I married someone, a patient. See?" I held up my hand with the onyx ring.

"Black," he said. "A black wedding." Then, "But you were married to me."

"You were listed as dead. Your mother brought me the telegram."

"And your heart said nothing? Your heart didn't tell you it was a lie?"

"I didn't know. I had no way of knowing. And there was no word from you."

There was a pause that couldn't be filled.

"You might have waited," he said simply.

Yes. I might have waited.

I felt his hand over mine, firm, dark, sinewy. "Never mind," he said. "It's done. Over with. We'll forget it."

I looked at him, bewildered. "What do you mean, forget it?"

"You made a mistake. I can understand it . . . you thought I was dead." The life that had been extinguished lit his eyes once more. "I forgive you." With that he gathered me into a strong embrace.

I managed to get my hand against his shoulder and shove with all my might. Crazy Dancer looked puzzled.

"I'm married. Can't you understand? I'm married."

"Yes," he agreed. "To me."

"Not to you. To someone else."

"But you can't. It's impossible. You're already married to me."

"I know we considered ourselves married. We were married, according to Iroquois tradition. But it's a marriage not recognized by Canadian law."

"What has Canadian law to do with you and me?"

"It sanctioned my present marriage. I'm someone you don't know anymore. I'm Mrs. Erich von Kerll."

"Von Kerll? German?"

"Austrian."

"What's the difference? He's still an enemy."

We stared at each other bleakly.

"I see how it is," he said in a low, toneless voice. "You love this other man."

"He's a very fine man, Crazy Dancer."

"He's a fool," he spat out, "if he loves you."

"Please don't hate me."

"Hate you? I want you to listen to me. I want you to come with me now. Now is the moment you leave your Austrian and come with the one who you married first and who loved you first. We will leave here and walk into the life we had."

"Crazy Dancer, Erich is a cripple. He only has one leg."

"That makes a difference? Then I'll cut off mine, both of mine. Come with me." With one light step he moved away from me. I stood rooted where I was.

He held out his hand. Mine was a heavy lump at my side. Another sudden movement and he was very close, but not touching. He spoke with controlled fury. "You called a Witigo to eat up your life. All that's left is lies, and faithlessness, and no love, no love at all. Throw out your guardian, he will not guard you any longer."

"If you are going to curse me, Crazy Dancer, don't hide behind guardians and Witigos. Do it yourself."

"Then I do, for throwing me away like a fish you don't want. For going against the promise of a life together, a promise made before my mother and my friends, a promise you tore in shreds and threw in my face."

"I have said all this to myself, Crazy Dancer. But when you think of me, besides everything you said, I want you to remember one other thing . . . I will be grateful all my life that you came back."

I turned away.

I half expected that with a glissade and a tour jeté he would land beside me. And if he did, I didn't know that I would have the strength a second time to walk away. Not like an unwanted fish. How could he think I would throw him away like that? A Witigo. Oh, dear God, I almost laughed. I knew from Elk Girl that a Witigo was a monstrous, hair-covered creature, who ate its young and lived below in an ice cave and had an ice heart. That's what he thought I had, an ice heart.

I didn't know where I was. I walked, taking streets at random. I sat in a little park. I sat there all day. I didn't think about Crazy Dancer and I didn't think about Erich. I watched a lady feeding pigeons, and children taking turns on a slide and rope swinging in tight circles. They called to each other in the quick voice pattern that is Canadian French. It was good to hear children play. I was glad for Anne Morning Light that her son was back. Would she also want a Witigo to attack my life?

I'd forced him to call the Witigo. I'd answered him in ways he couldn't strike back at or deny. "I'm married." I'd said it again and again. I used facts as my excuse, facts as my weapon. Fact: a husband. Fact: a ring. Fact: a legal marriage. Crazy Dancer used a different language. He spoke of love.

I watched the shadows of leaves as they danced on the walkway. I saw something surprising—a chameleon. Chameleons were not indigenous creatures in this climate, but they sold them at La Ronde. They came with a little gold chain and pin, to fasten to your collar. This small lizard had escaped the amusement park and lived here. As a result of his adventures he had only half a tail. Immediately I identified with him. I too had lost part of myself.

I went back to my room in the nurses' annex.

"Where on earth have you been?" Erich greeted me.

Fifteen

WE FOUND A small apartment. It was old French architecture and charming. Mme. Gosselin closed off three rooms of her home, and we rented them. There were no interior stairs, you had to go outside to get from one story to another. Erich had trouble at first, but by the third day had mastered the stairs. The largest room had been a library. There was a fireplace, and we curled up evenings in a Mackinaw blanket, the Hudson Bay kind with stripes of black and red, green and yellow. I didn't tell him about Crazy Dancer being alive, or that I'd seen him. I blocked it from my mind.

The bedroom was small. Once the double bed was in, there was no room for anything else. Erich was practicing his drafting skills and had a large drawing pad on the floor. It took up the entire space. He was able, with the aid of his crutch, to swing off the bed over the sketched plans to the bathroom, but I had to stand on the bed and jump.

I kept having flashbacks. Peering into fog, holding my end of a stretcher, not knowing where I was. . . . This kind of thing used to happen a good deal in the wards, it occurred in men who had seen combat. But it didn't have to be the war. In fact, it usually wasn't. Out of nowhere I'd hear his voice—*"I'll teach you to be an Indian."* I knew it was battle fatigue, but having a name for it didn't make it go away. Even when I was at work—cranking up a bed, assisting Dr. Bennett, or checking a chart—*"Watch it!" and the three-wheeler turned over and spilled us into the bank. "The center of gravity is too high."*

The announcement of our marriage didn't bring things tumbling down around our ears as we feared. It was taken philosophically, and we were even congratulated. Erich was being considered for a position with an architectural firm, and had been in for a second interview, which we took to be a favorable sign. We were already putting by for our surprise visit to Mama Kathy. I wasn't very original: I kept the money in the sugar bowl. We figured in about three weeks we could buy the tickets. Erich was very good about saving. He'd heard how fine the Montreal Symphony was. Desiré Dufauw directed, and Erich very much wanted to go, but deferred it for the sake of our trip.

"You'll love Mama Kathy. She spent her honeymoon traveling by dogsled."

—Sometimes it was the gesture of his hand at the railway station. Or the hurt look in his eyes—

I revived my cooking skills. For years I'd eaten in the hospital cafeteria. But no more. Between dispensing medication, changing dressings, and starting an intravenous feeding . . . I planned menus. Tonight I would prepare saschlik, a Polish dish Mama Kathy learned from a trapper's wife: lamb and tomatoes—*Or that first moment when he framed my face in his hands and looked at me with trust and love*—garnished with onion and apple and poured over a steaming potato.

Hiroshima. The dropping of the A-bomb brought an abrupt end to the war in the Pacific. Did it bring an end to man's humanity as well?

The technological aspect fascinated Erich. "A new energy source. Think of it! A teaspoon of U-235 will light the entire world. Submarines will be able to navigate the seven seas without needing to surface. The possibilities are unlimited."

One moment a human being, the next etched into cement like a trilobite. We had achieved world peace.

*   *   *

I ARRIVED HOME one evening to find Erich waiting for me on the stairs. He had a telegram in his hand. "I don't know whether it's good news or bad. It's from my mother. She's coming to visit us."

"All the way from Austria!" I ran up the remaining flight. "But that's wonderful, isn't it?"

"Of course it is. Only, the old life is so far away now. She'll bring it with her."

"Are you afraid she won't approve of me?"

"Nothing like that. Of course not. It's just that it was a lifetime ago I was her son."

"Yes, the Bodensee, the little boy in the sailor suit." I looked around at our three rooms. Each item we'd added had been a cause for celebration. The bud vase Egg gave us I'd tried in a dozen places—the table, the windowsill, by the kitchen sink. Finally it came to rest on the secondhand end table Erich had bought. Now I wasn't so sure—our home that looked cozy and just right, I saw with other eyes. Instead of being charming, its age seemed a defect. It needed paint, the ceiling flaked, and the walls were dingy. The bannister leading to the landing had buckled and the wood splintered. The wardrobes in his mother's home were undoubtedly larger than our bedroom.

"I don't think this place will be what she expects." And I don't think I will be either, I thought.

"Nonsense. You've done wonders with it. It's our home, pleasant, clean, comfortable—what else is needed?"

"Think of what she's used to."

"Remember, Mother's gone through a war. We don't know what she's used to."

"That's true," I said, relaxing a bit.

Erich laughed suddenly. "Of course if you mean it's not elegant, no it isn't."

His lightheartedness reassured me. After all, it was ours, brought together by borrowings, gifts, and castaways. Somehow it all fit together, and the result was warm and friendly. The china couldn't be so readily dismissed, two of the plates chipped and not all the same pattern.

Erich guessed my thoughts. "It isn't a crime to be poor and starting out. All Austrians have a touch of schmaltz in their nature, and Mother will think it romantic."

"It isn't only things, Erich. It's me. Your mother has never seen a First Nation person. Maybe she isn't prepared. Well, I am many skin tones darker than you."

"Once I get a good tan we'll be the same shade. Kathy, one of your amazing attributes is that you have no idea how beautiful you are."

"*Schön?*"

"*Sehr schön.*"

Now it was my turn to laugh at him. "I think the German language should be called *schön* talk. Everything with you is *schön. Sehr schön, bitte schön,* and *danke schön.* Any others?"

"Only you, *Liebchen.*"

ELIZABETH VON KERLL was coming by air transport, which she had somehow managed with the occupation authorities. The same skies that only four months ago had been deadly now accommodated a first trickle of traffic. Imagine looking *down* and seeing clouds, and, when they parted, the ocean! Soon, we were told, there would be commercial flights. The map of the world had shifted. The islands of the Pacific, so bloodily fought for, whose every inch was counted in human lives, suddenly were worthless. The war had passed over them, removing yesterday's values. Now everywhere, everyone was making a new start. What if—But there would be no more what-ifs. I was grown up and knew how tragically meaningless they were.

Erich and I took a streetcar to Boucherville, seven miles outside the city. Our guest was coming in on the flying boat *Caribou,* at Imperial Airways. It was rumored they intended to expand and form a transatlantic mail service. How quickly the mindset of the country changed; this had been an embarkation point for Hudsons, Liberators, Flying Fortresses, Mitchells, and Martin Marauders.

"Suppose," I asked, facing a fear I'd been struggling with, "suppose she wants us to go back with her to Austria?"

"We take a return flight, of course." Then, shaking me by the shoulders, "Don't look so stricken, *Liebchen.* Don't you know that nothing, nothing could pry me out of here?" And his fingers interlaced with mine.

Just before our stop I asked in panic, "What shall I call her?"

This gave him pause. "I think Elizabeth. Elizabeth will be best."

When I saw her I realized why. Young, blond, and beautiful, she gave no indication she had been in the air thirty-three hours with a stopover in Ireland, another in Newfoundland, and a midair refueling.

She stood still, letting crew members stream past as she took in her son. She seemed to inhale him, then inventory him, taking in the man. She came toward us smiling, allowing herself to be embraced, and then, catching sight of me, she made an instant assessment. Coming a step nearer, she clasped my hand and drew me to her.

"Kathy," she said; and to Erich, "She's lovely."

Then, if I remember, they both talked at once. "And how is father—?" But he scarcely paused when she shook her head in the negative. "—And uncle?"

"They both send their love. And Dorotea and Minna."

"And cousin Arthur?"

And so it went. Family members, friends, and relatives, all with a message for him, all wanting to be remembered. I watched his face. It was animated, flushed, and eager. His mind was back there, home, where he came from.

She hadn't mentioned the cane he used. She knew, of course, but she didn't mention it. They acted, both of them, as though he were exactly the same as when he'd left. But he wasn't. He knew and I knew that he was a cripple, with all that entailed—physical limitations, need for frequent rests, pain, and pain medication. Into their mélange of greetings, endearments, nicknames, and remembrances I inserted how pleased we were to have her.

She nodded, smiled at me, and went on talking to Erich. Her English was fluent, with a trace of accent that set certain words off in a lilting manner. Her *th*'s tended to *z*'s. It was charming. Everything about her was charming. She wore a fox fur, which had probably originated here. I took in her nylons. Silk stockings were out, nylons were in. Her traveling outfit was an understated, tailored brown suit. Small diamonds were set in her ears, I knew they were diamonds because of the one in my onyx ring—they had the same shifting centers.

Once or twice she lapsed into German, but Erich answered each time in English.

Elizabeth stepped into the cab without a clue as to the hole it made in our budget. How else did one get from here to there? She was interested in the city, exclaimed at the sight of Mont-Royal, whose massive volcanic upthrust dominated the city, while the cross blessed it. Elizabeth was impressed by the well-to-do homes along its higher terraces, identifying Gothic revivals, French provincial, Tudor, and Queen Anne villas. It pleased her that there were so many parks and bridges, but in spite of an occasional French mansard roof and crenelated parapet, she thought the downtown looked gray with its massive fieldstone fronts.

"Impressive," she said of the city, "more English than French. And the signposts, all English. I had thought of Montreal as a French city."

"Actually," Erich told her, "it's cosmopolitan, bilingual, and wonderfully old." He ordered the cabbie to drive out of our way so he could show his mother the sights.

"There seems to be a church every few blocks," she observed approvingly.

Erich pointed out the Place d'Armes with its monument to Paul Chomedy, Sieur de Maisonneuve, founder of the city, and the great basilica of Notre Dame. Then southeast to the St. Lawrence with its immense docking facilities going on block after block. "Fifteen hundred ships at a time could load here."

But Elizabeth was more interested in the shops on St. Catherine Street. I kept stealing sideways glances at her. She seemed too young to be Erich's mother, hardly older than I. We came to the lower-middle-class suburb where we lived, and Elizabeth was immediately intrigued by the exterior stairs. She pronounced them quaint.

It wasn't until she was ensconced in our best chair, with her stole hanging in my closet and a glass of sherry in her hand, that she began what she had crossed an ocean to say. It involved an acknowledgment of Erich's condition. I will say for her that she faced it directly. "One would not necessarily realize—a limp is distinguished these days, the mark of a soldier. As to the cane, almost every gentleman carries a cane. You must believe me, Erich, it is not that bad. I was afraid— one sees so much in the way of disfigurement among our veterans. Actually, I am quite relieved. I'm sure your rehabilitation is due in large part to the excellent nursing care you received." And she flashed me a brilliant smile.

I glanced at Erich. Usually, after he'd worn the prosthesis three or four hours, he would unstrap it and allow himself a period of relief. But with his mother here, he was determined to stick it out. The wound was still sensitive, and I was afraid of it becoming aggravated and inflamed. We had already gone through an ulceration, and I didn't want to deal with that again. But I couldn't say anything to embarrass him. Besides, seemingly he was tolerating it.

"Now tell me about Father," he said.

She shook her head. "Your father is in failing health. The war— at first we thought you were dead. Then the terrible financial reverses. There was so much for him to handle." She turned to me. "And now it must all be reassembled, the assets of the estate, everything, accounts in Switzerland, in the Caribbean, you've no idea. The bookkeeping alone is monumental. But," she added brightly, "not to burden you. You children have your own life. I can see how good it is. I see what a lovely wife you've chosen, Erich. Your home, so welcoming, so comfortable. I have a warm feeling when I look at the two of you."

When the sherry had been sipped, I suggested a rest for Elizabeth, which she was happy to take.

In this way I got Erich into our bedroom and helped him out of the prosthesis. The impacted area was inflamed, and I rubbed it with salve. This eased him, and he stretched out on the bed with a set of architectural drawings.

"Your mother is so pretty and so young."

He agreed. "One of the few people the war hasn't changed."

"Tell me more about your father."

"He doesn't capitulate. That's the main thing about my father. He belonged to the old Social Democratic Party. In your terms that would be the more liberal party. He didn't change when it became convenient not to belong to it, when promotions were going to the National Socialists. And he didn't change when it became dangerous to belong to it.

"During my teen years it got ugly. There were threats, there were incidents, I had fights at school. Things grew so bad that he resigned his commission. Mother wasn't happy about that. But he stood firm. He was like a rock around which waters boil and swirl. His convictions, that's all he knew."

Perhaps it wasn't as romantic as the Bodensee heritage, but it was, I thought, more substantial. And I pictured the old gentleman with side whiskers.

During dinner Elizabeth sketched in broad strokes the general tenor of her personal war. "Officially the war began in '39. For Austria it was 11 March 1938. I'll never forget it. They marched in from the east, through the Neusiedlersee Pass, which was still snowed in. Not only did they march, they skiied and trucked in, they came by rail through the Tyrol to Salzburg, and fanned out into Vienna and the farming districts, Bergenland, Steiermakki, Karnten, and Nieder-österreich.

"Everywhere our soft-spoken melodious German was replaced by harsh Northern dialect. What a distasteful sound!" She shuddered. "They took over everything, of course, the chemical plants, the ni-trogen plant in Linz, electrical power, crude oil, natural gas—but they aren't content with utilities—the National Bank of Austria is next, where, as you know, your father had a seat on the board. Fortunately, as it turned out, the commandant quartered on us was a career soldier, a gentleman of good family. It makes a difference. He saw to it that our larder remained full. We were not reduced to want, as so many of our friends and neighbors were. But our privacy was gone, our servants. We kept to our rooms while *they* had the run of the house."

She paused for a sip of port. "Then of course you were called up. You remember the initial euphoria. But a year and a half, two years later, the war news began to be punctuated, perhaps I should say *lacerated* by news that didn't fit. One heard things, a returned veteran, someone in hospital—delirious, of course, but . . . Here and there, it is rumored, a ship is sunk, and another—and then Russia . . . utterly defeated, we are told. Yet I heard a captain with the Hitler medal who had been at Stalingrad say our troops were starving, and winter would finish them. Nothing is official. It is all indirect. And from you, Erich, no more letters, nothing. But your father and I don't speak of it. Even with his connections, we didn't know are you alive or dead."

Elizabeth turned to me. "It is terrible to lose a child, an only son. Believe me, it is as bad not to know. To hope one day, despair the next, snatch the mail out of the postman's hands. It was then his father began to fail. I looked at him one day and saw an old man. But there—" She caught herself and turned back to Erich. "By a miracle you are returned to us."

Erich responded with a deprecating wave of the hand that took in his missing leg.

"What is that?" she said almost angrily. "You are with us, here, alive, when so many aren't."

"I feel that way too," I said, identifying with Elizabeth for the first time.

Erich was anxious to turn the conversation from himself. "The country," he asked, "will it recover?"

"Of course. Certainly. But it is heartbreaking. Half the railroads are gone, and the bridges over the Danube blown, in fact all bridges and roads are pockmarked by shells or completely destroyed. Life in the cities is just beginning to crawl out from the ruins. But," she said with resolution, "there are endless opportunities for someone with family, with connections, someone who was awarded the Iron Cross, someone like you, Erich."

"Not someone like me," Erich said firmly. "Someone who hasn't grown attached to a vast new country, someone who hasn't started a new life."

Had he wanted to say, someone who hasn't an aboriginal wife?

With a little laugh Elizabeth retreated. "Of course, you are quite right, my darling, to feel that way." Then, turning to me, "Your country is so large, so pristine and unspoiled. You must forgive me being stupid on the subject. But I know so little of it, and even less about your people. I did not even know that they are referred to as First Nation people. You bring such an exotic strain to our family, my dear. I must inform myself, I must learn something of your background, your fascinating heritage."

Erich intervened. "If you want to read up on Indians, fine. But Kathy can't tell you anything. With her, *background* and *heritage* are two different things. She was raised by a white woman, Katherine Mary Flannigan, and her husband, a sergeant in the Mounties. Her brother and sister are of French extraction, and she didn't know any Indians until she went to school."

I suppressed an impulse to tell her about the blanket ceremony and that I had married one of those exotic creatures known as First Nation people.

Erich must have felt uncomfortable too, for he declared we should leave the anthropology for another day. To another day also was left the question of his fealty. Was it, as his mother implied, to Austria?

Elizabeth continued to fill in the picture, emphasizing the very large hole Erich's defection made. His father, physically and mentally impaired, was no longer capable of attending to family interests. She herself, as she pointed out, was not a businesswoman. Yet she hesitated to rely on lawyers when so much was at stake.

Several days later, while Elizabeth was shopping, Erich and I had one of our private talks. "What would you think," he asked, "of going back briefly, for a fortnight or two? Just to straighten out the affairs of the estate, collect the proper documents, and put our claim for reparations before the new regime? Tidy things up, leave them in good hands?"

"It would certainly help Elizabeth out."

"How would you feel about it?" he persisted.

I countered this with "How would *you* feel about it?"

"What do you mean? I don't understand."

"I think you do."

"If it's that old obsession of yours about being Indian—"

"Erich, I *am* Indian. Your mother chooses to say 'exotic.' What about your friends, relatives, neighbors? The society your mother moves in? How will they see me, and how will they feel about me?"

"I fought on Hitler's side, simply because I am Austrian. Do you think that I or my family or friends have taken on any of his madness? That we believe in the special purity of the Aryan bloodline? Come on, Kathy."

Put like that it did sound stupid.

From then on it was assumed we were returning and would vacation in Austria. It did seem a marvelous opportunity, too good to miss. Especially as Elizabeth made it plain she was underwriting the entire trip.

I thought that perhaps, woman to woman, I would look for the right moment and confide some of my hesitation to her. That moment came as we walked through the Bio Exposition. I thought this exhibit was something she would enjoy. It was the second largest botanical garden in the world and housed, according to the brochure, twenty-six thousand different plant species. We passed thick rubbery stalks bursting with unlikely blooms and banked layers of savannah grasses where herds of papier-mâché elephant herds grazed, and came to a stop before delicate fan-shaped leaves with veins like those on our own hands. A zebra with a glass eye watched as I came out with it, asking if she thought that, once we got to Austria, I would fit in.

"Of course." And she gave me an impetuous hug. "Naturally you'll need a few things," she added.

My heart sank. There was nothing in our budget for clothes.

With wonderful intuition she guessed the problem. "There's a family fund that takes care of such necessities," she said, "so please, not to give it another thought."

But I did think about it and worry about it. Finally I asked Erich.

"Mother's right," he said. "There is a fund for such contingencies."

"Then it's all right," I asked, only half convinced, "to go shopping with her and let her buy me things?"

"You're my wife, aren't you?" And he dismissed the subject by kissing the tip of my nose.

Elizabeth had a list. From my feet to my head I was to be outfitted. We took a cab to St. Catherine Street. Next door to Eaton's department store we purchased a lovely pair of gray suede shoes with French heels. Inside Eaton's we looked at stylish suits and coats before settling on a black caracul. I refrained from looking at the price tag. Blouses and dresses went over my head in a small airless cubicle. I paraded them before Elizabeth for her approval.

On to Morgan's and then Simpson's. I liked a dirndl skirt cut on the bias, but Elizabeth dismissed it, insisting it did nothing for me—whatever that meant. I think it meant that I was totally lacking in taste, sophistication, and elegance.

When I thought we were through, we had merely stopped for what she called tea and I called lunch. She dragged me past a Kik stand, where you could get an economy cola, two glasses for a nickel. I found myself instead in the Ritz-Carlton having brunch in the Oval Room. I would have much preferred a quick sandwich at Ma Heller's. Elizabeth, I saw, was at home among sugar tongs and, in the evening I suppose, candle snuffers. While we waited for our shrimp canapes and watercress rolls, Elizabeth described shopping in Berlin. "I'm talking of the old days, of course. Tauentzienstrasse, corner of Kurfürstendamm. Marvelous shops, especially for jewelry."

As the luncheon progressed, the various items we had purchased were gone over. "I thought you looked very smart in the Worth."

"The Worth?"

"Yes, yes," she said with a touch of impatience, "the suit we decided on, the Suez rose designed by Worth."

I remembered gazing at myself in the large store mirror with its gilt frame. Who was that slim, dark girl? She wasn't me. I was sure of that. She was the girl Erich and Elizabeth planned to bring back to Austria, to introduce to high-bred relatives and friends as Erich's wife. Perhaps that's who the girl in the glass was—Erich's wife. The Suez rose suit was very becoming to her, it somehow minimized the copper tone of her skin.

I tried to focus on what Elizabeth was saying. "And I thought the periwinkle blue exceedingly becoming. Schiaparelli is for you, *Liebchen,* long simple lines. Yes, definitely, he had you in mind."

How charming she was, how generous. A fortune had been spent on me. The coat alone was a year's wages. How fairy-tale it seemed, misty, charming, and totally devoid of reality. But that girl in the looking glass, that Kathy that I would turn into, belonged to the periwinkle blue and the Suez rose. I saw her beside Elizabeth, acknowledging introductions, shaking hands, exchanging pleasantries. She was wearing the white kid gloves we had just purchased. They came to the elbows and closed with tiny seed pearl buttons. What if—?

With a start I came to myself.

The excursion did not end with the shopping. Elizabeth must see the French quarter. Old habit held me and a world of what-ifs. . . . What if Kathy Forquet von Kerll captured all hearts in her furs and her chiffons and her gray suede shoes? Erich was proud as he offered an arm and escorted her onto the floor of the grand ballroom. I could almost hear the strains of a Viennese waltz.

Coming out of Duprez Freres we passed by a touristy window in which a dark-colored mannikin was decked out in deerskin dress and moccasins with quillwork. She had a feather in her hair. Elizabeth stopped and stared.

The packages were delivered the following day. That evening we had a grand showing. I modeled item after item. Erich watched silently. I began to feel apprehensive. I had allowed his mother to spend too much. But at the end of the show he kissed me. "You'll knock them for a loop," he said. He loved picking up slang. To Elizabeth he said more formally, "You did well, Mother."

He considered the money well spent. It seemed I was dichotomized into two persons. The old Kathy, brought up by Katherine Mary Flannigan, and the new me, the one about to step from the mirror and take her place in a what-if world. I hung my wardrobe carefully in the chiffonier, but I didn't throw out the boxes. Instead, I folded the tissue paper into them and placed them on the highest shelf, which they occupied with my wolf talisman.

That says it all, I thought. Could they continue to reside side by side as they appeared to be doing?

The end of Elizabeth's visit was approaching. She had what she had come for. She had crossed the North Atlantic to bring us back with her. And we were going.

To make myself believe it, I went around after work to tell Egg. She looked up from her desk, and her face fulfilled its laugh lines. She was happy to see me and incredulous when I told her about a vacation in Austria.

"Such things don't happen to people I know," she said.

"It's wonderful, isn't it?"

She nodded that it was, but simultaneously made the sign of the cross over me.

I didn't phone Mama Kathy. I don't know why, except that she'd worry that I was visiting a country we had been at war with only months ago. Mama Kathy never worried about herself, it was just her kids. "Someday you'll know," she'd say.

I would write her, as I'd finally written of our marriage and our intention to visit. By return post she had answered with love and congratulations, but added that a civil ceremony such as I described seemed inadequate to her. It would be no trouble to arrange to repeat our vows in church with family present.

I spoke to Erich, and he was in agreement, he would be happy to do it. In large things and in small Mama was meticulous. One of the small, I explained to Erich, was saving foreign stamps. She used to save them for Georges. But I'm sure the habit was still with her, and she'd find some ten-year-old somewhere. . . .

In token of her farewell to Montreal Elizabeth decided we must have a suitable dinner, "at one of the better French restaurants." She had been reading the Divertissement section in *Le Devoir*. "The Chez Queux on Jacques-Cartier in the old French quarter sounds interesting. It says here, 'built on the fortifications of the original town.' According to this account, the chef has served the royal houses of France."

"He must be very old," Erich commented drily, "pre-Revolution."

Elizabeth ignored this. "And the same architect designed the palace of justice, the chapel of the Sacred Heart, and the church on Rue Bonsecours. We absolutely must dine there."

Later in the afternoon she slipped Erich money. That and the shopping expedition made me wonder if the family estate was in as desperate a condition as she depicted. But I dismissed the idea. Why else would she have made the crossing?

I dressed for the occasion in my elegant suit and felt like an Austrian aristocrat, until I saw a real one. Elizabeth took your breath away in a vaguely patterned, creamy material that gave the effect of sculpting her.

Erich's eyes passed from me to her. He bowed low but refrained from heel clicking, which he knew I detested. "What a privilege to escort two such beauties."

Snow White and Rose Red, I thought bitterly to myself.

As our cab pulled up to the restaurant, a liveried attendant sprang for the door. A fringed canopy led downstairs to an underground palace. The maitre d' hurried to precede us through subdued lighting in which sparkled the crystal of chandeliers and goblets. I glimpsed elegantly folded serviettes lying on the laps of ladies who had been appareled in the boutiques I'd come to know. Flowers drooped toward a central fountain. I felt I was in a play or an opera.

Exchanging a few words with Erich in French, the maitre d' left, sending a sous-chef to our table. An enormously large bill of fare was placed in my hands. I saw immediately that my French was not up to the challenge of these dishes. I planned to say, "I'll have the same."

Erich and the sous-chef embarked on a lengthy discussion of the menu. I looked it over more carefully, and translated *prix du marche* to mean "price on request." Good heavens! They didn't print the price.

Another conversation flowed around me, this one triangular as Erich enlarged the discussion to include his mother. He turned to me.

"It's between the entrecôte grillée aux trois poivres flambée au cognac, grilled steak in cognac sauce, or the Chateaubriand et sa suite, Chateaubriand for two with . . . with accompaniments."

"Accompaniments?"

"Soup, salad, appetizers."

"What are you having? Give it to me in plain English."

He laughed. "Filet mignon and potato pancakes in whiskey."

"Share the Chateaubriand with me," Elizabeth suggested.

I nodded, while Erich ordered from the wine list. A different waiter had appeared for this ritual. Kir Royals were decided on, to be followed by a Pinot noir Ramsey, and a Bordeaux la Grange Clairet. I was disturbed as I watched yet another waiter dutifully scribbling our preferences, a servant to the wines. But I had misjudged the profligacy of the establishment. Behind him, dinner napkin over his arm, was a second in command. His job was to listen, to smile, to nod approval, and, of course, the manual part of his job description, when the glasses arrived to set them on the table. I felt sad sitting there in Nile pink—no, no, Suez. It was Suez pink. At any rate I felt sad that a man should be a servant to a glass. But it seemed that if its contents had been pressed in the correct year the vintage was worth many times what he was.

The potage was served, bisque de crustace tuile parmesan, the salade d'endives au roquefort, avec noix. My champagne flute was removed and a wine goblet placed in front of me. A lightly smoked salmon in brandy marinade followed spiced duckling. I observed Erich carefully to see which of the array of forks he chose.

Elizabeth's color was heightened becomingly. They were speaking in English in deference to me, but of people and things I knew nothing of. "You remember Franz Werfel, he did many fine biographies. I read shortly before I came that he died. He was a Jew, you know. He escaped Hitler and fled to the United States."

"Yes, we played chess once. He beat me."

Then she was saying, "We lost the *Scharnhorst* early, so you would know about that. And the battleship *Gneisenau* in November of '39. And the merchant cruiser *Rawalpindi* in the North Sea. Each sinking was a blow to your father. Especially losing the pocket battleship *Deutschland* and the *Admiral Graf Spee*. Captain Langedorff's father was an old friend. You may remember him."

Erich had cast back his mind to the sinkings. "The focus was wrong," he said. "Time was wasted trying to produce an antiradar coating for U-boats, using strips of aluminum as a decoy against incoming missiles. Nonsense like that, when they should have been concentrating on measures to counter the search radar on Allied surface ships. When the Allies began to detect, we began to lose."

I didn't know these things still rankled. Erich had never spoken to me about them.

"Of course," he went on, "the main problem for a sub is air. It was solved by a German scientist, Helmuth Walter. He developed a turbine propulsion system using oxygen generated from hydrogen peroxide. His demonstration model, the type XXI and V-80, was already built in 1940. But the High Command fooled around with that damn tin foil. We lost battles simply because we couldn't breathe. Three hundred and twelve Axis U-boats were sunk by aircraft—on the surface. If we'd been able to dive—Now, when it's too late, I understand we have the snorkel breathing system. Stupid, stupid, stupid," he murmured at his caviar Beluga/Oscietre.

"Still," Elizabeth soothed, "you saw the last of the really big actions."

"Do you want to know what a big action looks like? There are no heroes, believe me. We were running on radio blackout, total silence, when we were stove in. You don't see it, you hear it. Exploding showers of sound, and a high whistling bursts your head. The next thing you are conscious of is cold, a paralyzing cold. I'd been ejected with scraps of metal, bodies, and tinned goods into a sea of oil. I remember wanting to report to Command that their chemically heated, wind-resistant flotation jackets didn't work."

As I looked across at Erich Helmut von Kerll and his mother, I saw, not the panels of the restaurant, but the great hall of Valhalla. There sat Odin with his mead and ale. He feasted where warriors had fallen. There he was, the horn of plenty at his side, dining on joints of pork from a boar whose flesh never gave out. He kept a wolf on a gold chain, and eagles and ravens came to dine. Two ravens he prized above the rest. They were named Thought and Memory. He sent them far and wide to bring him tidings. He sent them also deep into the recesses of his being. What if? he asked them.

What if this Erich, the Erich who was fluent in French and English, at home among menus and headwaiters, this sophisticated, charming man of the world, was more Erich than the Erich who was my husband? My eyes opened wide like the eyes on a china doll when you've screwed off the head and put your finger in to flick the metal rod. I saw everything, Elizabeth as a Valkyrie, her blond hair in braids, wearing armored breastplate, a fierce battling female. She had come from the sky to bring her son Memory, memory of his home, of his family, of his duty.

She had come to take him back.

Him.

Not me.

Memory was with me too. Memory of Mama telling the twins, "Kathy is to be included." But there was no way I would be included in Vienna. It wasn't their fault. It wasn't mine. I just didn't fit.

I'd been through a war. There I was wanted, needed—not tolerated. There I did fit. The war had changed me. Just to be included was no longer enough.

Elizabeth never had the least intention of introducing an Indian girl to Austrian society. I was not an acceptable wife. I was not an acceptable daughter-in-law. She had come with one mission in mind, to make me see for myself how out of place it would be, how inappropriate. We belonged to different worlds, and she had set herself to demonstrate this.

How did she do it? With gray suede shoes, tucked out of sight under the table, with a Worth suit now hunched miserably in a chair, wrinkled, the material crushed. And by an evening such as this. He was at home, I was an interloper.

The final delving brought new torment. Erich had never spoken to me of his pain at the sinking of each U-boat, of his analysis of the war. How could he? I was the enemy.

Was I? Had he thought of me like that? I had considered him in precisely that way. I remembered my reluctance to go near him when he lay helpless in my ward.

I pushed myself from the table and stood up. The room swam, wineglasses were filled with swirling faces, with solicitous waiters, with flowers and a fountain, with the twin birds . . . what if?

"Kathy, what is it?" Erich asked.

"I'm going to find the ladies' room."

"Shall I come with you?" Elizabeth asked.

She was so sweet to me, so kind. What if I was wrong? Wrong about the braids and the breastplate? A waiter whispered to me the direction, and I turned toward it.

It was the last I remember. Like Erich I was shot out of the water, scuttled not by a depth charge but by a Bordeaux la Grange Clairet. How humiliating.

Had I actually fallen to the floor? Poor Erich. Poor Elizabeth. How embarrassed they must have been. I couldn't understand it. I had never fainted in my life. I hid under the washcloth on my forehead and kept my eyes closed.

ixteen

ELIZABETH SAT BESIDE me for a long while.

"Don't worry," I said. "I'm not going back with you."

"Shh." She changed the wet cloth.

After a while her place was taken by Erich. "Are you feeling better?" he asked. Elizabeth was upstairs in the guest bedroom, packing—and repacking—her grips.

"I don't know what to say. It was the wine, I think, and the wonderful rich food, and—"

"You don't have to explain. It just happened, and I'm sorry."

"No, *I'm* sorry. You see, it was just too much. I'm not used to such—well, I'm not used to any of it. But I'm glad it happened."

He gave me a queer look. "What do you mean?"

"Erich, I'm not going with you."

"Of course you're going with us. Don't be ridiculous."

"Erich, I'm not."

"What are you talking about? It's our vacation."

"It's not. We both know it's not. We've all been pretending, you, Elizabeth, me. Once you are home in Austria, all this will fade as though it had never been."

He forced calm into his voice. Even so, it shook as he said, "You're crazy, Kathy. I don't know what you're talking about."

"You do. You know you do. And you know I'm right. I wouldn't fit in, just like at the restaurant. I hated every minute of it. I hated my wineglass having its own servant. How can a human being think so little of himself? To me, Erich, it's affectation, a charade, to consult for twenty minutes how a dish is to be prepared, whether or not to add a truffle garnish."

"I had no idea you were not having a good time," Erich said stiffly.

"I'm not criticizing, Erich. I'm just saying—for *me*. You understand, for *me* it is not a way of life. I couldn't get used to it. I don't want to get used to it."

Erich was regarding me intently. "And if I give up the trip?"

I was startled that he would suggest such a thing, and touched. "I don't think I want you to do that. I don't think I want to be responsible for your life, cut off from everything and everyone you knew."

"Let me understand, Kathy. You want me to go?"

"Yes."

"And you stay behind?"

I nodded.

"And our marriage? It's over just like that?"

I compressed my lips in an effort not to cry.

"You've been unhappy all these months? You were unhappy with this place that we found together and fixed up? You never, never—" He turned away.

"I did! I do! Oh, Erich, it has nothing to do with loving you."

"But it was a mistake?"

"Yes." I couldn't look at him, but rushed on. "It's my fault, Erich. Totally, completely my fault."

"Let me understand. You're saying it's one of those things, a wartime marriage, a mistake?"

"A mistake, yes. Remember how it was, Erich? I didn't think it was significant then, but looking back, a lot of things become clear. Almost from the beginning there was chemistry. You liked me, flirted with me. But it wasn't until you were recovering from the amputation that you thought of marriage. That was part of your decision never to go back, to make a new life. I was part of that new life. I'm not part of the old. Neither one of us ever intended that I should be."

There was a long silence, which he broke at last. "We've been happy."

"Yes," I acknowledged.

"Kathy, it's not fair on the basis of one evening to condemn an entire way of life."

"Not condemn, I don't mean it like that. I'm trying to say I'm a fish out of water. I don't fit in and I never will. And I'm not willing to cut you off, not only from your obligations, but from all those who asked after you and love you. . . . I saw your face when you inquired about your father, your cousin—and it isn't just one evening. There's the dress by Worth and the caracul coat, and the suit Elizabeth kindly, and I mean *kindly,* bought for me. They were all new dimensions, like trying to make a balloon into a certain shape. You press here, it bulges there."

I could see he wasn't angry anymore. His gray eyes were again thoughtful. He was considering what I was saying.

"You've been honest with me, Kathy. I can see I have been less honest with myself. I believed it was a vacation. I believed I was coming back. But you're right about the obligation part. My family needs me. There is no one else. But you're wrong about life there. It isn't just social whirl and glitter. It's being a player in the reconstruction of my country. I could influence the direction it takes, make the whole scene more open, more democratic. My voice would count."

"That's what I've been trying to say. You'd never forgive me if I held you back from all that."

A minute ticked between us.

"I can't give you up."

"And I can't go with you."

We heard the front door. Elizabeth had come down outside, from the guest bedroom above. "I've brought you tissue paper to put between the folds of your suit."

Erich stood up and faced her. "Kathy is not coming with us."

Elizabeth remained very still, looking from me to Erich. She did a strange thing: she kissed me. Then, with a small flutter of a laugh, "In that case I'll use the tissue paper for my jasmine scarf. It will travel better that way."

In the morning the three of us chatted amiably about the hardships of travel, the difficulty of crossing time zones. Erich explained it as the disruption of the circadian rhythm. None of us referred to the fact that I was staying behind. He had thought about it all night. So had I. Morning did not change anything.

When they left, Elizabeth took my hand and held it. "My dear."

I smiled back at her. She understood.

Erich said, "If you change—"

I put my finger against his lips. "Goodbye, Erich."

In response he bowed over my hand in his most Germanic manner and clicked his heels. It was good he did that, it reminded us both. Irreconcilable differences, those were grounds in some courts.

Elizabeth left a note for me, in which she promised to try for an annulment. I set about transferring my things from the bedroom Erich and I had occupied to the guest bedroom. I gave the Schiaparelli dress, the gray shoes, and the Suez pink to charity. I am ashamed to say I kept the coat. Winters are so cold here.

In moving to the second bedroom I uncovered my old wolf talisman. It was a bit mothworn, not so bushy as it had been. But the Cree believe that age implies wisdom. Perhaps the wolf tail had grown in wisdom. If so, why had it imparted none to me?

Actually I think it had, and I hadn't wanted to listen. I thought the loss of his leg would keep him here. I thought he needed me. It was I myself who had prepared him to leave, taught him day by day to be independent, to do for himself and not rely on me.

Had I known what I was doing? I think so. And yet I persisted. Day after day to care for the wound, to balance, to walk without crutches with only the help of a cane. And in mastering these physical impediments his confidence flowed back until at last he could face his family, his friends, and take up a career, take up his old life. He was the only son, and he was going home. In a way I was proud. It took good nursing skills and good psychological bolstering to accomplish what I had.

And what had it taken to undo a marriage, to break my vows? I stayed late at the hospital and after hours visited the little chapel. With a clicking of his heels he had shown me that he could leave me as easily as I could him. But it wasn't easy. It was one of the hardest things I'd ever done. It had made me sick. If I got up from a chair too quickly the whole room swam, just as in the restaurant.

I had always had perfect health. Mama Kathy used to say I was as strong as a little pony. What was this giddiness, this sudden faintness?

I was a nurse, and yet I didn't suspect. It didn't occur to me that I was pregnant. But a second missed period confirmed it, and thought disappeared down a black tarn.

I went to work. I changed the dressing for cot 4, checked that the acute dysentery case was responding, made a note that 12 was now urinating on his own. Suddenly I stood transfixed. I was going to have a baby.

That night I began my letter. *Dear Erich,* . . . I stopped. Dear Erich, what? Come back, we're going to have a baby? Remembering the final click of his heels, I wasn't at all sure he would come back.

What then? I've changed my mind, I'm joining you in Austria?

Austria was no longer the land of what if. It was as alien to me as the Martian plain or the ammonia atmosphere of Venus. Oh, God, what a mess! I stared at my blank letter with its standard opening— and tried to think. How had I come to make so many mistakes? I went back to the beginning trying to figure it out.

Katherine Mary Flannigan had done her best to ensure that my head was screwed on the right way. "Nothing should be worse because you were there," she'd told me more than once. And my sergeant Papa of the RCMP, what would he say of my impulse to leave things as they were, to not tell Erich? With a convulsive movement

I took hold of the pen. We'd talked about having a baby. Later on, at some unspecified time in the future. He'd said a boy would be Victor after his father. I smiled because I knew it would be a girl and that she would be Kathy.

My hand held its position above the page. *It's his child. He has a right to know.* The child would be part of the fantasy. The question was—which fantasy? Would we go into the woods, trap and fish and live close to nature? That had been his first fiction. He caught at anything not to go home, not to let them know he was a cripple, a man with one leg. Why hadn't I seen as plainly as I did now that phase would pass?

The other fantasy was mine—Austria of the waltzes, the Bodensee, and the little blond boy in the sailor suit. I would no longer be Kathy, and of Oh-Be-Joyful's Daughter there would not be a trace. In their place a Rhine maiden sipping rare vintages from the *cartes des vin* with the servant of the glass assiduously pouring.

But what deterred me mainly was a child of mixed ancestry growing up in Austria, subject to what slurs, what discrimination? And if the Naziism in Hitler's homeland was festering beneath the surface? Did I want my child imbibing that atmosphere?

I put the pen down without writing a word. Someday, someday I would sing little Kathy the Austrian folk songs her father had taught me. I'd tell her of our marriage, a wartime marriage which held a great deal of love, but not enough to make it right for either of us. I would tell her. And she would make the decision. If she wanted to write him, she would. If she wanted to visit him, she could do that.

This was probably a terrible decision, I told myself, but for that night at least I didn't go on with the letter.

IN THE FOLLOWING weeks my waistband expanded.

I thought Elizabeth might send me a card. She didn't.

What if she had sent a card? Perhaps—perhaps then . . .

Mental paralysis seemed to have taken over. I needed to talk, confide, tell someone. Egg came immediately to my mind. But how could Egg counsel me? She had never married, never been faced with the prospect of a child. But there was someone else close to me who had.

It took only two days to arrange a temporary leave, book my seat, and once again be on the long, silver-flashing train. As mile after mile was consumed and I approached my old life, I wondered if I could find my way back into it. I wanted to be Mama Kathy's little girl, and Connie and Georges's little sister. Only there was no

Georges. No Georges and no Papa. And my father—he was no longer that dark phantom shape, but I needed a woman. I needed my mother.

The silver and blue train sped on, swallowing the miles, swallowing the years. In Edmonton I left the Canadian Pacific and took a bus into the forests of Alberta. At the familiar crossroads I got out. There was no marker, not even a bench advertising the local mortuary.

Mama Kathy looked very small against the background of spruce and larch, yet somehow sturdy, timeless even, as she waved a bouquet of wayside flowers she had picked, tall lavender larkspur, fiery red paintbrush, and wild gold buttercups. She didn't exactly wave it, she shook it at me in her excitement.

I think I must have flung myself at her, for we rocked backward a moment, our arms tightly locked around each other. What we said was incomprehensible, because we talked at the same time, laughing, almost crying. She didn't notice I was pregnant. It seemed obvious to me by now, but people didn't notice.

She had borrowed a neighbor's car for the occasion. We bounced along the narrow, overgrown road, Mama Kathy, me, my suitcase, and my flowers, talking all the while. Then there it was, the small house where we had all fit so snugly, the fields I had scampered across searching for arrowheads, the step I preferred to jump over, the porch where I played jacks with Connie—it all burst on me.

The past refused to be relegated to the past. It was here, present, overwhelming. Only because I had made the pilgrimage before, when Mama Kathy was in Vancouver assembling replacement parts for planes, could I bring myself to realize she hadn't always been here in the old familiar setting. She too had been part of the war effort, and her life must have changed as drastically as mine. It was exciting, she told me, but demanding. "I felt the pressure after a while. I'm glad to be back home. My own things, everything familiar. The pace of city life gets to you after a bit."

Mama Kathy looked older, her red hair somewhat faded, her pretty face lined. "I suspect you're tired, Kathy, after such a trip. Your old room is ready for you. I'll call you for dinner, and afterwards you'll tell me what's on your mind."

I did as she said, just like the child I had been. And like that child, I put my shoes beside the bed and climbed under the quilt.

Oddly enough, when I began to talk, it was about Crazy Dancer. "He loved to have fun. He called me by my Indian name. And while I was with him I was Oh-Be-Joyful's Daughter. He rebuilt the toolbox of his three-wheel motorcycle into a sidecar, and we cracked up. He fitted out an old jalopy so it ran on kerosine. And he took me to an amusement park. When I was with him a kind of wildness took hold of me, and I was as crazy as he was. We sat on the moon, and afterwards he tied a handkerchief over my eyes, and I fed him ice cream."

Mama Kathy laughed, but when I joined in she looked at me sharply, and I realized my laughter had an edge of hysteria.

"He was a private. He drove trucks. When they sent him overseas, he asked me to marry him, Mama. And I did."

"Kathy . . ." The word was full of question.

"It was according to Indian ways, a Handsome Lake ceremony, an under-the-blanket marriage. We went to his mother, and she performed it, and neighbors and friends built a little tepee filled with boughs of leaves and flowers. Outside they left food and drink. It was beautiful. I want you to know that."

She rocked back and forth a few times. "But it wasn't a legal marriage? No priest, no church? It was not done in the sight of God."

"I think it was done in the sight of God. We made our vows to Him and to each other."

She continued to rock.

"We tried," I said. "We were going to invite you, and Connie and Jeff. But when I telephoned, you told me about Georges." My God, I was going out of my mind. I had mixed everything up, confused what happened with Erich and my days with Crazy Dancer. I burst into tears.

Mama Kathy reached for my hand and gave it a squeeze. "So what about your young man? They took him?"

"Yes, they took him."

"Was he killed?"

"I thought so. I didn't hear from him. There was a telegram, I heard the ship he was on was sunk."

"My poor Kathy."

"I've talked and talked, and haven't said it." I stood up, walked up and down the small living room, and came to a stop in front of her. "I'm pregnant."

In the silence I could hear Mama's intake of breath.

"And not by him," I said defiantly.

Mama's hand tightened over the arm of the old rocker. "You don't have to tell me anything you don't want to, Kathy."

"I wrote you. I married again."

"Yes, of course. That's why I'm so confused. But it's all right. The child is your husband's," she concluded with obvious relief. "The Austrian who was your patient, the amputee, is the father."

"You have the picture, but not all the pieces. His mother, Elizabeth Madeleine Hintermeister von Kerll, came after him."

"You mean, from Austria?"

I nodded. "She came to take him back."

"But—but—" It was too much for Mama Kathy. She started again, "But he had a wife and child. . . ."

"He doesn't know about the child."

"What?"

I took a deep breath and explained all the counts on which the marriage didn't work.

"I don't know, Kathy," she said as she listened.

I finished and she continued to rock. "I wish I were wiser, but I'm not. My best advice to you is—stay here where you grew up and where you are loved. Give your heart a chance to heal. Eventually your heart will answer you."

"You think so? You think there is an answer for me? Oh, Mama Kathy, I'm terrified. I don't know whether I can go forward, I know I can't go back, and I'm stuck right where I am. I don't know what's best for my baby."

IT'S AN AWESOME thing to be in charge of someone else's life, to make decisions for them. So I didn't. Gradually I absorbed the rhythm of the household. The daily cooking, the cleaning, the gardening, the occasional shopping. Evenings we sang the old songs, the songs we'd sung with Papa accompanying us on his accordion, the one he bought from Old Irish Bill. Then one evening Irish Bill himself appeared, an ancient gentleman who led us in "Kevin Barry" and "Polly Wolly Doodle Wally Day."

Some evenings we updated our songfest with the radio's hit parade. Once I forgot myself and found I was singing in German, "*Röslein, Röslein, Röslein rot, Röslein auf der Heiden.*" Mama Kathy gave me a surprised and quizzical look.

For the most part I mused. I felt very well. Why not, I was full of life. Life swelled my belly, hard and round. I remembered Crazy Dancer's word for soul, *ahcak*. I wondered if the new little Kathy possessed one yet. When does it fly in? At birth?

Connie came. She and Jeff drove up in their Ford. It was a fire-engine red sports car, with a canvas top they kept folded down. Jeff was the same nice guy I remembered, but somehow I had expected her to be with Georges. We took our sister walk. We went off together, leaving Mama Kathy to explain.

"It should be like old times," Connie said, "but it isn't."

"No, it isn't."

"Jeff's great," Connie said. "I really love him."

But he's not Georges, I finished in my mind.

We walked down by the pond, where the ducks migrated each year. They sailed the surface, miniature galleons, their wakes streaming out behind them. Others, who had foraged further, flew in feet first, braking. We watched heads go down and rears come up and shake with the delight of their catch. We watched the males rise from the water, ruffle their feathers, and preen themselves.

"Do you notice," Connie said, "they go in pairs."

Like twins, I thought.

Staring at the mallards, not seeing them, she looked as Erich had when he realized he had only one leg. They'd maimed her too, when they'd amputated her twin.

"I knew," she said, no longer conscious of me, speaking to the wind. "The weight of the world seemed to crash down on me. I was buried under rubble. I died, Kathy. I died when he did, at the exact moment."

I believed her. It can happen that way.

"I love Jeff," she went on. "I love being his wife. But I'm a ghost, Kathy, not here at all. I watch them together, Connie and Jeff. And I smile because it's very sweet. But her heart is dead."

I didn't dare put my arms around her, I didn't dare touch her.

"The War Office sent Mama the standard we-regret-to-inform-you letter, and his things. He had so little. It was a challenge to him to do without, get by on the barest minimum."

My stomach knotted, remembering.

"He left a diary. Mama's going to read it to us tonight. We'll know what he thought, what he felt. It will be Georges talking to us, saying goodbye. I always thought if I'd had a chance to say goodbye, it would be easier."

"Perhaps," I said, "there are special messages for each of us. Or at least for you."

"You think so?" She caught at my words so eagerly that instantly I was afraid I'd stirred up too much hope.

That evening as we sat together, I told them about the letter I'd received from Austria. Not from Erich, not even from his mother. His attorney wrote that a petition had been approved by the archbishop and cleared with the Vatican. There would shortly be papers of annulment for me to sign.

Connie was momentarily pulled from the endless repetitive grief that mired her. While she didn't comment directly on what I'd said, she did talk about the baby. She said over and over how excited she was to be an aunt, and agreed with me that it was a girl, and that of course she was Kathy. But I knew what was on her mind.

Mama Kathy took the diary from the pocket of the old leather chair. Connie went chalk white as Mama opened it and began to read. Connie's hands were clenched, and she leaned forward as though to draw the words out more quickly.

> *I have come to think that Germany was not equipped to fight a major war. The outcome, I believe, was determined before the first shot was fired. In my opinion it was the state of technology and the decisions made regarding which weapon systems to develop that decided things.*
>
> *The Germans began the war with a relatively small surface fleet, 57 U-boats, and the Z plan. This called for the building of 29 U-boats per month. A shortage of materiel scuttled this plan. As we discovered, it took them two years from the laying of the keel to the commissioning of a boat.*

Yes, yes, I thought, glancing at Connie. Get around to the family, Georges.

> *At first, Germany had things pretty much their way. The B-Dienst, the German intelligence headquarters, were successful in breaking into our Naval Cipher No. 3, which we used to send instructions to merchant shipping. The Jerries showed up at every rendezvous.*
>
> *In '41, however, there was an intelligence failure on their part, one which they persisted in with true German thoroughness. This was the belief that a transmission of under 30 sec. could not be picked up by our Directional Finder equipment. But by then we were able to mount HF/DF equipment on escorts, that allowed us to pick up a message as brief as 20 sec. From that time on the tables were turned, we knew every move they made. This invaluable device looked like a birdcage and was mounted on the top deck of our ships in plain sight. German agents in Spain took hundreds of photographs of it, but never figured out what the birdcage was for.*

There was a grunt of satisfaction and a wry laugh from Jeff. Connie's face was marble. A sense of panic began to rise in me. She was waiting for that special word, she was waiting for Georges to talk to her, and he went on and on about dry technical stuff that no one cared about now the war was over.

Mama had a sip of Coke and continued reading.

> *Bletchley Park, the hub where I work, is the tracking room. Our job: to detect U-boats. If I hadn't been so impatient, a similar transmission post was set up a year later in Ottawa. By that time we had established radio stations along the coast of Africa, the east coast of North America, Washington D.C., Iceland, Bermuda, and the Ascension Islands. At Bletchley we got so we could spot exactly who was transmitting. We even named them: Fritz had a strong even stroke, Hans was quick and nervous, and so on. Their styles are so distinct that we refer to them as fingerprints.*

Georges went on to describe special buddies. Steve, whose digs he had been on his way to when it happened. Alan Turing was another, a somewhat remote figure, but the undoubted genius of the operation.

> *It's quite likely that Turing or at least one of them knows at least one of the opponents he battles in this silent game, where lives and countries and civilization itself are at stake. Both Stephen and Alan, at different times, talk of vacations in Austria and Switzerland. They frequently met up with young Germans hiking the same trails, or in a rest hut on the side of the Matterhorn or Mt. Blanc. They'd share a sandwich, trade stories, laugh together, and talk of their studies. I'm sounding now like sister Kathy with her What-ifs.*

I made a gulping sound.

Connie jumped to her feet. "Don't read any more, Mama. I'd like to take it to my room."

"Of course," Mama started to say, but Connie talked through her words, "Did you hear what he said? Did you? He could have stayed right here in Canada. He said so himself. And done the same work. In Ottawa. Why didn't he wait? Why didn't he?"

Jeff started after her, but Mama motioned him to stay where he was. "They were very close," she said by way of explanation, and brought the diary in to Connie.

This worried me more because by now I was convinced that the word she wanted, the special thought for her, wasn't there. Georges had been caught up in the business at hand, fascinated by the deadly game he played for lives and ships and ultimately for the war itself. His twin was over here on the other side of the ocean. He'd kept his focus fixed. It was natural. It was natural for Georges, at any rate. And I worried.

I didn't sleep well. Too many dreams collided, broke apart, and couldn't be called back.

A faint sound disturbed what rest I had, and I found myself listening, not with my ears but with my pores. Something about it upset me, perhaps not being able to identify it. It came, I decided, from the living room.

I got up and very quietly stole across the room and opened the door. I don't know what Hell or Hades or any of those tormented places looks like, but it was there in front of me.

Connie was on her hands and knees, her hair falling in wild disarray around her. She searched through page after page of what had been Georges's looseleaf notepaper. The diary was scattered like a snowstorm. Scissors in hand, she was cutting out individual letters and pasting them on a large cardboard, her lips moving as she tried to press the letters into words.

The code. She was attempting to reconstruct the Twins' Code, like a psychic at a Ouija board, desperately trying to make sense of random letters, force meaning into them. But I could see they followed no pattern. Frantically she interchanged a letter here with a letter there. She was still working with every fifth word.

"Perhaps," she muttered, "perhaps I started in the wrong place. Perhaps I shouldn't have started at the beginning—" Her hands swept the letters lying in piles into new configurations.

"Nothing," she concluded. "He couldn't spare a word, a thought for me."

"Words, no. But thoughts—Connie, you told me yourself you knew in your own body the moment he died. What was that except his last, his very last thought? Be content with that."

She looked up. She hadn't heard me. "He could have stayed right here. He could have been in Ottawa the whole time."

I sat down beside her on the floor and began to gather the pages together.

"No, no," she said, stopping me. "It's here. I counted wrong. I'll start again. *I* is the first word. Count five. Second word is *that*. Count five. Third word is *to*. Count five. Fourth word is *The*. Count five.

Fifth word is *determined*. So, it's 'I that to The determined.' But the capital letter in *The*, that's our signal to switch from words to letters. Every fifth letter. But I'm not sure whether to go on, or go back to the beginning. If you go on, it's *b, e, i, u, w, r.* That starts out a word, *being,* and if you skip ahead you get *n* and *g,* but the count is wrong. Go back to the beginning. *I, c, o, k, G* . . ." She looked at me hopelessly.

"It's not in the diary, Connie."

"But I haven't gone through it all. Maybe it's not all here. Maybe the censors got at it, tore out some pages at the beginning. We've got to start the count right and not miss a single word or letter. If you help it will go twice as fast."

"It's not there, Connie."

This time the words reached her.

She rocked back on her heels and looked at me.

It was a full minute later that I reached out a tentative hand and continued collecting the pages. She watched me put them in a neat pile and fit them back in the notebook. Then with sudden decision she began painstakingly to gather individual letters from the floor. She folded them in a blank sheet of paper and tucked them into the notebook. "You were always so sensible, Kathy. Even when you were a baby, you were a sensible baby. I'm glad you said that, Kathy. I needed to hear it. If you hadn't said it just like that, so definitely, so positively, I think I'd spend all my life hunting through that diary for what isn't there. Why does there have to be 'last words'? That's kind of crazy, isn't it, to attach some special significance to last words. This is a diary. An ordinary diary. There's no code. It's just the day-to-day diary of a soldier."

I listened without saying anything as my sister put her life back. She was doing it methodically with grim determination, but she was doing it. I could do it too.

Connie and Jeff left in the morning.

Seventeen

WINTER MONTHS ARE deep and white and silent here. The snow lodges heavily in tree branches. When the sun shines you can see its structure, a honeycomb of crystals. I think I'd never taken time to notice before. Now things proceeded slowly, calmly, to a new rhythm. My baby grew, filling me. She would be born in the spring. That was when most new creatures arrive. I waited and watched for the first signs of budding.

One day Elk Girl came. Remembering her mysterious appearances at critical times in my life, I was not surprised to see her. She had left me on a stool eating eggs. I had been to war and come back, been married, and soon I'd have a baby. Elk Girl looked exactly the same. She had never been pretty, but from the time we were children, her face was filled with a great dignity.

She didn't want to sit and chat, but when she saw that tea and home-baked cookies would be served, she changed her mind. Elk Girl could always be moved by food. These days I was perpetually hungry and the smell of baking that so often filled the room was one of my pleasures. We sipped the green Irish tea Mama poured from the kettle with the cozy, and munched and talked, Mama inquiring minutely about her various friends on the reserve.

At last Elk Girl pulled back from the table. "Come to my house," she said. "I have to show you a few things."

"What things?"

She laughed and winked at Mama Kathy, who laughed back.

So I got my coat, put on my wool cap and muffler, pulled on mittens, fastened overshoes, and we started out. Any semblance of a road was obscured under snow, but we plowed through it. I knew I wouldn't flounder if I stuck close behind my guide.

Elk Girl neither paused or hesitated. It was as though she followed a broad avenue instead of trackless forest. The new life in me, instead of subtracting from my own health and strength, added to it. I had never felt so well, so alert to the day, the crisp weather, the gleam of an icicle hanging just out of reach. Life had doubled in me, and I took in more than my share.

Elk Girl had stayed on in Sarah's house after her death. That's where she lived. It was her house now. I was surprised, first to see a woman emerge from it, then on entering to find that in front of the cookstove a baby lay asleep under a beaver fur.

"Is he yours?" I gasped.

"Yes."

That was all, no other explanation. Whether he was hers biologically, or a foundling, or adopted, or simply acquired from someone who couldn't keep him I never knew. All I knew was there was no evidence of a father. If it is possible to share a lack, then it was a lack we shared.

"I brought you here to show you how to be a mother." She closed her eyes and went into her medicine place. "Your time," she enunciated oratorically, "is at the end of the popping of the trees. March. Or it could be when the leaves become large in the first part of April."

"I think that's right," I said.

"I will come then. I will bring *iskwao muskike*. That is a woman's medicine. It stops any bleeding."

"Good. Thank you."

"Now, about the baby. Do not wash it all the time. Use the oils that I will give you. And never wash it if it has fever, too much washing can kill it."

"My goodness," I said, thinking that Elk Girl and Mama Kathy were on a collision course regarding bathing.

"The kind of medicine you know was not the medicine that was here at the beginning. At the beginning medicine was made from natural things, things like maple sugar water mixed with pitch for a cough. And for a stomachache lard and charcoal with the head of the bullrush stirred in."

I thought of Mama Kathy's medicine chest: Smith Bros. cough syrup, milk of magnesia, and cod liver oil. I would guess the efficacy of the treatments to be about the same, if you excepted the washing. As a nurse I would also rate them as fairly interchangeable. I drew the line, though, at tobacco juice. It might, as Elk Girl firmly believed, be holy, but it did not stop infection as she claimed. There was a new wonder drug tried on the battlefield for that—penicillin.

Her baby smiled in his sleep.

"Such a pretty little boy. What's his name?" I asked.

She looked at me pityingly. "A baby is not named. A baby grows into its name. And when he is ready, I will make a blue sky trip and bring him a name."

"My baby's named already, even before she's born. Her name is Kathy."

Elk Girl considered this and then nodded. "There is a holy bond," she went on instructing me, "between named and namer."

"I know," I said. And it was true, I was beginning to know all manner of mysterious and unknowable things. Indian things such as Crazy Dancer dancing a path to the other world.

I went home with my head full of Elk Girl's remedies, choke-cherry pemmican and camas roots dried in the sun then stewed. But the important ingredient she had given me was her friendship. That and pushing wide open the door to my Indian self.

The smell of him had come back to me . . . the first day I met him, grease and gun oil and sweat and outdoors. What if—? But it was not his baby I carried.

MAMA KATHY TOLD me it was an easy birth. Elk Girl, as good as her word, was there to assist, and I heard her and Mama Kathy in the kitchen, arguing about the *iskwao muskike*. I held on to Mama Kathy, to Elk Girl, to the sides of the bed as the rending and tearing passed the baby along the birth canal. I remembered a black-and-white illustration of the process in my student textbook, how logical the various stages, how mechanically correct. But when it happened in your body, too large a being squeezed along too small a passage raised the pain to an intolerable pitch.

It wasn't going to get born. I regretted my decision to have a home birth. I should have gone back to the city, had the baby at the Daughters of Charity hospital. They could have given me a spinal block. Why hadn't I done that?

It was too big, I was too small. Oh, God, I cried, picturing the wooden Christ on the cross above my bed in Montreal.

A final, impossible effort and it was over. Kathy was laid in my arms. I looked into my daughter's little wrinkled face. "Hello, Kathy. We're going to be great friends."

"Newborns know things no one else does," Elk Girl told me, and it made sense. They are so recently here, just moments before on the other side.

The baby was white.

Elk Girl was disgusted. "You wouldn't know this child was Mé-tis."

No, you wouldn't. She looked like Erich and like Elizabeth. Only her eyes indicated Indian blood, not brown but black. It was arresting in a fair face.

Mama Kathy was a typical grandmother. According to her the baby was beautiful and perfect besides, with a straight, strong back and well-shaped head—she could go on and on. When Kathy's black eyes met mine, I asked her, "Who are you, Kathy?"

Elk Girl also fell in love with the newest Kathy and forgave her for looking like Austrian royalty. She too fell under the baby's spell and oohed and aahed over her with Mama Kathy and me. Secretly she fed me roots of cranberry with an admixture of powdered bark so that my milk would be nourishing.

Of course I was modern and sophisticated and knew better, but I enjoyed playing Indian. For whatever reason, my milk was abundant and the baby throve. Elk Girl's little son was a toddler now, and, as spring grew warm, we sat outside on the porch, me with my baby in my arms, she with one eye on her little boy. The days were wrapped in a lazy, timeless glow. Then there came one, with Mama Kathy putting up jam in mason jars, and Elk Girl chewing tobacco beside me, a day in fact no different from the others, when a sudden energy took over. What was I doing drowsing away the afternoon? There was a whole world out there, and I wanted to give it to little Kathy with both hands. I wanted to take her to Belmont Park, show her the harbor, the ships and bridges, take her to visit evenings, when Sister Ursula played piano and the girls sang. I wanted her to see the lights of the city and the traffic flowing by, hear the caroling of Notre Dame's great bells.

I had come home to Mama Kathy. I had taken refuge in my old home. I had found my strength and composure. I had had my child. She was a whole and complete person. As she filled out and grew, she was becoming simply more herself. This Kathy was no ordinary little body. I looked into her face, and wide-spaced black eyes laughed back at me one moment, but how stormy they could become. How imperious, how demanding she could be if I was a second late offering her the breast. I was getting to know her. Happy and jolly yes, but definitely her own person and, I suspected, a complex one. How fulfilling to be her mother. She reminded me constantly that I was finally Oh-Be-Joyful's Daughter.

"We'll be going back to Montreal." The words blew about in the air like a dandelion gone to seed and fell into the mulch of the heavily pine-twigged earth.

"You're a fool," Elk Girl said.

But I knew how to handle her by now. "Tell me something I don't know."

Mama Kathy came and sat beside me on the step. "You're going back to nursing?"

I nodded.

"It's a wonderful profession, that and teaching—the helping professions. I've always admired them."

I sat a while longer and Mama Kathy ventured, "If you need someone to look after the baby while you work—?"

I knew she was getting ready to brave sin city and nominate herself. But I couldn't let her do that, knowing how she felt. This was the home she'd shared with Mike.

"Don't worry, Mama, I have friends back there who will help out."

I went in to start dinner and think about my decision. There were advantages to growing up in a small place like this, you knew everyone, and they knew you. Little Kathy would run freer here, but the mission school could not compare to a big-city school. I smiled down at my baby—I was getting a few years ahead of myself. But one had to think of those things. I saw little Kathy in a school uniform, her light brown hair neatly braided. Myself I did not see at all.

I considered briefly that I no longer had anyone to go back to. I was no longer part of Crazy Dancer's life, and I had sent Erich away. He might be part of my little girl's future, but he was no longer part of mine. Two men, I thought, whom I had loved. And who had loved me. But the war turned everything upside down.

I had a profession, one I was proud of and that I worked hard at. It tired me out often, but at the end of the day I felt good about myself. Besides, it was a means of making my way. I belonged to a new generation of women for whom that was possible.

There were fears, there were questions, and plenty of what-ifs—but I brushed them aside. I was ready for the fray. I could make it on my own.

THE LARGE GRAY slabs of rough stone that made up the facade of the Daughters of Charity of St. Vincent de Paul Hospital were familiar and welcoming. My heart beat fast as it had the first time I entered it. I carried four-month-old Kathy in a laundry basket; with it I marched into Egg's office.

She looked up. Her glasses slid along her nose to the turned-up end. "Kathy! And . . . ?!"

"Little Kathy," I said promptly. "I want to come back, and I'm counting on you. I need to work," I said, slipping into the chair opposite.

She didn't hear me. She reached for the baby. "Will you look at her. Will you just look at her!" Then, glancing at me and through me, "She's the image of her father."

I heard the question. "Erich returned to Austria."

"How could he leave this little beauty, this—" She stopped. She looked at me carefully. "He doesn't know?"

"No," I said in a small voice, "he doesn't."

Sister's lips came together in a straight line.

"There are reasons, Sister."

"I'm sure there are." But her mouth did not relax.

"He's needed at home. His mother came for him. His family . . ." My voice trailed off.

"A baby needs a father."

"A baby needs a mother. And I can't live there, Egg. It's not my world, and I don't want it to be hers. It's old, and over here we're new and full of energy, and finding our own way. I can take care of her. I can. If I can bring her with me while she's nursing and leave her for a few hours with whoever is off duty, it will work out. She's a good baby. She hardly ever cries."

"Absolutely not," Egg said. "One of the girls indeed! She stays right here."

I reached across the basket and threw my arms around my rotund friend.

I found a small apartment adjacent to the hospital. When I had told Mama Kathy I'd have help, I hadn't anticipated that from the first I would be inundated with offers. The girls vied with each other to baby-sit. Sister Egg wound up organizing the volunteers into shifts. Little Kathy was never without her devoted court. When I wrote to Mama Kathy that I was afraid she would be spoiled rotten, Mama wrote back, "Love never hurt anyone."

The hours were long and grueling, but there was unexpected joy. Friends I didn't know I had rallied to support me. Emily was among them, an Emily no longer hesitant and unsure. She had never gotten over her habit of fixing and changing things. And in spite of it, or perhaps because of it, she had become Matron Norris's right hand.

Dr. Finch was an immediate ally. He said he didn't know how he had gotten along without me. "A surgical nurse is a rare and scarce item." I was part of the operating room team almost exclusively now.

At the end of the month I discovered my base pay had been increased. I felt it was justified. I worked with a will, and I was joyful.

Kathy was seven months, crawling into everything, dancing in her canvas swing with elastic attachments that allowed her chubby legs to push off from the floor.

It was Sunday, and after services we'd spent the day in the park. Kathy was asleep in her buggy, and I was weighing whether I was less apt to wake her if I bumped the carriage up the stairs, or lifted her out of it and carried her up. Occupied with this question, I didn't see him.

He stepped out of the shadow in front of me.

It was Crazy Dancer.

He kissed me before he said a word. "I've been wanting to do that for a long time."

There was a great rush of feeling in me that I didn't know how to give expression to. So I simply said, "Will you give me a hand with the buggy? I don't want to wake her."

"I'll go backwards. You lift up your end."

With two there was no problem, the baby slept on.

"I asked at the hospital. They told me you aren't married anymore."

"It was annulled."

"Kathy," he said, "I feel like I'm in a minefield. I'm afraid I'll say the wrong thing, make the wrong move."

"Come in," I said. "Sit down, and I'll fix tea. And jelly sandwiches," I added, remembering.

"I didn't die," he said, continuing the conversation we'd had more than a year ago, "because there was a sergeant waiting for me when I signed in. They put me on another ship. It turned out they wanted someone to look at these American torpedoes that had just been installed. They weren't firing accurately. For every hundred feet forward they fell about ten."

"Did you figure out what was wrong?"

"Not at first. We tried aiming higher, but all that accomplished was for the shell to hit the surface of the water before sinking. Then I thought—if they turn up the drive-planes to shoot higher . . . This worked short-range, but long-range—Oh, what the hell am I talking short-range, long-range? I want us to be together, Kathy. That's a real cute kid you've got there. Anyway, we went down off the French coast, and the Resistance saved my hide. I wrote, but I guess it was too risky, and they didn't send the letters."

"I understand," I said. "And you have to understand too."

"Right."

"So." I set the sandwich in front of him. "Were you able to diagnose the torpedoes?"

"Yeah. I found out from the gunner that to save money the Americans filled them with water for the test, instead of gunpowder."

"Water? You've got to be kidding."

"So what do you think?"

"About using water?"

"About us. You thought I was dead. Was the world supposed to stop on account of that?"

I sat on his lap and looked into eyes that mirrored mine. "Once you adjusted for the difference in weight, the torpedoes worked?"

It was a long warm kiss that turned time around.

"What did you say?"